# BREEDING GROUND FOR CORRUPTION
Revised Edition
by
T. A. Garrison

Ocala, FL

Zeta Publishing, Inc
3850 SE 58th Ave
Ocala, FL 34480
www.zetapublishing.com

Ordering Information:
Quantity sales. Special discounts are available on quantity purchases by corporations, associations, and others. For details, contact the publisher at the address above.
Orders by U.S. trade bookstores and wholesalers. Please contact Zeta Publishing: Tel: (352) 694-2553; Fax: (352) 694-1791 or visit www.zetapublishing.com

First Published by Xlibris in 2015

Rev. Date: 7/31/2017

ISBN: 978-1-947191-20-4 (sc)

ISBN: 978-1-947191-21-1 (e)

Library of Congress Control Number: 2017948821

Printed in the United States of America

To my husband, Steve, who gave his angel wings to fly and to my sons, Ryan and Matthew who keep me grounded.


ESTHER 4:14 "Perhaps this is the moment for which you were created"

TABLE OF CONTENTS


CHAPTERS




APPENDIX

This edition is dedicated to Jimmy.

# Chapter 1:

## History of American Police

Temptation has been an ever present demon since Adam and Eve entered the Garden of Eden. The unyielding relationship of the law enforcement family poses major scrutiny in the public eye. On the public sector, corruption among the law enforcement society is occurring at an astounding frequency. It is not a typical sign of the times, however, it has been a persistent feature "of human society, with the earliest references dating back to the fourth century BC" (Pinto, Leana, and Pil, 2008, pp. 686). For the purpose of this book, law enforcement society encompasses law enforcement officers (local, state, Federal, etc.), correctional officers (jailors, etc.), and others who have taken the oath to serve and protect. How can corruption be defined? It all depends on how it is looked upon. Corruption definitively faces debate because it refers to a broad range of conduct.

Distinguishing the definition of corruption isn't an exact science. IF one were to consider the definition of corruption in the

Stanford Encyclopedia of Philosophy, it is deemed as "the abuse of power by a public official for private gain" (2005). There is no hesitation that the abuse of power by a public official is paradigmatic of corruption. This strictly defines corruption as not phenomena, or an analytical fabric of society, but as exemplified acts carried out for personal gain. There are several sub categories of non-economic corruption. For the purpose of this book, the concentration of police corruption is addresses and emphasized.

Acts of corruption on have several areas of identity. These identified areas are procedural misconduct, corruption for financial gain, unconstitutional actions, direct criminal activities, and culpable negligence. All of these activities result in some failure of virtues and ethics.

The span of decades uncovers repetitive areas in which corruption continues to grow. As the moral deficiency continues to climb, it leaves one to question the fabric in which the oaths of office even are built upon. For a moment, let's examine a generalized law enforcement oath of office.

> "On my <u>honor</u>: I will never <u>betray</u> my badge, my <u>integrity</u>, my <u>character</u>, or the <u>public trust</u>. I will always have the <u>courage</u> to hold myself and others <u>accountable</u> for our actions I will always uphold the constitution, My <u>community</u> and the agency I serve"
>
> (Source: International Association of Chiefs of Police)

In a section of the International Association of Chiefs of Police (2000), it is suggested that when officer's take this oath, that the meaning behind key words are understood. The previous selection contains underlined words that meanings are more than just words.

Honor – means that one's word is given as a guarantee

Betray – defined as the breaking faith with the public trust

Badge – Symbol of Office

Integrity – Being the same person in both private and public life

Character – qualities that distinguish an individual

Public Trust – charge of duty imposed in faith toward those you serve

Courage – having the strength to withstand unethical pressure, fear, or danger

Accountability – being answerable and responsible for your oath

Community – the jurisdiction served

Yes, it is agreeable that law enforcement takes threat and suffers inconvenience in order to look after lives, defend liberty, and makes the general public safe. It is nonetheless a noble and selfless role. At what point do these values slip under the rug?
Surely, no officer will take the oath with a preconceived plan of totally corrupting themselves. Can we claim it is an occupational hazard or a paradigm of deviancy yet to come?

Police participate in a significant position in protection of the autonomous culture. A position of this respect compels police officers to maintain high moral principles of demeanor. Law enforcement must guard the constitutional rights of the general public, yet at the same time are charged with restricting the civil liberties of suspects in the furtherance of society's good. Police detain, explore, take into custody populace, and legitimately utilize the physical force necessary (including deadly force) when situations order. The acknowledgment of a representative weighs heavily in the discussions made by jurors when formulating the culpability, or virtuousness of defendants appearing in court.

When corrupt cops spoil the overall look of others in the field, ethical disciplinary action must be used. Police officers are required to take an oath of office (see above) and hold fast to a code of principles (see above) before entering the profession (Barry, 1999). Officers are under oath to adhere to ethical values and defend the general public as a provision of their service. The bulk of people in the US recognize the significance of police in the preservation of civic order and enforcing laws. Many are willing to allow an improved version of law enforcement that has trust, admiration, and respect by society. However, Police delinquency serves to destabilize this common bond. The predicament of police misconduct has been ever present in society since the establishment of law enforcement in America. Several high profile cases brought this topic to the vanguard of scholarly discussion. Revisiting the commentary of law delinquency in our nation affords us the chance to grasp how profoundly the crisis is deep-seated. The challenges facing police reformers of today are similar to the trials faced by their predecessors (Barry, 1999). It is significant to study how the law enforcement society has to the present state of affairs before we can plot a course to a better position. If we do not learn from our past mistakes, we are fated to replicate them.

European Influence on American Policing

American law enforcement influences can be traced back to the European model of law enforcement. Corruption was not born; instead it has been well documented back to France and England during the eighteenth century. The issues that both France and

England encountered are very similar to modern day American police corruption. "The challenges of hiring morally sound people and providing morally sound workplaces are the most obvious" (Sherman, 1974). Law enforcement transgression was a solemn issue that has been dated back to the 17th century. Sherman (1974) describes the early corruption that:

"Despite several attempts at reform, the Renaissance police of Paris were often said to be in a league with thieves. By the eighteenth century the mid-management job of a police inspector had become so corruptibly profitable that it was sold for twice the price of the head police administrator's office. And on the eve of the French Revolution, the police spent all their time off from political spying in sharing the profits of a large, illegal vice operation" Corruption was not as widespread when Napoleon French Monarchy was in charge; Sherman (1974) disclosed that the detective unit during that time coined the phrase "only a thief can catch a thief". Ultimately, the usage of thieves was utilized as detectives. Using thieves to catch thieves ultimately resulted in additional corruption, as it was initially predicted. The 'secret police' were responsible for many atrocities, including murder, rape and other felonies; they routinely falsely imprisoned people without justification (Sherman, 1974). In 1893, Louis Lepine became head of police administrators in France and made some improvements. He ensured that all detectives came from the uniform police. This ended the hiring of thieves as detectives, reducing some of the police corruption plaguing France. However, problems persisted in the area of enforcement of vice-related laws (Sherman, 1974). Prior to 1829, England primarily relied on citizens to protect them. The great separation between the classes resulted in frequent conflict on the streets. The wealthy could afford to pay for their own private security, but the same could not be said for the poor. Crime and violence were the norms on the streets of England.

From Norman times, the English position of a parish constable was to be performed by all citizens in rotation, a year at a time, in addition to one's regular occupation. As the statutory duties of the constables increased, wealthier citizens paid poorer ones to perform this onerous task in their stead. By the fifteenth century a permanent group of inept and dishonest substitutes filled the ranks of parish constables. More ambitious workingmen sought out the position of a high constable for even greater illicit profits (Sherman, 1974).The majority of citizens were deprived and lived in persistent fear from enforcement officials.  It was the responsibility of all males between the ages of 16 and 60 to enforce the law as they saw fit. Population shifts due to industrialization, migration and urbanization, resulted in rioting being commonplace. When turmoil grew too great military intervention was used. The military was hated by the majority of citizens because of their brutish tactics in order maintenance. The Crown of England realized that something needed to be done to ensure domestic tranquility without risking a coup d'etat.(Sherman,1974)

The suggestion to use a municipal law enforcement to handle domestic harmony was the way of thinking following the English reformers. "Establishing a police force, the Crown could eradicate much public scorn and provide tranquility in the streets" (Sherman, 1974) . In 1829, Sir Robert Peel created the London Metropolitan Police Department. The mission of the London Metropolitan Police was to "keep peace by peaceful means."  Sir Robert Peel was also known as the father of urbanized policing. He created the Metropolitan Police Act that created a force that operated on principles and guidelines. These guidelines also became the foundation of modern day law enforcement. The focus in Peel's viewpoint was to prevent crimes from happening instead of waiting until a response is needed. Thus, the proactive approach was developed. The first patrols, both day and night were formed and in a coordinated manner.

## American Policing

American Policing has its heredity in nineteenth century England. The predecessors were aware of the carnage committed by fraudulent French police and defused to incorporate that into American society. The newly formed English system seemed to have created domicile enforcement without the use of force via the military.

Early police departments in the United States resembled their English counterparts. The quasi-military foundation of American policing can be seen in contemporary policing. The wearing of identifiable uniforms, adherence to a formal chain of command, legally sanctioned use of force and isolation from the public are just some of the similarities between the military and police. Despite affinities with England's police, there were profound differences. England's police were created by national reformation; this was not the case in the United States. Local, instead of federal, government created American policing. Allowing local governments independence in creating their own police allowed for communities to have law enforcement that fit their own political needs. "Of all the factors that have shaped police departments in the United States, local political control and authorization have been pivotal." (Geller 3)

General management served as a proliferation position for law transgression in the nineteenth and premature twentieth century's. Local political control afforded police the chance to enhance populace being reactive to narrow requests. This also amplified police misconduct. In the nineteenth century the majority of police departments in the United States mirrored  the circumstances contiguous to municipal agencies. The police became a significant element in the corrupt opinionated political sectors. Officers brought into the force were "hired and promoted solely on the basis of political loyalties and payoffs" (Sherman, 1974). Law enforcements were free and protected against corruption assumptions because of the political umbrella that protected them. Towards the end of the  nineteenth century,  big city bureaucrats were predominately the leaders and director of mayoral, political causes, and law enforcement departments. This almost made a dictatorship of the entire law enforcement, judicial, and executive departments of many independent cities across the US.

Scandals were routine in countless law enforcement departments during the latter nineteenth century and early twentieth century's. "These early departments were so corrupt that even getting promoted to a higher rank, or a 'perk' assignment, required paying off superior officers" (Sherman, 1974). An example of the popularity of police bad behavior can be seen in the city of Boston. The salary officers received was insignificant, compared to the profits derived from payoffs. "Corruption was systemic, allowing the practice to continue without any form of deterrence" (Sherman, 1974).

As the 1870s and 80s entered the history books,  reformers began looking for remedies to deal with police misconduct. The immense exploitation of law enforcement power was accredited  the reality that  local politicians were using police to achieve their own agendas.


      Early restructuring pains recognized the danger of powerful political power above the police. The efforts ended with the creation of the Lexow Committee in 1894. This team was fashioned to compute the echelon of corruption contained by the New York Police Department. The examination exposed police officers getting wealthy through discerning enforcement of  crimes. The committee revealed t police delinquency was hard to calculate, because of reluctance of victims to testify as honest witnesses.  To add to this dilemma, the entire police force was involved in corruption.

*The Lexow investigation of 1894, an inquiry into the New York City Police Department conducted under the auspices of the Republican majority in the state legislature which was designed to embarrass the Democratic organization in New York City, showed $300.00 to be the accepted figure for an appointment as a patrolman; promotions to higher ranks required correspondingly higher payments. Therefore, from the rookie's first involvement with the department he was made aware of the systemic and pervasive impact of political influence and bribery. (Sherman, 1974, p. 48)*

The following are run-downs of the findings of the Lexow Committee:

- The Lexow Committee confirmed that officers were being paid off by selective enforcement of vice related crimes, such as prostitution, gambling and illegal alcohol sales. Saloons that did not pay bribes to the police soon realized that strict enforcement of the  law could cost them money. These payoffs were received by all ranks.


- The Lexow Committee revealed precinct captains had set prices that houses of prostitution had to pay. Depending on the number of prostitutes and clients, payoffs would vary from $25 to $500 per month. Captains would have 'bagmen' who would collect the money. 'Bagmen' were patrolmen or detectives who collected the payments from the businesses. The bagmen were usually transferred with the captain to new assignments.

• The findings of the Lexow investigation resulted in the election of a reform mayor in New York City, William Strong. Mayor Strong selected Theodore Roosevelt as Police Commissioner to clean up this troubled department. However, his efforts were unsuccessful because police corruption had become too widespread.

Examining nineteenth century law enforcement restructuring labors points to the  reasons for failures to be obvious.  Police sleaze served to benefit everyone involved. The suspects did not mind paying a fee to the police to avoid prosecution. Graft money allowed criminal enterprises to flourish, making payoffs a wise business investment for criminals. The policemen receiving the money benefitted financially (Sherman, 1974).  The broad-spectrum community seemed happy in that the majority of criminal activity was isolated to a small geographical area. Also, to the average citizen, knowing police were for sale, made his/her own transgression lawfully justifiable.. The police reformers of days gone by had to conquer obstacles analogous to  contemporary reformers. Thus the  difficulty in gaining information and unwillingness of witnesses to testify, are some of these similarities.

## 1920s

Prohibition in the 1920's became the undermining increase in corruption activity. Large amounts of cash were to be made bootlegging. Many law officers were paid to turn the other cheek to allow distribution. The Wickersham Committee was created by President Hoover in 1929 to look into the issues with Prohibition. It found that prohibition had caused an up rise in social, political, and law enforcement problems. It was recognized that prohibition was the greatest potential to corruption. The Wickersham Commission recommended reform, however, the attempts seemed pointless.

This trend reached a peak during Prohibition, when official corruption became the standard operating procedure of many American police departments. By the time Prohibition ended,however, the United States was deep in the Great Depression, and a constricted job market made policing an attractive career option to well-educated people who in better times would have gone into more traditional white collar and professional work. In many cases, this new breed was repulsed by old school corruption and sought to turn policing into a respectable undertaking" ( Sherman, 1974).

This era was decorated by deep rooted corruption and a very low public faith in American police. This resulted in improving the public's opinion of police officers. In the latter part of the 1920s, police began seeing slight difference with the new hiring's of police chiefs and officers. Police work was beginning to be seen as a respectable career, as opposed to "a group of thugs with badges."

## 1930s

The 1930s was a decade in which reform was made. The higher caliber of people entering the profession served to remove some of the political influence that had been so dominant. The leading police reformers during this decade were August Vollmer and O.W. Wilson. Their main contributions were removing local political control and shifting the police mission to law enforcement. This period of change is known as the Scientific Management period.  In his assessment, Vollmer emphasized the application of 'scientific' principles to organization deployment of personnel, criminal investigation and crime prevention. This emphasis on science and objectivity can be found in several dimensions of the reforms of the 1930s:

The federal government began assisting local departments. The Federal Bureau of Investigation served to help local departmentsby maintaining crime statistics from crime reports and supporting technical advances (i.e., radios, finger prints).

> *The Federal Bureau of Investigation played several roles in the diffusion of new thinking about police. Its public relations campaign disseminated a vision of policing. It administered the Uniform Crime Reports. In 1930 it created its own laboratory. And in 1935 it created the National Police Academy, where generations of police leaders would be trained. (Geller 8)*

Police were now being thought of as "crime fighters" instead of "political bullies." This shift increased the level of confidence citizens had in police departments. The direction of American policing moved away from the whims of local politicians toward protecting society.

"When the crime-related functions of the police were accented and political authorization was rejected, the character of U.S. Policing during the next half century was set: police aspired to be scientific crime fighters organized and administered according to objective principles." (Geller 7)  During this period of time, civil service boards were created to govern police personnel management. These boards were created to remove politicians from hiring, promoting and firing officers as a form of political pay back. Civil service resulted in restrictions being placed on police administrators in the area of personnel management.

0. W. Wilson anticipated problems with civil service reducing the autonomy of the police chief in managing his/her personnel. By having an outside board with authority over personnel selection, promotions and punishments, the police chiefs' power diminished.
*He opposed the creation of civilian review boards, since police leadership should be accountable for all officers' actions. He was concerned with punishing officers who used excessive force. As Gazell states in his excellent biographical article (1974:373), Chief Wilson was 'worried about what is sometimes called lawlessness in law enforcement.' He considered this to be a definite police management problem that should be handled internally.*[4]

The removal of politics from police departments and the creation of civil service protection created a major challenge for police administrators. Reduced political involvement resulted in less corruption. However, civil service boards limited the police chiefs' power to handle internal problems. The chief was responsible for the conduct of his officers, yet lacked power to ensure their decisions were implemented.

The challenges faced in the 1930s are still with us, almost 90 years later. This system also allows police managers to deflect blame onto the civil service boards, instead of taking responsibility. Police executives need to make ethically sound decisions without concerning themselves about the whims of civil service. Since decisions made by police management need to be approved by civil service boards, police executives often base decisions on appeasing civil service boards as opposed to moral soundness.

## 1940 - 1960

During the 1940s through the 60s, most police departments continued on their mission as 'crime fighters'. Police departments viewed themselves as professional organizations that resisted outside interference. This sort of thinking was seen in the television show 'Dragnet.' The only input that most officers sought from the public was, as Jack Webb often said, "just the facts Ma'am."

The thinking was that since only police were experts in fighting crime, 'Why get others involved?' This attitude enhanced police isolationism from the public. "Indeed, with rare exception police defined themselves as professional organizations that should be kept out of the purview of citizens, academics, researchers and other persons with an interest in police. Police business was just that: police business." (Geller 9)

The 1960's also served as a wakeup call to many Americans, concerning police misconduct. Police corruption was married with civil rights movements and widespread violations of constitutional rights and racial injustices were committed. The many demonstrations and riots during this decade showed police response as being brutal. Racial confrontations, Vietnam protests and the rioting in Chicago during the Democratic National Convention (1968), showed police reaction as being flawed. The public saw these fiascos in their living rooms, on their television sets. The image of police as professional crime fighters was replaced with that of 'keystone cops.'

Washington D.C. responded to the country's concern over police misconduct by forming several national commissions. These commissions sent the message to all police departments that the federal government was willing to intervene with conduct of officers within their jurisdictions. The days of local autonomy concerning police misconduct were over. The Kerner Commission was founded to suggest reform efforts, but there was again no long term solution to corruption.

- *One measure of the turmoil in U.S. cities and the controversy surrounding  police practices in the 1960's and early 1970's was the proliferation of blue-ribbon commissions during that period. Five national commissions were formed to examine various aspects of police services and the criminal justice process and make recommendations for reform.*

- *The President's Commission on Law Enforcement and Administration of Justice, which published its report in 1967 and 1968, was influenced by urban racial turmoil. Among the outgrowths of its work were the Safe Streets Act of 1968 and the Law Enforcement Assistance Administration, which provided significant funding for police related programs.*

- *The National Advisory Commission on Civil Disorders* (popularly known as the *Kerner Commission*) was similarly inspired by the riots and other disorders in many U.S. cities in the summer of 1967. Its report examined patterns of disorder and prescribed responses by the federal government, the criminal justice system and local governments.

- The National Commission on the Causes and Prevention of Violence was established after the assassinations of Martin Luther King and Robert Kennedy in 1968. Its report, *To Establish Justice, To Insure Domestic Tranquility*, was published in 1969. *The President's Commission on Campus Unrest was established following student deaths related to protests at Kent State and Jackson State universities in 1970.*

- *The National Advisory Commission on Criminal Justice Standards and Goals issued six reports in 1973 in an attempt to develop standards and recommendations for police crime control efforts.*

- *In addition to the work of these national commissions, the American Bar Association in 1973 published Standards relating to the Urban Police Function, the end product of a lengthy standard setting effort that began in 1963.*

- *The voluminous reports of these commissions contain insights that continue to have direct relevance to contemporary police concerns. Many of the most important recommendations in the commission reports can be seen, in retrospect, to be the seeds of important strategic, technological and operational initiatives that will command the attention of policing into the twenty-first century. (Geller 14)*

The case of Frank Serpico demonstrated to the nation that misconduct was accepted behavior within the largest police department in our country, the New York City Police Department (NYPD). In this case Serpico had to go outside the department seeking justice. This case demonstrated corruption became accepted behavior within the NYPD, and almost proved fatal to a morally sound officer. In this case Serpico was set up by fellow officers and nearly killed. He had to prematurely retire from "New York's Finest" to save his own life. As a result of the efforts of Frank Serpico, the Knapp Commission was formed to investigate the NYPD. Their findings horrified the entire nation. The corruption within the NYPD had become so systemic that honest officers feared coming to work. This fear was not about the hoodlums on the streets, but stemmed of possible retaliation they may encounter from corrupt coworkers.

*The corruption in the system was able to thrive not only because of the abuses of high-ranking officials, but also because the police demanded loyalty from their peers. Honest officers learned to turn away if they were to survive on the force.*

*They could avoid becoming involved, but they were forbidden to interfere with a partner's corrupt activities. 'Never hurt, another cop' was a by word of the force. In one social science study of police, officers were asked whether they would perjure themselves to protect their partners - a question to which many respondents were so hostile that they refused to cooperate further with the researcher. Of those who did reply, the majority affirmed that they would rather perjure themselves than expose a fellow officer.[5]*

As a result of the Knapp Commission's findings, many policies and procedures were changed throughout the nation. The code of silence was identified as being a major factor influencing police misconduct. Due to all the negative attention received during the 1960's, police departments needed to restore public trust.

## 1970-2000
### Liberation to a new millennium in policing

Liberation and free will laid the foundation for outside aspects in the policing and its logic.  The televised sitcom in American living rooms provided a fairy tale career.  Anyone born before the mid 1980's can appreciate the nonchalant whistling of "Andy Griffith" theme song.  The turn of the times resulted in a vast influence of research and well-funded research into the inner code of policing.  Keep in mind; policing was very primitive even in the 1980's simply because one could never prove corruption, misconduct, or shenanigans.

Big brother eyes and the creation of community style policing that were intended to gain the support of the community.  Bringing policing to the streets on a more personal approach appeared to be the new foundation of policing with the turn of the century approaching.

Sir Robert peel's mission of 'maintain peace by peaceful methods' appeared to be the new future of American policing (Barry, 1979). As with dormant volcanoes, the quiet did not last long and the explosion of police misconduct and corruptive behaviors came to the A Erica's forefront with infamous cases such as Rodney King, NYPD of the 90's, just to name a few.

The problems with law enforcement are the same as they were a hundred years ago. It would be unimaginable to address them all. The change of the century brought about integrity, corruption, scandals, abuse of conduct, And every other societal issue to the forefront. Many blame the left society and politicians. The eye-opening liturgical society has brought about a sense of justice to some;however, the most vast social media outlets leave everlasting scars by repetitive incidences that continue to plague policing, society, and future generations.

# **Chapter 2:**

## Defining corruption and the Code of Silence

The term corruption basically means "utterly broken".  The word was first introduced by Aristotle and later by Cicero who considered the term to identify with "bribe" and "abandonment of good habits".  Hauben (n.d.) describes the totality of corruption:

*He realizes that, "corruption brought by bad habits is so great that it extinguishes, so to speak, the sparks given by nature and allows corresponding vices to spring up and flourish."  Cicero does not explain the cause of 'bad habits' except to point to self interest as "the source of everything pernicious."(Ibid.)  But despite the corruption, "we are born for justice and that what is just is based, not on opinion, but on nature."(L I.28)*

With this definitive answer to what is corruption, we can deduce it is the illegitimate use of power, granted by authority, for a private benefit. Generally, corruption can be scaled into three categories. Petty corruption is typically small favors among people; grand corruption affects government functions; where systemic corruption is so prevalent that it begins to disrupt daily society. For the purposes of this book, the term systemic corruption will be applied to corruption of law enforcement. Systemic corruption is primarily due to a weak process within an organization. For example, law enforcement, correctional officers, and the like. Factors that encourage a systemic system include incentives, discretionary powers, lack of transparency, and a culture of silence.

What is typically referred to as the Blue Code of Silence (also referred to as the Blue Shield or Blue Wall) is an unspoken rule among law enforcement that prohibits the whistleblower of errors, misconduct, or crimes. If an officer is questions about it, ignorance is bliss. The Blue Code is perhaps a contemporary term for police corruption or misconduct. Officers who engage themselves in a discriminating fashion are considered to be corrupt. This includes the harassment and pulling over of a predominant race or nationality. All acts outside of the oath of office should, and perhaps is in many areas, grounds for immediate termination. However, it is unlikely due to the unwritten laws of conduct.

Simply, all law enforcement departments have a written code of conduct that parallels with policy and procedures. New recruits and seasoned officers are generally investigated when civilian complaints are made. Although Federal law exists to strongly extinguish police corruption, there are many gray areas and a legion to protect the Blue. One sticking point that protects wrongdoers is the US Supreme Court Decision that asserts police officers are generally given the benefit of the doubt that they lawfully carried out their day-t-day duties (Saucier v. Katz, 2001).

The history of police corruption goes back many centuries. However current police culture has resulted in barriers between law enforcement and the general community. A secondary set of 'values' within the police family also has evolved over the centuries. The unique demands put on law enforcement officers, including danger and scrutiny, tightens the binding on the family. Thus creating values that lead corrupt officer into isolation, solidarity, and producing an at-war-with-society attitude. Police corruption, for the purposes of this books, is a form of conduct in which law enforcement seek personal gain through bullying, excessive force, abuse of power, selective pursuance, and unjustified arrests. One common form of corruption is soliciting or accepting bribes to protect local drug rings from facing prosecution. Earlier in the book, it was stated how corruption is an entangled web in which once a law enforcement penetrates, it is very unlikely they can find a way out. This is important to notate: Falsifying evidence, and deliberately secure potential convictions based on false evidence, and participating in unapproved procedures is solely unconstitutional.

The sort of corrupt acts that are generally committed by law enforcement officers can be broken down into the following categories:

- Corruption of authority: receiving free drinks, meals, and other gratitude's. ( In my hometown, a local McDonald's often gave deputies free meals; Exxon would give officer's free coffee, another local store would give free doughnuts and coffee)

- Kickbacks: getting paid for referring others to a particular business
- Opportunistic theft:  stealing of items from arrestees, crime victims, and yes, even corpses.
- Shakedowns:  accepting monies or bribes in exchange for not pursuing a criminal violation
- Protection of illegal activity:  accepting payments from owners of illegal organizations such as drug dealers, back room casinos, etc.
- "fixing":  the purposeful withholding of evidence or failing to appear at a court hearing in order to undermine the judicial process
- Direct criminal activities.Framing"  planting or adding evidence, especially in large-level drug cases
- Hazing:  from within law enforcement groups
- Ticket fixing:  cancelling tickets as favors to friends, family, or to protect criminals
- Excessive force:  the use of force beyond the scope of what is truly needed in a particular situation.

Collecting accurate details in police corruption data is difficult, since corruption is only visible to the public when it has been published or brought before a judge.  Where corruptions subsist, the ever precedent Blue Code of Silence also resides.  However, a corruption that is non-typical of this book is labeled as noble cause corruption.

"Noble cause corruption in policing is defined as "corruption committed in the name of good ends, corruption that happens when police officers care too much about their work. It is corruption committed in order to get the bad guys off the streets…the corruption of police power, when officers do bad things because they believe that the outcomes will be good."[2] Examples of noble cause corruption are, planting or fabricating evidence, lying on reports or in court, and generally abusing police authority to make a charge stick" ( Martinelli, 2014).

The preconceived notion that committing crimes in the interest of making the world a better, or safer place, is astonishingly an arrogant viewpoint of an officer's duties to society.

# References


Hauben, J. (n.d.). A basis for democracy in Cicero's: The republic and the Laws. Retrieved from: http://www.columbia.edu/~jrh29/geneva/cicero.

Martinelli, T. (2014). Unconstitutional policing: The ethical challenges in dealing with noble cause corruption. Police Chief. Retrieved from: http://www.policechiefmagazine.org/magazine/index.cfm?fuseaction=display&article_id=1025&issue_id=102006

*Saucier v. Katz*, 533 U.S. 194 (2001), was a United States Supreme Court

CAUSES OF CORRUPTION:
## TOWARDS A CONTEXTUAL THEORY OF CORRUPTION

# Chapter 3:

Procedural misconduct:

Procedures are set forth to ensure employees, in this case, law enforcement offices, understand their roles (within clearly defined limits) within an organization.  In the terms of corruption,  procedural misconduct becomes criminal when state and federal laws are broken.  Procedural misconduct also can become unconstitutional when the rights of others are violated.  Typical descriptions of procedural misconduct are excessive force, physical and verbal harassment, selective enforcement, bribery, sale of drugs, false arrest, malicious prosecution, and many others. Procedural Corruption also involves abusing police powers for personal gain.

Guidelines against misconduct are noted throughout the law books.  The "books" even further gives examples throughout different levels within the department.  Protections can also be located within

State jurisdiction. These laws allow for civil charges to bring up against law enforcement officers for damages. Although both criminally and civilly law enforcement officers are well aware of the circumstances, corruption charges of sis nature are also federally prosecution. Federal laws are applicable to all state, county, and local offices, including those in the correctional field (Colon, 2011). According to section 18 of the US Code, it is illegal to deprive or consprire to deprive another of their constitutional rights; this includes discrimination (Section 18 U.S.C. Section 241, 2000).

It isn't cut and dry to prove procedural misconduct. According to West's Encyclopedia of American Law, significant obstacles such as protections under the law for law enforcement officers (2008) The common obstacle is to prove an officer was acting in a willfully negligent manner and purposely broke the rules of procedural conduct. West's Encyclopedia of American law also states police are protected by the defense immunity--an exemption from penalties and burdens that the ordinary citizen is required to adhere to (2008). Thus, this leeway allows for officers to do their jobs without fear of persecution, to some degree, based on their actions. In the US Supreme Court decision of Saucier V Katz (2001), decisions are generally assertive that officers of the law are given the benefit of the doubt regarding lawfully carrying out their duties.

Misconduct under the oath of law has always been pragmatic. In the latter 1800s, private police such as Pinkertons were commonplace as a heavy arsenal of law enforcement. At that same time, corrupt police vigilantes were part of the racially charged Ku Klux Klan. The foundation of constitutional rights was born from the civil rights act of 1871 that was directed at misconduct (West's

Encyclopedia of American law, 2008). Nearly a century later, the Supreme Court decisions gave way to evidentiary rules, tainted cases, and the establishment of the Miranda Warnings. As contemporary means of policing evolved, the ever probing media outlets have made procedural misconduct a watchful subject. The establishment of better regulations, better training, investigative techniques that were within constitutional constraints, and more control over officers attempted to fix the views the public had of law enforcement officers.

The Encyclopedia of American Law examines the most prolific examples of procedural misconduct as it has led up to contemporary policing.

"The system wide reform in policing was shown in New York City's responses to long-standing brutality, discrimination, and corruption within the New York City Police Department (NYPD). After flirting with civilian review of complaints against police in the 1960s, the city committed to it after video surveillance was used showing police beating citizens after curfew hours in 1988. In 1992, after further complaints of corruption, the Mayor of New York formed a commission to investigate allegations of police corruption. Two years later, the commission concluded that the city had alternated between cycles of corruption. Afterwards, Mayor Giuliani established a permanent, full time Commission to Combat Police Corruption (CCPC) as an entity established separately from the police department. The CCPC monitors the NYPD anti-corruption policies and procedures, conducts audits, and issues public reports" (2008).

Although safeguards have been put in place, not only in New York City, police involved in procedural misconduct has continued to plague the headlines of newspapers and online blogs daily. The National Institute of Justice accepted a report claiming many corruption incidents involving procedural misconduct do not get reported (2004). There is a broad range of examples highlighting procedural misconduct. For the purposes of this book, it is only descriptive. Any cases contained within the text, whether old or current, do not reflect views of the author nor does it contend guilt.

Highly publicized cases in New York, Texas, Detroit, and Cleveland exposed a new trend: police drug corruption ( Farlex, 2014). The author specifies 42 officers arrested from five agencies for cocaine distribution. Farlex (2014) also discussed a 1998 report to the US Congressman Charles Rangel of the federal General Accounting Office that there was a growing trend in theft of drugs from evidence, lies on amounts actually retrieved in arrests, theft of money and drugs from drug dealers, and perjury. Traditionally, the acts of corruption have always been a single incident involving individuals, not a group within same department, as the example above just examined.

## Case examples

*The cases listed from here on throughout the text are used for reporting and statistical research. It does not in any way imply guilt or personal views from the author. Case examples were pulled directly from media outlets, as cited.*

**John Burge - procedural corruption in torture**
John Burge was been into a blue collar family in Chicago. Although he attended college and eventually dropped out, he became a

deck rested Army Veteran with much recognition for heroism and valor. Burge was sworn in 1970 to the office of law enforcement (Chicago tribune, 2011). During his 20 year tenure, he received accommodations during his career, including serving as commander. Within the polished jacket, there was a deep loathsome side. Burge was accused of torturing suspects for over two decades and coercing dozens of fallacious confessions. The Chicago Tribune reported over 200 individuals was in the wake of his corruption (2011). Allegations of torture began to develop in 1972, with a prominent example in 1982 where a defendant received bruises, lacerations, and burns to his chest. Others claim they were beaten into confession by the use of telephone books, slamming arrestee's heads into table, cattle prods, and electrical torture to the genitals of suspects (Chicago Tribune,2011). Excerpts from Burge's trial stated "Burge cites a dismal failure of police leadership" and "how can anyone trust that justice will be served when the justice system has been so defiled" (Chicago Tribune, 2011). Those who were affected by Burge's sadistic tactics received new trials and/or charges were dropped. Burge faced many criminal charges and ultimately was fired in 1993. He served four years.

**Antonio Figueroa and Robert Bayard - violation of civil right**
Two Camden, New Jersey police officers were arrested for falsifying evidence in drug cases in what is expected to have impacted more than 200 cases. The cases involved some individuals serving haphazard jail sentences. Both officers were actively involved with the special operations unit assigned to police hotspots for open air drug markets (Fox News, 2010). According to the report by Fox News, 210 cases were forced to be dropped. Approximately six dozen federal lawsuits are pending stemming from false arrest issues. Figueroa and Bayard face charges of conspiracy to violate the civil rights of a citizen,

which can be punishable of up to the years in prison. Evidence further showed three other officers were involved in depriving individuals of their due process privileges.   The Attorney General for New Jersey told Fox News (2010) that "it places dishonor to the tens of thousands of law enforcement personnel who are out there day and night, basically doing the right thing".  David madden of CBS Philadelphia reported that Robert Bayard was acquitted of charges and Antonio Figueroa was charged three of the five charges (2011).  It is unclear if Bayard has decided to return to law enforcement.  US attorney Fishman was quoted saying " corrupt police officers undermine the dedicated men and women who put their lives on the line everyday and betray the trust the public is entitled to have in those that serve it....we will not hesitate to pursue allegations of this kind of conduct in the future"(CBS, 2011).

## Jennifer Baran - Carnal Knowledge

A former Henrico, Virginia Sheriff's deputy was arrested in late 2013 on three feeling accounts of having carnality knowledge with an inmate (WTVR, 2013).  The attempted flushing of a cell phone by an inmate prompted the discovery of the relationship with Baran. Further investigation led to love letters written to the inmate inside his cell. Sexual encounters were documented between January and April 2012, according to the WTVR news report.  Baran resigned from her position as of May 2012, was arrested, and placed temporarily in the jail she worked for. While as a deputy she was in charge of the jail laundry room.  The Henrico County Undersheriff told WTVR that it is their duty and responsibility to provide a service for these inmates and a deputy having sex with them compromises things (2013). This case is currently under further investigation.

## Correctional officer and inmates - carnal knowledge

This is not secluded to one state, these instances happen every day, everywhere. Taking a look back, Virginia opened an investigation in 1999 to probe into guard-inmate sex at a state prison for women. The ACLU reported on the organizational webpage regarding 25 complaints in nine months from when the prison opened in 1998. Inmate bobinette fearce told the associated press that "tip of the iceberg....in this little cesspool of seductions" (1999). Inmates interviewed by the AP said they were afraid of reporting abuse because of retribution. Authorities in Virginia prepared to make a law carrying a five year maximum sentence for employees taking indecent liberties with female inmate, or male inmates for that matter. Consensual sex is not permitted with inmates because they do not have reserved rights to agree because they are wards of the state. ACLU representatives suggest an all female staff at female institutions to combat this problem; however, it would be impossible because of equal employment laws (1999).

## Undercover in New York - hyper aggression and excessive force

West's Encyclopedia of American Law gives another example of procedural misconduct.

> "The controversy involving the killing of an unarmed man in 1999 created a further hit to the New York police integrity. Four undercover police officers shot Amadou Diallo 41 times after stopping the immigrant while he was in the vestibule of his apartment building. The officers reported he reached into his back pocket. Protests attracted activists such as Susan Sarandon and former New York mayor David Dinkins, who argued the departments so called Aggressive Street Crime Unit, was indeed too aggressive. In 2000, the four officers

were acquitted in a trial that supporters said vindicated them but which critics blame it on lax prosecution" (2008).

Mounting resentment and procedural misconduct leads to massive recourse for law enforcement officers. Police departments, legislatures, and federal governments attempt to look at ways to bring reform to the law enforcement society. Critics argue that corruption is not a new phenomenon. Public policy has been blamed because the emphasis of aggressive policing is forced. Whatever the cause, the finger pointing will continue. Each new headlines, creates further destruction of public ale enforcement.

# Chapter 4:

## Excessive Force

The authority of the police to use force represents one of the most misunderstood powers granted to representatives of government. Police officers are authorized to use both psychological and physical force to apprehend criminals and solve crimes. Alpert and Smith (1994) wrote: The United States Civil Rights Commission reviewed police use of force in the early 1980s and reported:Police officers possess awesome powers. They perform their duties under hazardous conditions and with the vigilant public eye upon them. Police officers are permitted only a margin of error in judgment under conditions that impose high degrees of physical and mental stress. Their general responsibility to preserve peace and enforce the law carries with it the power to arrest and to use force-even deadly force (p. 481-482).

Alpert and Smith continued to stipulate that police are not required to report the amount of physical force required to handle situations as they come about.  One of the obvious problems created by a reasonableness standard is determining the appropriate level of reasonableness.

When the first publically alert to excessive force can be contributed to the Rodney King incident in Los Angeles.  Since, the contentious issue of excessive force, use of force, and protective measures has grown in social and media outlets. Without a doubt, it is the most controversial issues in law enforcement.  The occurrence of excessive force continues to climb even with mechanisms, research and new technology is available to combat these issues.  Perhaps, the rise in excessive force rates has climbed because the 'respect' forpolice is down.  When I was younger, we were taught to respect the police.  Today, police receive ridicule and no respect simply because the actions they take is not a totality of the oath they swore to uphold. It is these reminders that determine the overall look into excessive force cases, court-battles, and liabilities that use of force creates.

There's no concrete definition of excessive force. Police have to use force to subdue suspects every day. Reasonable levels of force are guessed by cops on the street, second-guessed by police review boards and sometimes tested in civil lawsuits and criminal prosecutions on a case-by-case basis.  Excessive force is a slippery metaphor: experts say it's any force beyond what's necessary to arrest a suspect and keep police and bystanders safe. There are some moves, like choke holds, which are altogether barred in certain jurisdictions. "'Excessive' will have different meanings in different jurisdictions," says Mark Henriquez, project manager for the National Police Use of Force Database Project at the International Association of Chiefs of Police. (Segan, 2014).  According to Segan, Alison Collins, who wrote a report on police brutality in the U.S. for the group Human Rights Watch, has different numbers. She says the Justice Department receives "12,000 complaints every year of law enforcement abuse," fewer than 50 of which result in convictions — often the fault of the legal system, not the complainants, according to her. It's generally up to cops to weigh whether they're being threatened, whether bystanders are being threatened, and what force the suspect is using to resist arrest, experts said. The goal is to get a suspect to "comply" — to be subdued enough not to resist arrest (2014).In a survey by the Bureau of Justice Statistics (2008), an essential element in law enforcement is the potential for suspect resistance and police use of or threatened use of force. In the Police Public Contact Survey (PPCS), persons who had contact with police during the previous 12 months, whether as a driver in a traffic stop or for some other reason, were asked if the police officer(s) used or threatened to use force against them during the contact. Survey respondents who reported more than one contact during the year were asked about the use or threat of force by police during their most recent contact.

***Summary findings***

- Among persons who had contact with police in 2008, an estimated 1.4% had force used or threatened against them during their most recent contact, which was not statistically different from the percentages in 2002 (1.5%) and 2005 (1.6%).

- Males were more likely than females to have force used or threatened against them during their most recent contact with police during 2008, and blacks were more likely than whites or Hispanics to experience use or threat of force.

- Of persons who had force used or threatened against them by police in 2008, an estimated 74% felt those actions were excessive.

- Of those individuals who had force used or threatened against them in 2008, about half were pushed or grabbed by police. About 19% of persons who experienced the use or threat of force by the police reported being injured during the incident.Among persons experiencing police use or threat of force in 2008, an estimated 22% reported that they argued with, cursed at, insulted, or verbally threatened the police.

- About 12% of those involved in a force incident reported disobeying or interfering with the police.

- Among individuals who had force used or threatened against them in 2008, an estimated 40% were arrested during the incident.

- An estimated 84% of individuals who experienced force or the threat of force felt that the police acted improperly. Of those who experienced the use or threat of force in 2008 and felt the police acted improperly, 14% filed a complaint against the police.

The U.S. Commission on Civil Rights has stated that "…in diffusing situations, apprehending alleged criminals, and protecting themselves and others, officers are legally entitled to use appropriate means, including force." In studies of police use of force there is no single, accepted designation amid the researchers, analysts, or the police.

The International Association of Chiefs of Police (IACP) in its study, *Police Use of Force in America 2001*, defined use of force as "The amount of effort required by police to compel compliance by an unwilling subject." The IACP also identified five components of force: physical, chemical, electronic, impact, and firearm. To some people, though, the mere presence of a police officer can be intimidating and seen as use of force. The Bureau of Justice Statistics (BJS) in *Data Collection on Police Use of Force,* states that "…the legal test of excessive force…is whether the police officer *reasonably* believed that such force was *necessary* to accomplish a legitimate police purpose…" However, there are no universally accepted definitions of "reasonable" and "necessary" because the terms are subjective. A court in one jurisdiction may define "reasonable" or "necessary" differently than a court in a second jurisdiction. More to the point is an understanding of the "improper" use of force, which can be divided into two categories: "unnecessary" and "excessive." The unnecessary use of force would be the application of force where there is no justification for its use, while an excessive use of force would be the application of more force than required where use of force is necessary.

**Excessive force can be a complex issue**
**Roger Owens – Printed with permission**

Many who are not intimately familiar with  the nuances and complexities of law enforcement excessive force issues may be overly influenced by high profile death-involved cases. Excessive force may exist anytime more force is used than is reasonable in the circumstance.  Questions which should be answered are: (1) Why were non-lethal weapons — such as Tasers — not used in some of these situations? (2) What is the appropriate situation to use non-lethal and lethal force, and what are the specific guidelines?

A Use of Force Continuum is a standard that provides law enforcement with use-of-force guidelines. Such models clarify the complex subject of force by law officers. Various agencies have developed models; there is no universal standard. They are often presented in "stair-step" fashion, with each force level commensuratewith subject resistance. An officer need not progress through each force level before reaching the final level. One use-of-force progression model is: (1) physical presence, (2) verbal commands, (3) empty-handed submission techniques, (4) intermediate weapons (baton, pepper spray, Taser, beanbag rounds, Mace, etc.) and (5) lethal force.

Case law also controls use-of-force policies and practices. The U.S Supreme Court, in Graham v. Conner (1989), held that "When engaged in situations where the use of force is necessary, a law enforcement officer must act as other reasonable officers would have acted in a similar, tense, rapidly evolving situation." This is known as the "Reasonable Person" standard.

While there is a degree of consensus on the use of the standard, there is no universally accepted, technical definition. The standard is a composite of a relevant community's judgment as to how a typical law enforcement representative of that community should behave when confronting situations that might pose a threat or harm to law officer(s) and others. What is excessive force? The Greenville Police Department General Order on Force Response identifies three elements which must be present to justify lethal force:

1. Ability: The assailant must have the means to inflict death or serious injury to another.
2. Opportunity: The assailant must be close enough to use any weapon(s), instrument(s), or physical ability which would inflict death or serious physical injury to the officer or another person.
3. Jeopardy: Both ability and opportunity must be present at the same time, and serious and real intent to cause death and serious physical injury is being demonstrated. Thus excessive force may be defined as "Physical force that exceeds the degree permitted by law, or the policies and guidelines of the law enforcement agency." Excessive force may be presumed when the officer continues to apply physical force after the person has been rendered incapable of (or not actively) resisting arrest.

U.S. Supreme Court decision Thomas v. Nugent (2014) exemplifies the complexity of some excessive force cases. A Louisiana police officer, Scott Nugent, tasered Baron Pikes, at least eight times within 14 minutes, with 50,000 volts of electric shock, while Mr. Pikes was handcuffed and lying on the ground — for not responding to commands to get up and walk to the patrol car. Mr. Pikes died shortly thereafter. Officer Nugent was tried for manslaughter and found not guilty. Pike's son sued in federal court for civil rights damages, and the 5th U.S. Circuit Court of Appeals ruled that the officer was entitled to qualified immunity and could not be sued for allegedly violating the civil rights of the handcuffed prisoner. In May 2014, the U.S. Supreme Court over-ruled the 5th Circuit's decision, and required the appellate court to give the proper weight to evidence offered by those suing the police. A Taser is designed to be a non-lethal weapon, but obviously can be lethal if used irresponsibly.

Ultimately law enforcement will reflect the values of the community and law enforcement leadership. The reasonable person standard is reduced to an abstract idea when legal justice proceedings as well as community sentiment are not reasonable. Shooting an unarmed person 11 times when he is 20 to 30 feet away and no active threat, as officer Darren Wilson apparently did in Ferguson, Mo., is not reasonable. All officers who kill suspects should *not* be tried, butthose who kill *unarmed* suspects in such a manner should be.

## Case Examples

### Hammond, Indiana

A 14 year-old boy perhaps carries a viral video that shows how his family was victims of excessive force by the Hammond, Indiana police. It is important to note, that the video did not begin until some thirteen minutes after the initial stop. This leaves to question the entire story; nonetheless, it is evident that the overall picture was not looked at when the police pushed their way into the car. Allegedly, the driver of the car was pulled and presented her identification as requested. The passenger did not have an ID on him. The passenger did present a ticket he had as form of identification; however, the on-scene officer felt it was not a justified form of identification. After several verbal attempts to have the passenger exit the car, the second police officer smashed the passenger side window as glass flew across two minors in the back seat. Lastly, he was tasered and removed forcibly from the vehicle. I have seen the video several times. There is a two-sided issue here. First, Indiana does have a law that requires persons pulled over to identify themselves. In which the driver successfully did. The infraction however, was on the passenger for not wearing a seatbelt. According to the article written by Lutz, Relerford, and Wojciechowski, The complaint alleges that the police had no reason to use such force, stating:

> *The actions of the individual defendants created a reasonable apprehension of imminent harm by and constituted harmful or offensive contact with each Plaintiff. The actions of the individual defendants were objectively unreasonable under the circumstances and were undertaken intentionally with malice, willfulness, and reckless indifference to the rights and safety of Plaintiffs.*

In response, the Hammond Police Department released a statement arguing instead that the officers "were at all times acting in the interest of the officer's safety and in accordance with Indiana law." (2014). According to the U.S. Supreme Court in *Pennsylvania v. Mimms*, the police have the authority to ask a driver to step outside the vehicle during the course of a stop. The Court has also held in *Maryland v. Wilson* that an officer may order passengers to get out of the car pending completion of the stop. The purpose of this request is to protect both the driver and the officer from the surrounding traffic, and "diminishes the possibility, otherwise substantial, that the driver can make unobserved movements; this, in turn, reduces the likelihood that the officer will be the victim of an assault (Lutz, Relerford, and Wojciechowski, 2014).

It is interesting to establish a foundation in this particular case. Although state law allows police to request identification from passengers inside a car that they've stopped, two Indianapolis officers shouldn't have arrested a man for refusing to identify himself when there was no reasonable suspicion he'd done anything wrong. The Indiana Court of Appeals addressed that issue in a six-page opinion today in *Adam Starr v. State of Indiana*, No. 49A04-0912-CR-677, which overturned a ruling by Marion Superior Judge David Certo. In September 2009, officers from the Indianapolis Metropolitan Police Department arrested Adam Starr for refusing to identify him, a Class C misdemeanor as defined by Indiana Code 34-28-5-3.5. Two officers pulled over a vehicle driven by Starr's girlfriend, who'd made an illegal turn. After determining her identity, the officers questioned Starr about his identity. He denied having any ID, claimed he couldnot remember his Social Security number, and said his name was "Mr. Horrell."

According to Hoskins, after police found a photo ID in the vehicle, he claimed the person pictured was his "identical cousin." Officers determined his real identify and that an active protective order prohibited any contact between Starr and his girlfriend, and police arrested him on charges of privacy invasion and refusal to identify himself (2010).  Starr was acquitted on the privacy invasion charge, but convicted on the refusal charge and received an eight-day sentence in the Marion County Jail. On appeal, he argued that the statute criminalizing the refusal to identify oneself is directed toward the driver of a vehicle stopped for a traffic offense and not to the passengers. The appellate court determined that the legislature had not categorically excluded passengers from the statute's scope and that police are able to detain passengers in certain circumstances during and as a result of those stops. But this case didn't present circumstances, such as resistance, that allowed the police conduct. Though most will comply with an officer's request, the police power to request and obtain this identification isn't unlimited, the appellate court pointed out. "In the context of a traffic stop for a vehicular violation, the Good Faith Belief statute provides for detention of a person who, in the 'good faith' belief of the officer, 'has committed an infraction or ordinance violation,'" Judge L. Mark Bailey wrote. "The Refusal to Identify Self statute then criminalizes the refusal to comply with an officer's lawful request under the statute authorizing detention. In this instance, although Starr was 'stopped' when the vehicle in which he was a passenger was 'stopped,' there is no showing that Starr was stopped as a consequence of any conduct on his part. There was no reasonable suspicion that he had committed an infraction orordinance violation, giving rise to an obligation to identify himself upon threat of criminal prosecution." As a result, he didn't fall within the scope of the state statute and his conviction must be reversed, the court ruled.

But the question of whether the police are authorized to remove a passenger from a vehicle must be balanced against whether the officer's use of force was justified. According to the U.S. Court of Appeals for the Seventh Circuit in *Lester v. City of Chicago*, an officer's use of force is unconstitutional if, "judging from the totality of circumstances at the time of the arrest, the officer used greater force than was reasonably necessary to make the arrest."

Thus, the Hammond police officers must establish, based upon the totality of the circumstances leading up to and concurrent with the arrest, that their actions were both *reasonable* and *necessary*. Several factors are pertinent to this analysis. The basis for whether excessive force was used is derived from a three-part test articulated by the Supreme Court in *Graham v. Connor*. This objective test examines:

1. The severity of the crime at issue;
2. Whether the suspect posed an immediate threat to the safety of the officers or others; and
3. Whether the suspect was actively resisting arrest or attempting to

evade arrest by flight.

If the Hammond police can successfully show that their decision to break into the car to remove Jones was justified, either because they perceived he was reaching for a weapon or engaging in threatening behavior, they will have an easier time in court defending this incident, although there is little evidence from the video thatbe the case.  However, what if the passenger had respectfully rolled his window down further, or perhaps, slowly moved. What if the passenger had stepped out as asked? Would this have gone any further?

**Knoxville, Tenn.**
**© News Sentinel.  All Rights Reserved.  Reprinted with permission**

Knoxville Police Chief David Rausch should be commended for crushing a cover-up among his officers regarding a brutal beating in February of a homeless man in North Knoxville.

The three officers involved in the beating have confessed, entering guilty pleas last week to misdemeanor assault and felony official oppression charges. Former Knoxville Police Department officers Jeremy Jinnett, Ty Compton and Chris Whitfield face an Aug. 8 sentencing hearing.

The officers beat a homeless man, Michael Allen Mallicoat, after he had been detained and hog-tied at the intersection of Grainger and Luttrell avenues on Feb. 9.

Other officers and supervisors attempted to cover up the incident, which was captured on in-cruiser video and witnessed by people who live in the North Knoxville neighborhood where the incident occurred. One of the supervisors, Lt. Brad Anders, also is a Knox County commissioner.

Internal Affairs Unit Capt. Kenny Miller investigated the incident, and his report shows KPD supervisors tried to protect the officers involved. Capt. Eve Thomas, Sgt. John Shelton and Anders approvedwhat turned out to be deceitful use-of-force reports without having viewed the incriminating video. Thomas received an oral reprimand, while Anders and Shelton received written reprimands.

Officers Richard Derrick White and Nicholas Ferro also were found at fault in Miller's probe of excessive force against Mallicoat, while the original two responding officers to the scene that day — Haley Starr and Cynthia LeeAnn DeMarcus — were labeled in Miller's report as willfully blind and deceitful. Each was suspended without pay.

"It's just completely inappropriate," Rausch said at a news conference about the incident. "I feel sorry it happened. We're sorry to Mr. Mallicoat this happened. I tell people all the time, unfortunately we have to recruit from the human race."

The officers who beat Mallicoat certainly should bear the brunt of the blame for the incident, and the three should receive jail time, but those who would have given them a free pass also have violated their duty to the public. Anders' participation in particular is disturbing. As a county commissioner, he should be held to a higher standard of behavior. His participation in the cover-up is without question a stain on his service, both as a police officer and an elected official. At the very least, Anders needs to issue a public apology for his role in this episode of police brutality.

The vast majority of police officers are conscientious and dedicated public servants who do not let the considerable stresses of the job lead them to brutalize people taken into custody. A few, however, abuse their power, and there should be a zero-tolerance policy for them. Rausch is sending the right message to his troops and to the general public — brutality will not be tolerated. Knoxvillians should be proud of their police chief and confident that in the future he will make sure the officers under his command conduct themselves in a humane and honorable fashion.

In addition to the dash cam video, KPD interview more than half a dozen witnesses of the incident. The witnesses were at various locations on Grainger Avenue but all seven saw different parts of the arrest of Mallicoat, from the punching to the kicking to the slamming of his head on the patrol car. In the summary provided by KPD, witness Elliot Granju said "they dropped him on the concrete and then they just started beating him and hitting him and kicking him and they were stomping on him." While other neighbors saw the aftermath of the incident.

"The pool of blood was there and the blood staining on the concrete was there for about a week," said Lynda Evans, a resident of the neighborhood. In the summary it says because the witnesses were able to observe force from a distance, it had to have been obvious to the officers standing right there. But Evans says she understands the tough job of KPD officers. "This is not an easy black and white situation, our police are essential to us. On the other hand we don't need police brutality so I know there is a fine, fine line that police walk and it's very difficult when someone is very out of control,"

Evans said. Four of the officers were reprimanded for failing to stop the actions of the others, actions that have some in the neighborhood wary of police."I want people to understand in our community a lot of people don't trust the police and I think it's time to fix that," said Ricky Stallings, a resident of the neighborhood as well as the director of the Neighborhood Watch. Stallings emphasized he is sad they have lost officers in the area when they are so desperately needed but says more should be done to help the community."If anything we need a stronger support in this community," Stallings said. "We need more officers that show they care.

## Petersburg, Virginia

Witnesses on the scene were filming them, and it appears once the cops realized it, they more than lost their cool and attacked them for filming. At one point you can see an officer reach up over the porch and put one man in a headlock. The video was published by NBC 12 and was filmed in Petersburg, VA on July 8, 2o14: Cell phone video shows JaQuan Fisher, 17, standing on his own front porch recording the arrests happening on Rome Street. In the video, an officer is heard saying, "Unless you want me to take your phone from you," before there is a struggle and video goes to black. "I was right here. I pulled out my phone," JaQuan said, pointing to where he was standing. "Petersburg Police had just busted several people at a home next door. They were handcuffing the suspects in front of Fisher's home. He walked out onto the porch and his cousin—who was one of the people being arrested–yelled, "Start recording.""[The officer] came off the porch and said, 'You want me to take your phone?'" Fisher said. "I put my phone in my pocket and then when he tried to take my phone, I guess he thought he was going to get my phone and he shoved me. I shoved him back."The agency pointed out Debra Fisher was charged with obstruction and found guilty in a court of law. The agency went on to say, "All subject resistance reports are reviewed by the department and no officers were disciplined or transferred to other positions within the department because of the case. Officers are trained to use the least amount of force. No complaints have been filed and the event happened nearly 3 months ago. Officers do not hinder the public from recording video as it is their right to do so."

## St. Petersburg, Florida

A St. Petersburg police officer was fired after a review board said he used excessive force during a DUI arrest. Officer Kenneth Pienik also tried to hide dash cam video of the arrest, according to a report released by the St. Petersburg Police Department. The arrest took place on January 31. According to the report, officers found a man sleeping in a running car in the North Shore Park parking lot. They woke him up, suspected he was intoxicated, and called the DUI unit, which Officer Pienik worked with. Pienik arrived and positioned his car so the dash cam would record his investigation. According to the report, the DUI suspect became "uncooperative" and "argumentative," and asked for a supervisor.

At that point, video showed Pienik losing his temper, saying "I am my supervisor."He then used profanity, flung his clipboard away, and threw the man to the ground. The video also shows what appeared to be Pienik using a stun gun on the man while he was on the ground. The report goes on to detail a meeting with Pienik and an assistant state attorney. The report says Pienik told the attorney the dash cam video was "of no evidentiary value and it would 'disappear.'" The state attorney reported the comment to a supervisor, and the office issued a request for it. The report said Pienik then provided video of the suspect being transported, but not of the arrest.

**Portland, Oregon**



A Multnomah County jury ruled Monday that the city of Portland must pay a 27-year-old man nearly $306,000 after police used a stun gun and pepper spray on him, punched him and dog-piled on top of him before they unlawfully arrested him for criminally trespassing on a downtown sidewalk. The money represents one of the bigger jury awards in recent excessive force cases against police, who. are revising their Taser policy after federal investigators found officers often misused stun guns, especially against mentally ill people.

Jurors found that police falsely arrested, battered and maliciously prosecuted Gallagher Smith after he quarreled with a doorman on Nov. 13, 2010, at the Aura nightclub on West Burnside Street. The doorman told Smith he'd have to wait at the end of a long line again even though he'd just been in the club and had gotten a stamp on his hand before stepping outside. The doorman eventually flagged down police. Smith walked away from the club as police followed. Smith questioned police about what law prevented him from standing on a public sidewalk. Both sides agreed that police wouldn't explain why. As officers tried to handcuff Smith, he pulled his arms into his chest. Smith said he was immediately punched in the face. The scuffle that ensued was his attempt to protect himself, he said.

But one of the officers testified during the four-day trial that Smith clenched his fists from the beginning and his body language indicated he was looking to pick a fight. Smith never hit or kickedpolice, his attorneys said. Officer Patrick Johnson fired his Taser at Smith, but the probes didn't pierce his skin. Officer Sean McFarland then used his Taser and hit his mark. Police said Smith was defying orders to stay on the ground. Johnson pepper-sprayed Smith twice and police punched him in the back before half a dozen officers piled on top of him. Smith was handcuffed with his feet tied to his wrists and charged with criminal trespass, interfering with a police officer and resisting arrest.

Smith said he had smoked pot and was drinking that night, but his attorneys argued that had no bearing the officers' overreaction. Smith said he wasn't ignoring police orders, but simply trying to crawl out of traffic after he ended up in the street during the encounter. He suffered a black eye, road rash on his face and Taser marks on his abdomen. He also was diagnosed with post traumatic stress disorder and said he's lost his trust in police. Jurors awarded nearly $16,000 in legal fees for his criminal defense, medical bills and counseling. They also awarded $290,000 for his pain and suffering. After the verdict, juror Patty Smith said police were wrong to rough up and arrest Smith, and most of the verdict was an acknowledgement of his lasting psychological injuries. In June 2011, a jury found Gallagher Smith not guilty of all criminal charges. But a judge found him guilty of second-degree attempted criminal trespass, a violation similar to a traffic citation and not a crime.

During closing arguments, Smith's attorney Jason Kafoury contended that police hoped to win a criminal conviction against his client to forestall a lawsuit when they learned Smith had a clean record and they were wrong to rough him up. Deputy City Attorney

David Landrum told jurors that he accepts the earlier decision byJudge Youlee You that police didn't have probable cause to arrest Smith. But Landrum said police try to use their best judgment during difficult situations. "We get these ideas that police officers are these automatons -- they're robots, right?" Landrum said. "... They're just people, and we put them in this position when you're having trouble, when something is going wrong, it's as simple as ordering a pizza. You dial them up. ... They've got to figure out what's going on and 'What do I do about it?'" The Police Bureau's internal affairs unit investigated the confrontation and cleared the officers of wrongdoing, police spokesman Sgt. Pete Simpson said after the verdict. Kafoury applauded Smith for courage in standing up to police when he asked them what law he was breaking by standing on the sidewalk. "Some of you may be wondering '...Why don't you just say, 'Yes, sir,' and keep on moving?" Kafoury said. "There's one thing that history has proved: If we don't defend our rights, we lose them." After the verdict, Smith hugged his attorneys. He summed up his feelings in one word: "Relieved." This article has been revised to reflect the following correction:

*A jury, not a judge, found Gallagher Smith not guilty of all criminal charges. A judge found him guilty of the non-criminal violation of attempted second-degree criminal trespass.*

**Police brutality or "reasonable force"? Research review and statistics on law enforcement, violence and the role of race - John Wihbey**



Allegations of the use of excessive force by police departments in America continue to generate media headlines, more than two decades after the 1992 Los Angeles riots brought the issue to mass public attention and prompted law enforcement reforms. In Ferguson, Mo., a St. Louis suburb, the fatal shooting of teenager Michael Brown by a police officer in August 2014 has triggered unrest and protests. In New York, the July death of Eric Garner because of the apparent use of a "chokehold" by an officer has also sparked outrage. This follows other recent incidents and controversies, including an April 2014finding by the U.S. Department of Justice, following a two-year investigation, that the Albuquerque, N.M., police department "engages in a pattern or practice of use of excessive force, including deadly force, in violation of the Fourth Amendment."

Surveys in recent years with minority groups — Latinos and African-Americans, in particular — suggest that confidence in law enforcement is relatively low, and large portions of these communities believe police are likely to use excessive force on suspects. A 2014 Pew Research Center survey confirms stark racial divisions in response to the Ferguson police shooting, as well, while Gallup provides insights on historical patterns of distrust. According to a Pew/ *USA Today* poll conducted in August 2014, Americans of all races collectively "give relatively low marks to police departments around the country for holding officers accountable for misconduct, using the appropriateamount of force, and treating racial and ethnic groups equally."

Still, from a police perspective, law enforcement in the United States continues to be dangerous work — America has a relatively higher homicide rate compared to other developed nations, and has many more guns per capita. Citizens seldom learn of the countless incidents where officers choose to hold fire and display restraint under extreme stress. Some research has shown that even well-trained officers are not consistently able to fire their weapon in time before a suspect holding a gun can raise it and fire first; this makes split-second judgments, even under "ideal" circumstances, exceptionally difficult. But as the FBI points out, police departments and officers sometimes do not handle the aftermath of incidents well in terms of transparency and clarity, even when force was reasonably applied, fueling public confusion and anger.

How common are such incidents, both lethal and non-lethal, in the United States? Has there been progress in America? Without a doubt, training for police has become more standardized and professionalized in recent decades. A 2008 paper in the *Northwestern University Law Review* provides useful background on the evolving legal and policy history relating to the use of force by police and the "reasonableness" standard by which officers are judged. Related jurisprudence is still being defined, most recently in the 2007 *Scott v. Harris* decision by the U.S. Supreme Court. But inadequate data and reporting — and the challenge of uniformly defining excessive versus justified force — make objective understanding of trends difficult.

For perhaps the best overall summary of police use-of-force issues, see "A Multi-method Evaluation of Police Use of Force Outcomes: FinalReport to the National Institute of Justice," a 2010 study conducted by some of the nation's leading criminal justice scholars.

## Published federal statistics

The Justice Department releases statistics on this and related issues, though these datasets are only periodically updated: It found that in 2008, among people who had contact with police, "an estimated 1.4% had force used or threatened against them during their most recent contact, which was not statistically different from the percentages in 2002 (1.5%) and 2005 (1.6%)." In terms of the volume of citizen complaints, the Justice Department also found that there were 26,556 complaints lodged in 2002; this translates to "33 complaints per agency and 6.6 complaints per 100 full-time sworn officers." However, "overall rates were higher among large municipal police departments, with 45 complaints per agency, and 9.5 complaints per 100 full-time sworn officers." In 2011, about 62.9 million people had contact with the police.

In terms of the use of lethal force, aggregate statistics on incidents of all types are difficult to obtain from official sources. Some journalists are trying to rectify this; and some data journalists question what few official national statistics are available. The Sunlight Foundation explains some of the data problems, while also highlighting databases maintained by the Centers for Disease Control (CDC). The available data, which does not paint a complete national picture, nevertheless raise serious questions, Sunlight notes:

[A]ccording to the CDC, in Oklahoma the rate at which black people are killed per capita by law enforcement is greater than anywhere else in the country. That statistic is taken from data collected for the years 1999-2011. During that same time period, Oklahoma's rate forall people killed by law enforcement, including all races, is second only to New Mexico. However, Oklahoma, the District of Columbia, Nevada and Oregon are all tied for the rate at which people are killed. (The CDC treats the District of Columbia as a state when collecting and displaying statistics.) In Missouri, where Mike Brown lived and died, black people are killed by law enforcement twice as frequently as white people. Nationwide, the rate at which black people are killed by law enforcement is 3 times higher than that of white people.

The FBI publishes statistics on "justifiable homicide" by law enforcement officers: The data show that there have been about 400 such incidents nationwide each year. But news investigations suggest that the rates of deadly force usage are far from uniform. For example, Los Angeles saw an increase in such incidents in 2011, while Massachusetts saw more officers firing their weapon over the period 2009-2013.

**Academic estimates**

A 2008 study from Matthew J. Hickman of Seattle University, Alex R. Piquero of the University of Maryland and Joel H. Garner of the Joint Centers for Justice Studies reviewed some of the best studies and data sources available to come up with a more precise national estimate for incidents of non-lethal force. They note that among 36 different studies published since the 1980s, the rates of force asserted vary wildly, from a high of more than 30% to rates in the low single digits. The researchers analyze Police-Public Contact Survey (PPCS) data and Bureau of Justice Statistics Survey of Inmates in Local Jails(SILJ) data and conclude that an estimated 1.7% of all contacts result in police threats or use of force, while 20% of arrests do. Researchers continue to refine analytical procedures in order to make more accurate estimates based on police reports and other data.

## Characteristics of suspects

Research has definitively established that "racial profiling" by law enforcement exists — that persons of color are more likely to be stopped by police. But while the cases of Rodney King in 1991 and Amadou Diallo in 1999 heightened the country's awareness of race and policing, research has not uniformly corroborated the contention that minorities are more likely, on average, to be subject to acts of police force than are whites. A 2010 paper published in the *Southwestern Journal of Criminal Justice* reviewed more than a decade's worth of peer-reviewed studies and found that while many studies established a correlation between minority status and police use of force, many other studies did not — and some showed mixed results.

Of note in this research literature is a 2003 paper, "Neighborhood Context and Police Use of Force," that suggests police are more likely to employ force in higher-crime neighborhoods generally, complicating any easy interpretation of race as the decisive factor in explaining police forcefulness. The researchers, William Terrill of Northeastern University and Michael D. Reisig of Michigan State University, found that "officers are significantly more likely to use higher levels of force when encountering criminal suspects in high crime areas and neighborhoods with high levels of concentrated disadvantage independent of suspect behavior and other statistical controls." Terrill and Reisig explore several hypothetical explanations and ultimately conclude:Embedded within each of these potential explanations is the influence of key sociodemographic variables such as race, class, gender, and age. As the results show, when these factors are considered at the encounter level, they are significant. However, the race (i.e., minority) effect is mediated by neighborhood context. Perhaps officers do not simply label minority suspects according to what Skolnick (1994) termed "symbolic assailants," as much as they label distressed socioeconomic neighborhoods as potential sources of conflict.

In studying the Seattle and Miami police departments, the authors of the 2010 National Institute of Justice report also conclude that "non-white suspects were less likely to be injured than white suspects … where suspect race was available as a variable for analysis. Although we cannot speculate as to the cause of this finding, or whether it is merely spurious, it is encouraging that minority suspects were not *more likely* to be injured than whites."

**Use of Tasers and other weapons**

A 2011 report from the National Institute of Justice, "Police Use of Force, Tasers and Other Less-Lethal Weapons," examines the effectiveness and health outcomes of incidents involving CEDs (conducted energy devices), the most common of which is the Taser. The report finds that: (1) Injury rates vary widely when officers use force in general, ranging from 17% to 64% for citizens and 10% to 20% for officers; (2) Use of Tasers and other CEDs can reduce the statistical rate of injury to suspects and officers who might otherwise be involved in more direct, physical conflict — an analysis of 12 agencies and more than 24,000 use-of-force cases "showed the odds of suspect injury decreased by almost 60% when a CED was used"; and (3) A review of fatal Taser incidents found that many involved multiple uses of the device against the suspect in question.

Other recent research has documented trends in the use of non-lethal force by officers in recent years, concluding that CED use has indeed been on the rise, while the use of hands and batons has declined.

**Further reading**: The coverage of such incidents by mass media has been studied by researchers, some of whom have concluded that the press has often distorted and helped justify questionable uses of force. A 2012 study in the Criminal Justice Policy Review analyzed the patterns of behavior of one large police department — more than 1,000 officers — and found that a "small proportion of officers are responsible for a large proportion of force incidents, and that officers who frequently use force differ in important and significant ways from officers who use force less often (or not at all)." Other research also finds that officers with more experience and education may be less likely to use force, while a review of case studies suggests that specific training programs and accountability structures can lower the use of violence by police departments. Finally, survey data continue to confirm the existence of undercurrents of racism and bias in America, despite demonstrable social progress; a 2014 Stanford study shows how awareness of higher levels of black incarceration can prompt greater support among whites for tougher policing and prison programs.

- See more at: http://journalistsresource.org/studies/government/criminal-justice/police-reasonable-force-brutality-race-research-review-statistics#sthash.JLlLNK8C.dpuf

## Discussion

A fourth amendment inquiry would be a wholly objective of whether the "totality of the circumstances" justified the officer's actions. The cases above only reflect a mere handful of the excessive force issues that are out there in contemporary society. In Johnson V. Gleck (1973), the officer must consider, along with other reason, whether or not excessive force was necessitated in good-faith. This good faith effort would be to maintain or restore the discipline of a suspect(s). These courts have applied this standard mechanically-to the claims of inmates, pretrial detainees, suspects and free citizens alike-regardless of the surrounding circumstances or the specific constitutional right implicated by the use of force. The normal consequence of this practice has been to produce an intangible, lawful right, to be liberated of extreme power.

Resources

Alpert G. & Smith, W. (1994). How Reasonable Is the Reasonable Man: Police. *Journal of Criminal Law*

    *and Criminology, 85*(2), 481-501. doi:00914169/94/8502-0481

*Bureau of Justice Statistics*. (2011, June). Retrieved from Bureau of Justice Statistics:

    http://www.bjs.gov/

CBS. (2014, October 10). Lawsuit: Ind. police used excessive force in traffic stop. Hammond, Indiana.

    Retrieved from http://www.cbsnews.com/news/lawsuit-indiana-police-used-excessive-force-in-

    traffic-stop/

Fox. (2014, August 8). SPPD: Officer fired for excessive force, attempted cover-up. Tampa, FL. Retrieved

    from http://www.myfoxtampabay.com/story/26235627/2014/08/08/officer-fired-for-

    excessive-force-attempted-cover-up

Freyermuth, R. W. (1987). Rethinking excessive force. *Duke Law Journal*, 692-711.

Graham v. Conner, 87-6571 (The United States Court of Appeals October 3, 1988).

Green, A. (2012, December 10). City of Portland must pay $306,000 to man in excessive force case.

    (Oregonian, Ed.) Portland, OR, USA. Retrieved from

    http://www.oregonlive.com/portland/index.ssf/2012/12/city_of_portland_must_pay_3060.htm

Johnson v. Glick, 481 F.2d 1028 (United States Court of Appeals June 29, 1973).

Lester v. City of Chicago, 86-2008 (United States Court of Appeals; Seventh Court December 17, 1987).

Maryland v. Wilson, 95-1268 ( court of special appeals of maryland February 19, 1997).

Owen, R. (2014, October 10). *Excessive force can be a complex issue*. Retrieved from Geenville
Online:

http://www.greenvilleonline.com/story/opinion/contributors/2014/10/10/excessive-force-
can-

complex-issue/17046729/

Pennsylvania v. Mimms, 76-1830. (The Supreme Court of Pennsyclvania December 5, 1977).

Segan, S. (2014, July 14). What Is Excessive Force? USA. Retrieved from

http://abcnews.go.com/US/story?id=96509

Solomon, B. (2014, June 23). Group to rally following arrest of Petersburg teen. Petersburg, VA:
NBC 12.

Retrieved from http://www.nbc12.com/story/25773571/group-to-rally-following-arrest-
of-

petersburg-teen

Starr v. State of indiana, 49A04-0912-CR-677 (Court of Appeals of Indiana June 22, 2010).

Thomas v. Nugent, 12-30527 (United States Court of Appeals, Fifth Circuit. July 1, 2014).

Knoxville Sentenil. (2013, June 10). 3 former officers take plea deals; dashcam video released in

excessive force  case. Knoxville, Tennessee, USA. Retrieved from

http://www.wate.com/story/22550959/3-

former-officers-take-plea-deals-dashcam-video-released-in-excessive-force-case

Wihbey, J. (2014).  Police brutality or "reasonable force"? Research review and statistics on law

enforcement, violence and the role of race. *Journalists Resource.*

Retrievedfrom:http://journalistsresource.org/studies/government/criminal-justice/police-

reasonable-force-brutality-race-research-review-statistics#sthash.JLlLNK8C.dpuf

# Chapter 5:

Negligence

Case Examples

REPORT: FAMILY SUES FAIRFAX COUNTY POLICE
DEPARTMENT FOR $12 MILLION FOR GROSS NEGLIGENCE
IN 2013 FATAL SHOOTING

M. Barton, Patch.com © 2014 patch.com All rights reserved.
Reprinted with permission

The longtime partner of a man who died after being shot by a Fairfax County police officer is suing the police department, according to a report by The Washington Post.

Maura Harrington is suing the department, the chief of police and three unnamed officers for gross negligence and is seeking $12 million related to the Aug. 29, 2013 incident that left John Greer dead. The officer who fired the shot is reportedly on paid desk duty, the Post reported.

The incident took place in Greer's townhouse complex in a Springfield neighborhood.

In the year since John Geer was fatally shot by a Fairfax County police officer, his family has struggled to cope with the sudden loss. His younger daughter, now 14, cried for weeks after the Aug. 29, 2013, incident.

His older daughter, now 18, marks the 29th of every month with some remembrance of her father. For years, he took her to every travel and high school softball practice and game, so his absence was obviousalmost every day. The other fathers of her South County High team walked her onto the field on Senior Night, because hers couldn't be there.

For Geer's partner of 24 years and his parents, the grief was accompanied by waiting, they say. For information. For action. For answers from the prosecutors or police as to why a man who witnesses say was unarmed was shot in front of his home.

Police and federal investigators have not released any information publicly about the case. They have not said whether they think the shooting was justified and have not released the names of the officers involved.

"It's been hell," said Don Geer, John Geer's father. "Frustrating to say the least — not knowing anything and having a feeling of helplessness, sadness, anger. Just wondering what's going on and why nobody would tell us anything."

On Tuesday, Maura Harrington, Geer's longtime partner, sued the Fairfax County police department, the chief and three unnamed officers for gross negligence. The suit is seeking $12 million, but the family also wants "to get answers," said Harrington. "For our daughters. They've lost theirfather."

The Fairfax County police homicide unit investigated the shooting and provided its file to Fairfax Commonwealth's Attorney Raymond F. Morrogh in late 2013. In February, Morrogh said he had an unspecified "conflict of interest" and shipped the case to the U.S. attorney's office in Alexandria for a federal review.
U.S. Attorney Dana J. Boente declined to confirm whether his office is investigating the shooting.

But Geer's family and best friend were interviewed months ago by an assistant U.S. attorney and lawyers from the Justice Department, family members said.

The officer who fired the fatal shot has been on paid desk duty for months, according to police officials. Fairfax Police Chief Edwin C. Roessler Jr. said he spoke to the officer and Geer's father last week, just before the one-year anniversary of the shooting, "letting them know I'm thinking about both of them."

But Roessler declined to release the officer's name, per his department's policy of withholding such information until a criminal investigation is complete. He said he did not know why the county and federal prosecutors have taken so long.

"The stress that it puts everybody under," Roessler said, "not knowing when anything will happen, it's not a good place to be."

There has been no public uproar, no protests over the shooting of John Geer, in part because his family trusted the justice system to do its job, they said.

## 'Way too much'

Harrington is speaking publicly for the first time; the family had declined interview requests for months. "I just felt things were going to work out," Don Geer said. "I don't think you should be out demonstrating. People have their job to do. But a year is enough. Definitely. Way too much."

Don Geer and Jeff Stewart, John Geer's best friend, were standing together, about 70 yards from John Geer's front door, and watched in horror as he was shot. Harrington and her teenage daughters were in a nearby townhouse as police swarmed their Springfield neighborhood.

Geer's family and friend said that as they pleaded with the Fairfax police for help, the officers took no action to assist the wounded man for an hour. When police broke down Geer's front door about 4:30 p.m., officers had to step over the 46-year-old man's body just behind the door. According to an autopsy, he bled to death.

That night, Harrington and her daughters wanted to retrieve belongings and their cat from their home. Police said no. Geer's body was still on the floor at 9 p.m. "I was dealt another blow," Harrington said. "I had no idea he was still in there."

Fairfax police will not discuss their actions before or after the shooting, saying the case is under investigation.

John Geer, a Northern Virginia native, was a graduate of J.E.B. Stuart High School. He liked to hunt and fish, play volleyball, watch the Redskins and his fantasy football scores, and listen to the Grateful Dead and James Taylor.

But spending time with his daughters and their sports activities was his main leisure occupation, Harrington said. His older daughter, Haylea, led South County High to the Virginia state 6A championship last spring. Geer had attended every practice and game but did notlive to see his daughter launch a home run in the state final.

Harrington said she met Geer at a party in 1989. They began dating and moved in together that year, to the townhouse on Pebble Brook Court in the Pohick Hills neighborhood.

Harrington and Geer never married, and by the summer of 2013, Harrington had decided to move out. "Everything was fine," she said. "He wasn't happy about it, but he wasn't outraged. He understood."

But last Aug. 29, after Harrington told him that she had signed a lease for an apartment, Geer erupted. He began drinking, Stewart said, and then throwing Harrington's belongings out onto the small front yard of their townhouse.

Harrington rushed home from Washington, arrived about 2:30 p.m. and found Geer in the front yard, "very upset." "I said, 'You've got to stop this.' We were talking calmly," she said.

## A call to police

Geer went back in the house. Harrington said she walked in, and Geer threw a suitcase down the stairs. "I screamed," she said. "I decided to call the police, have somebody tell him he couldn't do this." She dialed 911 from the kitchen phone. An operator asked her whether there were guns in the house, and she said that Geer had guns for hunting but that they were locked in a safe.

Harrington said she then went back outside, where Geer followed her. Two police officers arrived at 2:40 p.m. Geer spoke to them, then turned and went back inside even as the officers asked him to stayoutside. "He told them he didn't have to come out," Harrington said. "He has every right to stay in his own house, and they're not welcome to come in."

He stood behind a storm door with a screen on the top half and glass on the bottom, his hands resting above his head on the top of the door. The officers aimed their weapons at him from a distance of about 20 feet, photos show. Harrington took the girls to a neighbor's house, and called Stewart and Don Geer. More officers arrived and took up positions around the neighborhood.

Morgan Geer, then 13, opened the neighbor's door and yelled at one officer, "Don't you hurt my daddy!" Harrington said the officer barked at her: "Don't come out. Keep the door closed."

John Geer stood, in a white shirt and shorts, empty-handed, for almost 50 minutes. "He's talking to them very calmly," Stewart said. "All of a sudden," at 3:30 p.m. "he starts lowering his hands. His hands move down the door, level with his face, and the cop shot him once in the chest."

Don Geer said he was "in a state of shock." He said his son's hands "were always above his shoulders. Almost simultaneous, you heard the shot, and he spun around and closed the door."

Officers retrieved Harrington from a neighbor's home, but as she watched, no one went to help Geer, according to the family. "I was saying, 'Why isn't anyone going in there? He's just in there bleeding to death,' " she said.At 4:30 p.m., an armored vehicle with a long battering ram blasted open Geer's door. Geer's body was just inside. A gun in a holster was on a stairway landing not far away, but photos of the blood stains show Geer did not move more than a step or two before collapsing.

The wrongful death lawsuit filed by attorney Michael Lieberman alleges gross negligence and failure to supervise the patrol officer who fired.

If the officer felt Geer was reaching for a weapon, why did he fire only one time, and why did no other officer fire? Lieberman asked.
He also questioned police's failure to summon a trained negotiator to deal with Geer.

# Chapter 6:

Mental illness = Corruption

Thinking about police corruption, there are so many commonalities between actual corruption and predetermining factors of the cause. What I mean is, the levels of PTSD, depression, and hyper-agression are all indicative to corruption. There are no statistics as of this publishing that quantify that statement. However, think about the correlation. The next few chapters will dive into causes of corruption, through a disabling viewpoint, and focus on theories that are comparative to police corruption.

## PTSD

In the recent years, law enforcement related PTSD is as common as military personnel having it. The result is that many years of many levels of PTSD (PTSD can occur at each incident) can cause law officer's to crack. Throughout the training phases of law officers, characteristics are brainwashed into their minds to be strong …while the stage is being set for a break later in the career. As a former correctional officer, the methodology of preparing one's mind to face the daily career altercations is taxing. In the academy, I was taught to never wear my heart on my sleeve, be strong, and never show emotion. Over time, the comradely of fellow correctional officer's becomes the only place where venting of daily events can occur, the erasing of the day's events are a common thing to do, ensuring that the family never hears or is a part of the daily grind is normal in law enforcement. The inability to deal with work stressors such as these can no doubt cause issues later on. Populations of law enforcement officers that are prone to PTSD suffer from a degree of mental illnesses that at some point begins to impact the basic sense of right and wrong. Many officers avoid the onset of symptoms because they will feel as a failure to thepeers, sick, or weak. Further, they fail to seek outside help because mental health personnel as perceived as those who lock people away. Bottom line – law enforcement personnel would most likely be the last to seek out any professional assistance.


According to the American Psychological Association (1980) the symptoms of PTSD can include:

Intense fear

Helplessness

Numb to trauma

Avoidance of stimuli

Sleep disturbances

Irritability

***Hyper vigilance***

***Depression***

***Excessive anger***

Withdrawal

***Alcoholism/Drug Abuse***

Beyond the obvious signs listed previously, the highlighted words are symbolic to this author's theory of PTSD, Depression, Alcoholism, and excess anger/hyper vigilant attitudes that lead to corruption. The following case examples are indicative of this theory.

## Case Example 1:

James Michael Ford (name changed to protect family) was 40 years old when he was captured for robbing three banks in about a 6-month span.  Mr. Ford was a resident of Columbus, Georgia who was facing many issues.  Mr. Ford was prosecuted and served out his time in a Federal penitentiary.  Looking back, Mr. Ford sufferedfrom depression, hyper-aggression, and alcoholism.  What is more important within this text is that Mr. Ford was a former police officer in Virginia.

Mr. Ford was a post-military law enforcement officer who was charismatic and deeply rooted in family values.  At some point, he had applied for a federal position and was denied ultimately because of issues with his wife.  It was said that this refusal started the spiraling into the web of corruption. Mr. Ford began withdrawing into himself and soon files of complaints lined his jacket.  Excessive force, threatening, and assault became the characterization in which Mr. Ford was noted for. After leaving the force, he went to Georgia as part of a job transfer (non- law enforcement). Things did not do as expected and Mr. Ford sank deeper into depression, financial troubles, and alcohol. At some point, Mr. Ford allegedly robs two banks and a Phoenix City, Alabama bank.  His wife eventually turned him in. In examining Mr. Ford's career, lifestyle, and personality, it would become very clear that he suffered from issues beyond those one could see on the outside.  Depression, PTSD, and alcoholism were dark demons that Mr. Ford contemplated with while an officer. The background issues so no exonerate the totality of the crimes; however, it offers insight to a phenomenon that connects PTSD and depression with police corruption.

### Case Example 2:

Minnesota SWAT Officer T. Carson entered an Apple Valley Bank on January 6, 2010 and robbed the bank at gunpoint. Following a string of similar robberies, the police were able to link Officer Carson with other unsolved robberies that had occurred. He was charged with 12 counts of robbery (attempted aggravated and aggravated robbery). Underneath financial problems, PTSD from serving in Iraq, a deceptive wife, and allegations that someone had molested his daughter; Mr. Carson's world seemed to "fall apart" FoxNewss, 2010) and he felt there was no other alternative than to die and leave his wife and child with life insurance money. According to an article by Lemagie, the officer's wife lied about having a form of cancer and threatened suicide if he left her (2010). In a plea agreement, Carson was sought to be sentenced of 9-10 years. The lawyer requested leniency as the defender for Mr. Carson stated "Can you imagine going through all of that, all at once" (Lemagie, 2010). Mr. Carson was diagnosed with PTSD from a 2004 mortar attack and major depressive disorder.

### Case Example 3:

A Hartford police officer was charged in a bank robbery attempt in 1994. The officer brought in a briefcase and ordered teller to give to the manager. He never asked for any money, however, the Officer was described as having marital and financial troubles. During the trial, the officer was diagnosed with PTSD and the psychologists felt the officer was unaware of his actions (Pazniokas, 1994). Furhter, the officer's PTSD was diagnosed from being involved in on-duty shootings during his career. The defense argued that the officer was suicidal and this attempt was nothing more than a cry for help. The prosecutor in this case argued the officer knew what he was doing. The jury was deadlock.

**Case Example 4:**

A former Wisconsin police officer was convicted in 2010 of bank robbery while on the force. He was sentenced to nine years. At the time of the incident, Officer Brooke was 44 years old suffering from pain killer addiction and a distraught divorce (Vielmetti, 2014). The former officer held a gun to woman's head threatening to shoot her if she did not open the vault. That woman happened to be Brooks' wife. Mr. Brooks had been decorated as officer of the year in 2002 and serviced as a student resource officer in a local high school. PTSD was not noted as a concurrent issue, however, severe stress, financial and personal relationships remains a common back drop in this case as well.

O'Hara and Levenson suggest that the stigma related o mental illness is the leading factor in why many police officials are reluctant to the idea that police work ultimately can lead to PTSD (n.d.). This unfortunate misinformation is a direct result of the American public viewpoint that mental illness is dangerous. O'Hara and Levenson further indicate that factors such s hyper-aggression, traumatic brain injury, and substance abuse are part of PTSD diagnosis' (n.d.).

The average law enforcement career is essentially 20 years. Twenty years of repetitive violence, disturbing calls, and a significant stress to social and emotional relationships/ other factors that correlate with PTSD and law enforcement duties include a high divorce rate, alcoholism, and suicide (American Psychiatric Association, 1980). This is not to excuse the actions of police officer for their corrupt behavior; instead, a validated insight into issues that plague officer's lives. It almost seems convenient to consider law enforcement as superheroes (Shilling, 1993). The public either loves them or hates them. The mental equation behind PTSD and police corruption provides an imperative argument into further research to fill in the gaps of knowledge.

## Resources

American Psychiatric Association. (1980). Diagnostic and statistical manual of mental health disorders. 3rd edition. Washington, DC: Author. P. 236-238

Fox News. (2010). Lawyer:  Minn. SWAT officer who robbed bank saw life crumbling, sough death for insurance cash.  Retrieved from: http:// www.foxnews.com/us/2010/06/11

Lemagie, S. (2010).  Rogue Minneapolis cop fought many demons, his attorney says. Star Tribune.

O'Hara, A. & Levenson, R. (n.d.).  Does PTSD cause violence? Article from Badge of Life.

Pazniokas, M. (1994).  Deadlocked jury in officer's trial to deliberate more.  Hartford Courant.

Shilling, R. (1993).  On coping. The Washington Police Officer, p. 4-6.

Vielmetti, B. (2014).  Decorated ex-Mukwonago police officer gets 9 years for bank robbery.  Journal Sentinel.

# Chapter 7:

Garrison Deviance Conformity Theory

Thinking about police corruption, there are so many commonalities between actual corruption and predetermining factors of the cause. What I mean is, the levels of PTSD, depression, and hyper-aggression is all indicative to corruption. There are no statistics as of this publishing that quantify that statement. However, think about the correlation. The next few chapters will dive into causes of corruption, through a disabling viewpoint, and focus on theories that are comparative to police corruption.

The theory of police corruption is a well research area in which police stress attributes to many issues. The physical and psychological demands of police stress have been explored throughout this text. The review of this book was to determine the likelihood of a coincidence of police corruption and PTSD (including depression, alcoholism, etc.) created a need for further examination of this subject matter. The next chapter will look into theories involving the likelihood a person/law officer can become corrupt. Factoring in

PTSD in with theories creates a phenomenon that police work creates the foundation for corruption. Although the upcoming appendix will show police stressors, many researchers have agreed that police stressors and corruption are methodological errors and no directly a result of the job demands. Police stress research has offered a diverse look into personality characteristics. At the same time, the nature of police work is stressful enough to cause psychological, emotional, and physical changes. There remains a need for research to uncover the different types of stressors and how they relate to corruption behaviors. Only clearly defined stressors can be proactively attended to help stop the corruption web. Perhaps future research can identify the root cause of both police stressors and corruption. According to Abdollahi (2002), a suggested efforts to unravel these issues should begin as follows (1) Understand the issue, (2) Discover the cause and effect, and (3) Implement a solution. Using a simple foundation will help both researchers and police to understand this phenomenon of corruption. The decrease work performance and lack of integral decision making can assumedly be connected to mental impairments and a manifestation of continuous corruption behavior.

**Background**

Deviance, as it pertains to this theory involves behaviors that violate the socially accepted norms of law enforcement, civil rights, and social norms. Conformity is considered the social construction many of us consider normal. Without a basis of conformity, our behaviors would direct our deviant behaviors. Many organizations develop policies practices, and laws based from on codified acts of deviance. Further, criminal justice agencies develop codes of ethics or standards of what is acceptable practices.

It is important to understand the two basic epistemological terms associated with this theory. First, the definition of corruption has been defined over and over .throughout this text as the intentional desecration of organizational norms ( e.g. rules, policies, and laws) by those who hold public office for personal gain. These corrupt behaviors are, but not limited to, embezzlement, theft, and abuse of authority to name a few. Second, deviance is a subset of corrupt practices (Ross, 2010). The basis of this theory entails how deviance occurs when police, or other law enforcement, acts in a way that is varying with the officer's authority, organizational authority, and the standards of ethical conduct (Ross, 2010).

**Nature of Deviance**

It is overly time-consuming to determine how much deviance exists in law enforcement. This makes the task of measuring deviance even harder. Little acts of deviance, even as simple as not adhering to "small" policies, like texting and driving, is one example of how law enforcement officer's violate at least one regulation during their career.

**Conceptions of Deviance and Corruption**

Informal prevalent beliefs consider that deviance and corruption as one of the same, all stemming from the "rotten apple theory". Further, a conglomerate of popular beliefs feels that the officer's that fall into one of these two categories are considered "weak" and somehow slipped through screening processes (Ross, 2010). Other considerations look at these "weak" individuals as those who deem to construe their behaviors into the law enforcement career. Temptations increase and the creation of ample opportunities to continue a deeper deviant behavior exists. However, the Garrison

Deviance conformity theory defines itself that deviance exists in some fashion in all law enforcement officers, however, the depth of elements that also exists make a considerable impression on the corruption/deviance action. Continual practices and environmental conformity factors also play a role in this theory.

Current research suggests that simple explanations such as low pay scales, economic deficits, reinforcement, and tolerance is the leading factors in deviance. The Garrison Deviance Conformity theory combats this explanation fixing on the idea that polices are constantly exposed to situations that create the ethical decision process flaw. These decisions can have a positive or a negative impact on a law enforcement officer's concept of what is considered "okay". Does perpetuity and laying one's life on the line allow for such a misconception? It shouldn't. Neither should the allowance of brotherhood interaction and history allow for the deviance to continue.

However, underlying conditions create a phenomenon where deviance begins to control the law enforcement officer's ability to conform in a positive way. PTSD, recurrent violent acts and violent situations, underlying mental illness, underlying personal stressors, and a confirmative environment lead to law enforcement deviant behavior.

In an attempt to develop a new theoretical approach to understanding, and labeling theories designed for police corruptive behaviors; the name (proposed by the author of this book) "Deviance Conformity Theory" will be used to explain the confounding parallels between corruption and law enforcement. These deviant behaviors are those in which law enforcement officers become corrupt. Further, artificial norms, which are produced by the culture of law enforcement creates artificial norms that are illegal, however, considered acceptable among cultures of this cohort. These actions or activities, outside of cultural norms or expectations assume many forms.

Additionally, the addition of external stressors from the demands of the job and internal factors such as post-traumatic stress syndrome contribute to the disillusioned confirmative values. Verifying the foundation of the Deviance Conformity Theory is established through B.F. Skinner's operant conditioning theory. This theory is based upon the idea that learning (including behavior) is a function of change in overt behavior. Changes in behavior is the individual's response to events (stimuli) that occurs in the person's environment. Recurrent exposure to stress/stimuli/events in a daily career of law enforcement officer can be directed to the onset of post-traumatic stress syndrome. Further, this consideration can be inductive to Skinner's operant conditioning theory. Lastly, the elements of PTSD; continuous exposure to stimuli/stressful events; cultural conformity in law enforcement; and personal economic/marital issues outlines the breeding ground of corruption.

## Discussion of Deviance Descriptivism

Although not one single character is a deviance conformity issues, it is important to understand the foundation of the pitfalls of police work that ultimately furthers the ability of corruption. One of the first issues in this is that the job precedes family. It is common that the family takes a second place to the career of police work. It is very often that the deeds of the day are not discussed at home creating an alienated type of feeling with the officer. Many officers begin to share less and less of their career with significant others and family; keeping most of the stress to themselves.

Also, officer's frequently refuse to show emotions at work as part of a strength structured administration. This act often falls into the home as well. Research and studies show that a lack of emotion also brings about lack of intimacy as well. This closed-off perception often leaves both children and wives wondering what has caused this. Many times, the stress of the job is directed towards family members when pent-up anger rushes outward. This collectively can lead to domestic violence among families of officers.

Some officer's deal with the stressors of financial issues, PTSD, hyper-aggression, etc with drugs and or alcohol. Stress is a subjective issue and drug or alcohol abuse only suppresses the issues for a short time. Before long, the suppression is required most of the time, leading to abuse. Further, this abuse also leads to a para-military style lifestyle at home. Because police see the worst side of society, most believe their own families are as suspect as those they deal with on a daily basis. Many enter the field with the thought of changing the world and making a difference in the community. Usually hardened attitudes create the perception that they cannot change the world. A deep-rooted cynicism evolves from these perceptions and leads to corruption. When officer's respond to the same area of town, to answer the call for the same type of problem all of the time, it creates a prejudice that goes beyond comprehension. After many years of constant déjà vu, police from troubled areas begin to automatically consider socioeconomic group as troublemakers. The average police officer learns through the lens of experience. It is not a basis of who the person is, it is the job that breeds these behaviors.

A typical us against them scenario. Finally, temptation are in many forms for police officers. Law enforcement officer's today typically deal with cover ups, lying, gifts, excessive force, and discretionary enforcement issues every day on the job. Recognizing the specific stressors for corruption is an important factor in successfully taking ·down the web of corruption that has challenged police for decades.

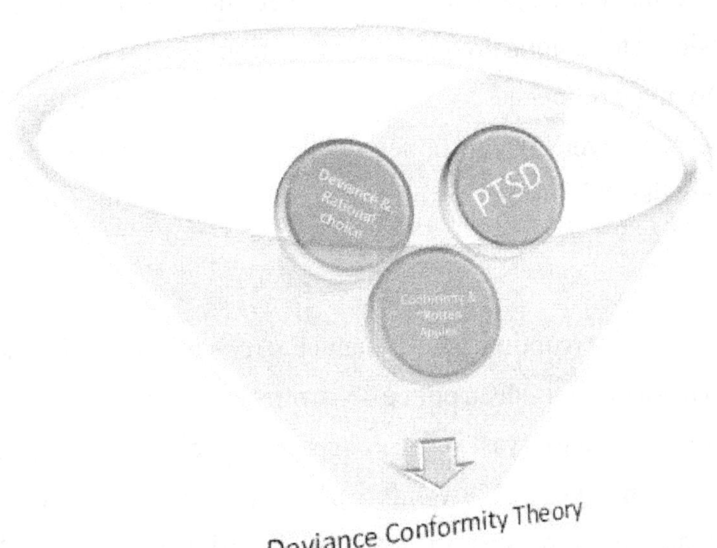


Throughout this book, many cases and examples have highlighted the actions of law enforcement officers. However it is important to understand that many of those who committed these crimes held underlying issues in which could, and perhaps, contributed to the onset of deviance and corruption. Further research into this area is being conducted by the author to determine more finite areas in which this theory can be applied to realistic proactive approaches in law enforcement behaviors. There is no evidentiary way to produce deviant free law enforcement officers unless they are assembled in a factory and pre-programmed. By this, it is assumed that each and every law enforcement officer conforms, or reacts to situations so differently, that it is impossible to be deviance free. Current research further indicates a large  frame of research supporting the fact the law enforcement officers are confronted with very erratic behavior intem1ittent and ongoing that exposes the officer's to high-stress situations. There is a rate of 4% -14% of police officers who develop PTSD during their law career, or have it entering the job. Further depression rates among law officer's range from 12% of female officers to 6% for male officers. Law enforcement officers also have the highest divorce rate. Over 20% of police officers are also problem drinkers. Numbers like this further enforce the Garrison Deviance Conformity Theory's existence.

Police corruption isn't a nuance of media induced concerns. Instead it is a major issue in police departments across the world. Police corruption is a major waste of resources, financial resources, creates a modem day mockery of law enforcement in general and undermines the foundations on which police/security is designed to employ. Why? Simply because law enforcement is the primary institution of social establishment. When that line is crossed, how can the foundation be rebuilt? It stops the establishment of the rule of law. The lessons about police corruption continue to break the basic building blocks of the nation. The many variations of police corruption undoubtedly effects perceptions of law as a legitimate establishment. One issue looms in the definition of corruption across the vast cultures within the United States. Suggestively, solutions to police corruption can be reduced by enlisting basic, cross-cultural, mass police department policies and procedures. Efforts to lower police corruption should be based on the selective differences between the individuals that cause it.

One major influence in reducing corruption can be enforced by longer investigations that include a correlative background on the individual, reasons, etc. Most police investigations interagency consists of internal review boards and once complete, the investigation is over. Perhaps not enough emphasis is put on the tort that corruption creates. The causal sweeping under the rug does nothing to reestablish the sanctity of law enforcement.

Second, creating a responsibility of supervisors to the actions of their subordinates would create a more hands on knowledge of officer actions. Many precincts operate on a basis in which supervisors claim to not know what their subordinates do. Perhaps this ignorance is also a key to understanding why so many corruption cases erupt in larger departments. This willful ignorance sparks a further divide among the police culture. Further, this divide create reluctances to report fellow officer transgressions. It becomes a never ending web of corruption that becomes harder and harder to get away from.

Underscoring police culture will also change the direction in which corruption can occur. One suggestion to thwarting of the usual compliances of corruption can be done through constant revision in rosters, assignments, and precincts. Research has shown that comfortable environments breed corruption. Less likely will the occurrence of corruption happen when the environment isn't so concrete? When the action of producing unknown "practice" can allow supervisors to vigilant and able to notice potentially corrupt behaviors ahead of time.

Police reform on corruption also lies upon the external. Evironment in which police culture exists. A solid existence of sufficient numbers of personnel to maintain a level of public safety is also another measure to reduce corruption. Infrequency of staff in assigned areas reduces the levels of trust among officers and the general public. This existence can create a better trust among officers and less association between officer's and the public they serve. An external impact on the reduction of police corruption can be stipulated by enforcement by state and federal law instead of an inter-agency bureaucratic investigation. Also, encouraging policy makers and budget holders to increase the overall pay to reduce the likelihood of financial hardships reasons for corruption.

The point within this text is to point out likely advances of impeding corruption. It cannot be totally eliminated. As this blemish in society is ever-present. However, maintaining a level, consistent, and perhaps a more deeply embedded analysis will brings the levels of corruption down. Prioritizing a selective process begins with leadership from the top. Lazy, inactive leadership does not count in running a department. Not knowing the names of all of the fellow officer's creates an· unsupportive atmosphere. If leadership is not readily visible from the top, how could society expect it to be any other way? It cannot be made from the bottom to the top. Clear and concise expectation of what is expected among officers in respective situations aligns departments on the same page. Imagine if only one department in every state changed to a reformed way that prevents police from becoming conformed to the blue culture? Change is made at a slow pace. However, change over time is a step in the right direction. More emphasis needs to be placed on departments getting their policies and procedures in line with all departments, instead of a multi-discipline approach.

Figuring out what actually causes police corruption is a difficult task to say the least. The examination of the consequences of police corruption is even more difficult. But when we consider the issue of potential signs of corruption in context about what we know about corruption, ideas begin to emerge as far as developing theories to contrast the outlasting effects of corruption. Normally, corruption is only noticed when someone is caught and media attention is directed towards that organization. The costs at whatever level, points a demolishing light towards police departments. Within this text, a discovery among contemporary theories cycled the daily stress from the job along with personal attributors to corruption. Theoretically, the underlying causes of corruption can affect the viewpoint of the public.

Perceptions, attitudes, and association are effected by corruption at any level. Because of the powers that are given to police officers, corruption is even more significant in the eyes of society. Whenever police go beyond their governed authority, they begin to lose their moral abilities to act in accordance with integrity. The ability of all police at some point becomes decimated with the acts of a few. Public confidence suffers and society no longer consider the police a figure of authority. The public, no less, expects a high level or moral servitude and professionalism that creates a legitimate environment. What is important to note is that there is a diminished trust and confidence in not just the officer or the department, it becomes an institution of mistrust. Therefore giving confidence that a few bad apples do spoil the barrel. Restoring confidence from this point requires a more focused reformation from the top down.

There is no operative device that can screen out potential

corruptive behavior. Mainly because corruptive behavior occurs at different points in an officer's career. Therefore, the determining model in this books considers constant stress, violence, and personal issues contributes to corruption happening at a more frequent rate.

The organizational culture also brings a prevalence of corruption. One way to referee potential corruption is to develop psychological intervention in very frequent intervals to establish issues and concerns. Perhaps intervention of this type can help officers who deal with depression, PTSD, family issues, and marital discourse. Further, the reaction by leaders on stopping corruption is also a vital instrument in developing official strategies to stop corruption t all levels Australia, for example has an internal and external board that look into all complaints and discusses them in a forum like structure. Influences from supervisors, outside review boards, and internal review boards can cooperatively offer a cultural change that can break down the wall of silence in the blue culture.

However, law enforcement in itself, creates a breeding ground of corruption. It is undoubtedly going to take time and a lot of effort to bring an inclusive resolution to the ending of corruption. However, since corruption can be traced for hundreds of years, it may take equally as long for it to see an end.

It is not only the United States that faces corruption among law enforcement. In fact, many corrupt law enforcement division in other countries pose a far greater issue than those here in the United States. The law enforcement position, regardless of geographic location is to protect the public. It is a bad thought when those who are hired to protect and serve cannot even do that. The corruption , in essence, effects society and endangers the citizens everywhere, Haiti is notoriously knows as a most corrupt in police forces around the world. Unethical leadership have allowed human rights infractions and kidnapping to be an everyday part of the job. Unlawful actions are catastrophic and resistance in helping maintain peace is a recipe for disaster.

In Mexico, crime is at an all-time high. I interviewed a Mexican national who exclaimed that police are the criminals themselves. For instance, when you are pulled over for a ticket, you had your license to the police with cash underneath. The pay in Mexico is so low that corruption is a means to make ends meet in an impoverished society. Drug trafficking works with police to ensure a daily flow of activates. Uzbekistan is also known as a historically corrupt country. Detaining of citizens and extortion are only among the corrupt charges. Bribery is a way of life for police in this area. There have been instances where access to higher education institutions has been held back without payment to police. Protection in this country, like many others, is not without a price.

Iraq, Somalia, and Afghanistan are notorious as well in corrupt police. Extortion, bribery, theft, and kidnappings are the ways to make extra money for police. Since many cannot stand up to these agencies without retribution, it is only an easy way to answer the demands. International efforts continuously try to alleviate these issues. However,.a watchful eye is not present 24/7.  To gain a holistic understanding of the factors that lead to deviance among law enforcement, it is important to look at how these cases have common factors that develop a theme. The next section will highlight these factors.  The premise of the Garrison Deviance Conformity Theory posits that specific characteristics and factors influence the change to deviance in police officers.

## Understanding Common Factors in Case Examples

*The cases listed from here on throughout the text are used for reporting and statistical research. It does not in any way imply guilt or personal views from the author. Case examples were pulled directly from media outlets, as cited. Further, these case examples will highlight underlying conditions that create a potential grounded theory in police corruption.*

## Case Example: John Burge - procedural corruption in torture
## Underlying conditions: Hyper aggression, Violence, veteran officer*

John Burge was been into a blue collar family in Chicago. Although he attended college and eventually dropped out, he became a deck rested Anny Veteran with much recognition for heroism and valor. Burge was sworn in 1970 to the office of law enforcement (Chicago Tribune, 2011 ). During his 20-year tenure, he received accommodations during his career, including serving as commander. Within the polished jacket, there was a deep loathsome side. Burge was accused of torturing suspects for over two decades and coercing dozens of fallacious confessions. The Chicago Tribune reported over 200 individuals was in the wake of his corruption (2011). Allegations of torture began to develop in 1972, with a prominent example in 1982 where a defendant received bruises, lacerations and burns to his chest. Others claim they were beaten into a confession by the use of telephone books, slamming arrestee's heads into table, cattle prods, and electrical torture to the genitals of suspects (Chicago Tribune, 2011). Excerpts from Burge's trial stated "Burge cites a dismal failure of police leadership" and "how can anyone trust that justice will be served when the justice system has been so defiled" (Chicago Tribune, 2011). Those who were affected by Burge's sadistic tactics received new trials and / or charges were dropped. Burge faced many criminal charges and ultimately was fired in 1993. He served four years.

## Case Example: Antonio Figueroa and Robert Bayard -violation of civil right Underlying Conditions: Veteran

Two Camden, New Jersey police officers were arrested for falsifying evidence in drug cases in what is expected to have impacted more than 200 cases. The cases involved some individuals serving haphazard jail sentences. Both officers were actively involved with the special operations unit assigned to police hot spots for open air drug markets (Fox News, 2010). According to the report by Fox News, 210 cases were forced to be dropped. Approximately six dozen federal lawsuits are pending stemming from false arrest issues. Figueroa and Bayard face charges of conspiracy to violate the civil rights of a citizen, which can be punishable of up to the years in prison. Evidence further showed three other officers were involved in depriving individuals of their due process privileges. The Attorney General for New Jersey told Fox News (2010) that "it places dishonor to the tens of thousands of law enforcement personnel who are out there day and night, basically doing the right thing". David Madden of CBS Philadelphia reported that Robert Bayard was acquitted of charges and Antonio Figueroa was charged three of the five counts (2011). It is unclear if Bayard has decided to return to law enforcement. US attorney Fishman was quoted saying " corrupt police officers undermine the dedicated men and women who put their lives on the line every day and betray the trust the public is entitled to have in those that serve it.... we will not hesitate to pursue allegations of this kind of conduct in the future" (CBS, 2011).

## Case Example: Carnal Knowledge
## Underlying Conditions: Unknown

A fonner Henrico, Virginia Sheriff's deputy was arrested in late 2013 on three feeling accounts of having carnality knowledge with an inmate (WTVR, 2013). The attempted flushing of a cell phone by an inmate prompted the discovery of the relationship with sheriffs deputy. Further investigation led to love letters written to the inmate inside his cell. Sexual encounters were documented between January and April 2012, according to the WTVR news report. The officer resigned from her position as of May 2012, was arrested, and placed temporarily in the jail she worked for. While as a deputy she was in charge of the jail laundry room. The Henrico County Under sheriff told WTVR that it is their duty and responsibility to provide a service for these inmates and a deputy having sex with them compromises things (2013). This case is currently under further investigation.

## Case Example: Correctional officer and
## inmates - carnal knowledge
## Underlying Conditions: Control

This is not secluded to one state, these instances happen every day, everywhere. Taking a look back, Virginia opened an investigation in 1999 to probe into guard-inmate sex at a state prison for women. The ACLU reported on the organizational web page regarding 25 complaints in nine months from when the prison opened in 1998. The inmate told the Associated press that "tip of the iceberg ... .in this little cesspool of seductions" (1999). Internees interviewed by the AP said they were afraid of reporting abuse because of retribution. Authorities in Virginia prepared to make a law carrying a five-year maximum sentence for employees taking indecent liberties with female inmate or male inmates for that matter. Consensual sex is not permitted with inmates because they do not have reserved rights to agree because they are wards of the state. ACLU representatives suggest an all-female staff at female institutions to combat this problem; however, it would be impossible because of equal employment laws (1999).

## Case Example: Undercover in New York
## Underlying Condition: hyper aggression

West's Encyclopedia of American Law gives another example of procedural misconduct.

> "The controversy involving the killing of an unarmed man in 1999 created a further hit to the New York police integrity. Four undercover police officers shot Amadou Diallo 41 times after stopping the immigrant while he was in the vestibule of his apartment building. The officers reported he reached into his back pocket. Protests attracted activists such as Susan Sarandon and former New York mayor David Dinkins, who argued the departments so called Aggressive Street Crime Unit, was indeed too aggressive. In 2000, the four officers were acquitted in a trial that supporters said vindicated them but which critics blame it on lax prosecution" (2008).

Mounting resentment and procedural misconduct lead to massive recourse for law enforcement officers. Police departments, legislatures, and federal governments attempt to look at ways to bring reform to the law enforcement society. Critics argue that corruption is not a new phenomenon. Public policy has been blamed because the emphasis of aggressive policing is forced. Whatever the cause, the finger pointing will continue. Each new headlines, creates further destruction of public enforcement.

## Case Example: Hammond, Indiana
## Underlying Condition: Control, hyper aggression

A 14 year-old boy perhaps carries a viral video that shows how his family was victims of excessive force by the Hammond, Indiana police. It is important to note, that the video did not begin w1til some thirteen minutes after the initial stop. This leaves to question the entire story; nonetheless, it is evident that the overall picture was not looked at when the police pushed their way into the car. Allegedly, the driver of the car was pulled and presented her identification as requested. The passenger did not have an ID on him. The passenger did present a ticket he had as form of identification; however, the on-scene officer felt it was not a justified form of identification. After several verbal attempts to have the passenger exit the car, the second police officer smashed the passenger side window as glass flew across two minors in the back seat. Lastly, he was tasered and removed forcibly from the vehicle. I have seen the video several times. There is a two-sided issue here. First, Indiana does have a law that requires persons pulled over to identify themselves. In which the driver successfully did. The infraction however, was on the passenger for not wearing a seatbelt. According to the article written by Lutz, Relerford, and Wojciechowski, The complaint alleges that the police had no reason to use such force, stating:

*The actions of the individual defendants created a reasonable apprehension of imminent harm by and constituted harmful or offensive contact with each Plaintiff. The actions of the individual defendants were objectively unreasonable under the circumstances and were undertaken intentionally with malice, willfulness, and reckless indifference to the rights and safety of Plaintiffs.*

In response, the Hammond Police Department released a statement arguing instead that the officers "were at all times acting in the interest of the officer's safety and in accordance with Indiana law." (2014). According to the U.S. Supreme Court in Pennsylvania v. Mimms, the police have the authority to ask a driver to step outside the vehicle during the course of a stop. The Court has also held in Maryland v. Wilson that an officer may order passengers to get out of the car pending completion of the stop. The purpose of this request is to protect both the driver and the officer from the surrounding traffic, and "diminishes the possibility, otherwise substantial, that the driver can make unobserved movements; this, in turn, reduces the likelihood that the officer will be the victim of an assault (Lutz, Relerford, and Wojciechowski, 2014).

It is interesting to establish a foundation in this particular case. Although state law allows police to request identification from passengers inside a car that they've stopped, two Indianapolis officers shouldn't have arrested a man for refusing to identify himself when there was no reasonable suspicion he'd done anything wrong. The Indiana Court of Appeals addressed that issue in a six-page opinion today in Adam Starr v. State of Indiana, No. 49A04-0912-CR-677, which overturned a ruling by Marion Superior Judge David Certo. In September 2009, officers from the Indianapolis Metropolitan Police Department arrested Adam Starr for refusing to identify him, a Class C misdemeanor as defined by Indiana Code 34-28-5-3.5. Two officers pulled over a vehicle driven by Starr's girlfriend, who'd made an illegal turn. After determining her identity, the officers questioned

Starr about his identity. He denied having any ID, claimed he could not remember his Social Security number, and said his name was "Mr. Horrell."

According to Hoskins, after police found a photo ID in the vehicle, he claimed the person pictured was his "identical cousin." Officers determined his real identify and that an active protective order prohibited any contact between Starr and his girlfriend, and police arrested him on charges of privacy invasion and refusal to identify himself (2010). Starr was acquitted on the privacy invasion charge, but convicted on the refusal charge and received an eight-day sentence in the Marion County Jail. On appeal, he argued that the statute criminalizing the refusal to identify oneself is directed toward the driver of a vehicle stopped for a traffic offense and not to the passengers. The appellate court determined that the legislature had not categorically excluded passengers from the statute's scope and that police are able to detain passengers in certain circumstances during and as a result of those stops. But this case didn't present circumstances, such as resistance, that allowed the police conduct. Though most will comply with an officer's request, the police power to request_ and obtain this identification isn't unlimited, the appellate court pointed out. "In the context of a traffic stop for a vehicular violation, the Good Faith Belief statute provides for detention of a person who, in the 'good faith' belief of the officer, 'has committed an infraction or ordinance violation,'" Judge L. Mark Bailey wrote. "The Refusal to Identify Self statute then criminalizes the refusal to comply with an officer's lawful request under the statute authorizing detention. In this instance, although Starr was 'stopped' when the vehicle in which he was a passenger was 'stopped,' there is no showing that Starr was stopped as a consequence of any conduct on his part. There was no reasonable suspicion that he had committed an infraction or ordinance violation, giving rise to an obligation to identify himself upon threat of criminal prosecution." As a result, he didn't fall within the scope of the state statute and his conviction must be reversed, the court ruled.

But the question of whether the police are authorized to remove a passenger from a vehicle must be balanced against whether the officer's use of force was justified. According to the U.S. Court of Appeals for the Seventh Circuit in Lester v. City of Chicago, an officer's use of force is unconstitutional if, "judging from the totality of circumstances at the time of the arrest, the officer used greater force than was reasonably necessary to make the arrest." Thus, the Hammond police officers must establish, based upon the totality of the circumstances leading up to and concurrent with the arrest, that their actions were both reasonable and necessary. Several factors are pertinent to this analysis. The basis for whether excessive force was used is derived from a three-part test articulated by the Supreme Court in Graham v. Connor. This objective test examines:

1) The severity of the crime at issue;
2) Whether the suspect posed an immediate threat to the safety of the officers or others; and
3) Whether the suspect was actively resisting arrest or attempting to evade arrest by flight.

If the Hammond police can successfully show that their decision to break into the car to remove Jones was justified, either because they perceived he was reaching for a weapon or engaging in threatening behavior, they will have an easier time in court defending this incident, although there is little evidence from the video that this appeared to be the case. However, what if the passenger had respectfully rolled his window down further, or perhaps, slowly moved. What if the passenger had stepped out as asked? Would this have gone any further?

## Case Example: Homeless in Tennessee
## Underlying Condition: hyper aggression, Control

Tennessee officers were charged with beating a homeless man. This case involved three officer s who attempted to cover up their crimes. The homeless man had been detained and was "hog-tied" and beaten. The officer's incident was caught on the dash camera of their vehicle, as well as witnessed by other bystanders. Further, it was discovered that supervisors attempted to cover for the officer's as well. It was stated that "His participation in the cover-up is without question a stain on his service, both as a police officer and an elected official. There are a few who abuse their powers, however, the conduct here is inhuman and intolerable.

## Case Example: Portland, Oregon
## Underlying Condition: Hyper aggression, control

Police used a stun gun and pepper spray on a man who had an altercation with someone else. This gentleman was beaten and illegally arrested after he was punched by police officer's who responded. Further, police antagonized the man after he questioned his ability to stand on a public sidewalk. The officer's stated the suspect refused direction and would not obey orders.

## Case Example: Spiraling Out of Control
## Underlying Condition: Alcohol abuse, depression, financial issues, hyper aggression

James Michael Ford (name changed to protect family) was 40 years old when he was captured for robbing three banks in about a 6-month span. Mr. Ford was a resident of Columbus, Georgia who was facing many issues. Mr. Ford was prosecuted and sented out his time in a Federal penitentiary. Looking back, Mr. Ford suffered from depression, hyper-aggression, and alcoholism. What is more important within this text is that Mr. Ford was a former police officer in Virginia.

O'Hara and Levenson suggest that the stigma related o mental illness is the leading factor in why many police officials are reluctant to the idea that police work ultimately can lead to PTSD (n.d.). This unfortunate misinformation is a direct result of the American public viewpoint that mental illness is dangerous. O'Hara and Levenson further indicate that factors such as hyper aggression, traumatic brain injury, and substance abuse are part of PTSD diagnosis' (n.d.).

The average law enforcement career is essentially 20 years. Twenty years of repetitive violence, disturbing calls, and a significant stress to social and emotional relationships/ other factors that correlate with PTSD and law enforcement duties include a high divorce rate, alcoholism, and suicide (American Psychiatric Association, 1980). This is not to excuse the actions of police officer for their corrupt behavior; instead, a validated insight into issues that plague officer's lives. It almost seems convenient to consider law enforcement as superheroes (Shilling, 1993). The public either loves them or hates them. The mental equation behind

PTSD and police corruption provides an imperative argument into further research to fill in the gaps of knowledge.

## Case Example: NYPD busy playing spy?
## Underlying Condition: Control

I thought the streets of NY were preeminently occupied for police to playing around. An off duty officer was charged with using a surveillance camera to spy on a neighbor in the building in which they shared (Kemp, 2013) .. The officer had been on the force for eight years. Most of his career was located in the Bronx area of New York. The accused police officer's mother defended him. Further, there was no information if the surveillance was recorded or if it was police department property that way used.

## Case Example: 'Cannibal cop'?
## Underlying Condition: Control

A former NYPD police officer was convicted of a heinous act, not particularly described through the text of this book. The conviction was overturned in a plot to kidnap and eat women. His was charged with conspiring online to abduct, torture, and eat his wife along with other women, according to Riley (2014). The sentence was overturned and he was released for time served after 21 months in jail. The finalized conviction was using a police database to research women. Outside of receiving mental health evaluations and counseling, this former police officer now aspires to become a criminal defense attorney.

*Unconstitutional Stops?*

In Newark, NJ, a three-year investigation ended following the US Department of Justice inquiry on unconstitutional behavior by police. According to Hamilton, the extensive review of the practices of the departments shows an astounding 75% rate of pedestrian stops that were deemed unconstitutional. Further, black makes made up nearly 54% of the population in Newark ... 85% of the pedestrian stops and nearly 80% of the arrests were all black males.

### Case Example:"Marquette "
### Underlying condition: Drug Abuse

This case, often referred to as the Marquette 10, is an example of how drugs and police work do not work. In the early 80's, an investigation of drugs in Chicago prompted the arrest of a large amount of drug dealers. Ten officers from that district were arrested and convicted. The majority of the charges included accepting bribery and exchanging money for goods. The entire officer's received prison sentences, However, this example shows how corruption is not a solitary officer event. It is a continuous web.

### Case Example: Veteran Officer
### Underlying Conditions: Financial (gambling addiction), PTSD

A 20 year Baltimore police officer was charged and received 14 years for robberies. During the trial, the officer reflected on many cases in which he still saw in his dreams nightly. Further, he was known as a 'good cop'. The judge in the case was reported as calling the case a tragedy. "This profession that you love and devote yourself to makes you a victim of your own actions". The judge's reaction is true to so may cases today. The officer had previously received accommodations for efforts earlier in his career.

## Case Example: Proud Officer
## Underlying Condition: Financial and Depression

As what is described as a proud uniformed officer, a young New York police officer was found to be a serial bank robber. He was charged with three accounts of felony robbery in order to buy a new car, an engagement ring for his fiancé. And pay off student loan debt. Following his arrest, he made the statement he was not paid enough to afford those luxuries. Prior to his arrest, this officer has no criminal record. Prior to his arrest, colleagues claim there were no indicators that he was losing himself. However, it was noted that the officer was depressed at the issue of not being able to afford these items on his salary.

## Case Example: Robbing Sergeant
## Underlying Condition: Financial and Depression

A police sergeant was arrested in connection to a bank robbery. He worked a moonlighting position as a second source of income as the security officer for the bank. The 20+ year veteran showed little warning signs of financial or emotional woes. Texas precinct constable states" when somebody falls down like this, it hurts all of us .. but we are not all the bad guys here".

## Case Example: Kentucky
## Underlying Condition: Financial

A Kentucky officer was sentenced to 16 months for the theft of evidence and property of victims. During a drug bust, the officer was accused and later charged with taking a watch and a ring. This officer intent was to pawn the jewelry for extra money

## Case Example: High ranking
## Underlying Condition: Control

A captain and a detective in Tennessee were charges with assaulting an individual's while in restrains.

## Case Example: Drugs for Delivery
## Underlying Condition: Drug Abuse

A captain and a detective were given 36 months probation for the delivery and possession of controlled substances. These drugs were bought and traded while the officers were on duty. Both officers' were also positive for drug use.

## Case Example: Corrupt Cop as a Drug Dealer
## Underlying condition: Financial

A long-term police officer, decorated with accolades, found himself in a world of robbing the criminals that infest the neighborhoods. Robbing drug dealers was a quid-pro-quo type of action against the drug dealers in the street. He would rob them of their cash and drugs, and resale the drugs. The money received allowed him to buy two homes and an additional rental property. It also came as a cost of losing two marriages. After the department received more than 20 complaints against him, the officer resigned on his own. However, continues to do drug busts on his own vigilante style. Dealers wised up and pressed charges on him and he was prosecuted in court.

## Case Example: Double Theft
## Underlying Condition: Financial

Two officers in California were part of a scandal that entailed two officers posing as thieves. They were accused of stealing property and cash from drug suspects to line their own pockets. They were further charged with conspiracy to deprive the public trust. Over 100 criminal cases were dropped as a result of the officer's charges. The jurors felt there were consequences for those who victimize the powerless under the color of authority. At one of the officer's homes, it was a large amount of money found buries in the yard.

## Case Example: Cell Phone Assault
## Underlying Condition: Control

In Petersburg Virginal, a local man was beaten and assaulted by police for capturing a domestic response on cell phone .. The officer asked the man to put down his phone and go back inside of his home. He refused, hence, more than one officer was a part of the assault.

# APPENDIX I: CAUSES OF CORRUPTION: TOWARDS A CONTEXTUAL THEORY OF CORRUPTION

# CAUSES OF CORRUPTION:
## TOWARDS A CONTEXTUAL THEORY OF CORRUPTION

**GJALT DE GRAAF**
Vrije Universiteit Amsterda

## ABSTRACT

The more we know about the causes of corruption, the better we can decide which policy instruments to use to combat corruption. The primary question of this article is: how can the causes of corruption in Western countries be studied? Here, an overview is presented of the causes of corruption mentioned in the literature using the kind of causality of explanations of corruption as an organizing principle. Six groups of theories are distinguished concerning causes of corruption, paying attention to the discourse on corruption control these groups of theories lead to. A primary conclusion is that there are not many studies on actual, individual corruption cases. It seems, therefore, that we need more contextual corruption research; many current studies lack contingency. The overview also makes clear that the theoretical model chosen determines, for a large part, the direction of the proposed solutions. Different causal chains lead to different discourses on corruption prevention and corruption control.

## INTRODUCTION

In October 1994, Piet Neus, former alderman of the Dutch city of Maastricht, received a one-month suspended prison sentence and was fined 10,000 Dutch guilders (about 5,000 US dollars) for accepting gifts valued at 42,000 Dutch guilders (about 21,000 US dollars) from

from three local companies in the form of household renovations (Dohmen 1996: 237). Just after his conviction, Neus commented, "I still believe I did nothing wrong. Society apparently disagrees. The judge considered the postponed payment for the renovation of a kitchen a gift. I have to respect that verdict" (Dohmen 1996: 218).

With that incident in mind, the primary question of this article is: how can the causes of corruption in Western countries be studied? The more we know about them, the better we can decide which policy instruments to use to combat corruption. But what are causes? Let's look at the example of Piet Neus again: why did it occur? This question seems straightforward for students of Public Administration. On closer inspection, it is not. To answer it, we first have to ask ourselves: what do we really want to know? After all, the 'why' question can be interpreted in many different ways.

Maybe we mean to ask: why did this corruption case start? In that case, we seek out the immediate causes and circumstances of the corrupt transactions and decisions. We look directly at the corrupt acts themselves.

Or do we want to know why the corruption case continued over a period of time, possibly in connection with other cases? (This is in fact what happened; see Dohmen 1996.) If so, we are less interested in the exact conditions by which the corruption case occurred than we are in the readiness of Piet Neus to become corrupt.

Perhaps we want to know why this particular corruption case occurred rather than not. Were there alternatives for Piet Neus, or was he 'forced' to do what he did? Was corruption, given the causes and conditions, his only course of action? This raises questions concerning the 'determinism vs. freedom' debate, which here will be left aside.

Maybe we are looking for the causes of this particular case of corruption, which gets most attention in corruption research (and in this article). In this context, are we interested in the causes of corruption that are external to the corrupt act itself? Or are we interested in the actual process of Piet Neus's corruption? The first interpretation is the most popular in the literature – not surprisingly, since social sciences usually deal with concepts rather than processes and thus 'freeze' reality (Schinkel 2004: 8). Corruption is then studied in an abstract sense, looking for the governing laws of corruption at a meso or macro level. As we shall see later in this article, in individual corruption cases, it is quite tricky to identify causal links.

Another possible interpretation of the 'why' question is: are we interested in the reasons and motives for Piet Neus to become corrupt? In Neus's statement, he expressed amazement about his conviction. He claims that he did not know he was corrupt, but that "society apparently disagrees." This brings us to an issue often raised in philosophy, that is, whether reasons for action can or should be seen as causes of action and, if so, in what sense can they be treated (Schinkel 2004: 8). This debate, too, will be left aside here.

As we shall soon discover, there is a tension in corruption research (as in other social research) between actors being regarded as autonomous agents making (bounded) rational means-end calculations, and explaining corrupt behavior by *causes* beyond individual control. In the latter case, the corrupt agent 'disappears' along with the corruption that is being studied: even though the corrupt agent is the source of the corruption, he or she is reduced to background characteristics, translated into variables. This leads to certain factors that can be relevant to understanding the motives for corruption, but it draws attention away from the corrupt practices and the corrupt agent. The central argument of this article is therefore that we need more contextual corruption research; many current studies lack contingency.

However we interpret the question of what the causes of Neus's corruption were, it implies *a kind of causality*. In this article, I give an overview of the causes of corruption mentioned in the literature using the *kind of causality* of explanations of corruption as an organizing principle. I distinguish six groups of theories concerning causes of corruption, paying attention to the discourse on corruption control these groups of theories lead to. The overview leads to a call for more contextually-based research on corruption, for which we need a theoretical model. In constructing one, a synthesis of the six groups of theories on the causes of corruption would be interesting, but two problems arise: the theory groups employ different levels of variables, and they have different implicit or explicit causal models. We will later discuss these problems and possible solutions.

Instead of synthesizing the theory groups, one could look for an alternative causal theory. One such possibility, Pierre Bourdieu's theory of social action, will be briefly discussed in this article. Bourdieu's theory is suitable to study the case of Piet Neus and similar cases. By combining macro and micro factors and everything in between, it would be well suited as a theoretical model for corruption case studies.

Before discussing the causes of corruption, we should heed the words of Caiden (2001: 21): "Just as there are many varieties of corrupt behavior, so there are multitudinous factors contributing to corruption … So many explanations are offered that it is difficult to classify them in any systematic manner." Adds Heywood (1997: 426): "The complexity of the phenomenon makes it impossible to provide a comprehensive account of the causes of political corruption." Caiden (2001: 21-26) mentions the following 'sources' of corruption: psychological, ideological, external, economic, political, socio-cultural and technological. Factors that contribute to corruption, however, are of course not the same as *causes* of corruption. "In sum, corruption can be attributed to almost anything … But while the opportunities exist everywhere, the degree of corruption varies widely among individuals, public agencies, administrative cultures, and geographic regions." (Caiden 2001: 26). Fijnaut and

Huberts remark: "Research shows that a conglomerate of social, economic, political, organizational and individual causal factors are important to explain cases of public corruption" (2002: 8).

*Six Kinds of Causes of Corruption*

In much literature (e.g., Fijnaut and Huberts 2002), a distinction is made between the causes of corruption in lower income countries and the causes in higher income countries; low salaries and poor working conditions greatly improve the chances of corrupt instances occuring. In this article I concentrate on the causes of corruption in Western (i.e., high income) countries, where corruption is much the exception (Caiden 2001: 27).

Great attention has been paid to the question of what corruption is (e.g. see Rose-Ackerman 1999: ch. 6). It seems that every article on corruption starts with an overview of the many definitions. Here, I choose the following definition: "behavior of public officials which deviates from accepted norms in order to serve  private ends" (Huntington 1989: 377).1 What is noticeable about this much-used definition is its emphasis on social constructivism: corrupt is that which is considered corrupt at a certain place and at a certain time. After all, 'accepted norms' change over time. Remember also that Neus disagrees with his conviction. Yes, in his eyes, 'corruption' (in general) is wrong, but he claims that what he did was not corrupt. Being corrupt is not always a matter of black and white. The norms at a certain place and at a certain time are not shared by everyone. Officials can also be 'more' or 'less' corrupt. A public official illicitly receiving 5000 euro is 'more' corrupt than one receiving 500 euro. And, research shows, people regard a police officer who *asks* for 20 euro from a speeding driver so he can 'forget' a ticket as being more corrupt than a police officer who accepts 20 euro when it is *offered* to him. A comparison of research on public attitudes towards corruption concludes that: "Over and over, the research found that respondents judged elected officials more severely than they judged appointed officials; judges more severely than police officers; bribery and extortion more harshly than conflict of interest, campaign contribution, and patronage; and harmful behavior more harshly than petty behavior" (Malec 1993: 16). What is consistent in all discussions about corruption, however, is that corruption is wrong; it is always a deviation from right moral conduct. People disagree about the norms that determine whether someone is corrupt, not about the reprehensiveness of 'corruption'. So as soon as someone is labeled 'corrupt,' he or she is morally judged in a negative way. Corruption is a morally loaded term. Just like 'integrity' is a (morally) positive label and everyone seeks it, corruption is a negative label. Since our views about morality differ in many respects, corruption is also a contested label. Neus does not state that he was corrupt, but that his acts of corruption were permissible (morally and legally); he disagrees that he was corrupt.

Table 1

| | Causal chain | Level of analysis of causes (independent variables) | Level of analysis of corruption (dependent variables) | The context | Most common research methods |
|---|---|---|---|---|---|
| 1. Public choice theory | A 'free' official making a (bounded) rational decision that leads to a more or less predetermined outcome. | Individual | Micro and Macro | Situational aspects mostly ignored; they cannot account for triggering causes. Starts from the moment the actor makes a calculation | Mostly theoretical |
| 2. Bad apple theories | A causal chain from bad character to corrupt acts. | Individual | Individual | Attention to individual background | Theoretical |
| 3. Organizational culture theories | A causal path from a certain culture – a certain group culture – leads to a mental state, which leads to corrupt behavior. Facilitating factors are described which, in some cases, strengthen a causal chain. | Organizational | Organizational | Organizational structure and culture; correlates to number of corruption cases. Situational aspects and contingencies mostly ignored. | Mostly theoretical |

| | Casual Chain | Level of analysis of causes (independent variables) | Level of analysis of corruption (dependent variables) | The context | Most common research methods |
|---|---|---|---|---|---|
| 4. Clashing moral values theories | The causal chain starts with certain values and norms of society, which directly influence the values and norms of individuals. These values and norms influence the behavior of individual officials, making them corrupt. | Societal | Societal | Situational aspects reduced to moral conflicts of individuals. | Mostly theoretical; some case studies |
| 5. The ethos of public administration theories | A causal path from societal pressure – often though the level of organizations on officials to perform and lack of attention to integrity issues – leads to a focus of the official on effectiveness, making him or her corrupt. | Societal and organizational | Societal and organizational | Situational aspects mostly ignored; no explanation of why some officials become corrupt and others do not. | Theoretical |
| 6. Correlation 'theories' | No causal model, only correlations. | All levels | All levels | Situational aspects and contingencies ignored; focus is on variables. | Surveys, expert-panels |

When looking  at the literature on corruption we notice a difference between studies that put forward propositions about the causes of corruption (in other words, studies that theorize about the causes of corruption) and those that empirically try to establish the causes of corruption. The latter sort of studies is by far outnumbered by the former.

Before I give an overview of the kinds of literature on the

kinds of causality of corruption, I would like to stress that every classification has its blind spots. Of course there is overlap, and maybe some theories resist the classification given here, but the overview should make clear that the concept of causality differs in the wide literature on corruption.

## *Public Choice Theory*

First, there is rational choice theory: public choice theory. For the independent variables to explain corruption, it primarily looks at the level of the indidual.

The causal chain is that of an individual making a (bounded) rational decision that leads to a predetermined outcome. Central to the public choice literature is the individual corrupt official who tries to maximize his or her utility. The individual (usually male) is portrayed as a rationally calculating person who decides to become corrupt when its expected advantages outweigh its expected disadvantages (a combination of possible penalty and the chance of being caught). This group of causal theories is made popular by Rose-Ackerman (1978), who claims that public officials are corrupt for a simple reason: they perceive that the potential benefits of corruption exceed the potential costs. Or as Klitgaard (1988: 70) states, if the benefits of corruption minus the probability of being caught times its penalties are greater than the benefits of not being caught, then an individual will ratio-nally choose to be corrupt. Of course, the theory can be expanded when conditions that influence the cost-benefit calculations are taken into account. For example, trust can play an important role. When the state cannot be trusted to manage private property transfers, cor-ruption might become more appealing (Gambetta 1993). Also, trust within  close personal relationships increases the chance of getting thethe benefits from the delivered corrupt 'services' or reduces the chance of getting caught. In this kind of theory, actions of corrupt officials are caused by a rational, conscious and deliberate weighing process of an individual. In its purest form, autonomous agents are assumed to make more or less rational means-end calculations. This contrasts with most of the other theories we will consider, where behavior is explained by causes beyond individual control. In organization sciences, this is closely related to decision theories. The reason is that just how 'choices' (which have the character of volition) cause actions (of a physical nature) must be made clear. In some theories, rational choice is combined with game theory and ideas that agent choice is bound by both the decision-making capacities of individual agents and a surrounding structure of political, economic and cultural rules (institutions), leading to a so- called institutional choice framework (Collier 2002). When we try to picture the causal chain in the case of Piet Neus, we would see him weighing the advantages of the promised gifts against the chances of being caught and the possible negative impact that would have for him. Apparently, Piet Neus made the conscious decision that the benefits were worth the risk.

The advantage of public choice theory is that it has relatively close focus (Schinkel 2004: 11). Instead of looking for general determining factors, it concentrates on a specific situation of an agent (a corrupt official) who calculates pros and cons. In that sense however, it is insensitive to the larger social context (which is something public choice in general has often been criticized for). It cannot account for triggering causes within the situation. The theory starts from the moment an official calculates whether to become corrupt or not. The question then becomes: why are some officials corrupt in many Western countries while most are not? If some calculate that corruption is a good deal, are the others, by not becoming corrupt, making 'bad' calculations? In other words, what have we explained with rational choice theories alone?

Public choice theories lead to a discourse on corruption control that maximizes the costs of corruption and minimizes the benefits.[2] Since the benefits of corruption are much harder to influence, most of the focus is on the costs of corruption. These costs can be made higher by improving the chances of getting  caught and imposing steeper penalties. This can easily lead to a discourse asking for a comprehensive system of control based on surveillance, massive information gathering, auditing, and aggressive enforcement of a wide array of criminal and administrative sanctions (Anechiarico and Jacobs 1996).

### *Bad Apple Theories*

Second, bad apple theories, like public choice theories, primarily look at the level of the individual corrupt agent for the causes of corruption.

These studies seek the cause of corruption in the existence of people with faulty (moral) character, the so- called 'bad apples'. There is a causal chain from bad character to corrupt acts; the root cause of corruption is found in defective human character and predisposition toward criminal activity. Causes are rooted in human weaknesses such as greed. When the focus is on the faulty character of an official, morality is assumed to determine behavior (like in the forthcoming clashing moral values theories):  people are assumed to act on the basis of moral values. 'Wrong' values are therefore the cause of corruption. Of course, one can question whether people act on the basis of moral values (see de Graaf 2003). But the focus on individual corrupt officials and their motives can also be of a different nature.

When we think of the case of Piet Neus, the causal chain in his case would start with moral vices on Neus's part. His 'wrong' moral values directly influenced his behavior toward corruption. Of course, if we believe in such a causal chain, new and interesting questions surface: how did Piet Neus acquire these moral vices? Did he have a bad childhood, or does he have a genetic propensity toward corruption?

'Bad apple' theories are less popular than they used to be. Punch (2000: 317) writes on police corruption: "In the past there was a tendency to think of corruption as a temporary, exceptional 'problem' to be removed by 'surgical' treatment, as if it was a malignant cancer, to restore an otherwise healthy agency (the 'bad apple' metaphor). Conventional wisdom has shifted recently to see corruption as near universal and as forming a permanent concern." We see the assumption of the 'bad apple' often made explicitly or implicitly in the literature, but hardly ever based on empirical claims: the assumption is most often theorized.

What is clear from research using criminological theories (which are somewhat related to the bad apple theories – more on this later) is that stating that the corrupt official is merely after material gain (public choice theories) is too much of a simplification. The official could also be seeking a higher social standing, excitement, work pleasure or a cure for frustration (Nelen and Nieuwendijk 2003: 43/44). For example, Cusson (1983) distinguishes thirteen goals of perpetrators of crime. Literature shows that the agent rationalizes and legitimizes the corrupt behavior and does not regard the behavior as corrupt. Recall, for example, the statement of Piet Neus.

In contrast to the following theories, these (criminological) theories do not lead to an emphasis on ethics management. The particular discourse on corruption controls they lead to is determined by the particular (criminological) theory that is used. Social control theory (seeing in the delinquent a person relatively free of intimate attachments, aspirations, and the moral beliefs that hold most people to a life within the law (Hirschi 1969)), focuses on factors that should *keep* people from criminal activities. One could imaginecorruption control based on such a theory. However, I know of no study combining criminological theories on individual motives for corruption with public administration and concrete suggestions for corruption control. When the root cause of corruption is sought in human weaknesses, 'strong moral values' are named as an antidote (Naim 1995: 285), but designing a policy to combat corruption with this medicine seems improbable.

### *Organizational Culture Theories*

Third, some literature is not so much interested in the background or motives of the corrupt official, but in the culture and structure of the organization within which the agent is working. For the first time, we are looking not the micro level of individual corrupt agents, but the meso level of their respective organizations.

The underlying assumption seems to be that a causal path from a certain culture – a certain group culture – leads to a certain mental state. And that mental state leads to corrupt behavior. Failure in the "proper machinery" of government, not faulty character, leads public officials to act corruptly. Therefore, it accounts for the context corrupt acts occur in. For example, Punch claims (2000: 304) (when talking about corruption within police departments around the world): "If we scan these activities then it is plain that we are no longer dealing with *individuals* seeking solely *personal gain* but with group behavior rooted in established arrangements and/or extreme practices that have to be located within the structures and culture  of police work and the police organization." Punch concludes (2000: 317): "The implication is that in tackling corruption and other forms of police deviance, it is vital to focus on group dynamics, the escalation from minor to serious deviance, and on the negative elements in the police culture." PietNeus's case would be explained by a culture within his municipality (Maastricht) in which everyone is corrupt. This influences Piet Neus in such a way that he 'cannot help' but become corrupt himself.

Once again, in these theories there is a causal path from a certain culture, a certain group culture, that leads to a mental state. And that mental state leads to corrupt behavior. But we could question whether this is a causal link at all, since not all people in the described organizations become corrupt. At best, we could say that these theories describe certain conditions under which corruption occurs. But that, too, is probably saying too much. It is more a matter of describing 'facilitating factors' which, in some cases (not all people in the organization become corrupt), strengthen a causal chain. These types of theory are not so much interested in the corrupt official, but in the contextual features that make for the setting of corruption. In that sense, these theories are not really about the causes of corruption. Implicit in most of these theories is the contention that people in organizations act on the particular dynamics of the organization. Of course, many good arguments involving economic, natural or social forces, for instance, show that institutions (not in the sense of organizations or buildings, more in a sense of collective ways of thinking, feeling and doing) determine, in large part, the decisions and behavior of people. There are dynamics that transcend individuals. In that sense this group of research distances itself from methodological individualism.

This brings us to a related group of theories of corruption that should be grouped here, those that see corruption as 'contagious' (e.g. Klitgaard 1988; Caiden and Dwivedi 2001; Hulten 2002). These theories state that once an organizational culture (or country) iscorrupt, every person who comes in contact with it also runs a big risk of becoming corrupt. Therefore (and interestingly enough) corruption itself seems to be the 'cause' of corruption (even though the specific causal relationship is hard to define). These theories sometimes use the metaphor of the 'slippery slope' (Punch 2000). Not becoming corrupt in certain organizational cultures means betraying the group (Jackall 1988, Punch 2000).

These theories lead  to a discourse on  corruption control in which the emphasis is on influencing the culture of an organization, the so-called 'cultural instruments' by, for  example,  altering  the organization's   leadership (Trevino, Weaver et al. 1999; Trevino, Hartman et al. 2000; Huberts, Kaptein et al. 2004).

## *Clashing Moral Values Theories*

A fourth branch of literature makes a distinction between the public role and private obligations of corrupt officials. As distinguished from the previous theories, corruption is considered on a macro level, more precisely, the level of society. Since the culture of an organization is also influenced by society at large, there is an overlap between this group and organizational culture theories.

The causal chain in these theories starts with certain values and norms of society  that directly influence the values and norms of individuals. These values and norms influence the behavior of individual officials, making them corrupt.

In many societies no clear distinction exists between one's private and one's public roles. Rose- Ackerman: (1999: 91): "In the private sector, gift giving is pervasive and highly valued, and it seemsnatural to provide jobs and contracts to one's friends and relations. No one sees any reason not to carry over such practices into the public realm. In fact, the very idea of a sharp distinction between private and public life seems alien to many people." Private appropriation of the spoils of office is not regarded as morally reprehensible or illegitimate. Here, as in the second group of theories, morality has an opportunity to cause behavior and thereby cause corruption. In many of these theories, values are assumed to determine behavior. Because of a clash of values connected to one's private and one's public role, choices have to be made. And certain values lead to corruption. Out of obligations to friends or family (which can be very important in certain cultures), officials take bribes. Thus it is not so much selfish personal gain the corrupt official is after, but rather the agent feels a need to be  corrupt to  fulfill important personal (moral) duties, like ensuring loyalty to friends and family.

In the case of Piet Neus, his personal ties with the contractors was such that he felt obliged to help them with commissions, just as they felt obliged to help their friend with the renovations. And friends do not charge each other for such things. So the consience of Piet Neus was the direct cause of his corrupt behavior.

In this group of theories, the antagonism between two value systems is central, like in the theories of Weber (1921) and Habermas (1984). Hoffling (2002: 71) speaks of micro morality and macro morality. Micro morality has to do with connections to people in our social circles (family, friends). It is about values, norms and moral obligations in our daily personal and social lives. Even though obligations from the micro morality are based on informal norms, they are very strong – much stronger than our moral obligations towardsstrangers. Moral obligations in our personal lives are characterized by reciprocity: we help friends and family just as we expect them to help us. The macro morality, by contrast, emphasizes the universal. It is the product of the process, as described by Nelson (1949), of universalizing morality and claims the legitimacy of its norms on institutions of the law, a universal system of formal norms. The macro morality is characterized by the complementarity of rights and duties as the primal modus of social ties. For its existence, it depends on societal trust in the compensating mechanisms of social institutions. A problem of the macro morality is its higher level of abstraction, which limits the chances of internalizing its norms. Conflicts in society arise when persons see themselves in two social roles with opposing moral obligations: the macro morality of public officials requires them to treat different persons equally, where the micro morality requires them to favor friends wherever possible. Especially in the vast literature on Third World countries (Williams and Theobald 2000), a popular theme is patrimonialism, leading to patrimonial administration in which the private-public boundary (micro versus macro morality), central to the (Western) concept of public administration (Weber), is blurred. Corruption is often seen (ethnocentrically) as a phase developing countries have to through before reaching maturity. Despite widespread agreement in the literature (Theobald 1999) that neo- patrimonial character is the root cause of corruption in the Third World, Theobald issues a warning (1999: 473): "There is a danger that we are simply describing symptoms rather than identifying underlying causes. There is after all a certain lack of specificity in the concept in the sense that it has been employed in such a range of empirical contexts – from Brazil to Zaire, from Paraguay to the Philippines – which raises serious questions about its analytical utility." Since instances of this group of theories for explaining corruption are mostcommon in studies of lower income countries, I leave it aside here. We do know, however, that even though the obligations from macro morality might be stronger in Western countries, micro morality is also very strong (Jackall 1988, Bauman 1993). We can also think of hypothetical cases, say, a sick child, in which large sums of money are needed for a public official, leading him or her to become corrupt. Also, certain patronage ties can be identified in Western countries that are sometimes connected to the causes of individual corruption cases (e.g., Dohmen 1996). Think of 'old-boy networks', alumni networks, Rotary clubs, fraternities and the like (see Perkin 1996).

These theories lead to a discourse on corruption control in which codes of conduct and their enforcement play an important role.

'Ethical training' also is popular. In general, attention is paid to ethics in these models (Kaptein 1998; Kaptein and Wempe 2002) rather than rules, threats, surveillance or coercion. In the Third World literature, the discourse is on the elimination of patronage and cronyism, and calls for merit-based principles in administration. Of course, when underdevelopment of a country is seen as the cause of corruption, development is the cure. However, it is clear that economic development is by no means a guarantee for eliminating corruption. In current literature, corruption is often seen as deep-rooted, common and permanent; it is in all social systems, organizations, age and gender groups (Alatas 1990; Williams 2000: x).

*The Ethos of Public Administration Theories*

The fifth group of literature is closely related to the third group (organizational culture), but varies in that the major concern is the culture within public management and society in general. Like the previous (fourth) group, we are mainly looking at corruption from asocietal level. Like the third group, the  organizational level plays an important role: the macro factors (unlike the previous group) work through the level of organizations instead of the individual.

In these theories, political and economic structures are studied. Officials' performance has a causal path from societal pressure through the level of organizations. This, combined with a lack of attention to integrity issues, leads to a focus of the official on 'effectiveness,' making him or her corrupt. It is feared, for example, that public sector reforms, under the influence of New Public Management (NPM), change the culture within public management (the meso level) in such a way that standards of ethical probity within public services are affected negatively, leading to more instances of corruption. Thus the impact of NPM is on the organizational level, which influences the officials; from this point, the causal path of the third group of theories is followed. Economist approaches that do not address the ethical dimension of public service or support virtues like public interest, guardianship, integrity, merit, accountability, responsibility and truth, have, according to some, subverted the ethos of public organizations (e.g. by undermining public trust) , thus leading to more corruption. What Heywood calls 'the structural approach' (1997: 427) to political corruption, in which the emphasis is on the nature of state development (with administrative organization and efficiency as key variables), would also fall into this group of theories. Also, arguments are put forward that developments like NPM, deregulation and privatization (Doig and Wilson 1997) have created significant structures for influence-peddling (Heywood 1997: 429) and have removed agencies that provide for public accountability.Let us say that Piet Neus's constituency and political superiors stressed to him that what mattered most was achieving his policy objectives; his responsibility was to build roads and preferably at a fast pace. This led Neus to focus on result which, in turn, led to frequent consults with building contractors (over dinner, at the golf course, or even on the French Riviera) on how practical problems could be solved as quickly as possible. This in turn led to good contacts with certain contractors and roads being built quickly, but also to Piet Neus paying less attention to personal integrity, accountability and legitimacy of his decisions. In fact, the causal chain used in Dohmen's 1996 book describing the case of Piet Neus is similar. Factors at the macro level – huge sums of money funneled from central government into Neus's province of Limburg, a feeling of 'being different' in the province, a political culture in which one political party (CDA) was always in power, small social circles – led to a culture and structure in public organizations that nurtured corrupt practices.

Literature from a subgroup of this fifth type focuses on the morality of a society that can be 'wrong', leading to corruption. We see this causal model most often in (older) literature on corruption in the Third World (e.g. Wraith and Simpkins 1963). "Why does the public morality of African states not conform to that of the British? Their answer seems to boil down to one simple cause: avarice!" (Theobald 1999: 471). In other (economic) literature on corruption in underdeveloped countries, social and political characteristics of nation states are part of the 'explanation of corruption' (Leys 1965).

Empirical research in this group seems non-existent, probably because the causal link, like in the previous group of theories, is so indirect that the claim, *as true as it may be*, is hard to supportempirically. To discuss corruption in this way is of course complex and multifaceted. Theoretically the claim is powerfully supported by many; see, for example, Frederickson (1993, 1997) and Gregory (1999). Gregory claims (1999: 63): "Especially where such reforms have been largely underpinned by the new institutional economics and public choice theory, they may tend to counter more piecemeal efforts to maintain standards of ethical integrity in the bureaucracy. These efforts may need to be reinforced by new approaches to the rebuilding of institutionalized public service, based on a fuller understanding of the important distinctions between public and corporate management."[3]

When talking about the structure of the organization and the machinery of government, we quickly refer to the discourse of Scientific Administration (Taylorism). The goals of scientific administration are 'effectiveness' and 'efficiency', but the theory also holds that administrative integrity could be achieved through administrative control. However, scientific administration is out of fashion. Like empirical research, corruption control based on these theories is quite hard. After all, the culture of a society is difficult to influence. It is clear however, that those who argue that New Public Management leads to more corruption (Gregory 1999) use a discourse advocating the abandonment of (some) methods and techniques of NPM. A more concrete example of success in trying to control corruption at the societal level is influencing the culture of emerging democracies. Seligson (2001) shows that a public awareness campaign in Nicaragua was a success; it helped raise concern about the negative consequences of corruption and had a measurable impact in reducing its incidence.

## Correlation 'Theories'

The sixth (and last) group of literature puts forth not so much a theory on the causes of corruption as it does a collection of (very popular) research with certain common characteristics. The analysis of the causes of corruption is at all levels.

Correlation theories do not start from an implicit or explicit theoretical explanation model (like the previous five groups), but from specific factors. The research has in common that certain social, political, organizational or individual factors are highlighted. The variables considered are on all possible levels: individual, organizational and societal. For example, campaign finance practices in the United States (Williams 1995), or longevity in power by elected officials (Heywood 1997: 431), or economic development and 'being a former British colony' (Treisman 2000). Then it is often claimed that these factors are somehow 'causes' of corruption. Usually this is done on the basis of percentages or explained variance. If we were to add up all the claimed variance of these factors in all the research that can be grouped here, it would not be surprising if we found a causal construction in which well over 100 percent of variance would be explained (Schinkel 2004: 11). This can be explained of course by the varying circumstances between and within countries. Once again, we are warned about making strong general claims on the causes of corruption.

This group of theories does not study (the contingencies of) individual cases and would  therefore have a hard time providing a causal chain for Neus's corruption. Based on these theories, however, one could say that it is not surprising that Piet Neus became corrupt, considering, as hypothetical examples, the fact that  his party was inpower over a long period, voter turnout was low, his job was long-held, control structures in his organization were weak, his personality dominating, etcetera, etcetera.

These kinds of studies are usually not explicit on the causality of corruption. How exactly the causal link between macro-variables and the act of corruption should be seen often remains unclear. In social science, the causal path generally remains in the dark. Often, statistical significance is used to signify active causality without actual evidence. Noticeable in this regard is the frequent correlation between 'income' and  'corruption'. It seems that the lower the income of a country, the higher the occurrence of corruption. But as Huberts (1998b: 213) notices: "it is not clear whether this relationship is of a causal nature. The income of a country is for example directly related with political system characteristics, e.g., with the score on political democracy. Further research is necessary to find out how democracy, wealth and corruption are related." In general, of course, we must be careful when concluding causality from correlations.

An example of research of this sixth group is Holbrook and Meier (1993). Based on a quantitative comparison of registered cases of corruption in the fifty American states (conducted by the United States Department of Justice's (1988) Public Officials Integrity Section), the level of corruption is correlated with several factors. Four categories of explanations are offered. Among the historical and cultural variables, urbanization and education are concluded as important influences on corruption. Among the political explanations, voter turnout and, to a lesser degree, party competition stand out as relevant influences. The size of the public sector and gambling arrests are considered important bureaucratic explanations of corruption.

Some research of Huberts (1995, 1996, 1998a, 1998b) is based on an international expert panel survey. Questions about public corruption and fraud were answered by 257 respondents from 49 countries. Within research on corruption, methodologies that use expert panels are very popular. The research done by Transparency International and its corruption perception-indices are  famous in this regard. In this type of research, causality is not explicitly assumed on the basis of percentages of explained variance, yet the reasoning is similar. Experts are asked which social, economic, political, organizational and individual factors are, in their opinion, important for the explanation of cases of corruption which occur in their country (Huberts 1996: 46). Experts are thus asked which factors correlate, in their opinion, with corruption. In that sense, not so much the real causes of corruption are discussed. Huberts concludes (1998) that the three most important causes of corruption are identical for higher and lower income countries. Corruption is associated with the values and norms of individual politicians and civil servants, the lack of commitment to public integrity of leadership, organizational problems and failures, the relationship between the public sector and business, and the strength of organized crime.

This type of theories leads to a discourse on corruption control related to the respective correlations. These variables often do not offer much to go by. If research shows that urbanization and education of the general public are always important influences on corruption, how does it then lead to policy recommendations?

*The context of corruption.*

The clearest theory on the causes of corruption of the six groups seems to be public-choice related theories, but in exchange for this clarity, the theory offers contextuality. But what is exactly a 'cause' in social theory? A (very) short reflection is warranted in this article.

In the philosophy of causality, an epistemological and an ontological tradition can be distinguished (Schinkel 2004). In the first tradition, a cause is the coinciding of phenomena where, because the 'cause' always precedes the 'consequence,' a belief exists that there is a cause (Hume, 1990). In the six theory groups that were discussed above, this kind of causality was not found because no cause was identified that always coincided with the consequence 'corruption'. Causes identified in corruption research are never assumed to always lead to corruption. (The so called 'necessity' criterion, often named as a criterion for causation – in which if A is the cause of B, B must occur when A occurs – is such a strong one that it is not used in the corruption theories considered here.)

In the ontological tradition, causality is seen as something that 'actually' happened. Since in social science this is often hard to identify, this is also unhelpful in corruption research. In what way does 'GNP' or 'leadership' exist, and how can that 'cause' a particular corruption case? Bourdieu is an example of someone who warned against ascribing intrinsic aspects to social phenomena since it would amount to naturalization of what is socially constructed (Schinkel 2004: 14). A general problem for corruption research, as noted before, is that rarely are individual corruption cases studied. Therefore, the identified causes are not the triggering causes in a particular situation, but most often the predisposing causes. This makes it difficult to explain corruption. My aim is not to criticize all theoretical models on causation in corruption research for not having a hard causal criterion from the philosophy of causation. I merely wish to reflect on the claims made when we talk about the causes of corruption; general problems with causality and explanation cannot be ignored. In some cases it is perhaps better to speak of studies trying to 'understand' corruption rather than 'explaining' it (compare Weber 1921). The theories discussed thus far have given us valuable insights. Poverty probably has something to do with corruption. Such a macro variable has its influence on an individual level. We should nonetheless be careful with the assumed causality of poverty on corruption. And, more importantly, there seems to be a need for close analyses and studies of actual corruption cases along with the many existing studies on macro variables.

A substantial amount of literature states the conditions of

culture and structure of organizations under which corruption is more likely to occur (the sixth group of theories). But since these studies are based on panel surveys or regression analyses, they are not really about the causes of corruption. They are helpful because they can help us design organizations and influence their culture in such a way that lessens corruption. The problem is, however, that the literature suggests many such devices and it is not clear under what circumstances which device is best used. What works under what conditions at what costs? When is what kind of leadership important? How do we make sure public ethos continues to support traditional public values? Since these theories do not offer a theory about the cause of corruption, and are based on general research and broad correlations, they do not say  much about contingency, which is so important for social research – especially corruption research because of the aforementioned complexity of the phenomenon. This point is an important one Anechiarico and Jacobs (1996) make in their comprehensive classic study of New York City. It is rich in detail and insights; the authors document and analyze the manifold liabilities of a vast range of corruption control projects. They show how corruption control mechanisms, which might make sense when based on general research, might not work in a specific  context. "You name the anticorruption reform, the authors point out its severe organizational liabilities" (Silverman 1998: 182).

The conclusion is that to say more about the causes of corruption in Western countries, more research is needed in actual corruption cases,4 research with special attention to the necessary and sufficient conditions of corruption in a particular case. Based on a multiple case study research design, theory can be built on the causes of corruption (Herriott and Firestone 1983; Eisenhardt 1989; Yin 1989). The focus should be on understanding the dynamics present within single cases. Case studies offer the advantage of richer details of actual cases and their contextuality. Anechiarico and Jacobs (1996: 198): "Using focus groups and case studies would generate a mass of data that, when analyzed and organized, will probably provide a way to move forward with policy experiments." In case studies, attention can be paid to the individuals within their culture and organization. What are the rationalizations and justifications of those who are labeled 'corrupt'? We already know that the lack of a concrete victim in most corruption cases is often mentioned as mitigating circumstances (by the corrupt officials), just as 'economical necessity' is often mentioned to develop a tight network of relations in which a 'necessity' exists for 'wheeling and dealing' (Nelen and Nieuwendijk 2003: 44/45). Dohmen (1996: 218) noticed in his book on corruption in a Netherlands province that none of those convicted by law showed any kind of regret. Statementslike "Everyone was doing it" or "It was a favor for a friend" or "I still think I did nothing wrong" were echoed. Also, among the befriended elite who were not convicted, there was not much understanding for "the hanging of someone for a small foreign trip." Here, again, we see that corruption can only be established based on norms, which are by definition local and contextual. Therefore, studies on the causes of corruption in Western countries should study the specific context of corruption cases. Since I am speaking of qualitative research, the concentration should be on the validity as a trust in the results of the study rather than looking for absolute certainty. It should pay attention to both the process of data collection and of story telling. By conducting such a study, the contextuality of ethics is taken seriously. What many ethnographers have revealed is that moral decision-making is situational. Understanding it means understanding the particular circumstances (possibilities, etc.) of a certain situation. The most important contribution of detailed case studies is that they would give content to the vague notion of 'putting moral problems into context' (Hoffmaster 1992: 1427).

Why does Piet Neus think that what he did should not be labeled as 'corruption'? What justifications does he give? How did he get in contact with those he took bribes from? What was his relationship with them (for example, in terms of 'trust' and 'reputation')? What did the rest of the city officials know about it? And so on.

Since corruption literature on high income countries is often divided in different categories –USA, northern Europe (which includes Scandinavia, the Netherlands and Britain), southern Europe (whichincludes Scandinavia, the Netherlands and Britain), southern Europe (which includes Italy, Spain, Greece), Australia/New Zealand, and Japan – it would be interesting to repeat such a study in these different countries to see whether the causes of corruption differ.

When we have a richer theory on the causes of corruption, the hope is that we know better what medicine to prescribe for a particular patient. In that sense it could help fill the gap noticed by Van Hulten (2002: 182): almost no empirical studies offer conclusions about which anti- corruption methods work under what circumstances. Currently there is much confusion in the literature. "The right mix of corruption controls will undoubtedly differ from governmental unit and from agency to agency within the same governmental unit. Moreover, the optimal mix changes over time" (Anechiarico and Jacobs 1996: 198). It is safe to say we know next to nothing about which corruption controls are most efficient under different circumstances. Take as an example the installment of something like 'integrity systems'.

Would it have stopped Piet Neus from becoming corrupt? Perhaps. Gilman (2000) and Huberts (2000) seem to think so. Others, however (Anechiarico and Jacobs 1996; Cooper 1998; Brown 1999), certainly disagree and would probably maintain that these programs would be ineffective at best. The call for rich case studies is in accordance with the conclusion of Menzel (2003: 35) after reviewing the body of empirical research conducted on ethics and integrity in governance: "The research strategies for ethics scholars should include greater methodological rigor with perhaps less reliance on survey research methods. Such rigor, of course, could include contextually rich case studies as well as trend or longitudinal analyses that were largely absent from the studies examined in this paper."

*Pierre Bourdieu's theory of action: disposition analyses.*

Menzel (2003) concludes in the aforementioned research on the state of the art of empirical research on ethics and integrity in governance that most of the research on ethics and governance is not sturdily grounded on philosophical/theoretical foundations. Much of the research is survey-based with conclusions about correlations between variables. The same can now be concluded about the research on corruption. For contextually based research on corruption, we thus need a theoretical model.

Since the six groups of theories described in this article all had interesting insights into the background of corruption, a synthesis of them would be interesting. But doing so involves two problems:

3. The different theories deal with different levels of variables.
4. The different theories have different implicit or explicit causal models.

Huberts (1998a) offers an interesting way out of the first problem. When discussing fraud and corruption in the police force, he states that three levels of factors are at play. At the micro level are those that deal with individuals and their work. At the meso level are characteristics of the organization, which are distributed among leadership, organization structure, personal policy and organization culture. Third, there is a whole range of factors on the macro level, including changes in criminality, rules and laws, and so on. Table 2 illustrates Huberts's model.

In this model we see many factors from the overview of the six groups of theories, bringing together, in a sense, the differentlevels. Of course, on all three levels, factors can be added from other theories. With Huberts's model, however, the second problem remains: how do the variables at the different levels lead to corrupt behavior? Causality is always based on a theory and its concepts. How do the variables determine actions of public officials? How do the variables at the different levels influence each other and how do they influence officials? How, exactly, did the political-administrative system make Piet Neus a corrupt official?

If it turns out that a synthesis between the six groups of theories is not possible because their different implicit or explicit causal models are too dissimilar, a choice needs to be made. Current and future case studies on corruption could be used to answer the question: which of the six models helps us best explain corruption in these cases?

Table 2

*Types of Causes of Corruption and Fraud*

Individual and Work
1. individual: character and private circumstances
2. work: type, colleagues, contacts

Organization
1. leadership
2. organization structure
    - size, complexity
    - control, auditing
    - separation of responsibilities
3. organization culture
    - goals/mission
    - values and norms
    - operational code
4. personal (policy)
    - training and selection
    - rewarding

Environment
1. juridical/law
2. political-administrative
3. societal (e.g. criminality)

Source: Huberts 1998a: 35

Which causal chain makes most sense, and leads to the most interesting insights? Of course, we could also look for an alternative contextually based causal theory on corruption. One such possibility is Pierre Bourdieu's theory of social action (1977; 1990; 1992; 1998). By combining macro and micro factors and everything in between, it would be well suited as a theoretical model for corruption case studies (Table 3).

With the mental schemata of Bourdieu, causality is easier to understand. I cannot do justice to the rich work of the anthropologist and sociologist Bourdieu in this article, and limit myself to why I think Bourdieu's theory of action is helpful for corruption research as outlined in the previous section. (For a prolegomena to Bourdieu's work, see Bourdieu and Wacquant, 1992. For an account in the field of organizations, see, for example, Oakes, Townley et al., 1998; Everett, 2002.)

Bourdieu was not happy with the dualistic nature of much of sociological thinking with a choice of focus on either structure or agency,[5] micro or macro (Everett 2002: 57); here lies the attractiveness of his theory for our purposes. Bourdieu dismisses both methodological individualism (like much of the rational actor theories in corruption research[6]) and holism; micro and macro is to Bourdieu a false antimony. Instead he uses a relational perspective. *Bourdieu's theory of action provides a means of linking the otherwise isolated factors of the micro, meso and macro level.* Bourdieu's theory of action establishes an *incorporation* of macro and micro levels: mental schemata are the embodiment of social divisions. An analysis of objective structures logically carries over into an analysis of objective dispositions (Everett 2002: 58). With the concept of 'habitus', Bourdieu links the global with the local. Habitus is the mediating link between social structure (macro) and individual action (micro). Individual cases of corruption can very well be analyzed with Pierre Bourdieu's concepts of 'habitus', 'symbolic capital', 'practice' and 'disposition'.

A *disposition* is a concept that Bourdieu uses to analyze the immediate, lived experience of agents to explain the categories of perception and appreciation that structure their action from inside (Wacquant 1992: 11). Dispositions are carried by 'natural persons' or human agents (Bourdieu 1977: 80). Human agents use perceptional and evaluative schemata (definitions of their situations) in their everyday lives.

To Bourdieu there exists a correspondence between social structures and mental structures, the schemata; between objective divisions of the social world, and the vision and division that agents apply to it.

Table 3

| | Causal chain | Level of analysis of causes (independent variables) | Level of analysis of corruption (dependent variables) | The context | Most common research methods |
|---|---|---|---|---|---|
| Bourdie u-research | A person within a certain habitus, and having certain dispositions and predispositions is triggered into corruption. | All levels | Individual | Contingencies of individual cases is central | Case studies |

In social research it is important to escape from the realism of structures (Bourdieu 1990: 52): we often see in research that objective social (macro) relations are constructed and treated as realities in themselves, outside of the history of the group. Yet we should also watch out for subjectivism, with which it is impossible to give an account of the necessity of the social world (Bourdieu 1990: 52): Bourdieu proposes that social divisions and mental schemata are structurally homologous because they are generally linked: the latter are nothing other than the embodiment of the former. Cumulative exposure to certain social conditions instills in individuals an ensemble of durable and transposable dispositions that internalize the necessities of the extant social environment, inscribing inside the organism the patterned inertia and constraints of external reality. If the structures of the objectivity of the second order (habitus) are the embodied version of the objectivity of the first order, then "the analysis of objective regularities logically carries over into the analysis of subjective dispositions, thereby destroying the false antinomy ordinarily established between sociology and social psychology" (Wacquant 1992: 13)

For corruption research, this means that we should study not only regularities of corruption, but also the process of internalization of these regularities, or how the mental schemata of officials are constituted.

Human beings operate from 'mental schemata', for example, definitions of the situation, typifications and interpretive procedures. A primary assumption of Bourdieu's sociology is: "There exists a correspondence between social structures and mental structures, between the objective divisions of the social world – particularly into dominant and dominated in the various fields – and the principles of vision and division that agents apply to it" (cited in Wacquant 1992: 12). In Bourdieu's theory, the level at which a factor manifests itself is unimportant, so long as it leaves a trace in an individual. With all the factors at all three different levels, it was often unclear how exactly they worked, how they could lead to corruption. But with 'mental schemata' this is clearer; we understand how that works. A specific trigger in the presence of certain dispositions will lead to corrupt behavior. To Bourdieu (1990: 53), stimuli do not exist for practice in their objective truth, as conditional, conventional triggers, acting only on condition that they encounter agents conditioned to recognize them. Whether an official becomes corrupt depends on his or her disposition to become corrupt. This is not to say that (societal or cultural) regularities are absent in the behavior of officials: there are social factors that work through the individual.

Dispositions then are a reformulation of we earlier called 'factors of corruption', which allow more fine- tuning. One can distinguish several levels  of predispositions. Contextual research can establish dispositions that *can* lead to corruption. Since these dispositions do not always lead to corruption, they cannot be called causes in the strictest sense of the word. What is important is the receptiveness of an individual to corruption, and whether that receptiveness is triggered.

Now we can also 'explain' something about corrupt cultures. For example, Piet Neus was an official who saw himself surrounded by corrupt officials (Dohmen 1996). Dispositions can be so strongly determined by the social context that it is hard to escape the behavior of that context. When consistently reinforced in certain ideas and acts, it is difficult for an agent to step outside that culture. This can be compared to subcultural delinquency theory: once individuals live in a group culture where violence is the norm, it is hard for them to not become violent themselves. The research on corruption using Bourdieu's theory of action should focus on the categories of perception, appreciation and the lived experience (Wacquant 1992: 7-9) of corrupt officials. This can be called a disposition analysis, in which the habitus of the corrupt official  is analyzed. Bourdieu and Wacquant (1992: 105):

One must analyze the habitus of agents, the different systems of dispositions they have acquired by internalizing a determinate type of social and economic condition, and which find in a definite trajectory within the field under construction a more or less favorable opportunity to become actualized. Adds Everett (2002: 71): One might also suggest that habitus can be investigated by examining its structuring components, that is, by examining the language and discourse of social agents, and the struggles over these components.

Everett mentions that discourse (de Graaf 2003) and other textual analyses can be used as insightful research techniques for analyzing the habitus. Drummond (1998) suggests that the habitus can be seen as a collection of stories. This makes narrative analyses (de Graaf 2003: chapter 6) a technique that can be used for disposition analysis. Everett (2002: 71) states:

For organizational researchers, this suggestion provides not only an opening for an investigation of "organizational habitus" (through an investigation of organizational narratives) but also a more general link between Bourdieu's theory and the concepts of organizational culture, leadership, conflict and change. These, Drummond says, can be usefully rewritten as organizational habitus (culture), enacted habitus (leadership), the imposition and resistance of habitus (conflict) and the destruction and replacement of habitus (change).

Were we to make a dispositional analysis of Piet Neus, we would first of all listen to his stories. His reasons, habitus, and dispositions would become clearer from the way he thinks. We would then study his dossier to see what mental schemata of dispositions towards corruption were present. In other words, what field of considerations was present in this case? We would also look for the more or less favorable opportunities that actualized the corruption on this case. What triggered it? By studying more of such cases we will come to an understanding of what dispositions, under what specific circumstances, lead to corruption. How was the susceptibility towards corruption and under what circumstances was it triggered? A predisposing factor could be a cup of coffee. Out of multiple (dispositional) case analyses will come regularities about and understandings of the causes of corruption. A view will present itself of predispositional factors, a scheme of dispositions. Causality will then be of such a nature that certain determining factors will not always leads to corruption. In that sense, we cannot speak of causality in the strictest sense of the word.

## Criminology

Recall from the discussion of the 'bad apple' theories that criminological theories can be used to study corruption (see Nelen and Nieuwendijk 2003: 43-48). Many different criminological theories exist on the causes of delinquency, like strain theories (Merton 1967) and social deviance theories (Cohen 1967). In these theories, the cause of criminal (corrupt) behavior is not so much about values as it is about various individual backgrounds and motives. The strong points of criminological theories in general, and especially for students of corruption, is that they offer models to explain (1) behavior; and (2) 'criminalizing', or why something is called a criminal (corrupt) act. As interesting as this last aspect is for corruption research, because of the many different definitions and interpretations of 'corruption,' it is beyond the scope of this article. When explaining behavior, criminological theories mostly focus on (1) the motive of the official;

and (2) opportunity. The latter aspect falls beyond the scope of 'bad apple' theories. Of course, in order to research 'opportunity' in corruption research, models from organization science are required to describe (1) the characteristics of an organization; and (2) the surroundings of an organization. All criminological theories that are used in corruption research need adaptation and some sort of 'translation.' Interestingly enough for students of corruption, lack of attention given to so-called 'white collar' criminality is a criticism. It is not surprising that many elements of criminological theories can be found in the six kinds of literature distinguished here, since criminology also contains many different causal models. It is a so-called 'object-science': the only thing that unites the many different criminological theories is the research object. Therefore, many different portrayals of the agent can be found in different theories. Homo economicus is currently popular in criminological theories, a view of the corrupt agent also present in rational choice theories. In all six groups of literature described here, some traces of criminological theories were found and some sort of criminological variant existed. Most traces however, were found in the 'bad apple' theories. Especially in the older criminological theories, criminality is seen as deviating behavior that needs to be explained: bad apple theories. The current trend (roughly from the 1980s) within criminology, however, is not to view criminal acts as deviating behavior. Social control theory for example, explains why people do abide by the law (Korn and McCorkle 1959; Hirschi 1969).

## CONCLUSION

Interesting to students of public administration is that, as it turns out, much confusion exists in the literature on which anti-corruption methods work best under which circumstances. The overview made clear that the theoretical model chosen determines, for a large part, the direction of the proposed solutions. Different causal chains lead to different discourses on corruption prevention and corruption control. We know little of what corruption control works best and most efficiently. More corruption case studies should help us with prescription and give us more information on what the right mix of corruption control is under specific circumstances. After all, proposed corruption control mechanisms should not be based on the logic of the theory of empirical research, but on what works best under what conditions.

The main question of this article was: how can the causes of corruption in Western countries be studied? Six groups of theories, each with an implicit or explicit theoretical model on the causation of corruption, were distinguished. A primary conclusion was that there are not many studies on actual, individual corruption cases. It seems, therefore, that we need more contextual corruption research; many current studies lack contingency. As a possible theoretical model on the causation of corruption, Pierre Bourdieu's theory of social action seems promising; it is suitable, for instance, to study the case of Piet Neus. The study of several of these cases in their context should lead to additional theories on the causes of corruption. Alternative explanations and understanding of corruption in particular countries can help us reconsider the effectiveness of existing policy instruments to combat corruption.

NOTES

1.  Public officials are corrupt when they act (or fail to act) as a result of receiving personal rewards from interested outside private partners.

2.  Interestingly enough, those public choice theorists in the field of Public Administration in favor of NPM also often use rational choice as its theoretical base, but argue for less regulation. This can be explained by the fact that NPM usually ignores integrity violations in its analysis, something NPM has been oft criticized for (e.g. Lane 1999; Frederickson 1993, 1997.)

3.  Incidentally, there are also those who stress that common values between public and private sector organizations are important too. For example, "the major actors on the world stage are gradually realizing that there cannot be two different codes of ethics or standards of conduct – one in the private realm and the other in the public realm. One cannot have a public sector free of corruption when the private sector actually tolerates if not rewards corrupt practices. Nor can there be a moral business sector when the public sector, the government, and the political system condone, not condemn, corruption." (Caiden, and Dwivedi 2001: 245-255

4.  What is and is not corrupt is already heavily under debate. To understand the social construction of corruption, the context in which the label is used is important. Only that can teach us under what conditions in specific cases the label 'corruption' is used.

5.  Bourdieu sees objectivism and subjectivism, structural necessity and individual agency as false antinomies (Wacquant 1998).

Bourdieu transcends these dualities with a social praxeology which weaves together structuralist and constructivist positions.

6.  "Bourdieu does not deny that agents face options, exert initiative, and make decisions. What he disputes is that they do so in the conscious, systematic (in short: intellectualist) and intentional manner expostulated by rational-choice theorists. He insists to the contrary that deliberate decision making or rule following "is never but a makeshift aimed at covering up misfirings of habitus" (Wacquant 1998: 24)

## REFERENCES

Alatas, S. (1990). *Corruption: Its Nature, Causes and Functions*, Avebury: Aldershot.

Anechiarico, F., & Jacobs J. (1996). *The Pursuit of Absolute Integrity. How Corruption Control Makes Government Ineffective*, The University of Chicago Press: Chicago.

Bauman, Z. (1993). *Postmodern Ethics*, Blackwell, Oxford.

Bourdieu, P. (1997). *Outline of a Theory of Practice*, Cambridge University Press: Cambridge.

Bourdieu, P. (1990) .*The Logic of Practice*, Polity Press.

Bourdieu, P. (1998). *Practical Reason*, Polity Press: Cambridge.

Bourdieu, P., & Wacquant L. (1992). *An Invitation to Reflexive Sociology*, The University of Chicago Press: Chicago.

Bourdieu, P., & Wacquant L. (1992). The Purpose of Reflexive Sociology (The Chicago Workshop). In *An Invitation to Reflexive Sociology*, Bourdieu, P.; Wacquant L., (Eds.), The University of Chicago Press: Chicago.

Brown, G. (1999). The Ethics Backlash and the Independent Counsel Statute, *Rutgers Law Review*, 51, 467.

Caiden, G. (2001). Corruption and Governance. In *Where Corruption Lives*, Caiden, G.; Dwivedi O.; Jabbra J.Eds., Kumarian Press: Bloomfield.

Caiden, G., & Dwivedi, O. (2001). "Official Ethics and Corruption". In *Where Corruption Lives*, Caiden G.; G. Dwivedi; Jabbra J., (Eds.), Bloomfield: Kumarian Press.

Cohen, A. (1967). *Delinquent Boys: The Culture of the Gang.* Glencoe: Free Press.

Collier, M. (2002). Explaining Corruption: An Institutional Approach. Crime, *Law & Social Change,* 38, 1-32.

Cooper, T. (1998). *The Responsible Administrator.* San Francisco: Jossey-Bass.

Cusson, M. (1983). *Why Delinquency?* Toronto: Toronto University Press.

Dohmen, J. (1996). *De Vriendenrepubliek.* Nijmegen: Sun. Doig, A., & Wilson J. (1997). What Price New Public Management? *Political Quarterly,* 69 (3), 267-276.

Drummond, G. (1998). New Theorizing about Organizations: The Emergence of Narrative and Social Theory for Management. *Current Topics in Management,* 3, 93-122.

Eisenhardt, K. (1989). Building Theories from Case Study Research. *Academy of Management Review,* (14), 532-550.

Everett, J. (2002). Organizational Research and the Praxeology of Pierre Bourdieu. *Organizational Research Methods*, 5, 56-80.

Fijnaut, C. & Huberts, L. (Eds.). (2002). *Corruption, Integrity and Law Enforcement*. Den Haag: Kluwer Law International.

Fijnaut, C., & Huberts L. (2002). Corruption, Integrity and Law Enforcement: An Introduction. In *Corruption, Integrity and Law Enforcement*, Fijnaut C.; Huberts L., (Eds.) Den Haag: Kluwer Law International, 3- 34.

Frederickson, H. G., (Ed.). (1993). *Ethics and Public Administration*. Armonk: M.E. Sharpe.

Frederickson, H. G. (1997). *The Spirit of Public Administration*. San Francisco: Jossey-Bass.

Gambetta, D. (1993). *The Sicilian Mafia*. Cambridge: Harvard University Press.

Gilman, S. (2000). An Idea Whose Time Has Come: The International Experience of the U.S. Office of Government Ethics in Developing Anticorruption Systems. *Public Integrity*, 135-155.

Graaf, G. de. (2003). *Tractable Morality. Customer Discourses of Bankers, Veterinarians and Charity Workers.* Rotterdam: Erim.

Gregory, R. (1999). Social Capital Theory and Administrative Reform: Maintaining Ethical Probity. Public Service, *Public Administration Review*, 59, 63-76.

Habermas, J. (1984). *The Theory of Communicative Action.*
London: Heinemann Polity Press.

Herriott, R., & Firestone W. (1983). Multisite Qualitative Policy
Research: Optimizing Description and Generalizability.
*Educational Researcher*, 12, 14-
19.

Heywood, P. (1997). Political Corruption: Problems and
Perspectives. *Political Studies,* XLV, 639-658.

Hirschi, T. (1969). *Causes of Delinquency.* Piscataway:
Transaction Publishers.

Höffling, C. (2002). *Korruption als Soziale Beziehung.*
Opladen: Leske+Budrich.

Hoffmaster, B. (1992). Can Ethnography Save the Life of
Medical Ethics? *Social Science and Medicine*, 35, 1421-
1431.

Holbrook, T, & Meier K. (1993). Politics, Bureaucracy, and
Political Corruption: A Comparative State Analysis. In
*Ethics and Public Administration*, H. Frederickson (Ed.).
Armonk: M.E. Sharpe.

Huberts, L. (1995). Western Europe and Public Corruption.
*European Journal on Criminal Policy and Research*, 3, 7-
20.

Huberts, L., Kaptein M., & Lasthuizen, K. (2004). Leadership and
Integrity Violations at Work: A Study on the Perceived

Impact of Leadership Behavior on Integrity Violations within the Dutch

Police Force. Paper presented at IRSPM VIII, Budapest.

Huberts, L. (1996). *Expert Views on Public Corruption Around the Globe. Research Report on the Views of an International Expert Panel*. Amsterdam: PSPA.

Huberts, L. (1998a). *Blinde Vlekken in de Politiepraktijk en de Politiewetenschap*. Gouda: Gouda Quint.

Huberts, L. (1998b). What Can Be Done Against Public Corruption and Fraud: Expert Views on Strategies to Protect Public Integrity. *Crime, Law & Social Change*, 29, 209-224.

Huberts, L. (2000). Anticorruption Strategies. The Hong Kong Model in International Context. *Public Integrity*, 211-228.

Hulten, M. van, (2002). *Corruptie, Onbekend, Onbemind, Alomtegenwoordig*. Amsterdam: Boom.

Hume, D. (1990). *A Treatise of Human Nature*. Hammondsworth: Penguin.

Huntington, S. (1989). Modernization and Corruption. In *Political Corruption. A Handbook*. Heidenheimer, A.; Levine, V., (Eds.), New Brunswick: Transaction Publishers, 377-388.

Jackall, R. (1988). *Moral Mazes: The World of Corporate Managers.* New York: Oxford University Press.

Kaptein, M. (1998). *Ethics Management.* Dordrecht: Kluwer Academic Publishers.

Kaptein, M., & Wempe J. (2002). *The Balanced Company: A Theory of Corporate Integrity.* Oxford: Oxford University Press.

Klitgaard, R. (1988). *Controlling Corruption.* Berkeley: University of California Press.

Korn, R., & McCorkle, L.. (1959). *Criminology and Penology.* New York: Holt-Dryden.

Lane, J. (1995). *The Public Sector Concepts, Models and Approaches.* London: Sage.

Lane, J. (1999). *The Public Sector Concepts, Models and Approaches.* London:Sage.

Leys, C. (1965). What Is the Problem about Corruption? *The Journal of Modern African Studies,* 3, 215-230.

Malec, K. (1993). Public Attitudes toward Corruption: Twenty-five Years of Research. In *Ethics and Public Administration,* Frederickson. H., (Ed.) Armonk, NY: M.E. Sharpe, 13-27.

Menzel, D. (2003). State of the Art of Empirical Research on Ethics and Integrity in Governance, Paper presented at the Annual Conference of The European Group of Public Administration, Oeiras, Portugal, 3-6 September, 2003.

Merton, R. (1967). *Social Theory and Social Structure.* New York: Collier-Macmillan.

Naim, M. (1995). The Corruption Eruption. *Brown Journal of World Affairs*, II, 245-261.

Nelen, H., & Nieuwendijk A. (2003). *Geen ABC: Analyse van Rijksrechercheonderzoeken naar Ambtelijke en Bestuurlijke Corruptie*. Den Haag: Boom Juridische Uitgevers.

Nelson, B. (1949). *The Idea of Usury: From Tribal Brotherhood to Universal Otherhood*. Princeton: Princeton University Press.

Oakes, L., Townley, B., & Cooper, D. (1998). Business Planning as Pedagogy: Language and Control in a Changing Institutional Field. *Administrative Science Quarterly*, 43, 257-292.

Perkin, H. (1996). *The Third Revolution: Professional Elites in the Modern World*. London: Routhledge.

Punch, M. (2000). Police Corruption and Its Prevention. *European Journal on Criminal Policy and Research*, 8, 301-324.

Rose-Ackerman, S. (1978). *Corruption: A Study in Political Economy*. New York: Academic Press.

Rose-Ackerman, S. (1999). *Corruption and Government: Causes, Consequences and Reform*. Cambridge: Cambridge University Press.

Schinkel, W. (2004). The Will to Violence. *Theoretical Criminology*, 8, 5-31.

Seligson, M. (2001). Corruption and Democratization: What Is To Be Done? *Public Integrity*, 221-241.

Silverman, E. (1998). The Price of Controlling Corruption.

*Public Administration Review*, 58, 182-185.

Theobald, R. (1999). So What Really Is the Problem about Corruption? *Third World Quarterly*, 20, 491-502.

Treisman, D. (2000). The Causes of Corruption: A Cross-National Study. *Journal of Public Economics*, 76, 399.

Trevino, L., Hartman L., & Brown. M.. (2000). Moral Person and Moral Manager: How Executives Develop a Reputation for Ethical Leadership. *California Management Review*, 42, 128-142.

Trevino, L., Weaver, G., Gibson, D.,& Toffler, B. (1999). Managing Ethics and Legal Compliance. *California. Management Review*, 41, 131-151.

Wacquant, L. (1992). Toward a Social Praxeology: The Structure and Logic of Bourdieu's Sociology. In *An Invitation to Reflexive Sociology*, Bourdieu, P.; Wacquant L., (Eds.), Chicago: The University of Chicago Press, 1-59.

Weber, M. (1921). *Economy and Society: An Outline of Interpretive Sociology.* Berkeley: University of California Press.

Williams, R. (1995). Private Interests and Public Office: The American Experience of Sleaze. *Parliamentary Affairs*, 48, 632-549.

Williams, R., (Ed.). (2000). *Explaining Corruption.* Cheltenham: Edward Elgar.

Williams, R., & Theobald, R., (Eds.) (2000). *Corruption in the Developing World*. Cheltenham: Edward Elgar.

Wraith, R., & Simpkins. E. (1963). *Corruption in Developing Countries*. London: Allen and Unwin.

Yin, R. (1989). *Case Study Research*. Newbury Park: Sage Publications

# APPENDIX II: STATISTICS

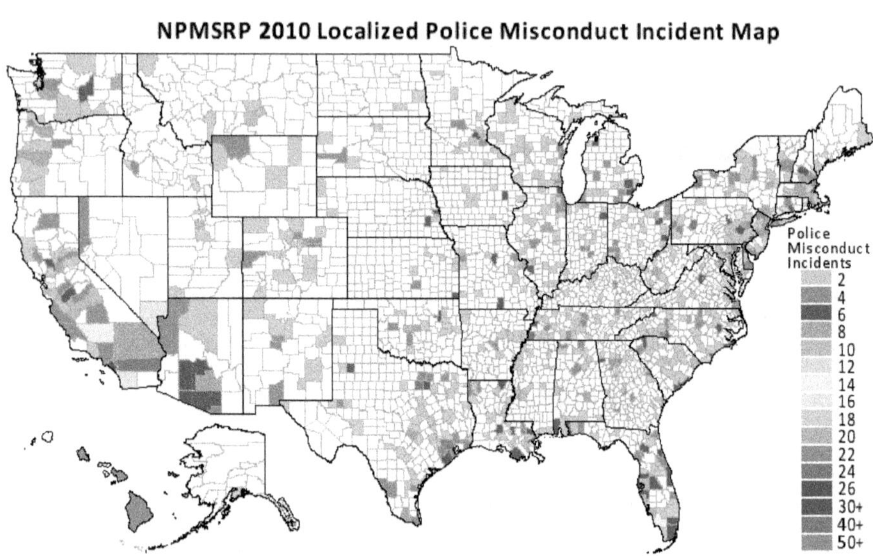


*SOURCE: PACKMAN, D. (2010). 2010 Q2 NPMSRP NATIONAL POLICE MISCONDUCT STATISTICAL REPORT.*

*http://www.policemisconduct.net/2010-q2-npmsrp-national-police-misconduct-statistical-report/*

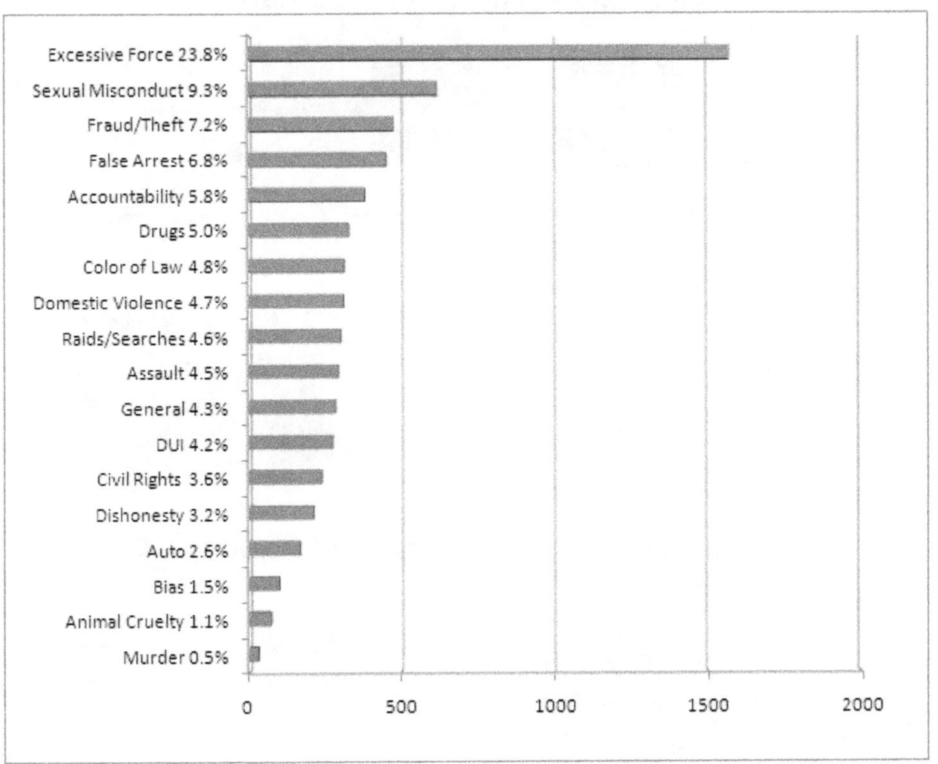


*SOURCE: CATO INSTITUTE. (2010). 2010 ANNUAL REPORT HTTP://WWW.POLICEMISCON-DUCT.NET/STATISTICS/2010-ANNUAL-REPORT/*

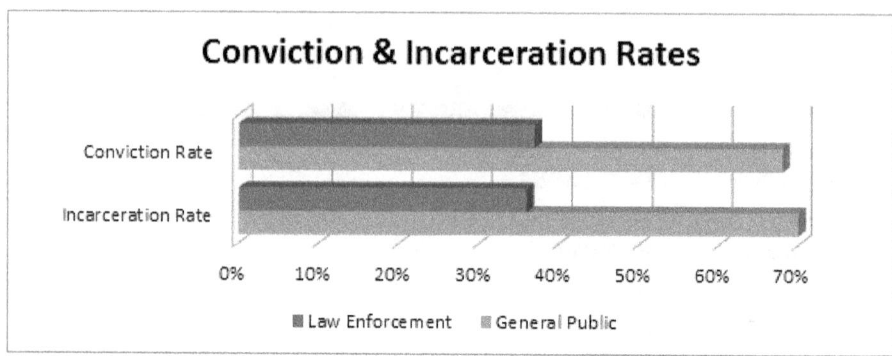



*SOURCE:  EVERETT, S. (2014).  POLICE BRUTALITY REPORT.  HTTP://QUIETMIKE. ORG/2014/07/16/POLICE-BRUTALITY-STATISTICS/*

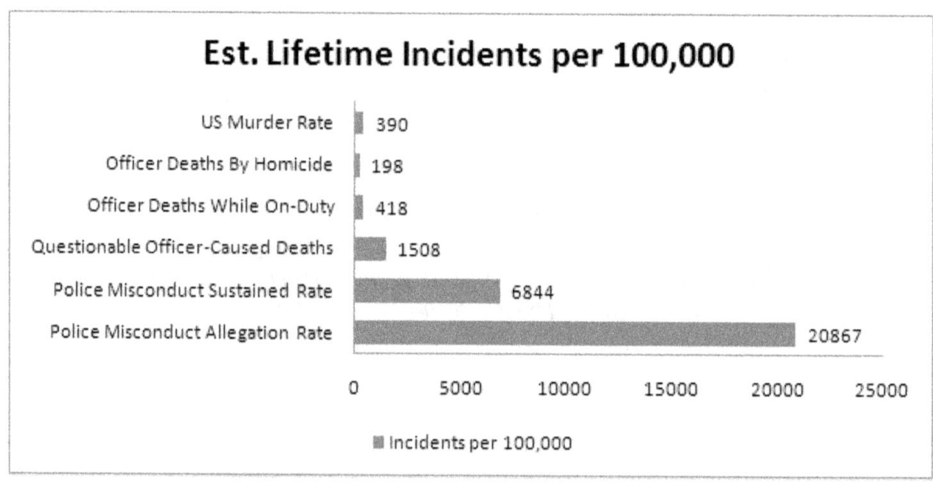



*SOURCE:  PACKMAN, D. (2009). ABUSED BY THE STATE: POLICE BRUTALITY STATISTICS. HTTP://QUIETMIKE.ORG/2014/07/16/POLICE-BRUTALITY-STATISTICS/*

**Most Corrupt States**

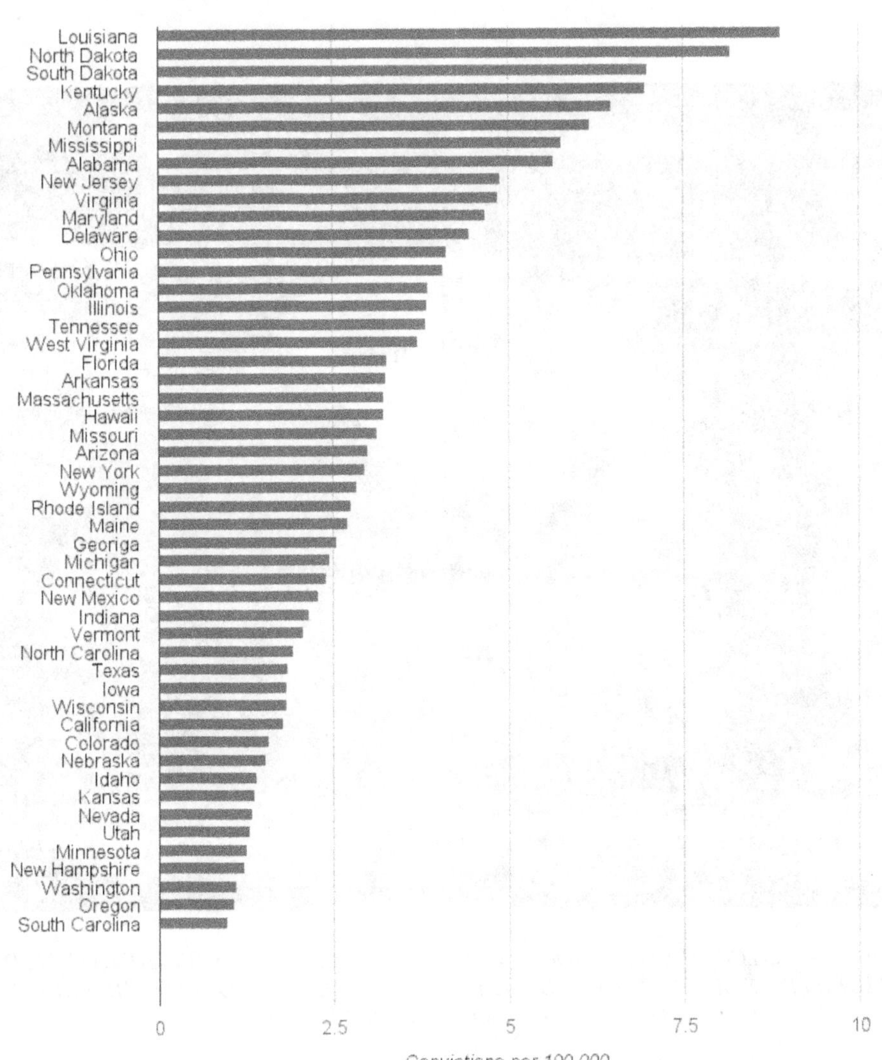


SOURCE: WASHINGTON POST. (2014). THE MOST CORRUPT STATES IN AMERICA. HTTP://WWW.WASHINGTONPOST.COM/BLOGS/GOVBEAT/WP/2014/01/22/THE-MOST-CORRUPT-STATES-IN-AMERICA/

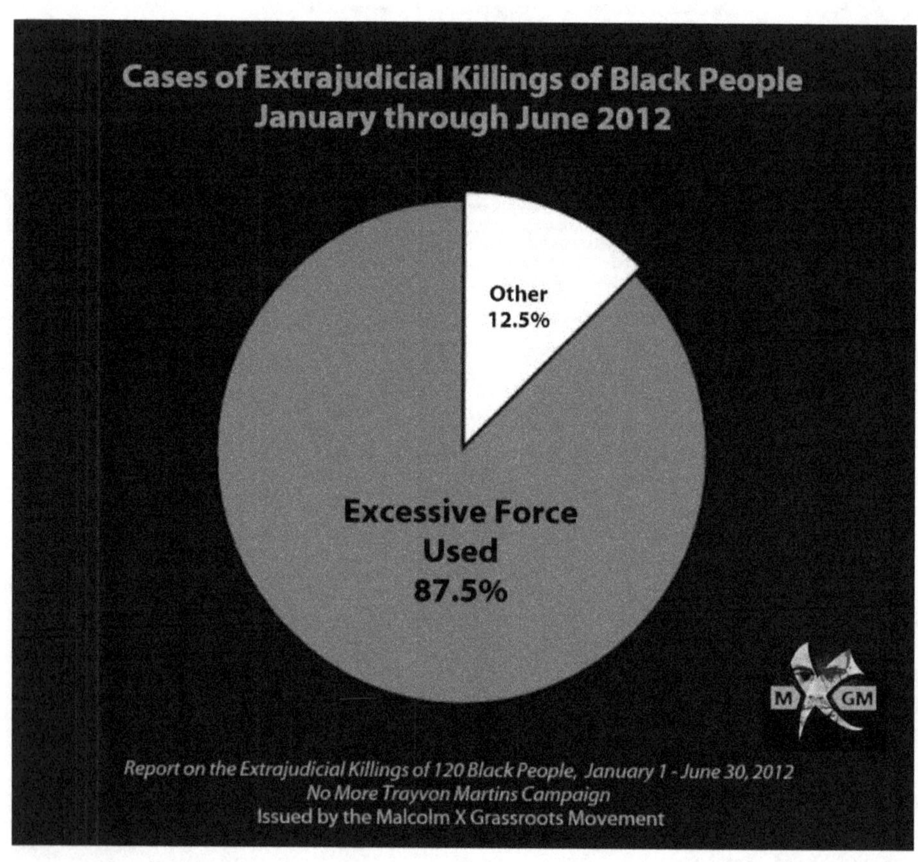



SOURCE:  MALCOLM X GRASSROOTS MOVEMENT. (2012). REPORT ON THE EXTRAJUDI-CIAL KILLINGS OF 120 BLACK PEOPLE. HTTP://MXGM.ORG/REPORT-ON-THE-EXTRAJU-DICIAL-KILLINGS-OF-120-BLACK-PEOPLE/

## TABLE 20
## Types of force used or threatened by police, 2008

| Type of force police used or threatened | Percent of contacts with police in which— | |
|---|---|---|
| | Force was used or threatened | Excessive force was used or threatened |
| Pushed or grabbed | 53.5% | 60.2% |
| Kicked or hit | 12.6 | 17.2 |
| Sprayed chemical/pepper spray | 4.9 ! | 5.6 ! |
| Electroshock weapon (stun gun) | 4.1 ! | 5.6 ! |
| Pointed gun | 25.6 | 28.4 |
| Threatened force | 76.6 | 84.9 |
| Shouted at resident | 75.5 | 76.6 |
| Cursed at resident | 39.1 | 44.0 |
| Number (in thousands) | 574 | 417 |

*SOURCE: WALTON, F. (2014). HOW OFTEN ARE UNARMED BLACK MEN SHOT DOWN BY POLICE. HTTP://WWW.DAILYKOS.COM/STORY/2014/08/24/1324132/-HOW-OFTEN-ARE-UN-ARMED-BLACK-MEN-SHOT-DOWN-BY-POLICE*

TABLE 18

Contacts with police in which force was used or threatened, by demographic characteristics, 2002, 2005, and 2008

| Demographic characteristic | Residents experiencing use or threat of force during most recent contact | | | | | |
|---|---|---|---|---|---|---|
| | Number (in thousands) | | | Percent[a] | | |
| | 2002 | 2005 | 2008 | 2002 | 2005 | 2008 |
| Total | 664 | 716 | 574 | 1.5% | 1.6% | 1.4% |
| Sex | | | | | | |
| Male | 520 | 514 | 390 | 2.2% | 2.2% | 1.8% |
| Female | 144 | 202 | 184 | 0.7 | 1.0 | 1.0 |
| Race/Hispanic origin | | | | | | |
| White[b] | 374 | 406 | 347 | 1.1% | 1.2% | 1.2% |
| Black or African American[b] | 173 | 183 | 130 | 3.5 | 4.3 | 3.4 |
| Hispanic/Latino | 103 | 105 | 68 | 2.5 | 2.6 | 1.6 |
| Other[b,c] | 15 ! | 3 ! | 19 ! | 1.1 ! | 0.2 ! | 1.1 ! |
| Two or more races[b] | ~ | 19 ! | 11 ! | ~ | 4.0 ! | 2.4 ! |
| Age | | | | | | |
| 16–19 | 152 | 168 | 78 | 3.6% | 4.0% | 2.4% |
| 20–19 | 230 | 271 | 253 | 2.1 | 2.5 | 2.5 |
| 30–39 | 117 | 135 | 122 | 1.2 | 1.6 | 1.5 |
| 40–49 | 95 | 66 | 61 | 1.0 | 0.7 | 0.8 |
| 50–59 | 50 | 39 | 33 ! | 0.8 | 0.6 | 0.5 ! |
| 60 or older | 21 ! | 38 | 27 ! | 0.4 ! | 0.8 | 0.6 ! |

*SOURCE: WALTON, F. (2014). HOW OFTEN ARE UNARMED BLACK MEN SHOT DOWN BY POLICE. HTTP://WWW.DAILYKOS.COM/STORY/2014/08/24/1324132/-HOW-OFTEN-ARE-UN-ARMED-BLACK-MEN-SHOT-DOWN-BY-POLICE*

**Table 1 • *Perceptions and Experiences of Police Misconduct***

| | Neighborhood | | | City | | |
|---|---|---|---|---|---|---|
| | Whites (%) | Blacks (%) | Hispanics (%) | Whites (%) | Blacks (%) | Hispanics (%) |
| Perceptions of misconduct | | | | | | |
| 1. How often do you think police officers stop people on the streets of your [neighborhood/city] without good reason?* | | | | | | |
| Very often | 2 | 18 | 12 | 5 | 27 | 18 |
| Fairly often | 5 | 18 | 15 | 11 | 27 | 20 |
| On occasion | 46 | 46 | 46 | 62 | 36 | 51 |
| Never | 46 | 19 | 27 | 23 | 11 | 11 |
| N = | 613 | 554 | 600 | 613 | 558 | 604 |
| 2. How often do you think police officers, when talking to people in your [neighborhood/city], use insulting language against them?* | | | | | | |
| Very often | 3 | 11 | 7 | 4 | 17 | 9 |
| Fairly often | 4 | 14 | 11 | 5 | 18 | 13 |
| On occasion | 36 | 44 | 33 | 48 | 45 | 41 |
| Never | 57 | 31 | 48 | 43 | 20 | 37 |

*SOURCE: WALTON, F. (2014). HOW OFTEN ARE UNARMED BLACK MEN SHOT DOWN BY POLICE. HTTP://WWW.DAILYKOS.COM/STORY/2014/08/24/1324132/-HOW-OFTEN-ARE-UN-ARMED-BLACK-MEN-SHOT-DOWN-BY-POLICE*

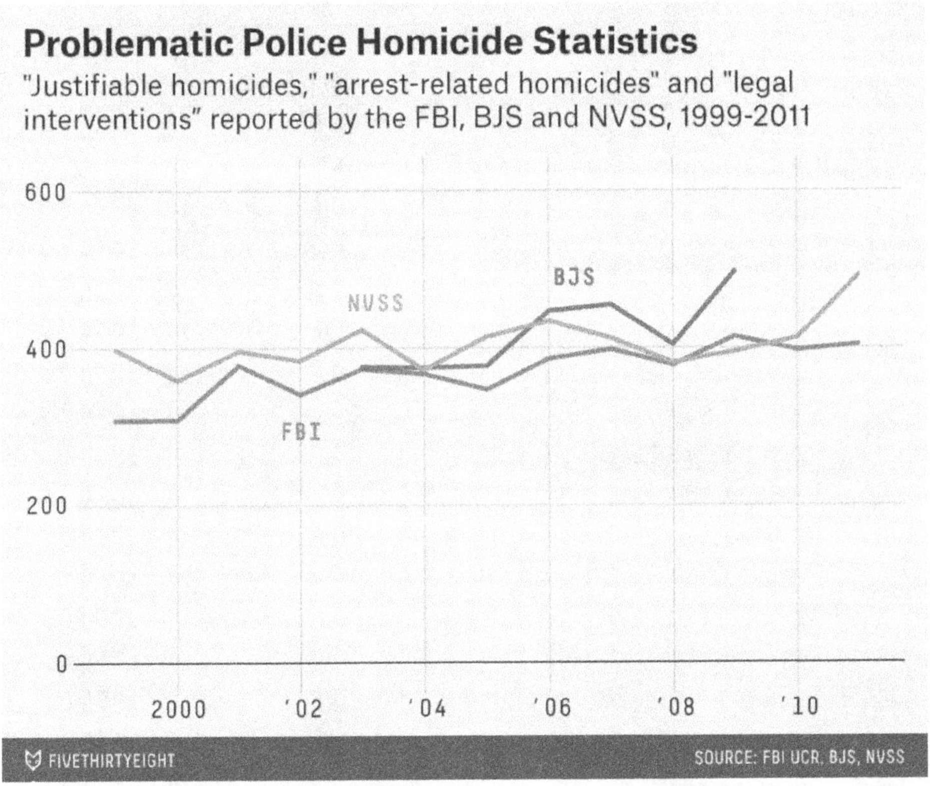
Problematic Police Homicide Statistics
"Justifiable homicides," "arrest-related homicides" and "legal interventions" reported by the FBI, BJS and NVSS, 1999-2011
600
400
200
0
2000
'02
'04
'06
'08
'10
BJS
NVSS
FBI
FIVETHIRTYEIGHT
SOURCE: FBI UCR, BJS, NVSS

*SOURCE: WALTON, F. (2014). HOW OFTEN ARE UNARMED BLACK MEN SHOT DOWN BY POLICE. HTTP://WWW.DAILYKOS.COM/STORY/2014/08/24/1324132/-HOW-OFTEN-ARE-UNARMED-BLACK-MEN-SHOT-DOWN-BY-POLICE*

## 500 – 999 Officer Agency Rates

The following chart displays the 20 agencies with between 500 to 999 sworn law enforcement officers with the highest misconduct rates for that group of agencies:

| | Agency | State | Officers Involved | Projected PMR |
|---|---|---|---|---|
| 1 | Pittsburgh | PA | 53 | 7731.58 |
| 2 | Lee County | FL | 32 | 7538.28 |
| 3 | Tulsa | OK | 42 | 6896.55 |
| 4 | Minneapolis | MN | 31 | 4654.65 |
| 5 | Oakland | CA | 18 | 3026.48 |
| 6 | Marion County | IN | 11 | 2933.33 |
| 7 | Maricopa County | AZ | 16 | 2859.70 |
| 8 | Collier County | FL | 13 | 2846.20 |
| 9 | West Virginia Highway Patrol | WV | 13 | 2827.62 |
| 10 | Montgomery | AL | 10 | 2661.34 |
| 11 | Portland | OR | 16 | 2229.19 |
| 12 | Fresno | CA | 12 | 1934.70 |
| 13 | Mobile | AL | 7 | 1718.85 |
| 14 | Kern County | CA | 11 | 1713.40 |
| 15 | Buffalo | NY | 10 | 1675.04 |
| 16 | Toledo | OH | 7 | 1545.25 |
| 17 | Shelby County | TN | 6 | 1538.46 |
| 18 | St. Petersburg | FL | 6 | 1481.48 |
| 19 | Syracuse | NY | 5 | 1320.13 |
| 20 | Orlando | FL | 7 | 1287.36 |

*Source: Walton, F. (2014). How often are unarmed black men shot down by police. http://www.dailykos.com/story/2014/08/24/1324132/-How-Often-are-Unarmed-Black-Men-Shot-Down-By-Police*

**Figure 2: Types of complaints (excluding deaths as a result of police action or in custody) received by ICD, April 1997-March 2002**

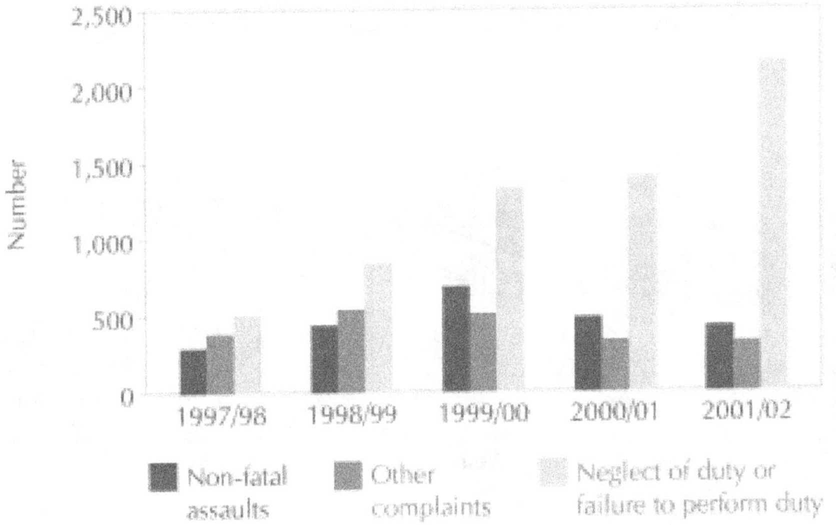

Source: ICD

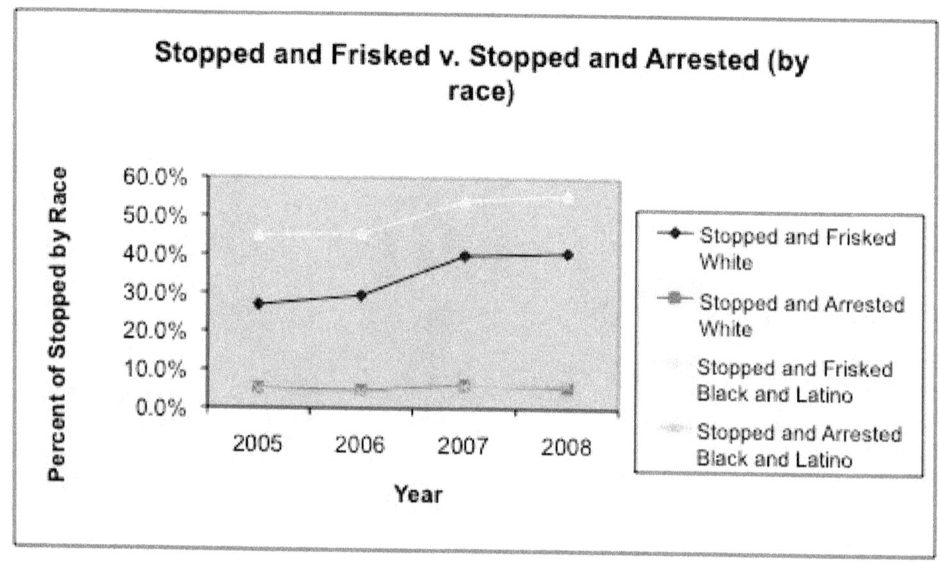



*Source: Center for Constitutional Rights (CCR). (2009). CCR Reports: Racial Disparity in NYPD Stop and Friskshttp://ccrjustice.org/ccr-reports%3A-racial-disparity-nypd-stop-and-frisks*

# POLICING THE POLICE

*2008 analysis of sustained cases statewide vs. Newark*

| TYPE OF COMPLAINT | STATE CASES | SUSTAINED* | NEWARK CASES | SUSTAINED* |
|---|---|---|---|---|
| Excessive force | 1,024 | 3.9% | 55 | 0% |
| Improper arrest | 308 | 3.9% | 15 | 0% |
| Improper entry | 43 | 2.3% | 0 | 0% |
| Improper search | 203 | 6.4% | 32 | 0% |
| Different treatment | 503 | 4.6% | 4 | 0% |
| Demeanor | 2,315 | 11.4% | 123 | 7.3% |
| Other rule violation** | 5,262 | 53.4% | 616 | 42.2% |
| Other criminal violation | 774 | 27.9% | 25 | 52.0% |

* Sustained complaints resulted in criminal charges filed or disciplinary actions.
** Other violations include insubordination, sleeping on duty and making false statements.
2008 is the most recent comparison available

THE STAR-LEDGER

*Source: Newark Police Department*

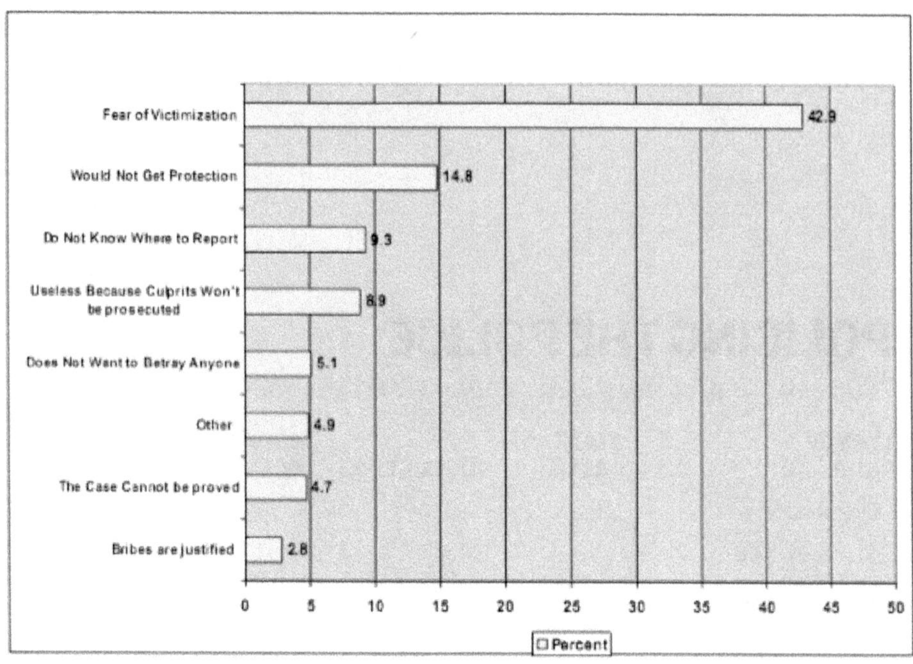



*Source: The King's Diary: The Importance of Fighting Corruption. (2011). http://mikochenireport. blogspot.com/2011/05/kings-diary-importance-of-fighting.html*

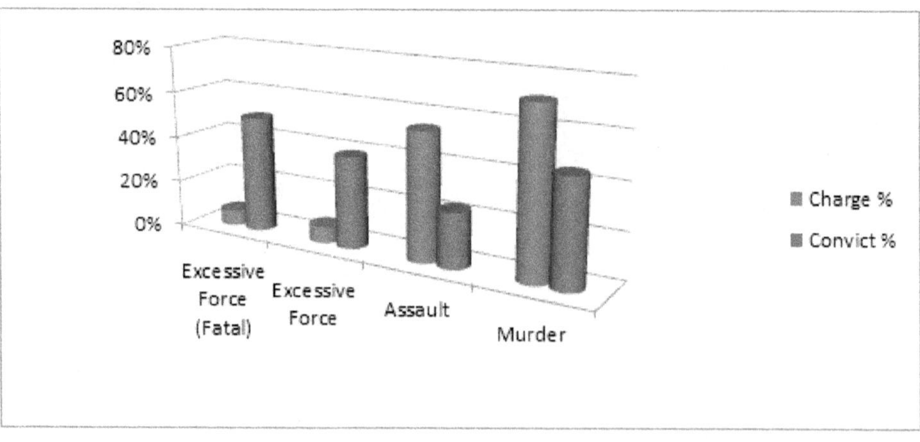



*Packman, D. (2011). The Problem with Prosecuting Police in Washington State. http://www.police-misconduct.net/the-problem-with-prosecuting-police-in-washington-state/*

Five states with the lowest prosecution rates for law enforcement officers in the US (AVG 32%):

1.    Washington DC      05%

2.    Washington      16%

3.    Vermont      18%

4.    West Virginia      20%

5.    Oregon      20%

Five states with the worst law enforcement conviction rates (AVG 37%):

1.    Alaska      14%

2.    Washington      17%

3.    Connecticut      18%

4.    Colorado      19%

5.    Georgia      19%

6.    New Mexico      19%

*SOURCE:  SOURCE:  PACKMAN, D. (2011). THE PROBLEM WITH PROSECUTING PO-LICE IN WASHINGTON STATE. HTTP://WWW.POLICEMISCONDUCT.NET/THE-PROB-LEM-WITH-PROSECUTING-POLICE-IN-WASHINGTON-STATE/*

# APPENDIX III: CRIME, CORRUPTION AND COVER-UPS IN THE CHICAGO POLICE DEPARTMENT

# Crime, Corruption and Cover-ups

## *in the Chicago Police Department*

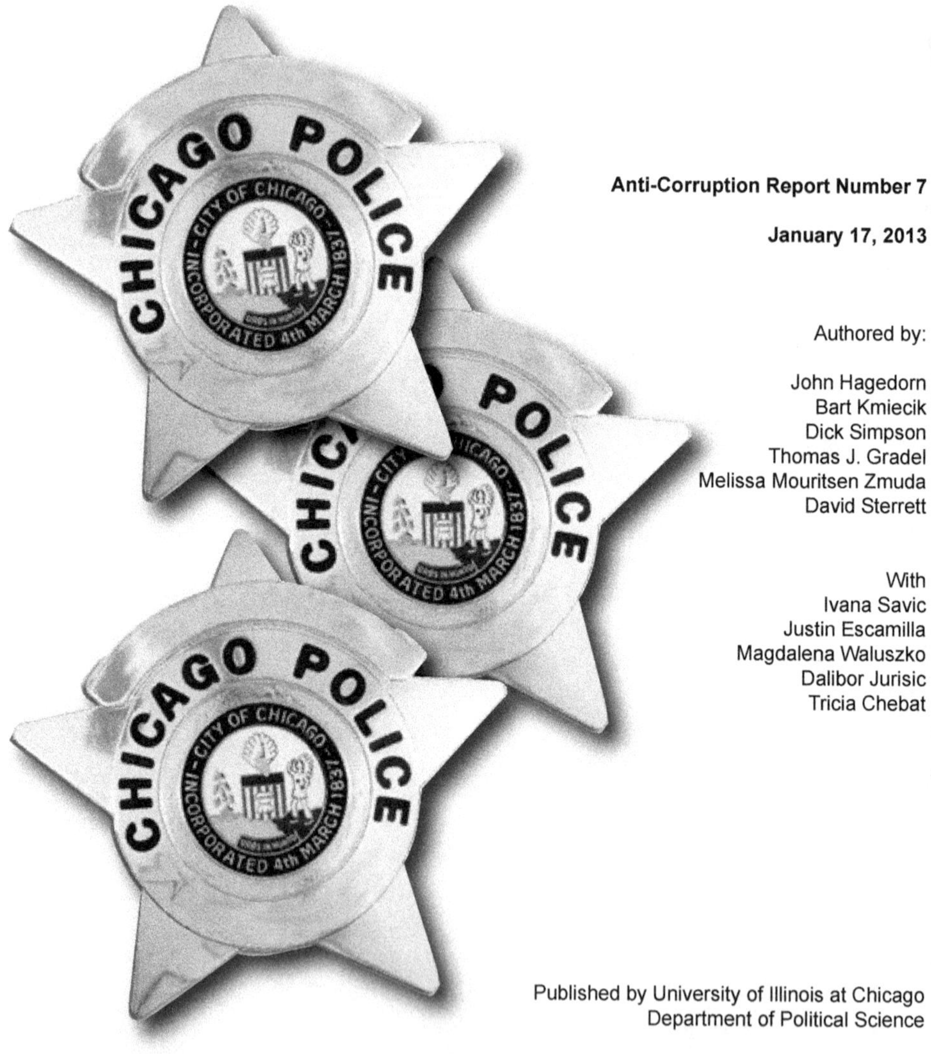


**Anti-Corruption Report Number 7**

**January 17, 2013**

Authored by:

John Hagedorn
Bart Kmiecik
Dick Simpson
Thomas J. Gradel
Melissa Mouritsen Zmuda
David Sterrett

With
Ivana Savic
Justin Escamilla
Magdalena Waluszko
Dalibor Jurisic
Tricia Chebat

Published by University of Illinois at Chicago
Department of Political Science

1

The Chicago Police Department has a legacy of both heroism and corruption. On the one hand, the department's officers risk their lives on a daily basis to enforce the law, protect the public and preserve the peace. On the other hand, Chicago has a checkered history of police scandals and an embarrassingly long list of police officers who have crossed the line to engage in brutality, corruption and criminal activity.

An analysis of five decades of news reports reveals that since 1960, a total of 295 Chicago Police officers have been convicted of serious crimes, such as drug dealing, beatings of civilians, destroying evidence, protecting mobsters, theft and murder.

Moreover, the listing of police convicted of crimes undoubtedly underestimates the problem of corruption in the Chicago Police Department (CPD). The list does not include undetected and unreported illegal activity, serious misconduct resulting in internal disciplinary action, and officers who retire rather than face charges.

Our analysis of police corruption in Chicago yields four major findings.

First, corruption has long persisted within the CPD and continues to be a serious problem. There have been 102 convictions of Chicago police since the beginning of 2000.

Second, police officers often resist reporting crimes and misconduct committed by fellow officers. The "blue code of silence," while difficult to prove, is an integral part of the department's culture and it exacerbates the corruption problems. However last November, a federal jury found that the City of Chicago and its police culture were partially responsible for Officer Anthony Abbate's brutal beating of a female bartender. After the civil trial to assess damages, the victim's attorney declared, "We proved a code of silence at every level in the Chicago Police Department."[1]

Third, overtime a large portion of police corruption has shifted from policemen aiding and abetting mobsters and organized crime to officers involved with drugs dealers and street gangs. Since the year 2000, a total of 47 Chicago law enforcement officers were convicted of drug and gang related crimes. The department's war on drugs puts police officers, especially those working undercover, in dangerous situations where they must cooperate with criminals to catch criminals. These endeavors require that CPD superiors provide a high degree of leadership and oversight to keep officers on the straight and narrow.

Fourth, internal and external sources of authority, including police superintendents and Mayors, have up to now failed to provide adequate anti-corruption oversight and leadership.

The case of Lieutenant Jon Burge, Commander of Area 2 Detective Division, accused of torturing suspects to extract confessions is the most notorious, high-profile example of the lack of accountability in the department involving several state's attorneys and mayors. The "blue wall of silence" protected Burge and his many accomplices. Despite numerous courts overturning convictions and several media exposés, the CPD leadership and Mayor's office denied and evaded evidence that Burge and 64 other officers tortured more than 100 African-American suspects over several decades. In addition, dozens, if not hundreds, of police officers, who were present at the stations while the torture occurred or who heard about it from co-workers, failed to report the torture to the proper authorities.

The Cook County State's Attorney never prosecuted a single officer for any crimes related to torture. And, there is no evidence that the Police Department ever disciplined any officer for failing to come forward with information about the tortures.

Finally, the United States Attorney stepped in and prosecuted Jon Burge. Last year, he was convicted in federal court, not for torture but for lying about it under oath. The dozens of other police officers involved in the torture cases were not prosecuted. By 2012, the statute of limitation had expired.

In this report, as well as in the previous six anti-corruption reports published by the Political Science Department, public corruption has been defined as an illegal or unethical act committed by a public official for his or her self interest rather than for the public good.

While we relied on a set of 295 criminal convictions of police offices to analyze and classify police corruption, it should be noted that most unethical behavior and non-criminal misconduct also fits the definition of corruption. Also while some non-criminal misconduct committed by individual officers may not its self be "corruption," it is often swept under the rug or covered-upped by the department to avoid embarrassment. Toleration of such misconduct is definitely "corruption."

Toleration of corruption, or at least resigned acceptance, appears to be the order of the day for at least the past 50 years. The department's Internal Affairs Division (IAD), the Independent Police Review Authority (IPRA), Police Board (PB), the department's top brass, the Mayor's office, and State Attorneys have all failed to aggressively and effectively reign in police corruption. In recent years, only the U.S. Attorney's Office has made a serious effort to curb police corruption.

In 2007, police consultant Lou Reiter testified in court that the department's lack of effective oversight was the product of "deliberate indifference" by CPD leaders.[2] The lack of an effective crackdown on police misconduct can be inferred from a 2007 study by University of Chicago law professor Craig Futterman.[3] He found that only 19 of 10,149 (or less than 2%)

civilian complaints of excessive force, illegal searches, racial abuse, sexual abuse and false arrests between 2002 and 2004 led to police suspensions of a week or more.

The listing in our report of the 295 convicted police officers and their illegal activities demonstrate that corruption in Chicago Police Department is not confined to a few isolated cases. While people can debate whether the CPD has a culture that promotes corruption, the findings clearly show that the CPD has at the very least a culture that tolerates police misconduct and corruption.

Police corruption not only undermines public trust in law enforcement, but also corruption related prosecutions, lawsuits, defense and settlements cost taxpayers millions of dollars. Jon Burge cases have cost local taxpayers more than $53 million since 1998.[4] Moreover since 2003, the City of Chicago has spent more than $82.5 million to defend police against misconduct charges with about a quarter of that total related to Burge.[5] In addition, the city paid $21 million in 2009 for compensatory damages in a wrongful conviction case involving Juan Johnson[6], and $18 million in 2001 to settle a case involving an unarmed woman shot by police[7].

The city also spends hundreds of thousands of dollars investigating police misconduct each year. Clearly these cases of police abuse and corruption have cost taxpayers several hundreds of millions of dollars at a time when all levels of government have to cut services and raise taxes.

The CPD's heavy focus on drug and gang activity, and the "blue code of silence" both present serious obstacles to reducing police corruption. Police officers loyalty to their colleagues understandably runs deep, but law enforcement officials should not ignore the criminal acts of their co-workers. Speaking out against a fellow officer can be difficult, and even dangerous. Only a few years ago a high profile police officer, Jerome Finngean, hired a gang hit man to kill fellow officers who were preparing to testify against him.[8] Encouraging officers to report corrupt or criminal acts of their colleagues and increasing oversight over officers is not easy. Nor will it be easy to reduce corruption when police are so heavily involved with gangs and lucrative drug dealing networks.

Proposals in the last section of this report recommend a combination of external review and internal incentives. They are based the experience of police departments from around the world and on academic studies. These proposed reforms are designed to create effective oversight structures and a culture of honest service within the CPD. If adopted, these reforms would help alleviate the serious problem of corruption in the police department.

# History of Chicago Police Department Corruption

For nearly a century, Chicago's political machines included police protection for gambling and prostitution and for vice lords like Mike McDonald and Big Jim Colisimo. In the 1920s, prohibition led to beer war violence and an alliance of Capone's mob with Republican Mayor William Hale Thompson. While the 1930s New Deal saw the Democratic Party taking power while the alliance between City Hall and Frank Nitti's Outfit continued to reign.

Reports from many sources, including Landesco's *Organized Crime in Chicago*, Lindberg's *To Serve and Collect*, Drake & Cayton's *Black Metropolis*, and Karen Abbot's *Sin in the Second City,* document rampant police corruption in the first half of the 20th century.

After the 1960 Summerdale scandal, where a police unit worked as a burglary crew, Mayor Richard J. Daley hired Orlando W. Wilson as his new Superintendent of Police. Wilson, a criminologist from The University of California Berkeley, was told to professionalize and clean up the CPD. According to Ovid Demaris in his corruption classic, *Captive City*, Wilson remarked to Congress in 1962 that of the 985 mob murders since the 1920s, only two had been solved. The Outfit, as the Chicago mob was also commonly known, was getting away with murder. Neither Superintendent Wilson nor the state's attorney went after the Outfit in a systematic way. With rare exception, the Cook County's State's Attorneys have avoided investigating the Outfit, which has always had highly placed friends in the machine. At the end of his term Wilson told Life Magazine, "Cosa Nostra in Chicago was so entrenched that he had barely scratched its surface. Nor had he been able to eradicate corruption in Chicago's police force."[9]

Beginning in the 1960s, when the Chicago Outfit was still the nation's second most powerful criminal organization, the CPD and the state's attorney turned their attention away from organized crime to the new street gangs. Street gangs, not the Outfit, began to control the retail distribution of drugs, gambling and prostitution. A "War on Gangs" declared in 1969 by Mayor Richard J. Daley and State's Attorney Edward Hanrahan, took aim at black and Latino gangs. At the same time, Chicago's Outfit sought greater profits from its operations in Las Vegas and Hollywood, and through control of the Teamsters Pension Fund. But while Outfit's vice operations were protected by its still cozy relationship with the Chicago political machine, the

> *"The 'rotten apple' theory won't work any longer. Corrupt police officers are not natural-born criminals, nor morally wicked men, constitutionall  different from their honest colleagues. The task of corruption control is to examine the barrel, not jus  the apples –the organization, not just the individu  in it –because corrupt police are made, not born."*
> -NYC Police Commissioner Patrick Murphy

street gangs had to cut their own deals with dirty cops. As the war on drugs progressed, more and more individual police officers were corrupted.

In the 1980s, police corruption again became front-page news. In 1982, ten officers in the Marquette police district were among the first Chicago police officers to be convicted of drug–related corruption charges. "The Marquette 10" arrests were followed by Operation Greylord, a federal investigation into the Cook County court system that swept up several corrupt police officers along with numerous judges, court bailiffs and attorneys. In the 1980s and 1990s, Joseph Miedzianowski, a member of the department's Gang Crimes Unit, ran a drug operation with several gangs.

The conviction of CPD Chief of Detectives and Assistant Police Superintendent William Hanhardt in 2001 for using secret police information to direct a mob-connected jewelry theft ring showed that organized crime could still reach into the CPD even in the 21$^{st}$ Century. The drug/gang connection continued into the current decade. In 2007, the U.S. Attorney's arrested of Keith Herrera and Jerome Finnegan of the Special Operations Squad for corruption and attempted murder.

Human rights violations have long plagued Chicago. At the end of the 1960s in the aftermath of anti-war protests, the Chicago Police Department's Subversive Activities Unit, known as the "Red Squad," spied on legitimate, non-criminal protesters, political activists and community organizations. Originally the "Red Squad" was supposed to provide surveillance of groups such as Communists, or Reds, thought to be plotting to overthrow the United States government. Later, however, the "Red Squad" spied on law-abiding individuals, officials and groups who opposed Mayor Richard J. Daley and the Democratic machine. Like many other secret police units, the Chicago "Red Squad" investigated and infiltrated dissenting political groups but when a group threatened those in power, the "Red Squad" would try to destroy it, directly or indirectly. Allegedly "Red Squad" officers committed criminal acts such as burglary, theft, and destruction of documents and equipment, all blatant violation of the First Amendment, according to the American Civil Liberties Union (ACLU).

Besides the ACLU, some of the groups targeted by the "Red Squad" were the National Association for the Advancement of Colored People, National Lawyers Guild, and Operation PUSH. By the end of the1960s, the "Red Squad" had collected information on approximately 117,000 Chicagoan, 141,000 out-of-town individuals and 14,000 organizations.

In 1974, the Red Squad reportedly destroyed 105,000 individual and 1,300 organizational files when it learned that the Alliance to End Repression planned to file a lawsuit against the unit for violating the U.S. Constitution.[10]  The ACLU then filed a lawsuit on behalf of 25 organizations and individuals including one of this report's authors, former Chicago Alderman Dick Simpson.  After many years of litigation, a 1981 court decree ended the Chicago Police Department's "Red Squad's" unlawful surveillance of political dissenters and their organizations. Then to settle the lawsuit, the City of Chicago agreed to pay a total of $335,000 to the plaintiffs and nearly $20,000 in attorneys' fees. And on the last day of 1985, a federal judge ordered the city to pay an additional $51,000 to two organizations and a civil rights activists who were illegally spied on by the "Red Squad."

The CPD also has a history of violating the human rights of African-Americans and other minorities. State's Attorney Edward Hanrahan orchestrated the infamous 1969 police raid that resulted in the shooting deaths of Fred Hampton and Mark Clark. Jon Burge headed up a team of officers in the 2nd Police District where many young, African-American men were tortured over several decades.

## Conviction Analysis

In order to study the extent of police corruption in Chicago, we focused on reports of criminal convictions of police in newspapers, magazines, books and various other sources. Data on corruption that did not result in convictions was not available.  Other officers are brought formally to the Police Review Board and some resigned to avoid formal charges. Some police misconduct is handled through a grievance process conducted by the department management and the police union. Generally, such cases are not reported in the news media. As a result, our information, which primarily is based on media reports of criminal convictions, very likely underestimates the breadth and severity of the police corruption problem.

However, the conviction statistics are the most concrete data available to assess and analyze the continuing problem of police corruption in Chicago. In addition, a more detailed look at the conviction cases reveals the strong connections between corruption and the war on drugs, the code of silence and the lack of internal and external oversight.

For each instance of police corruption or misconduct found, the following information was recorded:

- Officer's name
- Rank, title, position
- Date of conviction

- Type of incident
- Description of the crime and related corruption
- Source and citation

Three hundred cases of police crime were documented. After compiling the database of police crime, all of the cases were collapsed and coded into the following categories with the frequencies with which they occurred:

Civil Right Violations (CRV) – 10 police officers guilty of illegal search and seizures, false arrests, malicious prosecutions and extended detentions.

Off Duty Crime (ODC) – 53 police officers committed crimes while off duty.

General Police Crime (GPC) – 114 officers involved in scams, tax fraud, stealing, extortion, lying, bribery, and theft.

Drugs, Guns and Gangs cases (DGG) -- 95 cases including gang-related illegal drug dealings, weapon sales and gang activity.

Brutality, Torture and Sex Abuse cases (BTX) – 23 cases involving brutal beatings, torture, sexual abuse and excessive force.

## The War on Drugs

In studying corruption and in the war on drugs we find David Carter's typology to be useful, distinguishing between what he calls Type 1 and Type 2 acts of drug-related corruption. Type 1 is the drive for private gain, illegitimate acts that misuse the public status of an officer for his/her private gain, and illegitimate goals.

Type 2 corruption has the legitimate goal of prosecuting the bad guys, but uses illegitimate means of falsifying evidence, selling confiscated drugs from one gang to another in order to build a larger case, or lying under oath to get a prosecution.[11]

> *Those officers who engage in misconduct and violate citizens'*
> *constitutional rights would do so with the perception that their misconduct would*
> *go undiscovered or investigated in such a deficient manner or subjected to*
> *prolonged delay in adjudication that they would not be held accountable or*
> *sanctioned.*[12]
>
> Lou Reiter, Police Consultant

TABLE 2

OPPORTUNITY FOR DRUG CORRUPTION BY ASSIGNMENT

| Assignment | Drug Exposure | Type 1 Corruption | Type 2 Corruption |
|---|---|---|---|
| Patrol officers | Street dealers<br>Arrests of persons in possession of drugs<br>Response to calls where drugs are involved | Street bribes<br>Street confiscation of drugs<br>Protection money | Perjury with respect to the facts of the arrest<br>Perjury of facts of the drug seizure |
| Drug and vice officers | Undercover (UC) Operations Generally<br>Drug and money possession for role playing<br>Social interaction with dealers and users in UC role | Suppressing evidence and information learned in UC operations in exchange for bribes/money<br>"Ripoffs" of money and drugs from dealers during drug deals | Overt entrapment of suspected drug offenders<br>Perjury and falsifying evidence and incriminating statements<br>Planting drugs in drug raids |

Drug trafficking in Chicago is a multi-million dollar operation and gang members are often more than willing to pay for protection. Police officers can make deals with one gang or drug dealer in order to catch another. This can be both good police work as well as a major temptation for corruption. For example, Joseph Miedzianowksi, although he conspired with multiple gangs to import and sell drugs "took the witness stand in his own defense and claimed that he had never betrayed his oath. He said his seeming friendships with members of the Imperial Gangsters and other street gangs were merely designed to coax out inside information. "[13] However, Miedzianowksi's arguments did not resonate with the jurors during his trial as he was convicted and sentenced to life in prison for his crimes.

Both Type 1 and Type 2 corruption cases exist in our database. In addition, the war on drugs produces what the London review of the literature calls the "almost impossible" nature of drug-related policing:

* It is usually 'secretive, duplicitous and quasi-legal;
* The use of informants is widespread;
* It is extremely difficult to regulate;
* The 'war on drugs' rhetoric often increases pressure for results;

* Securing sufficient evidence to convict is often difficult ;

* Officers may be required to buy or, occasionally, use drugs in the course of their work; and

* Very large sums of money may be available to the corrupt officer. Tim Newman summarizes the problem concisely:

> *Here, then, is possibly the major problem now faced by those seeking to control police corruption. Those areas of police work that have the strongest link with, or are closest to, the 'invitational edge' are also those which are generally subject to the least managerial scrutiny and, in the specific case of drugs, are increasingly associated with extraordinarily large sums of money and therefore very high levels of (financial) temptation.[14]*

## The Code of Silence

It is clear from previous research that supervision of drug and gang squad officers must have the highest priority. However, even honest police officers have difficulty reporting misconduct, and the lack of oversight on the police drug war is a major problem. Lou Rieter, a consultant to the Chicago Police and former Deputy Chief of Police in Los Angeles, testified that:

> *The Code of Silence exists to varying degrees in all police agencies in the United States. The failure of the Chicago Police Department to acknowledge its potential and take affirmative steps to eliminate or minimize the influence of the Code of Silence, in my opinion, is a conscious choice various Chicago Police managers and executive officers have taken and, in my opinion, represents a position of deliberate indifference by the Chicago Police Department to this disruptive issue within the agency [15]*

In the Joseph Miedzianowski prosecution, Brain Netols, Assistant U.S. Attorney testified that he believed that the Code of Silence was involved in all 18 criminal trials of Chicago police officers that he prosecuted a devastating indictment of CPD oversight, according to Reiter's affidavit,

> "Netols *testified that he believed the Chicago Police Department was in the RICO conspiracy with Miedzianowski and in the wiretaps of the case which he played in court officers stated that they 'were not concerned about investigations by the Internal Affairs Division.' When the search warrant was served on Miedzianowski's home there were 'thousands of documents were taken from his home...,' which appeared to be from Internal Affairs investigations .*" [16]

In short, police officers do not fear being investigated by the Internal Affairs Department. Reiter concludes:

> *These deficiencies in the administrative investigations of complaints, employee discipline and the adverse impact of the Code of Silence, has been noted by, documented for and relied upon managers and administrators within the Chicago Police Department. The failure to modify this systemic deficiency in the process by successive Police Superintendents, in my opinion, is indicative of a conscious choice by the Police Department to continue this practice of indifference to allegations of misconduct and police abuse including Constitutional violations.*[17]

The code of silence obviously played a role in the recent case of Officer Anthony Abbate beating up a female bartender.

 It should be clear we do not ascribe to the "bad apple" theory of police misconduct. New York's famous Knapp Report explains:

> *According to this theory, which bordered on official Department doctrine, any policeman found to be corrupt must promptly be denounced as a rotten apple in an otherwise clean barrel. It must never be admitted that his individual corruption may be symptomatic of underlying disease... A high command unwilling to acknowledge that the problem of corruption is extensive cannot very well argue that drastic changes are necessary to deal with the problem.*[18]

Rather than focus on individual police or a wholesale indictment of CPD officers, most of whom are honest public servants, this report targets the "practice of indifference" in CPD leadership and the mayors' offices in providing effective oversight.

# Case Studies

The following cases highlight CPD corruption from the 1970s to the present day. Together, these cases, document the pervasive and persistent nature of corruption and the incapacity or unwillingness of the CPD to provide effective oversight. All of the cases are also subjects of controversy, including charges of entrapment, pious denunciations of "bad apples," and a failure to seriously address systemic issues. Nonetheless, these cases illustrate the different types of police corruption and abuses and demonstrate the severity and breadth of the problem.

### Case Study # 1 "Marquette 10"

The "Marquette 10" case is a prime example of police involved in Drugs, Guns and Gangs. In 1982, U.S. Attorney Dan Webb's investigation into drug dealers in Chicago's west side led to the arrest of 10 Marquette District officers for accepting bribes from drug dealers. The 10 officers were convicted for protecting two large drug-dealing networks in exchange for money and goods for more than three years. The officers warned the dealers of police raids and even beat up competing dealers, according to court records. The Marquette 10 officers were Thomas Ambrose, Frank DeRango, Curtis Lowery, John De Simone, Robert Eatman, Joseph Pena, James Ballauer, William Guide, William Hass and Dennis Smentek. They each received prison sentences ranging from 10 to 20 years.[19]

### Case Study # 2 "Austin 7"

The "Austin 7" case highlights the need for greater police oversight. The seven were Austin District tactical police officers and plainclothes cops assigned to root out gangs and drugs on the West Side. They were indicted on December 20, 1996 by a federal grand jury for allegedly stealing and extorting $65,000 from undercover FBI agents posing as Chicago drug dealers.

The seven officers indicted and tried were Edward Lee "Pacman" Jackson Jr.; Gregory S. Crittleton; Alex D. Ramos; M.L. Moore; Lennon Shields; James P. Young; and Cornelius Tripp. They were indicted on 21 different counts of extortion, illegal use of firearms and the conspiracy to commit robbery. The investigation of these officers was initiated after authorities received numerous complaints from neighborhood residents. After the officers were indicted, prosecutors had to drop more than 120 narcotics cases against suspects because of the involvement of at least one of these officers.

The "Austin 7" officers were prosecuted and convicted of racketeering for shaking down drug dealers for cash and cocaine, for providing protection for large narcotics deliveries and for robberies, home invasions and extortions of narcotics dealers in 1995 and 1996.[20]

In addressing the issue of police oversight at the time of the convictions in May 1998, the Mayor's Commission Report on Police Integrity urged that the CPD better monitor misconduct complaints from individuals and neighborhood groups if it hoped to avert similar patterns of abuse in the future.[21]

## Case Study # 3 Miedzianowski

Joseph Miedzianowski, a decorated member of the Gang Crimes Unit, was convicted in 2001 of racketeering and drug conspiracy for running an interstate drug ring between Miami and Chicago, shaking down drug dealers, fixing criminal cases, hiding a wanted murderer and undermining his fellow police officers. In 2003 he was sentenced to life in prison.

M iedzianowski's criminality continued for more than a decade and involved at least eight different gangs and dozens of gang members. Miedzianowski's lengthy record of corruption raises questions about the capacity or will of the CPD or any of the oversight bodies to effectively supervise drug and gang related misconduct.[22]

## Case Study# 4 "SOS"

The brazen behavior of the Special Operations Section of the CPD was well known, and both state and federal authorities investigated the unit. Prompted by evidence that police bosses knew of a pattern of misconduct over at least four years, the U.S. Attorney's office took over the Cook County state's attorney's investigation of the elite Special Operations Section (SOS) in 2007, and began investigating the conduct of department bosses and the Internal Affairs Division.[23]

In the previous year, 2006, the Cook County State's Attorney's Office indicted 10 members of the CPD's SOS for aggravated kidnapping, theft, burglary, home invasion, armed violence and false arrest. The officers indicted were: Jerome Finnigan, Keith Herrera, Carl Suchocki, Thomas Sherry, BartMaka, Brian Pratscher, Donovan Markiewicz, Guadalupe Salinas, Stephen DelBosque and EricOlsen. These indictments were the result of a federal investigation of SOS by the US Attorney's office."[24] Charges against Officers Thomas Sherry and Carl

Suchocki were dropped in February 2009, because they could not be placed at the scene of the crime. Officers Stephen DelBosque and Eric Olsen pleaded guilty in April 2011 to conducting illegal searches and lying about it before a grand jury or in court. Officers Bart Maka, Brian Pratscher, and Guadalupe Salinas pleaded guilty to charges of felony theft, and Officer Donovan Markiewicz pleaded guilty to charges of official misconduct in September 2009.[25]

Officer Keith Herrera told Katie Couric on "60 Minutes" that they "pulled over motorists without cause, grabbed their keys and stormed into their homes, falsified reports, pocketed huge sums of money and even shook each other down for money." Herrera sought to place the blame on team leader Jerome Finnigan who pleaded guilty in April 2011 to conspiracy to commit murder for hire as he hired a former hit-man to kill former SOS member Herrera.[26]

The charges allege that Finnigan's share of the money stolen in 2004 and 2005 was approximately $200,000, while Herrera allegedly netted approximately $40,000 in 2005 – all of which came from a larger pool of approximately $600,000 that allegedly was stolen in five separate episodes in 2004 and 2005. Finnigan was sentenced to 13 years in prison; Herrerais still awaiting sentencing, but could see up to 13 years in prison as well. Officers Bart Maka, Brian Pratscher, Guadalupe Salinas, and Donovan Markiewicz were sentenced to 6 months in jail, and Officers Stephen DelBosque and Eric Olsen pleaded guilty to lying on police reports.[27] Moreover, Finnegan named 19 other officers who took part in illegal activities, and said that commanding officers knew about the stealing and condoned civil rights violations. Finnegan said SOS officers' criminality was an "open secret" and while many officers did not steal, they signed off on false reports.[28]

### Case Study # 5 Guerrero and Martinez

Police corruption related to drugs and gangs continues to surface in Chicago.  In 2011, the U.S. Attorney's office filed indictments against two Chicago police officers for helping a gang steal. The officers Alex Guerrero and Antonio Martinez Jr., were accused of taking orders from gang leaders and using their authority to pull people over or enter houses. The indictment alleges the officers received at least $10,000 to steal guns, hundreds of pounds of drugs and tens of thousands of dollars. Martinez pleaded guilty in December 2011 to charges of conspiracy and racketeering, and Guerrero pleaded guilty to similar charges in July 2012.[29]

## Case Study # 6 Lewellen

The corruption case of Glen Lewellen highlights both the problems of paid informants and the lack of oversight in the CPD.  Lewellen, oversaw a federal informant, Saul Rodriguez, from 1996 to 2001. During that time, Rodriguez was paid $807,000 by the U.S. Attorney for information on drug dealing with his former gang, La Raza.[30]

But behind the scenes, Lewellen had hatched a secret, unauthorized deal with Rodriguez, where the drug trafficker would keep breaking the law and the cop would help him, joining Rodriguez's drug organization — which prosecutors contended was behind multiple violent kidnappings and robberies.[31]

According to the indictment filed in November of 2010, Lewellen and Rodriguez founded the "Rodriguez Drug Trafficking Organization" in 1996.  The Chicago cop and his paid informant allegedly worked together to rip off other drug dealers, splitting millions of dollars. In addition, Rodriguez was involved with three killings – in 2000, 2001 and 2002 - and Lewellen repeatedly invented excuses to keep his informant out of jail and benefit their drug trafficking organization. "[32]

Even after Lewellen retired in 2002, he managed to obstruct a separate Drug Enforcement Administration investigation of Rodriguez, prosecutors said.  Rodriguez testified that in 2006, Lewellen warned Rodriguez not to speak to a drug courier whose phone was wiretapped. Prosecutors pointed out that at the time, the DEA was investigating Rodriguez's ties to a cocaine wholesaler.[33]

The prosecutors' case against the 55-year-old Lewellen included evidence of a 2004 rip-off of 70 kilograms of cocaine from a man who delivered the drugs in a tractor-trailer to Lewellen's warehouse in south suburban Frankfort. Lewellen allegedly drove up in a fake squad car outfitted with police lights and the man ran away, allowing Lewellen and other crew members to steal the drugs.[34]

Last year in February, a federal jury convicted Lewellen, a former narcotics officer, of joining Rodriguez's massive drug conspiracy. [35]

## Case Study # 7 Osbourn and Gibson

Since 1970, 36 officers have been convicted on civil rights violations in cases similar to the arrest of Felicia Tolson in 1998. Officer Kevin Osbourn and Sgt. Mark Gibson entered her West Side home when looking for a teenager who had earlier escaped arrest. They disregarded her requests for identification and Officer Osbourn arrested Tolson for aggravated battery after she allegedly pushed him.[36]

Tolson, at the time a correctional officer at the Cook County Jail, was held in custody for 30 hours and was later acquitted of the aggravated battery charge. She stated that due to the incident she suffered post-traumatic stress and depression, along with humiliation, which lead her to quit her job as a correctional officer at Cook County Jail. In 2001, a federal jury found that the two officers falsely arrested Ms. Tolson and awarded her $300,000 in damages.[37]

### Case Study # 8 Abbate

On 19 February 2007, off-duty Police Officer Anthony Abbate attacked and punched Karolina Obrycka while she was bartending at Jesse's Shortstop Inn, a bar on the Northwest side of Chicago. The incident was caught on a bar videotape on which Officer Abbate can be seen repeatedly punching and kicking the visibly smaller bartender. He later claimed it was self-defense. Officer Abbate was apparently under the influence of alcohol. He stated that the bartender pushed him first and that the fight started after she refused to serve him more drinks. Abbate was convicted in 2009 in state court of aggravated battery and sentenced to community service, anger management counseling and two years of probation.[38]

On November 14, 2012, federal jury found both the City of Chicago and Abbate responsible and awarded the bartender, Karolina Obrycka, $850,000 in damages.[39]

The jury found that the police culture of impunity was "a moving force" in causing Abbate to attack Obrycka as she worked behind the bar. Abbate attacked Obrycka in part because he believed that, as a police officer, he wouldn't be punished, the jury found.[40]

During the trial, Obrycka's lawyer had argued that police brass have denied for decades that a "code of silence" protecting policemen who commit crimes runs all the way from the street to the top of the police department. They also argued that Abbate acted with impunity. That he was unafraid of consequences was the result of the blue wall of silence as well as department's history of ineffective discipline action against wayward officers.[41]

Officers who responded to the bar the night of the attack failed to include Abbate's name, the fact that he was a police officer and that there was a video in their police report. This further solidified arguments supporting the existence of blue wall of silence.[42]

**Case Study # 9 & # 10 Doyle and Hanhardt**

The cases of Officer Anthony Doyle and Chief of Detectives William Hanhardt hark back to an earlier time when The Outfit, Chicago's version of the organized crime syndicate or Mob, had its tentacles deep into the Chicago Police Department.

At the end of the federal "Family Secrets" trial in 2007, Doyle, was convicted of racketeering conspiracy for passing sensitive information to the Mob about a bloody glove left at the scene of the murder of mobster John Fecarotta in1986.[43] Doyle was a police officer working in the Evidence Department in 1999 when he pulled up information on evidence that turned out to be a bloody glove.[44] Doyle was sentenced to 12 years in prison in 2009.[45]

Hanhardt, the highest-ranking Chicago police official to be convicted of corruption, pleaded guilty in October 2001 to running a sophisticated jewelry theft ring that operated in several states and stole more than $5 million in diamonds and other gems. Hanhardt, who had a 33-year police career, worked directly with Chicago organized crime syndicate from the early 1980s to 1998. Hanhardt used law enforcement computers and other databases to get information on traveling jewelry sales representatives.[46]

## History of CPD Oversight

*"...police corruption cannot exist unless it is at least tolerated at higher levels in the Department."*

Frank Serpico, Undercover New York Police Officer

The Chicago Police Department has a long history of failing to curb police abuse and corruption.

### 1960 - Summerdale Scandal; Police Board Created; Superintendent Hired,

News exposure of a crew of policemen engaged in burglary of legitimate businesses, which became known as the Summerdale Police Scandal, caused public to question the integrity of the Chicago Police Department. The loud criticism and calls for greater accountability led to the resignation of the Police Commissioner, Timothy O'Connor.

To help select a new police chief, Mayor Richard J. Daley created a commission, which included O.W. Wilson, a former police officer and then Dean of the University of California's criminology school. After a month-long search, the committee selected Wilson.

Wilson was hired, given the title of Police Superintendent and told to reform the department. Mayor Daley promised to keep political influence out of the department. He appointed a five-member "nonpartisan Police Board, to govern the force."[47] The Board was given power to oversee the new superintendent and to enforce the department's rules. In essence, the board acted as the head of the department.

In 1961, the board's rules were revised. Its authority "to administer or direct the operations of the police department and superintendent" was not included in the new system. Powers were restored to the superintendent. However, the Police Board acquired the power to hear officer disciplinary cases that were previously handled by the Chicago Civil Service Commission.

### 1966 - ACLU develops reform plan; Mayor creates Citizens Committee

In 1966, the ACLU presented the police department with a reform plan calling for the Chicago Bar Association to review citizen complaints against the police. In response O. W. Wilson asked Harold Smith, a past president of the Chicago Bar Association, evaluate the work of the Internal Investigation Division (IID). Smith concluded that there was no need for a review of complaints by a Chicago Bar Association committee.[48]

In July of that year, Mayor Daley created a 23-member citizens' committee to evaluate and study police-community relations and to recommend programs to improve these relations.[49] The committee concluded that there were no faults with the IID's operations.[50]

### 1967 - Superintendent reorganizes IID

In 1967, then Police Superintendent James Conlisk Jr., reorganized IID and combined it with the Inspections Division, the unit responsible for inspecting departmental operations. The new unit, the Internal Inspections Division was expected to detect corruption and not just wait for it to be reported by others.[51] The reorganization of IID came soon after detective Jack Muller went to the Superintendent with information alleging tire theft. Muller said he did not go to the IID with this information due to the lack of action in previous reports he made with the IID.[52]

### 1970 - Creation of the Internal Affairs Division (IAD)

A police raid on the Black Panthers' headquarters in December 1969 resulted in the shooting deaths of two African-American men in their beds. There were newspaper exposures of false police reports, charges from the public that the police used excessive force, and allegations from some that the police murdered the victims. The ACLU renewed its call for civilian involvement in police oversight.[53]

Superintendent Conlisk nixed the idea of including civilian employees in the IID, and based on a study by the International Association of Chiefs of Police, once again reorganized IID. In 1970, a new Internal Affairs Division (IAD) was created with the task of investigating allegations of police misconduct. A separate Inspections Division was created to execute the inspectional function.[54]

## 1972 - Commission on Human Relations given a role

Due to increasing community dissatisfactions with how police oversight was handled, in 1972 the Mayor called a conference of civic leaders to discuss the problem of police-community relations. At the conference Superintendent Conlisk said the Chicago Commission of Human Relations would be assigned to review IAD files and if necessary re-investigate certain cases. This is the first time a civilian entity was given the opportunity to review and perform its own investigations of the Chicago Police Department. The Commission was not given direct disciplinary authority, only the power to recommend possible disciplinary actions.[55]

## 1973 - Knoohuizen Report

In 1973, the Chicago Law Enforcement Study Group analyzed the Police Board and how it was performing its four main functions: 1) Budget adoption; 2) adoption of rules and regulations; 3) nominating superintendent candidates; and 4) police officer discipline. The report, authored by Ralph Knoohuizen found that the Board only effectively handled discipline and that its other duties were mostly for show.[56]

## 1974 - The Office of Professional Standards created

In 1974 Superintendent James Rochford created the Office of Professional Standards (OPS) again combining investigative and inspectional functions in a single agency. OPS did not have subpoena power, did not hold public hearings, and was not asked to make policy recommendations.[57]

Superintendent Rochford proposed that the handling of police misconduct cases be placed directly under his command, and that OPS hire civilian investigators.[58] However, the investigators could be ex-police officers as long as they were not from CPD. OPS relied on the police department to notify them when they received complaints. OPS and CPD homicide detectives collaborated on shooting investigations. Critics claimed that OPS often adopted the homicide detectives' investigative findings as their own.[59]

OPS failed for two decades to bring charges against Jon Burge, although multiple victims and civil rights groups had demanded action.

## 1992 – Five year statute is implemented

In response to complaints about the charges against Burge, in 1992, the State Legislature passed a five-year statute of limitations for administrative proceedings.[60]

## 2006 - Futterman documents "Chicago Police Department's Broken System"

Craig B. Futterman, a professor at the University of Chicago Law School and two colleagues, published a report in 2006 analyzing 10,149 complaints of excessive force, illegal searches, racial abuse, sexual abuse and false arrest filed by civilians between 2002 and 2004. Futterman and his team found that:

- only 19 of the 10,149 complaints led to a suspension of a week or more
- the chance of meaningful discipline for a police brutality complaint was less than 3 in a thousand
- only 1 of 3,837 charges of illegal searches led to meaningful discipline
- over a three-year period, not a single charge of false arrest - planting of drugs, guns, etc.- led to an incident of meaningful discipline.

## 2007 - Independent Police Review Authority created

Mayor Richard M. Daley in 2007 responded complaints about police misconduct and how the Police Department handled them. He created the Independent Police Review Authority (IPRA) to replace OPS. The IPRA was assigned to investigate allegations against police officers, including excessive force, domestic violence, coercion, and biased-based verbal abuse. It also was given the responsibility to investigate discharges of firearms and Tasers, and extraordinary occurrences involving individuals in police custody, regardless of the existence of a complaint. IPRA was also given the intake responsibility for all complaints, from within the department and from community members.[61]

**2009 - Value of the Police Board doubted by the Chicago Justice Project**

The Chicago Justice Project studied Police Board decision in 310 cases in which the Superintendent sought termination of either sworn officers or civilian employees over a 10-year period from 1999 through 2008. The study was authored by Tracy Siska, the project's executive director, and by research assistant Sherie Arriazola. They found that the Police Board upheld the recommended discipline of the Superintendent in agreement with IAD or IPRA in only 37 percent of the cases of sworn officers. They also found that in 20 percent of the cases involving sworn officers, the policemen were returned to work without any discipline at all.

The authors questioned why police discipline is still the responsibility of the Police Board. "Looking at the numbers generated in our study," they said, "it is hard to see how the board serves the public interest by retaining two thirds of the officers the Superintendent is trying to fire." [62]

**2013 - Police Board still struggling**

Today there are still major concerns of accountability and transparency for the Police Board. It still has problems of transparency and difficulty earning a reputation as a fair and just decision maker.[63] However, even if the Police Board were effective, efficient, transparent, and accountable, it only addresses one aspect of police oversight, the individual officer. Though this is important and necessary, there is more to police oversight than the specific behavior of an individual officer. Every aspect that influences an officer needs to be addressed, from training to advancement to discipline.

# Discussion of Reform Approaches

Ignascio Cano, who researched ways to fight police corruption in Brazil and South Africa, recommends both External Review and Internal Incentives.[64] He proposed that:

1. Internal affairs units must report to bodies outside the bureaucratic hierarchy of the police.

2. Officers who report misconduct need substantial financial and professional rewards and strict protection from retaliation within the department.

3. The process of making complaints within the department must be strictly confidential.

4. Internal reviews need to be complemented by external bodies with power of subpoena and a process to turn complaints into prosecution.

In South Africa their anti-corruption report stressed three major themes for policing:

1. Enhancing internal accountability by establishing effective systems to receive and deal with public complaints, through dedicated internal capacity to investigate allegations of police abuse and criminality, and improve the management of discipline throughout the organization.

2. Promoting organizational integrity by fostering a culture that adheres to the South African Police Service Code of Conduct and Code of Ethics, that respect the Constitution and that puts service to the people first.

3. Mobilizing community support by encouraging communities to promote professional, honest, corruption-free policing by recognizing and supporting good police conduct and reporting all incidences of poor service or police criminality.[65]

We have incorporated these international experiences in dealing with police corruption in making our recommendations for reform of the Chicago police department.

## Summary of the Chicago Problem

The problem of police corruption in Chicago is not simply that there are occasional flawed police officers. Nearly all officers join the police force because they desire to serve and protect not serve and collect. By far, most officers are law-abiding, dedicated public servants.

The real problem is that an embarrassingly large number police officers violate citizens' rights, engage in corruption and commit crimes while escaping detection and avoiding discipline or prosecution for many years. The "code of silence" and "deliberate indifference" have prevented police supervisors and civilian authorities from effectively eliminating police corruption.

Today, the major source of police corruption is the war on drugs. While the public has many different ideas on the solution to the drug issue, the strong demand for drugs means that many people will risk the dangers of trafficking. Violence will continue as a way to settle disputes. The large amounts of money involved mean that police corruption will remain endemic as long as current policies continue.

Police superintendents and mayors typically denounce each new case as another "bad apple," and have failed to establish meaningful internal reforms or effective oversight. Fraternal Order of Police leadership and members of the City Council have repeatedly opposed establishing a powerful independent Police Review Board.

# Recommendations for Chicago

## *Internal Leadership, Reforms and Incentives*

1. The Police Superintendent must take the lead in promoting professional behavior through out the police force. He should make curbing police corruption a priority and create rules and procedures that punish corruption and reward integrity.

2. The Police Board should provide greater transparency by explaining its decisions in plain English on its web site. Currently the decisions are on the web site but they are often expressed in legal language that can be difficult for the average person to comprehend. The full legal findings should also be posted on the web site.

3. Independent Police Review Authority should report on the status of its investigations and Bureau of International Affairs should report the cases referred to the state's attorney for prosecution.

4. The Police Department should provide special recognition, accommodations and promotions, to officers for providing information leading to the successful prosecution of police officer corruption. "Meritorious Promotion" currently used within the department should include promotions for officers who report criminal conduct of police officers. Officers who choose to serve in the Bureau of Internal Affairs will be prioritized for promotion and will not be compelled to return to their old units after their service in BIA is complete.

5. CPD must punish officers who do not report police corruption, brutality, and other misconduct they observe. The Police Code of Ethics and Department Rules should be strengthened to require that officers must promptly report any crime or unlawful action committed by a fellow police officer. Article Five, Rule 21 of the Rules and Regulations of the Chicago Police Department should be amended to read: "Failure to report promptly to the Department any information *including violations of the law by police officers.*"

6. The Department should require and provide more extensive ethics training for officers. Training in issues of accountability for sergeants and front-line supervisors should be increased. This training needs to teach sergeants how to quickly recognize ethical problems of officers, particularly in the war on drugs, how to advise them, and how to hold them accountable.

### *External Review and Oversight*

1. The Mayor and City Council should enact legislation to replace the current appointed Police Board with either:

        A. a democratically elected civilian Police Board, or

B. a new appointed board with such high caliber members as good-government advocates and civil right leaders, former federal prosecutors, inspector generals, or respected former public defenders or eminent retired judges.

In either case, the new board's purview must not be limited to cases referred by the Superintendent or IPRA and appeals from individual officers. It also should have the power hire special inspectors to conduct investigations.  And, it must be empowered to refer cases to the State's Attorney and U.S. Attorney.

A call for a democratically elected police board is supported by groups such as the Chicago Alliance Against Racist and Political Repression. (See Appendix VI.)


2. The Cook County State's Attorney must allocate sufficient resources for its public integrity unit to improve its prosecution of police corruption. The State's Attorney should issue an annual report on its efforts to curb police corruption and establish better procedures to encourage residents to confidentially report criminal police misconduct.


3. The Mayor and City Hall should report to the public the cost of police corruption and make information about police corruption cases easy to access.  It should report the cost of investigating, defending and settling police corruption cases in its annual city budget and make it available on the city's web site along with a searchable database with all indictments and convictions of police officers.

**Appendix I, Database of Convicted Chicago Police Officers, 1960 - 2012**

| Year | First Name | Last Name | Title/ Position | Event | Code | Notes | Citations |
|---|---|---|---|---|---|---|---|
| 2011 | Anthony | Abbate | Police Officer | Convicted | ODC | Found guilty of aggravated battery related to punching and kicking a female bartender | Chicago Tribune, May 25, 2011 |
| 1999 | Manuel | Acevado | Police Officer | Convicted | BTX | Found guilty of causing paralyzing injury, excessive force, and failure to provide medical care | Chicago Tribune, Oct 26, 1999 |
| 2006 | Michael | Acosta | Commander | Convicted | GPC | Pleaded guilty to one count of fraud for stealing $4000 from police award fund. | Chicago Tribune, Jan 18, 2006 |
| 2007 | Michael | Allegretti | Police Officer | Convicted | BTX | Pleaded guilty to attempted intimidation charges. He asked women whom he pulled over to expose their breasts to avoid traffic tickets | Chicago Sun Times, Sep 7, 2007 |
| 1982 | Thomas | Ambrose | Police Officer | Convicted | DGG | Found guilty of accepting bribes to allow two heroin rings to operate in the Marquette District | Chicago Tribune Jul 1, 1982 |
| 1986 | Ramon | Anderson | Sergeant | Convicted | GPC | Pleaded guilty to bribery related to shaking down a tavern owner | Chicago Tribune, July 17, 1986 |
| 1987 | John | Antonucci | Police Officer | Convicted | GPC | Pleaded guilty to two counts of making false statements | Chicago Tribune, March 24, 1987 |
| 1973 | Daniel H. | Armstrong | Police Officer | Convicted | GPC | Found guilty of conspiracy and perjury related to shakedown of tavern owners | Chicago Tribune, Oct 6, 1973 |
| 2005 | Rafael | Balbontin | Police Officer | Convicted | ODC | Found guilty of stabbing his wife to death with a knife while off duty | Chicago Tribune, Oct 6, 2007 |
| 2002 | Sydney | Barber | Police Officer | Convicted | ODC | Found guilty of first-degree murder while off duty | Chicago Tribune, Sep 26, 2002 |
| 1973 | Edward J. | Barry | Sergeant | Convicted | GPC | Found guilty of conspiracy related to shakedown of tavern owners | Chicago Tribune, Oct 6, 1973 |
| 1973 | Thomas D. | Batastini | Police Officer | Convicted | GPC | Found guilty of conspiracy and perjury related to shakedown of tavern owners | Chicago Tribune, Oct 6, 1973 |
| 2003 | Turan | Beamon | Police Officer | Convicted | DGG | Pleaded guilty to charges that he stole cash and narcotics from a drug dealer | Chicago Tribune, Nov 23, 2003 |

| 1992 | William F | Beck | Police Officer | Convicted | GPC | Pleaded guilty to two counts of income tax fraud related to extorting bribes from truck drivers | Chicago Tribune, April 2, 1992 |
|---|---|---|---|---|---|---|---|
| 1997 | Gregory | Becker | Police Officer | Convicted | ODC | Found guilty of shooting a homeless man, and leaving him on the street to die | Chicago Tribune, May 12, 1997 |
| 1961 | Peter | Beeftink | Police Officer | Convicted | GPC | Found guilty of conspiracy to commit burglary and conspiracy to receive stolen property while in uniform and on duty | Chicago Tribune, Aug 24, 1961 |
| 1986 | Timothy | Belec | Police Officer | Convicted | BTX | Pleaded guilty to aggravated battery and one count of official misconduct for beating a man arrested for loitering | Chicago Tribune, Oct 9, 1986 |
| 2003 | James | Benson | Police Officer | Convicted | DGG | Pleaded guilty to drug conspiracy and narcotics smuggling | Chicago Tribune, Feb 1, 2003 |
| 2009 | Christopher | Berlanga | Police Officer | Convicted | ODC | Pleaded guilty to charges of causing death while operating a vehicle while intoxicated | Post Tribune, August 13, 2009 |
| 2007 | Eural | Black | Police Officer | Convicted | DGG | Found guilty of racketeering and conspiracy related to drug sales committed while armed with a gun | Chicago Tribune, May 12, 2007 |
| 1989 | Phillip | Blackman | Police Officer | Convicted | DGG | Found guilty of charges related to taking bribes to protect the activities of South Side gamblers and a drug dealer | Chicago Tribune, July 12, 1990 |
| 1984 | Ira | Blackwood | Police Officer | Convicted | GPC | Found guilty on one count racketeering/bribery and 10 counts of extortion. | Chicago Tribune, Aug 11, 1984 |
| 2009 | Richard | Bolling | Police Officer | Convicted | ODC | Found guilty of reckless homicide, drunk driving and leaving the scene of the accident that killed a youth | Chicago Tribune, January 12, 2012 |
| 1995 | Roland | Borelli | Police Officer | Convicted | GPC | Pleaded guilty to 1 count extortion and 2 counts of filing false tax returns | Chicago Tribune, May 10, 1995 |
| 1974 | Joseph | Bouse | Police Officer | Convicted | GPC | Found guilty of attempted bribery and official misconduct | Chicago Tribune, Sep 10, 1974 |

| 1973 | Clarence | Braasch | Captain | Convicted | GPC | Pleaded guilty to two counts of tax fraud. | Chicago Tribune, Oct 6, 1973 |
|---|---|---|---|---|---|---|---|
| 2002 | Corey | Braddock | Police Officer | Convicted | ODC | Found guilty of solicitation of a sex act | People v. Braddock, Case No.1-03-0404, March 24, 2004 |
| 1992 | Anthony | Brandys | Police Officer | Convicted | GPC | Pleaded guilty to two counts of tax fraud | Chicago Tribune, March 16, 1992 |
| 1961 | Allan | Brinn | Police Officer | Convicted | GPC | Found guilty of conspiracy to commit burglary and conspiracy to receive stolen property | Chicago Tribune, Aug 24, 1961 |
| 1992 | Kenneth | Brown | Police Officer | Convicted | GPC | Pleaded guilty to a charge of official misconduct | Chicago Tribune, July 1, 1992 |
| 2011 | Victor | Brown | Police Officer | Convicted | GPC | Pleaded guilty to extortion stemming from charges that he accepted $4500 bribe money from other officers to fix Police Board cases | Chicago Tribune, May 10, 2010 |
| 1988 | Philip | Bruno | Detective | Convicted | GPC | Pleaded guilty to accepting bribes from vending machine operators | Chicago Tribune, Oct 1, 1988 |
| 1967 | Raymond | Burford | Police Officer | Convicted | ODC | Pleaded guilty to voluntary manslaughter in the shooting of a police informant | Chicago Tribune, June 14, 1967 |
| 2010 | Jon | Burge | Lieutenant | Convicted | GPC | Found guilty of perjury and obstruction of justice related to torture of witnesses into giving confessions in the 1970s and 1980s | Chicago Tribune, Dec 29, 2010 |
| 1992 | Robert A | Burke | Police Officer | Convicted | GPC | Found guilty of lying to a grand jury when he denied giving a handcuff key to an inmate who killed two officers during an escape attempt | Chicago Tribune, Feb 1, 2003 |
| 2004 | Willie C. | Caldwell | Police Officer | Convicted | GPC | Pleaded guilty to attempted extortion for demanding a payoff to return an impounded vehicle to a citizen | Chicago Tribune, Dec 21, 2004 |
| 1973 | Natale R. | Cale | Police Officer | Convicted | GPC | Found guilty of conspiracy related to shakedown of tavern owners | Chicago Tribune, Oct 6, 1973 |
| 2010 | Gerald | Callahan | Police Officer | Convicted | ODC | Found guilty of battery for punching a 61-year-old man and a 50-year-old while he was off duty. | Chicago Tribune, Feb 12, 2010 |
| 2008 | Scott | Campbell | Police Officer | Convicted | ODC | Pleaded guilty to income tax evasion and mail fraud charges stemming from towing scam | Chicago Tribune, April 22, 2009 |

| 1985 | Thomas | Capparelli | Police Officer | Convicted | GPC | Pleaded guilty to accepting bribes to sidetrack investigations of motorists involved in hit-and-run accidents | Chicago Tribune, May 30, 1985 |
|------|--------|------------|----------------|-----------|-----|--------------------------------------------------------------------------------------------------------------------|------------------------------------|
| 2006 | Kevin | Carey | Police Officer | Convicted | ODC | Pleaded guilty to the DUI charge related to a road rage while off duty | Chicago Sun-Times, Jan 23, 2012 |
| 1989 | John | Carpenter | Police Officer | Convicted | DGG | Found guilty of charges related to taking bribes to protect the activities of gamblers and a drug dealer | Chicago Tribune, July 12, 1990 |
| 2004 | Rodney | Carriger | Police Officer | Convicted | CRV | Found guilty of home invasion and aggravated unlawful restraint and multiple counts of armed violence, bribery and official misconduct | Chicago Tribune, Sep 15, 2004 |
| 2006 | Jason | Casper | Police Officer | Convicted | ODC | Pleaded guilty to charges stemming from reckless homicide and aggravated drunken driving | Chicago Tribune, Jan 18, 2008 |
| 2002 | Xavier | Castro | Police Officer | Convicted | DGG | Found guilty of illegally entering the homes of suspected drug dealers and lying under oath to conceal improper searches | Chicago Tribune, July 12, 2002 |
| 1973 | John | Catalano | Police Officer | Convicted | GPC | Found guilty of conspiracy related to shakedown of tavern owners | Chicago Tribune, Oct 6, 1973 |
| 2003 | Alonzo | Caudillo | Police Officer | Convicted | ODC | Found guilty in the death of a 19 year old female whom he hit and killed while driving his Jeep | Chicago Tribune, Feb 8, 2005 |
| 1992 | Gregory | Chambers | Police Officer | Convicted | ODC | Found guilty of shooting and killing his girlfriend while off duty | Chicago Tribune, Nov 15, 1992 |
| 1985 | Anthony | Chiavola Sr. | Police Officer | Convicted | ODC | Pleaded guilty to conspiring to carry money skimmed from the gambling receipts | Chicago Tribune, July 30, 1985 |
| 1982 | Anthony | Chiavolo Jr. | Police Officer | Convicted | ODC | Pleaded guilty to serving as courier who delivered the skimmed cash from Las Vegas casino to various mob bosses | Chicago Tribune, June 23, 1982 |
| 2009 | Michael J | Ciancio | Police Officer | Convicted | GPC | Pleaded guilty to extortion related to soliciting bribes from tow truck drivers | Chicago Sun Times, Feb 12, 2011 |

| 1961 | Allen | Clements | Police Officer | Convicted | GPC | Found guilty of conspiracy to commit burglary and conspiracy to receive stolen property while in uniform and on duty | Chicago Tribune, Aug 24, 1961 |
|---|---|---|---|---|---|---|---|
| 2009 | William | Cozzi | Police Officer | Convicted | BTX | Pleaded guilty that he used excessive force related to beating a man who was handcuffed and shackled in a wheelchair | Chicago Sun Times, June 20, 2009 |
| 2002 | Matthew | Craig | Police Officer | Convicted | CRV | Pleaded guilty to violating a defendant's civil rights by lying about evidence against arrested people | Chicago Sun Times, April 13, 2002 |
| 2001 | Gregory S. | Crittleton | Police Officer | Convicted | DGG | Pleaded guilty to racketeering and weapons charges related to robbing money from gang members | Chicago Sun Times Oct 19, 2001 |
| 1990 | Kenneth | Cullen | Police Officer | Convicted | ODC | Found guilty of fatally shooting a man after a traffic altercation while off-duty | Chicago Tribune, March 24, 1995 |
| 2012 | Sean | Dailey | Police Officer | Convicted | GPC | Pleaded guilty to DUI when his blood alcohol content registered .14 | Chicago Sun Times, Feb 29, 2012 |
| 1972 | Timothy | Danaher | Sergeant | Convicted | GPC | Pleaded guilty to extorting money from taverns and a south side pharmacy | Chicago Tribune July 27, 1972 |
| 2007 | Aaron | Del Valle | Police Officer | Convicted | GPC | Found guilty of lying to a grand jury in case of patronage hiring at city hall | Chicago Tribune, March 29, 2007 |
| 1985 | Michael | Delany | Police Officer | Convicted | GPC | Pleaded guilty to committing burglaries while on duty | Chicago Tribune, May 3, 1985 |
| 2011 | Stephen | DelBosque | Police Officer | Convicted | DGG | Plead guilty to conducting illegal searches and lying about it, in court or before a grand jury | CBS Chicago, April 7, 2011 |
| 1972 | George | DeMet | Sergeant | Convicted | GPC | Found guilty of extorting money and liquor from tavern operators | Chicago Tribune, Jun 21, 1972 |
| 1982 | Frank T. | Derango | Police Officer | Convicted | DGG | Found guilty of accepting bribes to allow two heroin rings to operate in the Marquette District. | Chicago Tribune, July 1, 1982 |
| 1982 | John F. | DeSimone | Police Officer | Convicted | DGG | Found guilty of accepting bribes to allow two heroin rings to operate in the Marquette District. | Chicago Tribune Jul 1, 1982 |

| 1973 | Robert | Devitt | Lieutenant | Convicted | GPC | Found guilty of perjury related to receiving bribes from tavern owners | Chicago Tribune, May 5, 1973 |
|---|---|---|---|---|---|---|---|
| 1995 | William | Devoney | Lieutenant | Convicted | ODC | Pleaded guilty to insurance fraud | Chicago Tribune, June 7, 1995 |
| 2008 | Richard | Doroniuk | Police Officer | Convicted | DGG | Pleaded guilty to racketeering, admitting he robbed drug dealers of cash , planted drugs on people he arrested and used fake informants to secure search warrants | Chicago Tribune, June 4, 2008 |
| 2003 | Anthony | Downing | Police Officer | Convicted | BTX | Found guilty of official misconduct and bribery for engaging in a sex act with a young prostitute | Chicago Tribune, Feb 22, 2003 |
| 2009 | Anthony | Doyle | Police Officer | Convicted | GPC | Found guilty of racketeering conspiracy related to passing on confidential information about the federal probe to a mob friend | Chicago Tribune, March 12, 2009 |
| 1972 | Brian | Duffy | Police Officer | Convicted | GPC | Pleaded guilty to perjury related to ambulance chasing scheme | Chicago Tribune, Oct 21, 1972 |
| 1964 | Thomas | Durso | Police Officer | Convicted | ODC | Found guilty of shooting and killing handcuffed police informant | Chicago Tribune, Oct 30, 1974 |
| 2002 | Daniel | Durst | Police Officer | Convicted | BTX | Found guilty of excessive force and failure to stop beating | Chicago Tribune, Oct 23, 2002 |
| 1993 | James E. | Dvorak | Detective | Convicted | GPC | Pleaded guilty to bribery and income tax charges | Chicago Sun-Times, Aug 31, 1993 |
| 1979 | Patrick A. | Dwyer | Police Officer | Convicted | ODC | Found guilty of attempted robbery of a grocery store | Chicago Tribune, Jul 10, 1979 |
| 1981 | Fred | Earullo | Police Officer | Convicted | BTX | Found guilty of fatally beating up a mental patient after he was arrested and in custody. Suspect that was beaten by the officer had massive brain swelling, two broken legs, broken neck and nine broken ribs after his arrest | Chicago Tribune, Jan 26, 1984 |
| 1982 | Robert L. | Eatman | Police Officer | Convicted | DGG | Found guilty of accepting bribes to allow two heroin rings to operate in the Marquette District | Chicago Tribune Jul 1, 1982 |

| 1989 | Elbert | Elfreeze | Police Officer | Convicted | DGG | Pleaded guilty to charges related to taking bribes to protect the activities of gamblers and a drug dealer | Chicago Tribune, Jan 10, 1990 |
|---|---|---|---|---|---|---|---|
| 1973 | Martin D. | Eshoo | Police Officer | Convicted | GPC | Found guilty of conspiracy and perjury related to shakedown of tavern owners | Chicago Tribune, Oct 6, 1973 |
| 1961 | Frank | Faraci | Police Officer | Convicted | GPC | Found guilty of conspiracy to commit burglary and conspiracy to receive stolen property while in uniform and on duty | Chicago Tribune, Aug 24, 1961 |
| 1973 | Edward F. | Finn | Police Officer | Convicted | GPC | Found guilty of conspiracy related to shakedown of tavern owners | Chicago Tribune, Oct 6, 1973 |
| 2011 | Jerome | Finnegan | Police Officer | Convicted | DGG | Pleaded guilty to the murder-for-hire charge, robbery and a tax-evasion charge related to stealing of cash from drug dealers | Chicago Tribune, May 5, 2012 |
| 2006 | Corey | Flagg | Police Officer | Convicted | DGG | Pleaded guilty to racketeering for shaking down drug dealers for cash and cocaine and providing protection for large narcotics deliveries | Chicago Tribune, May 9, 2007 |
| 1973 | Carl | Flagg | Sergeant | Convicted | GPC | Found guilty of conspiracy and perjury related to shakedown of tavern owners | Chicago Tribune, Oct 6, 1973 |
| | | | | | | | |
| 1998 | Tyrone | Francies | Police Officer | Convicted | DGG | Found guilty of robbing undercover agents posing as drug dealers | Chicago Sun Times, June 9, 1998 |
| 2012 | Joseph | Frugoli | Police Officer | Convicted | ODC | Pleaded guilty to aggravated driving under the influence for crashing into a car and killing two men | Chicago Tribune, Nov 16, 2012 |
| 1992 | Michael | Gallagher | Police Officer | Convicted | ODC | Found guilty of weapons charges related to illegal possession of silencer | Chicago Tribune, Dec 17, 1992 |
| 2002 | John | Galligan | Police Officer | Convicted | DGG | Pleaded guilty to extortion, the theft of 2.2 pounds of cocaine from a drug dealer and supplying 3 grams of cocaine to a police informant | Chicago Sun Times Feb 27, 2003 |
| 1989 | Victor | Garcia | Police Officer | Convicted | GPC | Pleaded guilty to burglarizing a residency of a retired police officer | Chicago Tribune, April 6, 1989 |

| | | | | | | | |
|---|---|---|---|---|---|---|---|
| 1982 | Jerome | Garrison | Police Officer | Convicted | ODC | Found guilty of possession of a stolen motor vehicle with an altered vehicle identification numbers | Chicago Tribune, Jan 1, 1982 |
| 1973 | John M. | Geraghty | Sergeant | Convicted | GPC | Found guilty of conspiracy and perjury related to shakedown of tavern owners | Chicago Tribune, Oct 6, 1973 |
| 1999 | Aaron | Gibson | Police Officer | Convicted | ODC | Pleaded guilty to identity theft. He used other officer's identity to fraudulently obtain instant credit and make illegal purchases in the amount of $20,000 | Chicago Tribune, July 22, 1999 |
| 1989 | James | Ginani | Police Officer | Convicted | GPC | Pleaded guilty to extorting bribes from trucking companies to overlook trucks exceeding weight limits | Chicago Tribune, April 2, 1992 |
| 2002 | Robert | Gloeckler | Police Officer | Convicted | CRV | Pleaded guilty to a misdemeanor civil-rights violation related to lying under oath while testifying in court | Chicago Tribune, March 5, 2002 |
| 1985 | Willie | Grady | Police Officer | Convicted | DGG | Found guilty of conspiracy, three counts of distribution of cocaine and one count of distribution of heroin | Chicago Tribune, Sep 6, 1985 |
| 1985 | Ralph G. | Graham | Police Officer | Convicted | ODC | Found guilty of mail fraud for receiving about $15,000 in checks fraudulently issued, participated in a scheme to receive illicit Blue Cross/Blue Shield insurance benefits | Chicago Tribune, Feb 1, 1985 |
| 1973 | Philip R. | Grana | Police Officer | Convicted | GPC | Found guilty of conspiracy and perjury related to shakedown of tavern owners | Chicago Tribune, Oct 6, 1973 |
| 1985 | Ronald J. | Green | Police Officer | Convicted | GPC | Found guilty of accepting bribes to sidetrack investigations of hit-and-run accidents | Chicago Tribune, June 6, 1985 |
| 2009 | Joseph | Grillo | Police Officer | Convicted | ODC | Pleaded guilty to income tax evasion and mail fraud charges stemming from towing scam | Chicago Tribune, March 04, 2009 |
| 1961 | Patrick | Groark | Police Officer | Convicted | GPC | Found guilty of conspiracy to commit burglary and conspiracy to receive stolen property | Chicago Tribune, Aug 25, 1961 |

| 2011 | Alex | Guerrero | Police Officer | Convicted | DGG | Pleaded guilty to racketeering, related to using his law enforcement status to commit armed robberies of drug traffickers for the Latin Kings | Chicago Tribune, Dec 02, 2011 |
|---|---|---|---|---|---|---|---|
| 2006 | Richard | Guerrero | Lieutenant | Convicted | GPC | Found guilty of misdemeanor telephone harassment for taking a phone number of a police report and harassing a woman | Chicago Sun Times, March 1, 2006 |
| 1982 | William A. | Guide | Police Officer | Convicted | DGG | Found guilty of accepting bribes to allow two heroin rings to operate in the Marquette District | New York Times Jan 18, 1983 |
| 1989 | Everett | Gully | Sergeant | Convicted | DGG | Found guilty of charges related to taking bribes to protect the activities of South Side gamblers and a drug dealer | Chicago Tribune, July 12, 1990 |
| 2007 | Larry | Guy Jr. | Police Officer | Convicted | BTX | Pleaded guilty to misdemeanor battery related to beating a handcuffed shoplifting suspect | Chicago Tribune, Jan 24, 2009 |
| 1997 | Timothy | Hampton | Police Officer | Convicted | DGG | Found guilty of cocaine possession, armed violence and official misconduct late | Chicago Tribune, Dec 06, 1997 |
| 1992 | Paul | Hardin | Police Officer | Convicted | GPC | Found guilty of aggravated assault, official misconduct and theft | Chicago Tribune, July 1, 1992 |
| 2005 | Larry | Hargrove | Sergeant | Convicted | DGG | Found guilty of shaking down drug dealers for cash and narcotics over a period of six years | Chicago Tribune, June 23, 2005 |
| 1982 | William L. | Hass | Police Officer | Convicted | DGG | Found guilty of accepting bribes to allow two heroin rings to operate in the Marquette District | Chicago Tribune Jul 1, 1982 |
| 1995 | David | Hayes | Police Officer | Convicted | ODC | Pleaded guilty to leaving the scene of an accident after he crashed a car into another car | Chicago Tribune, March 7, 2008 |
| 2005 | Darek | Haynes | Police Officer | Convicted | DGG | Pleaded guilty to racketeering for shaking down drug dealers for cash and cocaine and providing protection for large narcotics deliveries | Chicago Tribune, May 12, 2007 |
| 1986 | James | Hegarty | Police Officer | Convicted | GPC | Pleaded guilty to 1 count of tax fraud | Chicago Sun Times, March 1, 1986 |
| 2008 | John | Herman | Police Officer | Convicted | BTX | Found guilty of aggravated criminal sexual assault, aggravated kidnapping and misconduct | Chicago Tribune Dec 04, 2007 |
| 2011 | Marcos | Hernandez | Police Officer | Convicted | GPC | Pleaded guilty to improperly accessing motorists' information and pocketing payoffs from tow truck operators | Chicago Tribune, Aug 16, 2011 |

| 2011 | Keith | Herrera | Police Officer | Convicted | DGG | Pleaded guilty to civil rights and tax-related charges and admitted he stole cash from suspected drug dealers and other citizens after making illegal traffic stops or home searches | Chicago Tribune, May 5, 2012 |
|---|---|---|---|---|---|---|---|
| 1998 | Eric | Holder | Police Officer | Convicted | ODC | Found guilty of resisting arrest following a fight while Holder was off duty at the time | Chicago Tribune, March 7, 1998 |
| 2009 | Margaret | Hopkins | Police Officer | Convicted | DGG | Pleaded guilty to official misconduct related to falsifying a police report after her colleagues illegally searched drug dealers and others for drugs | Chicago Sun-Times, Sep 23, 2009 |
| 2012 | Edward | Howard Jr. | Sergeant | Convicted | BTX | Found guilty of felony aggravated battery and official misconduct charges for slapping a handcuffed teen in an unprovoked attack | Chicago Tribune, July 20, 2012 |
| 1999 | Rayshawn | Hudgins | Police Officer | Convicted | BTX | Found guilty of aggravated kidnapping, unlawful restraint related to rape and sexual abuse of teen boys | Chicago Tribune, Jan 15, 1999 |
| 2004 | Ernest | Hutchinson | Police Officer | Convicted | CRV | Found guilty of home invasion and aggravated unlawful restraint and multiple counts of armed violence, bribery and official misconduct | Chicago Tribune, Sep 15, 2004 |
| 1996 | Sonia | Irwin | Police Officer | Convicted | DGG | Found guilty of aiding and abetting the Gangster Disciples street gang | Chicago Tribune, Feb 15, 1996 |
| 2001 | Edward Lee | Jackson Jr | Police Officer | Convicted | DGG | Found guilty of racketeering for shaking down drug dealers for cash and cocaine and providing protection for large narcotics deliveries | Chicago Sun-Times Oct 19, 2001 |
| 2002 | Eugene | Jennings | Police Officer | Convicted | GPC | Pleaded guilty to bribery, solicitation of sex and official misconduct | Chicago Sun Times, Sep 25, 2002 |
| 2005 | Erik | Johnson | Police Officer | Convicted | DGG | Pleaded guilty to conspiracy charges related to shaking down drug dealers for cash and cocaine and providing protection for large narcotics deliveries | Chicago Tribune, May 12, 2007 |

| 1970 | Walter | Johnson | Police Officer | Convicted | GPC | Pleaded guilty to theft in the amount of $3,000 | Chicago Tribune, July 8, 1970 |
|---|---|---|---|---|---|---|---|
| 2005 | Broderick | Jones | Police Officer | Convicted | DGG | Pleaded guilty to racketeering for shaking down drug dealers for cash and cocaine and providing protection for large narcotics deliveries | Chicago Tribune, Jan 28, 2005 |
| 1979 | Wilton | Jones | Police Officer | Convicted | DGG | Found guilty of conspiracy related to Chicago based heroin distribution ring | Chicago Tribune, March 9, 1979 |
| 1971 | John J. | Jordan | Police Officer | Convicted | GPC | Found guilty of bribery charges stemming from payoffs the officer took from ambulance drivers for calling them to the accident | Chicago Tribune, April 20, 1971 |
| 1961 | Alex | Karras | Police Officer | Convicted | GPC | Found guilty of conspiracy to commit burglary and conspiracy to receive stolen property while in uniform and on duty | Chicago Tribune, Aug 24, 1961 |
| 1961 | Sol | Karras | Police Officer | Convicted | GPC | Found guilty of conspiracy to commit burglary and conspiracy to receive stolen property while in uniform and on duty | Chicago Tribune, Aug 24, 1961 |
| 1971 | Edward J. | Kavale | Police Officer | Convicted | ODC | Found guilty of reckless conduct related to shooting a 19- your old youth while off duty | Chicago Tribune, May 13, 1971 |
| 2010 | John | Killackey | Police Officer | Convicted | ODC | Found guilty of stiffing a cabdriver of an $8 fare and then threatening him at gunpoint | Chicago Tribune, May 28, 2010 |
| 1975 | Thomas | King | Police Officer | Convicted | GPC | Pleaded guilty to bribery and official misconduct | Chicago Tribune, Oct 15, 1975 |
| 2010 | Richard | Kleinpass | Police Officer | Convicted | ODC | Pleaded guilty to violation of owner's duties in animal neglect case | Chicago Sun-Times, May 22, 2010 |
| 1981 | Louis | Klisz | Police Officer | Convicted | BTX | Found guilty of fatally beating up a mental patient after he was arrested and in custody. Suspect that was beaten by the officer had massive brain swelling, two broken legs, broken neck and nine broken ribs after his arrest | Chicago Tribune, Jan 26, 1984 |
| 1963 | Gregory | Kouvelis | Police Officer | Convicted | ODC | Pleaded guilty to auto theft | Chicago Tribune, Feb 26, 1963 |

| 2005 | John | Krass | Police Officer | Convicted | ODC | Found guilty of aggravated drunken driving and reckless homicide related to a car crash while he was off duty that killed a 20-year-old man | Chicago Sun-Times, April 28, 2005 |
|------|------|-------|----------------|-----------|-----|------|------|
| 1992 | Anthony | Kreiser | Police Officer | Convicted | DGG | Found guilty of conspiring to distribute cocaine | Chicago Tribune, May 24, 1992 |
| 1988 | Clarence | Kujawa | Detective | Convicted | GPC | Pleaded guilty: tax charges, accepting payoffs to make sure bar owners received liquor licenses | Chicago Sun Times, Apr 22, 1988 |
| 1991 | Roy | Kummer | Police Officer | Convicted | ODC | Found guilty of aggravated battery in connection with the fatal beating committed while off duty | Chicago Tribune, April 14, 1991 |
| 1988 | Leonard | Kurz | Police Officer | Convicted | BTX | Found guilty of charges stemming from robbery and severely beating a businessman who filed a complained against him for harassment | Chicago Tribune, July 30, 1995 |
| 1981 | Thomas | Kurz | Police Officer | Convicted | GPC | Found guilty of mail fraud and attempted extortion | Chicago Tribune, Feb 27, 1981 |
| 2000 | John | Labiak | Police Officer | Convicted | CRV | Found guilty of home invasion and aggravated unlawful restraint and multiple counts of armed violence, bribery and official misconduct | Chicago Tribune, Sep 15, 2004 |
| 1992 | Edward | LaCourse | Police Officer | Convicted | GPC | Pleaded guilty to extorting bribes from trucking companies to overlook trucks exceeding weight limits | Chicago Tribune, April 2, 1992 |
| 1984 | James | LaFevour | Police Officer | Convicted | GPC | Pleaded guilty to 3 counts of tax fraud | Chicago Tribune, April 30, 1985 |
| 1974 | Arthur | LaGace | Police Officer | Convicted | GPC | Found guilty of bribery and shaking down a motorist during a traffic stop | Chicago Tribune, June 14, 1974 |
| 1987 | Michael | Lambesis | Investigator | Convicted | GPC | Pleaded guilty to corruption charges and admitted he passed $17,500 in bribe money. On the separate change he also pleaded guilty to selling two machine guns and two silencers to the undercover FBI agent | Chicago Tribune, Aug 11, 1987 |

| 1993 | Milton | Lancaster | Police Officer | Convicted | BTX | Found guilty of official misconduct and criminal sexual abuse for molesting a woman he pulled over for a traffic stop | Chicago Tribune, Aug 19, 1993 |
|------|--------|-----------|----------------|-----------|-----|---------------------------------------------------------------------------------------------|-------------------------------|
| 1991 | Patrick | Lawrence | Police Officer | Convicted | ODC | Found guilty of sexual assaulted and abuse of a 15-year-old boy while off duty | Chicago Tribune, Sep 20, 1991 |
| 2007 | Edward | Leak | Police Officer | Convicted | ODC | Found guilty of masterminding a plot to have his friend and business associate killed to collect on a $500,000 insurance policy | Chicago Tribune, Oct 19, 2007 |
| 1994 | Reginald | Lee | Police Officer | Convicted | DGG | Found guilty of charges related to possession of a controlled substance and sale of narcotics | Court Case 392 F.3d 909, Docket No. 04-1402 |
| 2012 | Glenn | Lewellen | Police Officer | Convicted | DGG | Found guilty of providing members of the drug ring with information concerning ongoing federal investigations into its operations | Chicago Tribune, Feb 1, 2012 |
| 1980 | Peter | Lipa | Police Officer | Convicted | ODC | Found guilty of stealing $100,000 in state toll-way revenue during the armed robbery of a toll-road collection truck while off duty | Chicago Tribune, Oct 6, 1980 |
| 1998 | Marvin | Little | Police Officer | Convicted | GPC | Found guilty of theft and official misconduct perpetrated during warrantless search | Chicago Tribune, Jan 13, 1998 |
| 1998 | Richard | Lopardo | Police Officer | Convicted | DGG | Pleaded guilty to charges that he pocketed payoffs in return for providing sensitive details about a police investigation of a drug dealer | Chicago Tribune, Oct 23, 1998 |
| 1982 | Curtis A. | Lowery | Police Officer | Convicted | DGG | Found guilty of accepting bribes to allow two heroin rings to operate in the Marquette District. | Chicago Tribune Jul 1, 1982 |
| 2003 | Kenny | Lunsford | Police Officer | Convicted | CRV | Found guilty of wrongful death of an unarmed man he shot in the back | Chicago Tribune, Aug 08, 2003 |
| 1988 | Duane | Lyle | Police Officer | Convicted | CRV | Found guilty of violating the civil rights of a South Side man he shot in the head after a traffic accident | Chicago Tribune, Nov 16, 1988 |
| 1981 | Richard | Madeja | Police Officer | Convicted | ODC | Pleaded guilty to possession and manufacture of silencer | Chicago Tribune, Nov 10, 1981 |
| 2009 | Bart | Maka | Police Officer | Convicted | DGG | Pleaded guilty to felony theft related to illegal searchers of drug dealers and gang suspects and stealing their money and narcotics | Chicago Sun Times, Sep 18, 2009 |

| 1985 | Steve | Manning | Police Officer | Convicted | GPC | Found guilty of conspiracy and burglarizing a jewelry store in Pilsner where $260,000 were stolen in jewels | Chicago Tribune, March 11, 1987 |
|------|-------|---------|----------------|-----------|-----|------|------|
| 2009 | Donovan | Markiewicz | Police Officer | Convicted | DGG | Pleaded guilty to official misconduct related to illegal searchers of drug dealers and gang suspects and stealing their money and narcotics | Chicago Sun Times, Sep 18, 2009 |
| 1994 | Thomas | Marquez | Police Officer | Convicted | BTX | Pleaded guilty  to a charge of extortion | Chicago Tribune, Jan 27, 1994 |
| 1985 | Louis J | Martin | Police Officer | Convicted | GPC | Found guilty of racketeering and mail fraud related to soliciting bribes from motorists who were under investigation for leaving the scenes of accidents | Chicago Tribune, Oct 3, 1985 |
| 2011 | Antonio | Martinez Jr | Police Officer | Convicted | DGG | Pleaded guilty to conspiring to participate in racketeering activity, conspiring to possess cocaine and marijuana, interfering with commerce by threat or violence and using a firearm during a crime of violence and drug trafficking | Chicago Tribune, Dec 02, 2011 |
| 2000 | Pedro | Mataterrazas II | Police Officer | Convicted | DGG | Pleaded guilty to narcotics conspiracy charges | Chicago Tribune, Oct. 7, 2000 |
| 2003 | Peter L. | Matich | Police Officer | Convicted | DGG | Pleaded guilty to drug charges of stealing 7 kilograms of cocaine from a drug dealer | Chicago Sun-Times, Feb 14, 2003 |
| 1984 | Arthur W. | McCauslin | Police Officer | Convicted | GPC | Pleaded guilty to income tax fraud | Chicago Tribune, Aug 22, 1985 |
| 2001 | Brian M. | McCluskey | Police Officer | Convicted | DGG | Pleaded guilty to being part of a network that sold ecstasy to teenagers | Chicago Tribune, Nov 8, 2001 |
| 1996 | Ralph | McCue | Police Officer | Convicted | GPC | Found guilty of two counts of official misconduct related to robbery of a videocassette and $12 | Chicago Tribune, Feb 8, 1996 |
| 1973 | Edward | McGee | Police Officer | Convicted | GPC | Found guilty of conspiracy related to shakedown of tavern owners | Chicago Tribune, Oct 6, 1973 |

| 2009 | James | McGovern | Sergeant | Convicted | DGG | Pleaded guilty to misdemeanor charge of attempted obstruction associated with illegal drug sales | Chicago Tribune, Sep 26, 2009 |
|---|---|---|---|---|---|---|---|
| 2007 | Charlton | McKay | Police Officer | Convicted | ODC | Found guilty of trying to conceal his role in the reckless homicide by filing a false police report | Chicago Tribune, June 20, 2007 |
| 1986 | Lawrence | McLain | Police Officer | Convicted | GPC | Pleaded guilty to two counts of tax fraud | Chicago Sun Times, May 29, 1986 |
| 1989 | Edward J. | McMahon | Police Officer | Convicted | ODC | Pleaded guilty to misdemeanor election code violations in connection with the 1986 petition drive for a nonpartisan mayoral election | Chicago Sun-Times, Aug 17, 1989 |
| 1998 | Gerald | Meachum | Police Officer | Convicted | DGG | Found guilty of robbing undercover agents posing as drug dealers | Chicago Sun-Times, June 9, 1998 |
| 1982 | Erskine | Melchor | Police Officer | Convicted | DGG | Found guilty of possession and delivery of cocaine | Chicago Tribune, Feb 1, 1984 |
| 1995 | Christopher | Messino | Police Officer | Convicted | DGG | Found guilty on two tax counts stemming from charges related to narcotics sales | Chicago Tribune, Oct 4, 2000 |
| 1995 | Clement | Messino | Police Officer | Convicted | DGG | Found guilty of narcotics conspiracy, money laundering and tax charges | Chicago Tribune, April 14, 2000 |
| 2003 | Joseph | Miedzianowski | Police Officer | Convicted | DGG | Found guilty of RICO conspiracy, distribution of cocaine, extortion, possession with intent to distribute cocaine & illegal possession of a firearm | Chicago Sun Times Feb 27, 2003 |
| 1990 | Nedrick | Miller | Sergeant | Convicted | DGG | Pleaded guilty to running a million-dollar, round-the-clock drug ring operating out of an apartment building he managed | Chicago Tribune, Dec 20, 1996 |
| 2001 | Steven G. | Miller | Police Officer | Convicted | GPC | Pleaded guilty to official misconduct related to shaking down immigrants | Chicago Tribune, Aug 14, 2001 |
| 1984 | Raymond | Mills | Police Officer | Convicted | DGG | Found guilty of sale of a quarter ounce of cocaine | Chicago Tribune, March 29, 1984 |
| 1989 | Thure | Mills | Police Officer | Convicted | DGG | Pleaded guilty to charges related to taking bribes to protect the activities of South Side gamblers and a drug dealer. | Chicago Tribune, Jan 10, 1990 |

| 2012 | Kallatt | Mohammed | Police Officer | Convicted | DGG | Pleaded guilty to extorting payoffs from heroin and crack dealers | Chicago Tribune, Nov 2, 2012 |
|---|---|---|---|---|---|---|---|
| 2001 | M.L | Moore | Police Officer | Convicted | DGG | Found guilty of racketeering for shaking down drug dealers for cash and cocaine and providing protection for large narcotics deliveries | Chicago Sun Times Oct 19, 2001 |
| 1996 | Martin | Moore | Police Officer | Convicted | GPC | Found guilty of two counts of official misconduct related to robbery of a videocassette and $12 | Chicago Tribune, Feb 8, 1996 |
| 1972 | Walter | Moore | Police Officer | Convicted | GPC | Found guilty of trying to shake down Austin area tavern owners for $50 a month | Chicago Tribune, June 20, 1972 |
| 2004 | Mario | Morales | Police Officer | Convicted | DGG | Pleaded guilty to stealing 220 pounds of marijuana and more than $10,000 in cash from a drug dealer | Chicago Tribune, Jan 22, 2004 |
|  |  |  |  |  |  |  |  |
| 1961 | Henry | Mulea | Police Officer | Convicted | GPC | Found guilty of conspiracy to commit burglary and conspiracy to receive stolen property while in uniform and on duty | Chicago Tribune, Aug 24, 1961 |
| 1973 | Lowell E. | Napier | Police Officer | Convicted | GPC | Pleaded guilty to one count of conspiracy to commit extortion of tavern owners | Chicago Tribune, Jan 24, 1973 |
| 1989 | Ronald | Nash | Police Officer | Convicted | GPC | Pleaded guilty to charges stemming from taking bribes in an FBI auto-theft sting | Chicago Sun Times, Oct 15, 2012 |
| 2002 | Thomas P | Nash | Police Officer | Convicted | GPC | Pleaded guilty to a single misdemeanor count of theft related to disability scam | Chicago Sun Times, Oct 15, 2012 |
| 1985 | John | Novack | Police Officer | Convicted | GPC | Found guilty of mail fraud and racketeering related to accepting bribes from motorists involved in hit and run accidents | Chicago Tribune, May 30, 1985 |
| 1969 | Richard L. | Nuccio | Police Officer | Convicted | ODC | Found guilty of murder of a 19-year old youth whom he shoot in the back | Chicago Tribune, May 22, 1969 |
| 1989 | Daniel | O'Connor | Police | Convicted | GPC | Found guilty of taking $950 in bribes for | Chicago Tribune, |

| | | | Officer | | | providing confidential information | Oct 24, 1989 |
|---|---|---|---|---|---|---|---|
| 1988 | Robert | O'Donnell | Police Officer | Convicted | GPC | Pleaded guilty to income tax evasion related to accepting payoffs to make sure bar owners received liquor licenses | Chicago Sun-Times, Apr. 22, 1988 |
| 2003 | Ruben | Oliveras | Police Officer | Convicted | DGG | Pleaded guilty to misdemeanor civil rights violation | Chicago Tribune, May 29, 2003 |
| 2011 | Eric | Olsen | Police Officer | Convicted | DGG | Plead guilty to conducting illegal searches and lying about it, in court or before a grand jury | Chicago Tribune, April 20, 2011 |
| 1975 | Peter | Orciuoli | Police Officer | Convicted | GPC | Found guilty on charges of theft of $90,000 worth of cigarettes | Chicago Tribune, Jan 15, 1975 |
| 2011 | Donald | Owsley | Police Officer | Convicted | ODC | Found guilty of financial exploitation of the elderly and forgery while off duty | Chicago Sun-Times, June 18, 2011 |
| 1972 | James V. | Pacente | Police Officer | Convicted | GPC | Found guilty of extortion and perjury related to tavern shakedown | Chicago Tribune, Oct 13, 1972 |
| 2009 | John | Pallohusky | Sergeant | Convicted | GPC | Pleaded guilty to one count of felony theft related to stealing of about $1 million from the union fund | Chicago Tribune, June 6, 2012 |
| 1995 | Fred | Pascente | Detective | Convicted | ODC | Pleaded guilty to mail fraud involving a false insurance claim while off duty | Chicago Tribune, Nov. 28, 1995 |
| 1992 | Robert | Passeri | Police Officer | Convicted | GPC | Pleaded guilty to extorting bribes from trucking companies to overlook trucks exceeding weight limits | Chicago Tribune, April 2, 1992 |
| 2002 | William M. | Patterson | Sergeant | Convicted | DGG | Found guilty of conspiracy and attempting to possess cocaine with intent to distribute the drugs after stealing $20,000 and five bricks of fake cocaine planted by government investigators | Chicago Tribune, May 3, 2002 |
| 1998 | Falandes | Peacock | Police Officer | Convicted | ODC | Found guilty of stealing from a Super K-Mart while off duty | Chicago Tribune, Sep 2, 1998 |
| 1992 | William | Pedersen | Detective | Convicted | ODC | Pleaded guilty to selling criminal histories and employment and earnings information stolen from federally protected computer files | Chicago Sun Times, January 23, 2011 |

| 1982 | Joseph R. | Pena | Police Officer | Convicted | DGG | Found guilty of accepting bribes to allow two heroin rings to operate in the Marquette District. | Chicago Tribune, Jul 1, 1982 |
|---|---|---|---|---|---|---|---|
| 1998 | Gilberto | Perez | Police Officer | Convicted | BTX | Pleaded guilty to aggravated criminal sexual assault and kidnapping | Chicago Tribune, May 10, 1998 |
| 1981 | Anthony | Pesha | Police Officer | Convicted | GPC | Found guilty of mail fraud and extortion related to police car repair schemes and phony billing to the city of Chicago | Chicago Tribune, Feb 27, 1981 |
| 1993 | Samuel | Pesoli | Police Officer | Convicted | GPC | Pleaded guilty to 2 counts of perjury | Chicago Sun-Times, May 4, 1993 |
| 2002 | James | Petruzzi | Police Officer | Convicted | GPC | Pleaded guilty to lying to a supervisor related to shaking down immigrants for money | Chicago Tribune, May 10, 2002 |
| 1981 | Tyrone | Pickens | Police Officer | Convicted | GPC | Found guilty of charges stemming from burglarizing home while in uniform, official misconduct and possession of marijuana | Chicago Tribune, Sep 7, 1981 |
| 2003 | Edgar I. | Placencio | Police Officer | Convicted | DGG | Pleaded guilty to concealing a civil rights felony | Chicago Tribune, May 29, 2003 |
| 2012 | Juan | Prado | Police Officer | Convicted | GPC | Pleaded guilty to extortion-related to pocketing money in payoffs from a tow truck operator | Chicago Tribune, July 1, 2010 |
| 2009 | Brian | Pratscher | Police Officer | Convicted | DGG | Pleaded guilty to felony theft related to illegal searchers of drug dealers and gang suspects and stealing their money and narcotics | Chicago Sun Times, Sept 18, 2009 |
| 1991 | Robert | Purtill | Lieutenant | Convicted | GPC | Pleaded guilty to three felony tax charges of depriving the government out of in excess of $100 by not reporting the bribes on his tax returns | Chicago Tribune, Feb 15, 1991 |
| 2001 | Alex D. | Ramos | Police Officer | Convicted | DGG | Found guilty of racketeering for shaking down drug dealers for cash and cocaine and providing protection for large narcotics deliveries | Chicago Sun Times Oct 19, 2001 |
| 1994 | Michael | Randy | Police Officer | Convicted | ODC | Found guilty of mail fraud and money laundering related to sale of fraudulent certificates of deposit | Chicago Tribune, Jan 5, 1994 |

| 1998 | Herbert | Redmond | Police Officer | Convicted | GPC | Found guilty of theft and official misconduct perpetrated during warrantless search | Chicago Tribune, Jan 13, 1998 |
|------|---------|---------|----------------|-----------|-----|-------------------------------------------------------------------------------------|-------------------------------|
| 1982 | Vincent R. | Rizza | Police Officer | Convicted | DGG | Found guilty of conspiring to sell cocaine valued at $120,000 | Chicago Tribune, May 22, 1982 |
| 1992 | Nickolas | Rizzato | Police Officer | Convicted | DGG | Pleaded guilty to conspiring to possess and distribute cocaine | Chicago Tribune, Jan 20, 1992 |
| 1961 | Daniel | Rizzo | Police Officer | Convicted | GPC | Found guilty of accepting a $10 dollar bribe from a motorist whom he stopped for driving through a stop sign | Chicago Tribune, Jan 18, 1961 |
| 1973 | Stanley B. | Robinson | Sergeant | Convicted | CRV | Found guilty of depriving two citizens of their rights to life, liberty, and property without due process | Chicago Tribune, Aug 7, 1973 |
| 2002 | Norberto | Rodriguez | Police Officer | Convicted | DGG | Pleaded guilty to possession of heroin with intent to sell | Chicago Tribune, Nov 23, 2010 |
| 1995 | Lloyd | Roe | Police Officer | Convicted | DGG | Pleaded guilty to extorting money from a drug dealer | Chicago Tribune, Aug 24, 1995 |
| 2000 | John | Rose | Police Officer | Convicted | DGG | Pleaded guilty to selling crack cocaine stolen from drug dealers | Chicago Tribune, June 30, 2000 |
| 1973 | James | Ross | Patrolman | Convicted | GPC | Found guilty of extortion and one count perjury for lying to the court | Chicago Tribune, Jan 12, 1973 |
| 1988 | Rick | Runnels Sr. | Police Officer | Convicted | BTX | Found guilty of charges related to robbery and beating of a businessman who filed a complained against him for harassment | Chicago Tribune, July 30, 1995 |
| 1973 | Edward | Russell | Police Officer | Convicted | GPC | Found guilty of conspiracy and perjury related to shakedown of tavern owners | Chicago Tribune, Oct 6, 1973 |
| 1973 | Emmons P. | Russell | Police Officer | Convicted | GPC | Found guilty of conspiracy and perjury related to shakedown of tavern owners | Chicago Tribune, Oct 6, 1973 |
| 2010 | Sean | Ryan | Police Officer | Convicted | DGG | Pleaded guilty to charges that he sold a semi-automatic assault rifle to a gang member who was a convicted drug dealer | Chicago Tribune, Jan 13, 2010 |
| 2009 | Guadalupe | Salinas | Police Officer | Convicted | DGG | Pleaded guilty to felony theft related to illegal searchers of drug dealers and gang suspects and stealing their money and narcotics | Chicago Sun Times, Sep 18, 2009 |

43

| 1973 | Harry R. | Salvesen | Police Officer | Convicted | GPC | Found guilty of conspiracy related to shakedown of tavern owners | Chicago Tribune, Oct 6, 1973 |
|------|----------|----------|----------------|-----------|-----|------------------------------------------------------------------|------------------------------|
| 1990 | Fred | Sanders | Patrolman | Convicted | DGG | Found guilty of charges related to taking bribes to protect the activities of gamblers and a drug dealer | Chicago Sun Times, Jan 10, 1990 |
| 1977 | Richard | Scanlon | Sergeant | Convicted | CRV | Pleaded guilty to official misconduct stemming from charges that he lied on a stand when he testified that a defendant shot him while the truth was that the officer shot himself during a struggle. | Chicago Tribune, Aug 17, 1977 |
| 1973 | Joseph A. | Schillinger | Sergeant | Convicted | GPC | Found guilty of conspiracy and perjury related to shakedown of tavern owners | Chicago Tribune, Oct 6, 1973 |
| 1972 | Thomas | Schmidt | Police Officer | Convicted | BTX | Found guilty of depriving a suspect of civil rights by beating him with a night stick and kicking his teeth out | Chicago Tribune, Nov 27, 1972 |
| 1973 | Steve L. | Seno | Police Officer | Convicted | GPC | Found guilty of conspiracy related to shakedown of tavern owners | Chicago Tribune, Oct 6, 1973 |
| 1974 | Gerald | Sepka | Police Officer | Convicted | GPC | Found guilty of bribery and shaking down a motorist during a traffic stop | Chicago Tribune, June 14, 1974 |
| 1985 | Robert M. | Sepulveda | Police Officer | Convicted | GPC | Pleaded guilty to accepting bribes to sidetrack investigations of motorists involved hit-and-run accidents | Chicago Tribune, May 30, 1985 |
| 1990 | Mitchell | Shacter | Lieutenant | Convicted | CRV | Pleaded guilty to a misdemeanor charge of harassment by telephone | Chicago Tribune, Feb 10, 1990 |
| 2009 | Mahmoud "Mike" | Shamah | Police Officer | Convicted | DGG | Found guilty of racketeering and conspiracy charges related to stealing of drugs from drug dealers | Chicago Tribune, July 3, 2009 |
| 1960 | James | Shannon | Police Officer | Convicted | GPC | Pleaded guilty to aiding robbers in holdups and collecting payoffs from them | Chicago Tribune, May 25, 1960 |

| 2001 | Lennon | Shields | Police Officer | Convicted | DGG | Found guilty of racketeering for shaking down drug dealers for cash and cocaine and providing protection for large narcotics deliveries | Chicago Sun Times Oct 19, 2001 |
|---|---|---|---|---|---|---|---|
| 1998 | Alex | Sierra | Police Officer | Convicted | GPC | Pleaded guilty to conspiracy to commit a robbery | Chicago Tribune, Feb 14, 1998 |
| 2002 | Michael | Simpson | Police Officer | Convicted | GPC | Pleaded guilty to charges of lying to a supervisor related to shaking down immigrants | Chicago Tribune, May 10, 2002 |
| 1992 | Raymond | Siwek | Detective | Convicted | DGG | Found guilty of possession with intent to deliver more than 500 grams of cocaine | Chicago Tribune, May 5, 1995 |
| 1982 | Dennis L. | Smentek | Police Officer | Convicted | DGG | Found guilty of accepting bribes to allow two heroin rings to operate in the Marquette District. | Chicago Tribune Jul 1, 1982 |
| 1982 | Dennis | Smetanka | Police Officer | Convicted | DGG | Found guilty of accepting bribes to allow two heroin rings to operate in the Marquette District. | Chicago Tribune, April 11, 1995 |
| 2004 | John L. | Smith | Police Officer | Convicted | DGG | Found guilty of narcotics conspiracy, money laundering and three counts each of tax evasion and filing false tax returns | Chicago Tribune, Nov 11, 2004 |
| 1989 | Willie | Smith | Patrolman | Convicted | DGG | Pleaded guilty to charges related to taking bribes to protect the activities of South Side gamblers and a drug dealer. | Chicago Tribune, Jan 10, 1990 |
| 2002 | Daryl L. | Smith | Police Officer | Convicted | GPC | Found guilty of theft of government property | Chicago Tribune, May 3, 2002 |
| 2000 | Richard | Sobotta | Police Officer | Convicted | ODC | Pleaded guilty to contempt of court for helping a superior try to wiggle out of a speeding ticket | Chicago Sun-Times, Oct 24, 2000 |
| 1987 | William | Sorice | Police Officer | Convicted | GPC | Found guilty of conspiring and burglarizing a jewelry store where $260,000 were stolen in jewels | Chicago Tribune, March 11, 1987 |
| 1992 | Gloria | Steele | Police Officer | Convicted | DGG | Found guilty of charges that she aided in her son's large-scale heroin operation | Chicago Tribune, May 9, 1992 |
| 1989 | Robert | Stephenson | Sergeant | Convicted | DGG | Found guilty of charges related to taking bribes to protect the activities of gamblers and a drug dealer | Chicago Tribune, July 12, 1990 |
| 1995 | Tyrone | Stevenson | Police Officer | Convicted | DGG | Pleaded guilty to charges of extortion where he extorted $150,000 from an Indiana drug dealer | Chicago Tribune, Aug 24, 1995 |

45

| 1989 | Orville | Stewart | Patrolman | Convicted | DGG | Found guilty of charges related to taking bribes to protect the activities of South Side gamblers and a drug dealer | Chicago Tribune, July 12, 1990 |
|---|---|---|---|---|---|---|---|
| 1986 | Vito | Stonis | Police Officer | Convicted | BTX | Pleaded guilty to aggravated battery and one count of official misconduct for beating a man arrested for loitering | Chicago Tribune, Oct 9, 1986 |
| 1998 | Baxter G. | Streets | Police Officer | Convicted | DGG | Found guilty of robbing undercover agents posing as drug dealers | Chicago Sun-Times, June 10, 1998 |
| 1966 | John | Sullivan | Detective | Convicted | DGG | Found guilty of sale of narcotics | Chicago Tribune, Nov 11, 1966 |
| 2003 | Vondale | Sullivan | Police Officer | Convicted | ODC | Pleaded guilty to a federal bank robbery charge | Pantagraph, Nov 15, 2003 |
| 1995 | John | Summerville | Detective | Convicted | BTX | Pleaded guilty to sexually assaulting several women during traffic stops | Chicago Sun Times, July 28, 1995 |
| 1973 | William D. | Swallow | Police Officer | Convicted | GPC | Found guilty of conspiracy and perjury related to shakedown of tavern owners | Chicago Tribune, Oct 6, 1973 |
| 1973 | William | Taylor | Police Officer | Convicted | DGG | Found guilty of smuggling narcotics | Chicago Tribune, Aug 5, 1973 |
| 1966 | Sheldon | Teller | Sergeant | Convicted | DGG | Found guilty of sale of narcotics | Chicago Tribune, Nov 11, 1966 |
| 1979 | Mary Ann | Terry | Police Officer | Convicted | GPC | Found guilty of welfare fraud and perjury while on active duty | Chicago Tribune, Sep 14, 1980 |
| 1974 | Mark | Thanasouras | Captain | Convicted | GPC | Pleaded guilty to charges stemming from corruption and shaking down of tavern owners | Chicago Tribune, Feb. 5, 1974 |
| 1991 | Daniel | Thanos | Police Officer | Convicted | ODC | Found guilty of aggravated battery in connection with the fatal beating committed while off duty | Chicago Tribune, April 6, 1991 |
| 1989 | Fred | Tilford | Patrolman | Convicted | DGG | Found guilty of charges related to taking bribes to protect the activities of gamblers and a drug dealer | Chicago Tribune, July 12, 1990 |

| 1975 | John | Toner | Sergeant | Convicted | GPC | Found guilty of perjury in connection with shakedown of operators of parking lots | Chicago Tribune, March 14, 1975 |
|---|---|---|---|---|---|---|---|
| 2001 | William | Tortoriello | Police Officer | Convicted | GPC | Pleaded guilty to official misconduct related to shaking down immigrants | Chicago Tribune, Aug 14, 2001 |
| 2001 | Cornelius | Tripp | Police Officer | Convicted | DGG | Pleaded guilty to racketeering for shaking down drug dealers for cash and cocaine and providing protection for large narcotics deliveries | Chicago Sun Times, Oct 19, 2001 |
| 1984 | James | Trunzo | Police Officer | Convicted | GPC | Pleaded guilty to two counts of tax fraud | Chicago Tribune Jan 6, 1986 |
| 1984 | Joseph | Trunzoi | Police Officer | Convicted | GPC | Pleaded guilty to two counts of tax fraud | Chicago Tribune Jan 6, 1986 |
| 1998 | Samuel | Turks | Police Officer | Convicted | BTX | Found guilty of official misconduct related to fondling of women while conducting routine traffic stops | Chicago Tribune, June 12, 1998 |
| 1991 | John A. | Vercillo | Police Officer | Convicted | ODC | Found guilty of RICO charges related to series of illicit trades while off duty | Chicago Tribune, Jan 10, 1991 |
| 2000 | Costantino | Verre | Lieutenant | Convicted | ODC | Pleaded guilty to contempt of court related to perjury in court over a speeding ticket | Chicago Sun-Times, Oct 24, 2000 |
| 2009 | Frank | Villareal | Police Officer | Convicted | DGG | Pleaded guilty to a felony theft charge stemming from illegal searchers of drug dealers and gang suspects and stealing their money and narcotics | Chicago Tribune, Sep 26, 2009 |
| 1980 | Donald | Vogwill | Police Officer | Convicted | DGG | Pleaded guilty to conspiracy related to smuggling of cocaine into US | Chicago Tribune, Sep 5, 1980 |
| 1980 | James | Vogwill | Police Officer | Convicted | DGG | Found guilty of conspiracy to smuggle cocaine into US | Chicago Tribune, Sep 5, 1980 |
| 1984 | Carl | Walston | Police Officer | Convicted | DGG | Found guilty of official misconduct for selling fake heroin to a government informant out of his police car | Chicago Tribune, Feb 25, 1984 |
| 1981 | Stephen | Webster | Police Officer | Convicted | GPC | Found guilty of charges stemming from burglarizing home while in uniform, official | Chicago Tribune, Sep 7, 1981 |

| | | | | | | misconduct and possession of marijuana | |
|---|---|---|---|---|---|---|---|
| 1986 | Walter | Wells | Police Officer | Convicted | BTX | Found guilty of aggravated sexual assault, and sexual abuse of an 11 year old girl | Chicago Tribune, Dec 18, 1986 |
| 1973 | Thomas D. | West | Sergeant | Convicted | GPC | Found guilty of conspiracy and perjury related to shakedown of tavern owners | Chicago Tribune, Oct 6, 1973 |
| 1991 | Gerald | Williams | Police Officer | Convicted | ODC | Found guilty of fatally shooting his physically disabled wife while off duty | Chicago Tribune, Sep 18, 1991 |
| 1989 | Clarence | Wilson | Police Officer | Convicted | DGG | Found guilty of charges related to taking bribes to protect the activities of gamblers and a drug dealer | Chicago Tribune, July 12, 1990 |
| 2012 | James | Wodnicki | Police Officer | Convicted | GPC | Pleaded guilty to charges stemming from extortion-related to tow scam | Chicago Tribune, June 19, 2012 |
| 2003 | Jon F. | Woodall | Detective | Convicted | DGG | Pleaded guilty to conspiring to distribute cocaine | Chicago Sun Times Feb 27, 2003 |
| 1989 | Thomas | York | Police Officer | Convicted | ODC | Found guilty of mail fraud, arson, and conspiracy | Chicago Sun-Times, July 8, 1989 |
| 2001 | James P. | Young | Police Officer | Convicted | DGG | Found guilty of racketeering for shaking down drug dealers for cash and cocaine and providing protection for large narcotics deliveries | Chicago Sun-Times Oct 19, 2001 |
| 1973 | Mike | Zakoian | Police Officer | Convicted | GPC | Found guilty of conspiracy related to shakedown of tavern owners | Chicago Tribune, Oct 6, 1973 |
| 1990 | Dennis | Zancha | Police Officer | Convicted | BTX | Found guilty of aggravated criminal sexual assault for the attack on a 22 your old woman | Chicago Tribune, Feb 27, 1990 |
| 1992 | Jerry | Zywicki | Police Officer | Convicted | GPC | Pleaded guilty to conspiring with two other officers to rob a tavern owner and two bartenders | Chicago Tribune, Dec 23, 1992 |

## Appendix II: Police Reform in South Africa

Policing the police in Chicago is similar in many ways to problems in other international settings. For example, here is an excerpt from the Executive Summary of an anti-corruption report "Protector or Predator: Tackling Police Corruption in South Africa." In many ways the problems of Chicago's police are similar to post-Apartheid South Africa. Note the similar use of "bad apples" as a way to deflect more serious inquiry. As the South African reports says: "A rotten barrel breeds rotten apples, not the other way around."

Despite the positive changes that have occurred within the South African Police Service (SAPS) since the birth of democracy in 1994, police corruption remains a substantial challenge for the organization. While the extent of police corruption cannot be easily or accurately measured, there is evidence that the problem is a widespread and systemic one. This is not to say that most or a majority of police officials engage in corruption. However, the prevalence of the problem is such that it substantially hinders the extent to which to the SAPS is able to achieve its constitutional objectives and build public trust. This is not a unique challenge facing the SAPS. Corruption is a challenge throughout the country's public and private sectors and is a specific occupational hazard of policing agencies worldwide. Given the nexus of power, discretion and inadequate accountability that often arises in policing, this profession is particularly prone to the problem of corruption.

Typically, police management will respond to incidents or allegations of corruption as a problem of a few 'bad apples' who must be punished or removed from the organization. Yet, international research and commissions of inquiry into police corruption consistently emphasize that corruption is more a manifestation of organizational weaknesses than a challenge of bad employees. As such, punitive action against individuals who commit acts of corruption, while necessary, will on its own do little to change the factors that allow for police deviance and corruption to occur in the first place. To address corruption effectively a more holistic approach is required that focuses on strengthening the integrity of both the organization and its employees.

## Appendix III: Illinois Law on Misconduct in Public Office

The *Illinois Criminal Code of 1961* (ILCS720/33-3) indicates that any public officer or employee commits misconduct when, in her official capacity, she does any of the following:

$ Intentionally or recklessly fails to perform mandatory duty as required by law;

$ Knowingly performs an act the employee is forbidden by law to perform;

$ Performs an act in excess of their lawful authority with intent to obtain a personal advantage for herself or another; or solicit or knowingly accept for the performance of any act a fee or reward which the employee knows is unauthorized by law.

## Appendix IV
## PETITION FOR A DEMOCRATICALLY ELECTED
## CIVILIAN POLICE ACCOUNTABILITY COUNCIL

We, residents of Chicago, Illinois, do hereby petition the Chicago City Council and Mayor Rahm Emanuel to enact legislation such as that proposed by the Chicago Alliance Against Racist and Political Repression to establish a democratically elected Civilian Police Accountability Council (CPAC). This Council will be empowered to make policy, hire and fire police, petition for the appointment of a Special Prosecutor to investigate and prosecute police accused of crimes such as battery, unlawful arrest, racial profiling, torture and murder, and the use of force to suppress the democratic rights of the people to organize and protest.

**NAME**          **ADDRESS**                              **EMAIL**

---

Return petitions to
Chicago Alliance Against Racist and Political Repression
1325 S. Wabash Ave. Suite 105
Chicago IL 60605
For information; contact@naarpr.org, 312-939-2750
www.StopPoliceCrimes.com http://www.naarpr.org

# ENDNOTES

[1] Janssen, Kim. " 'We proved a code of silence'." Chicago Sun-Times. November 14, 2012.

[2] Lou Reiter, police consultant in testimony in US District Court, Northern District of Illinois, Eastern Division. Klpfel and Casalis vs City of Chicago. Case No. 94 C 6415. Feb 23, 2007. This case resulted in a $9.75 million judgement against the City of Chicago. p. 9.

[3] Futterman, Craig et al. "The Use of Statistical Evidence to Address Police Supervisory and Disciplinary Practices: The Chicago Police Department's Broken System." November 14, 2007.

[4] "Police Misconduct's Legal Tab." Chicago Sun-Times. July 30, 2012.

[5] Ibid.

[6] Meyerson, Ben. "Record verdict: Former gang member awarded $21 million for wrongful conviction." Chicago Tribune. June 23, 2009,

[7] Lighty, Todd and Gary Washburn. "City to pay Haggertys $18 million." Chicago Tribune. May 8, 2001.

[8] This was part of the SOS scandal which we will report on below. On Finnegan attempting to hire a 2-6 gang member to "hit" a fellow officer, see Sun-Times, March 20. 2012: "From jail, cop who admitted guilt in murder-for-hire plot proclaims innocence," by Frank Main.

[9] Life Vol. 65, No. 23. Dec. 6, 1968

[10] http://encyclopedia.chicagohistory.org/pages/1049.html

[11] Carter, David A. Journal of Criminal Justice Vol. 18. pp. 85-98 (1990) p 92

[12] Lou Reiter, police consultant in testimony in US District Court, Northern District of Illinois, Eastern Division. Klpfel and Casalis vs City of Chicago. Case No. 94 C 6415. Feb 23, 2007. This case resulted in a $9.75 million judgement against the City of Chicago.

[13] Journal Gazette (Mattoon, IL) - Tuesday, April 24, 2001

[14] Newman, Tim. Understanding and Preventing Police Corruption. Lessons from the Literature. Research Development Statistics. London. 1999

[15] Reiter, op cit. p. 9

[16] Reiter, op cit. p 17.

[17] Reiter op cit. p 19-20.

[18] Knapp, 1972:6-7

[19] Hanna, Janan, John O'Brien and Bill Crawford. " 'Marquette 10' cop celebrates freedom with 500 backers." Chicago Tribune. April 11, 1995.

[20] O'Connor. "Austin cops sent to prison; 5 former officers sentenced in '96 corruption probe." Chicago Tribune. October 19, 2001.

[21] Ibid.

[22] Lighty, Todd and Matt O'Connor. "Rogue cop gets life." Chicago Tribune. January 25, 2003.

[23] Heinzmann, David and Annie Sweeney. "Federal prosecutors say 4 Chicago police officers from elite SOS unit will plead guilty." Chicago Tribune. April 7, 2011.

[24] Heinzmann, David Todd Lighty and Jeff Coen. "Feds join in probe of city's elite police; Stakes get higher for accused officers." Chicago Tribune. August 16, 2007.

[25] Meisner, Jason. "What happened to the elite officers charged." Chicago Tribune. September 9, 2011.

[26] Heinzman, David. "Indicted city cop to be on '60 Minutes.'" Chicago Tribune. May 30, 2008.

[27] Meisner, Jason. "What happened to the elite officers charged." Chicago Tribune. September 9, 2011.

[28] Marin, Carol and Dan Moseley. "Jailed former cop speaks out about murder scandal." NBC 5 Chicago

News. March 21, 2012.

29 Tompkins, Sarah. "Ex-Chicago cop plead guilty to racketeering in Latin King case." The Times of Northwest Indiana. July 26, 2012.

30 Sweeney, Annie. "Ex-cop convicted of joining conspiracy." Chicago Tribune. February 01, 2012.

31 Ibid.

32 Main, Frank. "Drug-dealing killer: Chicago cop stopped DEA investigation." Chicago Sun-Times. October 4, 2011.

33 Ibid.

34 Main, Frank. "Ex-cop, four others guilty of participating in drug crew." Chicago Sun-Times. January 31, 2012.

35 Sweeney, Annie. "Ex-cop convicted of joining conspiracy." Chicago Tribune. February 01, 2012.

36 O'Connor, Matt. "Police lose false arrest lawsuit." Chicago Tribune. November 18, 2001.

37 Ibid

38 Babwin, Bob and Michael Tarm. "Will Chicago act on verdict in cop beating trial." NBC News. November 14, 2012.

39 Sweeney, Annie and Jason Meisner. "Jury finds in favor of bartender in cop bar beating case, 'Justice was served." Chicago Tribune. November 14, 2012.

40 Ibid.

41 Ibid.

42 Janssen, Kim. "Bartender beaten by drunken Chicago cop wins $850,000 verdict." Chicago Sun-Times. November 13, 2012.

43 Coen, Jeff. "Ex-cop testifies of code, bloody glove." Chicago Tribune. August 23, 2007.

44 Coen, Jeff. "Ex-cop testifies of code, bloody glove." Chicago Tribune. August 23, 2007.

45 Coen, Jeff. "Ex-cop Anthony Doyle gets 12 years for aiding Outfit." Chicago Tribune. March 13, 2009.

46 Schlikerman, Becky. "High-ranking crooked cop released to halfway house." Chicago Tribune. July 19, 2011.

47 UNITED PRESS INTERNATIONAL. "CHICAGO CHOOSES A CRIMINOLOGIST TO HEAD AND CLEAN UP THE POLICE." THE NEW YORK TIMES. FEBRUARY 23, 1960.

48 Knoohuizen, Ralph. Public Access to Police Information: A Report of the Chicago Law Enforcement Study Group. 1974.

49 "Chicago names police panel but refuses a review board." New York Times. July 26, 1966.

50 Ibid.

51 Ibid.

52 Chicago Tribune December 6th, 1967

53 Ibid.

54 Ibid.

55 Ibid.

56 Knoohuizen, Ralph. Public Access to Police Information: A Report of the Chicago Law Enforcement Study Group. 1974.

57 http://www.columbia.edu/itc/journalism/cases/katrina/Human%20Rights%20Watch/uspohtml/uspo55.htm#TopOfPage

58 Knoohuizen, Ralph. Public Access to Police Information: A Report of the Chicago Law Enforcement Study Group. 1974.

59 http://www.columbia.edu/itc/journalism/cases/katrina/Human%20Rights%20Watch/uspohtml/uspo55.htm#TopOfPage

60 Conroy, John. "Town without pity." Chicago Reader. January 11, 1996.

---

[61] Independent Police Review Authority. "Annual Report 2007-2008." City of Chicago. September 2008

[62] Siska, Tracy and Sherie Arriazola. Chicago Police Board: A 10-Year Analysis. 2009. The Chicago Justice Project.

[63] Siska, Tracy and Sherie Arriazola. Chicago Police Board: A 10-Year Analysis. 2009. The Chicago Justice Project.

[64] Cano I. (2005) Police Oversight in Brazil International Conference on Police Accountability and the Quality of Oversight: Global Trends in National Context, The Hague, The Netherlands.

[65] Gareth Newham and Andrew Faull. Protector or predator? Tackling police corruption in South Africa. ISS Monograph. No 182.

APPENDIX IV:  INVESTIGATION OF THE NEW ORLEANS
POLICE DEPARTMENT

# Investigation of the
# New Orleans Police Department

United States Department of Justice
Civil Rights Division

March 16, 2011

## TABLE OF CONTENTS

iii

Appendix: Recommendations to the New Orleans Police Department

## I.    <u>EXECUTIVE SUMMARY</u>

The NOPD has long been a troubled agency.  Basic elements of effective policing— clear policies, training, accountability, and confidence of the citizenry—have been absent for years. Far too often, officers show a lack of respect for the civil rights and dignity of the people of New Orleans.  While the majority of the force is hardworking and committed to public safety, too many officers of every rank either do not understand or choose to ignore the boundaries of constitutional policing.  Some argue that, given the difficulty of police work, officers must at times police harshly and bend the rules when a community is confronted with seemingly intransigent high levels of crime.  Policing is undeniably difficult; however, experience and study in the policing field have made it clear that bending the rules and ignoring the Constitution makes effective policing much more challenging.  NOPD's failure to ensure that its officers routinely respect the Constitution and the rule of law undermines trust within the very communities whose cooperation the Department most needs to enforce the law and prevent crime.  As systematic violations of civil rights erode public confidence, policing becomes more difficult, less safe, and less effective, and crime increases.

The deficiencies in the way NOPD polices the City are not simply individual, but structural as well.  For too long, the Department has been largely indifferent to widespread violations of law and policy by its officers.  NOPD does not have in place the basic systems known to improve public safety, ensure constitutional practices, and promote public confidence. We found that the deficiencies that lead to constitutional violations span the operation of the entire Department, from how officers are recruited, trained, supervised, and held accountable, to the operation of Paid Details.  In the absence of mechanisms to protect and promote civil rights, officers too frequently use excessive force and conduct illegal stops, searches and arrests with impunity.  In addition, the Department's culture tolerates and encourages under-enforcement and under-investigation of violence against women.  The Department has failed to take meaningful steps to counteract and eradicate bias based on race, ethnicity, and LGBT status in its policing practices, and has failed to provide critical policing services to language minority communities.

The problems in NOPD developed over a long period of time and will take time to address and correct.  The Department must develop and implement new policies and protocols, train its officers in effective and constitutional policing, and institutionalize systems to ensure accountability, foster police-community partnerships, improve the quality of policing to all parts of the City, and eliminate unlawful bias from all levels of NOPD policing decisions.

Recommendations on achieving these changes are attached to this Report.  We look forward to working with NOPD and the City of New Orleans to address the violations of constitutional and federal law that we identified, by developing and implementing a comprehensive blueprint for sustainable reform that will: (1) reduce crime; (2) ensure respect for the Constitution and the rule of law; and (3) restore public confidence in NOPD.

v

We find reasonable cause to believe that NOPD engages in patterns of misconduct that violate the Constitution and federal law.[1] We find further that NOPD practices and deficiencies cause or contribute to these patterns of misconduct. The following is a summary of these findings.

A.      Patterns and Practices of Unconstitutional Conduct

1.      Use of Force

Police-civilian interactions only rarely require the use of force. In the small portion of interactions where it is necessary for officers to use force, the Constitution requires that officers use only the amount of force that is reasonable under the circumstances. We found that officers in NOPD routinely use unnecessary and unreasonable force in violation of the Constitution and NOPD policy.

Our investigation did not include consideration of widely reported allegations of officer misconduct related to NOPD's response to Hurricane Katrina in 2005. Many of these incidents have been, or are currently being, prosecuted by the Criminal Section of the Civil Rights Division and the United States Attorney's Office for the Eastern District of Louisiana. We deliberately kept our civil investigation separate from the criminal investigation and prosecution of any NOPD officer, and this Report does not discuss any incident that is the subject of ongoing federal criminal proceedings. Nonetheless, our investigation, which covered incidents that occurred within the past two years and assessed practices as they exist currently, revealed a clear pattern of unconstitutional uses of force by NOPD officers.

Our review of officer-involved shootings within just the last two years revealed many instances in which NOPD officers used deadly force contrary to NOPD policy or law. Despite the clear policy violations we observed, NOPD has not found that an officer-involved shooting violated policy in at least six years, and NOPD officials we spoke with could recall only one out-of-policy finding even before that time.

We found a pattern of unreasonable less lethal force as well. We found that NOPD's canines were uncontrollable to the point where they repeatedly attacked their own handlers, compelling us to recommend immediate suspension of NOPD's use of canines to apprehend suspects. We found that officers use force against individuals, including persons in handcuffs, in circumstances that appeared not only unnecessary but deliberately retaliatory. We reviewed instances in which NOPD officers used significant force against mentally ill persons where it appeared that no use of force was justified.

---

[1] Our investigation found reasonable cause to believe that NOPD has engaged in a pattern or practice of conduct that deprives individuals of rights, privileges, or immunities secured or protected by the Constitution or laws of the United States. Under 42 U.S.C. § 14141, this finding authorizes the United States to obtain appropriate equitable and declaratory relief to eliminate the pattern or practice. We did not conduct a criminal investigation, which requires the government to show guilt beyond a reasonable doubt, of any NOPD officer or any other person. We make no assertions regarding the culpability of any individual.

NOPD, for at least the past several years, has been all too frequently indifferent to its officers' improper use of force. The Department has few meaningful controls to ensure that force is used appropriately. Officers are not properly trained on using force or alternatives to force. Policies regarding use and reporting of force are inconsistent, incomplete, and routinely disregarded. To the extent officers do report force, supervisors do not conduct investigations sufficient to determine whether the force was justified. Instances of clearly unjustified force are routinely approved by supervisors and ratified up the chain-of-command, resulting in no accountability. Officers even encourage each other to use force as retaliation. Indeed, when one NOPD officer reacted calmly after being spit on by another NOPD officer he had stopped for DWI, fellow NOPD officers told the arresting officer he was a coward for not at least punching the officer.

Even the most serious uses of force, such as officer-involved shootings and in-custody deaths, are investigated inadequately or not at all. NOPD's mishandling of officer-involved shooting investigations was so blatant and egregious that it appeared intentional in some respects. For a time, NOPD had a practice of temporarily assigning officers who had been involved in officer-involved shootings to the Homicide Division, and then automatically deeming the statements officers provided to homicide investigators to be "compelled," effectively immunizing the use of these statements in any subsequent criminal investigation or prosecution. It is difficult to interpret this practice as anything other than a deliberate attempt to make it more difficult to criminally prosecute any officer in these cases. We reviewed incidents where investigative missteps could not be explained by deficient training, such as where investigators failed to even attempt to lift fingerprints from a handgun found on the scene of shooting, where the ownership of the handgun was in dispute, and then misrepresented witness statements in their investigative report so that it appeared the presence of the weapon on-scene was not disputed. During our inquiry, we learned that many Homicide Division investigations of officer-involved shootings had never been provided to NOPD's Professional Integrity Bureau ("PIB"), which is charged with determining whether these shootings are consistent with NOPD policy. Some of these investigations were provided to PIB only following our inquiries, and the appointment of new leadership in NOPD's Homicide Division. Several still have not been located.

NOPD's use of force practices present a significant threat to the safety of the public and NOPD officers, and create a substantial obstacle to strong community-police partnerships. As we conducted our investigation, NOPD had begun to make significant and long overdue changes to its force policies regarding how officers will be trained to use force, and how force will be reported, investigated, and reviewed. NOPD will need to build on these initial steps with more comprehensive changes to policy and practice to end the pattern of unconstitutional use of force by NOPD.

2.      Stops, Searches and Arrests

We find reasonable cause to believe that NOPD officers engage in a pattern of stops, searches, and arrests that violate the Fourth Amendment. Detentions without reasonable suspicion are routine, and lead to unwarranted searches and arrests without probable cause. Our review of 145 randomly-sampled arrest and investigative reports confirmed a pattern of unlawful conduct.  Of the arrests that NOPD initiated, we found that a significant portion reflected on their face apparent constitutional violations, in that officers failed to articulate sufficient facts to justify stops, searches, and arrests.

A previous DOJ investigation noted almost ten years ago that some NOPD officers could not articulate proper legal standards for stops, searches, or arrests.  We recommended then that NOPD provide annual in-service training to officers on this critical topic.  As discussed below, NOPD still does not provide meaningful in-service training to officers on how to properly carry out stops, searches, and arrests.  NOPD's failure to train officers or otherwise provide guidance on the limits and requirements of the Fourth Amendment contributes directly to the pattern of unconstitutional stops, searches, and arrests we observed.  Throughout the Department, and among other stakeholders in the criminal justice system, we heard broad and emphatic consensus that officers have a poor understanding of how to lawfully execute searches and seizures.

Additionally, the Department's organizational focus on arrests, particularly in combination with its poor training and policies, encourages stops without reasonable suspicion, illegal pat downs, and arrests without probable cause.  NOPD's focus on statistics, such as generating Field Interview Cards ("FIC"s) and arrests, amplifies the risk that officers will execute illegal searches and seizures.  NOPD patrol officers and many members of the command staff described a Department that has long been statistics-driven—one that measures "productivity" by quantity, rather than quality, of encounters and arrests.  As one commander told us, "[t]hese officers are under the gun to make arrest, arrest, arrest, which leads to civil rights violations and complaints."  We observed that arrests, *Terry* stops, and FIC numbers were the predominant focus of the Department's weekly COMSTAT meetings, and many officers described a strong and unyielding pressure to increase numbers.

Detached as it is from problem-oriented policing, community partnerships, or long term strategies, there is no indication that NOPD's emphasis on arrests results in better crime prevention or safer communities.  To the contrary, NOPD recently acknowledged that the Department's staggering volume of arrests for low-level offenses is counter-productive.  In November 2010, according to the New Orleans Times-Picayune, the Superintendent advised the City Council that officers would no longer make arrests based on outstanding traffic or misdemeanor warrants from neighboring parishes, noting that to do so "simply does not make sense, economical or common."

We believe that with this pledge, the Department has taken a significant and positive step.  Nonetheless, we found NOPD's emphasis on "activity," defined as numbers of encounters such as stops, FICs, and arrests—at the expense of a more deliberate focus on problem-solving—to be an ingrained part of NOPD's organizational culture.  Although the Superintendent's commitment to ensuring that officers are engaged, observant, and productive is commendable and appropriate, the Department must recognize that its tactics and chosen police strategy, together with lapses in training and policy, cultivate an atmosphere where officers cut corners and make too many errors that result in constitutional harm and compromise effective law enforcement.

viii

3.    Discriminatory Policing

We find reasonable cause to believe that NOPD engages in a pattern or practice of discriminatory policing in violation of constitutional and statutory law. Discriminatory policing occurs when police officers and departments unfairly enforce the law—or fail to enforce the law—based on characteristics such as race, ethnicity, national origin, sex, religion, or LGBT status. Discriminatory policing may take the form of bias-based profiling, in which an officer impermissibly decides whom to stop, search, or arrest based upon one of the above-mentioned characteristics, rather than upon the appropriate consideration of reasonable suspicion or probable cause. Failing to provide police services to some persons or communities because of bias or stereotypes, or by not taking necessary steps to enable meaningful communication, also constitutes discriminatory policing. Discriminatory policing may also result when a police department selects particular enforcement and crime prevention tactics in certain communities or against certain individuals for reasons motivated by bias or stereotype.

NOPD has failed to take sufficient steps to detect, prevent, or address bias-based profiling and other forms of discriminatory policing on the basis of race, ethnicity, or LGBT status, despite widespread concern and troubling racial disparities in arrest rates and other data. We further find that the Department fails to adequately investigate violence against women, including sexual assaults and domestic violence. Additionally, we find that the Department fails to provide critical policing services to New Orleans residents with limited English proficiency.

> *a)    Discriminatory Policing on Basis of Race, Ethnicity or LGBT*
> *status*

Subjecting individuals to differential treatment—based on a belief that characteristics such as race, ethnicity, national origin, sex, or religion signal a higher risk of criminality or unlawful activity—constitutes unlawful discrimination, often called "profiling" or "biased policing." During our investigation, many members of the community—particularly African Americans, ethnic minorities, and members of the lesbian, gay, bisexual, and transgender ("LGBT") community—reported that the Department subjects them to harassment and disrespectful treatment, and unfairly targets them for stops, searches, and arrests. Many members of NOPD echoed these concerns.

We found a clear failure by NOPD to implement adequate policies and provide appropriate training on how to identify and articulate suspicion based on behavior and other permissible factors. This critical lapse raises the risk that NOPD officers, without sufficient guidance and training on how to properly carry out stops and arrests, will instead rely on inappropriate factors such as racial stereotypes and bias in their decision-making. NOPD's failure to acknowledge the potential for stereotypes and bias to taint police work, on both an individual and an organizational level, and to take steps to prevent this, further cultivates an atmosphere in which discriminatory policing can occur unchecked.

Indeed, the limited arrest data that the Department collects points to racial disparities in arrests of whites and African Americans in virtually all categories, with particularly dramatic disparity for African-American youth under the age of 17. Arrest data provided by NOPD

ix

indicates that in 2009, the Department arrested 500 African-American males and eight white males under the age of 17 for serious offenses, which range from homicide to larceny over fifty dollars. During this same period the Department arrested 65 African-American females and one white female in this same age group. Adjusting for population, these figures mean that the ratio of arrest rates for both African-American males to white males, and African-American females to white females, was nearly 16 to 1. Although a significant disparity in arrest rates for this age group exists nationwide, it is not nearly as extreme as the disparity found in New Orleans. Nationally in 2009, among those agencies reporting data, the arrest ratio of African-American youth to white youth, for the same offenses, was approximately 3 to 1. The level of disparity for youth in New Orleans is so severe and so divergent from nationally reported data that it cannot plausibly be attributed entirely to the underlying rates at which these youth commit crimes, and unquestionably warrants a searching review and a meaningful response from the Department.

NOPD use of force data also shows a troubling racial disparity that warrants a searching inquiry into whether racial bias influences the use of force at NOPD. Of the 27 instances between January 2009 and May 2010 in which NOPD officers intentionally discharged their firearms at people, all 27 of the subjects of this deadly force were African American. In our sample of resisting arrest reports documenting uses of force between January 2009 and May 2010, we found that in 81 of the 96 uses of force we reviewed (84%), the subject of the force was African American.

We also found reasonable cause to believe that NOPD practices lead to discriminatory treatment of LGBT individuals. In particular, transgender women complained that NOPD officers improperly target and arrest them for prostitution, sometimes fabricating evidence of solicitation for compensation. Moreover, transgender residents reported that officers are likelier, because of their gender identity, to charge them under the state's "crimes against nature" statute—a statute whose history reflects anti-LGBT sentiment. Multiple convictions under the "crimes against nature" statute, unlike Louisiana's general prostitution statute, require registration as a sex offender. Persons convicted of soliciting crimes against nature make up nearly 40 percent of the Orleans Parish sex offender registry. NOPD is charged with monitoring all registrants' compliance with sex offender registry requirements, raising questions about efficient and effective use of resources to ensure public safety. Further, for the already vulnerable transgender community, inclusion on the sex offender registry further stigmatizes and marginalizes them, complicating efforts to secure jobs, housing, and obtain services at places like publicly-run emergency shelters. Of the registrants convicted of solicitation of a crime against nature, 80 percent are African American, suggesting an element of racial bias as well. Indeed, community members told us they believe some officers equate being African American and transgendered with being a prostitute.

Both bias and the perception of bias erode citizens' inclination to trust and cooperate with law enforcement, impeding effective and safe policing. Nonetheless, NOPD has failed to take steps to counteract bias and promote impartial policing through proactive policies, clear messages from leadership, effective supervision, and quality training. The Department does not have a sufficiently comprehensive policy regarding discriminatory policing and fails to adhere to the policies that are in place. In addition, the Department has no way to track allegations and

x

complaints of racial profiling, and does not collect, analyze, or report race or ethnicity data for most citizen encounters with police.

> *b)      Gender-Biased Policing: Failure to Adequately Investigate*
> *Allegations of Sexual Assault and Domestic Violence*

Law enforcement may not selectively deny protective services to certain groups, including women. This principle applies to the under-investigation of violence against women, including sexual assault and domestic violence. Nonetheless, in many cities reports have surfaced of law enforcement agencies undercounting and failing to investigate allegations of sexual and domestic violence. Such under-enforcement appears to stem in part from cities' reluctance to acknowledge the extent of serious crime in their communities, and in part from stereotypes and misapprehensions about sexual assaults and the victims of sex crimes.

We find that NOPD has systematically misclassified large numbers of possible sexual assaults, resulting in a sweeping failure to properly investigate many potential cases of rape, attempted rape, and other sex crimes. Additionally, we find that in situations where the Department pursues sexual assault complaints, the investigations are seriously deficient, marked by poor victim interviewing skills, missing or inadequate documentation, and minimal efforts to contact witnesses or interrogate suspects. The documentation we reviewed was replete with stereotypical assumptions and judgments about sex crimes and victims of sex crimes, including misguided commentary about the victims' perceived credibility, sexual history, or delay in contacting the police. NOPD has recently acknowledged its serious deficits in responding to sex crimes, and has taken some significant remedial steps. NOPD and the City will need to build on these efforts to bring about the extensive and sustained change necessary to effectively and appropriately respond to these serious violent crimes.

We also find systemic deficiencies in NOPD's handling of domestic violence cases. In recent years, the New Orleans Family Justice Center ("NOFJC"), a federally funded center designed to provide comprehensive services to victims of domestic violence by integrating law enforcement, prosecution, civil legal services, and advocacy in one location, has had a salutary effect on NOPD's handling of domestic violence complaints. Nonetheless, we find significant weaknesses in Department policies and practices in responding to these cases.

> *c)      National Origin Discrimination: Failure to Provide Effective*
> *Policing Services to Persons with Limited English Proficiency*

Failing to take reasonable steps to ensure meaningful access to services for limited English proficient ("LEP") persons is a form of national origin discrimination. We find that NOPD is dangerously limited in its capacity to communicate effectively and accurately with LEP victims, witnesses, suspects, and community members in the Latino and Vietnamese communities. Language barriers, and the often closely related cultural barriers, can put cases and lives at risk and create safety, evidentiary, and ethical challenges for officers and others. Such barriers can prevent LEP individuals from understanding their rights, complying with the law, assisting law enforcement and receiving meaningful access to law enforcement services and information.

xi

NOPD has virtually no capacity to provide meaningful access to police services to LEP community members, who in New Orleans are predominantly Latino or of Vietnamese descent. The Vietnamese community has been an established presence in New Orleans since the mid-1970s, and since Hurricane Katrina the City has seen a significant influx of Latino immigrants. Both communities represent growing shares of the City's population, and a significant segment of each has limited proficiency in English. NOPD relies primarily upon just two officers, one fluent in Spanish and one fluent in Vietnamese, to assist on calls for service and investigations throughout the Department, in addition to performing their regular duties. The Department does not compensate these officers for interpreter services performed while off-duty or provide them with enhanced pay for language fluency; nor does the Department have protocols to assess the fluency of its multilingual officers and train them in carrying out their duties.

Community members described significant consequences resulting from language barriers in their dealings with NOPD—including delays in or denial of services, incidents where victims were mistaken for suspects, and situations where encounters escalated unnecessarily due to gaps in communication. At one community meeting, a monolingual Spanish speaker reported calling police on four different nights regarding domestic violence, but receiving a response only once.

During an August 2010 ride-along, we observed firsthand a delay in response to a call for service from a victim of domestic violence, apparently because she was a monolingual Spanish-speaker. It further appeared that the officer may not have responded at all if not pressed by the DOJ investigator and if the DOJ investigator had not happened to be bilingual. After the officer continued to patrol the district for 30 minutes following receipt of the complaint, the DOJ investigator inquired about what calls had come in through dispatch. The officer initially skipped over the domestic violence call, but then asked the DOJ investigator whether he spoke Spanish. When the investigator replied that he did, the officer responded to the call. Upon arrival at the scene, the victim, who had visible injuries, said she had been waiting more than an hour for a response. Later, the officer explained that there was only one person on the shift capable of serving as an interpreter, and that the individual was often difficult to reach.

NOPD's lack of capacity to serve LEP communities undermines public safety, crime prevention, and crime-solving, and results in inferior police services to LEP community members. Although the Department has recently signaled its commitment to improving access to its services to LEP community members, NOPD has significant work ahead to ensure it can effectively serve the entire New Orleans community.

B.      Systemic Deficiencies Causing or Contributing to Unconstitutional Conduct

A number of longstanding and entrenched practices cause or contribute to the patterns or practices of unconstitutional and discriminatory conduct we observed. The Department's failure to provide sufficient guidance, training, and support to its officers, as well as its failure to implement systems to ensure officers are wielding their authority effectively and safely, have created an environment that permits and promotes constitutional harm. We found deficiencies in a wide swath of City and NOPD systems and operations, including failures to: adopt and enforce appropriate policies; properly recruit, train, and supervise officers; adequately review and investigate officer uses of force; fully investigate allegations of misconduct; identify and respond to patterns of at-risk officer behavior; implement community policing; oversee and control the system of Paid Details; provide officer assistance and support; or enact appropriate performance review and promotional systems. NOPD has recently begun making changes in each of these areas, but more, and more fundamental, change is necessary.

Alongside police practitioners, Courts have long acknowledged that deficiencies in systems and operations can unequivocally lead or contribute to constitutional violations. In *City of Canton, Ohio v. Harris*, 489 U.S. 378 (1989), the Supreme Court held a municipality liable for failing to adequately train its law enforcement officers, recognizing that a law enforcement agency's practices and decision-making can cause constitutional harm. *Id.* at 387. The Fifth Circuit has extended the *City of Canton* rationale to recognize that a broad range of systemic deficiencies can result in constitutional harm, including: inadequate disciplinary measures, *Deville v. Marcantel*, 567 F.3d 156, 171 (5th Cir. 2009) (citing *Piotrowski v. City of Houston*, 237 F.3d 567, 581 (5th Cir. 2001)); inadequate officer stress management programs, *Snyder v. Trepagnier*, 142 F.3d 791, 798-799 (5th Cir. 1998); and faulty screening of new officers, *Brown v. Bryan County*, 67 F.3d 1174 (5th Cir. 1995).

The deficiencies identified below must be corrected for legitimate, sustainable reform to occur. Without this comprehensive reform, the patterns and practices of unconstitutional conduct within NOPD will continue.

    1.    Policies

Clear and well-drafted policies are essential to ensuring constitutional police practices. Officers need to know what is permitted and what is prohibited. Police managers need policies to guide their work and hold officers accountable.

In every area we reviewed, we found that NOPD policies do not provide sufficient guidance. Policies are outdated, inconsistent, and at times, legally inaccurate. Policies do not, for example, provide officers adequate guidance regarding stops, searches, and arrests that are lawful, safe, and effective. Use of force policies are incomplete, out of date, and often contradictory. NOPD does not have in place policies or protocols for how first responders (usually patrol officers) should respond to individuals experiencing a mental health crisis. NOPD policies do not require sufficient collection of data to permit NOPD to track, assess, and respond to problems in a number of areas, from bias-based profiling, to use of force. Policies that do require NOPD to collect and analyze data are ignored. Policies related to complaint investigation facilitate the under-investigation of whole categories of complaints. There is a general lack of adherence to policy, exacerbated by pervasive tolerance by NOPD supervisors and commanders for officers' routine failure to comply with policy.

We do not discuss policies in a stand-alone section in this Report, but rather discuss policies pertaining to specific areas, such as use of force, supervision, or complaint intake, in each corresponding section of the Report.

xiii

2.	Recruitment

NOPD's longstanding failure to prioritize the recruitment of high-quality candidates contributes to the chronic, Department-wide problems we observed, including inappropriate and disrespectful conduct in the community, corruption, unnecessary uses of force, and improper stops and searches.  We found NOPD's recruitment program to be anemic, entirely passive, and lacking clear goals, plans, or accountability.  NOPD's Recruitment and Applicant Unit, which has a staff of six commissioned law enforcement officers, has no plan to seek out and recruit qualified candidates.  Recruiters were unclear about the scope of their authority or obligations, and report having done little since Hurricane Katrina to find or attract highly-qualified applicants, apart from distributing literature at job fairs, colleges, and universities.

The Department has been aware of deficiencies in its recruitment efforts, yet for years failed to act meaningfully to address them.  Recently, NOPD has begun to make changes to its recruiting process to ensure a stronger pool of applicants is selected to attend the academy.  Although the Department has a great deal of work ahead to attract the most highly-qualified workforce possible, we commend its recent focus on these efforts.

3.	Training

The training NOPD has for the past several years provided to its officers is severely deficient in nearly every respect, compromising officer and public safety, effective crime reduction, and the credibility and reputation of the Department as a whole.  Shortcomings at the recruit, field, and in-service stages of training have left NOPD officers ill-equipped to perform their duties in a safe, constitutional, and respectful manner.  We found systemic problems in training of every type, including tactical, operational, legal, ethical, and professionalism training.  Officers receive an insufficient amount of training—there has been almost no in-service training for the past five years—and the instruction officers do receive is often out-of-date, conflicts with NOPD  policies or current legal requirements, or fails to address officers' most pressing training needs.  Our investigation found direct links between inadequate training and serious, systemic problems in use of force; stops, searches, and arrests; supervision; interacting with and building partnerships with members of the community; and racial, ethnic, and gender bias in policing.

We found no disagreement that NOPD training is inadequate.  NOPD officers of all ranks told us they want more and better training, and strongly expressed this sentiment in their responses to a recent NOPD employee survey.  In that survey, only 24% of NOPD employees agreed that they have sufficient opportunities for training, and overwhelmingly reported that existing training needs improvement.  NOPD leadership likewise has acknowledged that its training systems are in need of repair, and the Superintendent has prioritized the wholesale remaking of training in his organizational strategy to improve NOPD.

4.	Supervision

Front line supervision, especially of officers patrolling and responding to calls in the field, is a lynchpin of effective and constitutional policing.  Field supervisors provide the close and consistent supervision necessary to guide officers' conduct and to help them learn from their mistakes. They are in best position to recognize a problem with an officer's conduct and intervene immediately to ameliorate or prevent harm. When a supervisor is on-scene and realizes that a patrol officer has made an arrest without probable cause, the supervisor can instruct the officer to release the arrestee and immediately counsel the officer about what the officer did wrong. When a community member is upset about how an officer responded to a call, a supervisor can immediately take a complaint—or sometimes address the concern to prevent a complaint. How a field supervisor conducts him or herself, and whether he/she requires adherence to policy and ethics, sets a tone of accountability and integrity—or not.

Field supervisors also are in the best position to ensure that street level crime prevention efforts are as effective as possible; they know how productive their officers are, and what they need to be more effective. Properly trained and deployed, field supervisors can identify the strengths and weaknesses of each officer under their command, adjusting their level and type of supervision accordingly.

NOPD fails to provide the supervision necessary to prevent or detect misconduct and ensure effective policing. Supervisors frequently sign off on arrest reports that fail to articulate probable cause, and conduct use of force investigations that are grossly deficient. They also frequently ignore obvious misconduct and poor officer performance in conducting internal investigations.

Our investigation further showed a lack of accountability throughout the chain of command sufficient to ensure that field sergeants are properly supervising their subordinates. Much of the work supervisors do requires review or approval by the chain of command. Commanders seem to take no notice of, much less hold accountable, supervisors who approve egregious uses of force without question, conduct obviously flawed investigations, sign off on clearly deficient arrest reports, or who simply do not supervise.

A number of systemic deficiencies within NOPD appear to contribute to this poor supervision. Supervisors are poorly trained and poorly guided by policy. The ratio of supervisors to officers (span of control) is too high, and unity of command (allowing for close and knowledgeable supervision by ensuring that each officer has one supervisor to hold them fully accountable) exists on paper only. Supervisory accountability is undermined by NOPD's practice of broadly assigning supervisory responsibilities and then failing to ensure these responsibilities are carried out by anyone.

     5.      Paid Details

There are few aspects of NOPD more broadly troubling than its Paid Detail system. NOPD's Detail system, as currently structured: 1) drastically undermines the quality of NOPD policing; 2) facilitates abuse and corruption by NOPD officers; 3) contributes to compromising officer fatigue; 4) contributes to inequitable policing by NOPD; and 5) acts as a financial drain on NOPD rather than fulfilling its potential as a source of revenue for the City and Department.

The Detail system is essentially a form of overtime work for officers. Officers may work *ad hoc* Details providing, for example, extra security for special events or individuals visiting

xv

245

New Orleans.  Or an officer may have a regularly-scheduled Detail, such as being hired by a business to provide security in a retail establishment or by a neighborhood association to patrol the neighborhood.  When on Detail, however, officers are paid and largely controlled by entities other than NOPD.  Many police departments allow officers to work outside law-enforcement jobs, but few if any large police departments have a system of Details as entrenched and unregulated as in NOPD.  Between August 2009 and July 2010, 69% of all officers, almost 1000 in all, submitted a request to work at least one Detail.  This number includes 85% of all Lieutenants and 78% of all Captains.  Virtually every officer works a Detail, wants to work a Detail, or at some point will have to rely on an officer who works a Detail.  The effects of Details thus permeate the entire Department.  It is widely acknowledged that NOPD's Detail system is corrupting; as stated by one close observer of the Department, the paid Detail system may be the "aorta of corruption" within NOPD.  Our interviews with NOPD officers, meetings with other New Orleans-based law enforcement agencies, criminal justice system stakeholders, and the public, revealed that NOPD's Detail system was a significant contributing factor to both the perception and reality of NOPD as a dysfunctional organization.

In the last few months, Superintendent Serpas has begun to implement measures meant to correct and prevent some of the negative impact of the Detail system.  In August 2010, the Superintendant banned cash payments.  But officers are still expected to negotiate their compensation with the Detail employer and officers who coordinate Details still wield inordinate influence including, in some instances, over their superiors.  In December 2010, the Superintendent initiated a program to try to centralize Detail information by setting up a single telephone number for all officers to call to report working a Detail, and a web-based application for officers to enter additional Detail information.  While these are undoubtedly improvements, it is too early to assess whether they are effective and, regardless, they are a small part of the wholesale remaking of the Detail system that is necessary.

6.      Performance Evaluations and Promotions

NOPD's evaluation and promotion practices are deficient to the point that it may be impossible to correct patterns of constitutional misconduct without also correcting the failings of these systems.  NOPD's promotional system does not adequately assess or consistently reward the officers who are best able to police effectively and constitutionally.  Promotional decisions do not adequately consider misconduct by officers or their ability to lead with integrity and diligence.  Performance evaluations do not sufficiently assess officers' conduct or value constitutional policing.  As they currently function, NOPD's performance evaluation and promotion systems erode public confidence in the Department and facilitate officers' unconstitutional conduct.

People inside NOPD and in the broader New Orleans community view NOPD's promotion and performance evaluation systems as broken.  In November 2010, a NOPD employee satisfaction survey ranked promotions and performance evaluations among the areas about which employees expressed the most dissatisfaction.  While a slight majority of respondents agreed that the Department punishes unethical behavior, a mere 17% agreed that the Department rewards ethical behavior.  Research shows that departments that reward officers who display exemplary leadership qualities with promotion foster the growth of a values-based,

xvi

246

ethical culture in the department. The NOPD survey also found that only 13% of respondents believed that "promotions are handled fairly."

Our review similarly showed significant problems with both NOPD's performance evaluations and its system of promotions. NOPD's performance evaluations do not assess an officer's crime prevention skills and abilities. There are no specific goals for the officers, and no assessment of an officer's progress in achieving stated goals. Likewise, there is no assessment of an officer's ability to build effective community partnerships or problem-oriented policing efforts. According to City officials, the city-wide performance evaluations have not changed in 20 years and are badly in need of updating. Consistent with recommendations from outside reviews, Civil Service Commission staff and police officials reported a need for more task-specific evaluations, but recognize that this would require the creation of different evaluations for different City departments, for which the City currently has allocated no funding. However, each department, including NOPD, already has the authority and ability to create their own performance evaluation overlay to the City-wide performance evaluation form. NOPD has not done this. In addition, training for supervisors on how to most effectively evaluate employees' performance under the current system is insufficient, and performance evaluations are infrequent and intermittent, rather than part of an ongoing process. There is no formalized system of on-going, documented, supervisory evaluation of subordinates' work, and we saw very little evidence of informal evaluation.

Similarly, NOPD's promotional system policies and practices are highly process related, too infrequently held, and include insufficient substantive assessment of candidates. NOPD's promotional policies have not been revised in nearly ten years and, until very recently NOPD's promotional exam had not been revised in years and was, by all accounts, woefully out of date. The infrequency of exams causes good officers to leave when they learn they have missed a promotion exam and it will be years before they have even an opportunity to compete for promotion. Infrequent exams mean also that officers who scored relatively low on the last exam are promoted over other officers who were not given a chance to compete.

Nor does NOPD's current promotions system provide for appropriate assessment of promotional candidates. There is little consideration of community policing or ethics (reportedly, promotional candidates in the past "did not do so well" on the ethical scenarios that were incorporated into the exam). Current NOPD policy further undermines adequate consideration of an officer's disciplinary history. By policy, only sustained violations for conduct with an *incident date* within the previous year of the promotion, and which resulted in a penalty greater than a Letter of Reprimand, are considered, and denial on even this ground appears discretionary.

We found that these problems directly impact NOPD's ability to assess and promote officers who are effective and ethical.

> 7.    Misconduct Complaint Intake, Investigation, and Adjudication

NOPD's system for receiving, investigating, and resolving misconduct complaints, despite many strengths and recent improvements, does not function as an effective accountability

xvii

measure.  Policies and practices for complaint intake do not ensure that complaints are complete and accurate, systematically exclude investigation of certain types of misconduct, and fail to track allegations of discriminatory policing.  Field supervisors are not sufficiently trained or supported in conducting misconduct investigations.  Deficiencies in policies, resources, training, and oversight weaken investigations and result in findings that are unsupported by the evidence.

Discipline and corrective action are meted out inconsistently and, too often, without sufficient consideration of the seriousness of the offense and its impact on the police-community relationship.  Louisiana State law requiring that internal administrative investigations be completed within 60 days is laudable in intent, but in practice has allowed officers to commit egregious misconduct and get away with it.  Apparent criminal misconduct by officers is inadequately investigated and has in the past too rarely been prosecuted.

There is a lack of transparency in the Civil Service Commission's review of officer appeals of NOPD disciplinary decisions, making it difficult to fully assess whether troubling reversals of disciplinary decisions are due to the Commission's failure to stay within the appropriate bounds of review, as is widely perceived.  Our review of several years of Commission decisions indicates that, while there may be legitimate concerns about particular Commission decisions, significant weaknesses in NOPD's investigation of officer misconduct, and in NOPD's and the City's defense of disciplinary decisions, unquestionably contribute to many poor outcomes.

These deficiencies render NOPD's system for investigating and responding to allegations of officer misconduct ineffective at changing officer behavior or holding officers responsible for their actions.  Consequently, the system has little legitimacy in the Department or in the broader New Orleans community.

NOPD is making efforts to improve its complaint investigation process.  The Department has made innovative changes, such as appointing a civilian to lead PIB, and has implemented long-overdue corrections to basic policies, including clarifying an employee's duty to be honest and truthful and to cooperate with investigations; making dismissal the presumptive penalty for not being truthful; and requiring employees who become aware of misconduct to immediately report it to a supervisor.  These changes mark a good beginning; however neither the public nor the police have confidence in NOPD's current system for investigating and responding to allegations of police misconduct.  A fundamental transformation of the processes for investigating and responding to allegations of police misconduct must occur in order to regain the trust of the public and officers, and correct the pattern of constitutional misconduct we observed.

8.      Community Oriented Policing

Community policing strategies balance reactive responses to calls for service with thoughtful and proactive problem-solving.  This problem-solving is achieved in large part by forging robust relationships in the community.  The Department's policies, training, and tactics support neither a community policing orientation, nor the ultimate goal of proactively addressing problems to reduce and prevent crime, rather than merely reacting to it.  Within NOPD, the

xviii

concept of community policing is poorly understood and implemented only superficially. Outside the Department, community members, especially members of racial, ethnic, and language minorities, and the LGBT communities, expressed to us their deep distrust of and sense of alienation from the police. This crisis of confidence and credibility serves as both a barrier to an effective community oriented policing program, and as a compelling reason to prioritize its implementation.

NOPD has publicly acknowledged the need to repair and cultivate community partnerships to more effectively fight crime and increase respect for police officers throughout the New Orleans community. Indeed, in August 2010, the Superintendent released a 65-point plan to reform the Department, which opened with a commitment to prioritize community policing and to "listen, collaborate, and respond proactively." The Department has implemented or announced plans to implement a number of community outreach programs, including: citizen callbacks regarding quality of service; Community Outreach Coordinator sergeants in each district; an expanded citizen academy; a partnership with clergy; and a program for bilingual outreach on public safety issues. While these initiatives are either in the planning stages or too new to have allowed for close assessment, we commend the Department's stated interest and focus on genuinely assessing current attitudes toward the police, reaching out to diverse segments of the City, and enhancing community relations.

Nonetheless, considerable work lies ahead if community policing is to be a central feature of NOPD's culture, decision-making, and organizational structure, consistent with the Department's commitment. The Department does not adequately encourage or promote meaningful partnership, interaction, and communication with diverse stakeholders, which is critical to learning about and collaboratively addressing problems in the community. Indeed, community groups nearly uniformly said that the police rarely reach out to them; one member of a Vietnamese community organization reported that "[a] lot of the young Vietnamese people who get shot in this community, we know who shot them but the New Orleans police don't do anything. They don't talk to us. They don't build community relationships." We found that some NOPD officers tend not to view members of the public as potential collaborative partners or sources of information and insight about their communities, but rather as potential problems, cultivating an "us vs. them" atmosphere of mutual distrust.

NOPD has also failed to implement policies, training, and accountability measures to truly integrate and embed community- and problem-oriented policing principles into each aspect of its management, structure, and use of resources. Consequently, few in the Department believe they bear any responsibility for implementing community policing strategies, or even have a clear sense of what specific strategies would look like. Further, officers consistently reported that pressure to conduct stops and arrests diverts attention and resources from quality arrests, community engagement, and more considered problem-solving.

Now that NOPD has identified community policing as a priority, it will need to ensure that change is sustained and more than superficial. This will require review of the Department's leadership, policies, climate and culture, systems of accountability, training and deployment of personnel, to ensure that they reflect and integrate community-oriented and problem-oriented strategies and practices.

xix

9.    Officer Assistance and Support

Officer assistance and support services are a significant component of a department's accountability system. The demeanor, judgment, and physical abilities that make an officer effective in carrying out law enforcement duties can be dangerously impaired when officers work under inordinate stress levels or while grappling with symptoms of mental illness. Police executives owe a duty to their community and officers to provide the services necessary to ensure the mental and physical wellness of their officers. NOPD is failing to provide such critical officer assistance and support services.

Stress is not an excuse for police misconduct, but officers who are mentally and physically fit generally are more productive; use fewer sick days; and importantly, may receive fewer complaints regarding demeanor or use of force. There is little question that NOPD is in need of officer assistance and support services. We found that a comprehensive system of officer assistance and support services for NOPD officers has never been in place, and that efforts to create a system have been faltering, even after Hurricane Katrina underscored the need. NOPD can better serve its officers and protect the public by implementing a centralized and comprehensive range of officer assistance and support services to address the stress and mental health needs of its employees.

10.    Interrogation Practices

NOPD's custodial interrogation practices reflect many of the same problems we found throughout NOPD: inadequate policies, poor or non-existent training, weak supervision and accountability, and inadequate facilities and equipment. As a result of these problems, NOPD does not adequately use custodial interrogations to build cases. NOPD detectives conduct relatively few interrogations and the interrogations they do conduct are often perfunctory.

We found that NOPD's policies about what constitutes a constitutional interrogation are inadequate, as is NOPD's training and selection of detectives. NOPD practice further undermines the effectiveness and integrity of NOPD interrogations. Audio and video recordings of interrogations reflect that detectives do not conduct, or at least record, full interrogations. Documentation of interrogations is poor due to a number of deficient practices and systems. Most districts lack dedicated space and video recording equipment; officers only record a final summary statement by subjects and/or witnesses; officers generally destroy notes from unrecorded portions of interviews with subjects and witnesses after completing investigative reports; and taped interviews in the Districts are preserved inconsistently, if at all. Taken together, these deficiencies not only undermine NOPD's efforts to build strong criminal cases, but could also facilitate and hide constitutional violations of criminal suspects' rights. Indeed, we found credible allegations that such violations have occurred.

While we did not reach a conclusion on whether there is a pattern or practice of unconstitutional interrogations at NOPD, we did find that as NOPD increases its efforts to build more effective cases and improve the reliability and integrity of its criminal investigations,

xx

current interrogation policies, training, and practices should be improved to ensure constitutional and effective interrogations.

11.    Community Oversight

The City of New Orleans and NOPD have a long history of efforts to provide effective civilian oversight of the Department. For decades, the City's Office of Municipal Investigation served as an alternative to NOPD's PIB, accepting and investigating individual complaints of misconduct against NOPD officers (and other City employees), before it was defunded in 2008. A thoughtful and comprehensive report in 2001 by the Police-Civilian Review Task Force, which was comprised of well-regarded and prominent community advocates as well as NOPD representatives, considered whether and what type of civilian oversight might be appropriate for NOPD. The Task Force determined that an Independent Monitor who would review policies, procedures, complaint patterns, and the quality of complaint investigations, as well as make regular reports to elected officials, NOPD and the public, would "create the impetus and the focus for correcting problems," "empower citizens with the information necessary to effect change," and would in this way "increase the ability of citizens and the NOPD to identify, address, and correct problems, thereby improving the department and building citizen confidence and support." *Report of the Police-Civilian Review Task Force* at 5. As noted in the Task Force report, this type of "quality control monitoring" has been used in other communities and has had beneficial results. *Id.* at 6.

Almost a decade later, in August 2009, New Orleans created the Office of the Independent Police Monitor ("IPM") as an independent, civilian police oversight agency. According to the IPM, its mission is to: improve cooperation and trust between the community and NOPD through objective review of police misconduct investigations; provide outreach to the New Orleans community; and make thoughtful policy recommendations to the NOPD and the City Council. The IPM recently reached an agreement with NOPD to help ensure it has access to the information it needs to fulfill these responsibilities. Last year, the IPM volunteered to use its own funds to develop a new early warning system for NOPD, and is currently working with NOPD to implement this new system. We have met with the IPM's Police Monitor several times and have been impressed with her dedication to building genuine reform and a constructive relationship with NOPD and the community.

In addition, with assistance from DOJ's Community Relations Services, community leaders in New Orleans have contributed significant time and effort to develop a community advisory board in conjunction with NOPD and the Mayor's office. This board would serve as a sustainable mechanism for ongoing dialogue to understand and address concerns from the community as well as opportunities for the community and police department to work together to achieve common goals.

There are myriad types of civilian oversight and each is capable of improving police-community relations, preventing unconstitutional conduct, and helping to ensure a constructive response when such misconduct does occur. Because the type of oversight appropriate for any given community is circumstantial, deference should be given to the oversight mechanisms a community has chosen for itself. Regardless of the type of oversight chosen, it is critical that

xxi

oversight mechanisms be sufficiently resourced and empowered. We have some concerns regarding whether the IPM has received sufficient resources and latitude to carry out its duties effectively. Adequate staffing, as well as the ability and authority to promptly obtain internal NOPD records on officer conduct, will be critical to the IPM's success as an oversight mechanism. Additionally, while it is still in a nascent state, we are encouraged by the steps to develop a community advisory board and hopeful that this will be an important bridge in communications between NOPD and parts of the community most concerned about police misconduct.

When combined with practices that ensure appropriate transparency in police department decisions related to misconduct and tactics, and with tools to measure, assess, and respond to changing community attitudes towards policing over time, civilian oversight can help create a powerful form of community engagement that will ensure that reforms are sustained over time, even after court-ordered oversight has ended.

C.	Summary of Recommendations

In conjunction with our experts, we developed recommendations for correcting the deficiencies that led to the patterns and practices of constitutional violations we observed. These recommendations are listed in the attachment to this Report.

The recommendations center on our key findings related to unconstitutional policing and its causes, and concern:

- Policies and procedures in each area we reviewed;
- Training for recruits, new officers, experienced officers, and supervisors;
- Supervision for officers in the field, including patrol and task force officers, and for detectives;
- Mechanisms of accountability, including force reporting and investigation, complaint intake and investigation, and discipline;
- Tracking and analyzing data to improve police practices, including an early warning system;
- Moving from policing to increase the number of arrests to an integration of community and problem-oriented policing strategies;
- Measures to address discriminatory policing;
- Paid Details;
- Officer assistance;
- Recruitment, performance evaluations, and promotions; and
- Community Oversight

## Conclusion

The City of New Orleans took a critical step by asking the Civil Rights Division to conduct a thorough, independent investigation of the Police Department in an effort to bring about the "complete transformation" of NOPD. The Department of Justice's investigation, involving extensive community engagement and in-depth review of NOPD practices, has

xxii

provided a fuller understanding of the systemic problems within the Department and the extent of the resulting harm.  This understanding serves as the foundation upon which to build sustainable reform that will reduce crime and prevent crime more effectively, police all parts of the New Orleans' community fairly, respect the rights of all New Orleans' residents and visitors, and prepare and protect officers.  Past reform efforts underscore the need for long term commitment and meaningful engagement of all key stakeholders to fundamentally and permanently transform the Department in this way.  The incredible optimism and desire for change expressed by the people we met tells us that this transformation is within reach.  We look forward to working with the City, the Police Department and the broader New Orleans community to ensure that this effort is successful.

xxiii

## <u>ACKNOWLEDGEMENTS</u>

In addition to the cooperation and assistance of Mayor Mitch Landrieu and his staff and Superintendant Ronal Serpas and his officers, we received important contributions from other public stakeholders, including the Orleans Parish District Attorney's Office, the Orleans Public Defenders, the New Orleans Civil Service Commission and the City's Office of the Independent Police Monitor. We also appreciate the willingness of members of the State and Municipal Courts, New Orleans City Council, Louisiana State Legislature, Business Council of New Orleans & the River Region, New Orleans Police and Justice Foundation, and the New Orleans Crime Coalition to meet with us and share their perspectives. Likewise, the insights and experiences shared by the many interested individuals and community groups with whom we met throughout our investigation were invaluable.

We worked closely with United States Attorney Jim Letten and the United States Attorney's Office for the Eastern District of Louisiana, which provided extensive assistance to Division attorneys throughout the investigation. DOJ's Community Relations Service ("CRS") coordinated many of the community meetings, working closely with grassroots New Orleans community organizations and enabling community members to express their concerns and proposals for improving public safety in New Orleans. Additionally, Ellen Scrivner, Deputy Director of the National Institute of Justice, and a former police deputy superintendent and chief psychologist, and Steve Parker, Assistant United States Attorney for the Western District of Tennessee, and a former police officer, each provided extensive assistance.

During our investigation, we coordinated closely with other components of DOJ, in part to enhance our understanding of NOPD and the City of New Orleans, and in part to identify areas of need in which DOJ had already provided or could immediately begin to provide assistance. We worked with the Office of Justice Programs; the Office of Community Oriented Policing Services; the Office on Violence Against Women; the Office on Juvenile Justice and Delinquency Prevention; and the Access to Justice Initiative. We also spoke to supervisors with the Federal Bureau of Investigation; the United States Marshal Service; and the Bureau of Alcohol, Tobacco, Firearms and Explosives, about ways to improve federal-local cooperation and coordination. The National Virtual Translation Center expanded the reach of our work by translating the Executive Summary of this Report into Spanish and Vietnamese.

This collaboration has allowed us to provide the City of New Orleans with substantial assistance. The City of New Orleans has availed itself of a number of other DOJ criminal justice system trainings, programs and initiatives, including but not limited to: A Comprehensive Homicide Assessment (U.S. DOJ, Bureau of Justice Assistance ("BJA")); An Integrated Justice Information System Technology Assessment (BJA); Conflict Resolution, Sensitivity and Cultural Competency Training (CRS); Domestic Violence/Sexual Assault First Responder Training (OVW); an Orleans Parish Prison Jail-size Facilities Assessment (ATJ); and Integrated Ballistic Information System Training (ATF). We further provided assistance that allowed NOPD to begin addressing its considerable backlog of rape kits awaiting testing (NIJ/OVC).

It is our hope that as we continue to work together to develop and implement these initiatives, we will help New Orleans create a criminal justice system that is both more effective and respectful of civil rights.

xxiv

## GENERAL METHODOLOGY

The investigative team consisted of lawyers and other staff from the Civil Rights Division's Special Litigation Section. Throughout our investigation, our understanding was informed by the expertise of law enforcement professionals (current and former police chiefs and supervisors) and other experts working alongside Division attorneys. These professionals provided in-depth knowledge about how to detect and respond to law enforcement challenges.

We gathered information through many interviews and meetings with NOPD officers, supervisors and command staff, as well as members of the public, City and State officials, and other community stakeholders. Our investigation included on- and off-site review of documents, including policies and procedures, training materials, incident reports, use of force reports, crime investigation files, data collected by the Department, complaints of misconduct, and misconduct investigations. We also participated in ride-alongs with officers and supervisors, attended COMSTAT meetings, observed police activity, and met with representatives of police fraternal organizations and several larger group officer "round tables" to elicit officer concerns and ideas about how to improve services provided by NOPD.

We participated in over 40 community meetings, including meetings held at our request as well as regularly scheduled community meetings, including New Orleans Neighborhood Police Anti-Crime Council ("NONPACC") and Rape Crisis Network meetings. We met with judges from the State and Municipal Courts and members of the District Attorney's Office, the Public Defender's Office, the Civil Service Commission, the Office of the Independent Police Monitor, City Council, Louisiana State Legislators, the Business Council of New Orleans & the River Region, the New Orleans Police and Justice Foundation, and the New Orleans Crime Coalition.

## <u>ABBREVIATIONS</u>

| | |
|---|---|
| NOPD | New Orleans Police Department |
| DOJ | United States Department of Justice |
| ADA | Assistant District Attorney |
| ATF | U.S. DOJ, Bureau of Alcohol, Tobacco, Firearms and Explosives |
| ATJ | U.S. DOJ, Access to Justice Initiative |
| AVL | Automatic Vehicle Location |
| BOP | Black Organization of Police (NOPD Fraternal Organization) |
| BJA | U.S. DOJ, Bureau of Justice Assistance |
| CAD | Computer-Aided Dispatch |
| CoCo | Community Outreach Coordinating Sergeant |
| COPS | U.S. DOJ, Office of Community Oriented Policing Services |
| CVSA | Computerized Voice Stress Machine |
| DWI | Driving While Intoxicated |
| DA | District Attorney |
| ECD | Electronic Control Device |
| FBI | U.S. DOJ, Federal Bureau of Investigation |
| FIC | Field Interview Card |
| FOP | Fraternal Order of Police (NOPD Fraternal Organization) |
| ICO | Integrity Control Officer |
| LEP | Limited English Proficient/Proficiency |
| LGBT | Lesbian, Gay, Bisexual, Transgender |
| MCTU | Mobile Crisis Transportation Unit |
| NOFJC | New Orleans Family Justice Center |
| NONPACC | New Orleans Neighborhood Police Anti-Crime Council |
| NOPJF | New Orleans Police and Justice Foundation |
| OC | Oleoresin Capsicum |
| OIS | Officer Involved Shooting |
| OJJDP | U.S. DOJ, Office on Juvenile Justice and Delinquency Prevention |
| OJP | U.S. DOJ, Office of Justice Programs |
| OVW | U.S. DOJ, Office on Violence against Women |
| PANO | Police Association of New Orleans |
| PD | Public Defender |
| PIB | Public Integrity Bureau |
| PPEP | Personnel Performance Enhancement Program |
| RAR | Resisting Arrest Report |
| SOD | Special Operations Division |
| UCR | Uniform Crime Reports |
| UOF | Use of Force |

**II.**     <u>**USE OF FORCE**</u>

We find reasonable cause to believe that NOPD engages in a pattern or practice of unconstitutional force.

     A.      Legal Standards

The Fourth Amendment guarantees "the right of the people to be secure in their persons, houses, papers, and effects, against unreasonable searches and seizures." U.S. CONST. amend. IV. Force used by a law enforcement officer while conducting an arrest or investigatory stop is evaluated under the Fourth Amendment, and use of excessive or unnecessary force during an arrest or stop is considered an "unreasonable" seizure that violates the Fourth Amendment. *Graham v. Conner*, 490 U.S. 386, 394 (1989).

The assessment of reasonableness, and therefore constitutionality, of an officer's use of force is an objective one. Just as an officer's bad intentions will not render an objectively reasonable use of force unconstitutional, an objectively unreasonable use of force is unconstitutional, even where the officer had good intentions. *Id.* at 397. Judging the reasonableness of the force used to effect a seizure requires a careful balancing of the nature and quality of the intrusion on the individual's Fourth Amendment interests against the countervailing governmental interests at stake. *Id.* at 396. The analysis "requires careful attention to the facts and circumstances of each particular case" to determine whether the force used was reasonable. *Goodman v. Harris County*, 571 F.3d 388, 397 (5th Cir. 2009) (internal quotation marks omitted) (citing *Graham*, 490 U.S. at 396).

The most significant and "intrusive" use of force is the use of deadly force, which can result in the taking of human life, "frustrat[ing] the interest of . . . society in judicial determination of guilt and punishment." *Tennessee v. Garner*, 471 U.S. 1, 9 (1985). Use of deadly force is permissible only when an officer has probable cause to believe that a suspect poses an immediate threat of serious physical harm to the officer or another person. *Id.* at 11. An officer may employ deadly force against someone who is attempting to evade arrest only where there is probable cause to believe: 1) a suspect has committed a crime involving the infliction of serious physical harm; 2) deadly force is necessary to prevent the suspect's escape; and 3) if feasible, the officer has warned the suspect. *Id.* at 11-12. In the words of the Supreme Court, "[i]t is not better that all felony suspects die than that they escape." *Id.* at 11.

     B.      Findings

        1.      Overview of Force Findings

While police-civilian interactions only rarely require the use of force, there are times when officers must use force to enforce the law, prevent serious injury, or protect life. The Constitution requires that officers use force only when necessary and that, when necessary, the force used is reasonable under the circumstances. Our review showed that officers in NOPD routinely use unnecessary and unreasonable force in violation of the Constitution and NOPD

- 1 -

policy.  We noted particular problems with NOPD's use of deadly force; force against restrained individuals, including retaliatory force; and the use of canines.

Our investigation did not include consideration of widely reported allegations of officer misconduct related to NOPD's response to Hurricane Katrina in 2005.  Many of these incidents have been, or are currently being, prosecuted by the Criminal Section of the Civil Rights Division and the United States Attorney's Office for the Eastern District of Louisiana.  We deliberately kept our civil investigation completely separate from the criminal investigation and prosecution of any NOPD officer, and this Report does not discuss any incident that is the subject of ongoing federal criminal proceedings.  Nonetheless, our investigation, which covered incidents that occurred within the past two years and assessed practices as they exist currently, revealed a clear pattern of unconstitutional uses of force by NOPD officers.

Our review of officer-involved shootings within just the last two years revealed many instances in which NOPD officers used deadly force contrary to NOPD policy or law.  We found a pattern of unreasonable less lethal force as well.  We found, for example, that NOPD's canines were uncontrollable to the point where they repeatedly attacked their own handlers, compelling us to recommend immediate suspension of NOPD's use of canines to apprehend suspects.  We found that officers used force against individuals, including persons in handcuffs, in circumstances that appeared not only unnecessary but deliberately retaliatory.  We reviewed instances in which NOPD officers used significant force against mentally ill persons where it appeared that no use of force was justified.  Our review showed further that officers likely report only a small fraction of the force they actually use.

While many of the instances of unreasonable force we reviewed cannot be explained or excused by a lack of policies or training, it is also true that police departments have the ability and responsibility to prevent and detect the use of unreasonable force by their officers.  The components of an effective and accountable use of force system are largely settled.  Police departments must ensure appropriate training in how and when to use force, and provide the supervision necessary for sufficient oversight of officers' use of force.  Departments must also provide officers clear and consistent guidance on when and how to use and report force, in the form of clear and comprehensive policies.  Departments must implement systems to ensure that force is consistently reported and investigated thoroughly and fairly.  The force investigation serves as the basis for reviewing the force incident to determine whether the officer acted both lawfully and consistent with departmental policy, as well as to determine whether the incident raises policy, training, tactical or equipment concerns that need to be addressed for officer and civilian safety.  Use of force aggregate data and trends should be monitored to enable a department to identify and address emerging problems before they result in significant or widespread harm.  We discuss below deficiencies in each of these components of an effective and accountable use of force system, including inadequate:  1) use of force policies; 2) use of force training; 3) force reporting and investigation; 4) use of force review, including reviews of officer-involved shootings; and 5) tracking, analysis, and response to use of force data and trends, including use of an early warning system.

As detailed below, we found that NOPD for years has acted with indifference to whether its officers are using force unconstitutionally and that, as a result, none of the components necessary to prevent unreasonable force are functioning. NOPD has allowed the systems and practices that were once in place to prevent and detect excessive force to languish. NOPD has failed to ensure that policies are accurate, up to date, and consistent, and has not provided adequate force-related academy or in-service training. NOPD has tolerated and condoned widespread and routine violation of policy and has allowed supervisors and commanders to ignore mechanisms previously established to investigate and review use of force and respond to problematic incidents or trends.

We observed no indication that supervisors or commanders take steps necessary to ensure that officers report force, despite evidence that force is widely underreported at NOPD. Nor does NOPD conduct meaningful investigation and review of any type of force. We discuss below specific incidents and types of unreasonable force that NOPD consistently has failed to investigate. We found that the deficiencies in NOPD's investigations of officer-involved shootings were, in some instances, so blatant and severe that the mishandling appeared intentional. We found further that NOPD's oversight of its officers' use of deadly force has been so perfunctory that until we inquired, NOPD did not know where some officer-involved shooting investigation files were located and did not initially provide officer-involved shooting investigative files for approximately one-half of the incidents that occurred during the time period we were reviewing. Several officer-involved shooting investigations are still missing.

As a result of these deficiencies, there is little accountability for officers who use force contrary to law or NOPD policy. We found repeated instances where officers used force, including deadly force, in a manner that plainly contradicted NOPD policy or the Constitution, and that endangered the lives of civilian bystanders and other police officers, yet no one in the chain-of-command held officers accountable.

We fully recognize the many dangers faced by law enforcement officers and that officers sometimes have to use force to enforce the law, defend themselves, or to protect others. However, NOPD's use of force practices present a significant threat to public and officer safety, and create a substantial obstacle to building the strong community partnerships necessary to prevent crime. As we were completing our investigation, NOPD began to make significant changes to force policies, including how officers will be trained to use force, and how force will be reported, investigated, and reviewed. These changes are urgently needed and long overdue. They are also only a small part of the comprehensive reform necessary to ensure that NOPD officers use force in a manner that is consistent with the Constitution.

2.      Unreasonable Use of Force

The prevalence and nature of the force-related misconduct we observed indicates that NOPD officers' use of unreasonable force in violation of the Constitution is widespread. The incidents of unreasonable force we reviewed reflected generally poor tactics and lack of adherence to all use of force policies, rather than problems with force of a particular type or in particular circumstances. Moreover, within NOPD, unless there is an injury requiring medical attention, there is little to prevent an officer from not reporting force, and it does in fact appear that a significant number of force incidents are unreported at NOPD. We noted particular problems in some areas, including the use of less lethal force,[2] particularly against restrained persons; the use of canines; and the use of deadly force.[3]

> *a)*      *Less Lethal Force, Force against Restrained Persons, and Retaliatory Force*

Our review of non-deadly use of force incidents included a review of almost 100 NOPD Resisting Arrest Reports ("RARs") documenting uses of force by NOPD officers between January 2009 and May 2010.[4] We found that in a number of instances officers used force that appeared unreasonable in light of the described resistance and other relevant circumstances. In many of the incidents we reviewed, the resulting injuries were inconsistent with the force as described and this inconsistency was not explained. There was no indication that the reviewing supervisor probed the apparent inconsistencies or established critical facts, and the report was approved as written.

In some instances it was not necessary to look beyond the officer's own description of force to determine that the force used appeared excessive. In one incident, an officer at central lock-up punched an apparently handcuffed arrestee in the jaw with a closed fist after the arrestee spit on the back of the officer's head. After being punched in the face by the officer, the arrestee fell back and hit his head on the wall, sustaining what the RAR described as a "small laceration." The arrestee was then "put in the back of the [transport] wagon," where, according to the RAR, he began "rolling around," cutting himself above the right eye. The arrestee was taken to the hospital for treatment, where a sergeant arrived and had other officers take over to "remove [the] officer [who used force] from the situation." The supervisor approved the officer's admitted use of force, even though, if used as described by the officer, the force was clearly retaliatory and excessive. The supervisor did not document that the arrestee was handcuffed, which under any set of police practices he would have been, and did not probe any of the subsequent injuries. The

---

[2] NOPD uses the term "Less than lethal" to describe intermediate level force. In our view, the term "less lethal" is more accurate and provides clearer guidance to officers. "Less lethal" is a term of art that refers to weapons and tactics that are *designed* to temporarily disable or stop a suspect without killing, thereby providing law enforcement with an alternative to lethal force. These weapons and tactics should not be referred to as "less than lethal" because they have resulted in fatalities and in general have a greater potential for lethality than lower level uses of force such as, for example, soft hands or hard hands.

[3] Our review of NOPD force was based almost entirely upon information provided by NOPD, primarily reports written by NOPD officers and ratified by NOPD supervisors. We did not "look behind" these materials by, for example, interviewing the individuals against whom force was used or the involved officers, or by reviewing primary source evidence such as audio or video recordings or other forensic evidence. Because our findings are largely based on NOPD's self-reporting, it is reasonable to believe that further inquiry would reveal additional problems with NOPD's use of force.

[4] We reviewed 96 RARs involving force incidents that occurred between January 1, 2009, and May 31, 2010. This sample included an over-representation of reports involving Electronic Control Device (ECD) discharges. During the time period we reviewed, NOPD had a greater organizational commitment to, as well as clearer protocols about, reporting ECD use. Recognizing this, we make no finding regarding whether ECDs are over-used within NOPD as compared to other weapons. We did, however, for each ECD incident reviewed, assess whether the use of the ECD in that instance was justifiable.

- 4 -

supervisor failed even to document the injuries, interview any witnesses, or make any attempt to determine what force was used and how that force resulted in the described injuries.

The above described incident raises also the issue of retaliatory force by NOPD officers. Based on our review of this incident and others, the use of retaliatory force, which is by definition unconstitutional, appears widely accepted within the Department. Indeed, when one NOPD officer reacted calmly after being spit on by another NOPD officer he had stopped for DWI, fellow NOPD officers told the arresting officer he was a coward for not at least punching the officer, according to reports of the arresting officer's testimony in court in December 2010. It is reasonable to believe that if officers find it appropriate to hit another officer in retaliation for disrespectful behavior, and if an officer will be ridiculed for not using unnecessary force in such situations, that NOPD officers will be at least as likely to use unlawful retaliatory force against civilians who show similar disrespect.

We found that the use of significant force against restrained persons by NOPD officers is relatively frequent and approved with little inquiry by supervisors. The use of significant force against handcuffed suspects should always be subjected to great scrutiny because such force is generally unnecessary. Particularly where officers repeatedly justify force against restrained suspects on losing control of the suspect, as they do at NOPD, officer-safety and accountability demand that an agency immediately investigate and then either correct dangerously poor tactics, or hold accountable officers found to have claimed falsely to have lost control of a suspect.

The reports we reviewed indicated that instead of increased scrutiny, supervisors generally accepted without question officers' loss-of-control justification for using significant force. In the incidents we reviewed, there was no clear explanation of how officers lost control of the individual or why the force used was reasonable under the circumstances. In one instance, for example, two officers deployed an Electronic Control Device ("ECD")[5] against a handcuffed arrestee who reportedly attempted to flee after being arrested for drug offenses and possession of a firearm. When he was taken to the hospital, the arrestee was treated for injuries that included a broken nose, as well as abrasions, bruises, and swelling. Despite the level of injuries and the fact that the man was handcuffed during at least part of this use of force, there was no real investigation, or even report, of the incident. The RAR, which is supposed to be written by the sergeant and incorporate the sergeant's investigation of the incident, and the Incident Report, which is supposed to be written by the officer, are identical (a frequent occurrence in our review). Neither indicates how the suspect was able to escape; how he sustained a broken nose; or why a lesser force option was not available. In another incident, officers deployed an ECD against a handcuffed man while re-apprehending him after a foot chase. The officers were arresting him for auto burglary and he had already been apprehended once after a foot chase (any force used to effect the first apprehension was not reported). The officers deployed an ECD when the handcuffed man "struggled" during the re-apprehension. The officers did not explain what force they used to apprehend the suspect the first time; how a handcuffed subject had managed to escape from them; the nature of the resistance they encountered justifying the use of

---

[5] We use the term ECD (Electronic Control Device) because this is the term used in NOPD policy. Other common terms for the weapon more commonly known by the brand name TASER, include Conducted Energy Device ("CED") and Electronic Control Weapon ("ECW").

- 5 -

an ECD; or what injuries, if any, the man sustained.  The reviewing sergeant did not interview the subject, or in any way investigate these issues.

In other instances, significant force, including ECD force, was used on restrained individuals where the circumstances, as described by the involved officers themselves, did not justify the level of force they used.  In one such incident, an officer used his ECD to drive-stun[6] a handcuffed woman being arrested for public intoxication after she "attempted to strike [an] officer with [her] body" while several other officers were attempting to put her in the back of a police vehicle.  There is no indication that any lesser degree of force was attempted or that the level of resistance required use of this level of force.  Rather, the incident report states, "[d]ue to the subject not following any of the officers commands she was drive tazed by [the officer]."  As described by the officers, the force used was excessive.  There is no indication that the sergeant reviewing the force questioned why officers did not attempt a lesser degree of force, or why basic evidence, such as witness interviews, was not gathered.  In a similar incident, three officers patrolling in one vehicle used their ECD in drive-stun mode twice against a handcuffed man who was being arrested for driving with a suspended license, so that they could more easily retrieve marijuana that the handcuffed man was attempting to hide.  Using an ECD to retrieve evidence, particularly under the circumstances described in the RAR, is unreasonable.

We also reviewed instances in which NOPD officers unreasonably deployed ECDs in circumstances that increased the potential lethality of the ECD.  In one incident, for example, officers deployed an ECD against an individual riding a bicycle who had been shining a hand-held flashlight into the windows of vehicles parked on the street and fled when officers approached him.  The Incident Report (but not the RAR) states that the ECD struck the bicyclist in the back.  The individual "immediately stopped pedaling and released the bike."  There is no description of the injuries the subject incurred, only that "the subject was transported to university hospital for medical attention, then transported to central lock-up to be booked accordingly."  It is contrary to accepted police practice to deploy an ECD against an individual riding a bike, as falling off a bike with no motor control (and thus no ability to break a fall by putting hands out, etc.) creates a risk of serious, potentially lethal, injury.  In the circumstances described by the officers in their reports, this use of force was excessive.  It also violated NOPD policy, which states that "[p]roper consideration and care should be taken when deploying the ECD on subjects who are in an elevated position or in other circumstances where a fall may cause substantial injury or death."  *See* Ops. Man. Chapter 1.7.1.

### b)       Canines

At the time of our investigation, NOPD's canines and their handlers were so poorly trained that handlers were not able to adequately control their canines, substantially increasing the risk that canines would bite individuals, even after those individuals were complying or trying to comply with officers' orders.  Our on-site observation of each dog and its handler undertaking drills that are routine at other police departments revealed that some dogs were almost completely uncontrollable and the rest were not consistently controllable.  One dog

---

[6] The drive-stun function of an ECD, also known as "pain compliance" mode, delivers non-incapacitating pain through direct contact of the ECD with the body.

attacked its handler twice over the period of a few hours while we were on site in October 2010. During our review of documents, we learned that there were at least three additional incidents between December 2009 and October 2010 where NOPD canines bit NOPD officers. Our review indicated that NOPD canines bite subjects approximately six out of ten times they apprehended a suspect—over twice as high as the three out of ten rate one would expect to see in a well-run canine unit.[7] NOPD's own analyses found that NOPD canines bite subjects more than 68% of the time they apprehend a suspect.[8] Especially concerning was the level of obedience demonstrated in an exercise termed "recall." In this exercise, a dog is taken off leash and ordered to attack an officer in a protective suit. After the dog has been released and is charging the subject, the officer commands the dog to stop the attack. It is essential that a canine/handler team be able to perform this exercise with precision. Many of the handlers were unable to recall their dog during the exercise and most had never previously executed this exercise.

Our observations indicated that the handlers' inability to control their dogs was a result of inadequate training and supervision rather than poor social disposition of the dogs (with the exception of one dog). We learned that none of NOPD's canines were certified to engage in criminal apprehension by any nationally recognized organization, and that there was no other assessment in place to provide adequate assurance of the Canine Unit's proper training and conduct. NOPD policy requires that canine teams attend two days of training per month, which comports with the industry standard of 8 hours every four weeks, or 16 hours every 4-6 weeks. NOPD policy also calls for canine handlers to maintain their own training records and, as a result, NOPD does not centrally maintain training records for its canines or their handlers. The Canine Unit was unable to provide any record of any dog's initial certification or of any subsequent recertification or training. Canine handlers informed us that, they had only trained with the canine trainer twice during the calendar year, contrary to industry standard and NOPD policy. Moreover, the Canine Unit's current trainer lacks sufficient training, experience, and certification to train the dogs and their handlers, and the Unit as a whole lacks supervision. The Unit's current supervisor appeared dedicated and well-meaning but was unfamiliar with conventional training practices and unaware of what training the dogs under his supervision have.

We found also that canine deployments and apprehensions are so poorly documented that appropriate oversight is not possible. When an apprehension results in a bite, an RAR is completed and approved by the sergeant supervising the Canine Unit. We reviewed 52 canine RARs covering the period from January 2009 through March 2010 and found every report deficient. These RARs were extremely short and used boilerplate language that was not tailored

---

[7] We base this 30%—or less—bite rate on the opinion of our canine expert as well as review of related research and case law. *See, e.g.*, *Kerr v. City of West Palm Beach*, 875 F.2d 1546, 1551 (11th Cir. 1989) (recounting expert testimony that "less than thirty percent of apprehensions should, on average, result in a bite" in a "properly trained and supervised canine unit").

[8] The information NOPD provided regarding bite ratio reflected an inaccurate understanding of how to calculate bite ratios. In addition to the information noted above, in response to a request for their canine unit's "bite ratio," NOPD informed us that their canines bit subjects 41 times in 109 deployments. It is widely accepted that when calculating a bite ratio, the number of apprehensions, not deployments, must be used as the denominator. Using deployments as the denominator decreases reliability, as "deployment" can be more widely defined than can "apprehension" and creates an incentive to deploy one's canine unnecessarily.

to the specific incident and did not describe with particularity the events leading up to the decision to deploy the canine. Such language included that the canine "apprehended the subject," that the subject "received minor dog bites," and that the canine "made physical contact" with the subject. Particularly since the handlers are not required to write Incident Reports or otherwise document their canines' use of force first-hand, it is not clear from where the sergeant obtained the information that is contained within the RAR. None of the reports described the nature or severity of the wounds and no photographs were taken to document injuries received. There was no indication that the sergeant who approved the use of force reviewed any of the corresponding Incident Reports.

The only reporting requirement of the Canine Unit is contained within the "New Orleans Police Department K-9 Unit Policy and Operating Procedures." It requires that, when a canine bites a suspect during an apprehension, "a departmental 'USE OF FORCE' report shall be completed and distributed by Canine Unit Supervisor within a 24 hour period." The key term "Use of Force report" is never defined, but use of this term indicates that this policy has not been substantively updated since at least before NOPD began using RARs rather than Use of Force reports. Canine patrol policy specifies that "canine officers shall complete only those reports required by the Canine Unit." Ops. Man. Ch. 41.22. Based on the documentation we reviewed, it appears that when a Canine Unit conducts a search and no bite results, the handler subsequently fills out a form entitled "N.O.P.D. Patrol K-9 Data," which is then approved by the Unit Commander. However, there is no written policy requirement that this documentation be completed, and therefore no accountability for failing to do so, raising concerns about whether this reporting is completed consistently.

Our concerns regarding NOPD's canine program were serious enough that we immediately asked the Superintendent to suspend the use of canines for suspect apprehension until NOPD was able to ensure that the canines and their handlers were properly trained and able to apprehend suspects lawfully and without unnecessary injury. We further recommended that each canine be assessed for suitability for criminal apprehension work. To the Superintendent's credit, he immediately suspended the use of canines for criminal apprehensions. We have been working, and will continue to work, with NOPD to implement both short and long term remedies to NOPD's canine program.

### c)       *Officer-Involved Shootings*

Our review of NOPD officer-involved shootings revealed unconstitutional uses of deadly force, repeated violations of NOPD policy, and critical officer safety issues.[9]

Many of the officer-involved shooting incidents we reviewed involved shooting at vehicles in circumstances that did not justify the use of deadly force or were contrary to NOPD policy. Shooting at vehicles is generally a poor tactical choice because it is difficult to fire effectively; if the driver is disabled by the shot, the vehicle becomes a potentially more

---

[9] We reviewed all identified officer-involved shootings for the time period covering January 2009-May 2010. We were provided with 46 reports that involved an officer discharging a firearm during this time period. Of those, we analyzed 27. The remaining nineteen consisted of five accidental discharges, thirteen shootings at dogs, and one incident in which an officer discharged his weapon to escape a vehicle after an accident.

dangerous unguided missile; and there is a high risk of significant injury or death to bystanders. NOPD's Use of Force policy acknowledges these dangers and states that, "Police Officers shall not discharge a firearm from a moving vehicle or at a moving vehicle, unless the occupants of the vehicle are using deadly force, other than the vehicle, against the member or another person, and such action is necessary for self-defense or to protect the other person." *See* Ops. Man. Ch. 1.2.

Nonetheless, we reviewed a number of incidents in which NOPD officers fired their weapons at moving vehicles in direct violation of this policy, in some instances after the vehicle had passed by, at which point the use of lethal force was not reasonable under the circumstances. In several instances, officers shot at vehicles after the officers had placed themselves or their squad cars directly in front of fleeing vehicles, a practice contrary to sound tactics and NOPD policy. *See* Ops. Man. Ch. 41.5. In one case, where an officer placed himself in front of a vehicle and was thrown over its hood, several officers responded by shooting and killing the vehicle's driver. In another instance, an officer fired at the tires of a fleeing vehicle, a clear and dangerous violation of NOPD policy. In still another case we reviewed, an officer fired at a driver purportedly accelerating towards the officer, instead of the officer getting out of the path of the vehicle, as required by NOPD policy. The officer suspected the driver was breaking into cars.

A number of the problematic shootings we reviewed were carried out by sergeants. In one of several shootings involving sergeants, a sergeant, who has been involved in six officer-involved shootings in four years, fired several shots at individuals fleeing from him on foot in a residential area. The sergeant gave conflicting accounts as to why he fired his weapon, and the sergeant's decision to engage in a foot pursuit was tactically questionable, given that he was by himself, at night, and the only infraction he had cause to believe the subjects had committed was failure to wear seatbelts (although he stated he suspected them of selling drugs).

As discussed below, we find reasonable cause to believe that deficiencies in NOPD's investigation and review of officer-involved shootings contribute to officers' use of deadly force that is contrary to policy or excessive. Moreover, NOPD's failure to adequately investigate and review officers' use of deadly force likely endangers officers by failing to detect and correct deficiencies in NOPD policy, training, tactics, and equipment.

      3.      Failure to Implement Measures to Prevent Unreasonable Force

The patterns of unreasonable force we observed are rooted in a number of longstanding systemic deficiencies within NOPD, including a failure to implement adequate: 1) use of force policies; 2) use of force training; 3) force reporting and investigation; 4) use of force review, including reviews of officer-involved shootings; and 5) tracking, analysis, and response to use of force data and trends, including use of an early warning system.

      *a)*      *Use of Force Policies*

We found that many officers, supervisors, and commanders have a poor understanding of use of force policies. When we asked, for example, what level of force should be used against a handcuffed subject who is inside the back of a police car kicking, one sergeant (who heads a task

- 9 -

force) told us, contrary to generally accepted police practice and NOPD policy, that an ECD should be the first level of force used.

While this poor understanding of how to use force appropriately is due to a number of factors, including insufficient training and poor supervision, its foundation lies in the extensive deficiencies of NOPD's force-related policies.  We found that NOPD has made little attempt to ensure that its use of force policies provide necessary guidance to officers.  NOPD's policies regarding what constitutes force, when various levels of force may be used, and when force must be reported, are incomplete, outdated, contradictory, and often incorrect.  NOPD's force policies are scattered through a number of directives[10] and have not been substantively updated in many years, in some instances over a decade.  In many instances policy "revisions" appear to involve nothing more than changing the date.  When NOPD has implemented new use of force policies, it has been done with little thought to how they will integrate with existing policies and practices.  As a result, force policies conflict with each other and, taken as a whole, leave significant gaps.  No NOPD policy, for example, provides guidance for how first responders (usually patrol officers) should respond to individuals experiencing a mental health crisis.

In many instances, key terms used throughout policies are not defined, or defined in conflicting or inaccurate ways.  NOPD's primary use of force policy fails to provide definitions for key terms such as "non-lethal," "physical force," and "bodily force" and contains two different definitions for "deadly force."  The definition of "excessive force" is convoluted and misleading, noting that serious injury or death is not "absolutely" necessary for force to be excessive.  The policy quotes Louisiana law extensively, but does not define any of the terms included, such as "imminent danger" and "violent or forcible felony."  Nor is there any explanation of how these state law requirements or terms interact or whether they are integrated into the rest of NOPD's force policy.

In some respects, NOPD's force policy implies that NOPD uses a force continuum.  For example, the skills and equipment that are included are listed in ascending order of seriousness, and the baton is referred to as an "intermediate level of force."  But, the policy does not include the guidance that would make a use of force continuum useful to officers, such as identifying all levels of force and the types of resistance against which such force can be expected to be effective.  Related force policies are similarly deficient.  The ECD policy provides officers no guidance about when an ECD, as opposed to another type of force, is appropriate, or what types of resistance justify ECD use.  In general, it appears that the ECD policy (which refers to ECDs as TASERs, the brand name, throughout) has been largely cut and pasted from vendor materials, and that little if any attempt has been made to integrate it into NOPD's use of force policies.

NOPD is currently rewriting its use of force policies.  To be effective, this effort must be comprehensive and ensure that force policies are integrated, consistent, and complete.

---

[10] *See* Ops. Man. Ch. 1.2, *Use of Force*; Ch. 1.13, *Policy on the Use of Force*; Ch. 1.7, *Oleoresin Capsicum Spray*; Ch. 1.7.1, *Electronic Control Device (ECD)*; Ch. 41.4, *Response to Police Calls*; Ch. 41.5, *Vehicle Pursuits*; Ch. 41.22, *Canine Patrol.*

- 10 -

    *b)*     *Use of Force Training*

    (1)    General Use of Force Training

The impact of NOPD's deficient force policies is substantially exacerbated by the deficient use of force training NOPD provides its officers. Police departments have long recognized the importance of training in preventing excessive force, yet NOPD does not provide necessary training on how to use force effectively, or on tactics to avoid using force. NOPD's use of force training is insufficient in amount and quality. NOPD does not prepare new recruits in how to use force effectively and appropriately. Nor does NOPD provide sufficient in-service training to ensure that officers refresh and refine their skills or understand new tactics and changes in the law.

Once recruits become officers, use of force "training" within NOPD consists primarily of annual firearms and ECD recertification. Training Division staff reported that firearms recertification is scheduled for one to two hours per year but, because of travel time and other logistical issues, the actual training lasts about thirty minutes. There is thus no actual training attached to firearms recertification. Officers thus do not receive critical training in deadly force judgment or role-play or scenario-based training. Nor has there been routine and mandated training on Oleoresin Capsicum ("O.C.") spray, the baton, or hand-to-hand encounters. There is no training on critical use of force legal or policy issues, force options, the appropriate application of deadly force or less lethal force, or the practical application of the use of force tools and techniques.

Since there is no use of force training, there is no written testing to determine whether officers understand the limits imposed by the law and NOPD policy, or performance testing to determine whether they can properly use and apply NOPD approved physical control techniques and weapons. NOPD officers also are not trained on what constitutes reportable uses of force, and NOPD supervisors are not trained in use of force report writing and investigation.

NOPD's failure to adequately train its officers leaves officers ill-equipped to deal with dangerous situations in the field. Without the skill set to de-escalate or control volatile situations, officers are more likely to lose control of situations and resort to force. They are more likely to feel unsafe and to be unsafe. The unreasonable uses of force and tactical errors we observed in our review of use of force incidents were consistent with this lack of training.

NOPD officers at all ranks acknowledged the lack of adequate use of force training, and nearly every officer expressed a desire for more and better training in using force. The Superintendent has been making efforts to increase and improve force training, recently announcing, for example, a plan to dedicate one and a half days per year to specifically focus on new arrest techniques, including training officers to safely avoid using force in making arrests. This force training is a positive initial step to ensuring that all NOPD officers are trained adequately in using, reporting, and investigating force.

- 11 -

(2)      Training in Mental Health or Behavioral Crisis Response

Crisis intervention policies and training can change officers' preconceived notions of mental illness, decreasing officers' use of force, and improving officer safety when responding to individuals in mental health crises.  NOPD in recent years has experienced both the tragedy of an officer being killed by an individual in apparent mental health crisis, as well as the tragedy of killing an individual in apparent mental health crisis.  While it is not always possible to determine conclusively in retrospect the impact of better policies and training on such incidents, these deaths underscore the importance of policies and training to minimize the potential for harm in interactions between officers and individuals in mental health crisis.

In several of the use of force incidents we reviewed involving officers using significant force against persons in apparent mental health crisis, it appeared that if officers had been trained in responding to such persons, they might have avoided the use of force altogether.  In one incident, NOPD officers responded to a scene where a man was on his own property in a large tractor trailer, claiming to be a "member of the secret police" with "an affidavit to prove it." Under circumstances in which the use of any force was questionable, officers deployed an ECD twice against the man to little effect.  A sergeant arrived on the scene and was "able to convince [the man] to come to the front of the trailer and display his secret police affidavit to him."  The man was then apprehended without further incident.  Unlike the officers who first responded to the scene, the sergeant employed tactics that involved no force and were effective.

In addition to incidents we learned of during our review of documents, we heard many concerns about NOPD's response to mentally ill persons in our conversations with the broader New Orleans community.  Mental health professionals as well as community advocates in New Orleans characterized NOPD interactions with subjects suffering serious mental illness as resulting in avoidable or excessive uses of force and lacking in sensitivity.  One mental health community advocacy organization explained the problem "of police being called on by families for assistance in getting a loved one who is mentally ill, depressed or in emotional crisis to a hospital for care, only to have their loved one injured or killed by responding police officers."

While all police encounters involve some level of risk that force may be necessary to apprehend the subject, police encounters with subjects suffering serious mental illness and experiencing a behavioral crisis involve a greater risk that the officers will employ force.  Such incidents may involve a suspect that does not immediately respond to the directives of the officer, and who may perceive the officer as a threat.  Such incidents may also involve officers that misinterpret the behavior of the subject as deliberately threatening, or who have not been trained in de-escalating such crises without resorting to force.

While NOPD provides limited mental health crisis intervention training to officers on its hostage negotiation team and to the Mobile Crisis Transportation Unit ("MCTU"), it does not provide adequate crisis intervention training to patrol officers, who are often the first-responders. Reportedly, the only training on crisis intervention is provided during basic academy training when the officers learn about the function of the MCTU, and some ad hoc roll call training provided by the Director of the MCTU.  As a result of this lack of policies and training, it appears that NOPD is not identifying many of the individuals they encounter that suffer from

- 12 -

mental illness;[11] sometimes uses more force than necessary in such encounters; and is not taking full advantage of emerging community resources to divert persons in mental health crisis directly to medical treatment where appropriate.

We found some recent successes in this area at NOPD, including the innovative and expanding MCTU. NOPD's MCTU is an innovative unit staffed with well-trained and dedicated community volunteers to assist NOPD patrol units in processing and transporting subjects with serious mental illness to a hospital emergency room or other available mental health treatment center. The officers and volunteers of this Unit are working with NOPD leadership and the community to develop new models of crisis intervention and training. This work in developing models of crisis intervention for first responder patrol officers is critical, as the function of the MCTU is limited to the post-apprehension transfer of the subject. The MCTU has tremendous value but should not replace the need for crisis intervention training targeted at first-responder patrol officers.

*c)*      *Use of Force Reporting and Investigation*

To help ensure that unsafe tactics and misconduct are identified and can be prevented in the future, the facts of every use of reportable force must be established accurately, and reviewed fairly and thoroughly. For the lowest levels of force, sometimes referred to as "soft" control techniques[12] where there is no complaint of injury and no discrepancy in the descriptions of the force used, a report fully describing the force used may be sufficient. However, for even moderate levels of force, such as hand strikes and pushes, and in particular where there is a complaint of injury or a discrepancy in the description of the force used, some level of investigation and review is required, even in the absence of a formal misconduct complaint.

NOPD policy purports to provide for such force reporting, investigation, and review, but does not provide sufficient guidance for when and how to report or investigate force, or set up a realistic framework for meaningful review. As a result of this, in combination with inadequate training and little accountability, investigations of reported force are generally of too poor quality to serve as the basis for useful force review, and many uses of force are never reported at all.

---

[11] Data provided by NOPD appears to show approximately 200 calls-for-service per month related to a mental health crisis. For a city the size of New Orleans, attempting to take into account the increase in mental illness post-Katrina, this number would be expected to be three to four times higher than this reported 200 calls for service.

[12] "Soft" control techniques usually include techniques such as wrist locks and arm twists and, performed correctly, present a minimal risk of injury. Generally, these techniques are used to control passive or defensive resistance. However, soft control techniques can be utilized for any level of resistance if tactically possible and legally permissible. By comparison, "hard" control techniques include striking techniques using the hands or feet, and are more likely to cause injury. The forceful direction of the suspect to the ground, sometimes called a "take-down," is generally considered a "hard" control technique. Generally, hard control techniques are used to counter defensive resistance, active aggression, or aggravated active aggression.

- 13 -

1)      Unreported Force

We found that NOPD tolerates widespread underreporting of force by its officers. Underreporting appears to be due in part to poor understanding of what force must be reported by policy; as discussed below, many officers reported to us that they would report force only where the subject of the force was injured or complained that the force was excessive, even though NOPD policy requires broader force reporting. Underreporting also appears to be the result of systemic failure to hold officers accountable for not reporting force, or to even acknowledge the extent to which NOPD officers use force. Some District Commanders reported to us that no officer in their entire District had used force in weeks or, in one instance, months. One sergeant told us his task force, a unit that tends to have higher than average arrests and force encounters, did not have a single incident of reportable force in the previous three month period. Given the number of arrests NOPD officers make, such claims lack credibility and indeed, officers, supervisors, and commanders at all ranks expressed to us a lack of confidence that force is consistently reported.

A snapshot of force reporting for one month further indicates that officers do in fact report only a small fraction of the force they actually use. We reviewed all uses of force reported by NOPD officers for the month of June 2010, 34 reports in all. During this same month, NOPD effectuated 6,787 arrests. Nationwide, estimates of force rates vary, but generally range from approximately 2-5% (*i.e.* for every 100 arrests, officers use reportable force in approximately 2-5 arrests).[13] Thus, in the month of June 2010, if NOPD officers were using force at the national average rate, one would expect to have seen between approximately 135 and 340 uses of force, rather than the 34 NOPD reported. This underreporting appeared to be prevalent throughout the Department. In every district there were a substantially lower number of uses of force reported than one would expect based on the numbers of arrests. In one district, officers made 647 arrests in June 2010 and did not report a single use of force. Our conversations with NOPD staff reported similarly incredible use of force rates.

Our dataset of a random sample of RARs had fewer reports related to hands, fists, or other bodily force than would be expected in a department that by policy requires reporting this type of force. In our view, this is at least partially explained by the fact that NOPD has more structured protocols for how to report ECD deployment, and to some extent the use of O.C. spray, resulting in more accurate reporting of these types of force.

---

[13] *See, e.g.*, Edward R. Hickey & Joel H. Garner, *Rate of Force Used by the Police in Montgomery County, Maryland*, U.S. Dep't Just. Nat'l. Inst. Just. 199877 (2002) (reporting a force rate of 6.4 percent); William Terrill, Ph.D, *City of San Antonio, Texas Police Department Use of Force Analysis July 1, 2001-December 31, 2002*, (2003), *available at* www.sanantonio.gov/SAPD/pdf/UOFcomplete.pdf. (reporting a force rate of 2 percent); Dr. Steven Brandl, *An Overview of Milwaukee Police Department Use of Force Incidents: January 1, 2010 to June 30, 2010*, Rept. Fire and Police Commission (2010), *available at* www.ci.mil.wi.us/ImageLibrary/.../ 2010_ MidYear _Use_of_Force_Report.pdf (reporting a force rate of 1.12 percent). We found no evidence that NOPD officers use force at less than the average rate. It is likely that the variance in force/arrest ratios is due in part to different requirements among law enforcement agencies of what force must be reported. NOPD policy requires generally broad force reporting.

- 14 -

270

Widespread underreporting of force by officers means that NOPD has no opportunity to learn from use of force incidents.  It also means that NOPD does not learn of some uses of force that were unjustified and should have resulted in officers or supervisors being held accountable.  It appears that part of the reason that force is reported at very low rates within NOPD is that its force reporting policies do not require, or at least are not understood to require, reporting some of the force that officers use.  However, the larger problem appears to be that within NOPD many officers simply do not report the force they use, despite knowing that policy requires that they do so, and that NOPD does not hold officers accountable for failing to report uses of force.

(2)      Force Reporting Policies

NOPD's policy on use of force reporting, Ops. Man. Ch. 1.3, *Resisting Arrest Report,* states that force reporting: "shall benefit the Department by identifying training improvements; problem assignments, activities or locations; potential liability issues and situations; the cause of confrontation and conflict resolution; and statistical data to assist in the planning and the development of policies and procedures."  This is a good policy but it is not being followed.  We saw no evidence that force was being reported, reviewed, or analyzed in a way that would realize any of these stated benefits.

NOPD's Use of Force and RAR policies each address when and how force must be reported, but conflict with each other and, even read together, contain signification gaps.[14]  One critical deficiency is that neither chapter defines "reportable use of force" or otherwise provides clarity on what types of force must be reported.  The RAR policy states that a RAR "shall be prepared when an employee of the Department is involved in any situation where lethal and/or less than lethal force is used by or toward an employee."  However, "less than lethal force" is not defined in the NOPD Operations Manual and it is unclear whether reportable "less than lethal force" is meant to encompass only the devices explicitly specified as less than lethal in NOPD's Use of Force policy (batons and chemical agents), or is meant to cover *all* types of force besides lethal force, including, for example, bodily force such as hits, kicks, and leg sweeps.

Another provision of NOPD's force policy is likely responsible for the erroneous opinion we heard voiced more than once by NOPD officers; that force need only be reported if it results in injury.  The policy states that "in all instances where physical force is used to control an individual and the individual is injured or complains of injury, the supervisor shall complete an offense report covering the circumstances surrounding the incident."  The terms "offense report" and "physical force" are not defined in either the Use of Force or RAR policy, further confusing how and when to report force.

Not surprisingly, officers and commanders at all levels expressed confusion or contradicted each other when describing what NOPD considers reportable force, and NOPD's definition of less than lethal force.  One Captain who currently commands a District told us that an officer need only report force when the officer used more force that the officer thought

---

[14] NOPD policy on use of force reporting is captured primarily in its *Use of Force* policy, Ch. 1.2, and its *Resisting Arrest Report* policy, Ch. 1.3, and to a lesser degree in Ch. 1.6, *Police Firearms Discharge,* and Ch. 1.24, *In Custody Deaths.*

necessary. During a visit to another District station, we observed an arrestee who was bleeding from his forehead. An officer stated that the man had injured his head after officers dragged him out from under a house; the arrestee stated that an officer had pulled him off a fence by his ankle, causing him to fall and hit his head. While the officers and subject disagreed on what type of force led to the injury, all parties agreed that the officers had used force and that the man was injured. Yet we received conflicting answers from the officer, his sergeant, and the lieutenant, about whether a use of force report would be completed, and whether the man would be taken to the hospital, even though NOPD policy clearly required both.

Officers also displayed inconsistent and erroneous understandings of when officers must notify NOPD's Public Integrity Bureau ("PIB") of a use of force. Some told us PIB would be notified only where there is a discrepancy between an officer's and subject's description of a force event. Others told us PIB would be informed if a supervisor thought excessive force had been used. NOPD's RAR policy in fact requires that the completed RAR "shall be forwarded" to PIB within 24 hours from the time of the force incident, and does not appear to limit this to RARs involving only more serious or questionable uses of force.

Neither the Use of Force nor RAR policy makes clear that an employee observing a use of force has a responsibility to report that force. In fact, NOPD's RAR policy appears to release employees from that responsibility, stating that "[r]esponsibility for the notification of an appropriate supervisor within his chain of command to handle the report shall rest with the employee involved in the incident." It is appropriate to place the primary responsibility for reporting force on the officer that used the force, but any reporting policy should make clear that all employees have a responsibility to ensure that force is reported, especially where the employee believes the force used was unreasonable.

(3)    RAR Investigations

Our review of RARs and related policies, as well as conversations with NOPD officers, supervisors and commanders of all ranks, make clear that NOPD does not routinely investigate the uses of force that officers do report. Further, we saw no accountability for supervisors who conduct inadequate force investigations. By tolerating supervisors' failures to investigate uses of force NOPD gives up the opportunity to correct dangerous behavior, and instead sends the message that there is little institutional oversight or concern about officers' use of force.

Pursuant to NOPD policy, a supervisor is required to respond to the scene to "conduct the necessary follow-up investigation" of each "resisting arrest incident." As discussed above, NOPD policies do not make clear what constitutes a "resisting arrest incident" requiring supervisory follow-up. However, even in circumstances where a RAR is completed, we generally did not find evidence of the "follow-up investigation" required by policy. We found that in many instances it does not appear that the supervisor even responds to the scene as required by policy and, even when a supervisor did respond, the supervisor appears to have done little more than complete the RAR, taking few if any investigative steps to establish the facts related to the officer's use of force. We found that, despite the clear policy requirement that supervisors interview officer and civilian witnesses, conducting such interviews is the exception rather than the rule. We reviewed incidents in which one supervisor responded to the scene of a

- 16 -

272

use of force and a different one conducted the interviews.  Often, interviews were conducted days after a use of force had already been approved by a different supervisor.  While many departments recognize the value of ECD cameras but cannot afford the expense, NOPD has purchased this much more expensive version of ECD, but supervisors do not routinely review— or at least document their review of—the video capture of an ECD deployment.  Similarly, we rarely saw reference to whether a sergeant had reviewed in-car camera recordings of an incident, or what the recording showed.

In many instances, it appeared that the officer who used the force simply wrote the RAR and gave it to the supervisor to sign.  Often, the language in the RAR, which is by policy meant to document the supervisor's investigation of the use of force, was identical to the incident report, which is meant to document the arresting officer's version of events.  Both types of reports often included general language that the subject was "violently resisting," or that the officer "took the suspect down," which does not describe the level of resistance or the type of force used with the specificity necessary to permit meaningful assessment of the incident.  Yet, supervisors consistently approved, and in some cases wrote, force reports replete with such language.

Similarly, we observed many instances in which a single officer wrote an Incident Report to document the actions of all involved employees, rather than having each employee document their observations in supplemental reports.  The Incident Reports documenting force were nearly always written in the third person, making it impossible to discern whose version of events was being reported, or to hold any one officer accountable for his or her actions; and, consequently building into any investigation based on the Incident Report the assumption that all officers saw and heard the same things.  As only one officer is required to sign the report, there is no indication that the other named officers agreed with or even saw the version of events described in the Incident Report.  It was often unclear when supervisors reviewed and approved officers' reports.  In many instances, the signature blocks on reports were not clear, making it difficult or impossible to discern who investigated the use of force and who approved the report.  We also reviewed reports in which the signature blocks were not signed or dated.

Upon completion of the force "investigation," supervisors generally do not document whether the force used indicated a failure of training or tactics and whether it was consistent with NOPD policy.  This was true even where the use of force clearly demonstrated inappropriate conduct, such as an ECD discharged at a range too close to be effective, necessitating multiple ECD cycles.  Even in cases of such clear policy violations, we found that supervisors marked "Yes," to the question "Was departmental policy followed?"

NOPD policies and protocols further fail to provide the structure for reliable and credible force investigations.  NOPD policy does not require that the RAR be completed, and the use of force investigated, by a supervisor who was uninvolved with the use of force, or who is of a higher rank than the officer who used force. Indeed, we saw many uses of force reported and investigated by supervisors who weere present when the force occurred, and thus had already tacitly approved the action of the officer, raising the potential of a self-serving RAR.  We reviewed some cases in which supervisors reviewed their own uses of force.  We also saw several cases in which officers investigated the use of force of officers of the same or higher rank.

NOPD does not provide sufficient guidance to supervisors on conducting use of force investigations. No directive, training curricula, or other document provides direction on the purpose of the questioning and the appropriate line of questioning. No policy, protocol or training sets out how to conduct use of force investigation interviews, how to decide who to interview, or what issues need to be resolved. No policy requires that the supervisor gather evidence as necessary to resolve material discrepancies, or consider and document whether the description of the force used is consistent with the injuries sustained. NOPD policies do not require collecting forensic evidence, taking photographs, or gathering and reviewing any audio or video evidence.

(4) Officer-Involved Shooting Investigations

The systemic deficiencies in NOPD's investigation and review of officer-involved shootings are so egregious that they appear in some respects to be deliberate. NOPD officer-involved shooting investigations consistently fail to gather evidence, establish critical facts, or fairly analyze the evidence that is readily available. As a result, despite clear and systemic problems with how NOPD officers use deadly force, NOPD has not found that an officer-involved shooting violated policy in at least six years, and NOPD officials we spoke with could recall only one out-of-policy finding even before that time.

To prevent the unconstitutional use of deadly force, build credibility with communities, protect officer safety, and manage risk, every use of deadly force, including all officer-involved shootings, should be promptly and comprehensively investigated and reviewed. To be complete, this investigation must be conducted from the criminal and administrative perspectives. Neither investigation depends upon whether anyone has complained about the use of force. These investigations may be conducted at the same time or sequentially, depending upon departmental policy and the circumstances of the incident.

The criminal investigation assesses whether the use of deadly force was lawful, and is often conducted by a specialized force investigation team, or by an outside entity such as the state police, a neighboring jurisdiction, or the DA's Office. In many departments the homicide division conducts the assessment of whether the officer's use of deadly force was justified; doing so necessitates specific policies, training and supervision to ensure investigations are credible, complete, and reliable. If the criminal investigation indicates that the shooting may have been unlawful, the incident should be referred to local prosecutors to determine whether to seek prosecution.

The administrative investigation of the use of deadly force assesses whether the involved officers or others violated departmental policies, and whether the incident raises tactical, policy, training, or equipment concerns. This administrative investigation is often conducted by a department's internal affairs division, by a specialized force investigation team, or, particularly in controversial cases, by an independent, skilled, and credible outside investigative team. As discussed in the next section, once the administrative investigation of the use of deadly force is

- 18 -

completed, the department must make use of the information, reviewing the incident to determine the appropriate response to any identified policy violations or tactical, policy, training, or equipment concerns.

NOPD does not have a legitimate system in place for investigating uses of deadly force by its officers. Where a firearms weapons discharge results in death or injury, the Homicide Cold Case Unit has the primary responsibility to investigate. In such circumstances, PIB's administrative investigation is, pursuant to written policy, to "ask the assigned Homicide Investigator if there are apparent violations of law or departmental regulations on the part of the involved officer." This and other NOPD directives divest PIB of any real authority or ability to conduct an administrative investigation and place that authority instead with the Homicide Division, whose detectives have no training in conducting administrative investigations, nor independence from the criminal investigation. Our conversations with NOPD officials confirmed that, counter to good policing practice, NOPD conducts an administrative investigation only of officer-involved shootings where no one is injured or killed.

Adding to the harm caused by NOPD's failure to conduct focused administrative investigations of officer-involved shootings in which someone is injured or killed, is the consistent extremely poor quality of the investigations of these incidents conducted by NOPD's Homicide Division. As noted above, we reviewed all identified officer-involved shooting investigations for the time period covering January 2009-April 2010. We found each of the investigations of these shootings to be deeply flawed. The investigations generally did not include the investigative steps or analysis necessary to make a credible determination of whether the use of force was lawful. In addition, the Homicide Division investigations made no attempt to determine whether the use of force was consistent with policy, or even to conduct an investigation that would allow anyone else to make this determination. For a time, NOPD even had a practice of temporarily assigning the officers who had been involved in officer-involved shootings to the Homicide Division, and then automatically deeming the statements officers provided to Homicide investigators to be "compelled." As discussed more fully below, this practice effectively immunized the use of these statements in any subsequent criminal investigation or prosecution. It is difficult to view this practice as anything other than a deliberate attempt to make it more difficult to criminally prosecute any officer in these cases, regardless of the circumstances.

We found that, in addition to broad practices and policies that undermine the efficacy of NOPD's officer-involved shooting investigations, individual investigations are severely deficient as well. In one officer-involved shooting incident we reviewed, a sergeant endangered bystanders and other officers when shooting at a fleeing vehicle after unnecessarily placing his vehicle in front of it. Officers were attempting to stop the vehicle for traffic violations, although they suspected the car was stolen. After a lengthy vehicle pursuit in which the subject rammed several police cars trying to escape, the sergeant pulled his squad car directly in front of the vehicle, violating NOPD policy and exposing himself and his partner to danger. The sergeant fired four shots at the car, hitting the driver once. The shooting would have clearly violated policy except that the sergeant reported that he saw the driver of the car raise a handgun. Clearly the statement that the driver was holding a gun was a crucial fact in determining whether the shooting was consistent with NOPD policy, and perhaps whether it was excessive.

- 19 -

The credibility of the investigation was undermined by the investigator's failure to take basic but critical investigative steps and by a report that appeared designed to confirm the involved sergeant's version of events and gloss over admissions of clear violations. Though a gun was found in the car, no officer besides the sergeant who fired said that he saw a gun during the incident. The driver and three passengers each stated that the driver did not have a gun. The investigating sergeant did not make any attempt to determine why none of the officers saw the weapon, despite lighting that the investigator called "excellent." While investigators successfully lifted prints from the car, they did not attempt to take prints from the gun. NOPD's efforts to talk with the gun's registered owner, whose home address the detectives had, are also unclear and described only as meeting with "negative results." In addition to these troubling facts, the homicide investigator's report implied that the driver admitted that there was a gun in the car but that it was not his. However, the transcript of the driver's statement makes clear that the homicide investigator's characterization of the driver's statement is misleading. The driver told investigators clearly that he did not have a gun, that he never saw a gun in the car that night, and that he had no knowledge that anyone in the car had a gun with them. The driver told detectives that the female passenger had spoken of a gun that she owned in the past, but that he had never seen her with one. A fair and thorough investigation would have resolved these discrepancies rather than obscured them.

We found that even in instances where officers' use of deadly force resulted in the death of an individual, basic investigative steps were not taken and key facts remain unresolved. One such incident involved officers who shot and killed the fleeing suspect of a car-jacking. The man was unarmed and was ramming vehicles in an attempt to evade officers. When an officer placed himself in front of the man's truck, the officer was struck and thrown over the hood of the car. Officers shot and killed the man while still in his truck. Officers gave different rationales as to why they fired and witnesses stated that the driver was attempting to surrender when the officers shot him. The Homicide Division investigation did not attempt to establish whether the facts mitigated officers' decision to shoot at the driver, in violation of NOPD policy, rather than get out of the path of the truck. The criminal investigator did not resolve the conflict between witness statements, or even interview a number of "reluctant" witnesses. The investigator did not account for all shots fired; determine which officer fired the fatal shot; or interview the officer who was struck by the truck. The officers apparently were not separated before they were interviewed, and investigators compelled officers' statements (immunizing the use of such statements in any criminal prosecution) without first attempting to obtain voluntary statements.

Officer-involved shooting investigations conducted by PIB (because no one was struck or injured) appeared largely pro forma. Often in response to the question on the Administrative Shooting Notification Form, "Follow up Administrative Investigation to be Conducted," the investigator did not even check either "Yes" or "No." In many of the investigations where an administrative investigation was purportedly conducted, the administrative investigator did not indicate whether the force was within policy or presented training concerns, leaving the answer to that question blank as well.

In one officer-involved shooting investigated by PIB, an officer shot at a moving vehicle, reporting that he had done so because the driver was about to hit him with the car and that he was unable to get out of the way.  The recording from the officer's in-car video system showed this to be false.  The officer's supervisor claimed to have watched the in-car video, but did not question the officer's account.  According to the PIB lieutenant that investigated the incident, the video showed that the car was not heading towards the officer when he shot at it; there were no visible obstructions that prevented the officer from retreating; and the officer was not in danger when he fired the shot.  The PIB investigator also discovered that several officers in the District turned off their in-car video cameras during the vehicle pursuit that preceded the shooting.  Inexplicably, the formal investigation found the violations associated with the shooting to be "not sustained," a finding that is supposed to indicate that the policy violation could be neither proven nor disproven.  Neither the supervisor who failed to identify the apparent policy violation, nor the officers who turned off their in-car video cameras were held accountable.

NOPD has acknowledged the problems with its investigations of officer-involved shootings, and reports that it is fundamentally remaking its systems for investigating them.  Already, NOPD has made some changes, including reportedly revising its previous practice of not allowing PIB investigators behind the tape in an officer-involved shooting—although this change has not yet been memorialized in policy.  This change is significant.  We reviewed officer-involved shooting scene sign-in sheets that documented over seventy officers and City officials allowed on-scene following shootings, making it appear as though everyone within NOPD except PIB was allowed on-scene.  Access to the scene of any major crime, especially the scene of an officer-involved shooting, should be kept to as few personnel as possible, and PIB investigators conducting the administrative investigation of the shooting should always be included among those few.

More broadly, NOPD has reported that it is developing a system under which both the administrative and criminal investigations of officer-involved shootings, as well as of other critical incidents, will be conducted by a force investigation "team."  This team will report to PIB, which in turn will report directly to NOPD's Superintendent.

(5)     In-Custody Death Investigation

To minimize and appropriately respond to unreasonable force, police departments must thoroughly investigate the deaths of detainees or arrestees that occur while in police custody, regardless of whether these deaths appear to have occurred proximate to the use of deadly force.  Neither Ops. Man. Ch. 1.24, *In Custody Death*, nor any other NOPD directive, provides for sufficient investigation and review of in-custody deaths.  Indeed, that policy is little more than a list of who must be notified.  Our conversations with NOPD officials confirmed that there is no specific guidance or training for NOPD criminal or administrative investigators regarding how to investigate an in-custody death.

One of the two in-custody death investigations in the data set we were provided was sufficiently complete to review. [15]  This investigation by NOPD's Homicide Division raised significant concerns about the adequacy of NOPD's in-custody death investigations.  NOPD investigated the death of a man arrested for a family-related disturbance of the peace.  According

---

[15]  We did not review an in-custody case file that was provided to us that included a handwritten note stating that the file "was recreated as much as possible," and noting that "perhaps the FBI has the case file."

- 21 -

to police reports, the man was belligerent during the arrest and had to be forcefully subdued. The man was taken to the hospital twice during the evening of his arrest, first because the jail refused to accept him because he had sustained a laceration above his eye when officers arrested him (the investigation report notes the laceration was "very minor," although it required "several stitches" to close); the second time because of high blood pressure. Approximately three days later, while still in jail custody, the man died. According to the investigation, the coroner determined that the man died of a laceration to the spleen that occurred approximately 48 hours prior to the man's death. The investigator concluded that NOPD officers did not cause the man's death.

This investigation leaves critical questions unanswered. The case file includes no documentation of the coroner's conclusion that the man died due to injuries sustained approximately 48-hours prior to death, or indication that the investigator talked with the coroner to determine how wide a time-span might be included in this "approximate" time frame. Rather, the only document in the investigative file from the coroner notes a final diagnosis of, among other things, "multiple recent injuries of blunt impact," does not mention an injury to the spleen, and classifies the death as "undetermined." In addition, the investigator did not record, or even take a formal statement from, the deceased man's mother, who witnessed the event. The mother, according to interview notes, believed that her son was unconscious after officers arrested him, while officers state that the man, who moments earlier had been belligerently threatening to shoot officers, was conscious but "passively resisting" by not moving when they took him to the squad car. The report notes that the mother was extremely upset and that a formal statement would be "forthcoming," but, as we observed in other investigations by NOPD's Homicide Division, the follow-up interview of a witness whose statement appeared to conflict with officers' versions of events was not conducted or recorded. Without taking any investigative steps to verify facts, the report concluded that the man likely died after thrashing on the floor of the jail or a "physical encounter with another inmate." But the investigator did not interview any jail inmates or staff. We found it impossible to draw any firm conclusions from this investigation regarding the circumstances of the subject's death. We did conclude however, that NOPD's investigation and review of the incident were clearly inadequate and are particularly concerned that there is no indication that NOPD command staff intervened to require a more thorough and reliable investigation of this death.

d)     Use of Force Review

A use of force investigation serves as the basis for a department's review of the incident to determine whether there were any policy violations or tactical, policy, training, or equipment concerns. This review is critical in enabling the department to learn from past incidents, prevent future misconduct, and improve officer safety. Reviewing aggregate force data allows a department to identify concerns and trends (including positive trends) with particular types of force, geographic areas, officers, supervisors, or units, and to enable an evidence-based response that may include policy changes, training, corrective measures, a shift in tactics, or new equipment. While NOPD nominally has in place systems to review use of force incidents and aggregate force data, we found that these systems are not functioning and these reviews do not take place.

- 22 -

(1)    Review of Officer-Involved Shootings and other Critical
       Incidents

NOPD policy does not set out a clear process for reviewing officer-involved shootings or other critical incidents.  Our conversations with NOPD officials indicate that PIB has in the past conducted administrative "hearings" that consisted primarily of the PIB commander meeting with the officer to discuss the shooting.  Even this "review" has in many instances been impossible because, in a number of instances, the Homicide Division failed for months or even years to provide its investigative report of the shooting to PIB, as required by policy.  Based on our conversation with NOPD officials, this failure by the Homicide Division to provide these files to PIB appears to have effectively prevented any review of these officer-involved shootings.

As of September 2010, there were fourteen firearms discharge reviews that could not be completed because PIB had requested but not received the Homicide investigations or RARs for these cases.  After we inquired about these outstanding investigations, some of which dated back to 2005, PIB asked Homicide to provide them.  In November, Homicide's new commander provided PIB with every OIS criminal investigation she could find.  Still missing are NOPD's investigations of four officer-involved shootings that occurred between 2005 and 2007, and an additional two RARs regarding officer-involved shootings, one from 2006 and another from 2010.  NOPD's oversight of its officers' use of deadly force has been so perfunctory that until we inquired, PIB had not requested the Homicide Division to provide these long-overdue investigations.  Moreover, when we asked for all of NOPD's officer-involved shooting investigations during a given time period, NOPD initially provided investigations for only approximately one-half of the incidents.  It was only after repeated additional inquires that NOPD was able to locate and provide a list of all officer-involved shootings as well as the related investigative case files.

Even in the cases where it has a complete investigative file, PIB has not conducted "hearings" in a timely manner.  As of September 2010, in addition to the fourteen cases that could not be completed because Homicide had not provided the files to PIB, an additional eleven cases were completed but awaiting hearing.  One of these cases dated from 2008 and several were from 2009.  NOPD's failure to complete reviews of some officer-involved shootings in a timely manner unnecessarily compromises officer and civilian safety, and subjects the City and Department to substantial liability risks.

Alongside its efforts to improve investigations of critical incidents like officer-involved shootings, NOPD reports it is remaking its process for reviewing such incidents, moving towards an interdisciplinary force review "board."  Whether this board is effective at preventing misconduct and increasing officer safety will depend upon how NOPD structures and supports this board.

(2)    Review of Non-Deadly Force Incidents

In addition to failing to ensure that non-deadly force is reported and investigated, NOPD also fails to adequately review the non-deadly force used by its officers.  By policy, PIB is responsible for reviewing all NOPD uses of force, but we found this review has been deliberately, albeit implicitly, narrowed over the years and is currently largely ministerial. A number of PIB protocols, read together, provide for expansive use of force review. PIB Operations Directive #17 states that PIB's Professional Standards Section is responsible for complying with the requirements of Ops. Man. Ch. 1.3, *Resisting Arrest Report*,[16] by conducting a "continual analysis" of use of force reports received during the calendar year and submitting periodic reports. Chapter 1.3 provides that PIB is responsible for the "collection, review, analysis, and dissemination of information gained from the 'Resisting Arrest Reports.'" The policy further specifies that this review should determine: 1) whether Department policy and procedures were adhered to; 2) whether policy and procedures are clearly understandable to the employee and effective to cover the situation; 3) whether Department training is adequate; and 4) whether Department equipment is adequate. The PIB Directive further provides that reports analyzing use of force are to be submitted quarterly, or more frequently as needed, to the Deputy Superintendent of PIB. An annual report summarizing the quarterly reports is required to be submitted to PIB's Deputy Superintendent annually. Chapter 1.3 requires that a written, yearly analysis summarizing use of force incidents be submitted to the Superintendent.

The use of force review contemplated by NOPD policy is appropriate; unfortunately, none of this mandated use of force review or analysis is or has been occurring, at least for the past several years. Our interview of PIB staff and review of documents indicated that PIB's review of use of force, at least in recent years, has been limited to the narrow report review mandated by PIB Directive #27, which does not acknowledge the existence of the more expansive PIB Directive #17. PIB Directive #27 requires review of NOPD's use of force reports to ensure that they are "completed as required" and to correct "any deficiencies in the form completion." It appears that Directive #27 was added without consideration of Directive #17 and that no attempt has been made to update the former directive or to otherwise make consistent PIB's responsibilities pursuant to each directive. Our conversations with NOPD officials made clear that the sergeant PIB assigned to review use of force reports was given a narrow mandate for reviewing force. He did not appear aware of any responsibilities beyond the minimal facial review required by Directive #27, nor had he been trained in the more substantial force review contemplated by Directive #17 and Chapter 1.3. Accordingly, this sergeant reported providing some ad hoc feedback to supervisors regarding their officers' use of force, but stated that generally feedback is related to ensuring that use of force reports are filled out completely.

NOPD's use of force review is further undermined by NOPD policies and practices that diffuse responsibility for reviewing force while not demanding accountability to ensure that review by anyone actually occurs. Thus, while some policies nominally place responsibility for use of force review, tracking, and reporting on PIB, other NOPD policies and practices act to divest PIB of some of its authority to review and determine the propriety of force. Integrity Control Officers ("ICOs"), who report to District Commanders, not PIB, are required to review two in-car camera videos per day and "note any deficiencies and [counsel] officers as needed." Our interviews with staff throughout NOPD confirmed that there is no consultation with PIB by the Training Division or ICOs when making these determinations. The RAR form itself contains a distribution list for the completed report, which includes PIB, the Unit Commander, the

---

[16] PIB Operations Directive #17 refers to this Chapter as "Use of Force Report," but this reference appears outdated, as this Chapter is currently called "Resisting Arrest Report."

- 24 -

Division Commander, the Bureau Assistant Superintendent, and the Superintendent, but there is no indication of what, if any responsibility for review any of these offices besides PIB has.

*e)     Force Data Review and Response*

NOPD has implemented a number of systems that require the review of aggregate force data to identify concerns and positive and negative trends, including NOPD's early warning system, called Personnel Performance Enhancement Program ("PPEP"), and the collection and review of force data by PIB. Neither of these systems is functioning as necessary to be effective, or as required by policy.

(1)     Early Warning System

The development and implementation of NOPD's new early warning system will better enable NOPD to track and analyze force data. NOPD's current system, set out in Ops. Man. Ch. 13.27, *Professional Performance Enhancement Program (PPEP)*, is outdated and essentially exists in name only. Officers of every rank and throughout the Department told us that information is only haphazardly submitted for inclusion in the database, and being subjected to the program's single intervention—a one-size-fits all course commonly referred to as "bad boy school"—reportedly is seen by some as a badge of honor. There has been only one of these classes in the past eight months while NOPD implements a new program that will provide more individualized interventions and will make a professionalism and courtesy course part of in-service training for every employee.

To be effective, NOPD's early warning system should be re-tooled so that it is a single-source of real time information that can assist line supervisors and upper level commanders alike in identifying officers who may need closer supervision or particular interventions. Interventions developed based on early warning system data should be tailored to the specific problem presented, and the intervention should be monitored and refined as necessary until the problem is resolved. Part of this function should be identifying use of force outliers, determining whether the aberration is meaningful and needs correction, and monitoring interventions to determine that any use of force problems have been resolved.

NOPD, in conjunction with the Independent Police Monitor, is currently working to implement new software and hardware to create a more comprehensive and current early warning system. Alongside this effort, NOPD must ensure that the appropriate policies and training related to the early warning system are developed and implemented, and that provisions are made to ensure the ongoing maintenance of the hardware and database. More generally, NOPD should work closely with the Independent Police Monitor to analyze and respond to force trends.

(2)     PIB Data Collection

PIB collects a broad variety of complaint, investigation, and use of force data and reports this information in lengthy annual and statistical reports. These reports, required by NOPD policy, are quite detailed, including, for example, types of complaints by assignment, district and

- 25 -

281

rank; identifying the officers with the most complaints, including the type and resolution of each complaint; and listing a breakdown of complaints by race and gender of the officer. This information, however, is unaccompanied by any analysis or discussion of how this raw data might be used to help decrease misconduct complaints through, for example, prioritizing training areas or changing oversight mechanisms. It is significant and laudable that NOPD is gathering and tracking this data. However, without analysis of the data for such purposes as developing policy and identifying training needs, collecting and aggregating this data amounts to a substantial amount of work with little tangible benefit.

(3)    COMSTAT

COMSTAT provides another opportunity for NOPD to prevent force misconduct by discussing use of force trends and directly comparing the use of force rates of various units, Districts, and other strata with their similarly situated peers; their respective arrest rates; the rate of misconduct complaints; and the quality of arrests, i.e. whether and what type of prosecutions result from the arrests. ICOs are required to report to COMSTAT each week a variety of integrity related data. In the several COMSTAT meetings that we attended we never saw this data presented. Use of force data can be included in the data ICOs compile for COMSTAT and substantively discussed at COMSTAT meetings.

## III.    <u>STOPS, SEARCHES AND ARRESTS</u>

Our investigation also provided reasonable cause to believe that NOPD officers violate the Fourth Amendment by engaging in a pattern or practice of stopping, searching, and arresting individuals without the requisite reasonable suspicion or probable cause.

A.    Legal Standards

The Fourth Amendment guarantees in part, "the right of the people to be secure in their persons, houses, papers, and effects, against unreasonable searches and seizures." U.S. CONST. amend. IV. Generally, a search or seizure is unreasonable "in the absence of individualized suspicion of wrongdoing." *City of Indianapolis v. Edmond*, 531 U.S. 32, 37 (2000). Under the Fourth Amendment, "[a] person is seized if 'taking into account all of the circumstances surrounding the encounter, the police conduct would have communicated to a reasonable person that he was not at liberty to ignore the police presence and go about his business.'" *United States v. De Jesus-Batres*, 410 F.3d 154, 160 (5th Cir. 2005) (quoting *Kaupp v. Texas*, 538 U.S. 626, 629 (2003)).

Probable cause supporting an arrest exists only where the facts and circumstances within the arresting officer's knowledge "are sufficient to warrant a prudent person . . . in believing, in the circumstances shown, that the suspect has committed, is committing, or is about to commit an offense." *Club Retro L.L.C. v. Hilton*, 568 F.3d 181, 204 (5th Cir. 2009). The facts "must be particularized to the arrestee," *Id.* (quoting *Ybarra v. Illinois*, 444 U.S. 85, 91 (1979)), and "must be known to the officer at the time of the arrest; post-hoc justifications based on facts later learned cannot support an earlier arrest." *Id.*

- 26 -

Absent probable cause, the Fourth Amendment permits law enforcement officers to briefly detain individuals for investigative purposes if the officers possess reasonable suspicion that criminal activity is afoot. *Terry v. Ohio*, 392 U.S. 1, 21 (1968). Reasonable suspicion must be supported by articulable facts particular to the detained individual, which, combined with "rational inferences from those facts, reasonably warrant an intrusion." *United States v. Michelletti*, 13 F.3d 838, 840 (5th Cir. 1994). To justify a *Terry* stop, officers must possess "more than a hunch" that an individual may engage in wrongdoing. *Id.* at 840. Notably, the suspected behavior must constitute an actual violation of the law. If a police officer incorrectly interprets the law in seizing a person, a Fourth Amendment violation has occurred even if the officer's factual observations were correct or the officer's interpretation of the law was made in good faith. *See United States v. Lopez-Valdez*, 178 F.3d 282, 288 (5th Cir. 1999) (finding that stop reliant upon officer's mistaken interpretation of state traffic law violated the Fourth Amendment because "the legal justification [for a stop] must be objectively grounded," internal quotation marks omitted).

Under limited circumstances, an officer may briefly search a detained individual for weapons incident to a valid *Terry* stop. A *Terry* weapons search must be premised on "individualized suspicion" derived from "specific and articulable facts" that a suspect "is armed and dangerous" or "may gain immediate control of weapons." *Maryland v. Buie*, 494 U.S. 325, 332-334 (1990). *See also Arizona v. Johnson*, 129 S. Ct. 781, 784-786 (2009); *United States v. Rideau*, 969 F.2d 1572, 1575 (5th Cir. 1992). During a lawful *Terry* weapons search, a law enforcement officer may also seize objects whose incriminating nature is immediately apparent. *Minnesota v. Dickerson*, 508 U.S. 366, 375-376 (1993). Nonetheless, courts are "sensitive to the danger . . . that officers will enlarge a specific authorization, furnished by a warrant or an exigency, into the equivalent of a general warrant to rummage and seize at will." *Id.* at 378. Thus, to seize evidence under the "plain feel" exception, an officer must first have probable cause to believe that the item is contraband. *Id.* at 376-377.

B.     Findings

NOPD's policies and training on warrantless searches and seizures are highly inadequate, leaving officers with little guidance regarding the Fourth Amendment's limitations on their authority to detain, search, and arrest. A previous DOJ investigation noted almost ten years ago that some NOPD officers could not articulate proper legal standards for stops, searches, or arrests. We recommended then that NOPD provide annual in-service training to officers on this critical topic. As discussed below, NOPD still does not provide meaningful in-service training to officers on how to properly carry out stops, searches, and arrests. Throughout the Department, and among other stakeholders in the criminal justice system, we heard broad and emphatic consensus that officers have a poor understanding of how to lawfully execute searches and seizures. NOPD's failure to train officers or otherwise provide guidance on the limits and requirements of the Fourth Amendment contributes directly to the pattern of unconstitutional stops, searches, and arrests we observed. Additionally, the Department's organizational focus on arrests encourages stops without reasonable suspicion, illegal pat downs, and arrests without probable cause.

1.      Inadequate Policies and Training

NOPD's written policies governing warrantless search and seizure provide insufficient detail and explanation to adequately guide officers' conduct.  A clear example is Ops. Man. Ch. 41.3, regarding field interviews and stops and frisks.  The policy, which was placed in effect August 29, 1999 and last updated on October 5, 2003, is just four pages long, and only two paragraphs provide officers with direction on the appropriate legal standards for initiating an investigatory stop and/or frisk under *Terry*.  While the policy provides a canned list of recognized facts used to justify a *Terry* stop, it does not instruct officers that most of these facts standing alone are insufficient—effectively glossing over the requirement that to establish reasonable suspicion under *Terry*, officers must have articulable facts that, when considered together, provide evidence that a crime is about to be, is being, or has been committed.  Overall, the policy fails to provide clear and comprehensive guidance on stops and frisks, while its tone serves to minimize the *Terry* standard in a manner that may promote improper stops.

We also found officer training on search and seizure to be deficient in both content and frequency.  Officers, including uniform patrol, detectives, and members of narcotics and task force units, consistently reported to us that they received search and seizure training in their original recruit class, but no yearly in-service training to update and reinforce their understanding of the law and of NOPD policy.  NOPD's recruit training schedule reflects that a current patrol officer with a law degree teaches several legal blocks related to search and seizure.  Typically, however, training divisions secure outside instructors who have a current and thorough knowledge of Fourth Amendment issues, such as law school professors or attorneys regularly encountering search and seizure issues in court.  As discussed in the Training section of this Report, NOPD's Fourth Amendment training curriculum does not reflect either current or thorough knowledge of this critical area.  The USAO has in the past offered free search and seizure instruction to the Department, but only a small fraction of the force took advantage of the training.  Indeed, only recently has NOPD leadership appeared receptive and welcoming of outside training opportunities.

We saw no evidence of efforts to reinforce or build upon what officers learn in the Academy related to search and seizure, or to provide officers with legal updates on this constantly-evolving area of law.  Officers at all levels, criminal court judges, and prosecutors uniformly pointed to a need to augment and enhance NOPD's search and seizure training.  Indeed, one district commander told us: "This gets us in so much trouble," pointing to the need for training in "justification for detaining someone, when you have PC [probable cause], when you put your hands on someone."  The same commander observed that what cadets "learn at the Academy is sucked right out of their heads as soon as they leave," reflecting the reality that once in the field, officers forget what they learned due to non-use and/or other officers exchanging common misconceptions of law.  Without regular refresher courses to correct misconceptions and mistakes, NOPD risks institutionalizing common legal errors and converting them into de facto operating methods.

The consequences of the Department's lapses with respect to training were evident in our interviews with officers who displayed a profound lack of understanding of the limits of *Terry*.  For example, one officer, when asked about the appropriate length of time for a *Terry* stop,

- 28 -

responded that he had the right to detain a person for a period of one hour. He did not identify any particularized circumstances that might justify a detention of that length, but rather appeared to believe it was presumptively appropriate. In another exchange, several officers were queried about the circumstances under which they could conduct a pat down for weapons. The officers responded that they had the right to check anyone detained to ensure the officer's safety. In fact, the law is clear that an officer can only conduct a pat down when he has reasonable articulable facts to support that the subject is armed and dangerous. Deficiencies in NOPD's policies and training have left officers with an unacceptably poor understanding of how to constitutionally execute warrantless searches and seizures.

2.        Organizational Focus on Arrests

Additionally, we found that NOPD's focus on statistics, such as generating Field Interview Cards ("FIC"s) and arrests, amplifies the risk that officers will execute illegal searches and seizures. As one commander told us, "[t]hese officers are under the gun to make arrest, arrest, arrest, which leads to civil rights violations and complaints." NOPD patrol officers and many members of the command staff described a Department that has long been statistics-driven—one that measures "productivity" by quantity, rather than quality, of encounters and arrests. We observed that arrests, *Terry* stops, and FIC numbers were the predominant focus of the Department's weekly COMSTAT meetings, and many officers described a strong and unyielding pressure to increase numbers.

Officers throughout NOPD told us that pressure to make arrests and engage in sufficient "activity" to satisfy command staff and NOPD brass encourages aggressive enforcement of low-level infractions, and diverts attention and resources from quality arrests leading to significant convictions. Indeed, in 2009, NOPD made nearly 60,000 arrests, of which about 20,000 were of people with outstanding traffic or misdemeanor warrants from neighboring parishes for such infractions as unpaid tickets. By mid-2010, the Department had made nearly 10,000 arrests on outstanding warrants, about two-thirds of which were for minor out-of-parish warrants, according to reports from the Metropolitan Crime Commission, a New Orleans-based non-profit organization.

Additionally, NOPD's database of documented field interviews appears to reflect a dramatic recent uptick. For four months, from June 1, 2010 through October 1, 2010, NOPD recorded in its FIC database nearly 24,000 field interviews, compared with about 29,800 for three and a half years, from 2007 through May 31, 2010. Of course, this increase may partially reflect both better reporting and increased use of the electronic database (although some officers continue to use physical field interview cards and store them in individual districts). Nonetheless, it is consistent with reports from both officers and the community of more intense field-interview activity in recent months. At the same time, it was apparent during our interviews that officers lack a uniform understanding regarding the completion, use, and preservation of FICs. Some officers stated they prepared FICs only in "special cases," while others said they prepared FICs on people they encountered during traffic stops and calls for service.

- 29 -

The pressure to achieve a high volume of field interviews comes with little correlative emphasis on gathering and using quality intelligence. Officers reported that they rarely, if ever, find FIC data useful. Moreover, NOPD retains FIC data longer than such information could be considered relevant or timely; the Department appears not to have ever expunged sensitive information from the database, though it is available to all sworn officers and contains personal data such as social security numbers. FIC cards and the FIC database are also of little use as documentation of *Terry* stops. Although a *Terry* stop requires a factual basis to establish that a crime is about to be or has been committed, neither the physical FIC card nor database has any place to list the suspected crime. Moreover, FICs lack a narrative portion for the officer to specifically articulate the basis for the stop. Overall, we found that the Department's exclusive focus on the number of FICs prepared may institutionalize and encourage officers to make illegal stops.

Recently, NOPD acknowledged that the Department's staggering volume of arrests for low-level offenses is counter-productive. In November 2010, according to the *Times-Picayune*, the Superintendent advised the City Council that officers would no longer make arrests based on outstanding traffic or misdemeanor warrants from neighboring parishes, noting that to do so "simply does not make sense, economical or common." We believe that with this pledge the Department has taken a significant and positive step. Nonetheless, we found the emphasis on "activity," defined as numbers of encounters such as stops, field interview cards, and arrests—at the expense of a more deliberate focus on problem-solving—to be an ingrained part of NOPD's organizational culture. Although the Superintendent's commitment to ensuring that officers are engaged, observant, and productive is commendable and appropriate, the Department must recognize that its tactics and chosen police strategy, together with lapses in training and policy, cultivate an atmosphere where officers cut corners and make too many errors that result in constitutional harm and compromise effective law enforcement. This was fully apparent in our review of NOPD arrest reports.

3.      Failure to Properly Justify Stops, Searches, and Arrests

We find reasonable cause to believe that NOPD's lack of adequate policy and training regarding search and seizure, along with the Department's emphasis on arrest numbers, contribute to the frequency of constitutional violations we found reflected in arrest reports. We reviewed 145 randomly-sampled arrest reports to determine whether the officers articulated sufficient facts to justify arrests, searches, or pat downs. Many of the reports that NOPD provided involved circumstances in which NOPD did not initiate the stop or arrest, for example where a store owner detained a suspect, and NOPD merely effectuated the arrest, or where the NOPD responded to a scene after learning of an outstanding warrant. Of those arrests that NOPD initiated—involving either warrantless search or seizure or execution of a search warrant—we found that a significant portion reflected constitutional deficiencies. Our review confirmed serious gaps in knowledge, and included examples of illegal detentions, searches, and pat downs, as well as arrests without probable cause to establish the elements of the crimes. Moreover, because our review encompassed only arrest reports, it would not capture stops and/or searches where the officer did not find contraband or effectuate an arrest, encounters which have a potentially higher rate of impropriety.

- 30 -

Each of these deficient reports reflected not only an NOPD officer's illegal search or seizure, but also a supervisor's failure to adequately review the arrest report, as required. For instance, in one case, while the officer had reasonable suspicion to make a *Terry* stop, the report referenced no information or facts to demonstrate reasonable suspicion that the subject was armed and dangerous. Nonetheless, the officer performed a *Terry* frisk and found a packet containing synthetic marijuana. The report failed to state any reason for the frisk, or what facts, upon feeling the packet, justified a search into the pockets to retrieve the drugs, using the "plain feel rule." In another case involving an apparently illegal search, officers opened the closed backpack of a suspect without consent, removed an iPod believed to be stolen, and arrested the juvenile suspect.

In another instance, an officer received a "suspicious person" call from the dispatcher, but the arrest records reflected no specific articulable facts to justify a *Terry* stop. Although the officer made a traffic stop based on the suspicious person call and found stolen property in the car, the report is totally devoid of facts demonstrating a reasonable suspicion to make the stop or probable cause to search the vehicle. A citizen complaint of a "suspicious person" alone is insufficient to authorize a *Terry* stop; the officer must still have the specific facts to articulate the justification for the detention. *See United States v. Gomez*, 623 F.3d 265 (5th Cir. 2010) (holding that in a *Terry* stop resulting from a citizen telephone caller the officer must have specific detailed information from the caller that would satisfy the articulable suspicion standard).

We also found examples of arrests for which the reports failed to state probable cause to support a criminal violation. In one case involving a juvenile arrest for curfew violation, the arrest report provides no narrative whatsoever describing why officers believed a curfew violation occurred, and therefore no facts to justify a stop, detention or arrest of the juvenile. In several situations, reports reflected that officers executed search warrants for narcotics at residences, and then transported individuals who were merely present at the scene to districts stations for interrogation, without stating any facts to justify their detention or arrest.

Overall, our review of arrest reports reflected what many within and outside of the Department told us during our review: that inadequate policies and training have left officers without the basic foundation to perform their duties within constitutional boundaries. Further, as discussed in the next section of this Report, these factors increase the likelihood that officers, unable to properly perceive and articulate reasonable suspicion and probable cause, may either stop individuals arbitrarily or rely on impermissible factors such as an individual's race, ethnicity, or national origin.


## IV.    <u>DISCRIMINATORY POLICING</u>

We find reasonable cause to believe that NOPD engages in a pattern or practice of discriminatory policing in violation of constitutional and statutory law. Discriminatory policing occurs when police officers and departments unfairly enforce the law—or fail to enforce the law—based on characteristics such as race, ethnicity, national origin, sex, religion, or LGBT status. Discriminatory policing may take the form of bias-based profiling, in which an officer decides whom to stop, search, or arrest based upon one of the above-mentioned characteristics,

- 31 -

rather than on the subject's behavior or on credible information identifying the subject as having engaged in criminal activity. Denying police services to some persons or communities because of bias or stereotypes, or failing to take meaningful steps to enable communication, also constitute discriminatory policing. Discriminatory policing may also result when a police department selects particular enforcement and crime prevention tactics in certain communities or against certain individuals for reasons motivated by bias or stereotype.

NOPD has failed to take sufficient steps to detect, prevent, or address bias-based profiling and other forms of discriminatory policing on the basis of race, ethnicity, or LGBT status, despite widespread concern and troubling racial disparities in arrest rates and other data. We further find that the Department fails to adequately investigate violence against women, including sexual assaults and domestic violence. Additionally, we find that the Department fails to provide critical policing services to New Orleans residents with limited English proficiency.

      A.       Legal Standards

      1.       Fourteenth Amendment

The Equal Protection Clause of the Fourteenth Amendment prohibits selective or discriminatory enforcement of the law. *Whren v. United States*, 517 U.S. 806, 813 (1996). Discriminatory policing may arise from an explicit classification or a facially neutral law or policy. *Id.* In the latter case, an Equal Protection violation occurs when the government's administration of the facially neutral law is motivated by a discriminatory purpose and results in a discriminatory effect. *See Washington v. Davis*, 426 U.S. 229, 239-40 (1976); *Taylor v. Johnson*, 257 F.3d 470, 473 (5th Cir. 2001). Evidence of discriminatory effect may include evidence of similarly situated individuals who were not subjected to the enforcement action, statistical evidence, or both. *United States v. Armstrong*, 517 U.S. 456, 467 (1996). To assess discriminatory intent, courts consider direct and circumstantial evidence, including contemporaneous statements by decision makers, the impact of the challenged policy or action on different groups, patterns of conduct, historical background, substantive departures from normal procedure, and the sequence of events leading up to the adoption of the policy or action. *Village of Arlington Heights v. Metro. Hous. Dev. Corp.*, 429 U.S. 252, 265-66 (1977). Further, a plaintiff may illuminate discriminatory motives by showing a "clear pattern, unexplainable on grounds other than race." *Id.* (citing *Yick Wo v. Hopkins*, 118 U.S. 356 (1886) and *Gomillion v. Lightfoot*, 364 U.S. 339 (1960)). The Fourteenth Amendment does not require proof that the government actor was motivated solely by a discriminatory purpose, but only that such purpose was a contributing factor. *Arlington Heights*, 429 U.S. at 265-66.

This admonition applies equally to discriminatory inaction – such as law enforcement practices that systematically under-serve certain communities. As the Supreme Court has explained, "the Fourteenth Amendment not only prohibits the making or enforcing of laws which shall abridge the privileges of the citizen, but prohibits the states from denying to all persons within its jurisdiction the equal protection of the laws. Denying includes inaction as well as action, and denying the equal protection of the laws includes the omission to protect." *Bell v. Maryland*, 378 U.S. 226, 311 (1964) (Goldberg, J. concurring). *See also DeShaney v. Winnebago County Dep't of Soc. Servs.*, 489 U.S. 189, 197, n.3 (states may not "selectively deny

- 32 -

its protective services" to certain protected groups without violating the Equal Protection Clause.). Many courts, including the Fifth Circuit, have extended this principle to under-enforcement of sexual and domestic violence where such under-enforcement adversely impacts women. *See, e.g., Shipp v. McMahon*, 234 F.3d 907, 916 (5th Cir. 2000); *Beltran v. City of El Paso*, 367 F.3d 299, 305 (5th Cir. 2004).[17]

Finally, we note that a number of factors weigh in favor of applying heightened scrutiny in the context of discrimination by law enforcement on the basis of sexual orientation and gender identity, including a long history of animus and deeply-rooted stereotypes about lesbian, gay, bisexual, and transgender ("LGBT") individuals. As the Attorney General recently noted, "there is, regrettably, a significant history of purposeful discrimination against gay and lesbian people, by governmental as well as private entities, based on prejudice and stereotypes that continue to have ramifications today. Indeed, until very recently, states have 'demean[ed] the[] existence" of gays and lesbians "by making their private sexual conduct a crime.'" Letter from Attorney General Eric Holder to the Hon. John A. Boehner (Feb. 23, 2011) (quoting *Lawrence v. Texas*, 539 U.S. 558, 578 (2003)). We found this dynamic clearly at work in New Orleans.

2.      Safe Streets Act

Discriminatory law enforcement activities are likewise prohibited by the Safe Streets Act, which provides that "[n]o person in any State shall on the ground of race, color, religion, national origin, or sex be excluded from participation in, be denied the benefits of, or be subjected to discrimination under or denied employment in connection with any programs or activity funded in whole or in part with funds made available under this title." 42 U.S.C. § 3789d(c)(1). NOPD is a program recipient under the Safe Streets Act. The statutory text and implementing regulations make clear that the Act applies not only to intentional discrimination, but also to any law-enforcement practices that disparately impact an identified group based on the enumerated factors. The non-discrimination regulation implementing Section 3789d(c) prohibits program recipients from "utiliz[ing] criteria or methods of administration which have the effect of subjecting individuals to discrimination under [§ 3789d(c)], or have the effect of defeating or substantially impairing accomplishment of the objectives of the program as respects individuals of a particular race, color, sex, national origin, or religion." 28 C.F.R. § 42.203.

3.      Title VI

Similarly, Title VI provides that "[n]o person in the United States shall, on the ground of race, color, or national origin, be excluded from participation in, be denied the benefits of, or be subjected to discrimination under any program or activity receiving Federal financial assistance." 42 U.S.C. § 2000d. NOPD is a program recipient under Title VI.

Title VI prohibits intentional discrimination, *see Alexander v. Sandoval*, 532 U.S. 275, 281 (2001), and the Title VI regulations proscribe law-enforcement activities that exert a discriminatory effect on the basis of race, color, or national origin. *See Sandoval*, 532 U.S. at

---

[17] While the cases following *Shipp* address domestic violence specifically, federal courts have adopted a substantially similar standard for § 1983 claims addressing failure to report and investigate allegations of sexual abuse. *See, e.g., Michels v. Greenwood Lake Police Department*, 387 F. Supp. 2d 361, 366 (S.D.N.Y. 2005).

281-282; *see also* 28 C.F.R. § 42.104(b)(2) (Title VI funding recipients may not "utilize criteria or methods of administration which have the effect of subjecting individuals to discrimination because of their race, color, or national origin.").

The Supreme Court has held that failing to take reasonable steps to ensure meaningful access for limited English proficient ("LEP") persons is a form of national-origin discrimination prohibited by Title VI regulations. *See Lau v. Nichols*, 414 U.S. 563 (1974). Executive Order 13166, issued in 2000, reinforced that mandate by directing federal agencies to publish LEP guidance for their financial assistance recipients, consistent with initial general guidance from DOJ. *See* 65 Fed. Reg. 50121 (Aug. 16, 2000). In 2002, DOJ issued final *Guidance to Federal Financial Assistance Recipients Regarding Title VI Prohibition against National Origin Discrimination Affecting Limited English Proficient Persons.* 67 Fed. Reg. 41455 (June 18, 2002) (DOJ Guidance).

    B.      Findings

        1.      Discriminatory Policing on the Basis of Race, Ethnicity, and LGBT Status

When law enforcement subjects individuals to differential treatment, based on a belief that characteristics such as race, ethnicity, national origin, gender, or religion signal a higher risk of criminality or unlawful activity, it constitutes unlawful discrimination, often called "profiling" or "biased policing." Law enforcement's consideration of the above listed characteristics in its decision-making is only permissible in very limited circumstances, such as when an officer has specific information, based on credible sources, to "be on the lookout" for specific individuals identified in part by race, ethnicity, or other personal identifying characteristics.

We find reasonable cause to believe that there is a pattern or practice of unconstitutional conduct and/or violations of federal law with respect to discriminatory policing. NOPD personnel at all levels of the Department not only acknowledged that the community perceives racial and ethnic profiling as a significant problem, but some also expressed their own belief that such discriminatory conduct occurs. Both bias and the perception of bias erode citizens' inclination to trust and cooperate with law enforcement, impeding effective and safe policing. Although both community members and officers told us that this dynamic is clearly at work in New Orleans, the Department has failed to respond with systems to prevent, detect, and respond to discriminatory policing, and to ensure that police officers are conducting themselves in accordance with constitutional guarantees of equal protection.

The Department's inadequate policies and training in conducting proper stops, searches, and arrests increase the likelihood that officers, without sufficient understanding of how to identify and articulate suspicion based on behavior and other permissible factors, will instead rely on inappropriate stereotypes and bias in their decision-making. At the same time, NOPD fails to acknowledge the potential for stereotypes and bias to taint police work, on both an individual and an organizational level, and to take steps to prevent this through proactive policies, messaging from leadership, supervision, and training. The Department does not have a sufficiently comprehensive policy regarding discriminatory policing, fails to adhere to those policies that are in place, has no way to track allegations and complaints of racial profiling, and

- 34 -

does not collect, analyze, or report race or ethnicity data for most citizen encounters with police. This failure to counteract bias and promote impartial policing further cultivates an atmosphere in which discriminatory policing can occur unchecked.

The data that we have been able to review, though haphazard and incomplete, points to troubling disparities in treatment of the City's African-American community, and an urgent need to implement systems to ensure that the Department is providing services and enforcing the law in a fair, equitable, and nondiscriminatory manner.

### a)      *Community Concerns*

NOPD's statistics-driven approach to policing appears to contribute to the strong community perception of bias in stops, arrests, and other encounters.  Individuals we spoke with, particularly youth, African Americans, ethnic minorities, and members of the LGBT community, told of frequent stops and of being targeted, booked, and arrested for minor infractions.  They consistently described how these tactics serve to drive a wedge between the police and the public, antagonizing and alienating members of the community.

Many individuals with whom we spoke directly linked biased policing to what they describe as a focus on maximizing arrests, as opposed to reducing serious crime.  In a complaint to PIB, one man alleged that he had been pulled over for "being a black man driving a nice car." The officers told PIB that they had stopped the man for following another car too closely, ran the driver's name, and arrested him for having an outstanding warrant for an unpaid seatbelt ticket in another city.  The driver, who was handcuffed and then booked into Orleans Parish Prison, wrote in his complaint: "Forgive me if I seem to be prehistoric, but I thought racial profiling was illegal.  One good thing happened, [the officer] got his arrest credit."

Regardless of whether this specific driver was in fact following a car more closely than allowed by law, the complaint clearly conveys the individual's frustration and belief that officers would never have stopped him for this type of infraction, much less handcuffed and jailed him, but for his race and the Department's emphasis on arrests for minor violations.  Whatever the reason for stops and arrests like this one, there is little question that the frequency and tenor of police encounters has deeply alienated many segments of the New Orleans community.  One Orleans Parish criminal court judge told us that "[i]f you are a black teenager and grew up in New Orleans, I guarantee you have had a bad incident with the police." African-American residents consistently cited negative encounters with police as a source of deep distrust of law enforcement, reporting experiences with discourtesy, harassment, and unwarranted stops, arrests, and uses of force.  Community members often raised specific concerns over task forces, whose members wear distinctive military-style uniforms and are referred to throughout the City (and colloquially within the police department) as "jump out boys." One sergeant, assigned to a community relations position, acknowledged that the task forces "are perceived by the community as jump out boys, dirty cops, the ones who are going to be brutal."

While task forces can play an important role in combating chronic and complex crime problems, we did not observe NOPD to be providing the kind of direction, hands-on supervision, monitoring, and training in problem-solving that task forces require.  The Department relies

- 35 -

heavily on task forces as the sole "enforcers" and agents of crime control for the City, while also measuring productivity by numbers of stops and arrests, and failing to provide officers with adequate training and supervision. This combination invites problematic encounters with citizens, and raises the risk that officers will rely on inappropriate considerations such as race in the course of discharging their duties. Although task forces and specialized units tasked with crime suppression typically generate more citizen complaints than other components of a police department, simply because there is a greater potential for negative encounters with members of the public, NOPD will not begin to repair the reputation of its task forces, particularly among the African-American residents in many of New Orleans' neighborhoods, without a shift in emphasis towards community policing and adequate training and supervision.

Latinos in New Orleans, especially young Latino males, reported that NOPD officers stop them for unknown reasons or for minor offenses that would not ordinarily merit police attention, and then question them regarding immigration status. Members of the Latino community also told us they believe they are pulled over at a higher rate than other drivers for minor traffic violations, because officers assume from their appearance that they are undocumented immigrants, and therefore driving without a valid license. NOPD's position on inquiring about immigration status has been in flux; recently, however, the Superintendent clarified that officers may not question victims of crime about whether they are lawfully present in the country. Nonetheless, members of the Latino immigrant worker community, who are frequently victimized because they tend to carry cash on their person, reported a deep reluctance to report crime—either as victims or witnesses. We heard reports of specific incidents in which immigrant workers called to request police assistance after being victimized by crime, but instead of providing assistance, NOPD officers questioned them about their immigration status. Consequently, we found a strong belief among some segments of the Latino community that reporting crime to NOPD may subject the reporter to unwanted attention or harassment. As one participant in a community meeting told us: "Out of fear, we stay quiet."

Members of the LGBT community complained that NOPD officers subject them to unjustified arrests for prostitution, targeting bars frequented by the community and sometimes fabricating evidence of solicitation for compensation. Moreover, transgender residents reported that officers elect to charge them under Louisiana's statute criminalizing solicitation of "crimes against nature," rather than the state's generic solicitation law. The crimes against nature statute, a statute whose history reflects anti-LGBT sentiment, in part criminalizes the solicitation of an individual "with the intent to engage in any unnatural carnal copulation for compensation." Louisiana Revised Statute § 14:89. Until August 2010, a first offense under this statute constituted a felony and required registration in the sex offender registry, unlike the general prostitution statute. Although the state legislature equalized penalties for a first conviction, a second conviction under the crimes against nature statute still requires registration as a sex offender. Persons convicted only of soliciting crimes against nature make up nearly 40 percent of the Orleans Parish sex offender registry. NOPD is charged with monitoring all registrants' compliance with sex offender registry requirements, raising questions about efficient and effective use of resources to ensure public safety. Further, for the already vulnerable transgender community, inclusion on the sex offender registry further stigmatizes and marginalizes them, complicating efforts to secure jobs, housing, and obtain services at places like publicly-run emergency shelters. Of the registrants convicted of solicitation of a crime against nature, 80 percent are African American, suggesting an element of racial bias as well. Indeed, community members told us they believe some officers equate being African American and transgender with being a prostitute.

Further, members of the City's LGBT community gave accounts of harassment and even sexual and physical abuse by law enforcement. The community cited a culture within NOPD of insensitivity and animosity, and our own interviews and observations of inappropriate joking underscored a need for sensitivity training and education regarding LGBT issues. A number of community members also complained of a long-standing failure by NOPD to take complaints by LGBT individuals seriously, with several reporting that PIB had failed to act on their complaints of officer misconduct. While NOPD has a policy prohibiting discrimination based on sexual orientation, PIB has no system or mechanism for tracking or analyzing complaints alleging bias or misconduct based on sexual orientation or gender expression.

### b)  Policies, Training, and Accountability

Although the Department acknowledges the perception of biased policing, and officers at the highest levels of the Department acknowledge that it sometimes occurs, NOPD has failed to put in place systems and measures to detect, prevent, and respond to allegations of profiling and other forms of biased policing. The Department's policies on biased policing contain many essential elements, but are not sufficiently detailed to guide officers' conduct, and do not contain a sufficiently clear or emphatic statement of purpose. A police agency's profiling policy should serve to embed principles of bias-free policing and set clear expectations for officers regarding their conduct. We also found that the Department fails to adhere to existing policy in many respects.

The Department's policy on "bias-based profiling," Ops. Man. Ch. 41.6, contains many appropriate elements, including a broad statement prohibiting "bias-based profiling," a restatement of the reasonable suspicion standard for investigatory detentions, and a directive that outside of a credible report, "an individual's race, gender, sexual orientation, or ethnicity or any combination thereof, shall not be a factor in determining probable cause for an arrest, the reasonable suspicion for a stop, or asset seizure and forfeiture efforts." Although this directive is appropriate, the policy is internally inconsistent in that it also defines profiling as reliance "solely" on one of the delineated characteristics—an inappropriately narrow construction.

Chapter 41.6 also requires the Education and Training Division to formulate a lesson plan on bias-based profiling, and to teach this course to each recruit class and to each commissioned employee during his or her yearly in-service training. Although recruits do receive a one-hour block at the Academy, many NOPD personnel until recently had received no in-service training since Hurricane Katrina. In the fall of 2010, DOJ's Community Relations Service trained more than 300 officers in mediation for law enforcement and responding to allegations of racial profiling. Attendees included sergeants, lieutenants, and command staff, as well as Community Coordinating sergeants and the NOPD Hispanic Liaison officer. The two-day training featured a joint class between officers and community members. The training is a significant step forward, but still leaves the Department far short of the training requirement appropriately required by policy, and from the overarching goal of inculcating attitudes of bias-free policing.

- 37 -

NOPD policies also include some accountability measures and requirements, to which the Department has not adhered. Chapter 41-6 requires PIB to submit an annual statistical summary of all profiling complaints received to the Assistant Superintendent of NOPD's Operations Bureau, and the Superintendent. The Assistant Superintendent is required to use the summary of citizen concerns, and the information received from the summary of profiling complaints received, to recommend changes to NOPD procedures, practices, in-service instruction, and disciplinary procedures. The policy requires the Assistant Superintendent to forward these recommendations to the Superintendent, with the goal of eliminating racial and ethnic profiling. NOPD has not completed this summary, conducted analysis, or formulated any recommendations pursuant to this policy.

PIB personnel told us they receive very few allegations of racial profiling. This conclusion is unreliable, given the poor systems in place to track racial profiling allegations, and is undercut by our review of PIB cases and policies. That review indicated that NOPD is likely systematically undercounting such complaints, as discussed in this Report's section on NOPD's complaint investigation process. Moreover, the perceived lack of integrity and effectiveness of the misconduct complaint process was a theme that we heard from many community members, who frequently expressed reluctance to make complaints against specific officers out of a fear of retaliation and reprisal. One citizen, at a Vietnamese community group meeting, said that "[y]our house gets burglarized and it may take 10, 12 hours from the police to show up. You get a cop in trouble and you'll see the whole force here." Another participant told us that "NOPD needs a code of silence to protect citizens, not each other." These comments point to underlying issues of trust and credibility that are pervasive among some communities, and that may prevent them from making complaints related to bias or other forms of misconduct.

NOPD's bias-based profiling policy also contains a requirement that when an officer makes a stop, he or she is to radio the dispatcher and provide a description of the subject. While the policy is not clear, the inclusion of this requirement in the policy on "profiling" suggests an intent to record data regarding such factors as race and ethnicity. Yet the Computer-Aided Dispatch ("CAD") data that we reviewed contained no information regarding subjects, apart from occasional observations regarding apparent race or ethnicity in a section for officer comments. Although the FIC database does contain race and ethnicity data, as discussed in section III of this Report, its use is inconsistent. The FIC card and database also fail to capture such important information as whether a frisk or other search took place, whether contraband was found, and the disposition of the stop. In any case, it is clear that the Department is not collecting data in a sufficiently useful or complete way, and is conducting little or no analyses of the data it does have.

c)     Arrest and Force Data

Among other reasons to question NOPD's crime data, the Department has not reported certain arrest data to the FBI's Uniform Crime Reports ("UCR") system for at least several years. This data typically includes the race and ethnicity of persons arrested. The internal arrest data that the Department provided to us upon request was limited and haphazard, but pointed to racial disparity in virtually all categories, with particularly dramatic disparity for African-American

- 38 -

youth under the age of 17.  For example, the Department provided recent arrest data for the eight UCR "Index" or "Part 1" offenses, which are the offenses that the FBI uses to produce its Crime Index: homicide, forcible rape, robbery, burglary, aggravated assault, larceny over $50, motor vehicle theft, and arson.  It recorded arrests, by age, in five different race/ethnicity categories: "Black," "White," "Spanish," "Orientals," and "Unknown."  For all age groups, the Department recorded no arrests for "Spanish" or "Orientals," itself a problematic omission.

NOPD's data indicates that in 2009, the Department arrested 500 African-American males and 65 African-American females under the age of 17 for these offenses.  For the same time period, the Department arrested eight white males and one white female in the same age group.  Adjusting for population, these figures translate to a ratio of arrest rates for both African-American males to white males and African-American females of nearly 16 to 1, a deeply concerning disparity.  In 2010, there were 419 arrests of African-American males and 61 of African-American females in this age group for Part 1 offenses, compared with eight of white males and three of white females, resulting in an overall arrest rate ratio of nearly 11 to 1 when adjusted for population.  Although a troubling disparity in arrest rates also exists nationwide, it is not nearly as extreme.  Nationally in 2009, among those agencies reporting data, the ratio of arrest rates for African American youth to arrest rates for white youth, for the same offenses, was approximately 3:1.

For non-UCR Part I crimes, which include such offenses as simple assault, curfew and loitering offenses, disorderly conduct, drug and drinking offenses, weapon offenses, and driving under the influence, there was a similarly striking level disparity for youth under the age of 17.  For example, the black to white arrest rate ratio for males was approximately 11:1 in 2009, and approximately 5:1 in 2010.  For both UCR Part I and Part II crimes, racial disparities exist for adult men and women as well, but are closer to or comparable to the level of disparity reported nationwide.

Although we are continuing to review the Department's data and practices regarding bias-based profiling, what we have found so far is strongly suggestive of differential enforcement for whites and African Americans, most clearly for New Orleans' youngest residents.  Certainly, a disparity in arrest rates between African-American males and white males is not unique to New Orleans, and many people with whom we spoke, both black and white, attributed the starkly different rates primarily to socio-economic factors.  However, the level of disparity for youth is so severe and so divergent from nationally reported data that it cannot plausibly be attributed entirely to the underlying rates at which these youth commit crimes, and unquestionably warrants a searching review and a meaningful response from the Department.

NOPD use of force data also shows a troubling racial disparity that warrants a searching inquiry into whether racial bias influences the use of force at NOPD.  Of the 27 instances between January 2009 and May 2010 in which NOPD officers intentionally discharged their firearms at people, all 27 of the subjects of this deadly force were African American.  In our sample of resisting arrest reports documenting uses of force between January 2009 and May 2010, we found that in 81 of the 96 uses of force that we reviewed (84%), the subject of the force was African American.

- 39 -

More generally, it is critical that Department and City leadership acknowledge community concerns regarding discriminatory policing, consider the ways its policies, training, and supervision may encourage bias, and implement adequate systems to detect, prevent, and remedy bias in its police practices.  These measures are essential if the Department is to rebuild itself as one that serves—and is perceived as serving—all segments of the community fairly, equally, and effectively.

2.	National Origin Discrimination:  Failure to Provide Police Services to Persons with Limited English Proficiency

NOPD is dangerously limited in its ability to communicate effectively and accurately with limited English proficient ("LEP") victims, witnesses, suspects, and community members, a deficiency that directly undermines public safety, crime prevention, and crime-solving, and results in inferior police services to LEP community members.  Language and cultural barriers can put cases and lives at risk by creating safety, evidentiary, and ethical challenges for officers and others.  Language and cultural barriers can prevent LEP individuals from understanding their rights, complying with the law, reporting crimes, and receiving meaningful access to law enforcement services and information.

While NOPD recently has taken steps to connect with LEP communities, including the "El Protector" program, which will involve bilingual outreach to Latinos on public safety issues, and a similar program directed to the Vietnamese community, the Department will need to undertake more concerted and comprehensive efforts to ensure that LEP individuals receive meaningful access to vital police services.

*a)	Failure to Develop a Language Assistance Plan*

NOPD has virtually no capacity to provide meaningful access to police services to LEP community members, who in New Orleans are predominantly Latino or of Vietnamese descent.  Although demographic data post-Katrina remains imperfect, the Vietnamese community has been an established presence in New Orleans since the mid-1970s, and since the storm the City has seen a significant influx of Latino immigrants.  A significant segment of each of these communities speaks little or no English and the presence of both communities in the City has been growing.  NOPD relies primarily upon just two officers, one fluent in Spanish and one fluent in Vietnamese, to assist on calls for service and investigations throughout the Department, in addition to performing their regular duties.  The Department does not compensate these officers for interpreter services performed while off-duty or provide them with enhanced pay for language fluency; nor does the Department have processes to assess the accuracy of its multilingual officers and train them in carrying out their duties.

Although the Department employs several Vietnamese-speaking officers and between fifteen and twenty Spanish-speaking officers, one member of NOPD leadership acknowledged that "there is no real incentive" for officers with language capacity to provide interpretation, making many "reluctant" to do so.  Indeed, the lack of a structured language assistance program has actually created disincentives for officers to utilize their language skills.  Those officers who do volunteer to assist with interpretation needs appear to be subject to receiving calls from units throughout the Department at all times of the day or night, while off duty or on vacation, and on their personal cell phones.

The Department's Bureau of Policy and Review has engaged in limited efforts to formalize Spanish-language interpretation for NOPD, and in December 2008 issued a General Order setting out official personnel policies with respect to scheduling an interpreter, appropriate compensation for interpreters, and interpreter responsibilities under a new program. This General Order also provided for overtime pay for Spanish-language interpretation, though the process for receiving overtime compensation was complex and cumbersome. But in April 2010, NOPD ceased paying any overtime. The General Order did not specify the interpretation policy for any non-Spanish language, the process for translating any vital documents, the training necessary for becoming an interpreter, or any required training for officers on how to work with interpreters.

For the period between December 2008 and April 2010, the Department's primary Spanish interpreter, who now also serves as the Hispanic Liaison officer, kept a log documenting that he assisted on more than 350 calls for service, illustrating the considerable demand for these services. There has been no comparable tracking of calls for service by monolingual Vietnamese speakers, nor any efforts to formalize Vietnamese-language interpretation and translation. The Department's few Vietnamese speakers have always provided interpreter assistance on an informal basis.

Apart from the December 2008 General Order, which contained very little substantive guidance, the Department has no formal language assistance plan, nor any policies or procedures for: determining the number of LEP individuals within its jurisdiction; determining the languages spoken by LEP individuals within its jurisdiction; collecting and recording primary language data for LEP individuals encountered; collecting and recording the number of LEP victims and witnesses who seek NOPD services; informing victims and witnesses of the availability of language assistance; interrogating and interviewing LEP individuals; or responding to and tracking citizen complaints filed by LEP individuals. The Department similarly lacks protocols to identify and train multilingual staff; assess the accuracy of multilingual staff's translation and interpretation skills; train NOPD officers on how to work with interpreters in the field; and train all NOPD personnel on providing language assistance services to LEP individuals. Finally we found no evidence of any systems to identify and translate vital documents such as: consent to search forms; witness and victim statement forms; citation forms; victim rights notification forms, and citizen complaint forms.

### *b)*      *Impact on LEP Communities*

NOPD's lack of a formal and comprehensive plan to serve individuals who have limited English proficiency results in the provision of inferior and, in some instances, no police assistance to a growing segment of the City's population. We spoke to many officers, both with and without foreign language capacity, who described communication barriers as a significant problem. Community members and individual officers also told us that a Department-wide lack of cultural competency further impedes communication and effective policing of the City's Latino and Vietnamese communities. No one in the Department was able to articulate how

NOPD serves LEP residents when one of the "unofficial" interpreters is off-duty, in court, or otherwise unavailable. Some officers said that when an officer who could interpret was not available they used gestures or drew pictures in an attempt to communicate. We heard from officers with language fluency that they receive frequent phone calls directly from language-minority members of the public who seek a more direct and efficient police response.

During an August 2010 ride-along, we observed firsthand a delay in response to a call for service from a victim of domestic violence, apparently because she was a monolingual Spanish-speaker. It further appeared that the officer may not have responded at all if not pressed by the DOJ investigator and if the DOJ investigator had not happened to be bilingual. After the officer continued to patrol the district for 30 minutes following receipt of the complaint, the DOJ investigator inquired about what calls had come in through dispatch. The officer initially skipped over the domestic violence call, but then asked the DOJ investigator whether he spoke Spanish. When the investigator replied that he did, the officer responded to the call. Upon arrival at the scene, the victim, who had visible injuries, said she had been waiting more than an hour for a response. Later, the officer explained that there was only one person on the shift capable of serving as an interpreter, and that the individual was often difficult to reach.

In addition to delaying or preventing response to complaints of serious violence, the Department's inability to provide language assistance, in situations where officers do respond, can lead to family members or children serving as interpreters. This can be especially dangerous in domestic violence cases where using a family member to interpret may discourage the victim from speaking or, in cases where the abuser is the interpreter, may further isolate an LEP victim whose words are purposefully misinterpreted.

The direct observation described above is consistent with reports we received not only from officers but also from members of the community. Community members described significant consequences resulting from language barriers in their dealings with NOPD— including delays in or denial of services, incidents where victims were mistaken for suspects, and situations where encounters escalated unnecessarily due to gaps in communication. At one community meeting, a monolingual Spanish speaker reported calling police on four different nights regarding domestic violence, but receiving a response only once. She attributed the lack of response to the Department's failure to understand her. At another meeting, a participant said that she was arrested in front of her small child after failing to comprehend and follow an officer's orders. This encounter began when she attempted to intervene on behalf of another person being arrested. Officers themselves recognized the dangers inherent in NOPD's lack of language capacity; one gave the scenario of a victim of a robbery, waving his hands in agitation, and unable to communicate with the responding officer: "So the victim gets cuffed or restrained."

We also heard accounts of Spanish-speaking individuals being cited or arrested themselves after calling police to report wage theft or other conflicts with employers, because an officer was unable to understand or sort out precisely what was taking place. Workers also perceived that officers were more likely to understand and consequently side with employers, who generally speak English. One worker, who filed a complaint with PIB in November 2009, alleged that he called police to report a physical assault by an employer, but that instead of fully investigating, the responding officers interrogated him about his immigration status and cited him for disturbing the peace. PIB sent the complainant a response letter in March 2010, stating that the allegations could not be substantiated. The investigation noted, however, that because the responding officers were "[u]nable to resolve the dispute at the time of the incident, the officers issued a summons to both men for disturbing the peace so the matter could be resolved in court," seeming to support the complainant's allegation that he was inappropriately cited. The investigation also pointed to some confusion over the officers' questions on the scene, which the PIB investigator attributed to the interpretation skills of a community organizer who was assisting the worker. Irrespective of whether the investigator's conclusion was valid, the incident reinforces the need for NOPD to develop its own capacity to provide LEP individuals with meaningful access to law enforcement services.

This complainant submitted his complaint to PIB with the assistance of a local community group that works with and represents Spanish-speaking day laborers. But in general, Spanish or Vietnamese speakers who wish to make a complaint regarding police conduct have very limited options. A monolingual Spanish or Vietnamese speaker attempting to make a complaint at a district could only do so if he or she were fortunate enough to find someone present to interpret. PIB officials said they would probably have to call in an officer from outside the bureau to interpret a complaint of misconduct from a non-English speaker. This raises serious concerns about the confidentiality of complaints and integrity of the investigation process when persons with limited English proficiency are involved.

> 3. Gender-Biased Policing: Failure to Investigate Sexual Assault and Domestic Violence

Inadequate policies and procedures, deficiencies in training, and extraordinary lapses in supervision have contributed to a systemic breakdown in NOPD handling of sexual assault investigations. NOPD has misclassified large numbers of possible sexual assaults, resulting in a sweeping failure to properly investigate many potential cases of rape, attempted rape, and other sex crimes. Additionally, in situations where the Department pursued sexual assault complaints, the investigations were seriously deficient, marked by poor victim interviewing skills, missing or inadequate documentation, and minimal efforts to contact witnesses or interrogate suspects. The documentation we reviewed was replete with stereotypical assumptions and judgments about sex crimes and victims of sex crimes, including misguided commentary about the victims' perceived credibility, sexual history, or delay in contacting the police. NOPD recently acknowledged its serious deficits in responding to sex crimes, and has taken some significant remedial steps. NOPD and the City will need to build on these efforts to bring about the extensive and sustained change necessary to effectively and appropriately respond to these serious crimes.

We also found systemic deficiencies in NOPD's handling of domestic violence cases, although not to the degree evident in sex crimes. The City benefits from the presence of the New Orleans Family Justice Center ("NOFJC"), a federally-funded center designed to provide comprehensive services to victims of domestic violence by integrating law enforcement, prosecution, civil legal services, and advocacy in one location. The NOFJC, which is managed by the non-profit Catholic Charities, opened two years after Hurricane Katrina and now houses NOPD's Domestic Violence Unit. Although the existence of the NOFJC appears to have had a

- 43 -

salutary effect on NOPD's handling of domestic violence complaints, we found significant weaknesses in the Department's policies and practices with respect to responding to and investigating these cases.

### a) *Sexual Assault Policies, Training, and Supervision*

The Department's policies covering sex crimes investigations are set forth primarily in Ops. Man. Ch. 42, *Criminal Investigations*. Department leadership acknowledged that these policies are outdated and in need of revision. The current policies are short on substantive content, failing to provide guidance with respect to such basic, essential functions as: initial and follow-up victim interview protocol; collaboration with victim advocates; protocols for forensic examinations of victims; suspect interviews and forensic examinations; evidence preservation and crime scene management in the sexual assault context; and services/assistance to be offered to victims.

Rape crisis advocates, representatives from the DA's Office, and officers themselves told us that additional training is urgently needed for sex crimes detectives and supervisors, as well as patrol officers, who are generally the first responders to a complaint of sexual assault. Sex Crimes Unit detectives described their training as having been largely "on-the-job" for the last several years. Although some reported attending courses on interviewing and interrogation on an ad hoc basis, the Department has not required in-service training for detectives for at least three years. Specialized training in such critical areas as victim interviewing skills, investigating non-stranger and drug and alcohol facilitated sexual assault, and documenting sexual assaults are essential.

We further found that supervision of the Sex Crimes Unit has been grossly inadequate. In the context of sex crimes, it is essential that supervisors clarify expectations of investigators; ensure that complaints are being classified, investigated, and cleared appropriately; enhance cooperation between rape-crisis centers and forensic examination programs; and communicate early and effectively with prosecutors. Community stakeholders, prosecutors, and officers alike reported that this type of supervision and leadership has been virtually absent from the Sex Crimes Unit, for at least several years. In June 2010, the Department took the long-overdue step of installing a new commander of the Sex Crimes Unit. The Unit's new commander has prioritized collaborative, victim-centered problem-solving with the DA's Office and rape-crisis advocates, who uniformly report improved working relationships with the Unit and its leadership.

### b) *Classification of Sexual Assault Complaints*

Under the FBI's UCR program, police departments provide statistics regarding reports of certain crimes, including forcible rape and attempted forcible rape. The UCR program defines forcible rape as the "carnal knowledge of a female forcibly and against her will," and specifies that "'[a]gainst her will' includes instances in which the victim is incapable of giving consent because of her temporary or permanent mental or physical incapacity (or because of her youth)." Many types of sexual assault that fall outside of the UCR's definition of forcible rape still

- 44 -

constitute felonies under Louisiana law, and the Sex Crimes Unit is charged with fully investigating these offenses.

Departments must include reports of forcible rape or attempted forcible rape in their UCR data irrespective of whether the victim cooperates or an arrest is made. In situations where investigators determine that a report is false or baseless—meaning that the evidence shows no crime occurred or was attempted—the department may designate a report as "unfounded." Departments must still include these reports in their UCR statistics for Index Crimes, under the category of unfounded crimes.

In 2009, NOPD reported 98 forcible rapes and 179 homicides, when in virtually every other city the number of rapes far outpace the number of homicides.[18] By mid-August 2010, the Sex Crimes Unit had investigated just 54 UCR rapes for the year, along with 49 non-UCR investigations, which include "carnal knowledge" or statutory rape, sexual battery, oral rape, rapes of males, and sexual assault complaints deemed "unfounded." These figures, particularly in a city with high tourism and multiple colleges and universities, are strikingly low. Based on our review of the documents and interviews with NOPD and other stakeholders, we concluded that the Department likely had diverted many complaints of possible sexual assault from being fully investigated by classifying them as non-criminal "Signal 21s," the Department's code for miscellaneous complaints. The *Times-Picayune* reported NOPD's extensive use of Signal 21 designation in June 2009, putting the Department on notice about the potential misclassification of sexual assault complaints.

Use of codes and signals for classification of complaints varies widely across police departments. There are often situations where it is appropriate to categorize a complaint with a "miscellaneous" or "non-criminal" type designation—namely, when the elements of a crime are clearly not present, or when a third party reports a crime but the reported victim denies that one occurred. Our review determined that NOPD has used the Signal 21 code far more expansively, effectively shutting down investigation for a significant proportion of possible sex crimes. In 2008, the Sex Crimes Unit of NOPD responded to 230 complaints of alleged sexual assault; of those 230 complaints, the Department classified 144 – or almost 63 percent – as "Signal 21" miscellaneous complaints. In 2009, NOPD used the miscellaneous complaint code for 112 of 261 total sexual assault complaints, or 43 percent. By mid-August 2010, the Unit had classified 81 out of 184 complaints of possible sexual assault received in 2010, or about 44 percent, as Signal 21s. In the vast majority of these cases, sex crimes detectives filled out a Major Offense Report Form ("MORF"), coded the disposition as "NAT," or "Necessary Action Taken," and undertook no further review, victim follow-up, or investigation.

The Department's practice, according to the Sex Crimes Unit's caseload reports, has been to give complaints the Signal 21 designation not only in situations where the elements of a crime do not appear to exist, but also where the detective concludes, after only an initial investigation, that there is: "an uncooperative victim;" "the victim is unsure of what occurred or unsure if she

---

[18] According to 2009 UCR data: In New York City there were 471 homicides and 832 rapes; Los Angeles 312 homicides and 903 rapes; Pittsburgh, Pennsylvania 39 homicides and 116 rapes; Austin, Texas 22 homicides and 265 rapes; Las Vegas, Nevada 111 homicides and 698 rapes; Louisville, Kentucky 62 homicides and 230 rapes; and Nashville, Tennessee 77 homicides and 262 rapes.

- 45 -

wants to report the incident;" "if the evidence refutes the allegation;" or if there are "conflicting statements." The caseload reports also note that "If we can prove that the allegation is false during the initial investigation that's a MORF."

Indeed, the Signal 21 reports that we reviewed clearly reflected a focus on and effort to, from the outset, "prove an allegation is false"—a conclusion that is virtually impossible to draw based on a cursory investigation or preliminary victim interview. Many of the reports emphasized the victim's inconsistent statements, gaps in knowledge or memory, or inability to give a good description of the perpetrator, none of which demonstrate that an allegation is false. Such reactions, common for sexual assault victims in crisis or suffering from posttraumatic stress, should not be used to label a report of assault as false. The determination that a report of sexual assault is false should only be made if the evidence, obtained in a thorough investigation, establishes that no crime was committed or attempted.

Additionally, the Signal 21 reports often expressed skepticism about victims' credibility, opined on victims' possible motivations for lying, and expressed judgments about delayed reporting, an extremely common dynamic in sexual assault cases. In many instances, the investigation seemed to focus on the trustworthiness of the victim herself, rather than on the alleged crime; indeed, in a number of reports the investigator noted checking the victim's criminal history. Among the justifications given for classifying a complaint as a Signal 21 were: history of prostitution; mental illness; having previously made a "similar" report in another city; having "lied" about being arrested in the past; and "a possibility that the victim lied to the police" in an unrelated matter. One investigator classified the signal as a 21 due to "the victim staying out at night knowing she has a live in boyfriend of 14 years, and the victim not really concern with the rape only the morning after pill."

In arriving at these conclusions, investigators appeared to rely on initial victim interviews in which detectives asked leading or blaming questions, or on stereotypes about how victims of sexual assault should behave. In many of the Signal 21 reports, detectives asked victims why they did not resist, why they put themselves in certain situations, and why they did not immediately disclose the assault to police, family, or friends. In one report, the detective asked the victim "if she screamed or resisted the perpetrator," and when the victim replied that she did not, he "then asked why she did not resist. The victim stated the perpetrator was aggressive and she was afraid, the victim then stated she did not think anyone would help her." In another report, the detective commented that the victim "seemed very calm and unrattled seeing as though the aforementioned account had just taken place." He also asked her why she did not leave the French Quarter earlier with some family members, "rather than walk alone in the cold on a dark street at that time in the morning." Later in the same interview, he asked her whether she had a cell phone on her, and when she replied that she did, he "asked her why she didn't try to call 911" during the assault.

In short, our review of Signal 21 reports found that NOPD routinely asks questions that are likely to heighten many victims' feelings of shame and self-blame, fear of not being believed, and lack of confidence in the criminal justice system. Such interview tactics, particularly at the critical initial stage of a sexual assault investigation, may well intensify a victim's reluctance to cooperate with an investigation or prosecution. This effect was clearly evident in a number of anonymous survey responses that victims completed after receiving treatment at area hospitals. One victim said she felt that detectives were "there to catch me in a lie, not to help. They were unconcerned and analyzing my story to find fault and not the truth." Another said the detective "seemed bored" while questioning her, and that she "got one thing out of sequence and he seemed annoyed." A third victim said she "felt pressured into not pressing charges/not cooperating," and another said the detective told her "there was nothing to report, that NOPD didn't have the manpower to handle my case, and I could go to the hospital or urgent care if I wanted."

In addition, the Signal 21 reports reflect an NOPD practice likely to discourage victims from pursuing prosecution. Files indicated that NOPD routinely has victims fill out and sign a document called a "Voluntary Victim/Witness" form, stating that they do not want to file charges or proceed with an investigation or prosecution. The form also includes information on the content and penalty of Louisiana's "Criminal Mischief" and "Injuring Public Records" statutes. Use of this form at such an early stage is a poor practice that may deter many from participating in an investigation and potential prosecution.

NOPD has acknowledged serious problems in the way it classifies sexual assault complaints, and recently provided 93 Signal 21 reports from 2009 to the Louisiana Commission on Law Enforcement ("LA Commission"). The state agency conducted an audit of the reports and concluded that 9 were reportable as UCR rapes or attempted rapes, and another two dozen could have been scored as a different UCR reportable offense (such as Assault or Aggravated Assault). The LA Commission's focus was on UCR-reportable offenses, excluding from review many other possible sex crimes that under Louisiana law may have been coded inappropriately and should be thoroughly investigated. The LA Commission's audit also listed several dozen complaints as "unfounded"—irrespective of the fact that they were never thoroughly investigated—without explaining why the unfounded designation was appropriate.

The Department, to its credit, recently reopened the nine rape/attempted rape complaints identified by the LA Commission, along with an additional 21 identified through internal review. The request for the audit and the performance of an internal review were significant and positive initial steps. Nonetheless, as described above, our review suggested that many more complaints may have been coded inappropriately and diverted from full and thorough investigation. More significantly, the underlying deficiencies—particularly in the areas of victim interviewing, sensitivity, documentation, and an understanding of the dynamics of sexual assault—are pervasive and have yet to be addressed.

*c)     Inadequate Sexual Assault Investigations*

We also found that even where assaults were properly classified, those investigations were inadequate in several important respects. As in Signal 21 documentation, the investigative reports suggested problematic interviewing techniques such as blaming or leading questions, and stereotypes regarding how a victim behaves in a "real" case of rape. In one interview, of a teenager who reported being assaulted by her mother's boyfriend, the detective wrote that the "victim was asked if she resisted and asked to explain. The victim stated that she told him to stop and he didn't. She stated she didn't yell or scream, nor did she try to use her cell phone to

- 47 -

call her mom or the police.  The victim states that the accused never threatened or implied to have a weapon or cause her physical harm.  In fact, the victim states that accused is smaller than her in weight and around the same height."  The detective also noted that the "victim's demeanor and her mother's were very nonchalant and unwavered by the police inquisition."

In some cases it was difficult to separate poor interviewing from poor report-writing.  Many reports omitted critical details, such as descriptions of victim injuries, or results of forensic exams or requested laboratory analysis.  Additionally, detectives wrote their reports in the third person, an unusual practice that results in confusing and hard-to-follow narratives.  In virtually every investigation we reviewed, victim and witness statements contained no first-person quotes, and were essentially a synopsis of what the detective believed he heard the victim or witness say.  Detectives appeared to routinely sanitize victims' accounts or used clinical language that civilians, and especially victims of sexual assault, do not typically use.  It is critically important that investigators learn to preserve a victim's own detailed statement.

Investigative reports also did not compile or contain any reports prepared by patrol officers or first responders.  We learned that patrol officers do not prepare any reports themselves when responding to a sexual assault complaint, although they do write reports for all other crimes, including major and violent offenses.  Instead, we were told that sex crimes detectives are called out to every complaint, and they interview patrol officers about what they observed, just as they would any other witness.  We found no evidence of such interviews in the investigative reports, however, which lacked the important information typically captured by first responders, such as "outcry" statements by the victim, appearance of the scene, or whether the victim required medical assistance.  Although patrol officers will need intensive training in dealing with sexual assault victims, conducting and recording preliminary interviews, and preparing reports, it is crucial to successful investigation and prosecution that first responding officers accurately document what they see, do, and hear.  Additionally, having a record of uniformed officers' actions in these cases will assist the Department in identifying training needs and ensuring that first responders and investigators treat victims appropriately.  Although detectives told us that patrol officers call them almost immediately to respond to a complaint of sexual assault, uniformed officers are still a victim's first interaction with law enforcement, an interaction that is likely to influence a victim's decision to participate in an investigation.

Detectives routinely failed to seek out and interview witnesses and interrogate suspects.  In fact, both officers and prosecutors told us that until recently the Sex Crimes Unit had an "unofficial" but clear policy of not conducting interviews of suspects, and instead built cases based on victim testimony.  Our review confirmed that detectives rarely questioned suspects, even in situations where a suspect was positively identified in a line-up and arrested.  In one report, although a suspect was identified, arrested, and waived his rights, the one and only statement that the detective documented was the suspect's denial of having been involved in any rape.  There was no evidence of any effort to question the suspect about the details of the incident or elicit any additional information.  Fortunately, the new commander of the Sex Crimes Unit has significant background and expertise in interrogations, and has prioritized changing policy and practice in this area.  We learned that he recently secured private funding to purchase video equipment for an interrogation room.

- 48 -

We also found that investigators failed to follow standard guidelines governing collection of physical and forensic evidence. In one case, the detective failed to bring the victim to University Hospital for a forensic examination due to the amount of time that had elapsed since the date of the assault – approximately 54 hours, which is well within the national standards for obtaining forensic examinations. In 2004, the National Protocol for Sexual Assault Medical Forensic Examinations (Adult /Adolescents) increased the time frame for forensic exams from 72 hours to 96 hours following an assault and many agencies collect biological evidence in a forensic exam up to 120 hours (5 days) after the assault. In another case, the detective informed the victim that "because she had reported the incident over 72 hours after it happened, there would be no chance of getting physical evidence." In addition to blaming the victim for her delay in reporting, the detective's statement overlooks the possibility of obtaining physical evidence from clothing or from the victim's car, where the assault allegedly occurred.

Another significant issue confronting NOPD's investigations of sexual assaults is its crime lab's lack of DNA analysis capacity. The Department has sent evidence to the state police crime laboratory for analysis, but at the time of our review, there were 800 untested forensic examination kits in NOPD's property room. NOPD recently announced an NIJ-sponsored partnership to transfer backlogged kits to Marshall University, at a rate of 60 per month. Additionally, the Department has sought funding to hire two DNA Criminalists to work at the state laboratory (pending funding and construction for their own DNA lab).

### d) Inadequate Domestic Violence Policies, Procedures, and Training

Ops. Man. Ch. 42.4 sets out basic procedures for making domestic violence arrests and carrying out investigations, and specifically requires that officers prepare a report documenting every domestic violence call for service. Additionally, the commander of the Domestic Violence Unit, who, like the Sex Crimes Unit commander, recently assumed his position, provided us with a second operations manual specific to his Unit. He indicated that he is revising the Unit's operations manual, which contains minimal guidance for detectives or other officers responding to domestic violence calls; it merely lays out the mission, goals, and broad responsibilities of detectives, listing such duties as "conduct[ing] follow-up investigation," "ensur[ing] that appropriate resources are provided," and "provid[ing] helpful information to victims."

Neither NOPD's Operations Manual nor the Domestic Violence Unit's manual contains specific guidance regarding such important functions as: protocols for 911 operators taking domestic violence calls; initial entry and preliminary investigation of domestic violence scenes; identifying and documenting victim injuries; or procedures for follow-up investigations. The absence of specific guidance for officers and detectives not only impedes effective response and investigation, but also creates potentially dangerous conditions for victims. As an example, the Department has no specific protocols regarding how to safely communicate with victims, either during initial encounters or future contacts, a serious deficiency in the domestic violence context. In a survey administered by the NOFJC, a victim noted that she "[i]nformed the dispatcher to inform the officers that were coming out not to let the batterer know I was the one calling or that I was inside the house. They did it anyway. He wasn't arrested but was asked to leave my property. I had plenty of reasons why I asked them to do it this way. They did the way they wanted to do it. What they did, I could have done myself. To me, they are the reason this has escalated."

### e) *Inadequate Domestic Violence Investigations*

At the time of our review, the Domestic Violence Unit was staffed by only three detectives, which was wholly inadequate to address the volume of the Department's domestic violence calls and provide appropriate follow-up and services to victims. In one NOFJC survey, a victim noted that the center "[r]eferred me to a detective who never called." As of July 2010, there had been 6,200 calls for service regarding domestic violence since the beginning of the year. Of those cases, about 1200 had been assigned to Domestic Violence Unit detectives for follow-up, while another 2700 were fully handled by officers in the individual districts, though subject to a superficial "review" by domestic violence detectives. We were told that at least 1500 reports were "missing" due to the recent transition to a new reporting system.

Due to the high volume of domestic violence cases, the three detectives assigned to the Domestic Violence Unit are not permitted to do field work, severely restricting their ability to conduct any meaningful follow-up investigation. And consistent with this, the reviewed reports did not reflect any follow-up interviews of witnesses. Although officers generally photographed and documented injuries at the scene, we did not find any evidence that they were returning to take photographs at a later point, when injuries might become more visible. Nor did we find that officers were seeking communication tapes of dispatch calls for inclusion in reports, though such follow-up appeared appropriate in many cases. In general, it appears that substantive follow-up investigation is largely handled by the Domestic Violence Prosecution Unit of the DA's office. As with sex crimes, the Department's involvement in investigating a case appears to end at the point of arrest, although both the DA's office and the Department reported that they are beginning to cultivate a more collaborative relationship on both sex crimes and domestic violence.

Patrol officers and district investigative officers handle the vast majority of on-scene investigations in domestic violence cases. Officers, prosecutors, and advocates reported that training for these officers has long been grossly inadequate, compromising the quality, completeness, and consistency of on-scene investigations and written reports. In some cases officers did a thorough job of documenting the appearance of the crime scene, describing injuries, and capturing spontaneous statements in direct quotes. In many others, however, officers failed to solicit or document key facts regarding past history of domestic violence or assault, or include sufficient information to identify the primary aggressor in a situation. Officers are also failed to note symptoms of strangulation or ask appropriate follow-up questions related to strangulation.

In most instances, efforts to find and interview witnesses were minimal. In one case, for example, the report reflected that a neighbor had heard screams and called 911, yet there is no indication that the officer interviewed or attempted to interview the neighbor. In another, the report suggests that a male friend of the victim's was present, and involved in the events that led to the disturbance, yet the report reflects no attempt to interview him or obtain his contact information.

Additionally, the reports reflect that officers virtually never interview child witnesses, even in cases where children are present at the scene and listed on the domestic violence reporting form. It may be that officers believe that children must be interviewed by a forensic interviewing specialist, but we found no evidence that such follow-up interviews were taking place, or that officers were obtaining even minimal statements from children. While very sensitive, properly-trained officers can interview child witnesses. Interviews of suspects are also the rare exception, and officers do not appear to interview suspects when they arrest on a warrant, despite routinely providing *Miranda* warnings. The reports do reflect that officers reliably pursue arrest warrants when suspects have left the scene.

NOPD has taken some recent significant steps to remediate deficiencies in its overall response to domestic violence. Over several months between April and December 2010, the Department sent nearly 300 officers to training on domestic violence, provided in a collaborative effort by the USAO, the State Attorney General's Office, and the Louisiana Supreme Court Protection Order Registry. Additionally, as in sex crimes, the Department named a new commander of the Domestic Violence Unit, who appears committed to partnering with advocates in the community to improve the Unit's performance.

Nonetheless, the Department has yet to fully leverage the considerable tools and resources available to enhance its response to domestic violence. For example, none of the reports we reviewed contained a victim referral to the NOFJC. Further, the NOFJC has urged implementation of an Integrated Protocol for Law Enforcement, which NOPD has reviewed but has yet to endorse or adopt as policy. The Integrated Protocol reflects best practices and contains the specific and detailed guidance that NOPD currently lacks. Additionally, the NOFJC's technical assistance provider, the National Family Justice Center Alliance, recently conducted a "Snapshot audit," a review of each aspect of the NOFJC's service provision designed to improve programs and identify training issues. The Snapshot, which involved record and data review, interviews with service providers, and focus groups with victims, made many findings consistent with ours and included a comprehensive set of recommendations that we urge NOPD to carefully review.

## V.   <u>RECRUITMENT</u>

NOPD's longstanding failure to prioritize the recruitment of high-quality candidates contributes to the chronic, Department-wide problems we observed, including inappropriate and disrespectful conduct in the community, corruption, unnecessary uses of force, and improper stops and searches. Good police officers possess problem-solving skills, emotional maturity, sound judgment, interpersonal and communication skills, and the ability to collaborate with a diverse cross-section of the community. If the Department is to attract a workforce capable of policing ethically and effectively, it will need to develop a strategic recruiting plan focused on attracting recruits with these qualities.

- 51 -

We found NOPD's recruitment program to be anemic, entirely passive, and lacking clear goals, plans, or accountability.  NOPD's Recruitment and Applicant Unit, which has a staff of six commissioned law enforcement officers, has no plan to seek out and recruit qualified candidates.  Recruiters were unclear about the scope of their authority or obligations, and report having done little since Hurricane Katrina to find or attract highly-qualified applicants, apart from distributing literature at job fairs, colleges, and universities.

City policy decentralizes recruitment efforts among various departments and functions, primarily NOPD's Recruitment Unit and the Civil Service Commission, and also delegates some informal authority to a non-profit entity, the New Orleans Police and Justice Foundation (NOPJF).  Consequently, recruiting efforts are unfocused and reactive, and there is little accountability for outcomes.  While NOPD recruiters told us they rely in part on the Civil Service Commission for recruiting, Civil Service employees told us recruitment was the NOPD's job; they described their primary responsibility as administering the Civil Service Exam and providing administrative oversight to the hiring process.  No one we spoke to identified, as their primary goal or responsibility, recruitment of high-quality applicants who share the Department's values and can help it achieve its mission.

The Department has long been aware of deficiencies in its recruitment efforts, yet for years failed to act meaningfully to address them.  In many ways, in fact, leadership decisions appear to have compounded these problems.  In the past, extremely noncompetitive entry pay reportedly impeded the Department's ability to attract strong candidates.  With entry pay increases several years ago, that obstacle has diminished (although it appears that noncompetitive pay increases for officers may still be hindering retention of good candidates).  In more recent years, the failure to attract strong candidates appears linked to NOPD's lack of any strategic recruiting plan, along with the pressure the Department was under to hire new police officers after Hurricane Katrina.  NOPD hired hundreds of officers during a relatively short time period; one estimate is that 400 officers were hired during the three year period following Katrina.  In its press to hire these officers, NOPD reportedly lowered its recruiting standards, essentially removing the physical agility requirement and asking the Civil Service Commission to score the written portion of the application less vigorously.

In 2006, NOPD asked the RAND Gulf States Policy Institute (RAND GSPI) to review its recruitment process.  RAND GSPI's 2007 report observed that Recruitment Unit officers spent most of their time on the internet performing background checks; that NOPD had no specific selection criteria to identify successful recruiters; and that the Department provided no training to members of its Recruitment Unit.  The study also found that NOPD made no attempt to collaborate with institutions that could be a source of well-qualified recruits.  After its review, the RAND GSPI made simple and common sense recommendations to NOPD to help establish a more successful recruitment process—recommendations that the Department has ignored until relatively recently.

Predictably, these deficiencies have hampered NOPD's ability to hire quality recruits.  At the time of our review, the attrition rate for the latest recruit class was nearly sixty percent.  Of the sixty-six recruits that successfully completed the recruitment and background investigation, thirty-nine were eliminated from the training class.  NOPD expended thousands of dollars to test,

- 52 -

train, and conduct background checks on what were clearly marginal applicants, a waste of funds that NOPD could have better used in a more targeted recruiting process. Nonetheless, NOPD's decision to eject unqualified candidates before they became officers was the appropriate one. In interviews with NOPD officers at all ranks, we heard the consistent complaint that the Training Academy routinely graduated police recruits who were sub-par and not fit for duty.

Recently, NOPD has begun to make changes to its recruiting process to ensure a stronger pool of applicants is selected to attend the academy. Working with the Civil Service Commission, NOPD has made the physical agility portion of the exam more stringent, and has instituted a requirement that applicants for police officer have at least 60 hours of college credits from an accredited college or university, or two years of full-time military service. The Department is also launching a partnership with a local community college, through which cadets will work twenty hours per week at NOPD while attending school. Once the cadets have earned sufficient college hours and completed certain requirements, including taking courses in a foreign language, they will be eligible to apply to NOPD's recruit academy. While research shows that most participants in junior cadet programs do not become police officers, these efforts appear to be cost-effective and can serve to improve police-community relations. Although the Department has a great deal of work ahead to attract the most highly-qualified workforce possible, we commend its recent focus on these efforts.

The Department will also need to focus on meeting its particular need for officers who can communicate and form partnerships with all segments of the New Orleans community—which includes efforts to attract a diverse applicant pool. NOPD's policies specifically require the involvement of minority employees in formal recruiting presentations and pre-employment counseling programs, as well as outreach to community organizations for recruitment assistance. *See Ops. Man. Ch. 32, Recruitment.* Although these guidelines make clear that NOPD acknowledges the value and importance of a diverse workforce, the Department's practices with respect to recruitment depart significantly from its policies. Members of the diverse community groups with whom we spoke consistently reported that the Department has not reached out to them for any assistance in recruitment efforts. Nor has the Department sought the assistance or leveraged the community contacts of employees such as the Hispanic Liaison Officer. Such outreach to community organizations and stakeholders, and efforts to elicit their active support, is critical to both strengthening and maintaining community ties, and ensuring that the Department is in the best possible position to serve all of its citizens.

As we discuss in section III.B.2 of this Report, NOPD is particularly ill-equipped to serve the City's significant Vietnamese and Latino populations. The Vietnamese community has long comprised a sizable minority within the City, and the Latino population has grown substantially in the last five years, with Latino laborers participating heavily in the City's post-Katrina rebuilding efforts. We heard from both community organizations and those within NOPD that recruiting officers with language skills and cultural awareness is critical to serving these communities. Although these qualities do not necessarily or exclusively flow from race and/or ethnicity, diversifying the applicant pool is one important way that the Department can seek to increase its language capacity and cultural fluency—along with providing pay incentives for any officers with language skills, and enhancing diversity training for all officers. Doing so through diverse stakeholder organizations serves the additional purpose of strengthening community ties and signaling the Department's commitment to being inclusive and representative.

## VI.  <u>TRAINING</u>

The training NOPD has provided to its officers during the last several years is severely deficient in nearly every respect.  NOPD's failure to train compromises officer and public safety, effective crime reduction, and the credibility and reputation of the Department as a whole. Shortcomings at the recruit, field, and in-service stages of training have left NOPD officers ill-equipped to perform their duties in a safe, constitutional, and effective manner.  We found systemic problems in training of every type, including tactical, operational, legal, and ethical. Officers receive an insufficient amount of training—there has been almost no in-service training for the past five years—and the instruction officers do receive is often out-of date, conflicts with NOPD  policies or current legal requirements, or fails to address officers' most pressing training needs.

We found no disagreement that NOPD training is inadequate.  NOPD officers of all ranks told us they want more and better training, and strongly expressed this sentiment in their responses to NOPD's employee survey.  In that survey, only 24% of NOPD employees agreed that they have sufficient opportunities for training, and overwhelmingly reported that existing training needs improvement.  NOPD leadership likewise has acknowledged that its training systems are in need of extensive repair.  NOPD's Superintendent has prioritized the wholesale remaking of training in his organizational strategy to improve NOPD.

Other sections of this Report address the impact of poor training in the areas of use of force; stops, searches, and arrests; investigating misconduct; supervision; community policing; and racial, ethnic, and gender bias in policing.  Our investigation found direct links between inadequate training and serious, systemic problems in each of these areas.  This section addresses our findings regarding NOPD's overall systems for developing and delivering training, including priorities and goals; curricula and lesson plan development; selection of training staff; facilities; and records management.

A.      Deficiencies in Developing and Delivering Training

1.      Inadequate Development of Priorities and Goals

NOPD lacks a strategic training plan that sets out the Department's training goals, establishes its training priorities, and reflects the Department's values.  Such training plans are essential to ensuring that a police department directs its resources to meeting its officers' greatest training needs, and provides officers and recruits with consistent messages regarding its mission and values.  The Department has not only failed to develop and implement a plan, but its leadership provided only minimal, sporadic executive input into the Training Division's activities.  This lack of focus and planning has had clear consequences; indeed, only 23% of respondents to NOPD's employee survey reported that NOPD provides the "right kind" of training to District officers.  Even fewer, 14%, believed that NOPD provides the "right kind" of training to detectives/investigators.

- 54 -

While NOPD has a centralized, staffed Training Division, the Division does not serve as an effective central management or coordination point for NOPD's training efforts. The Department's limited in-service training occurs on an ad-hoc basis. Specialized units in particular often formulate and carry out their own training. Much of the training offered at the District level is not communicated back to NOPD's Training Division. Further, the Department does not properly develop or review training curricula, evaluate instructor qualifications and abilities, or keep centralized training statistics. This near-total absence of coordination and planning results in poor quality control, inefficient training practices, and grossly inadequate documentation and record-keeping.

As the Department seeks to address the lack of coordinated strategy and planning in training, it should establish an executive training task force to advise the Superintendent and identify global training priorities and broad training goals. The Department should also take full advantage of the resources available outside of the Department, including the many colleges and universities in and around New Orleans. A public safety training consortium, comprised of the presidents/chancellors of local universities/colleges, as well as representatives from the public and private secondary school system, and the Louisiana POST, could provide NOPD with expertise in creating training strategy, course topics, curriculum development, classroom/facility use, instructor development, and training delivery.

2.       Weaknesses in Curricula, Lesson Plans and Presentation

Once a department establishes training goals and priorities, it must develop appropriate curricula and lesson plans, to ensure that officers receive instruction that is consistent with departmental policy and values, constitutional policing practices, and current law. NOPD has no formal curriculum development process. As a consequence, we found that NOPD training materials are not integrated with each other or NOPD policy; use or reference outdated materials; contain contradictory definitions; are poorly and inconsistently formatted; and do not reflect community involvement in their development.

As noted in section I of this Report, NOPD's use of force materials are particularly poorly integrated. They do not convey a complete or consistent message regarding how NOPD officers should use force. The use of force curriculum, for example, refers to a federal use of force curriculum that is no longer in use, and contains contradictory definitions. Similarly, NOPD's exclusionary rule training materials date back more than two years and reference material from more than a decade ago. The curriculum does not address the Supreme Court's ruling in *Arizona v. Gant*, 554 U.S. 941; 129 S. Ct. 24 (2009), and its important implications for how officers should conduct warrantless searches and seizures.

We further found that NOPD devotes an insufficient amount of time for instruction of some of the most critical and complex subjects in policing. The materials we reviewed reflect only eight hours of Academy training on the topic of use of force, which is wholly insufficient. Similarly, the Department provides recruits with two hours of training on the exclusionary rule, a critical piece of a police officer's training regimen. The amount of time devoted to weapons recertification is also grossly inadequate; NOPD reports that officers spend only 30 minutes on firearms requalification for the entire calendar year. The Department should be providing two eight-hour mandatory training sessions (16 hours per year), and incorporating a firearms/use of force requalification curriculum.

We also found that NOPD's over reliance on classroom lectures in delivering its training undermines the effectiveness of the instruction the Department does provide. The Department should be incorporating a variety of teaching strategies into its lesson plans, including scenario-based role play, video, case-study, local-example methods, and field trips. We noted that the *Police and the Community* curriculum did incorporate video, and the *Diversity in the Community* curriculum included viewing the movie *Crash*, but saw few other examples of teaching modes other than lecture. As with the development of training curricula, the Department should incorporate community involvement in the delivery of training to give officers a better understanding of community perspectives, and help build police-community partnerships.

One area in which a variety of teaching methods can be particularly helpful is in report writing. NOPD should use actual reports (redacted if necessary) as examples of both high quality and also low quality reports. Training should include a discussion of the impact that police reports have on the criminal justice system, including the repercussions of poor reports and the benefits of high-quality reports. Experts and guest speakers such as judges, prosecutors, and even crime victims can serve to complement a basic report writing lecture. Finally, as it relates to all reports, NOPD should offer various levels of writing, spelling, and grammar classes, with an emphasis on legal writing.

B.      Deficiencies in Staffing, Facilities, and Recordkeeping

1.      Failure to Develop Criteria for Instructor Selection and Review

A highly qualified training staff is critical to ensure that training is developed and delivered effectively. NOPD's training staff is comprised of twenty-one members—thirteen based at the Training Academy and eight at the firing range. In addition, adjunct instructors (temporary instructors from units within the Department, but not assigned to the Training Division) also provide training. Adjunct instructors are normally on loan to the Training Division for a short period to teach designated topics.

The Training Division staff appeared motivated and dedicated, and has attempted to fill gaps and compensate for the lack of upper-level command leadership and training strategy. However, the lack of established criteria for instructor selection, alongside a failure to provide regular reviews of Training Division personnel or adjunct instructors, means that the Department is not formally considering the quality of instructors' basic qualifications, past performance, their adherence to Department values, or their complaint or disciplinary history in deciding who will train NOPD officers. The Department should have set criteria for selecting qualified staff, including certain select-in criteria (i.e. college or special certifications), as well as disqualification criteria such as sustained excessive force, misconduct, or behavior violations. NOPD will also need to require annual reviews of all staff assigned to the Training Division to ensure they meet delineated criteria, as well as tailored annual training, including training on effective teaching and adult-learning techniques, as well as curriculum development.

- 56 -

2.      Inadequate Training Facilities

Although the Training Division recently moved into a new building that offers a clean, comfortable, and professional environment, the facility currently does not have the capacity to allow large groups to conduct physical skills training in defensive tactics and ground fighting techniques.  We observed some undeveloped space at the Training Academy that the Department could potentially convert into a space for such training, as well as some usable space in the lower level of the Third Police District building.

The Department has also suffered from the lack of a well-functioning firing range, since its own facility was damaged in Hurricane Katrina.  The Department has yet to repair the facility, and instead requires officers to use ranges operated by two other law enforcement agencies in order to recertify annually.  The arrangement creates serious logistical challenges for officers, and leaves them without adequate space, time, and facilities to qualify with weapons and learn other less-lethal tactics.  NOPD should provide officers access to a safe and modern firing range to ensure that their sworn members receive appropriate firearms training.

The current NOPD firing range facility is in disrepair and we were told the facility is located in a flood plain.  We were told also that there is a U.S. Coast Guard Facility, a NASA facility, and a refurbished New Orleans Fire Department facility adjacent to the police firearms range site and that the site has an excellent secure driving training area.  NOPD and the broader New Orleans community should consider whether to renovate this firing range facility for short-term use until a longer-term solution is realized.

3.      Lack of Effective Record Management

The Department lacks an effective record management system to monitor and track all training activity; a critical function to ensure that officers receive training and complete mandatory training requirements.  During our investigation, we learned that previously maintained records were destroyed during Hurricane Katrina, and the Department has since failed to re-establish a training record management system.  Training staff, NOPD leadership, and rank-and-file officers all expressed concern and dissatisfaction with the current system, which has left the Department unable to accurately determine what training classes have been offered to NOPD officers and which officers completed mandatory or voluntary training classes.

Recently, NOPD's Training Division has made efforts to track training manually, creating a centralized hard-copy training file with folders for all sworn members of the Department.  These records are stored in an upstairs file room and are maintained by a lone sergeant.  Our review of these training files revealed that they contained very little documentation and the information was not recorded in a consistent format.  More typically, with the exception of TASER certification records, records are maintained throughout the Department with little coordination to ensure that records are forwarded to the Training Division or any other centralized location.  Consequently, we found instances where officers had not yet completed mandatory training, the Department was apparently unaware of the lapse, and the officers were neither scheduled for training nor reprimanded for failing to complete the mandatory training.

  C.  Inadequate Recruit, Field, and In-Service Training

    1.  Problems in Recruit (Academy) Training

During our investigation, we did not have the opportunity to closely review recruit training. The recruit class had recently graduated and it was the last one scheduled for the year. However, the concerns we have expressed regarding NOPD's training apply fully to new recruits. In addition, we found that the unfocused recruit selection process discussed in section IV of this Report has an impact on academy training. The Department hired candidates as they became available and immediately placed them into the existing academy class, creating varied training levels within the class, and leading to considerable confusion and inefficiency. NOPD found itself with a class size of nearly 75 recruits, which was too large to be manageable, given the resources available and the structure of the training. Recruit class sizes should be kept to approximately 25-30 candidates.

Recruit selection problems also result in a high attrition rate at NOPD's academy. During just one week of NOPD's most recent Academy, five recruits were released after "behavioral red flags" were raised. It is appropriate to release recruits from the Academy when it becomes apparent that they are not suitable to be police officers. It is of course preferable not to admit unsuitable recruits in the first place.

We also found that, as in other areas of training, there did not appear to be a curriculum developed for each of the delineated topics. Also as in other areas of training, an overwhelming majority of officers, nearly 80%, according to NOPD's employee survey, said that they believe training for recruits needs to be improved.

    2.  Deficiencies in Field Training Program

Field training is an integral component of an effective training program, transitioning recruits from classroom theory to field practice. NOPD's process for selecting Field Training Officers ("FTOs") raises significant concerns. District Commanders have chosen the Department's more than 70 FTOs without any established criteria, reportedly leading to selection of some FTOs who are unqualified and unsuitable to supervise and train recruits. Most troubling, we learned of situations where District commanders were aware that FTOs were unqualified to supervise or train, yet failed to remove those FTOs from their positions. This lapse constitutes an egregious disservice to new recruits and risks liability to the Department, injury to officers and civilians, and damage to relationships in the community. We were told that unqualified FTOs typically were not removed because recruit assignments for Districts are predicated on the number of FTOs in each district. Thus, District Commanders have an incentive to keep as many FTOs as possible to ensure that new recruits are assigned to their districts. This dynamic underscores the need for established, centralized criteria for the FTO selection process.

- 58 -

We are also concerned that there does not appear to be any process for the Training Division or Field Training Coordinator to actively elicit feedback from recruits regarding their perspective on the quality of their field training, including the extent to which their field training was consistent with what they learned in the Academy. This can be a valuable way to learn what is working and what is not, as well as which FTOs may need additional instruction.

The failure to develop an adequate process for selecting, retaining, and removing FTOs, in combination with the generally poor state of training at NOPD, likely explains why officers throughout NOPD hold a poor opinion of the FTO program. NOPD's Employee Survey identified FTO training as a major weakness in NOPD, with over 80% of surveyed employees agreeing that training for FTOs needs to be improved. Officers described the FTO program as "defunct," telling us that officers without sufficient experience or competence are selected, and suggesting that FTOs receive more instruction before they are asked to train recruits.

Rehabilitating the program, and its reputation within NOPD, will require that the Department establish clear eligibility criteria for FTOs; develop and implement a FTO training curriculum that incorporates training on learning styles, generational differences, and adult instruction; and implement a mechanism to review FTOs, and remove them where appropriate.

NOPD has a good foundation upon which to build a credible and effective FTO program. The Department's program is based on the San Jose Field Training Model and involves seventeen weeks of intensive on-the-job training, including daily observations of recruits and bi-weekly reporting of recruit progress. This constant evaluation helps determine recruits' readiness for patrol duty. Training officers and sergeants are responsible for mentoring and advising recruits, as well as formally monitoring their progress. The structure of NOPD's FTO program is also good. FTOs receive tailored instruction, and are regularly updated on new items by the Training Division. There is a central FTO manager based at the Training Division, and each district designates a field training sergeant coordinator. The Training Division field training manager meets monthly with district-based field training sergeants to discuss the progress and training of each individual new officer in the program. This allows for early identification of problems and allows for timely adjustments so the new officer can be successful.

3.     Failure to Provide In-Service Training

NOPD's failure to provide a formal and mandatory in-service training program is a critical lapse. For many years, the Department has required only firearms re-qualification and driving training. Officers throughout the Department reported that they have not received in-service training since Hurricane Katrina, and overwhelmingly told us they needed and desired more training. While some in-service training does take place, attendee selection appears random, attendance is not documented, and training curricula are not preserved. There is no strategic planning to determine in-service training priorities, attendee selection, or delivery of training. Most importantly, there appears to be no accountability for failing to attend required training.

In-service training is the most effective way to prevent poor police tactics, incorporate best police practices, provide necessary training updates and refresh perishable skills. NOPD

- 59 -

315

leadership has committed to improving in-service training and the Superintendent has asked the Training Division to develop a 40-hour annual in-service training program. Critical in-service topics include: use of force, firearms, defensive tactics, integrity and ethics, community policing, communication skills (de-escalation training), cultural competency, search and seizure, policies and procedures, and current legal developments.

Recently, NOPD has offered valuable courses, including leadership and community relations, and has also stepped up its efforts to provide less-lethal force training to officers. There is still, however: no plan that sets in-service training goals or prioritizes training needs; no system for developing good in-service training curricula and lesson plans; and no system for tracking what has been offered and whether officers attended as required. These steps are critical as the Department moves forward with its plan to implement a mandatory in-service training program.

In concert with annual in-service training, NOPD will need to develop and implement a supervisory training program that specifically focuses on supervisory and managerial roles, with a specific emphasis on risk management. NOPD has not provided such training, at least in recent years. All newly-promoted officers should complete mandatory supervisory training prior to assuming a supervisory position. NOPD should also provide tailored training for all specialized units. The Department should consider that, as it develops and implements new policies, many of these policies will require structured, formal, in-service training.

In addition to structured in-service training, NOPD should provide meaningful daily roll call training, and consider incorporating distance-learning into its training delivery methods. Daily roll call training allows for continuing, effective daily instruction on less complex departmental policies and procedures, review of laws, and officer safety. These sessions are short in duration and intended to supplement other departmental training and allow for officer discussion. Daily roll call sessions typically occur at the beginning of each shift and are an essential part of a strategic training program. Daily roll call training at NOPD is not being used to its potential and may be another source of inconsistent communication of NOPD policies, procedures, and practices. While NOPD has what it calls "roll call" training, we found that the Training Division is not involved with developing topics, evaluating instructors, or even reviewing lesson plans. While we did observe one roll call training during a line up, an officer approached us immediately afterwards to tell us that what we observed was staged for our benefit and did not fairly represent NOPD's normal roll calls, in which officers regularly arrive late and little of substance is covered.

## VII.  FIELD SUPERVISION

Field supervisors, who at NOPD are sergeants, supervise NOPD field officers who work in the streets and neighborhoods of New Orleans. These field officers may be in a "platoon," assigned to patrol and respond to calls, or they may work in District-level task forces or narcotics units, usually assigned to non-patrol duties, but occasionally patrolling and responding to calls to supplement patrol operations. While their assignments vary, field officers have daily interactions with the public. These interactions provide the opportunity to solve problems and build community relationships, or to create or exacerbate divisions, making it more difficult for NOPD to police effectively.

Field sergeants, with critical support from their Lieutenants, provide the close and consistent supervision necessary to guide officers' conduct and to help them learn from their mistakes. Field sergeants should be in the best position to recognize a problem with an officer's conduct and intervene immediately to ameliorate or prevent harm. When a supervisor is on-scene and realizes that a patrol officer has made an arrest without probable cause, the supervisor can instruct the officer to release the arrestee and immediately counsel the officer about what the officer did wrong. When a community member is upset about how an officer responded to a call, a supervisor can immediately take a complaint—or intervene to prevent a complaint. How a field sergeant conducts him or herself, and whether he/she requires adherence to policy and ethics, sets a tone of accountability and integrity—or not. Field sergeants also are in the best position to ensure that street level crime prevention efforts are as effective as possible. Field supervisors know how productive their officers are, what they need to be more effective, and should be able to identify the strengths and weaknesses of each officer under their command, adjusting their level and type of supervision accordingly.

During our investigation, we encountered many excellent field sergeants and lieutenants. However, we found a number of systemic obstacles to effective field supervision and found that these obstacles are in fact preventing NOPD from providing officers the supervision necessary for accountability and effectiveness.

As in other areas of NOPD practice, with respect to field supervision there is a disconnect between policy and actual practice. In some instances, the policies are poor. But more often, supervisors simply do not follow policy and NOPD does not take steps to hold supervisors accountable for failing to adhere to policies or provide necessary supervision and guidance.

A.      Deficient Field Supervision Policies

By policy, NOPD allows for too few assigned supervisors. The number of officers a sergeant supervises—the sergeant's "span of control"—is a critical factor affecting the adequacy of supervision. At NOPD, a patrol supervisor may be responsible for directly supervising up to twenty officers. *See* Ops. Man. Ch. 11.0.1, *Authority & Responsibility-Unity of Command.* NOPD's Bureau Commander for Operations told us that each platoon "should" have one lieutenant, three sergeants, twenty officers and six detectives. However, as per policy, there is only a requirement that two "supervisors" work at a time on the weekend. *See* Ops. Bureau Policy #2. We have been told also that there are currently an insufficient number of platoon sergeants to staff each platoon with three sergeants, even on paper. The sergeant/officer ratio for District Task Forces is, by policy, 1:12. *See* Ops. Bureau Policy #2. The span of control for District narcotics units is 1:6 by policy, and, we were told by the Bureau Commander, the actual span of control for these units can be 1:10.

The 1:20 span of control allowed by NOPD policy for patrol units is too large to permit adequate supervision. We observed assigned spans of control at this ratio, generally where an assigned sergeant was off duty and another sergeant was handling two squads/platoons, although we also routinely saw far smaller spans of control, including 2:8 or 2:11. It is generally accepted practice that spans of control for patrol units should be no more than 1:10, and 1:5 is recommended. Any span of control should take into account the level of activity and type of assignment of the unit being supervised. As discussed below, given the considerable supervision challenges NOPD faces, a span of control at the lower end of this spectrum for all field units is necessary to ensure adequate supervision.

In some other respects, field supervision policies are sufficient as written. Supervisors are clearly required by NOPD policy to review, correct, and approve each arrest report, affirming that the report "is sufficient in form and content." *See* Ops. Man. Ch. 82.1, *Incident Report/Field Report Writing Manual* at p. 20. Similarly, another directive requires that the supervisor of the arresting officer, "review, correct, and approve" the arrest report, before forwarding. *See* Ops. Man. Ch. 42.15, *District Attorney Screening and Arrest Case Management.* Another policy requires that all District officers, including platoon (patrol), task force, narcotics officers, K-9, Mounted, Traffic, SOD personnel, and any other NOPD personnel working patrol, complete a Daily Activity Report. *See* Ops. Bureau Policy #19. Platoon and Task force supervisors are required to review and approve each Daily Activity Report completed by their subordinates, and to complete their own "Supervisors Daily Activity Report." According to this policy, supervisors "shall be responsible and accountable for counseling officers/supervisors whose Daily Activity Reports are disapproved." Where a Daily Activity Report is disapproved more than three times in a quarter the supervisor is required to discipline the officer, and document that discipline in a DI-2. If there are subsequent violations, the supervisor is required by policy to initiate a formal investigation of the officer.

NOPD policy requires sergeants to be in the field directly supervising patrol officers. Operations Bureau Policy #18 provides that, except at the beginning or end of a shift, only one platoon sergeant may stay in the station. All other platoon sergeants "shall remain on the street directing resources, supervising personnel, managing backlogs, responding to scenes, signing affidavits, etc." This policy further requires that at least one platoon sergeant respond to the scene of every UCR Part I crime in their district to "ensure the appropriate police action/response." Sergeants are also required by this policy to ensure that certain types of calls are responded to immediately, by a sergeant if no one else is available; that sergeants monitor calls for service backlogs and response times; and that sergeants "ensure that there are sufficient personnel on the street at all times." Platoon sergeants are further required by this policy to ensure that officers are logged into the Department's AVL system (which tracks squad car location) and in-car camera system, and ensure that their systems are functioning properly.

These policies comport with the standard practice of field supervisors reviewing, correcting, and approving the arrest reports of their subordinate officers, and confirming through documentation and observation that officers are actually active and productive in the field. However, other NOPD policies appear to place these responsibilities on only one sergeant in each District per shift, regardless of the number of officers working the shift, or whether the incident involves an officer under the direct command of that sergeant. Operations Bureau Policy #5, for example, requires platoon commanders (usually lieutenants) to delegate to each platoon sergeant specific job assignments and responsibilities. The policy requires that only a single sergeant review, track, and approve all reports and activity sheets for the entire platoon.[19] Depending upon the number of officers working and the activity in the District, it may not be possible for a sergeant to adequately review all arrest reports and activity sheets for accuracy and completeness, much less to do so in conjunction with the other activities patrol sergeants must undertake, such as responding to the scenes of certain arrests or uses of force, and handling misconduct complaints. Moreover, if a sergeant is reviewing, correcting, and approving arrest reports written by officers who officially report to another sergeant, this can undermine unity of command and make it more difficult to effectively supervise, counsel, and assist officers.

B.      Deficient Field Supervision in Practice

1.      Failures in First-line Supervision

Through our interviews, document review, ride-alongs, and other first-hand observations, we found that NOPD fails to provide the supervision that is necessary for accountability and effectiveness, and required by the Department's policy. We saw a pattern of arrest and use of force reports that had been approved by a supervisor even though they contained obvious flaws—a problem we discuss in more detail in other sections of this Report. We found that arrest reports sometimes appear to have not been reviewed at all, and use of force reports sometimes appeared to have been written by the involved officers, rather than by the supervisor as required by policy. Some reports were signed days after the incident, or not signed at all. As discussed in the Use of Force section of this Report, it is clear that supervisors do not always respond to the scene of a use of force incident, or conduct investigations of uses of force as required by policy. We saw little indication that Daily Activity Reports are being accurately and consistently filled out, or that counseling and corrective action occur when they are not. There is evidence that some supervisors do not even ensure that officers stay on-duty: local officials told us that officers have argued in litigation that it is consistent with Department "customs and practices," to leave early on a slow day while remaining on the clock, even though this clearly violates Department rules.

On ride-alongs, it was often our experience that only a single platoon sergeant was providing field supervision for an entire District. During one ride-along in the Eighth District, for example, the sergeant with whom we rode was the only supervisor in the field and was responsible for supervising the entire uniform patrol, as well as specialized units and a special task force assigned to Canal Street. Sometimes this situation was the result of having two sergeants on duty, with one sergeant remaining at the District station; in other instances, there appeared to be more sergeants staying at the station than supervising in the field. Exacerbating this lack of field supervision, sergeants in the field often responded to calls as if the sergeant were simply another officer in the platoon, rather than first determining whether an officer was available to take the call so that the sergeant could remain free to perform supervisory duties.

---

[19] Sergeants are assigned other platoon-wide tasks as well. One platoon sergeant is assigned the task of handling platoon scheduling and lineups, including reviewing and tracking attendance, sick leave and furloughs. One platoon sergeant is assigned the task of handling filing, correspondence and paperwork, and one, roll-call training. Ops. Bureau Policy #5. Many of these tasks are completed by civilian employees or non-supervisory officers in other Departments.

2.      Reliance on Integrity Control Officers

In many respects, NOPD relies on ICOs to conduct direct supervision duties. ICOs, for instance, are charged with conducting periodic on-scene observations to "monitor the quality of NOPD services;" checking summons issued by District personnel daily for errors; and talking with citizens about their experiences with NOPD officers. Officers' direct supervisors should be conducting such tasks in the first instance, and NOPD should not have to rely on ICOs for such duties. A similar example is NOPD's initiation of an "audit procedure" in which "field supervisors will randomly visit the scenes of calls to NOPD where the original officer recorded the disposition as Necessary Action Taken, Unfounded, or Gone on Arrival." Such supervisory response to calls, especially calls that are more complicated or prone to problems, should be a routine part of field supervision rather than part of a special "audit."

While ICOs and similar oversight mechanisms serve important functions, we found that NOPD's overreliance on these entities to perform functions that should be part of direct supervision leads to a number of problems. First, the surrogate supervision provided by these other mechanisms is too often ad hoc or random, and insufficient in scope or amount. We found that ICOs are the widely acknowledged but unofficial Assistant Commander for each District, as well as the Administrative Lieutenant for the District Commander, creating duties that are sufficient for at least one full time job. Consequently, ICOs spend relatively little time on direct, integrity-related activities that are, by policy, the core function of their assignment. We found that some ICOs rarely leave the station and do not, as required by policy, check off-duty detail locations or attend community meetings. Nor do ICOs conduct the document-based integrity checks as required by policy. Ops. Bureau Policy #8 requires that ICOs review at least two in-car camera videos each day and make two random citizen call-backs each day, completing a Daily Citizen Call Form for each. Our review of ICO COMSTAT weekly and year-to-date statistics made clear that ICOs, while reporting hundreds of call-backs and in-car camera video reviews over the year, are not keeping up with this requirement. ICO weekly reports routinely indicated between 2-5 citizen call-backs or in-camera videos reviewed per week, and sometimes these duties did not occur at all during the week. Although required by policy, we found that some Districts did not report their ICO's integrity related duties for COMSTAT, and we saw no evidence that ICOs' integrity related work is ever discussed or even referenced during Department-wide COMSTAT meetings.

It is clear that ICOs are not able to complete even the integrity related duties as required by policy. Not surprisingly, we found they are not effectively performing the additional direct supervision duties they have been assigned.

3.      Ineffective Alternative Mechanisms for Supervision

Other units assigned direct supervision-type duties are similarly unable to provide sufficient or consistent oversight. For instance, "A-case officers" are assigned to each District and are meant to act as a liaison between the District and the DA's office to ensure that arrest reports articulate probable cause and thus form a strong basis for prosecution. We found that this assignment had become largely moribund, although the DA's office reports recent attempts to revive the role of A-case officers. This is a good step but, even if performing as contemplated,

- 64 -

A-case officers cannot substitute for close and consistent supervision of field officers by their direct supervisors. Similarly, the Incident Report Review Section is tasked with monitoring the quality of reports "throughout the Bureaus" to ensure they are accurate; complete; include the correct signal and classification; comply with NOPD policy on Incident Reports; and comply with Louisiana criminal law, criminal procedure, and evidentiary law. This Section is required by policy to return reports that do not meet these standards to the originating officer's commander and Bureau Superintendent to meet the standards set forth [by policy]." *See* Ops. Man. Ch. 82.5. Such a unit is commendable if used as a backstop behind first-line supervisors who have already carefully reviewed every arrest report completed by officers under their command. However, our interviews with supervisors and officers, as well as the number of extremely poor arrests reports we reviewed, indicates that supervisors are routinely missing errors and problems with arrest reports. The Incident Report Review Section, while ripe with potential, is in practice of little use, particularly, since it is only staffed by a single officer, a lieutenant. Moreover, any unit set apart from the field, with no realistic opportunity to be on-scene and which does not review incidents until days or weeks later cannot provide the benefits of contemporaneous on-site review that field supervisors are meant to provide.

The second problem with NOPD's de facto reliance on specialized positions or units is that it confuses lines of authority and accountability. In doing so, it may encourage supervisors and officers to view oversight and direction that should be ongoing and routine (such as responding to the scenes of uses of force or particular arrests, and reviewing reports), as something intermittent and random—and someone else's responsibility. As discussed in other sections of this Report, we found this lack of responsibility and ownership throughout NOPD, and particularly evident in responsibilities related to direct supervision, such as use of force reporting and investigation, complaint intake, and report approval.

Finally, where direct oversight is shifted from officers' direct supervisors to others, the supervisor does not have the same opportunity to learn about officers' strengths and weaknesses, and may not always learn immediately of specific errors, depriving the supervisor of the ability to intervene, counsel, and work with their officers to improve their skills and conduct. Primary review and counseling by those more removed from the officer may be less informed, less efficient, and less effective.

We understand that NOPD's establishment of these various systems to act as accountability mechanisms is almost certainly motivated by a perceived need to provide closer oversight to officers and to identify problems that supervisors were missing. However, these systems currently are used as an alternative to effective direct supervision rather than to supplement it, and are a poor substitute for close, consistent supervision of officers by well-qualified supervisors.

By adopting the changes outlined below, NOPD can facilitate more effective and efficient direct field supervision, and allow these other oversight mechanisms to narrow and focus their efforts to better support NOPD's integrity, quality control, and accountability efforts.

C.     Implementing Effective and Accountable Field Supervision

- 65 -

Many of the recommendations made elsewhere in this letter apply equally to the area of field supervision. Inadequate training, poor recruitment, and the problems in NOPD's Field Training Officer program result in too many officers in need of inordinate levels of supervision. Problematic performance evaluations and constraints on promotions result in officers being promoted to supervisory positions when they are not ready or are unqualified to supervise. The lack of in-service training, particularly for new supervisors in areas such as use of force reporting and review, complaint intake and investigation, report writing, and stops, searches and seizures, further compromises field supervisors' ability to effectively supervise. Improvements in these areas will positively impact field supervision of patrol officers. Below, we discuss a number of additional changes to NOPD practice that are necessary to bring about adequate field supervision.

1.      Appropriate Span of Control and Staffing Allocation

In the context of current staffing allocations, field sergeants' span of control which, as noted above, can by policy be as high as one sergeant supervising twenty officers, is too wide to allow for effective supervision. Field supervisors should be able to respond to the scene to review uses of force and to approve certain arrests. They also should be available to handle the initial response to complaints about their subordinates. Supervisors should know their officers and assigned areas well enough to maximize the efficiency and effectiveness of their unit. They should be working closely enough with their officers to be able to comprehensively and credibly evaluate their performance.

In addition to specifically allowing for a wide span of control, NOPD policy and practice further encourages an overly broad span of control by requiring one sergeant to review, track, and approve all reports and activity sheets for the entire platoon. *See* Ops. Bureau Policy #5. While it is not unusual to assign one sergeant the duty of ensuring that all reports are collected at the end of a shift, it is unrealistic to expect one sergeant to conduct meaningful review of all reports and activity sheets for a platoon that may number over twenty officers, even if the sergeant is not assigned any other platoon-wide responsibilities. Even where only eleven officers are covering an entire District during a watch, which, as noted above, did not appear to be uncommon, what would be a manageable span of control of 2:11 is rendered a far more challenging ratio of 1:11, due to NOPD's approach of keeping one sergeant in the station house.

A smaller span of control on paper is thus meaningless if field supervisors are not actually responsible for fewer officers and given the opportunity to directly supervise them by responding to the scene, reviewing their reports, and providing counseling, redirection, and support where necessary. NOPD should review the current staffing allocation of platoon supervisors and restructure current allocations to permit sergeants to spend more time directly supervising officers. At the same time it deploys more sergeants to the field, NOPD should ensure that sergeants in the field do not become de facto patrol officers. NOPD should require that, where feasible, sergeants determine the status of each officer and attempt to identify an available officer before responding to a call to perform the duties of an officer.

2.      Unity of Command

- 66 -

NOPD policy requires that "all employees of the New Orleans Police Department shall be answerable to only one supervisor at a time." *See* Ops. Man. Ch. 41.01.05. This idea of "unity of command," is meant to ensure that officers have consistent supervision and that supervisors know their subordinates' strengths and weaknesses, allowing them to better direct and redirect their work. It appears, however, that large spans of control in patrol and the current allocation of sergeants undermine unity of command. Under NOPD's current approach to supervision, the supervisor to whom a patrol or task force officer reports can change on a daily basis. Officers may be assigned on paper to a particular supervisor to whom they submit leave requests and the like, but supervisors and their subordinates do not consistently work the same days, and supervisors do not necessarily respond to the calls of their own subordinates. There is no true unity of command that facilitates the development of a genuine supervisory relationship between sergeants and their subordinates. With the reported current shortage of platoon sergeants, this dynamic is exacerbated.

In even the best run departments, the absence or unavailability of an officer's supervisor will at times require that another supervisor respond to the scene, review reports, or take a complaint. However, this should be the exception, not the norm. NOPD should implement a true system of unity of command, in which officers and their supervisors have the same days off and the same schedules, and officers report consistently to one sergeant. Sergeants should respond to the scene of arrests and uses of force by the officers they supervise, and should closely review and approve their reports. This level of consistent interaction will allow field sergeants to develop a genuine supervisory relationship with their officers, allowing them to better learn and respond to each officer's strengths and weaknesses, and provide the appropriate level of direction and correction.

3.      Systems to Support Field Supervision

As discussed above, NOPD has in place a number of units and individuals that, properly used, can serve as a significant source of support to field supervisors. There are a number of additional systems that NOPD can implement that will facilitate supervision that is more efficient, effective, and accountable.

*a)     Chain-of-Command Accountability*

Our investigation showed a lack of accountability throughout the chain of command for ensuring that field supervisors properly supervise officers. As discussed throughout this Report, supervisors too frequently approve arrest reports that do not articulate probable cause and use of force reports that are grossly deficient; ignore obvious misconduct in conducting internal investigations; and approve timesheets that are inaccurate. Many, if not most, of these documents require review or approval up the chain of command. There seemed to be no notice taken, much less discipline imposed, for NOPD supervisors who approve egregious force without question; conduct obviously flawed investigations; approve clearly deficient arrest reports; or who simply do not adequately supervise officers. Even where officers are disciplined for misconduct, there is no consistent effort to determine whether supervisors played a role in condoning or turning a blind eye to the officer's conduct, or to hold supervisors accountable where they knew or should have known of the officer's misconduct.

- 67 -

NOPD should provide field supervisors the tools and training to effectively supervise and should consistently hold them accountable where they fail to provide appropriate supervision. This is true also for NOPD commanders. NOPD must hold accountable lieutenants, captains, and above for reviewing and correcting incomplete or inaccurate work by sergeants, and for ensuring that supervisors supervise.

*b)      Early Warning System*

As discussed in the Use of Force section of this Report, NOPD's early warning system, called PPEP, currently exists in name only, providing no real support or assistance to NOPD managers and supervisors. NOPD is currently working with New Orleans' Independent Police Monitor to develop and implement a new early warning system. If properly developed, implemented, and maintained, an early warning system can be an effective way of tracking uses of force and misconduct complaints, among other data. This tracking can assist departments in identifying those officers, supervisors, and units with uses of force or complaints that are unexpectedly high, even after taking into account the nature of the particular assignment. In addition, an early warning system can identify other warning signs, such as excessive sick leave or a sudden decline in performance. Early warning systems can also allow an agency to track trends based not only on individual officers, but also on individual supervisors and commanders.

Once an apparent problem is identified, the department can more closely analyze available data to determine whether there is in fact a problem, and implement appropriate interventions to address it. Interventions might include, for example: requiring additional or remedial training in de-escalation techniques; referral to an officer assistance and support program; transferring an officer to a more suitable assignment; breaking up a problematic unit; or providing training to a sergeant on how to better respond to complaints about her subordinates. By implementing non-disciplinary interventions—and monitoring or revising the intervention to ensure the problem is resolved—departments can prevent more serious misconduct, improve officer safety, avoid substantial liability, improve or repair police-community relationships, and sometimes save an officer's career.

Supervisors can be an invaluable part of providing an early warning about problematic officers, and early warning systems can be an invaluable part of effective supervision. In order for this to be so, early warning systems should be developed and implemented to provide supervisors access to information about their subordinates, as well as the ability to enter into the system their own supervisory observations. With a well-run and accessible early warning system, supervisors do not have to search for documents or rely on second-hand information and hallway conversations to gain complete and real-time information about the officers under their supervision. In order to ensure that early warning systems are accepted and effective, a department must ensure that they are user-friendly and useful to supervisors. This requires consideration of supervisory use at the development and policy stages, as well as training for supervisors on the system once it is implemented.

As it develops NOPD's new early warning system, NOPD should ensure that it can be used as a supervisory tool. NOPD also should provide the policy, training, and administrative support to ensure that the early warning system is maintained and the information included in it is accurate and timely, and that supervisors know how to use it.

### c)    *COMSTAT*

COMSTAT, if modified as recommended in other sections of this Report to include regular consideration and analysis of integrity-related data and the quality of arrests by NOPD officers, will become a more useful tool for supervisors. NOPD should modify COMSTAT in this way and train supervisors how to use this information to provide more effective supervision and direction to their officers.

### d)    *Recording Devices*

NOPD should also ensure that the technology it has implemented is maintained and actually used so that supervisors can better monitor and respond to their officers' actions. NOPD currently has ECD cameras, AVL, and in-car camera capabilities, but these technologies are reportedly underused and, particularly with in-car cameras, often in disrepair. By NOPD policy and generally accepted practice, it is a supervisor's responsibility to report equipment problems, seek to have the equipment repaired, and ensure that officers are properly caring for and using the equipment they are assigned. It is also a supervisor's responsibility to use the valuable information captured by these types of technology to determine the accuracy of reports and assist supervisory inspections of the unit.

Recordings of officer-civilian interactions nearly always exonerate an officer, and in any event they allow a department and a community a better opportunity to learn what really happened during controversial incidents. In the use of force and misconduct investigations we reviewed, there was rarely any indication that supervisors or investigators sought or reviewed audio or video recordings of incidents. NOPD should ensure that review of such information is a routine part of supervision.

NOPD also should consider providing officers with lapel cameras to document interactions, and providing supervisors with handheld audio recorders to permit supervisors to contemporaneously record interactions with community members and complainant statements.


## VIII.    **PAID DETAILS**

There are few aspects of NOPD more broadly troubling than its Paid Detail system. Between August 2009 and July 2010, 69% of all officers, almost 1000 in all, submitted a request to work at least one Detail. This number includes 85% of all Lieutenants and 78% of all Captains. Virtually every NOPD officer either works a Detail, wants to work a Detail, or at some point will have to rely on an officer who works a Detail. The effects of Details thus permeate the entire Department. It is widely acknowledged that NOPD's Detail system has a corrupting effect on the Department. Our interviews with NOPD officers, meetings with other New Orleans-based law enforcement agencies, criminal justice system stakeholders, and the public, revealed that NOPD's Detail system was a significant contributing factor to both the perception and reality of NOPD as a dysfunctional organization.

- 69 -

The Detail system is essentially a form of overtime work for officers.  When on Detail, however, officers are paid and largely controlled by entities other than NOPD.  Many police departments allow officers to work outside law-enforcement jobs, but few if any large police departments have a system of Details as entrenched and unregulated as in NOPD.  Most well functioning departments have far more checks in place to ensure that outside employment does not undermine the police mission or officer accountability.  NOPD's Detail system is a vestige of the days when starting pay for NOPD officers was among the lowest in the nation.  Details were created as a way to give officers maximum flexibility to find work to supplement their incomes.  But as NOPD starting salaries became commensurate with similar jurisdictions in the region (though salaries linked to promotions and years-on continue to lag), the Detail system remained largely unchanged.

In the last few months, the Superintendent has begun to implement measures meant to correct and prevent some of the negative impact of the Detail system.  In August 2010, the Superintendant banned cash payments.  *See* Gen. Order #828.  But, pursuant to this same policy, officers are still expected to negotiate their compensation with the Detail employer.  In December 2010, the Superintendent initiated a program to try to centralize Detail information by setting up a single telephone number for all officers to call to report working a Detail, and a web-based application for officers to enter additional Detail information.  *See* Gen. Order #848.  While these are undoubtedly improvements, it is too early to assess their effectiveness and, regardless, they are a small part of the wholesale remaking of the Detail system that is necessary.

A.     The Impact of the Detail System as Currently Structured

NOPD's Detail policy is set out in the NOPD Ops. Man. Ch. 22.8, *Paid Details* and defines a Detail as "off-duty employment, for compensation (anything of value, however slight, (tangible or intangible)) . . . by another individual, business, establishment, or organization where the employee is performing the duties of a police officer or a function of the police department."  The policy provides further that  "[e]mployees working paid Details do so as representatives of the New Orleans Police Department."  Officers working Details are "governed by all Department rules, orders and procedures."  Despite these mandates, NOPD's Detail system, as currently structured:  1) drastically undermines the quality of NOPD policing; 2) facilitates abuse and corruption by NOPD officers; 3) contributes to compromising officer fatigue; 4) contributes to inequitable policing by NOPD; and 5) acts as a financial drain on NOPD rather than a source of revenue.

1.     Negative Impact on Quality of NOPD Policing

The Detail system contributes to the poor policing that we observed.  There is evidence that some officers are more committed to their Details than their work for NOPD.  We heard accounts of "ghosting," where an officer shows up for roll call and then reports to his or her Detail, rather than his assignment for NOPD.  Law enforcement officers from outside agencies told us about NOPD officers leaving in the middle of investigations so as not to be late for their Details.  In the records of an October 2009 appeal of a disciplinary decision, it was shown that, for over two years, an officer worked his Detail thirty-eight times on the same days that he took sick leave before it came to the attention of NOPD officials via an anonymous tip.  In some cases, officers are paid by the City and are on a Detail for the same hours.  PIB, for example, found that two detectives worked Details that overlapped with their assigned shifts.  One of the detectives worked overlapping shifts for an eight month period, including eight times in two months.  The other worked four overlapping shifts.

Details can also decrease the quality of policing by leading to divided loyalties and attendant under-policing.  Even where officers working Details show up for their regular shifts, we found evidence that some officers are predominately concerned about their Details, with little regard for making good arrests or their other policing responsibilities.  For example, an officer may ignore potential criminal incidents that could have an adverse effect on the officer's Detail if addressing the apparent criminal violation would jeopardize the Detail (and income), or if there is a personal relationship with the business because of a friendship or a longstanding working relationship.  It is widely acknowledged in the policing field that some businesses hire officers on Detail with the expectation that officers will "look the other way" when faced with a conflict between enforcing the law and protecting the business's interest.  We reviewed one case, for example, in which an officer learned that a warrant had been issued for his Detail employer's arrest, and the officer called to notify the employer about the warrant and did not arrest him or send others to arrest him.  While the employer subsequently turned himself in, this can be seen as either preferential treatment for the Detail employer or a dereliction of duty by the officer but, regardless, is not the manner in which warrants should be handled.

The amount of money that officers can earn working Details increases the incentive for officers to emphasize their Details over their regular police duties.  We have, for example, heard of officers receiving as much as $300 to $500 a night to serve as private security guards for professional athletes.  We also heard of two motorcycle officers who insisted on $100 cash each for a one way escort from a New Orleans church to a New Orleans French Quarter hotel.  When officers can earn more money on their Details than they do as officers, they may feel a greater allegiance to their Detail employer than they do to the public they are sworn to protect, and they may look the other way rather than report criminal wrongdoing by their Detail employer.

NOPD's Detail system further undermines good policing by undermining the chain of command.  Although Chapter 22.8 bars lower ranked officers from supervising higher ranked officers, there is nothing to bar lower ranked officers from coordinating Details for higher ranked officers.  The Detail coordinators possess an inordinate amount of power.  The coordinator decides who works when, where, and for how much.  Some Detail coordinators officially receive extra pay from the businesses, while others are said to just "take a little off the top."  We were told that some coordinating officers get paid an extra five hours a week or receive as much as $200 per week just to coordinate Details.  Having lower ranked officers acting as coordinators puts supervisory officers who want to make extra income in a situation where they answer to a lower ranked officer.  This naturally affects the ability or willingness of the supervisor to question the performance of, or to discipline, an officer who is responsible for the supervisor's additional income.  This also leads to the appearance of, if not the reality of, favoritism.

It is also likely that the coordinating officer is coordinating the Details during regular work hours.  In order for a Detail coordinator to determine who will work, when officers will work, and how last minute absences will be staffed, that coordinator needs to be in regular contact with the officers and the business entity. It is highly unlikely that all of this work is done on non-NOPD time.

2.      Role of Details in Facilitating Abuse and Corruption

With poor documentation, no restrictions on officers soliciting work, and officers being allowed to negotiate their own compensation, it is easy for officers to extort businesses or individuals. We heard, for example, of many instances in which officers insisted on exorbitant sums of money, often in cash, for motor escorts. We learned of one instance in which officers told a business owner that if the business owner did not hire certain officers at a particular rate, the business would not receive *any* police protection from NOPD. The business owner reportedly was told, "You f*** with me and you will never see a police car again." When the business owner tried to speak to a supervisory officer about the issue, the supervisory officer told the business owner that there was nothing the supervisory officer would or could do about the threat. Because of the perceived need for the additional security, the business owner relented and hired the officers he was told to hire at the rates demanded.

We heard of officers receiving free or subsidized housing for doing nothing other than living, and possibly parking their police car, in a particular neighborhood. While subsidizing officer housing can be a progressive measure to enable and encourage officers to live in the cities and neighborhoods they police, such a program constitutes compensation and requires oversight to ensure it is administered fairly and effectively. We were told that some officers who were provided free or subsidized housing would not leave their residences when notified of an incident occurring right outside their doors.

Complaints about officers working Details might also be compromised. In some larger Details, such as the security for events at the Superdome, misconduct complaints are given to the Detail coordinator, and neither the Superdome nor the officer's regular supervisor has any way of knowing how or if the coordinator deals with these complaints.

3.      Increased Risk of Dangerous Officer Fatigue

Because NOPD Detail policy allows officers to work as many as 28 additional hours per week and has little oversight to ensure officers adhere to even this generous cap, it facilitates a system in which officers are so fatigued that it compromises their own safety, impacts their long term well being, and impacts the quality of their work. Until recently, NOPD had virtually no way to know if officers were keeping to the maximum allowable number of hours. NOPD's new web-based application allows NOPD to better track officers' Detail hours, but the Department has not put in place a system of accountability to ensure that officers do not work more than 28 hours, or that their Detail work does not compromise their work for NOPD. In speaking with Judges and other members of the criminal justice system, we heard complaints that officers were often too tired to perform their duties on the street and in the courtroom. There is nothing in the rules to prevent an officer from working an overnight Detail and then going directly to his/her NOPD job in the morning. Being sleep-deprived, especially chronically so, can contribute to an officer making dangerous tactical errors; missing potential evidence; taking investigatory short

- 72 -

cuts; writing incomplete reports; providing inaccurate testimony; and acting unprofessionally toward residents.

### 4. Role of Details in Contributing to Inequitable Policing

NOPD's Detail system contributes to the inequitable policing we observed in New Orleans. NOPD leadership should know how to best deploy its officer resources, but the Detail system as it is currently operating undermines that judgment. The breadth and prevalence of the Detail system has essentially privatized officer overtime at NOPD, resulting in officers working Details in the areas of town with the least crime, while an insufficient number of officers are working in the areas of New Orleans with the greatest crime prevention needs. Those with means in New Orleans are essentially able to buy additional protection, while those without such means are unable to pay for the services and extra protection needed to make up for insufficient or ineffective policing. When NOPD is able to do its job effectively, no community should feel that it has to pay extra to be secure. NOPD officers who work neighborhood Details do the same work—stand watch, patrol, investigate criminal activity—that the City pays them to do, but when they work these Details, they are not supervised by NOPD. While any community that wants extra security certainly has a right to pay for it, it raises troubling legal and ethical questions when that extra security might otherwise have been focused on parts of the City most in need of police assistance. We were told by NOPD officers that, pursuant to policy, when they work a Detail they have no obligation to respond to a crime reported near to, but outside, of their Detail area. *See* Ops. Manual Ch. 22.8.36 ("Commissioned members working paid details will investigate all incidents which occur within the boundaries of the detail area.").

### 5. Cost of Details to the City

The Detail system costs the City money it can little afford to spend, while the City could easily be making money for providing the same service. Officers are permitted and even expected to use their NOPD equipment while working Details. In most instances, neither the business nor the officer is charged for the private use of this equipment. NOPD's vehicle fleet is in significant disrepair, and yet the City pays for the additional maintenance on and gas for vehicles used during Details. If an officer gets injured while performing police duties on a Detail, or is successfully sued for misconduct while working a Detail, the City is potentially liable. Over the past three years, for example, three motorcycle officers who have been in accidents while working Details have had their workers' compensation claims paid by the City. In December 2009, a canine officer took his dog to his Detail assignment and took the opportunity to conduct a training exercise. The canine died when it fell down an open elevator shaft. The City bore the loss of the approximately fifteen thousand dollars it would cost to replace this trained canine.

### B. Fixing the Paid Detail System

It is uncertain whether NOPD's Detail system can or should be salvaged. What is certain is that the mechanisms currently in place to prevent the type of problems discussed above are insufficient, and far-reaching changes to the Detail system are necessary. As the examples noted above indicate, the mechanisms NOPD currently has in place to ensure officer accountability, including Detail checks by the Office of Compliance and ICOs, may not be significantly more effective than reliance on ad hoc anonymous tips. NOPD's ambivalence towards effective accountability in its Detail system is further evidenced by its lax enforcement of Detail related policies, such as Ops. Man. Ch. 22.8, which provides that officers are not permitted to work Details at ABOs. The definition of ABOs —"a place where the sale of alcoholic beverages is the primary source of revenue"— can be, and is, flexibly interpreted, and there is no guidance for supervisors approving the Detail in what "primary" means or how they are to make this factual determination.

Despite recent changes, NOPD's Detail documentation still does little to encourage accountability. Even with the recently added web-based data entry system, the Paid Detail Authorization Form is still used to initially approve Details. This means that Detail information is still kept on nearly three thousand pieces of loose paper divided among the different districts. This paper-based system undermines effective oversight, a dynamic that is further exacerbated by the fact that the individuals tasked with this assignment, ICOs, have almost no time to do it. An ICO told us that he had very little time for checking on Details when it was just one of dozens of areas of compliance for which he was responsible. While the supervisor said that he does random checks on Details, he stated that he has never thought to ask a business owner how the Detail came to exist or about officer performance on the Detail. With close to 1000 officers working Details, as they are currently structured, it would take a sizeable number of officers to ensure appropriate oversight, including making sure that officers are not working Details when or where they are not supposed to be, and are properly representing the Department when they are working Details.

NOPD needs to immediately stop the decentralized-system of self-negotiated and poorly monitored Details. In its place, the City should create a single office that arranges all outside employment requests. If done right, this office will pay for itself and more. In Miami, for example, such an office makes over one million dollars annually for the City. NOPD should establish a system with appropriately stringent criteria that will fairly assign officers to work paid Details, sending the message that Details are not an entitlement based on favoritism or friendship. NOPD should set Detail pay uniformly according to rank and include a reasonable fee that goes to the City to cover the expenses of the outside employment office, workers compensation, fuel, use of equipment, and any other actual or potential costs to the City. Officers who work outside employment should be required to log into CAD system and the District Commander will have the authority to pull officers to another assignment in the event of an emergency in the area. This new office will pay the officers and take out any applicable taxes in the same manner that taxes are taken out of officer salaries. The 28 hours per week maximum should be examined and likely lowered. In addition, officers with any sustained disciplinary actions should be ineligible to work these outside jobs.

There is no question that working a Detail is a privilege and not a right; a refusal to approve a Detail, or to withdraw approval, is not subject to appeal to the Civil Service Commission. While a significant number of officers expressed to us their desire that the Detail system remain unchanged, many others acknowledged the problems related to Details. We believe that the changes we recommend have the potential to provide officers better protection from the problems we found. The changes we recommend will help ensure that supervisors do

- 74 -

not play favorites based on Detail positions, or unfairly punish the non-favorites, and that everyone who wants to work extra-time can do so (except those whose behavior has made them ineligible). These changes should provide officers, some of whom told us they pay for their own supplemental insurance, greater assurance that they are covered by City insurance if they are injured while working a Detail. While some officers noted their concern that non-NOPD officers would not have to abide by any new rules and could price themselves below the NOPD officers, the experiences of officers in other cities indicate that this need not be the case.

NOPD already has models, albeit not perfect ones, for a better-regulated centralized Detail system. At the Superdome, the City's largest Detail, NOPD officers are paid according to rank: Officers make $29.00 per hour; Sergeants $33.00; Lieutenants $35.00; and Captains $39.00. Officers who want to work at the Superdome must fill out a separate employment application and fill out tax forms (I-9, W-4, L-4). The officers are then paid by check. While this Detail is currently coordinated by one NOPD Captain, a City office could and should take over this task.

Similarly, the New Orleans Police and Justice Foundation ("NOPJF") administers a media Detail for movie and television productions under which all of the officers are paid a predetermined amount (normally $25 an hour and up to $75 an hour during a City-wide special event such as Mardi Gras). An officer-administrator is paid 10% of that amount, and the NOPJF receives 4%. The business requesting the Detail pays the NOPJF which distributes the money and provides a 1099 tax form. That 14% in administrative fees could and should go to the City.

Fundamentally restructuring the current Detail system will also protect businesses. Currently, businesses sometimes feel they must pay for Details to obtain the police services that should be provided by NOPD as a matter of routine policing. In addition, businesses have no way to hold officers accountable when they do not show up for their contracted Detail or perform poorly while on Detail. A business owner described this problem in stark detail when he explained that there was nothing that he could do when officers showed up late, failed to show up at all, or failed to provide agreed upon services, all of which the business owner had experienced. Another employer described his frustration that he had no idea whether or not he would actually receive security because everything was handled casually over the phone and he was rebuffed when he requested written confirmation. A new, centrally-run system will help NOPD provide better policing for the City overall and ensure that its individual officers provide better policing as well.

## IX.   <u>PERFORMANCE EVALUATIONS AND PROMOTIONS</u>

NOPD's evaluation and promotion practices are deficient to the point that it may be impossible to correct patterns of constitutional misconduct without also correcting the failings of these systems. NOPD's promotional system does not adequately assess or consistently reward the officers who are best able to police effectively and constitutionally. Promotional decisions do not adequately consider misconduct by officers or their ability to lead with integrity and diligence. Performance evaluations do not sufficiently assess officers' conduct or value constitutional policing. As they currently function, NOPD's performance evaluation and promotion systems erode public confidence in the Department, facilitate officers' unconstitutional conduct, and fail to identify and develop officers with the capacity to lead with integrity.

People inside NOPD and in the broader New Orleans community view NOPD's promotion and performance evaluation systems as broken. City leadership, community members and NOPD officers share a deep concern about these systems. In November 2010, a NOPD employee satisfaction survey ranked promotions and performance evaluations among the areas about which employees expressed the most dissatisfaction. While a slight majority of respondents agreed that the Department punishes unethical behavior, a mere 17% agreed that the Department rewards ethical behavior. Research shows that departments that reward officers who display exemplary leadership qualities with promotion foster the growth of a values-based, ethical culture in the department. The NOPD survey also found that only 13% of respondents believed that "promotions are handled fairly." A report by the Business Council of New Orleans assessing the New Orleans Civil Service System noted similar problems in a report released in May 2010. Our review similarly showed significant problems with both NOPD's performance evaluations and its system of promotions. These problems directly impact NOPD's ability to assess and promote officers who are effective and ethical.

A.      Inadequate Processes to Assess Officer Performance

Performance evaluations are an important tool for a department to help employees improve their skills and effectiveness, and assess employees' ability for particular assignments. As with promotional assessments, performance evaluations must be carefully aligned to a department's values, mission, and needs, both as a signal to employees of what the department values and will reward, and to assess employees' ability to live up to those standards.

NOPD's performance evaluation system is insufficient in form, frequency and scope to achieve the goals of encouraging, assessing, and rewarding effective and constitutional policing. Our review of NOPD policy, as well as interviews with NOPD officers, supervisors and commanders, City officials, and Civil Service Commission employees, confirmed that the current performance evaluation process is not directly tailored to police work or to individual officer goals. We found that NOPD's performance evaluation system is out of date and focuses too much on process and too little on substance. NOPD's policy on Performance Evaluations, Ops. Man. Ch. 35.1, *Performance Evaluations,* was last updated in 2005. According to the Civil Service Commission, and the Business Council of New Orleans' report, performance evaluations are used primarily to prioritize which employees should be terminated, in the event that budgetary restraints necessitate a reduction in force. This is a gross-underutilization of a valuable tool.

NOPD's performance evaluations do not assess an officer's crime prevention skills and abilities. There are no specific goals for the officers, and no assessment of an officer's progress in achieving stated goals. Likewise, there is no assessment of an officer's ability to build effective community partnerships or problem-oriented policing efforts. According to City officials, the city-wide performance evaluations have not changed in 20 years and are badly in need of updating. Consistent with recommendations from outside reviews, Civil Service Commission staff and police officials reported a need for more task-specific evaluations, but

- 76 -

recognize that this would require the creation of different evaluations for different City departments, for which the City currently has allocated no funding. However, each City department, including NOPD, already has the authority and ability to create their own performance evaluation to overlay the City-wide performance evaluation form. NOPD has not done this.

In addition, training for supervisors on how to most effectively evaluate employees' performance under the current system is insufficient. Supervisors are offered three hours of non-mandatory training that consists of little more than how to complete the city-wide performance evaluation form. Formal performance evaluation appears to be an annual (at most) event, rather than an ongoing process. The Civil Service Commission encourages quarterly evaluations, but we found no evidence of NOPD consistently meeting this goal. There is no formalized system of on-going, documented, supervisory evaluation of subordinates' work, and we saw very little evidence of informal evaluation.

Performance evaluations should be both formal and informal, with formal evaluations occurring several times a year. Evaluations should be documented to track employees' progress and growth. Poor performance should also be documented. Documentation is critical so that a new supervisor can understand an employee's strengths and weaknesses and can build on previous efforts. Each supervisor of an employee during the time period being evaluated should provide input on the employee's performance.

More generally, NOPD should work with the City and the Civil Service Commission to modify the current City-wide system, or develop a more useful new system. Regardless of whether the current system continues, NOPD should develop its own specific and comprehensive system of evaluating officer performance. This system should recognize that ethical and effective policing are intertwined and assess both. Performance evaluations should build in consideration of the officer's productivity in all areas of law enforcement, including the officer's success at preventing crime, helping to build strong prosecutable cases, and engendering community trust. The performance evaluation system should be better integrated into ongoing supervision and should be documented.

B.      Inadequate Systems for Promoting Ethical and Effective Officers

A police department's mechanism for selecting officers for promotion is a critical component of effective and constitutional policing. As officers are promoted they gain wider impact and influence. Promotion decisions convey to other officers and to the community the department's values and the type of conduct that will be rewarded. To be effective and to ensure that officers and the community recognize the department's values, the department has a strong interest in ensuring that its promotional system identifies and selects for promotion the most capable and ethical officers, with the greatest capacity to grow and to lead others.

The challenge in developing and implementing a system of promotions that furthers a police department's effectiveness and integrity is two-fold. First, the promotions system must be thoughtfully tailored to measure the particular skills, values, and traits the department needs in its leaders. To do this, promotional tests and interviews must accurately assess officers' law enforcement knowledge and skills, including an officer's sense of ethics and ability to remain clear-headed under pressure, implement problem-oriented policing strategies, communicate professionally, and motivate others. Second, an effective promotional system must strike the difficult balance between structure and flexibility. A system of promotions must be sufficiently structured to ensure that the process identifies and rewards the values and abilities that the department needs to be effective, and does so in a manner that is fair for all employees. At the same time, a promotions system must be sufficiently flexible to ensure that the best officers are promoted despite the unavoidable imperfections of the assessment process, or unnecessary procedural obstacles. This is particularly true in organizations like NOPD, where a failure to promote the most highly capable and ethical officers both reflects broader systemic deficiencies and contributes to patterns of misconduct.

NOPD's promotions system does not include any of the components of an effective system. NOPD promotion policies, Ops. Man. Ch. 34.1, *Police Officer Classes and Promotional Criteria,* Ch. 34.2, *Promotion Committee,* and Ch. 34.3, *Promotional Examinations*, have not been revised since 2001-2002. In policy and practice, NOPD's promotions system is overly focused on process, with limited substantive assessment. Moreover, until very recently, the promotional exam had not been revised in years and was, by all accounts, woefully out of date.

The infrequency of NOPD's promotions exams narrows the pool of the most capable promotional candidates. Due to the Civil Service Commission's limited resources, there are too few opportunities for officers to sit for promotional exams. Officers may wait for several years after they are eligible before taking an exam. Recently, for example, the City decided not to fund a sergeant's promotion exam. Infrequent exams can have a dramatic impact not only the promotion but also the retention of good officers. As noted in a 2007 report by the RAND Corporation, because NOPD exams are infrequent, some officers who seek promotion will resign because, as quoted in the RAND report, "their timing was wrong," and they do not want to wait for years until the next examination is given. At the same time, when promotion exams are infrequent, old promotion lists remain in effect and higher-scoring officers may leave the Department, resulting in officers who score relatively low being promoted over newer officers who were not given a chance to compete.

NOPD's promotions system as currently structured does not provide for sufficient assessment to determine which officers should be promoted. There is little consideration of community policing or ethics (persons close to the process report that, promotional candidates in the past "did not do so well" on the ethical scenarios that were incorporated into the exam). The promotional examinations result in a relatively rigid system of employee "bands" that, particularly combined with problems caused by the infrequency of exams, may not enable the Superintendent to select the most appropriate candidates. NOPD's promotions policy ostensibly takes into account an officer's disciplinary history. However, NOPD's complaint investigation system renders this consideration ineffective. Many complaints are not formally investigated when they should be; investigations are not sustained when they should be; and sustained cases do not result in the discipline they should. Current NOPD policy further undermines adequate consideration of an officer's disciplinary history. By policy, only sustained violations for conduct with an *incident date* within the previous year of the promotion, and which resulted in a penalty greater than a Letter of Reprimand, are considered, and denial on even this ground appears discretionary.

NOPD should work with the City and Civil Service Commission to improve the promotions process in NOPD so that it is both equitable and flexible, allowing for promotions of NOPD's most effective and ethical officers. NOPD, the City, and the Civil Service Commission should also work to ensure that promotional exams are given more frequently. NOPD and the City should develop promotional criteria and assessment tools that ensure that NOPD promotional selection criteria both communicate NOPD's values and mission, and result in the promotion of officers who most closely adhere to these values and are capable of carrying out its mission. NOPD should require assessment of officers' community policing and problem solving efforts and abilities, as well as officers' professionalism, ethics, and integrity, as part of the promotions selection process. Officers with a disciplinary history that does not comport with the behavior that NOPD wants to model for other officers should be disqualified from promotion.

## X.   MISCONDUCT COMPLAINT INTAKE, INVESTIGATION, AND ADJUDICATION

An effective system for investigating complaints of officer misconduct can prevent constitutional violations and transform a community's perception of its police department. NOPD's system for receiving, investigating, and resolving misconduct complaints, despite some strengths and recent improvements, does not yet function as an effective accountability measure. Our review found significant weaknesses in policies governing complaint classification, documentation and investigation, as well frequent departures from existing policies. We found that NOPD's policies and practices exclude from investigation many categories of serious officer misconduct and fail to adequately investigate and track allegations of discriminatory policing.

In addition to the lack of clear policy guidance, we found deficiencies in resources, training, supervision, and accountability, which serve to weaken investigations and result in poorly-supported investigative outcomes. We found significant problems with how NOPD collects, documents, and analyzes evidence in misconduct investigations, including physical evidence and witness interviews.

Our review also found that the Department metes out discipline and corrective action inconsistently and, too often, without sufficient consideration of the seriousness of the offense and its impact on police-community relationships. As a consequence of these deficiencies and an accompanying lack of transparency, NOPD's system for investigating and responding to allegations of officer misconduct does not effectively change officer behavior or hold officers responsible for their actions, giving it little legitimacy within the Department or in the broader New Orleans community.

NOPD is making considerable efforts to improve complaint intake, investigation and adjudication. The Department has made both innovative changes, such as placing a civilian at the helm of PIB, and implemented long-overdue corrections to basic policies — such as clarifying an employee's duty to be honest and truthful at all times; making dismissal the presumptive penalty for not being truthful; and requiring employees to cooperate with investigations and report misconduct to a supervisor.  In making these efforts, NOPD has acknowledged that the objectivity, independence, and integrity of misconduct investigations are critical to police accountability.  However, NOPD will need to implement more fundamental and comprehensive change to achieve a truly effective system for investigating and responding to allegations of misconduct, and to restore community and officer trust in this critical accountability system.

A.  NOPD Misconduct Investigation Process and Background

PIB is commanded by a civilian Deputy Superintendent who is responsible for overseeing the timeliness and quality of NOPD's internal investigation process, from complaint intake through the imposition of discipline.  PIB's Administrative Division is responsible for complaint intake, administrative investigations (including assigning most administrative investigations for District-level investigation), and processing sustained investigations for hearings.[20]  The Bureau's Criminal Division conducts investigations of most criminal allegations against officers, and its Special Operations Section is responsible for conducting integrity checks, although PIB's last Annual Report noted that no such checks were conducted in 2009.  Allegations of rape, child abuse, and homicide by officers are investigated by the corresponding specialized NOPD Division.

PIB Directives provide that an accused officer's individual district or specialized component conducts investigations of administrative (non-criminal) allegations, except for those involving positive drug screening results; firearms discharge incidents resulting in formal investigations; criminal complaints occurring outside Orleans Parish, and unauthorized force complaints.  PIB Dir. #25.  The directives require PIB commanders to consider additional factors when deciding whether PIB should investigate a complaint that would normally be delegated to a District, such as:  whether there may be a perception of bias on the part of the subject employee's immediate supervisor; whether the complaint involves "sensitive issues" or "media attention;" whether the officer is also under criminal investigation in another matter; or at the request of field commanders.  A large proportion of NOPD's internal investigations are thus conducted not by PIB, but by the supervisor (usually a sergeant) of the officer alleged to have committed misconduct.  Each District has an ICO who is tasked with ensuring that misconduct complaints are properly and timely investigated.  However, as discussed in more detail in the Supervision section of this Report, ICOs and PIB report that ICOs have broad and diffuse responsibilities, and that those responsibilities are often expanded further by District commanders, leaving insufficient time for oversight of misconduct investigations.

Under Louisiana State Law, non-criminal, administrative investigations must be completed, and officers notified of the disposition, within 60 days, unless granted an extension by the Civil Service Commission.  *See* La. Rev. Stat. 40:2531.  Even with an extension, which is subject to challenge by the subject officer, the case must be completed within 120 days.  Under state law, without "complete compliance" with this timeline there can be "no discipline,

---

[20] In addition to its responsibilities directly related to investigating allegations of officer misconduct, PIB is responsible for administering a number of other accountability related systems including:  conducting administrative reviews of officer-involved shootings; reviewing and analyzing use of force reports; and administering NOPD's early warning system, known as the Personnel Performance Enhancement Program ("PPEP").  These additional accountability systems are discussed elsewhere in this Report.

demotion, dismissal or adverse action of any sort," regardless of whether the officer committed the misconduct. *Id.*

NOPD reports that most investigations are completed within two months, with more complex cases taking four months to complete. However, the term "complete" does not mean that the case is resolved, since if the complaint is sustained and discipline is proposed, the subject officer may appeal, thereby prolonging the process. Further, as discussed below, the Department designates many investigations as "complete" without appropriately resolving the allegations of misconduct. Thus, despite some success in this area, the intent of a due date—ensuring that investigation of each allegation is initiated and resolved in a timely manner—is not being met.

According to PIB's most recent Annual Report, it conducted 1,465 "case investigations" in 2009.[21] Of these, approximately 321 were formal investigations (called "DI-1s"), including 129 based on complaints from outside NOPD, and 192 based upon complaints initiated by NOPD. Another 342 of these "case investigations" were actually, by policy, documentation of "minor administrative violations" correctable by "simple counseling or minimal intervention by a supervisor" (called "DI-2s"). The vast majority of these DI-2s (291) were based upon internally-generated complaints. "INFO" cases, or documentation of information that does "not contain sufficient information to initiate an investigation," accounted for 168 "complaints." The remaining 634 complaints received and "investigated" by PIB, were resolved with one of the following designations: "NVO" (no violation observed); "NIM" (no investigation merited); or "NFIM" (no formal investigation merited). These classifications fall into NOPD's "DI-3" category, which, by Department policy, includes complaints that do not warrant formal investigation because, among other reasons: "the actions complained of have no basis in fact;" the complainant "challenges the legality of an arrest or a citation;" the allegation is being investigated by an outside agency; or for "other appropriate reason."

Significantly, when a complaint is classified as NVO, NIM, NFIM, or INFO, the allegation of misconduct remains unresolved, with no formal determination of whether the allegation should be "sustained," "not sustained," "unfounded," or "exonerated." Nor is an "informal" complaint finding included on an officer's "short form," the documentation used for decisions related to discipline, assignments, transfers, and promotions. In addition, some informally resolved complaints appear not to be tracked in NOPD's early warning system, called PPEP.[22] In addition, a complaint made to PIB may be "cancelled," but there is no clear instruction in policy regarding what the criteria are for cancelling a complaint. These many exceptions to the requirement that NOPD investigate misconduct complaints thus have the

---

[21] *See* PIB 2009 Annual Report, Appendix I. The count of complaints and the various sub-categories is not consistent throughout PIB's 2009 Annual Report. The actual number in any category often varied by a small amount—usually less than five.

[22] Ops Manual Chapter 13-27, states that PPEP tracks "personnel complaints (sustained, not-sustained, withdrawn, and pending cases)." It thus appears not to track, at least formally, even exonerated or unfounded complaints, as well as informally resolved complaints. PIB staff provided inconsistent answers regarding whether informal complaints are tracked by PPEP. Over a number of conversations, it became apparent that current use of PPEP is haphazard and inconsistent, and Departmental understanding of how it actually operates is similarly inconsistent and incomplete.

potential to affect not only the outcome of individual complaints of misconduct, but also the overall picture of officers' conduct over time.

NOPD reports that of 2325 charges[23] in 2009, it sustained 354, or 15.22%. Of these 354 sustained charges, approximately 128 came from sources outside the department. Thus, it appears that NOPD's rate of sustained allegations of misconduct by non-police civilians is approximately 5.5%. Our review of recent internal investigations similarly indicated that sustained allegations result more often from internally generated "complaints" such as a failure to appear in court, although other sustained charges included being intoxicated on duty, shoplifting, and charges related to an off-duty car accident. PIB's annual reports note that in many instances the final disposition in sustained cases was changed or was still pending, meaning that the allegation has not in fact been sustained and indicating that the actual sustained rate is almost certainly lower than the rate reported in PIB's annual reports.

B.    Deficiencies in Misconduct Complaint Intake and Investigation

1.    Outdated and Inconsistent Policies

NOPD policies and directives related to the receipt, investigation, and adjudication of misconduct complaints are in critical need of revision, updating and clarification. Current policies, most notably Ops. Man. Ch. 26.2, *Disciplinary Hearings/Penalties*; Ch. 52.1, *Internal Disciplinary Investigations*, and PIB Operation Directives, nominally updated in May 2010, include policies that fundamentally undermine NOPD's ability to fully and fairly investigate misconduct. In other instances, there is a disconnect between the policy as drafted and NOPD's operational structure or capacity, resulting in a policy with which NOPD officers literally cannot comply, and undermining the credibility of NOPD's written mandates overall.

Some PIB policy deficiencies appear to have a significant impact on the scope, quality, and effectiveness of NOPD's efforts to investigate and review officer conduct. Under PIB Operation Directive #3, for example, one of the most frequently complained of and serious types of misconduct in policing is outside the jurisdiction of PIB investigation: where the "complaint challenges the legality of an arrest or citation," the challenge "must be resolved in the appropriate court of law," and the complaint should be classified by PIB as "NVO," or No Violation Observed.

It is appropriate for an agency to decline to investigate complaints that truly challenge only the guilt or innocence of the complainant without alleging officer misconduct, and another PIB Directive does provide that "investigators shall obtain and review all pertinent documentation and information to ensure that no other violations exist." Furthermore, our review of PIB case files indicated that investigations of allegations of illegal arrest do occur. However, PIB's policy in this area likely discourages the investigation of allegations of serious misconduct. Indeed, our review of PIB case files confirmed that many allegations of illegal arrests and related misconduct, such as improper stops, detentions, searches, and seizures, are not fully investigated and are instead improperly closed with a "NVO" or similar "informal"

---

[23] Each case may include more than one charge, although the PIB reports we reviewed were not always consistent in presenting this information.

designation.[24]  In one investigation we reviewed, NOPD closed a case as an informal DI-3 where the complainant alleged that officers planted drugs on his stepson, subjected the stepson to a body cavity search (officers first obtained a warrant), and used unnecessary force in the arrest. When it closed the case informally, NOPD sent a letter to the complainant saying, "The matter of your son being arrested must be adjudicated in State Court."  This policy is particularly problematic given widespread concerns we heard from community members about allegedly illegal stops, searches, and seizures.

We also found a lack of clear guidance about when an investigation can be changed from a DI-1 formal investigation to a DI-3 informal investigation, or why this change was made in particular cases.  The ease with which complaints can be downgraded or resolved as NVO, NFIM or NIM undermines the integrity of NOPD's misconduct investigation process.  Our review showed a number of instances, beyond allegations related to searches and arrests, where a formal finding should have been reached but was not.  In one case closed without resolution as an informal DI-3, the complainant called 911 after her former boyfriend, an NOPD officer, allegedly tried to kick in her door after she refused to answer his knock.  In another case, resolved as INFO, the complainant alleged that an officer "bumped" him with his squad car and left the scene.  Other cases closed without resolution that should have been formally resolved include a complaint that an officer was alleged to be assisting criminals and a number of complaints that officers were rude and unprofessional when interacting with community members during pedestrian or traffic stops.

Because it prevents investigation of allegations of even serious misconduct, and results in a systemic failure to track complaints over time, this classification system needs to be fundamentally altered.  Complaint classification should be allegation-driven, not outcome-driven, so that all allegations of misconduct are investigated and given a formal disposition of sustained, not sustained, exonerated, or unfounded.  The level of investigation should be tailored to the requirements of the case including, for example, the seriousness of the allegations and the complexity of the case.

PIB policies and directives related to the assignment and investigation of misconduct complaints by field supervisors are also deficient in that they assign relatively serious and complex allegations for field investigation and do not provide sufficient guidance to field supervisors on how to fairly and completely investigate misconduct complaints.  It is common and acceptable in policing to have field supervisors investigate less serious allegations, such as those concerning demeanor, verbal abuse, neglect of duty and poor response to calls for service. Requiring field supervisors to investigate such complaints can be an important and beneficial component of a department's accountability system, since the field supervisor is in the best position to provide positive and constructive feedback to his/her subordinates, and in the best position to prevent recurrence of negative encounters between officers and community members.

---

[24] Consistent with the view that pursuant to this policy complaints of illegal arrests and related misconduct are often not investigated is the fact that none of the 2076 allegations listed in the 2009 PIB Annual Report were in a category that would appear to directly encompass false arrest, illegal stop, search or seizure, or other Fourth Amendment violations. There were only 152 allegations for the entire year in the four categories that, while broader, could conceivably capture such allegations:  Adherence to Law (121); Abuse of Position (6); False/Inaccurate Reports (21); and Acting Impartially (4).

- 83 -

However, without strong training, clear policy guidance, and close oversight — including by supervisors' own chain of command — field investigations of misconduct will be sub-par. At NOPD, none of these elements are in place, resulting in demonstrably poorer-quality misconduct investigations completed by field supervisors.

2.      Systemic Failure to Investigate and Track Allegations of Bias

Another policy failure that impedes NOPD's overall ability to investigate and track a significant area of misconduct is the lack of any policy or protocol that provides guidance or structure to the requirement that the Department track allegations of racial, ethnic, LGBT status, or other bias-based profiling. *See* Ops. Man. Ch. 41.6. Currently, PIB is not tracking allegations of racial profiling or other forms of bias-based policing because it does not have the ability to do so. To the extent that they are tracked at all, PIB complaints are tracked exclusively by rule number violation. Because there is no specific rule violation covering discrimination or bias, PIB personnel told us they would probably classify a racial profiling complaint under "Professionalism." Of the three types of classifications that PIB uses, DI-1, DI-2, and DI-3, only the DI-3 has a place to note that the complaint concerned discriminatory policing. This is particularly problematic since, as noted above, DI-3s are usually resolved with findings of NVO, NFIM, or NIM, which are not tracked in NOPD's early warning system and do not result in any formal determination of whether the alleged misconduct occurred.

PIB's inability to capture or track racial profiling/bias complaints prevents any meaningful study or analysis of those complaints. Indeed, although PIB's 2009 Annual Report states that there were zero racial profiling complaints that year, there is little question that NOPD does receive complaints of racial profiling and other forms of biased policing. In addition to the many complaints about bias we heard from community members, we found such allegations in the sample of investigative files we reviewed. In one case, a bus driver observed an officer doing a traffic enforcement detail and alleged that the officer cited only black drivers and gave white drivers warnings. PIB conducted an investigation of the case but closed the case with a NVO finding, even though the facts as alleged clearly would have violated NOPD policy. In a separate case that was formally investigated but not sustained, the complainant asserted that the officer used a racial epithet towards him, slapped him, and stole his computer when having his car towed. Consistent with PIB's statement that it does not track such allegations, these case files did not indicate that these allegations were recognized, or tracked, as allegations of racial profiling or biased policing.

3.      Inadequate Training for Complaint Intake and Investigation

Police personnel investigating allegations of misconduct should be among a department's best investigators and should receive training specific to conducting internal investigations. At NOPD, misconduct investigations are conducted by investigators within PIB and at the District level by supervisors, usually sergeants. Neither PIB nor District-level investigators receive sufficient training. District-level supervisors, despite being asked to investigate serious allegations of misconduct receive little to no training in conducting investigations at all, much less internal investigations. To ensure that all investigations meet a threshold of acceptability, a department must provide substantial and ongoing investigative training to field supervisors, as

- 84 -

well as additional guidance, including investigative templates and written investigation protocols, for "field" misconduct investigations, and thorough quality control checks. NOPD lacks each of these components necessary to ensure adequate District-level investigations.

Many of the investigators within PIB and the ICOs, tasked with oversight of misconduct investigations at the field level, have not been specifically trained in conducting administrative investigations. This training is essential because the rules and methods for internal investigations are often different than traditional criminal investigations. Consistent with our findings about training throughout NOPD, most investigators learn how to carry out their responsibilities through on-the-job experience, based primarily on information passed on from more experienced, but usually equally poorly trained, investigators.

In addition to investigative training, NOPD should train all personnel at every level on their role in taking misconduct complaints. NOPD should explain the mechanics of complaint intake and teach officers and supervisors how complaints can actually be turned into positive police-civilian interactions. NOPD should also make clear to all personnel the consequences of failing to take a misconduct complaint.

4.     Insufficient PIB Staffing

Throughout the course of our review, there were 32 total staff in PIB, including investigators, support staff, and managers. This staffing includes a total of fourteen investigators, not including commander/reviewers, or the five investigators in the Special Operations Section, responsible for conducting integrity checks. Four of these investigators are responsible for complaint intake; four are administrative investigators, and six are criminal investigators. As noted above, PIB reported that in 2009 it received 1465 complaints of misconduct and, by state law, has only 60 days (or 120 days if the Civil Service Commission grants an extension) to complete investigations. It is well-settled that NOPD may not discipline an officer if it exceeds this deadline. In one case, for example, NOPD found that an officer discharged his personal weapon during a domestic disturbance, suspended him for fifteen days, and demoted him from the rank of sergeant to officer. The Civil Service Commission denied the officer's appeal but the State appellate court reversed that denial on the grounds that the investigation exceeded both the mandated initial 60-day period and the maximum allowable 120-day period. *Davis v. New Orleans Police Dep't*, 899 So.2d 37 (2005). In another instance, NOPD terminated a sergeant because he and his wife took two police department vehicles on a personal vacation to Florida, contrary to NOPD rules and City policy. The State appellate court confirmed the Commission's decision to overturn the termination because the PIB investigation exceeded 60 days. *Dunn v. New Orleans Police Dep't*, 938 So.2d 217 (2006).

While we did not undertake a formal staffing study as part of our investigation, it appears that, particularly in light of state mandated deadlines, PIB needs additional investigators. Moreover, based upon our interviews and review of case files, it appears that this lack of investigators may be undermining the quality of investigations by encouraging the referral of serious or complex misconduct investigations to field supervisors; the downgrading of cases from formal to informal investigation; and giving short-shrift to investigations to ensure they are completed within the mandated timeframe.

- 85 -

It is critical that a law enforcement agency have sufficient numbers of specially trained and dedicated internal misconduct investigators to investigate more serious administrative complaints of officer misconduct. Likewise, criminal allegations of misconduct, when not investigated outside the agency, should be investigated by specially trained investigators who are kept separate from administrative investigators to avoid contamination of either process. These dedicated investigators, in addition to being well-trained, must also be sufficient in number to ensure that investigations are initiated and completed quickly. Long running or delayed investigations result in lost or stale evidence and are unfair both to the complainant awaiting vindication of his or her rights, and the officer who must endure the stress of an ongoing investigation. Because state law prohibits the disciplining of officers for misconduct if an investigation is not completed within strict state timelines, justice delayed is truly justice denied in instances where the complaint of misconduct was meritorious.

ICOs, if used to their potential, could be a critical adjunct to PIB investigators, allowing PIB to refer some cases for District-level investigation, and requiring less time and focus from PIB to ensure that District level-investigations are well-done and timely. Each District within NOPD is assigned an ICO, who reports to the District Commander. The ICO's duties are myriad but, at least by policy, all directly relate to ensuring that officers within the District abide by Departmental policy. Among many other responsibilities, the ICO is supposed to meet with community members, review randomly selected arrest reports, "ensure" that PIB cases are "properly investigated," manage the Field Training Officer Program, and personally inspect Detail sites. The ICO system is innovative and has enormous potential to assist NOPD with a number of its accountability systems. However, as discussed in the Supervision section of this Report, at present ICOs are spread thin, undertaking responsibilities that could be a routine part of supervisors' and even officers' daily activities, as well as acting as the administrative assistant to the District Commander. As part of ensuring adequate staffing to conduct misconduct investigations, NOPD should rethink how ICOs are deployed and determine how best to restructure so that they can play a more effective role in overseeing misconduct investigations and reduce the staffing pressures on PIB.

5.      Faulty Complaint Intake and Classification

Complaint intake is the critical first step of misconduct investigation. If an individual is afraid to make a complaint, or finds it exceedingly difficult to do so, the police department may never learn of the misconduct. As importantly, if the agency official taking the complaint does not properly and completely document the complaint, a fair and complete investigation will be compromised from the outset.

NOPD has many policies in place designed to ensure that there are no artificial obstacles to complaint investigation: third party and anonymous complaints are accepted, and supervisors are required to receive and document all complaints, even where the complaint does not appear to the supervisor to state a violation of Departmental rule. By policy, complaints can be provided via telephone or letter, and do not need to be written on any particular form. Complaints may be made to the Independent Police Monitor, or via the internet, and NOPD has a complaint brochure and form. PIB commanders told us that "when made aware of it" PIB will investigate allegations of police misconduct that are alleged in lawsuits against the Department or City (although we found no evidence to confirm this is occurring). NOPD has in place written requirements for documenting the circumstances under which an individual has decided to withdraw a complaint. Moreover, by policy, where an investigator determines that the "violations complained of are so egregious that the department would have an interest in pursuing the investigation without the complainant. . . . the investigation must continue to its logical conclusion." This policy of broad complaint acceptance is laudable.

We found that in practice, complaint acceptance does not match the promise of NOPD policy. NOPD's written complaint brochure and form are outdated and misleading. The brochure, which still includes on the cover the name of the former Superintendent, suggests that complaints can be made only to PIB, the DA's Office, the FBI, or the U.S. DOJ. There is no mention anywhere on the form that complaints can be made to any officer, or any supervisor, anywhere in the City. Nor is there mention that individuals may file complaints with the Independent Police Monitor. The form suggests further that complaints must be made in a particular format.[25] After visiting every District station, we noted that posters or other visual information about how to file a complaint were usually absent. Forms were often unavailable. Many District stations were locked and inaccessible even during daylight hours, making it difficult if not impossible for a civilian to file a complaint in person, or even determine how to file a complaint.

A bigger obstacle to ensuring that complaints are received and investigated is the lack of clear direction and variety of opinion among field supervisors over what constitutes a "complaint," and what "taking a complaint" requires. Pursuant to NOPD policy, misconduct complaints can be made to any officer or directly to PIB. PIB policy provides that PIB is open until 10 p.m. to take complaints, although PIB staff stated that PIB in fact was taking *calls* until 10 p.m., and now even that is not happening because the sergeant who took those calls was terminated and has not been replaced. It appears that complaints made at PIB will be received and documented. However, it is far less clear what happens to complaints made to individuals outside PIB. It appears that officers are to direct complainants to their supervisors or to PIB to take the complaint, although policy on this point is unclear. Nearly every supervisor we talked with understood that if an individual went to a District station and said they wanted to make a complaint, the supervisor should meet with them. Beyond that, there was little consistency. We received varying opinions from supervisors about whether supervisors must always formally initiate the complaint process or whether they are permitted in some circumstances to refer the person to PIB, or even informally resolve the complaint and not document it. For complaints made outside PIB, there is no documentation or tracking of when a complaint was made and to whom, and the complainant is not given any sort of reference or control number. According to PIB, if the supervisor does not take the complaint, "we probably won't know." PIB is aware of this problem and reportedly making efforts to correct it, telling us that it recently became aware of a supervisor's failure to take a complaint and initiated a formal misconduct investigation against the supervisor.

---

[25] The form notes that "If a complaint is not made *to the Public Integrity Bureau,* the NOPD will have no means by which to judge the effectiveness of the services it provides or the professionalism of its employees. Therefore, we strongly encourage citizens *to use the attached form* to file a complaint of police misconduct." (Emphasis added.)

- 87 -

The confusion about what "taking a complaint" requires appears due in part to a lack of clear policy.  NOPD policy on complaint intake is in some respects very specific, including, for example, the exact information the supervisor is to leave on PIB's voicemail when reporting a complaint.  However, overall, the policy is deficient.

Adequate complaint intake often requires ensuring that medical attention is provided, if warranted; taking photographs if the complaint involves use of force whether there is observable injury or not; preserving evidence such as video surveillance records; taking statements of on-scene witnesses who may be difficult to locate later; taking officer statements; and completing and attaching related reports.  At NOPD there is no apparent organizational dedication to requiring that supervisors take the steps necessary to establish the facts related to an allegation of misconduct.  Supervisors are given no clear direction or guidance in this area.  Policy is unclear regarding when a supervisor must or should take a complainant's statement, whether witnesses should be canvassed before they disburse, and whether photographs should be taken or any physical evidence (*e.g.*, camera tapes or clothing) collected.  Some supervisors told us they would always take the complainant's statement; others told us they never would.  Most told us they would not take pictures or interview witnesses, although a few said that they would.  We found that complaint statements are too often not recorded and the complainant's statement is often written by the supervisor, with no sign-off by the complainant to ensure that the supervisor accurately captured the entirety of the complaint.

The failure to have complainants write out, or at least review and sign, complaints is of particular concern given the large number of complaints that are resolved with NFIM or NVO findings, which are in many instances based upon the complainant's putative failure to state allegations which, if true, would constitute a violation of NOPD rules or directives.  Similarly, many of the DI-2 files we reviewed did not include documentation sufficient to determine the nature of the initial complaint.  There is thus no way for PIB (or anyone else) to ensure that the supervisor of the subject officer identified and investigated each potential rule violation alleged by the complainant.

Another area of particular concern is the delay between the field supervisor's receipt of the complaint and submitting documentation of the complaint to PIB.  For DI-1s, the supervisor must leave a message on PIB's recorder and submit the documentation related to the complaint within three calendar days.  It compromises investigation quality and sends the wrong message to officers to wait three days to initiate a complaint investigation.  Complaints of serious misconduct, especially misconduct that has just occurred, require an immediate response.  Leaving a message on a recorder minimizes the seriousness of a complaint and is an insufficient substitute for talking with a PIB investigator to ensure that an investigation is being handled appropriately from the outset.  For DI-2s, supervisors have four calendar days to submit documentation to PIB, and for DI-3s fourteen calendar days.  It is only after receiving this documentation that PIB can fully evaluate whether the field supervisor has properly initiated and classified the complaint.  Particularly in light of the 60 day deadline, as well as the insufficient training and lax oversight of field investigations, waiting fourteen days to determine whether a complaint has been properly initiated could significantly undermine any investigation, and is substantially out of line with accepted police practice.

- 88 -

6.  Investigations Inadequate to Support Reliable Findings

The quality of an internal investigation, including gathering evidence, analyzing that evidence, and making findings consistent with what a preponderance of the evidence shows, is the heart of misconduct investigations and, in many police departments, also the Achilles' heel. In addition to training, workload, and resource challenges, police departments often must contend with investigators who may have difficulty making findings against their colleagues, and with complainants who often do not engender investigators' sympathies. A strong culture of accountability and integrity, often combined with an infusion of outside perspective, can temper these tendencies and allow a police department to reach findings that are credible, reliable, and consistently supported by the evidence.

At NOPD, the mechanics supporting robust misconduct investigations are in some respects in place, and we reviewed many good investigations. The Superintendent's decision to put in place a civilian to head PIB demonstrates recognition of the importance of injecting a non-law enforcement perspective to strengthen the objectivity and credibility of investigations.

But, our review of investigative case files and on-going conversations with PIB command staff and investigators, NOPD officers, and community members, make clear that PIB is not yet working as it should. Policies are not followed; review of the completeness and quality of investigations is lax; findings at odds with the evidence are routinely accepted and affirmed through the chain of command; allegations of misconduct are often not investigated, or are improperly resolved without any determination of whether the conduct was within policy; evidence of misconduct, including physical evidence and witness statements, is frequently not gathered; and evidence is often not fairly analyzed, resulting in findings that are inconsistent with the evidence. In general, we found that investigations done at the District level were of poorer quality than those completed by PIB investigators.

While the deficiencies in the quality of misconduct investigations at NOPD have a myriad of causes, it does appear that, in a few instances, through no fault of its own, NOPD simply does not have sufficient time to complete a fair, thorough, and complete investigation. The purpose behind the state mandate that internal investigations be completed within 60 days is laudable, but in practice it has allowed officers to commit egregious misconduct and get away with it. In order to "complete" an investigation within 60 days, PIB investigators do not always gather and sufficiently analyze the evidence necessary for the investigation to withstand scrutiny. NOPD and the City should work with the State to modify the state law to allow for certain exceptions, as do similar laws in other states, such as where the alleged misconduct involves numerous officers or is particularly complex, or where evidence is newly discovered well into the investigation.

   *a)*  *Failure to Identify and Investigate all Allegations of Misconduct*

With some significant exceptions addressed above regarding the investigation of allegations of illegal arrests and biased policing, NOPD policies encourage the identification and investigation of all apparent misconduct, even if the allegation goes beyond the four corners of the complaint. This approach to investigation allows NOPD an opportunity to review the

- 89 -

officer's interaction with the public and evaluate not only whether policy was followed, but also whether the interaction indicates training and safety concerns that need to be addressed. Unfortunately, in the cases we reviewed, we found that this opportunity was often squandered, with very little consideration of training and safety concerns, and often, as discussed above, a failure to formally investigate and resolve even obvious policy violations. This was true even where the allegations of misconduct were quite serious, including use of unnecessary force, planting evidence, and untruthfulness. In one case involving all of these allegations, the investigator made little attempt to contact the alleged victim of the misconduct, and closed the case without ever interviewing him.

In addition to a pattern of allegations of misconduct not being investigated, we found also that in some instances allegations were extensively investigated, only to be closed without any determination of whether the conduct was within policy. We found that this was often done by reclassifying complaints from DI-1 formal investigations to DI-3 informal investigations well into the investigation with no documentation supporting the decision. We observed this practice even where the complainant requested a formal investigation and a formal investigation appeared warranted. Complaint classification should be allegation based, not outcome based, and any change in classification should be documented.

We saw little evidence in the files we reviewed of supervisory oversight of the quality and content of investigations. There was often a failure of the chain of command to sign off on an investigation, indicating that there was no meaningful review. The failure to identify and investigate all allegations of misconduct thus appears to be one of more than just policy, and reflects a failure by NOPD to review misconduct investigations and require that they be completed fairly and fully.

b)      Inadequate Collection and Analysis of Evidence

To be effective, administrative investigations must collect and analyze evidence. Available evidence is generally in the form of physical evidence, documentation, and information gained through interviews. We found problems with how NOPD collects and documents evidence in misconduct investigations.

Official documentation (*e.g.*, police reports, video documentation, dispatch records, shift assignment sheets and officer activity materials) pertinent to the investigation is not consistently gathered; nor do investigators consistently or thoroughly gather evidence through witness interviews. Although the complaint and related documentation will generally make clear what witnesses must be interviewed, a reasonable inquiry to determine whether there are other persons who may have information is a basic component of any investigation. This inquiry, depending on the nature of the complaint, may involve a canvass of the area of the incident, whether the area is a neighborhood or a police lockup, or review of surveillance videos. Whether a police agency conducts a complete search for witnesses is indicative of the police agency's dedication to determining the truth of misconduct allegations. We found not only a failure to canvass for witnesses but a failure to interview even known, highly relevant witnesses.

- 90 -

Where interviews were conducted, they appeared to be incomplete or even biased. Unbiased, professional, and thorough interviews of the involved persons and uninvolved witnesses are central to credible and effective evidence gathering. The investigator must be willing and able to appropriately question the version of facts offered by the interviewee, especially where that version conflicts with the physical evidence or information from other witnesses, whether the interviewee is a police officer or civilian. To help ensure all persons interviewed are treated in the same manner, police agencies often establish a consistent protocol for interviews during administrative investigations to ensure and reinforce proper execution of these protocols through training. In NOPD, interviews are not guided by a policy or practice to be consistent and thorough. Most interviews conducted by NOPD are documented in a narrative summary format, which is both very time consuming and difficult to do without letting some modicum of personal bias alter the interpretation of the information offered by the person being interviewed. Nor does it appear that interviews are consistently recorded or reviewed by the chain of command. To monitor and minimize these problems, the Department should develop interview protocols and should ensure that all interviews be audio recorded and reviewed as appropriate for investigative and audit/supervision purposes.

In the cases we reviewed, the analysis of evidence was often poor. We found instances where investigators used witnesses' statements to the extent they supported officers, but overlooked statements where they supported the complainant. We found that investigators often researched complainant backgrounds to determine credibility but did not document or appear to similarly consider officers' backgrounds. Factual assertions by officers were often not probed, even where the facts asserted in interviews were not included in contemporaneous official documentation.

c)  Findings Unsupported by a Preponderance of Evidence

The ultimate test of the quality of analysis and overall fairness of a misconduct investigation is whether the findings are supported by the evidence. In administrative investigations, the finding must be supported by a preponderance (often described as 51%) of the evidence. We found too many cases where the findings were not supported by a preponderance of the evidence. We found a failure to sustain allegations even where the officer admitted to the violation, and a failure to even list as allegations obvious violations that should have been sustained. In other cases, we found that PIB exonerated officers when the evidence dictated otherwise. This distinction is more than administrative—as noted above, exonerated allegations are not tracked in NOPD's early warning system or considered as broadly for personnel considerations as are "not sustained" findings. In general, the standard for sustaining a case appeared too high. One expert noted that the only sustained allegations in the cases he reviewed involved incidents where the officer was arrested.

It is widely believed that having a higher level commander, rather than the internal affairs or chain of command investigator, make the actual dispositive finding for each allegation (i.e. sustained; not sustained; exonerated; or unfounded) may result in findings more in line with the evidence. NOPD should explore this approach.

- 91 -

C.        Inadequate Investigations of Criminal Misconduct

Reducing and preventing criminal activity by NOPD officers will require transforming a number of NOPD systems, including recruiting, training, supervision, Details, and use of force investigation and review.  Along with these efforts, NOPD and the City must improve the system for investigating alleged criminal misconduct and assisting in the prosecutions of officers who commit crimes.  Current practices place significant obstacles to effective prosecutions of officers and their removal from the Department, and must be changed if NOPD hopes to effectively prevent criminal misconduct by its officers.

In 2009, according to PIB, eighteen officers were arrested and seven issued summonses for alleged criminal conduct including aggravated burglary, theft, false imprisonment, kidnapping, perjury, driving while intoxicated (DWI), domestic violence, aggravated rape and aggravated incest.  Some of these cases have resulted in convictions; others are awaiting trial.  These numbers count only once each of two NOPD officers who were arrested twice in 2009.  By comparison, NOPD's officer arrest rate of 1.3% to 1.8% (depending upon whether summons are included) compares to a New York Police Department officer arrest rate  that ranged between .25% and .36%  from 2001 to 2006.[26]  Moreover, the number of NOPD officers involved in criminal misconduct is likely greater than reflected in the data provided by PIB.  PIB's 2009 Annual Report noted that there was at least one instance where an officer was arrested by another jurisdiction, but did not report the arrest to NOPD as required.  Additionally, we reviewed instances where PIB investigated officer misconduct that appeared clearly criminal, but there was no indication of any arrest or summons, or referral to the DA's Office.

PIB criminal investigators investigate allegations of officer misconduct that are potentially criminal and are required to submit cases with apparent criminal violations to the DA's Office.  Pursuant to PIB Directive, the investigator must check the status of referrals to the DA's Office every thirty days and, after ninety days, inform the complainant that the matter is being reviewed by the DA.  If the investigator finds that there are no criminal violations but "suspects administrative violations may have been committed," the investigation is reclassified from criminal to administrative.  Upon reclassification from criminal to administrative, the 60-day clock for the completion of administrative officer misconduct investigations begins.  PIB does not have policies directly guiding administrative investigators on how to proceed if they discover apparent criminal misconduct in the course of conducting an administrative investigation.

Our review found three overarching problems with NOPD's internal investigations of criminal misconduct.  First, according to PIB and DA officials, as well as NOPD policy, in most instances NOPD does not initiate an administrative investigation until a criminal investigation is complete and the prosecutor has declined prosecution, or if the matter is prosecuted, unless and until a conviction is obtained.  Where a case is criminally prosecuted but the officer is acquitted, NOPD reportedly will not investigate whether the officer violated NOPD policies, despite the lower standard of proof and the fact that it is often the case that misconduct that is not criminal

---

[26] This calculation uses 1400 as the number of NOPD officers and 34,500 as the number of NYPD officers. According to NYPD IA reports, the number of NYPD officer arrests was: 2001: 124; 2002: 114; 2003: 103; 2004: 86; 2005: 91; 2006: 114.

- 92 -

nonetheless may violate agency policies. This practice results in a delay in the initiation of the administrative investigation in some cases for months or even years after the incident occurred. By this time, any additional evidence that might be needed is often impossible to obtain. In addition, the delay of appropriate administrative discipline undermines NOPD's accountability systems. In DWI cases, for example, where there is breathalyzer evidence (and often an admission) indicating the officer's guilt, there usually is generally no reason for NOPD to wait, often for months, until there is a conviction before completing the administrative investigation and administering discipline. Similarly, where an officer is accused of excessive force but the use of force is not found to be criminal, this same conduct nonetheless may violate numerous NOPD policies and warrant the officer's termination from the Department or imposition of other significant discipline. Acknowledging these concerns, PIB reports that it has begun to conduct the administrative investigation in some cases while the criminal investigation is ongoing, creating a firewall to keep cases separate. However, this practice, along with important accompanying protections, have not been memorialized in policy or guided by training.

Each internal investigation should be considered individually and where it becomes apparent that the case may in fact involve criminal conduct, it may be prudent to delay compelling interviews of subject officers, and sometimes other interviews as well. Conducting a full investigation short of compelling an interview generally does not compromise either investigation and is often critical to ensuring the later success of the administrative investigation. Regardless of whether or for how long a compelled statement is delayed, a meaningful and timely administrative investigation is particularly important in cases alleging criminal misconduct, given the usually egregious nature of the allegations, the often slow wheels of the criminal justice system, and the very low rate at which these cases are prosecuted (regardless of jurisdiction). Where officers are not guilty of committing the misconduct, they deserve to have the case adjudicated internally and be brought back to work; where an officer is guilty, the community and department have an interest in seeing the officer disciplined or removed from the force without having to wait months or years with the officer on paid or unpaid suspension. The DA's Office is supportive of this parallel approach to criminal and administrative investigations and the First Assistant reports he has requested that NOPD start taking this approach.

Our second concern regarding NOPD's criminal investigations of officer misconduct is the apparent lack of adequate bifurcation between the administrative and criminal investigations. Officers cannot be forced to choose between losing their jobs because they disobeyed an order to answer questions, and exercising their Fifth Amendment right to avoid self-incrimination. *Garrity v. New Jersey*, 385 U.S. 493 (1967). While an officer may be ordered (or "compelled") to provide a statement to police department investigators, that statement, and any other evidence that derives from that statement, may not be used against the officer in any subsequent criminal prosecution of the officer. Accordingly, whether administrative and criminal investigations are conducted sequentially or simultaneously, the processes, at least after compelled statements have been taken, should be kept bifurcated so that the criminal investigation is not compromised.

In cases where PIB is essentially conducting parallel administrative and criminal investigations—as noted above, without guidance in policy or training—PIB attempts to bifurcate the criminal and administrative investigations and asserts that it does not allow investigators handling the criminal charge to co-mingle their investigations with investigators conducting the administrative portion.  However, ensuring true separation is difficult in a PIB the size of NOPD's.  Indeed, in our review of DA's Office prosecutions of NOPD officers, we observed instances, including some quite serious, that were reportedly quashed because the criminal investigation had been infected by information gained directly or indirectly from compelled statements.  To avoid this result, and to ensure the fact and appearance of independence and impartiality, at least some criminal investigations of officer misconduct should be conducted by an outside agency.  In addition, PIB should immediately develop and implement policies and training to ensure that there is clear guidance and that investigators know how to follow that guidance to keep criminal and administrative investigations separate.

One positive change we observed in this area is that NOPD has ended the egregious practice of transferring officers who had been involved in officer-involved shootings to the Homicide Division and then having a Homicide investigator interview the officer and, at the end of the interview, state on the record that the officer was being compelled to provide a statement, regardless of whether the officer was willing to voluntarily talk about the shooting.  This practice not only undermined the normal dynamic in good departments of officers voluntarily talking about shootings they know are justified, it also sabotaged any criminal case in the usually rare instance where the officer's conduct may not have been justified.

Our third overarching concern about NOPD's investigations of criminal misconduct relates to how criminal referrals are made to the DA's Office and what has happened in the past once those referrals are made.  NOPD offers no written guidance to administrative investigators on when or how to contact a prosecutor for advice or declination when potentially criminal conduct becomes apparent in an investigation.  Currently the practice in PIB is to consult with the prosecutor when the investigator is "concerned" that there may be a criminal issue and the investigator believes the case will be sustained.  NOPD should provide written guidance and training to ensure that investigators identify, seek advice, and refer where appropriate, allegations of criminal conduct.

The flip side of this responsibility lies with the DA to prosecute cases where officers have committed serious crimes.  Our review of some DA's Office case files of NOPD officer prosecutions revealed a number of previous decisions which caused us to question whether the DA's Office investigated and prosecuted potential criminal acts by officers.  In one case, the DA's Office refused to prosecute a referral by NOPD of an officer for indecent behavior with a juvenile and two years later refused to prosecute a charge of simple rape against the same officer.  The current DA is now prosecuting a case of forcible rape and molestation of a juvenile against this officer—who remained on the force until this most recent prosecution.  It is critical that the DA's Office expand its efforts to work with NOPD in this area to ensure that criminal investigations are fair and thorough, and that officers who commit crimes do not escape accountability.

D.      Deficient System for Administrative Discipline

In any police department, it is vital that the leadership administer a disciplinary system that has the confidence of its police officers and the public.  Unfortunately, neither the force nor the public are confident that NOPD's disciplinary system is fair, and our investigation indicates that this lack of confidence is well-founded.  Internally, officers view NOPD's disciplinary system as arbitrary, or as unfairly targeting certain individuals, diminishing its ability to improve behavior.  Externally, NOPD's disciplinary system is seen as ineffectual and, in some instances, protective of bad actors within the Department.  This perception undermines the community's confidence in the Department overall.  There are measures NOPD can and should take so that its disciplinary system routinely metes out reasonable discipline and treats all similarly situated officers equally.  Once such a system is in place NOPD will, in time, regain the confidence of the public and its own officers.

In NOPD's administrative investigation, the investigator makes a finding and recommends a disposition for each identified allegation.  Once completed, the investigation is, according to policy, reviewed by a number of supervisors and commanders for "error checks," and "content checks," and then provided to the PIB Deputy Superintendent for final approval.  Where there are no sustained violations, the case is closed.  At the close of the investigation, PIB is required to send a letter to the complainant and any other involved party, notifying them of the disposition.

Where there is a sustained violation approved by NOPD's Superintendent, the case should be scheduled for a disciplinary hearing, according to NOPD policy.  Disciplinary hearings, pursuant to NOPD policy, are meant to determine the validity of the investigation; recommend a disposition; allow the subject officer to present mitigating circumstances; and recommend a penalty "if the investigation is validated." *See* Ops. Man. Ch. 26.2.  The Hearing Officer (who may be any of a number of commanders) documents the disposition and penalty recommendation and this information is provided to the Superintendent, who may approve, disapprove, or change any recommended disposition or penalty.  The Superintendent's disciplinary action is documented in a disciplinary letter to the officer.  The officer may appeal the disciplinary decision to the Civil Service Commission.

In making disciplinary determinations, NOPD nominally uses a penalty schedule.  This penalty schedule was recently updated to increase the penalties for dishonesty and interfering with investigations and to add failing to report misconduct as a rule violation.  This penalty schedule, while in need of some further updating and revision, has the potential to be a strong accountability tool.  It provides a disciplinary range for rule violations that increases with each recurrence and allows the decision maker to take into account various aggravating and mitigating circumstances to go outside the range.  However, officers at all levels acknowledged that the penalty schedule has not been adhered to or been particularly relevant for a number of years.

Currently NOPD has in place no policy regarding the production of PIB files that document disciplinary decisions that are potentially exculpatory to a defendant in a criminal case, such as findings that an officer lied during an investigation; provided false or misleading statements; or submitted a false police report.  We reviewed one case where an employee was disciplined for lying during the investigation.  Under current policy, this employee would likely be dismissed but, in any event, NOPD should be aware of every employee who may have credibility issues, and should establish a protocol for identifying and producing such materials where appropriate.

NOPD should update its penalty schedule and put in place policies to ensure its proper use (*e.g.* requiring that all deviations outside the prescribed range are documented in writing and that exceptions to the stated range do not become the rule).  More broadly, NOPD should revise its disciplinary hearing structure to provide a greater degree of consistency and integrity to the process by, for example, having a small, defined, and well-trained number of persons (or even one person) conduct disciplinary hearings and document the reasons for disciplinary recommendations.  In addition, the Superintendant should document the reasons for every decision to reverse an investigative finding as well as the reasons for accepting or changing any disciplinary recommendation.  Finally, the City Attorney's Office, which should play a larger advisory role at every stage of the investigative process, should provide close guidance at the disciplinary stage to ensure that NOPD's disciplinary decisions are as fair and legally defensible as possible.

E.      Role of the Civil Service Commission in Disciplinary Adjudication

Sworn and non-sworn permanent NOPD employees have a right to appeal the disciplinary decisions of the Superintendent to the city's Civil Service Commission, and, in adjudicating these appeals, the Commission has an independent duty to ensure that the discipline is in accordance with the rights granted under Louisiana's constitutionally-based civil service system.[27]

During our review, people from across the criminal justice system – from individuals in the Public Defender's office to longtime advisors to the NOPJF to former and current NOPD officials – stated their belief that the Civil Service Commission operates as an impediment to NOPD's ability to appropriately discipline its officers.  There is a shared belief that there are times when officers are rightfully terminated and the Superintendent gets "rolled over" by the Commission.  This sentiment was summarized in a 2010 study of the Commission conducted jointly by the Business Council of New Orleans and the Bush School of Government and Public Service: "[i]n addition to stories that expose wrongdoing [by public servants], the media also reports information detailing how disciplined civil servants often escape punishment, thanks to the city's appeals process... Rightly or wrongly, the public perception is that the city suffers from widespread corruption and a civil service system that is not functioning."

We reviewed many of the Commission's recent decisions in which it overturned or modified the discipline NOPD imposed.  While we disagreed with some decisions and believe that greater transparency is necessary to improve the Commission's credibility, we found:  1) that the Commission upholds the majority of NOPD's disciplinary decisions; 2) many examples in which NOPD itself appeared at fault for a decision being overturned; and 3) that NOPD has only rarely chosen to exercise its power to appeal an adverse decision of the Commission.

---

[27] The Louisiana Constitution states:  "No person who has gained permanent status in the classified state or city service shall be subjected to disciplinary action except for cause expressed in writing.  A classified employee subjected to such disciplinary action shall have the right of appeal to the appropriate commission pursuant to Section 12 of this Part.  The burden of proof on appeal, as to the facts, shall be on the appointing authority."  La. Const, Art. X, Sec. 8(A).  The relevant "appointing authority" here is NOPD.

- 96 -

Although there were Commission decisions that we found questionable, the problems we observed in NOPD's investigation and adjudication of officer misconduct, alongside a lack of transparency in the Commission's appeal process, made it difficult to fully assess the extent to which troubling disciplinary decisions are due to the Commission's failure to stay within the appropriate bounds of review, as is widely perceived, or are instead due to weakness in NOPD's investigations of officer misconduct and NOPD's and the City's defense of disciplinary decisions.

We heard concerns that recommendations to the Commission by past hearing officers were in some instances influenced by bias or favoritism. We found no evidence that such bias was widespread, indeed as discussed below, the Commission overwhelmingly affirms NOPD's disciplinary decisions. Nonetheless, it is clear that even a small number of notorious decisions by the Commission can delegitimize the process in the eyes of the officers and the public. Further, the almost complete lack of transparency in the way the Commission operates – none of its decisions are posted online, for example – has fostered an atmosphere where rumors can fester. Addressing this lack of transparency by posting Commission decisions in full and online, will give the public and NOPD officers the tools to better understand the Commission's decisions.

Ultimately, we found that while there may be instances where the Commission made the wrong decision, NOPD and the City should not lose focus on the very real problems in their complaint investigation and adjudication processes. Correcting these deficiencies will improve the Department's ability to prevail before the Commission to a greater extent than is commonly acknowledged.

1.    Commission's High Rate of Affirming NOPD Disciplinary Decisions

For at least the past four years, the Commission has upheld many more of NOPD's disciplinary decisions than it overturned or modified, and its rate of affirming NOPD is increasing. For the four years between 2006 and 2009, there was an average of 105 appeals per year of NOPD disciplinary decisions. There are, of course, many cases where discipline is not appealed. In recent years, it appears that roughly half of NOPD's disciplinary letters were appealed.[28] Of the 112 cases appealed in 2009, the NOPD employee won outright in thirteen cases. In addition to those thirteen, there were ten cases in which the Commission modified the Superintendent's judgment downward in some way.[29] In 2008, there were only 80 appeals, but there were twenty-four in which the employee either won outright or won a modification. Thus, in 2008, 30% of the decisions altered NOPD's judgment, but, in 2009, only 20% did.

---

[28] In 2007, there were 208 letters issued and 115 appeals decided. In 2008, there were 206 letters issued and 80 appeals decided. In 2009 there were 192 letters and 112 decisions. As of October 15, 2010, there were 158 letters issued in 2010. The number of disciplinary letters issued by NOPD does not correspond directly to the number of appeals heard each year because the appeal may be decided in a different calendar year.

[29] The Commission cannot increase the penalties assessed by the Department.

2.      Role of NOPD and the City in Reversal of Some Disciplinary Decisions

We found a number of examples where NOPD failed to support its disciplinary decisions with evidence, which left the Commission little choice but to find for the testifying employee. Indeed, a former high-ranking NOPD official told us that, in the past, some charges that clearly could not be adequately proven (but were believed to be true) were nonetheless brought against officers in order to put them through the difficult civil service appeal process. This type of action is exactly the harm the civil service system was designed to prevent.

Additionally, City Attorneys often do not join the investigation until too late in the process to ensure that the cases will withstand scrutiny and meet the City's burden of proof. For instance, in 2010, in a traffic accident case involving two police cars, NOPD failed to call any fact witnesses to contradict the appealing officer's version of events, even thought the witnesses were police officers and thus should have been easy for the City to locate. In addition, the officer who wrote the police report about the accident only interviewed the other driver-officer, and "provided no explanation for his failure to interview the Appellant even though he determined she caused an accident." Facing only hearsay to rebut direct evidence, the Commission overturned the discipline.[30]

In some cases it appears that NOPD's disciplinary decisions were overturned because they were, in fact, arbitrary. Four of the overturned cases we reviewed from the last two years involved NOPD questionably disciplining officers for failing to attend court. It is essential that officers attend court when asked to do so, and we are aware that NOPD has had a problem in the past because good cases have had to be dropped when officers failed to appear in court. However, in three of cases overturned by the Commission, officers were punished for not appearing in court even though they were excused in advance by the Assistant District Attorney ("ADA") prosecuting the case or were told by the ADA they were not needed. Under these circumstances, it is difficult to find that cause for the imposed discipline was sufficient.

In several cases we reviewed, commanders reviewing investigations appeared to change the disposition of the case or the level of discipline even where the evidence indicated that the original determination was correct. It is sometimes incumbent upon a reviewing official to modify the disposition or level of discipline in a case. However, this should only be done to correct an erroneous determination that is at odds with a preponderance of the evidence, and the rationale supporting the change should always be documented. Our review indicated that in cases where there was an increase in penalty for a documented reason, the increase was more likely to be upheld. In a case ultimately appealed to the state's Fourth Circuit, an officer was originally issued a letter of reprimand for making a traffic stop while off-duty, in civilian clothes, and in his own car. Then-Deputy Superintendent Serpas increased the penalty to a three-day suspension because it was the officer's second violation in three years—an increase that fit within the penalty schedule. This was upheld at both the Commission level and on appeal.

---

[30] *See* Docket No. 7624 (2010) and Docket No. 7447, 7448 (2009) for similar cases in which the Commission determined that the City did not meet its evidentiary burden.

- 98 -

However, in most of the cases we reviewed, these criteria were not met. For example, in a traffic accident case from 2009, there was no dispute over the facts, and the appealing sergeant's testimony was uncontested. There was no explanation in the record for why the investigating officer and the supervisor's report, both of which found the sergeant to be not at fault, were overruled by a captain on the Accident Review Board. In another traffic case, again both the investigating officer and the supervisor on the scene found no violation. Here, their findings were "overturned by the Superintendent, apparently based solely on the amount of damage." The then-Superintendent did not testify to provide another reason.

In another case, a letter of reprimand had been recommended, but a former NOPD Superintendent increased the penalty to a five-day suspension. There was no explanation for the increased discipline in the record, and the Deputy Superintendent who testified at the hearing stated that he had not been aware of the fact that the appealing sergeant had been acting on the advice of her supervisors. He testified that, had he known this, he would not have recommended even the letter of reprimand. Finding that the appealing Sergeant had been acting in good faith, as well as on the advice of her superiors, when she made her mistake, the Commission reduced the discipline back to the letter of reprimand.

We acknowledge that there may be cases where the Commission simply made the wrong decision and nothing that NOPD might have done would have altered that outcome; we certainly reviewed cases where we did not agree with the Commission's decision. However, it is the responsibility of NOPD and the City Attorney's Office to ensure that the record, both at the internal investigative level and then at the Commission level, includes all the evidence supporting their determinations. As stated in the 2010 study of the New Orleans Civil Service system, "[u]sually, when a department has its disciplinary action overturned, it is because the managers in the department were either unaware of proper procedure or failed to follow it."

It is the responsibility of the City Attorney's Office to advise NOPD so that inappropriate decisions at the investigation and internal review stages are less likely. Where NOPD's decisions are appropriate, it is the responsibility of the City Attorney's Office to vigorously defend those decisions before the Commission. Where NOPD and the City do not meet these responsibilities it is not surprising that the Commission finds for the appellant. Where the City and Police Department do meet these responsibilities they will better be able to defend their decisions—to the public and on appeal—in instances where the Commission's determination was incorrect.

3.     Infrequent Appeals of Unfavorable Commission Decisions

The decision whether to appeal an unfavorable decision involves consideration of a number of factors, and we do not make any findings as to whether the City should have appealed any particular unfavorable Commission decision we reviewed. However, we do note that the City and NOPD have asserted that Commission decisions are contrary to law and an abuse of their discretion, yet they have relatively rarely chosen to appeal those decisions. Between the years of 2004 and 2009, the City appealed between zero and nine Commission decisions, averaging fewer than 5 appeals per year. During this same time period, NOPD has received an average of 14.7 outright reversals by the Commission per year, and about seven modifications

- 99 -

355

per year.  The City thus has appealed fewer than a quarter of the unfavorable decisions handed down by the Commission.  As NOPD and the City improve their systems for investigating misconduct, including imposing discipline and defending disciplinary decisions, it is likely that alongside an increase in favorable Commission decisions the City's ability to successfully appeal erroneous Commission decisions to the Fourth Circuit will also improve.


## XI.  <u>COMMUNITY ORIENTED POLICING</u>

Community policing strategies balance reactive responses to calls for service with thoughtful and proactive problem-solving.  This problem-solving is achieved in large part by forging robust relationships in the community.  The Department's policies, training, and tactics support neither a community policing orientation, nor the ultimate goal of proactively addressing problems to reduce and prevent crime, rather than merely reacting to it.  Within NOPD, the concept of community policing is poorly understood and implemented only superficially.  Outside the Department, community members, especially members of racial, ethnic, and language minorities, and the LGBT communities, expressed to us their deep distrust of and sense of alienation from the police.  This crisis of confidence and credibility serves as both a barrier to an effective community oriented policing program, and as a compelling reason to prioritize its implementation.

A.  Need for Community Oriented Policing

NOPD has publicly acknowledged the need to repair and cultivate community partnerships to more effectively fight crime and increase respect for its officers.  Indeed, in August 2010, the Superintendent released a 65-point plan to reform the Department, which opened with a commitment to prioritize community policing and to "listen, collaborate, and respond proactively."  The Department has implemented or announced plans to implement community outreach programs, including:  citizen callbacks regarding quality of service; an expanded citizen academy; a partnership with clergy; and an "El Protector" program, which will involve bilingual outreach to Latinos on public safety issues.  Additionally, the Department has sought funding and is preparing a Request for Proposal to commission an independent and detailed survey of community attitudes and perceptions of NOPD.  While these initiatives are either in the planning stages or too new to allow for close assessment, we commend the Department's stated interest in genuinely assessing current attitudes toward the police, reaching out to diverse segments of the City, and enhancing community relations.

Nonetheless, considerable work lies ahead if community policing is to be a central feature of NOPD's culture, decision-making, and organizational structure.  As the U.S. Department of Justice's Office of Community Oriented Policing ("COPS") instructs, a true community oriented policing strategy rests on the key components of:  1) collaborative partnerships between police and the public to identify and solve public safety problems and increase community trust; 2) organizational transformation, that is, the alignment of a law enforcement agency's management, structure, personnel, and technology systems to support these partnerships and problem solving efforts; and 3) proactive and systematic examination of

- 100 -

356

identified problems to develop and rigorously evaluate effective responses.[31]  An effective community policing approach to crime-fighting should integrate these key tenets, and should hold accountable all members and components of the organization for their implementation.  We identified barriers that NOPD must address before it can institutionalize the core components of community policing:  collaborative community partnerships, organizational transformation, and systematic problem-solving.

B.      Lack of Collaborative Community Partnerships

NOPD does not adequately encourage or promote meaningful partnership, interaction, and communication with diverse stakeholders, which is critical to learning about and collaboratively addressing problems in the community.  The Department's Operations Manual addresses "Community Relations" in a 3-page policy, outlining the duties and responsibilities of the Department's Crime Prevention Unit, and of the designated "Crime Prevention Officers" assigned to each of NOPD's eight districts.  The policy states that Crime Prevention Officers will act as liaisons to community groups; assist in formulating community relations policies for the Department; identify training needs; and "relay information and concerns, through the chain of command, from community groups to the proper authority within the department."  The policy further requires each district's Crime Prevention Officer to hold a monthly New Orleans Neighborhood Police Anti-Crime Council ("NONPACC") meeting of neighborhood watch groups and other interested citizens.

Until recently, the functions of the "Crime Prevention" position had been the responsibility of Quality of Life officers in each district, but we were told that these officers were frequently pulled from those duties when the platoons were short on manpower.  In July 2010, the Department created the position of Community Outreach Coordinator Sergeant, also known as "CoCos," who have assumed some of the responsibilities described in the Operational Manual, and who appear to have more authority and autonomy than the Quality of Life officers.  Although the CoCo sergeants appeared engaged and committed to enhancing community relations, at the time of our review, they described themselves as essentially "self-taught" and in need of specialized training in community- and problem-oriented policing principles.

In November 2010, the CoCo sergeants, along with other supervisors and a number of advocacy organizations, attended CRS' training in basic law enforcement mediation and racial profiling.  Another participant in the training was the Department's Hispanic Liaison officer, a position the Department created in mid-2009 and that has improved dialogue between the Department and some groups in the community.  The officer conducts a weekly radio show in Spanish, makes public presentations, reaches out to Spanish-language media, and also serves as the Department's primary interpreter while on-duty.  Although creation of this position was a positive step, the Latino organizations we spoke with said broader and more extensive engagement and communication is sorely needed.

While CoCo sergeants have begun attending their districts' NONPACC meetings and neighborhood homeowners' association meetings, outreach to other sectors of the community,

---

[31]      See http://www.cops.usdoj.gov/Default.asp?Item=36, U.S. Department of Justice Office of Community Oriented Policing Services.

which have traditionally had less sustained and positive interaction with police, has been far more limited.  One CoCo sergeant, for example, described language barriers in engaging heavily immigrant communities.  He also noted that the CoCos tend to avoid more volatile neighborhoods out of fear of citizens labeling those contacted as "snitches."  He further observed, more generally, that in "high crime neighborhoods, officers may stay five minutes explaining a crime whereas in the rich part of town they might stay ten minutes.  Officers aren't inclined to listen to someone they believe is a suspect.  The culture here forgot that we are required to protect and serve."

Minority community groups nearly uniformly said that the police rarely reach out to them, for any purpose.  One member of a Vietnamese community organization reported that "[a] lot of the young Vietnamese people who get shot in this community, we know who shot them but the New Orleans police don't do anything.  They don't talk to us.  They don't build community relationships."  We found that some NOPD officers tend not to view members of the public as potential collaborative partners or sources of information and insight about their communities, but rather as potential problems, cultivating an "us vs. them" atmosphere of mutual distrust.  Some community members said that such assumptions and perceptions by the police are especially evident in their interactions with young people.  One young community organizer told us that, "Officers are on a power trip.  NOPD needs to learn how to talk to young people.  They get harassed like no other in New Orleans.  Whether you're white, black or Asian, or Latino [young people] get treated like crap.  They see us as a walking problem."

Many within and outside of the Department observed an NOPD "culture" of discourtesy, disrespect, and an unwillingness to listen.  This constitutes a significant barrier to successful outreach to the community and to the creation of constructive partnerships.  One community leader said that when officers engage with members of the community, they too often do so with an "arrogance, a hostility, a rudeness and vulgarity.  It's not everybody, some people know how to talk to people, but it's the culture."  The prevalence of discourtesy and disrespect was acknowledged at the highest levels of NOPD, with one member of the Department's leadership observing: "I don't know where this thing, this thing that we have to demoralize people in getting our point across ... I don't know where this disrespect thing came from ... I'm trying to get officers to understand that the public just wants to know why they are being detained, the purpose of the citation, what are my recourses and just show me some professionalism, and some courtesy, and some respect.  The public is hungry for this type of interaction."

He went on to recount being at the scene of a homicide and seeing a woman in her kitchen window, looking out.  "I went over to talk to her through the screen, talking about her living conditions and why she's still living back here, when they're going to tear this building down.  She said, 'You know, I tried to talk to the officers on the scene about what happened.'  I said, 'You know what happened?'  She said, 'Yeah, I did.'  I said, 'What did the officer tell you?'  She said, 'he said get the F off this scene.  Get behind the yellow tape.  So I got behind the yellow tape and went into my apartment.'  So we almost lost that witness who was wanting to help and the officer was being belligerent.  That's what I'm trying to get the officers to understand, that every contact is important, no matter how old, young, rich or poor, that person can be your biggest advocate."

- 102 -

Our review found that NOPD has a particularly long way to go to repair its reputation, build trust, and create community partnerships with the City's minority citizens.  Indeed, a recent survey by the Kaiser Family Foundation found that trust in the police, though lacking across the board, differed considerably by race.  For white respondents, 59 percent said they trusted the police to do what is right "almost always" (18 percent) or "most of the time" (41 percent).  At the same time, only 34 percent of African-American respondents said they could trust the police "almost always" (9 percent) or "most of the time" (25 percent).

Citizens, particularly youth, African Americans, ethnic minorities, and members of the LGBT community, spoke of discourtesy, harassment, unwarranted stops, and arrests for minor infractions.  They consistently reported that these tactics serve to drive a wedge between the police and the public, antagonizing and alienating members of the community.  In the Latino and Vietnamese communities, language barriers and a lack of cultural fluency further impede effective engagement with the police.  Encouragingly, however, participants in our community meetings consistently told us that they are ready to work with, and toward, a police department that is inclusive, respectful, and fair in its service delivery and enforcement of the law.  Improved relationships with the community will benefit the Department by enhancing people's willingness to report crime, work with the police in problem-solving efforts, and be the "eyes and ears" for the police.

C.      Challenges to Achieving Organizational Transformation

Organizational transformation requires that a police department integrate and embed community- and problem-oriented policing principles into each aspect of its management, structure, and use of resources.  To ensure that change is sustained and more than superficial, an agency must review its leadership, policies, climate and culture, systems of accountability, and training and deployment of personnel.

As an initial matter, we observed that outside of the CoCo sergeants, few others within NOPD could articulate the basics of community policing, especially its "problem solving" component.  Indeed, officers tended to describe community policing as the domain of the CoCo sergeants, rather than as a shared, Department-wide, responsibility.  Apart from the Operations Manual chapter on Community Relations, which lacks substance and primarily describes the responsibilities of "Crime Prevention Officers," there are no policies to require or guide patrol officers in integrating community policing strategies into their assignments.

We also found that training in community policing principles and techniques—for CoCo sergeants and even more critically for patrol officers—is both qualitatively and quantitatively deficient.  Currently, the Department offers just four hours of training on community policing to recruits at the Academy, and no mandatory in-service training to reinforce those skills and concepts. NOPD does not incorporate community policing concepts and strategies into the field training program or the "traditional" academy courses on patrol procedures, investigations, traffic enforcement, and use of force; nor does it offer training in problem solving techniques, such as the "SARA" (Scanning, Analysis, Response, Assessment) approach to identifying, assessing, resolving, and evaluating its collaborative efforts to reduce crime.  In-service training on verbal de-escalation of conflict, language barrier policing, and cultural sensitivity are

- 103 -

similarly lacking, though the Department did recently introduce a unit entitled "Latino Cultural Awareness," and plans to roll out an expanded version. Other than that course, which a Latino community organization helped to develop and present, the Department has not solicited community input in assessing training needs or developing curricula.

The Department also lacks systems and measures to ensure accountability for and to determine the impact of community policing efforts. Neither recruits' "Daily Observation Reports" nor patrol officers' performance reviews evaluate engagement with the community, and success in utilizing community policing strategies is not a criteria for promotion. Apart from NONPACC meetings, the Department does not report on community partnerships; or evaluate or measure how these meetings and partnerships help identify and effectively respond to public safety problems. COMSTAT, the weekly crime meeting that the Superintendent opened to the public in May 2010, has the potential to serve as a useful tool to hold commanders and supervisors accountable for implementing community policing. Although some of the CoCo sergeants reported that they now attend and present at COMSTAT, our observations of COMSTAT meetings and review of COMSTAT materials confirmed that its predominant focus remains the recitation of crime statistics. The Department does not presently utilize COMSTAT as an effective means to gauge what specific efforts are being made to improve community relations, or how these efforts are aiding in addressing crime.

As discussed above, officers consistently reported that pressure to conduct stops and arrests diverts attention and resources from quality arrests, community engagement, and more considered problem-solving. One commander observed that community policing had become a "buzzword" in the Department but "we have to go to COMSTAT and produce. I can't say I went out and shook 2000 hands. If I said that, someone else would be sitting in this chair." We heard this sentiment repeated often in our conversations with both patrol officers and supervisors. One Lieutenant could recite crime statistics for his district for the previous week, but could not provide basic information about the demographics or businesses in the district.

The Department's deployment of personnel reflects this emphasis on arrests and statistics; staffing is heavily concentrated into specialized units and task forces, which engage in the crime suppression tactics that the Department calls "proactive policing," as opposed to uniformed patrol platoons, which handle calls for service. The Special Operations Division ("SOD") also functions as essentially a city-wide task force unit, in addition to handling more typical SWAT duties such as hostage situations, barricades, and high-risk warrant service. SOD patrols the City in full SWAT uniform and gear on a daily basis, an unusual practice with strong potential to project hostility and intimidation. Some within NOPD, including supervisors, acknowledged this potential, recommending that SWAT be used only for special deployments because of this dynamic.

The emphasis on statistics-driven policing leaves officers with less time or opportunity to constructively engage with the community. Arresting people in situations where a warning or a citation would serve a tantamount purpose takes time away from more important law enforcement needs. Indeed, the Metropolitan Crime Commission estimated that each of the 20,000 NOPD arrests last year on misdemeanor or traffic warrants took an hour to 90 minutes of an officer's time, or between 35,000 to 40,000 hours. For their part, platoon officers told us that they spend their shifts traveling between calls for service throughout their districts, and are rarely able to cultivate relationships or meaningfully communicate with members of the public. Such dialogue is critical to identifying community problems and unique needs, gaining the trust of the public, determining strategic deployment of resources, and problem- and crime-solving. The Department plans to conduct a staffing allocation analysis, which should help identify whether such issues exist and how to re-deploy personnel to address them. It is critical that in conducting that review, the Department align its assessment with a community policing philosophy.

>     D.      Lack of Systematic Problem-Solving

The third major component of community policing involves proactive problem-solving, executed in a systematic and routine manner. COPS defines problem-solving, in the context of community policing, as follows: "Rather than responding to crime only after it occurs, community policing encourages agencies to proactively develop solutions to the immediate underlying conditions contributing to public safety problems. Problem-solving must be infused into all police operations and guide decision-making efforts. Agencies are encouraged to think innovatively about their responses and view making arrests as only one of a wide array of potential responses. A major conceptual vehicle for helping officers to think about problem solving in a structured and disciplined way is the SARA problem-solving model."

With the exception of just a few officers in command positions, those within NOPD were uniformly unfamiliar with proactive problem-solving methodologies and concepts. The district task forces are charged with carrying out "proactive" duties for the Department, yet their singular focus is on making arrests and cooling crime "hotspots" in a fundamentally reactive manner. Several officers observed that to date, NOPD's proactive efforts have not yielded sustainable change in volatile neighborhoods, yet the Department continues to repeat the same enforcement cycle. Daily deployments of resources appear to depend largely on the previous day's reports or tips received, rather than on any effort or plan to address identified trends and patterns. Although the Department has technologies like density mapping and visual mapping at its disposal, we did not see task forces using them to forecast crime patterns. Moreover, there is virtually no coordination among specialized units or process to avoid conflicts in operations, and uniformed patrol officers are largely unaware of what tactical units are doing in their districts, creating potential officer safety issues.

We also found that NOPD does not provide adequate direction, incentive, training and opportunity for uniformed patrol officers to engage constructively with the community. Officers have generally not been assigned to fixed geographic areas within their districts, although one commander, who was well-versed in the fundamentals of community and problem oriented policing, did say he had recently begun keeping patrol officers in specific zones. Some districts have also implemented walking beats, although their use appeared to be sporadic and subject to factors like manpower and weather. Patrol officers are viewed, and view themselves, as responsible strictly for responding to calls for service, and not for watching and listening to identify and assess problems within neighborhoods.

Although COMSTAT has the potential to advance problem-solving efforts, the Department does not currently use it for that purpose. COMSTAT does not encourage a

- 105 -

collective mission of reducing crimes in neighborhoods while minimizing friction and confrontation with citizens.  We observed no exploration at COMSTAT of issues underlying crime, potential collective solutions, or how to strategically align resources Department-wide to address a common crime problem.  We saw very limited use of crime mapping or similar technologies to visualize trends and patterns, other than to display number and location of arrests.  Additionally, we saw no evidence that the Department utilizes COMSTAT to hold supervisors accountable for their officers' performance – either to promote the use of community and problem-oriented policing strategies, or to identify performance and integrity issues.

## XII.   OFFICER ASSISTANCE AND SUPPORT SERVICES

Officer assistance and support services are a significant component of a department's accountability system.  The demeanor, judgment, and physical abilities that make an officer effective in carrying out law enforcement duties can be dangerously impaired when officers work under inordinate stress levels or while grappling with symptoms of mental illness.  Police executives owe a duty to their community and officers to provide the services necessary to ensure the mental and physical wellness of their officers.  NOPD is failing to provide such critical officer assistance and support services.

Stress is not an excuse for police misconduct, but officers who are mentally and physically fit generally are more productive; use fewer sick days; and importantly, may receive fewer complaints regarding demeanor or use of force.  There is little question that NOPD is in need of officer assistance and support services.  We repeatedly received reports of NOPD officers' unsuccessful efforts to seek out stress and mental health counseling.  Supervisors and command staff reported that officers have approached them with questions about the availability of services.  Representatives of the local chapter of the FOP and other law enforcement associations and training organizations relayed stories of NOPD officers seeking services.  Officers expressed to us directly their frustration about the lack of stress and mental health counseling available to officers and their families.

Some of the need relates to the daily stressors of police work.  There is also a continuing need to address the effects of NOPD officers' experiences during Hurricane Katrina.  An April 2006 report by the Centers for Disease Control found that one in five NOPD officers self-reported symptoms of Post-Traumatic Stress Disorder ("PTSD").  More than one in four NOPD officers self-reported symptoms of major depression.  And reminders of Katrina still remain throughout the City.  Many officers patrol areas devastated since 2005.  A NOPD mental health professional speaking of PTSD noted: "Where's the 'post' to this?  The effects of Katrina haven't ended, they go on and on."

There are few officer assistance and support services provided by NOPD, and those that exist are uncoordinated and difficult to access.  Mental health counseling to help officers and their families combat stress and cope with traumatic incidents, are available on an ad hoc basis at the District level, placing referral and approval control with the District commanders.  This lack of Department-wide direct access leads to less confidentiality and less accessibility, resulting in fewer officers seeking and obtaining services.

- 106 -

This lack of services forces officers, and associations like the FOP, to search outside of NOPD for stress and mental health treatment. The FOP, for example, is working with the Southern Law Enforcement Foundation to develop a peer counseling program. These services are potentially helpful and welcome, and NOPD's present leadership has appropriately embraced these efforts. However, these nascent programs are not a substitute for a comprehensive range of officer assistance services.

NOPD currently contracts with two mental health professionals, a psychiatrist and a psychologist, both of whom focus primarily on conducting fitness for duty ("FFD") evaluations on behalf of the Department. These FFD evaluators are often called upon to provide counseling and other support services. FFD evaluations identify officers with potential psychological difficulties that may manifest themselves in inappropriate police behaviors, and are thus critical to helping a law enforcement agency ensure that its officers are able to serve safely and effectively. Professionals conducting these evaluations owe a duty to the department and confidentiality to the officer generally is not guaranteed. When the FFD evaluators provide other services to officers, they may have a conflict of interest between what is best for the officer and what is best for the department. For this reason, both the American Psychological Association's Guidelines for Consulting Psychologists and the practice guidelines from the Police and Public Safety Section of the International Association of Chiefs of Police caution their membership to avoid assuming multiple roles with the same individual when at all possible. Nonetheless, the mental health professionals performing NOPD's FFD evaluations recognize the unmet need in NOPD, and attempt to meet that need as best they can.

At NOPD, the potential risk caused by the dual role its FFD evaluators play is exacerbated by a lack of clarity about what services they are being asked to provide. The FFD policy appears to be primarily focused on the use and or abuse of sick leave, not assessing the psychological fitness of employees. Yet, the mental health professionals' contracts state that they should conduct FFD evaluations. Without clear policies and protocols that clearly delineate professionals' roles and the services they are being asked to provide, the risk of conflicting duties and responsibilities is increased.

It appears that a comprehensive system of officer assistance and support services for NOPD officers has never been in place, and that efforts to create a system have been faltering, even after Hurricane Katrina underscored the need. NOPD can better serve its officers and protect the public by implementing a centralized and comprehensive range of officer assistance and support services to address the stress and mental health needs of its employees.

## XIII.  <u>INTERROGATION PRACTICES</u>

Custodial interrogations can be an integral part of police investigations. They may lead to a reliable confession, often the most important piece of evidence in a case. Even where they do not, they may result in leads that can be used to build present or future cases. However in their eagerness to obtain the evidence needed to make a case, or sometimes due to a simple lack of knowledge about what the law permits or how to protect their cases, detectives may use methods that run afoul of the Constitution — running the risk that the wrong person will be prosecuted, or that the prosecution of the right person will fail because of unlawful tactics used during the interrogation. Ensuring that custodial interrogations are robust but not abusive, leading to strong evidence and legitimate convictions, not false confessions and thrown-out cases, requires that the detectives that conduct them have skill, strong training, and integrity — and can document the propriety of their conduct.

Custodial interrogation involves the questioning of suspects by law enforcement officers under conditions that the suspect would not feel at liberty to cease the questioning and leave. *See Thompson v. Keohane*, 516 U.S. 99 (1995). The Constitution provides certain protections to suspects during custodial interrogations, including the right to counsel and the right to remain silent. *Miranda v. Arizona*, 384 U.S. 436 (1966). Not only do suspects retain such rights during custodial interrogations, but law enforcement officers are required to warn suspects of their rights, and provide an opportunity for the suspect to exercise or waive their rights. *Id.* The warnings that law enforcement officers are required to provide — known commonly as *Miranda* warnings—require that the suspect "be warned prior to any questioning that he has the right to remain silent, that anything he says can be used against him in a court of law, that he has the right to the presence of an attorney, and if he cannot afford an attorney one will be appointed for him prior to any questioning if he so desires." *Id.* at 478-79. The Constitution also provides suspects due process protections against coercive interrogation methods such as physical violence or the threat of physical harm; lengthy interrogations involving sleep and food deprivation; or lengthy incommunicado interrogations. *Colorado v. Connelly*, 479 U.S. 157 (1986) (due process protections); *Stein v. People of State of New York*, 346 U.S. 156 (1953) (physical violence); *Arizona v. Fulminante*, 499 U.S. 279 (1991) (threat of physical harm); *Ashcraft v. Tennessee*, 322 U.S. 143 (1944) (sleep and food deprivation); *Spano v. New York*, 360 U.S. 315 (1959) (lengthy incommunicado interrogations).

NOPD's custodial interrogation practices reflect many of the same problems we found throughout NOPD: inadequate policies, poor or non-existent training, weak supervision and accountability, and inadequate facilities and equipment. As a result of these problems, NOPD does not adequately use custodial interrogations to build cases. NOPD detectives conduct relatively few interrogations and the interrogations they do conduct are desultory. We did find practices that could facilitate and hide constitutional violations of criminal suspects' rights, as well as allegations that such violations in fact occur. Our overarching concern is that as NOPD begins to focus more on building strong cases, and thus presumably will be conducting a greater number of interrogations, it runs the risk that many of these interrogations may be neither effective nor legal. To ensure that this does not happen, NOPD should revise its interrogation policies and practices.

A.    Custodial Interrogations

Within NOPD, custodial interrogations are conducted by detectives assigned to specialized investigative units, such as Homicide and Sex Crimes, and by detectives assigned to the various Districts investigating property crimes and crimes of violence that do not involve homicides or sexual assaults. Reportedly, patrol officers do not typically conduct custodial interrogations. Instead, patrol officers will often conduct questioning before placing a suspect under arrest, thus removing the custodial aspect of the questioning and the necessity of *Miranda* warnings. Such on-the-scene questioning by patrol officers is often brief. In more serious cases, as when a patrol officer responds to the scene of a major crime, officers are trained to defer questioning of a suspect to the responding detectives.

Interrogations are conducted in various NOPD locations, depending on the unit or detective conducting the interrogation. The Homicide Unit, for example, has two interview rooms, each equipped with video recording technology. Both rooms are adjacent to a monitoring room, in which the recording equipment is stored and observers can view the interior of the interview rooms. Similarly, the Sex Crimes Unit now has a dedicated interview room with video recording technology and a monitoring room. The various Districts, however, struggle with dedicated space for interview rooms. Most District interview rooms double as storage rooms. All of the Districts have audio recording capability, but few are equipped with video recording technology. District 8, for example, has video recording technology, but this is largely due to the efforts of the detectives in the District who have set up the system themselves. District 8 uses VHS tapes to video record interrogations, as opposed to digital recording, and the detectives usually bear the costs of purchasing the necessary tapes.

In New Orleans, NOPD detectives refer to the fact-gathering interview phase of a custodial interrogation as the "pre-interview" phase, and the interrogation phase as "the interview" or "the confession."[32] NOPD detectives do not employ the phrase "interrogation." In reality, there appears to be very little actual interrogation conducted during the "interview" or "confession" phase. Any interrogation, in the traditional sense of the word, is actually taking place during the unrecorded "pre-interview" phase, and "the interview" or the "the confession" usually consists of only the suspect's recorded statement. As one of the NOPD detectives explained the process, "the pre-interview is everything we do before we turn on the tape."

It appears that the interrogation process routinely employed by NOPD is not unduly lengthy. In fact, most interrogations are reportedly concluded in under an hour. Rarely do interrogations continue for several hours, and in no case could we find interrogations lasting a day or longer.

Homicide detectives said that they attempt to obtain statements from every suspect arrested. The Homicide Division does not, however, track the number of cases that involve confessions. Until recently, the Sex Crimes Unit did not conduct interrogations at all. The practice within that unit was not to conduct interviews of suspects. Sexual assault cases were thus built largely on the testimony of the victims, particularly in light of problems with NOPD's crime lab, as noted earlier. This practice has since changed and interrogations are now viewed as an important part of sex crimes investigations.

NOPD will at times utilize a Computerized Voice Stress Analysis machine ("CVSA machine") and a polygraph. While we did not find any NOPD statistics indicating how successful NOPD has been using these devices, we were told that, in one District, officers

---

[32] Ironically, the only unit not employing this terminology was the NOPD Training Division. The training personnel we interviewed had never heard the phrase "pre-interview," and the training materials we reviewed referred to "interviews" and "interrogations." This is further evidence of a larger NOPD trend, in which what officers are taught during official NOPD training is contradicted by what they learn in the field.

- 109 -

primarily used the CVSA machine on "victims" where the officers suspected false reporting. We also noted that NOPD has very few trained examiners for either device.

Juveniles are rarely brought to NOPD District stations for questioning. Instead, juveniles are transported to the Juvenile Intake Unit, which is equipped with audio and video recording capability. Juvenile suspects are required to be accompanied by a parent or guardian during questioning. *Miranda* warnings are to be given to both the juvenile and the parent or guardian, and the juvenile is required to have adequate time to consult with the parent or guardian before choosing to invoke or waive his or her rights. Juvenile witnesses and victims are to be interviewed by trained forensic interview experts at a specialized facility in Children's Hospital.

B.       Problems with NOPD Interrogations

Our review found a number of problems with NOPD's interrogation practices. We found that NOPD's policies about what constitutes a constitutional interrogation are inadequate, as is NOPD's training and selection of detectives. NOPD practice further undermines the effectiveness and integrity of NOPD interrogations. Audio and video recordings of interrogations reflect that detectives do not conduct, or at least record, a full interrogation. Documentation of interrogations is poor due to a number of deficient practices and systems, including that: most of the Districts lack dedicated space and video recording equipment; officers only record a final summary statement by subjects and/or witnesses; officers generally destroy notes from unrecorded portions of interviews with subjects and witnesses after completing investigative reports; and taped interviews in the Districts are preserved inconsistently, if at all. Taken together, these deficiencies not only undermine NOPD's efforts to build strong criminal cases, they could also facilitate and hide constitutional violations of criminal suspects' rights. Indeed, we found credible allegations that such violations have occurred.

The current NOPD administration and the broader New Orleans' criminal justice system appear well aware of the problems with NOPD's interrogation practices. The DA's Office recently began working more closely with NOPD detectives in order to improve interrogation practices and documentation.

1.       Flaws in Interrogation Policies

NOPD policies provide very little guidance on appropriate methods of conducting interrogations. There are several particular omissions in NOPD policies on interrogations worth noting. First, the policies fail to discuss the basic purpose and importance of conducting interrogations, or the risks of employing certain interrogation methods, including the danger of eliciting a false confession. Second, the policies do not provide any legal references or constitutional standards to place the rules and procedures of interrogation into context for the detectives. Third, the rules and procedures regarding adherence to legal safeguards are inadequate, failing to, *inter alia*, address the rules and procedures to be followed when a suspect invokes constitutional or other legal rights, or how prosecutors' discovery obligations impact how detectives document and retain records of their interrogations. Fourth, the policies do not include any express prohibitions on interrogation methods, such as physical violence or threats of harm. Finally, the policies do not address the importance of documentation of the interrogations, and do not set forth procedures for documentation.

      2.      Insufficient Training and Selection Requirements for Detectives

NOPD does not adequately train or select detectives, impacting the quality of custodial interrogations. NOPD provides very little formal training to its detectives regarding custodial interrogations. We were told that during recruit training at the NOPD Training Academy, police recruits are taught basic differences between a police interview that seeks information about a crime, and a police interrogation that seeks to obtain a confession from a suspect. Legal issues involving *Miranda* warnings and waivers are reportedly also covered during basic recruit training. There is, however, no NOPD training specifically tailored for detectives conducting interrogations. Any training detectives receive is usually conducted through private outside courses. Using outside training courses can bring in needed outside expertise, but supervisors should carefully examine all outside training because some courses and instructors overstate their effectiveness, and encourage techniques that may violate constitutional safeguards, or that create a risk of obtaining false confessions and unreliable information.

NOPD also has too few personnel trained to properly use CVSA machines and polygraphs. NOPD does not provide adequate training to detectives on how to use these machines most effectively during an investigation, or on the dangers of overreliance on these machines.

The selection of detectives for Districts and specialized units appears inconsistent with policy and poorly understood throughout NOPD. It appears that to be a District detective, an officer must have at least two years of experience on the job, but this rule does not appear to be strictly enforced. One detective interviewed knew of several officers selected for detective immediately following their post-academy field training. Applicants for District detective positions do not undergo any special selection process or application procedure. For specialized units, such as the Homicide Division, the minimum experience is five years, but this rule too seems to be subject to exceptions. Specialized units require supervisor recommendations and samples of the officer's investigative reports.

      3.      Failure to Conduct Full and Complete Interrogations

NOPD does not conduct interviews and interrogations in a manner sufficient to build strong cases. Prosecutors attribute NOPD's failure to conduct full interrogations to a lack of ownership for the prosecution of a case after a suspect is arrested. Defense attorneys agreed with the notion that NOPD is driven by arrest statistics, but suggested a different reason for NOPD's lack of post-arrest interrogations: a desire to avoid discovering exculpatory information during the interrogation that would interfere with the arrest or prosecution of the suspect. Our finding that NOPD only conducts interrogations post-arrest and does not expend much legitimate effort to obtain confessions or investigative leads from interrogations, is consistent with both explanations.

- 111 -

4.      Deficient Documentation of Interrogations

NOPD does not adequately document its interrogations. *Miranda* warnings are reportedly provided at the start of the "pre-interview" and waivers are obtained prior to questioning. The "pre-interview," which appears to include the bulk of what would, under normal practice, be considered the interrogation, is not recorded with audio or video recording by NOPD detectives. In fact, the "pre-interview" is rarely documented in any significant manner at all. This means that any interrogation techniques and methods employed by the detectives during the "pre-interview" are not recorded or documented, making it difficult both to confirm that detectives are conducting proper pre-interviews, and to defend proper conduct when it is questioned.

The only video or audio recording appears to be that of "the interview" or "the confession." The recorded "interview" or "confession" in cases where the suspect is willing to make a statement is usually just a summary statement by the suspect of what was discussed during the "pre-interview." *Miranda* warnings are provided again at the start of the recorded confession. Documentation of the entire process is limited to a report prepared by the detective taken largely from the detective's notes from the interrogation process. In a practice our experts found particularly concerning, it is routine for NOPD detectives to then destroy their notes after preparing the report.

In addition to the audio or video recording, NOPD policy requires that recordings be transcribed. In the Homicide Division, an administrative staff completes the transcriptions, but in the Districts, this responsibility falls upon the detectives. The policy requiring the transcription of all recordings provides a strong incentive for detectives to limit the length of the taped portion of interrogations, or to not tape interrogations at all. Retention of the audio and video recordings depends on the unit and the storage space available. In the Homicide Division, the original recording is processed into evidence, a copy is provided to the DA's Office, and another copy is retained in the Division. In District 8, however, a lack of storage space prevents regular and systematic retention of the recorded video tapes in the District. Some Districts, and some rooms in the Homicide Division (due to equipment in disrepair), lack the capability to video record interrogations, further undermining good documentation and potentially impacting the decision whether to conduct an interrogation.

C.      Allegations of Constitutional Violations

NOPD employs practices that could facilitate and hide constitutional violations of criminal suspects' rights. We heard allegations that such violations do in fact occur, although we did not confirm them. According to well-regarded criminal defense attorneys, apparent constitutional violations frequently encountered in NOPD interrogations include: investigators waiting until incriminating statements are made before advising suspects of their *Miranda* Rights, rather than providing the rights at the start of the interrogation process; threats made during interrogations—most commonly against family members, such as threatening to "go to grandma's house, knock down the door, and search for drugs," or threats to women that they may lose their children to social services if they do not cooperate, or to spread a rumor in the suspect's neighborhood that the suspect is a snitch; and questioning that continues even after the suspect tells the interrogator that s/he does not want to talk anymore. Other allegations of improper interrogation tactics include promises of leniency, and, in juvenile cases, telling children, incorrectly, that their guardians have waived the suspect's *Miranda* Rights, and that is all that is required.

## XIV.  <u>COMMUNITY OVERSIGHT</u>

The City of New Orleans and NOPD have a long history of community engagement, including efforts to provide effective civilian oversight of the Department. For decades, the City's Office of Municipal Investigation served as an alternative to NOPD's PIB, accepting and investigating individual complaints of misconduct against NOPD officers (and other City employees), before it was defunded in 2008 after years of concern about its viability and effectiveness. A thoughtful and comprehensive report in 2001 by the Police-Civilian Review Task Force, which was comprised of well-regarded and prominent community advocates as well as NOPD representatives, considered whether and what type of civilian oversight might be appropriate for NOPD. The Task Force determined that an Independent Monitor, who would review policies, procedures, complaint patterns, and the quality of complaint investigations, as well as make regular reports to elected officials, NOPD and the public, would "create the impetus and the focus for correcting problems," "empower citizens with the information necessary to effect change," and would in this way "increase the ability of citizens and the NOPD to identify, address, and correct problems, thereby improving the department and building citizen confidence and support." *Report of the Police-Civilian Review Task Force* at 5. As noted in the Task Force report, this type of "quality control monitoring," has been used in other communities and has had beneficial results. *Id.* at 6.

Nearly a decade after the Task Force's recommendation, in August 2009, New Orleans created the Office of the Independent Police Monitor ("IPM") as an independent, civilian police oversight agency. According to the IPM, its mission is to:  improve cooperation and trust between the community and NOPD through objective review of police misconduct investigations; provide outreach to the New Orleans community; and make thoughtful policy recommendations to the NOPD and the City Council. The IPM lists as its specific responsibilities:  ensuring that all concerns regarding police misconduct are classified and investigated at the appropriate level and that those investigations are fairly, timely and thoroughly handled, and making this information available to the public; carefully considering aggregate data from complaints, investigations, community concerns and public policy in crafting recommendations aimed toward improving the quality services of the NOPD; reaching out to inform the community about the complaint process and IPM activities; and listening and responding to broader community concerns. The IPM recently reached an agreement with NOPD to help ensure it has access to the information it needs to fulfill these responsibilities. Last year, the IPM volunteered to use its own funds to develop a new early warning system for NOPD, and is currently working with NOPD to implement this new system. We have met with the IPM's Police Monitor several times and have been impressed with her dedication to building genuine reform and a constructive relationship with NOPD and the community.

In addition, with assistance from DOJ's Community Relations Services, community leaders in New Orleans have contributed significant time and effort to develop a community

- 113 -

advisory board in conjunction with NOPD and the Mayor's office.  This board would serve as a sustainable mechanism for ongoing dialogue to understand and address concerns from the community as well as opportunities for the community and police department to work together to achieve common goals.

There are myriad types of civilian oversight and each is capable of improving police-community relations, preventing unconstitutional conduct, and helping to ensure a constructive response when such misconduct does occur.  Because the type of oversight appropriate for any given community is circumstantial, deference should be given to the oversight mechanisms a community has chosen for itself.  Regardless of the type of oversight chosen, it is critical that oversight mechanisms be sufficiently resourced and empowered.  We have some concern regarding whether the IPM has sufficient resources to carry out its duties and it remains to see whether it will be given sufficient latitude in practice to be effective.  While still in a nascent change, we are encouraged by the development of the community advisory board and hopeful that this will be an important bridge in communications between NOPD and parts of the community most concerned about police misconduct.

When combined with practices that ensure appropriate transparency in police department decisions related to misconduct and tactics, and with tools to measure, assess, and respond to changing community attitudes towards policing over time, civilian oversight can help create a powerful form of community engagement that will ensure that reforms are sustained over time, even after court-ordered oversight has ended.

## XV.　<u>CONCLUSION</u>

The law governing officer conduct in many respects simply memorializes a basic code of ethics:  treat all individuals with dignity; treat people fairly regardless of their race, ethnicity, national origin, gender, sexual orientation, or religion; use only the force necessary to uphold the law and protect others and yourself; and act with integrity, honesty and diligence in enforcing the law.  The awesome authority we vest in law enforcement officers is contingent on adherence to these tenets.

Officers' dual responsibility to enforce the law even as they strictly abide by this code thus requires the responsible exercise of considerable discretion.  Too many officers at NOPD have chosen to exercise their discretion abusively or with little concern that their work effectively prevent crime.  This has been unfair both to the many officers within the New Orleans Police Department that act with diligence and selflessness each day, as well as to the people of New Orleans these officers are sworn to serve.  Until recently, City and Department leadership had largely acquiesced to wide-spread abuses by officers at all ranks.

The City of New Orleans took a critical step by choosing not to let the Police Department be defined by its past, and instead opening the operations of the Police Department for independent review and a public report.  This decision has already benefited the people of New Orleans by allowing for a fuller understanding of the systemic problems within the Department and the extent of the resulting harm.  This understanding serves as the foundation upon which to build a new Police Department that will prevent crime more effectively, serve all parts of the New Orleans' community more fairly, respect the rights of all New Orleans' residents, and better prepare and protect officers.  Past reform efforts underscore the need for long-term commitment and meaningful community engagement to fundamentally and permanently transform the Department in this way.  We look forward to working with the City, the Police Department and the broader New Orleans community to ensure that this effort is successful.

# APPENDIX

## Recommendations to the New Orleans Police Department

### Use of Force

1. Develop, train on, and implement an integrated and comprehensive set of use of force policies that are consistent with best practices and current law. Policies should comprehensively address the use of force; alternatives to force; reporting force; and reviewing and investigating force. Policies should provide clear guidance to all NOPD members who use force and observe uses of force, as well as supervisors and commanders who review and investigate force. All force policies should guide officers on how to avoid even justifiable force where it is safe and effective to do so, through the use of de-escalation techniques and solid tactics. This integrated set of use of force policies should include a primary use of force policy, as well as secondary policies specifically guiding the use of each type of force NOPD officers are permitted to use, including but not limited to ECDs, impact weapons, canines, and firearms.

2. Ensure that use of force policies explain what approved weapons may be used for and provide clear guidance regarding the circumstances under which various types and levels of force may be appropriate, including the crime at issue; the subject's level of resistance; the danger to the officer and others; the context of the force, including location, the size and apparent or known physical condition of the subject, and similar circumstances; and how the officer uses the weapon. An adequate force policy would thus, for example, state clearly that a baton is capable of inflicting lethal injuries, but may also be considered a lower level of force, depending on how it is used and the body part attacked. Whether this measured force policy is termed circular, quadrant, staircase, matrix, graduated, situational, or a continuum, it must provide clear guidance to officers regarding appropriate behavior, to better enable them to use force properly and to provide clear standards to which they may be held accountable.

3. Include input from high-level NOPD command representatives, as well as representatives from the Training Division, PIB, the City Attorney's Office, and community representatives in the use of force policy development process.

4. Require officers to report all force above un-resisted handcuffing.

5. Establish stringent penalties for officers who use or observe force and fail to report it, regardless of whether the force appears to be reasonable.

6. Require all officers on the scene of a use of force to write a report documenting their actions and observations. The report should include: a detailed account of the incident from the officer's perspective; the reason for the initial police presence; and a specific description of the acts that led to the use of force; the level of resistance encountered; and the force that was used.

7.	Ensure that all force incidents are investigated by uninvolved superior officers.  The investigator should determine:  whether the subject's actions precipitated the use of force; whether the officer's use of force was proportionate to the subject's actions or resistance; whether the injuries sustained by the subject are consistent with the amount of force claimed by the officer; and whether the officers', witnesses', and subject's versions of events reasonably agree.  Where they do not, the investigator should clearly describe the discrepancies and the evidence supporting different versions of events.

8.	Require investigators to collect and document all evidence—including officer and witness statements, and physical evidence, including but not limited to audio and video recordings, photographs and other documentation of injuries or the absence of injuries— to establish material facts related to the use of force.  If the supervisor cannot resolve a material discrepancy, elevate the investigation and require an immediate, on-site response by specialized force and/or misconduct investigators.

9.	Develop processes to review all uses of force, with the level and type of review tailored to the type of force used, the type of injury, if any, resulting from the use of force, and the particular circumstances of the incident.  For higher-level uses of force, including but not limited to officer-involved shootings, or where there is an in-custody death, develop and implement a process for more stringent criminal and administrative investigation and review.  Convene interdisciplinary force or roll out "teams," that include personnel specially trained in criminal and administrative force investigations, specially trained representatives of the Training Division, representatives of the City Attorney's Office, and others as appropriate, to investigate such uses of force from a criminal and/or administrative perspective.  Require these teams to determine not only whether the use of force was out of policy, but also whether it presented tactical, policy, training, or equipment concerns.  Require a senior commander, as part of this team, to immediately respond to the scene of the incident and take command of the inquiry.  This interdisciplinary group should report to a high level group of senior officers, sometimes called a use of force review "board," that should review investigatory findings and make disciplinary, policy, training, tactical, and equipment recommendations to the Superintendent as appropriate.

10.	Significantly increase mandatory recruit and in-service use of force training.  Include tactical, legal, and ethical training in all types of force NOPD officers are permitted to use, as well as training in de-escalation and other techniques to avoid the use of force where it is safe and effective to do so.

11.	Collect and maintain use of force data and analyze this data to identify trends and develop policy, training and operational recommendations.  Consider all recommendations that result from this analysis and adopt them where appropriate.  Document the decision not to adopt a recommendation and reason for the decision.  At least annually, report to the public findings from analyzing the previous year use of force data and the steps taken to correct problems and build on successes.

12.	Develop, train on, and implement a policy on the use of canines that is comprehensive, legally sound, and consistent with best practices.

- 2 -

13. Significantly improve and increase mandatory training of canines and their handlers. Training content and frequency should be consistent with best practices. No handler or canine should be deployed unless the handler and canine are current on all training requirements and the canine is fully controllable during exercises.

14. Collect and maintain all records on canine training, deployment, apprehension, and bites. Analyze canine-related data to develop, consistent with best practices, training and operational recommendations for individual dogs, handlers, and the unit as a whole.

15. Establish procedures for auditing canine training, deployment, and administrative documentation, to be performed by an entity outside the Canine Unit.

16. Develop, train on, and implement a policy on the use of force by SOD, including clear guidance on what tactics are permissible for the service of each type of warrant, and when SOD or other units will be used to serve warrants and perform other police functions. This policy should be comprehensive, legally sound and consistent with best practices. SOD should not be deployed for routine police work.

17. Require SOD to document its activities in detail, including preparing plans and after-action reports. Require review of SOD activities and deployments to identify any policy, training, or tactical concerns raised by the action.

18. Incorporate discussion of uses of force, including trends, arrest/force ratios, and outliers during weekly department-wide COMSTAT meetings.

19. Promptly input all force data into the early warning system. Develop and implement policy to ensure the early warning system functions as a source of real-time information that assists line supervisors and commanders in identifying officers in need of closer supervision or particular interventions.

20. Tailor interventions based on early warning system data to the specific problem presented, and monitor and refine the intervention as necessary until the problem is resolved. The early warning system should be used to identify use of force outliers, determining whether the aberration is meaningful and requires correction, and monitoring interventions to determine that any use of force problems have been resolved.

### Stops, Searches, and Arrests

1. Institute mandatory and comprehensive Fourth Amendment training, at the Academy and annually, for all officers. The training should include lectures as well adult learning methods that incorporate role-playing scenarios, where officers then prepare written reports to gauge comprehension of law. Classes should be taught by a competent legal instructor with significant experience litigating Fourth Amendment issues.

2. Institute policies and procedures to collect data on and to review stops and arrests to identify problem areas and ensure high quality arrests, searches and seizures that result in prosecutable cases.

3.      Include Districts' conviction rates and disposition of important cases at COMSTAT meetings.  Establish a formal system to coordinate with the DA's Office for input regarding the quality of the arrests by NOPD and to make operational changes based upon this input.

4.      Establish clear and comprehensive guidelines controlling the preparation, use and preservation of FICs.  The policy should dictate when it is mandatory, rather than discretionary, for officers to prepare a FIC, and guide officers in the use of completed FIC information.

5.      Revamp FICs to make them an analytically useful tool for both crime suppression and statistical analysis.  The cards should include the suspected crime relevant to any *Terry* or probable cause stop.  The cards should have a short narrative for the officer to list the facts that establish probable cause or articulable suspicion, and should include the length of time of the stop.  They should also include a comments section for the officer to list any investigative findings.

6.      Ensure that FIC information complies with all Federal and State privacy standards.

## Discriminatory Policing on the Basis of Race, Ethnicity, and LGBT Status

1.      Develop and implement policies that specifically and comprehensively address and prohibit discriminatory policing, including bias-based profiling.  The policy should clearly outline the very limited, suspect-specific circumstances in which officers may consider race, ethnicity, gender, LGBT status, religion, or national origin in discharging their duties.

2.      Provide coordinated training – academy, field, and in-service – that sends a clear, consistent and emphatic message that bias-based profiling and other forms of discriminatory policing are prohibited.  Include instruction on data collection protocols, relevant legal and ethical standards, how to handle stops effectively, and diversity and cultural awareness.  Provide training in how stereotypes and implicit bias may infect police work, making it less safe, less effective, alienating communities and violating the rights of individuals.  Provide training to supervisors and commanders in how to detect and respond to bias-based profiling and other forms of discriminatory policing.

3.      Begin collecting and analyzing data related to race and ethnicity of subjects of law enforcement actions, including:  traffic stops; pedestrian stops; searches; arrests; and uses of force.  Consider and implement operational changes based on this analysis. At least annually, report to the public findings from analyzing the previous year stop, search, and arrest data and the steps taken to correct problems and build on successes.

4.      Capture and track complaints alleging racial and other bias-based profiling, along with characteristics of the complainants.

5.      Develop and implement policies and protocols for responding to employees, units, assignments, or other components, that indicate a pattern of biased policing.  Consider

- 4 -

complaints of bias-based profiling and other potential indicators of biased policing in the Department's early warning system.

## Services for Limited English Proficient Communities

1. Establish a language assistance plan and policy that outlines such critical functions as: determining the number of LEP individuals within NOPD's jurisdiction; collecting and recording the number of LEP victims and witnesses who seek NOPD services; interrogating and interviewing LEP individuals; responding to and tracking citizen complaints filed by LEP individuals; identifying and training multilingual staff; and training all NOPD personnel on providing language assistance services to LEP individuals.

2. Communicate the language assistance plan and policy to police personnel, the City of New Orleans Human Relations Commission, and to the community, and provide training to personnel on the policies and the requirements of Title VI. The communication plan should include outreach to organizations representing LEP individuals.

3. Identify and translate official documents that are subject to public dissemination into Vietnamese and Spanish, at a minimum.

4. Prioritize recruitment of qualified bilingual personnel and provide incentives for assuming interpreter or translator duties for the Department.

## Sexual Assault Investigations

1. Revise policies and procedures governing response to and investigation of sex crimes, including specific guidelines covering: the respective duties of patrol, investigators, and supervisors; initial and follow-up victim interview protocol; collaboration with victim advocates; protocols for forensic examinations of victims; suspect interviews and forensic examinations; evidence preservation and crime scene management in the sexual assault context; and services/assistance to be offered to victims.

2. Require training for sex crimes detectives in topics including: overcoming the perceptions of false/unfounded allegations to successfully investigate non-stranger sexual assault; drug and alcohol facilitated sexual assault; victim interviewing skills; realistic dynamics of sexual assault; victim impact; report-writing; and discovery.

3. Require training for patrol/unformed officers with a focus on the dynamics of sexual assault; report writing, victim interviewing, and initial assessment of victim and crime scene.

4. Incorporate the recommendations of the National Protocol for Sexual Assault Medical Forensic Examinations (Adult / Adolescents), and other recognized criminal justice model policies, procedures, and training in the development and implementation of policies and procedures.

5.  Require patrol/uniformed officers to document calls for service involving sexual assaults, including their own observations and all actions taken, and any statements of victims, witnesses, and reporting persons.

6.  Implement more thorough and regular systems to audit and ensure accountability in the classification and reporting of sex crimes. The decision to code a report as a miscellaneous complaint should be submitted to a supervisor for close secondary review.

7.  Develop an understanding of the language and best policies regarding the definitions of "unfounded," "false," and "baseless" in the context of sexual assault. Track these different types of conclusions separately so that the agency can easily report them.

8.  Separately track and account for all felony sexual assaults, including those offenses not included in UCR counts, *e.g.*, Drug Facilitated Sexual Assault, Sexual Assaults involving persons with disabilities unable to consent, sodomy, and male victims of sexual assault. Collect data on the final disposition of investigations, including whether the DA charged the suspect, and if so, whether the case was eventually dismissed, pled, or tried, and the final outcome.

9.  In non-stranger sexual assault cases, where there is no belief that the suspect presents a danger to the victim or the community, may flee the jurisdiction of the court or destroy evidence, NOPD should consider delaying arrest so that the investigation can fully support prosecution. Such delay, when circumstances warrant, permits detectives to build a detailed and complete investigation. The Department should educate advocates and the public that this is a best practice for ensuring that police provide prosecutors with thorough and professional investigations.

## Domestic Violence Investigations

1.  Revise policies and procedures to include specific guidance for initial and investigative response to domestic violence, including: 911 dispatch procedures; initial entry and preliminary investigation of scenes; identifying and documenting victim injuries; referral of all victims to the NOFJC; and procedures for follow-up investigations.

2.  Implement the law enforcement "Integrated Protocol" developed by the NOFJC, and review and update protocols regularly. Continue collaboration with community providers to ensure that policies and protocols remain victim-centered and effective.

3.  Assign sufficient staff to the Domestic Violence Unit at the NOFJC to permit detectives to conduct appropriate follow-up investigation, including field work and coordination with the DA's Domestic Violence Prosecution Unit.

4.  Provide mandatory training to officers and detectives responding to reports of domestic violence. Specific training on identifying the primary aggressor in mutual combat situations, interviewing witnesses and suspects, and responding to and investigating strangulation in the context of domestic violence is strongly urged.

5.      Track dispositions of domestic violence investigations.  Such tracking should not stop at the point of an arrest, but should include information on whether the DA charged the suspect, and if so, if the case was eventually dismissed, pled, or tried, and the final outcome.

## Recruitment

1.      Refocus the Recruitment Unit on the primary goal of recruitment of high quality applicants who share the Department's values and can help it achieve its mission.

2.      Remove the background investigation function from the Recruitment Unit.  Place the Unit under the direct supervision of a Deputy Superintendent or similar level of management to ensure accountability.

3.      Task the Recruitment Unit with developing a plan for recruitment that will identify the skills and abilities NOPD needs, including, for example, the ability to think strategically, complex cognitive problem solving skills, interpersonal communication skills, capacity to use technology, emotional maturity, and the ability to collaborate with a diverse cross-section of the community.

4.      Develop clear and understandable goals for the Recruitment Unit that require maintaining detailed records and reporting of its activities.  Establish scheduled reviews of the Recruitment Unit and its personnel to ensure productivity.

5.      Staff the Recruitment Unit with full-time recruiters, as well as part-time recruiters who can be temporarily reassigned from elsewhere in the Department.  Establish job-related qualifications for members of the Recruitment Unit, and make Department-wide announcements for openings in the Unit to ensure qualified Unit members.

6.      Provide Recruitment Unit members with specific training for recruiting a qualified and diverse work force, including training on employment and discrimination law.

7.      Establish significant and sustained relationships with various institutions and community organizations that can serve as the source of qualified and diverse applicants.

8.      In conjunction with the Civil Service Commission, develop a recruitment process and testing procedure that addresses barriers for out of town applicants.  This process should permit initial testing, i.e. civil service exam, agility test, and psychological tests, to take place at the recruitment site.

9.      Explore and implement measures to better attract and reward individuals with fluency in languages other than English.

## Training

1.      Establish an executive training education task force to advise the Superintendent and identify global training priorities and broad training goals.  Include both law enforcement officials and community representatives as members.

2.      Consider establishing a public safety training consortium to provide expertise in creating training strategy, course topics, curriculum development, classroom/facility use, and instructor-development.

3.      Ensure that training priorities and goals reflect and incorporate NOPD's commitment to transforming the Department and incorporating community/problem-oriented policing into all aspects of policing.

4.      Make the Training Division the central coordination point for all NOPD training, including but not limited to recruit, in-service, use of force (firearms), roll call, leadership, special mission unit, and elective training.  The Training Division should also be responsible for tracking, maintaining, and reporting detailed, real-time training records and statistics.

5.      Develop an electronic database to create and maintain records for each recruit and each sworn and unsworn member of the Department, including a standard electronic training record and electronic copies of certificates and other materials.

6.      Create a full-time Department-Wide Training Liaison position within the Training Division, to coordinate training activities with designated liaisons in every police district and organizational unit.

7.      Establish a formal training curriculum development process that incorporates command staff input, recent research, subject matter expertise, and City Attorney review.  Require a full-time, specially-trained Curriculum Developer to formalize all curriculum development for the Department.  Develop written curricula for every training topic.

8.      Increase the number of hours allotted for training in priority subject matter areas, including use of force; the exclusionary rule; and weapons recertification.

9.      Establish eligibility criteria for all staff assigned to the Training Division, and conduct regular (at least annual) reviews of Training Division staff and adjunct instructors to ensure that they meet the delineated criteria.

11.     Provide tailored annual training to Training Division staff and adjunct instructors, including training on effective teaching, adult-learning techniques, and curriculum development.

12.     Consider designating a large enclosed climate-controlled area for physical training activities, such as defense tactics, ground fighting techniques, and baton requalification, as well as CPR recertification.  Provide ready access to a safe, modern, firing range to ensure sworn officers receive appropriate firearms training.

13.     Maintain recruit class sizes of no more than 25-30 candidates per class.  Hire candidates on a rolling basis and place them in non-sworn support roles until the desired class size is attained.

- 8 -

14. Require the Training Division to develop a Field Training Program Manual that describes the policies and procedures for the field training program.

15. Establish eligibility criteria for Field Training Officers and Field Training Sergeants, and conduct regular (at least annual) reviews of FTOs and Field Training Sergeants to ensure that they meet the delineated criteria. Give the Training Division authority to remove any FTO or sergeant from the program.

16. Provide a tailored annual field training officer/sergeant curriculum.

17. Create a mechanism to actively elicit feedback from recruits regarding the quality of their field training, including the extent to which their field training was consistent with what they learned in the Academy.

18. Establish a mandatory annual in-service training program of at least 40 hours. Identify critical in-service training topic areas based on analysis of officer safety issues, input from members at all levels of the Department, input from members of the community, community complaints, use-of-force statistics, internal affairs statistics, court decisions, and research reflecting the latest law enforcement trends.

19. Create tailored training tracks for command staff (captains and above); lieutenants and sergeants; detectives; narcotics and gang investigators; special mission units (SWAT, Task Force, Drug Enforcement, etc); and FTOs. Create a customized 40-hour training program for new promotees to all ranks, and develop upper-level managers and executives by supporting participation in executive development programs.

20. Strategically plan a daily roll call schedule consisting of brief training sessions conducted by the roll call sergeant at the beginning of each tour of duty.

## Supervision

1. Develop and implement policies for supervision that set out clear requirements for supervisors and are consistent with best practices regarding span of control and unity of command.

2. Develop and implement supervisory training of no fewer than 40 hours that each supervisor must complete before becoming a supervisor. This mandatory training should include: training in how to effectively direct and guide officers; legal standards and requirements; building community partnerships as a supervisor; reviewing officer uses of force; conducting investigations of complaints of misconduct; how to use supervisory tools such as an early warning system, audio and video recording, and AVL.

3. Develop and implement an annual in-service training program for supervisors of no fewer than 40 hours and provides all necessary updates and refreshers, as well as training in new skills.

4. Ensure adequate allocation of field supervisors so that field supervisors work the same days and schedules as their subordinates and can directly supervise them by responding

to the scene, reviewing their reports, investigating their uses of force, responding to complaints of misconduct; and providing counseling, redirection, and support as appropriate.

5. Consider whether some clerical duties currently assigned to supervisors should instead be assigned to civilian or non-supervisory staff.

6. Ensure that the early warning system can be used as a supervisory tool. Provide the policy, training, and administrative support to ensure that the early warning system is maintained and the information included in it is accurate and timely, and that supervisors know how to use it and are required to do so.

7. Ensure that COMSTAT includes regular consideration and analysis of integrity-related data and the quality of arrests and train supervisors on how to use this information to provide more effective supervision and direction to their officers.

8. Implement and maintain appropriate technology to assist officer supervision and accountability, including video and audio recorders and similar devices.

9. Hold supervisors accountable for the quality and completeness of their supervision, including their review of officers' reports and uses of force. Supervisory performance should be assessed in part on the productivity of their subordinates as well as their response to complaints received concerning their subordinates.

## Paid Details

1. Immediately remake the Paid Detail system. In its place, create a single office that arranges, coordinates and monitors all officers' outside law enforcement employment.

2. Underscore that the ability to work Details is a privilege.

3. Increase officer accountability and oversight of the Detail system.

4. Prohibit officers from soliciting Detail opportunities.

5. Establish a system with appropriately stringent criteria that will fairly assign officers to work Details.

6. Set Detail pay uniformly according to rank and include a reasonable fee that goes to the City to cover the expenses of the outside employment office, workers compensation, fuel, use of equipment, and any other actual or potential costs to the City.

## Performance Evaluations and Promotions

1. With the City and its Civil Service Commission, determine the usefulness of applying the current City-wide performance evaluation system to the Police Department, and revise the current system or develop and implement a new one.

- 10 -

2. Develop and implement an NOPD-specific, comprehensive system of evaluating employee performance. This system should recognize that ethical and effective policing are intertwined and assess both, and should assess employees' productivity not only by stops, citations, and arrests, but also by employees' success at preventing crime, building strong, prosecutable cases, and fostering productive community relationships. Performance evaluations should be integrated into ongoing supervision and should be documented.

3. Ensure that all supervisors are trained in and held accountable for completing timely and ongoing performance evaluations of every subordinate. Where an employee reports to more than one supervisor, or has had more than one supervisor during the rating period, all supervisors should provide written input regarding the employee's performance while under their supervision.

4. In conjunction with the City and Civil Service Commission, make NOPD's promotions process more fair, transparent, and flexible, allowing for promotions of NOPD's most effective and ethical officers.

5. Develop and implement promotional criteria and assessment tools to ensure that unqualified individuals are not promoted. Ensure that NOPD promotional selection criteria communicate NOPD's values and mission, and result in the promotion of officers who most closely adhere to these values and are capable of carrying out NOPD's mission. Require assessment of officers' community policing and problem solving efforts and abilities, as well as officers' professionalism, ethics, and integrity, as part of the promotions selection process. Officers with a disciplinary history that does not comport with the behavior NOPD wants to model for other officers and the community should be disqualified from promotion.

6. Advertise promotion opportunities widely. Give promotion exams for every position at least every 18 months, and recommend for promotion only the number of candidates for which there appear to be likely vacancies during the period before the next promotional exam.

7. Train all members and employees on performance evaluation and promotions policies that incorporate these recommendations.

### Misconduct Complaint Intake, Investigation, and Adjudication

1. Revise and update all policies related to the intake, investigation, and adjudication of misconduct complaints, including policies guiding complaint intake and investigation by officers, field supervisors, and PIB staff. Create protocols and directives for use by field and PIB investigators to improve investigative quality, thoroughness and consistency.

2. Revise policy so that complaint classification is allegation-driven rather than outcome-driven, and so that all allegations of misconduct against NOPD officers are investigated and given a formal disposition of sustained, not sustained, exonerated, or unfounded. The level of investigation should be tailored to the requirements of the case.

- 11 -

3.  Revise policy to ensure that allegations of misconduct related to arrests and discriminatory policing are investigated and specifically tracked.

4.  Provide significant and ongoing training to PIB investigators and managers, as well as to field investigators and their supervisors, including ICOs, in receiving, investigating, and reviewing misconduct investigations. Train all officers in how to properly handle complaint intake, including strategies for turning complaints into positive police-civilian interactions, and the consequences for failing to take complaints.

5.  Clarify officer and investigator responsibilities related to misconduct complaint intake and investigation and hold all investigators and officers responsible for adhering to these directives.

6.  Staff PIB with sufficient trained staff to complete thorough and timely investigations within the timeframes mandated by law. Create a PIB selection process that ensures that only officers with excellent investigative skills and who can fairly hold officers accountable become PIB investigators.

7.  Restructure the ICO position to allow ICOs to act more effectively as a liaison between the districts and PIB and as genuine accountability liaisons. Hold supervisors and commanders responsible for preventing, detecting, and responding to misconduct.

8.  Ensure that allegations of misconduct made in civil and criminal lawsuits are identified and promptly investigated by the Department. Establish a system to identify and investigate cases that are dropped for lack of probable cause, or instances where officers may have violated the law or policy, as identified by the DA's Office, the Courts, the PD's Office, or federal agents or attorneys working with NOPD.

9.  Implement systems to monitor and ensure that all allegations in a complaint are captured and investigated and that investigative reports accurately reflect the content of subject and witness interviews. Ensure that PIB and other NOPD managers thoroughly review misconduct investigations, signing off only on those in which all material evidence has been gathered, and in which all findings supported by a preponderance of that evidence.

10. Work with the State to modify the state law requiring that administrative misconduct investigations be completed within 60 days to allow for certain exceptions, such as where the alleged misconduct involves numerous officers or is particularly complex, or where evidence is newly discovered well into the investigation.

11. Consider having higher level commanders, rather than investigators, make investigative findings.

12. Update the Department's penalty schedule and enact policies to ensure its proper use (*e.g.* requiring that all deviations outside the prescribed range are documented in writing, and that exceptions to the stated range do not become the rule). Revise the disciplinary hearing structure to ensure consistency and integrity.

13.	Improve training for PIB investigators and commanders on New Orleans' civil service system requirements related to the imposition of discipline.

14.	Document and explain the rationale for all disciplinary decisions.  To ensure transparency in the system and ensure that decisions can withstand scrutiny, implement a requirement that all disciplinary decisions be within the range set out in the penalty schedule unless there is a justified and documented rationale for going outside the range.

15.	The Civil Service Commission should post all its decisions in full, online, and in a timely manner.

16.	Document the reasons for every decision to reverse an investigative finding as well as the reasons for accepting or changing any disciplinary recommendation.

17.	The City Attorney's Office, which should play a larger advisory role at every stage of the investigative process, should in particular provide close guidance at the disciplinary stage to ensure that NOPD's disciplinary decisions are as fair and legally defensible as possible.

18.	Implement a system to allow for the investigation of misconduct and imposition of administrative discipline prior to completion of criminal or civil suits against the officer. Enhance policies, protocols, and training to ensure bifurcation of criminal and administrative investigations.  Develop protocol for referring allegations of criminal misconduct to an outside agency where appropriate.

19.	Provide written guidance and training to ensure that investigators identify, seek advice, and refer where appropriate, allegations of criminal conduct.

20.	The DA's Office should continue and expand its efforts to work with NOPD to ensure that criminal investigations are fair and thorough, and that officers who commit crimes are held accountable.

## Community Policing

1.	Articulate, internally as well as externally, that the Department is adopting Community Policing as a philosophy, not as a series of projects or programs.  Ensure that the community policing philosophy is reflected in the Department' mission statement and set of cores values.

2.	Build the Community Policing philosophy into all aspects of the Department's operations, including policies and operating procedures, performance evaluations, incentives, recruitment, training, and promotional criteria.

3.	Review and reassess staffing allocation and personnel deployment to ensure that they support community policing and problem-solving goals.

4.	Implement a mandatory and robust training on community policing and problem-oriented policing methods, including training on contemporary approaches for all officers, to include supervisors, managers and executives. This training should focus on practical skills and ideally include a practicum out in the community.

5.  Require in-service training on skills that enhance the officer's ability to engage successfully in community policing, to include leadership, ethics, interpersonal skills, community engagement, crime prevention, conflict resolution, verbal de-escalation of conflict, and cultural awareness training. Train officers on how to establish formal partnerships and actively engage community organizations, including building trust with special population groups such as immigrant communities and LGBT communities.

6.  As part of the effort to rebuild credibility in the community, encourage officer outreach to a broad cross-section of community stakeholders to establish extensive problem-solving partnerships and develop cooperative strategies that build mutual respect and trusting relationships. Create a comprehensive community policing plan with community input that collaboratively identifies and implements strategies to address crime and safety problems. Consider programs such as citizen academies in languages other than English.

7.  Develop measurements to assess the effectiveness of the three tenets of community policing—partnerships, problem-solving and organizational transformation.

8.  Review and evaluate alternative COMSTAT models, with a focus on using COMSTAT to hold command staff and supervisors accountable for implementing community-policing strategies. Develop skills, knowledge and abilities for the analyst function to enhance mapping techniques, such as predatory mapping and predictive policing to support COMSTAT and community policing efforts.

9.  Provide data and information to the public in a transparent and public-friendly format to the greatest extent allowable by law. Revise the website to be user-friendly and provide more transparent data on the website from the community perspective, and in multiple language formats.

10. Consider working with members of racial, ethnic, and language minorities, immigrant communities, and the LGBT communities to develop a mechanism that would allow for regular communication and cooperation between the Department, the City, and community leaders, such as through the development of a community advisory panel.

## Officer Assistance and Support

1.  Design and implement a comprehensive range of mental health services for NOPD professionals through a centralized and adequately-staffed office. The range of mental health services should include: readily accessible confidential counseling services with both direct and indirect referrals; critical incident debriefings and crisis counseling; and stress management training.

2.  Provide the infrastructure for a peer counseling program (possibly in conjunction with neighboring jurisdictions), and incorporate mental health services into an overall department-wide health and wellness program. To this end, consider establishing a fitness center where such wellness programs and trainings could be offered, and

- 14 -

mandating an annual physical exam for officers where wellness issues can be addressed and discussed on an individual basis with medical professionals.

3.	Use mental health professionals to enhance training of NOPD officers on avoiding excessive force.  Topics that mental health professionals can address in such training should include:  cultural sensitivity and diversity; intervention by fellow officers to stop the use of excessive force; the interaction of human perception and threat assessment; decision making under highly charged conditions; psychological methods of situation control; patrol de-escalation and defusing techniques that not only provide a tactical response, but also respond to the fear stimulated by confrontations; anger management programs that use self-assessment and self-management techniques for providing individual feedback to officers on how variable levels of legitimate anger influence judgment; and training in verbal control and communication, including conflict resolution.  Provide academy and in-service training on mental health stressors related to law enforcement and the mental health services available to officers and their families.

4.	Ensure that mental health services to NOPD officers and their families are incorporated into any crisis response and emergency preparedness planning and actual response.

## Interrogations

1.	Revise interrogation policies to include discussion of legal standards and safeguards, as well as express prohibitions on certain interrogation methods.

2.	Revise interrogation policies to provide specific guidance on documentation of the interrogation process and discovery obligations of DA's Office.

3.	Revise and update interview and interrogation training for recruits.

4.	Formalize training for newly assigned detectives on interrogation procedures and methods.  Include legal standards, ethics, and causes for investigative failures and false confessions in all interview and interrogations training.

5.	Require video recording of all phases of interviews and interrogations.

6.	Require that detectives maintain their notes taken during interviews and interrogations and provide copies of the notes in the case file to the DA's Office.

7.	Revise selection standards for detectives in Districts and specialized units, requiring an appropriate tenure on the job, writing samples, supervisor recommendations, and an interview for qualification.

8.	Enlarge the applicant pool for detectives by posting all detective openings throughout the Department.

9.	Provide regular training to all detectives on changes to the law regarding interrogations and confessions.  Consider providing this training in partnership with the DA's Office and/or USAO.

- 15 -

10.    Designate interview rooms for all Districts and specialized units. Equip all interview rooms with audio and video recording technology.

## Community Oversight

1.    Work with the City and the City Council to ensure that the Office of the Independent Police Monitor possesses the authority and staffing necessary to fulfill its mission, and to further build upon this mission to ensure that the IPM is a truly independent, effective, and sustainable mechanism for police accountability.

2.    Work with a variety of community groups and individuals to develop additional mechanisms to ensure representative, active, and constructive community engagement in NOPD crime prevention and accountability efforts.

3.    Develop and implement mechanisms to ensure that NOPD data and decision making is as transparent as possible, including meaningful analysis and reporting of accountability and integrity related data and decisions.

4.    Develop and implement mechanisms, such as recurring community surveys, to assess recent experiences and current attitudes about NOPD among all communities throughout the City, and changes in these experiences and attitudes over time.

# APPENDIX V: NIJ: EARLY WARNING SYSTEMS: RESPONDING TO THE PROBLEM POLICE OFFICER

**U.S. Department of Justice**
Office of Justice Programs
*National Institute of Justice*

# National Institute of Justice

## R e s e a r c h   i n   B r i e f

*July 2001*

## Issues and Findings

*Discussed in this Brief:* A systematic study of early warning systems designed to identify officers who may be having problems on the job and to provide those officers with the appropriate counseling or training. The findings are based on a survey of 832 local law enforcement agencies and site visits to three departments with established early warning systems.

*Key issues:* A growing body of evidence indicates that in any police department a small percentage of officers are responsible for a disproportionate share of citizen complaints. Early warning systems help supervisors identify these officers, intervene with them, and monitor their subsequent performance.

Even though early warning systems are becoming more popular among law enforcement agencies, little research has addressed the effectiveness of such programs. This Brief reports on a study that establishes a baseline description of early warning system programs and asks some fundamental questions:

● Are early warning systems effective in reducing police officer misconduct?

● Are some types of early warning systems more effective than others?

● What impact do early warning systems have on the departments in which they operate?

● Do early warning systems have unintended and undesirable effects?

*Key findings:* Twenty-seven percent of local law enforcement agencies serving populations of at least 50,000 had an early warning

*continued...*

# Early Warning Systems: Responding to the Problem Police Officer

*by Samuel Walker, Geoffrey P. Alpert, and Dennis J. Kenney*

It has become a truism among police chiefs that 10 percent of their officers cause 90 percent of the problems. Investigative journalists have documented departments in which as few as 2 percent of all officers are responsible for 50 percent of all citizen complaints.[1] The phenomenon of the "problem officer" was identified in the 1970s: Herman Goldstein noted that problem officers "are well known to their supervisors, to the top administrators, to their peers, and to the residents of the areas in which they work," but that "little is done to alter their conduct."[2] In 1981, the U.S. Commission on Civil Rights recommended that all police departments create an early warning system to identify problem officers, those "who are frequently the subject of complaints or who demonstrate identifiable patterns of inappropriate behavior."[3]

An early warning system is a data-based police management tool designed to identify officers whose behavior is problematic and provide a form of intervention to correct that performance. As an early response, a department intervenes before such an officer is in a situation that warrants formal disciplinary gartion. The system alerts the department to these individuals and warns the officers while providing counseling or training to help them change their problematic behavior.

By 1999, 39 percent of all municipal and county law enforcement agencies that serve populations greater than 50,000 people either had an early warning system in place or were planning to implement one. The growing popularity of these systems as a remedy for police misconduct raises questions about their effectiveness and about the various program elements that are associated with effectiveness. To date, however, little has been written on the subject.[4] This Brief reports on the first indepth investigation of early warning systems. The investigation combined the results of a national survey of law enforcement agencies with the findings of case studies of three agencies with established systems.

## How prevalent are early warning systems?

As part of the national evaluation of early warning systems, the Police Executive Research Forum—funded by the National Institute of Justice and the Office of Community Oriented Policing Services—surveyed 832 sheriffs' offices and municipal and county police departments serving populations of 50,000 or

Support for this research was provided through a transfer of funds to NIJ from the Office of Community Oriented Policing Services. 

## Issues and Findings
*...continued*

system in 1999; another 12 percent were planning to establish such a program.

Larger agencies were more likely than smaller agencies to use an early warning system. Among agencies with 1,000 or more sworn officers, 79 percent had or planned to have an early warning system; only 56 percent of agencies with between 500 and 999 sworn officers had or planned to have such a program.

No standards have been established for identifying which officers should participate in early warning programs, but there is general agreement that a number of factors can help identify problem officers: citizen complaints, firearm-discharge reports, use-of-force reports, civil litigation, resisting-arrest incidents, and pursuits and vehicular accidents.

Data from the three case-study agencies (in Miami, Minneapolis, and New Orleans) indicate the following:

● In spite of considerable differences among the programs, each program appeared to reduce problem behaviors significantly.

● Early warning systems encourage changes in the behavior of supervisors, as well as of the identified officers.

● Early warning systems are high-maintenance programs that require ongoing administrative attention.

A caveat is in order about the findings reported here. The research design was limited in a number of ways, and each of the early warning systems studied operates in the context of a department's larger commitment to increased accountability. It is impossible to disentangle the effect of the department's culture of accountability from that of the early warning program.

***Target audience:*** State and local law enforcement administrators, planners, and policymakers; researchers; and educators.

more.[5] Usable responses were received from 571 agencies, a response rate of 69 percent. The response rate was significantly higher for municipal agencies than for sheriff's departments.

Approximately one-fourth (27 percent) of the surveyed agencies had an early warning system in 1999. One-half of these systems had been created since 1994, and slightly more than one-third had been created since 1996. These data, combined with the number of agencies indicating that a system was being planned (another 12 percent), suggest that such systems will spread rapidly in the next few years.

Early warning systems are more prevalent among municipal law enforcement agencies than among county sheriffs' departments.

## How does an early warning system work?

Early warning systems have three basic phases: selection, intervention, and postintervention monitoring.

**Selecting officers for the program.**
No standards have been established for identifying officers for early warning programs, but there is general agreement about the criteria that should influence their selection. Performance indicators that can help identify officers with problematic behavior include citizen complaints, firearm-discharge and use-of-force reports, civil litigation, resisting-arrest incidents, and high-speed pursuits and vehicular damage.[6]

Although a few departments rely only on citizen complaints to select officers for intervention, most use a combination of performance indicators. Among systems that factor in citizen complaints, most (67 percent) require three complaints in a given timeframe (76 percent specify a 12-month period) to identify an officer.

**Intervening with the officer.** The primary goal of early warning systems is to change the behavior of individual officers who have been identified as having problematic performance records. The basic intervention strategy involves a combination of deterrence and education. The theory of simple deterrence assumes that officers who are subject to intervention will change their behavior in response to a perceived threat of punishment.[7] General deterrence assumes that officers not subject to the system will also change their behavior to avoid potential punishment. Early warning systems also operate on the assumption that training, as part of the intervention, can help officers improve their performance.

In most systems (62 percent), the initial intervention generally consists of a review by the officer's immediate supervisor. Almost half of the responding agencies (45 percent) involve other command officers in counseling the officer. Also, these systems frequently include a training class for groups of officers identified by the system (45 percent of survey respondents).

**Monitoring the officer's subsequent performance.** Nearly all (90 percent) the agencies that have an early warning system in place report that they monitor an officer's performance after the initial intervention. Such monitoring is generally informal and conducted by the officer's immediate supervisor, but some departments have developed a formal process of observation, evaluation, and reporting. Almost half of the agencies (47 percent) monitor the officer's performance for 36 months after the initial intervention. Half of the agencies indicate that the followup period is not specified and that officers are monitored either continuously or on a case-by-case basis.

2

## Limitations of the survey findings

The responses from the national survey should be viewed with some caution. Some law enforcement agencies may have claimed to have an early warning system when such a system is not actually functioning. Several police departments created systems in the 1970s, but none of those appears to have survived as a permanent program.[8]

## Findings from three case studies

The research strategy for the case studies was modeled after the birth cohort study of juvenile delinquency conducted by Wolfgang and colleagues.[9] They found that a small group within the entire cohort (6.3 percent of the total) were "chronic delinquents" and were responsible for half of all the serious crime committed by the entire cohort. The early warning concept rests on the assumption that within any cohort of police officers, a small percentage will have substantially worse performance records than their peers and, consequently, will merit departmental intervention. The research was designed to confirm or refute the assumption.

Three police departments were chosen for the case study investigation: Miami–Dade County, Minneapolis, and New Orleans. The three sites represent large urban areas, but the size of each police force varies considerably: At the time of the study, Miami–Dade had 2,920 sworn officers, New Orleans had 1,576 sworn officers, and Minneapolis had 890 sworn officers.

The three sites were chosen for several reasons. Each has an early warning system that had been operating for at least 4 years at the time of the study.

Also, the three systems differ from one another in terms of structure and administrative history, and the three departments differ in their history of police officer use of force and accountability (see "Three cities, three stories").

One goal of the case studies was to evaluate the impact of early warning systems on the officers involved. In New Orleans, citizen complaints about officers in the early warning program were analyzed for 2-year periods before and after the initial intervention. Officers subject to early warning intervention participate in a Professional Performance Enhancement Program (PPEP) class; their critiques of the class were analyzed and a 2-day class was observed to determine both the content of the intervention and officer responses to various components.

Demographic and performance data were collected in Miami–Dade and Minneapolis on a cohort of all officers hired in certain years—whether or not they were identified by the early warning systems. The performance data included citizen complaints, use-of-force reports, reprimands, suspensions, terminations, commendations, and promotions. Other data were collected as available in each site.

These records were sorted into two groups: officers identified by the early warning system and officers not identified, with the latter serving as a control group. The performance records of the early warning group were analyzed for the 2-year periods before and after the intervention to determine the impact of the intervention on the officers' behavior. The analysis controlled for assignment to patrol duty on the assumption that citizen complaints and use-of-force incidents are infrequently generated in other assignments.

**Characteristics of officers identified by early warning systems.** Demographically, officers identified by the systems do not differ significantly from the control group in terms of race or ethnicity. Males, are somewhat overrepresented and females are underrepresented. One disturbing finding was a slight tendency of early warning officers to be promoted at higher rates than control officers. This issue should be the subject of future research, which should attempt to identify more precisely whether some departments tend to reward through promotion the kind of active (and possibly aggressive) behavior that is likely to cause officers to be identified by an early warning system.

**The impact of early warning systems on officers' performance.** Early warning systems appear to have a dramatic effect on reducing citizen complaints and other indicators of problematic police performance among those officers subject to intervention. In Minneapolis, the average number of citizen complaints received by officers subject to early intervention dropped by 67 percent 1 year after the intervention. In New Orleans, that number dropped by 62 percent 1 year after intervention (exhibit 1). In Miami–Dade, only 4 percent of the early warning cohort had zero use-of-force reports prior to intervention; following intervention, 50 percent had zero use-of-force reports.

Data from New Orleans indicate that officers respond positively to early warning intervention. In anonymous evaluations of the PPEP classes, officers gave it an average rating of 7 on a scale of 1 to 10. All of the officers made at least one positive comment about the class, and some made specific comments about how it had helped them. Officers in the PPEP class that was directly observed were actively engaged in those components they perceived to be related to the practical problems of police work, particularly incidents that often generate complaints or other problems. Officers were disengaged, however, in components that they perceived to be abstract, moralistic, or otherwise unrelated to practical aspects of police work.

This study could not determine the most effective aspects of intervention (e.g., counseling regarding personal issues, training in specific law enforcement techniques, stern warning about possible discipline in the future) or whether certain aspects are more effective for certain types of officers.

**The impact of early warning systems on supervisors.** The original design of this study did not include evaluating the impact of these systems on supervisors. Nonetheless, the qualitative component of the research found that these systems have potentially significant effects on supervisors. The existence of an intervention system communicates to supervisors their responsibility to monitor officers who have been identified by the program. The New Orleans program requires supervisors to monitor identified officers under their command for 6 months and to complete signed evaluations of the officers' performance every 2 weeks. Officials in Miami–Dade think that their system helps ensure

## Three cities, three stories

The three early warning systems in the sites selected for the case studies have different administrative histories and program structures, and the three police departments have different histories with regard to police officer use of force and accountability.

**Miami–Dade County.** The Miami–Dade Police Department (MDPD) currently enjoys a reputation for high standards of professionalism and accountability to reforms instituted following controversial racial incidents in the late 1970s and early 1980s.

As a result of the real and perceived problems between police and citizens, the Dade County Commission enacted legislation that opened to the public the internal investigations conducted by MDPD. In addition, an employee profile system (EPS) was created to track all complaints, use-of-force incidents, commendations, disciplinary actions, and dispositions of all internal investigations. As an offshoot of the EPS, MDPD created the Early Identification System (EIS) under the supervision of the Internal Review Bureau.

MDPD's EIS began operating in 1981. Quarterly reports list all officers who receive two or more citizen complaints that were investigated and closed or who were involved in three or more use-of-force incidents during the previous 3 months. Annual reports list officers who were identified in two or more quarterly reports. Monthly reports list employees who received two or more complaints during the previous 60 days, regardless of disposition.

The reports are disseminated through the chain of command to the supervisors of each officer identified. As one official described the system, supervisors use the reports "as a resource to determine if job stress or performance problems exist." [8] The information is intended to help supervisors evaluate and guide an employee's job performance and conduct in conjunction with other information.

The intervention phase of EIS consists primarily of an informal counseling session between the supervisor and the officer. The supervisor is expected to discuss the report with the officer and determine whether further action is needed. Such actions may include making referrals to employee assistance programs inside or outside the department, such as psychological services, stress abatement programs, or specialized training programs.

Postintervention monitoring of officers in the early warning system is informal and conducted by supervisors. Review of officers' performance records is designed to identify officers who continue to exhibit patterns of misconduct and to make the officers aware that their performance is being closely scrutinized. Additionally, the program puts supervisors on notice that their responsibilities include the close monitoring of those whose performance is problematic.

**Minneapolis.** When the study began, the Minneapolis Police Department (MPD) had a mixed reputation and was in transition under the leadership of a relatively new chief. MPD has long had a national reputation as a police department receptive to research. At the same time, however, MPD had a troubled local reputation with respect to the use of force by its officers. This reputation eventually brought a number of important political and administrative changes in the 1990s. The mayor declined to reappoint the incumbent police chief, who had failed to discipline the police officers. The new police chief began raising standards of accountability; among other reforms, he instituted a version of the COMPSTAT process. These changes have had direct implications for the system of accountability within the MPD and complicate any attempt to evaluate the impact of MPD's early warning system.

The program was established in the early 1990s and has undergone a number of significant administrative changes, including a period of slightly more than 1 year in the mid-1990s when the system ceased functioning altogether. After the data collection period for this study, a new procedure was instituted that calls for reviewing all reports of potentially problematic officer performance every that supervisors will attend to potential problem officers under their command. In this respect, the systems mandate or encourage changes in supervisor behavior that could potentially affect the standards of supervision of all officers, not just those subject to early intervention. Furthermore, the system's database can give supervisors relevant information about officers newly assigned to them and about whom they know very little.

**The impact of early warning systems on the rest of the department.** The original design of this study did not include evaluating the impact of these systems on the departments in which they operate. Nonetheless, the qualitative component identified a number of important issues for future research. The extent to which a system changes the climate of accountability within a law enforcement agency is not known, and identifying it would require a sophisticated research design. The qualitative findings suggest that an effective early intervention program depends on a general commitment to accountability within an organization. Such a program is unlikely to create or foster a climate of accountability where that commitment does not already exist

The data developed as a part of an early warning system can be used to effect changes in policies, procedures, or training. Presumably, such change

## Three cities, three stories (continued)

2 weeks. This procedure substantially heightens the intensity of the level of supervision. Thus, the findings reported here do not reflect current practices in the department.

The only selection criterion for the system is citizen complaints. The formal selection criteria have changed over the years, however. Currently, a quarterly report lists all officers with two or more citizen complaints, whether sustained or unsustained.

The intervention phase in Minneapolis consists of only an informal counseling session between the officer and his or her immediate supervisor. In the early years, supervisors were required to document their counseling session in the form of a memorandum to the commander. There is currently no documentation requirement, and MPD's program does not include any formal postintervention monitoring. Apart from the routine supervision applied to all officers, officers who are subject to intervention are not subject to formal monitoring and no special data are collected on their performance.

**New Orleans.** In the mid-1990s, the New Orleans Police Department (NOPD) had a national reputation for both corruption and use of force by its officers. Between 1995 and 1998, NOPD terminated an average of slightly more than 18 officers per year and imposed an average of more than 100 suspensions per year. At the same time, 97 officers resigned or retired while under investigation by the department and 105 officers were either arrested or issued a citation for a criminal law violation. These are extremely high figures compared with police departments of similar size.[b]

The officials associated with NOPD's Professional Performance Enhancement Program (PPEP) have a strong sense of identification with the program and are committed to maintaining and improving it. The department also conducts random integrity "stings" to identify possible corrupt activities by officers. Furthermore, PPEP does not limit its focus to individual officers, but also examines training, procedures, and supervision."[c]

As in Minneapolis, changes in the program occurred after the data collection period. It is likely that the administration of the program has weakened somewhat, due largely to the retirement or departure of key individuals. Thus, the findings reported here do not reflect current practices in the department.

Officers are selected for the program on the basis of three categories of performance indicators: incidents involving conflict in arrest and nonarrest situations and referrals from supervisors. However, intervention is not automatic; commanders review performance records and exercise discretion in selecting officers.

The PPEP class consists of an overview and explanation of the program and units on human behavior, stress management, conflict management, complaint avoidance, sensitivity training, "extraneous contributors to conflict" (such as substance abuse), and techniques and assessment (which includes training related to such police activities as tactical stops, situation assessment, handcuffing, and custodial security). Each class includes a private counseling session with the instructor, during which the officer's record is reviewed and the reasons for being selected for the program are explained.

Immediate supervisors are required to monitor each officer for a period of 6 months after the intervention. During that period, the supervisor is required to observe the officer interacting with citizens while on duty and to complete a bi-weekly evaluation of the officer's performance.

---

a. Charette, Bernard, "Early Identification of Police Brutality and Misconduct," Miami: Metro-Dade Police Department, n.d., p. 5.

b. "Disciplinary Action Breakdown," New Orleans Police Department, February 9, 1999.

c. New Orleans Police Department, Public Integrity Division, "To Whom It May Concern," May 5, 1998.

5

help reduce existing problems and help the department maintain and raise its standards of accountability. Thus, these systems can be an important tool for organizational development and human resource management.[10]

**The nature of early warning systems.** A second goal of the case studies was to describe the systems themselves. In all three sites, qualitative data gathered from official documents and interviews with key stakeholders yielded a description and assessment of the formal structure and administrative history of each program, along with an assessment of its place in the larger processes of accountability in the department.

In addition to finding that the early warning systems in the three sites vary considerably in terms of their formal program elements, the study documented that an effective system requires considerable investment of resources and administrative attention. Miami–Dade's program, for example, is part of a sophisticated data system on officers and their performance. The New Orleans program involves several staff members, including one full-time data analyst and two other full-time employees who spend part of their time entering data.

Early warning systems should not be considered alarm clocks—they are not mechanical devices that can be programmed to automatically sound an alarm. Rather, they are extremely complex, high-maintenance administrative operations that require close and ongoing human attention. Without this attention, the systems are likely to falter or fail.

**Limitations of the case study findings.** The findings regarding the impact of early warning intervention

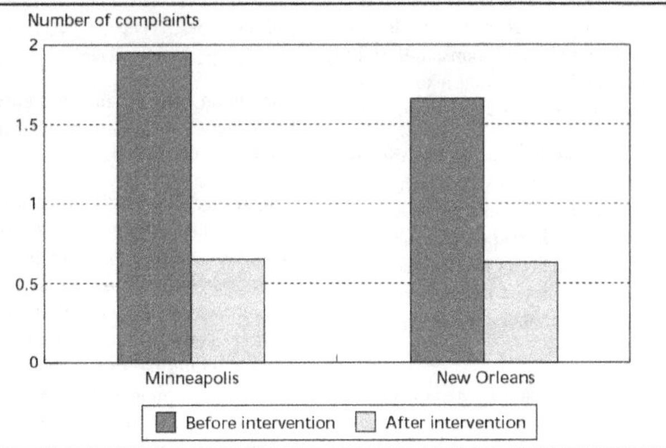

Exhibit 1. **Annual average number of complaints against officers, before and after intervention**



should be viewed with caution. As the first-ever study of such systems, this project encountered a number of unanticipated problems with the data. First, it was not possible to collect retrospectively systematic data on positive police officer performance (e.g., incidents when an officer avoided using force or citizens felt they had been treated fairly and respectfully). Thus, it is not known whether early intervention had a deterrent effect on desirable officer behavior.

Second, the early warning systems in each site studied operate in the context of a larger commitment to increased accountability on the part of the police department. Given the original research design, it is impossible to disentangle the effect of this general climate of rising standards of accountability on officer performance from the effect of the intervention program itself.

Finally, the early warning systems in two of the three sites experienced significant changes during the years for which data were collected. Thus,

the intervention delivered was not consistent for the period studied. Significant changes also occurred in two sites immediately following the data collection period. In one instance, the system was substantially strengthened. In the other, it is likely that the administration of the system has deteriorated significantly; this deterioration may have begun during the study, affecting the data that were collected.

## Policing strategies and legal considerations

**Early warning systems and policing strategies.** These intervention strategies are compatible with both community-oriented and problem-oriented policing. Community-oriented policing seeks to establish closer relations between the police and the communities they serve. Insofar as the systems seek to reduce citizen complaints and other forms of problematic behavior, they are fully consistent with these goals.[11]

Problem-oriented policing focuses on identifying specific police problems and developing carefully tailored responses.[12] Early warning systems approach the problem officer as the concern to be addressed, and the intervention is the response tailored to change the behavior that leads to indicators of unsatisfactory performance.

**Early warning systems and traffic-stop data.** The issue of racial profiling by police has recently emerged as a national controversy. In response to this controversy, a number of law enforcement agencies have begun to collect data on the race and ethnicity of drivers stopped by their officers.

An officer who makes a disproportionate number of traffic stops of racial or ethnic minorities (relative to other officers with the same assignment) may be a problem officer who warrants the attention of the department. Traffic-stop information can be readily incorporated into the database and used to identify possible racial disparities (as well as other potential problems, such as disproportionate stops of female drivers or unacceptably low levels of activity).

**Legal considerations of these systems.** Some law enforcement agencies may resist creating an early warning system for fear that a plaintiff's attorney may subpoena the database's information on officer misconduct and use that information against the agency in lawsuits alleging excessive use of force.[13] Several experts argue, however, that in the current legal environment, an early warning system is more likely to shield an agency against liability for deliberate indifference regarding police use of force. Such a system demonstrates that the agency has a clear policy regarding misconduct, has made a good faith effort to identify employees whose perform-

ance is unsatisfactory, and has a program in place to correct that behavior.[14]

## Policy concerns and areas for further research

Each of an early warning system's three phases involves a number of complex policy issues.

**Selection.** Although the selection criteria for most early warning systems consider a range of performance indicators, some rely solely on citizen complaints. A number of problems related to official data on citizen complaints, including underreporting, have been documented.[15] Using a broader range of indicators is more likely to identify officers whose behavior requires departmental intervention.

**Intervention.** In most early warning systems, intervention consists of an informal counseling session between the officer and his or her immediate supervisor. Some systems require no documentation of the content of that session, which raises concerns about whether supervisors deliver the intended content of the intervention. It is possible that a supervisor may minimize the importance of the intervention by telling an officer "not to worry about it," thus reinforcing the officer's behavior. Involving higher ranking command officers is likely to ensure that the intervention serves the intended goals. Further research is needed on the most effective forms of intervention and whether it is possible to tailor certain forms of intervention to particular categories of officers.

**Postintervention monitoring.** The nature of postintervention monitoring

varies among systems. Some systems rely on informal monitoring of the subject officers; others employ a formal mechanism of observation and documentation by supervisors. The relative impact of different postintervention monitoring systems on individual officers, supervisors, and departments requires further research.

## One tool among many

Early warning systems have emerged as a popular remedy for police misconduct. This study suggests that these systems can reduce citizen complaints and other problematic police behavior. Officers in the three departments investigated as case studies were involved in substantially fewer citizen complaints and use-of-force incidents after the intervention than before. In these three departments, however, the systems were part of larger efforts to raise standards of accountability. The effectiveness of such a system is reinforced by (and probably dependent on) other policies and procedures that enforce standards of discipline and create a climate of accountability.

An effective early warning system is complex, high-maintenance operation that requires a significant investment of administrative resources. Some systems appear to be essentially symbolic gestures with little substantive content, and it is unlikely that an intervention program can be effective in law enforcement agency that has no serious commitment to accountability. It can be an effective management tool, but it should be seen as only one of many tools needed to raise standards of performance and improve the quality of police services.

## Notes

1. "Kansas City Police Go After Their 'Bad Boys,'" *New York Time,* September 10, 1991; and "Waves of Abuse Laid to a Few Officers," *Boston Globe,* October 4, 1992.

2. Herman Goldstein, *Policing a Free Society,* Cambridge, MA: Ballinger, 1977: 171.

3. *Who is Guarding the Guardians?* Washington, DC: U.S. Commission on Civil Rights, 1981: 81.

4. Kappeler, Victor, Richard Sluder, and Geoffrey Alpert, *Forces of Deviance: Understanding the Dark Side of Policing,* Prospect Heights, IL: Waveland Press, 1998.

5. The first wave of the survey occurred in August 1998, with a second wave in October 1998 and followup in February 1999.

6. For discussions of recommended performance categories, see International Association of Chiefs of Police, *Building Integrity and Reducing Drug Corruption in Police Departments,* Washington, DC: U.S. Department of Justice, Bureau of Justice Assistance, 1989: 80; and Reiter, Lou, *Law Enforcement Administrative Investigations: A Manual Guide,* 2nd ed., Tallahassee, FL: Lou Reiter and Associates, 1998: 18.2.

7. Zimring, Franklin, and Gordon Hawkins, *Deterrence,* Chicago: University of Chicago Press, 1973.

8. Milton, Catherine H., Jeanne Wahl Halleck, James Lardner, and Gary L. Albrecht, *Police Use of Deadly Force,* Washington: The Police Foundation, 1977: 94–110.

9. Wolfgang, Marvin E., Robert M. Figlio, and Thorsten Sellin, *Delinquency in a Birth Cohort,* Chicago: University of Chicago Press, 1972.

10. Mathis, Robert L., and John H. Jackson, eds., *Human Resource Management: Essential Perspectives,* Cincinnati: Southwestern College Publishing, 1999: 98–102; and Poole, Michael, and Malcolm Warner, *The IEBM Handbook of Human Resource Management,* London: International Thomson Business Press, 1998: 93.

11. Alpert, Geoffrey, and Mark H. Moore, "Measuring Performance in the New Paradigm of Policing," in *Performance Measures for the Criminal Justice System,* Washington, DC: U.S. Department of Justice, Bureau of Justice Statistics, 1993: 109–142.

12. Eck, John E., and William Spelman, Problem-Solving: *Problem-Oriented Policing in Newport News.* Washington, DC: U.S. Department of Justice, National Institute of Justice, 1987.

13. Reiter, Lou, *Law Enforcement Administrative Investigations,* chapter 18.

14. Gallagher, G. Patrick, "The Liability Shield: From Policy to Internal Affairs," in Reiter, Lou, *Law Enforcement Administrative Investigations,* chapter 20; and Beh, Hazel Glenn, "Municipal Liability for Failure To Investigate Citizen Complaints Against Police," *Fordham Urban Law Journal* XXV (2) 1998: 209–254.

15. Walker, Samuel. *Police Accountability: The Role of Citizen Oversight,* Belmont, CA: Wadsworth Thompson, 2001.

Findings and conclusions of the research reported here are those of the authors and do not necessarily reflect the official position or policies of the U.S. Department of Justice.

*The National Institute of Justice is a component of the Office of Justice Programs, which also includes the Bureau of Justice Assistance, the Bureau of Justice Statistics, the Office of Juvenile Justice and Delinquency Prevention, and the Office for Victims of Crime.*

This study was conducted by Samuel Walker, Ph.D., Professor, University of Nebraska at Omaha; Geoffrey P. Alpert, Ph.D., Washington State University; and Dennis J. Kenney, Ph.D., Rutgers University. Support for the study was provided by NIJ grant number 98-IJ-CX-0002 through a transfer of funds from the Office of Community Oriented Policing Services.

**This and other NIJ publications can be found at and downloaded from the NIJ Web site (http://www.ojp.usdoj.gov/nij).**

**NCJ 188565**

---

**U.S. Department of Justice**

Office of Justice Programs

*National Institute of Justice*

*Washington, DC 20531*

Official Business

Penalty for Private Use $300

# APPENDIX VI:  NIJ:  THE MEASUREMENT OF POLICE INTEGRITY

**U.S. Department of Justice**
Office of Justice Programs
*National Institute of Justice*

# National Institute of Justice

## Research in Brief

*Julie E. Samuels, Acting Director*

*May 2000*

## Issues and Findings

***Discussed in this Brief:*** Research exploring police officers' understanding of agency rules concerning police misconduct and the extent of their support for these rules. The survey also considered officers' opinions about appropriate punishment for misconduct, their familiarity with the expected disciplinary threat, their perceptions of disciplinary fairness, and their willingness to report misconduct. The results of this survey have important implications for researchers and policymakers, as well as for police practitioners.

***Key issues:*** Until recently, most studies of police corruption were based on a traditional administrative approach—one that views the problem of corruption primarily as a reflection of the moral defects of individual police officers. This research, however, is based on the organizational theory of police corruption, which emphasizes the importance of organizational and occupational culture.

Researchers asked officers in 30 U.S. police agencies for their *opinions* about various hypothetical cases of police misconduct, thereby avoiding the resistance that direct inquiries about corrupt behavior would likely provoke. The survey measured how seriously officers regarded police corruption, how willing they were to report it, and how willing they were to support punishment. By analyzing officers' responses to the survey questions, researchers were able to rank the police agencies according to their environments of integrity. The capacity to measure integrity in this way is especially significant for police administrators, who, this research suggests, may be able to influence and cultivate

*continued...*

# The Measurement of Police Integrity

*By Carl B. Klockars, Sanja Kutnjak Ivkovich, William E. Harver, and Maria R. Haberfeld*

As the history of virtually every police agency attests, policing is an occupation that is rife with opportunities for misconduct. Policing is a highly discretionary, coercive activity that routinely takes place in private settings, out of the sight of supervisors, and in the presence of witnesses who are often regarded as unreliable. Corruption—the abuse of police authority *for gain*—is one type of misconduct that has been particularly problematic. The difficulties of controlling corruption can be traced to several factors: the reluctance of police officers to report corrupt activities by their fellow officers (also known as "The Code," "The Code of Silence," or "The Blue Curtain"), the reluctance of police administrators to acknowledge the existence of corruption in their agencies, the benefits of the typical corrupt transaction to the parties involved, and the lack of immediate victims willing to report corruption.

Until recently, police administrators viewed corruption primarily as a reflection of the moral defects of individual police officers. They fought corruption by carefully screening applicants for police positions and aggressively pursuing morally defective officers in an attempt to remove them from their positions before their corrupt behavior had spread through the agency. This administrative/

individual approach, sometimes called the "bad apple" theory of police corruption, has been subject to severe criticism in recent years.

This Research in Brief summarizes a study that measured police integrity in 30 police agencies across the United States. The study was based on an organizational/occupational approach to police corruption. Researchers asked officers for their opinions about 11 hypothetical cases of police misconduct and measured how seriously officers regarded police corruption, how willing they were to support its punishment, and how willing they were to report it. The survey found substantial differences in the environments of integrity among the agencies studied. The more serious the officers considered a behavior to be, the more likely they were to believe that more severe discipline was appropriate, and the more willing they were to report a colleague for engaging in that behavior.

## Contemporary approaches to corruption

Pioneered by Herman Goldstein,[1] contemporary theories of police corruption are based on four *organizational* and *occupational* dimensions. Each is described below.

## Issues and Findings

*continued...*

environments of integrity within their agencies.

*Key findings:* Based on officers' responses to questions relating to 11 hypothetical case scenarios involving police officers engaged in a range of corrupt behavior, the following conclusions emerged:

● In assessing the 11 cases of police misconduct, officers considered some types to be significantly less serious than others.

● The more serious the officers perceived a behavior to be, the more likely they were to think that more severe discipline was appropriate, and the more willing they were to report a colleague who had engaged in such behavior.

● Police officers' evaluations of the appropriate and expected discipline for various types of misconduct were very similar; the majority of police officers regarded the expected discipline as fair.

● A majority of police officers said that they *would not* report a fellow officer who had engaged in what they regarded as less serious misconduct (for example, operating an off-duty security business; accepting free gifts, meals, and discounts; or having a minor accident while driving under the influence of alcohol.

● At the same time, most police officers indicated that they *would* report a colleague who stole from a found wallet or a burglary scene, accepted a bribe or kickback, or used excessive force on a car thief after a foot pursuit.

● The survey found substantial differences in the environment of integrity among the 30 agencies in the sample.

*Target audience:* Criminal justice researchers and policymakers, legislators, police administrators, police officers, and educators.

**Organizational rules.** The first dimension concerns how the organizational rules that govern corruption are established, communicated, and understood. In the United States, where police agencies are highly decentralized, police organizations differ markedly in the types of activities they officially prohibit as corrupt behavior. This is particularly true of marginally corrupt or *mala prohibita* behavior, such as off-duty employment and acceptance of favors, small gifts, free meals, and discounts. Further complicating the problem, the official policy of many agencies formally prohibits such activities while their unofficial policy, supported firmly but silently by supervisors and administrators, is to permit and ignore such behavior so long as it is limited in scope and conducted discreetly.

**Prevention and control mechanisms.** The second dimension of corruption emphasized in contemporary approaches is the wide range of mechanisms that police agencies employ to prevent and control corruption. Examples include education in ethics, proactive and reactive investigation of corruption, integrity testing, and corruption deterrence through the discipline of offenders. The extent to which agencies use such organizational anticorruption techniques varies greatly.

**The Code.** The third dimension of corruption, inherent in the occupational culture of policing, is The Code or The Blue Curtain that informally prohibits or discourages police officers from reporting the misconduct of their colleagues. The parameters of The Code—precisely what behavior it covers and to whom its benefits are extended—vary among police agencies. For example, The Code may apply to only low-level corruption in some agencies and to the most serious corruption in others. Furthermore, whom and what The Code covers can vary substantially not

only *among* police agencies but also *within* police agencies. Particularly in large police agencies, the occupational culture of integrity may differ substantially among precincts, service areas, task forces, and work groups.

**Public expectations.** The fourth dimension of police corruption that contemporary police theory emphasizes is the influence of the social, economic, and political environments in which police institutions, systems, and agencies operate. For example, some jurisdictions in the United States have long, virtually uninterrupted traditions of police corruption. Other jurisdictions have equally long traditions of minimal corruption, while still others have experienced repeated cycles of scandal and reform. Such histories indicate that public expectations about police integrity exert vastly different pressures on police agencies in different jurisdictions. These experiences also suggest that public pressures to confront and combat corruption may be successfully resisted.

## Methodological challenges to the study of police corruption

Although many theories can be applied to the study of police corruption, the contemporary organizational/occupational culture theory has an important advantage over the traditional administrative/individual bad-apple theory: The organizational/occupational approach is much more amenable to systematic, quantitative research.

Corruption is extremely difficult to study in a direct, quantitative, and empirical manner. Because most incidents of corruption are never reported or recorded, official data on corruption are best regarded as measures of a police agency's anticorruption activity, not the actual level of corruption. Even with assurances of confidentiality, police officers are unlikely to be willing to report their own or another officer's corrupt activities.

Unlike the administrative/individual approach, an organizational/occupational culture approach to the study of police integrity involves questions of *fact* and *opinion* that can be explored directly, without arousing the resistance that direct inquiries about corrupt *behavior* are likely to provoke. Using this approach, it is possible to ask nonthreatening questions about officers' *knowledge* of agency rules and their *opinions* about the seriousness of particular violations, the punishment that such violations would warrant or actually receive, and their estimates of how willing officers would be to report such misconduct.

Moreover, sharply different goals and visions of police integrity characterize these two approaches to understanding corruption. The administrative/individual theory of corruption envisions the police agency of integrity as one from which all morally defective individual officers have been removed and in which vigilance is maintained to prevent their entry or emergence. By contrast, the organizational/occupational culture theory envisions the police agency of integrity as one whose culture is highly intolerant of corruption.

Methodologically, the consequences of these two visions are critical. For example, although it may be possible to use an administrative/individual approach to measure the level of corrupt behavior, the number of morally defective police officers, and an agency's vigilance in discovering misconduct, the obstacles to doing so are enormous. Using an organizational/occupational culture approach, by contrast, modern social science can easily measure how

seriously officers regard misconduct, how amenable they are to supporting punishment, and how willing they are to tolerate misconduct in silence.

In an effort to measure the occupational culture of police integrity, a systematic, standardized, and quantitative survey questionnaire was designed and pretested. The survey sought information in key areas that constitute the foundation of an occupational/organizational culture theory of police integrity. At the same time, the survey responses could be used to satisfy certain basic informational needs of practical police administration. The survey attempted to answer the following questions:

- Do officers in this agency know the rules governing police misconduct?

- How strongly do they support those rules?

- Do officers know what disciplinary threat they face if they violate those rules?

- Do they think the discipline is fair?

- How willing are they to report misconduct?

For a more detailed description of the survey methodology and samples, see Survey Design and Methodology. The actions taken to enhance the legitimacy of the survey results are discussed in Validity of Survey Responses.

## Survey results

The results of the survey, reported in exhibit 1, show that the more serious a particular behavior was considered by police officers, the more severely they thought it should and would be punished, and the more willing they were to report it. The extraordinarily high rank-order correlation among the

responses to the survey questions suggests that all six integrity-related questions measured the same phenomenon—the degree of police intolerance for corrupt behavior.

**Offense seriousness.** The 11 case scenarios fall into 3 categories of perceived seriousness. Four cases were not considered very serious by police respondents: Case 1, off-duty operation of a security system business; Case 2, receipt of free meals; Case 4, receipt of holiday gifts; and Case 8, coverup of a police accident that involved driving under the influence of alcohol (DUI). The majority of police respondents, in fact, reported that the operation of an off-duty security system business (Case 1) was not a violation of agency policy. Respondents considered four other cases of misconduct to be at an intermediate level of seriousness: Case 10, the use of excessive force on a car thief following a foot pursuit; Case 7, a supervisor who offers a subordinate time off during holidays in exchange for tuning up his personal car; Case 9, acceptance of free drinks in exchange for ignoring a late bar closing; and Case 6, receipt of a kickback. Respondents regarded the remaining three cases—those that involved stealing from a found wallet (Case 11), accepting a money bribe (Case 3), and stealing a watch at a crime scene (Case 5)—as very serious offenses.

**Discipline.** In general, police officers thought that the four cases they regarded as not very serious warranted little or no discipline. Officers thought that the four cases involving an intermediate level of seriousness merited a written reprimand or a period of suspension, and that the three very serious cases merited dismissal.

## Survey Design and Methodology

**Case scenarios.** The survey questionnaire presented officers with 11 hypothetical case scenarios. Displayed in exhibit A, the scenarios cover a range of activities, from those that merely give an appearance of conflict of interest (Case 1) to incidents of bribery (Case 3) and theft (Cases 5 and 11). One scenario (Case 10) described the use of excessive force on a car thief.

Respondents were asked to evaluate each scenario by answering seven questions (see exhibit B). Six of these questions were designed to assess the normative inclination of police to resist temptations to abuse the rights and privileges of their occupation. To measure this dimension of police integrity, the six questions were paired as follows:

- Two questions pertained to the *seriousness* of each case—one addressed the respondent's own view and the other concerned the respondent's perception of the views of other officers.

- Two related to *severity of discipline*—one addressed the discipline the respondent felt the behavior *should* receive and the other addressed the discipline the officer felt it *would* receive.

- Two concerned *willingness to report* the misconduct—one addressed the respondent's own willingness to report it, and the other concerned the respondent's perception of other officers' willingness to report it.

The remaining question asked respondents whether the behavior described in the scenario was a violation of the agency's official policy.

The incidents described in the scenarios were not only plausible and common forms of police misconduct, but ones that were uncomplicated by details that might introduce ambiguity into either the interpretation of the behavior or the motive of the officer depicted in the scenario. Some scenarios were based on published studies that had employed a case scenario approach.[a] Others drew on the experience of the authors. Respondents were asked to assume that the officer depicted in each scenario had been a police officer for 5 years and had a satisfactory work record with no history of disciplinary problems.

**Survey sample.** The sample consisted of 3,235 officers from 30 U.S. police agencies. Although these agencies were drawn from across the Nation and the sample was quite large, it was nonetheless a convenience sample, not a representative sample. The characteristics of the officers in this sample are summarized in exhibit C. The majority of the police officers surveyed were employed in patrol or traffic units (63.1 percent). The overwhelming majority of respondents were line officers; only one of five police officers was a supervisor. The mean length of service for the entire sample was 10.3 years.

---

*Exhibit A.* **Case scenarios**

**Case 1.** A police officer runs his own private business in which he sells and installs security devices, such as alarms, special locks, etc. He does this work during his off-duty hours.

**Case 2.** A police officer routinely accepts free meals, cigarettes, and other items of small value from merchants on his beat. He does not solicit these gifts and is careful not to abuse the generosity of those who give gifts to him.

**Case 3.** A police officer stops a motorist for speeding. The officer agrees to accept a personal gift of half of the amount of the fine in exchange for not issuing a citation.

**Case 4.** A police officer is widely liked in the community, and on holidays local merchants and restaurant and bar owners show their appreciation for his attention by giving him gifts of food and liquor.

**Case 5.** A police officer discovers a burglary of a jewelry shop. The display cases are smashed, and it is obvious that many items have been taken. While searching the shop, he takes a watch, worth about 2 days' pay for that officer. He reports that the watch had been stolen during the burglary.

**Case 6.** A police officer has a private arrangement with a local auto body shop to refer the owners of cars damaged in accidents to the shop. In exchange for each referral, he receives payment of 5 percent of the repair bill from the shop owner.

**Case 7.** A police officer, who happens to be a very good auto mechanic, is scheduled to work during coming holidays. A supervisor offers to give him these days off, if he agrees to tune up his supervisor's personal car. Evaluate the *supervisor's* behavior.

**Case 8.** At 2:00 a.m., a police officer, who is on duty, is driving his patrol car on a deserted road. He sees a vehicle that has been driven off the road and is stuck in a ditch. He approaches the vehicle and observes that the driver is not hurt but is obviously intoxicated. He also finds that the driver is a police officer. Instead of reporting this accident and offense, he transports the driver to his home.

**Case 9.** A police officer finds a bar on his beat that is still serving drinks a half-hour past its legal closing time. Instead of reporting this violation, the police officer agrees to accept a couple of free drinks from the owner.

**Case 10.** Two police officers on foot patrol surprise a man who is attempting to break into an automobile. The man flees. They chase him for about two blocks before apprehending him by tackling him and wrestling him to the ground. After he is under control, both officers punch him a couple of times in the stomach as punishment for fleeing and resisting.

**Case 11.** A police officer finds a wallet in a parking lot. It contains an amount of money equivalent to a full day's pay for that officer. He reports the wallet as lost property but keeps the money for himself.

---

4

The sample has some biases, including overrepresentation of particular types of police agencies and particular regions of the country. Because it includes no State police agencies, only one sheriff's agency, and only one county police agency, the sample overrepresents municipal police agencies. The sample also overrepresents police agencies from the Northeast. Although the sample does include agencies from the South, Southeast, and Southwest, it does not include agencies from the West, Northwest, or Midwest.

The sample likely has another bias because not all agencies that were asked to participate in the study accepted the invitation. The reason for an agency's refusal to participate could include a fear of revealing something untoward. Agencies declined to participate despite assurances that their participation in the survey would be kept confidential; that all individual respondents would remain anonymous; and that respondents would be asked about only their opinions, not any actual misconduct.

Nevertheless, the sample includes some seriously troubled police agencies. Key contacts in a number of such agencies, including senior officers and high-ranking union officials, exercised sufficient influence to arrange the participation of these agencies in the survey.

a. A number of studies of police corruption have employed a research strategy that asked police officers to evaluate hypothetical corruption scenarios. These include Fishman, Janet E., *Measuring Police Corruption*, New York: John Jay College of Criminal Justice, 1978; Martin, Christine, *Illinois Municipal Officers' Perceptions of Police Ethics*, Chicago: Illinois Criminal Justice Information Authority, 1994; Huon, Gail F., Beryl L. Hesketh, Mark G. Frank, Kevin M. McConkey, and G.M. McGrath, *Perceptions of Ethical Dilemmas*, Payneham, Australia: National Police Research Unit, 1995; and Miller, Larry S., and Michael C. Braswell, "Police Perceptions of Ethical Decision-Making: The Ideal vs. The Real," *American Journal of Police* 27 (1992): 27–45.

*Exhibit B.* **Case scenario assessment options**

1. How serious do YOU consider this behavior to be?
   Not at all serious                 Very serious
       1          2          3          4          5

2. How serious do MOST POLICE OFFICERS IN YOUR AGENCY consider this behavior to be?
   Not at all serious                 Very serious
       1          2          3          4          5

3. Would this behavior be regarded as a violation of official policy in your agency?
   Definitely not                 Definitely yes
       1          2          3          4          5

4. If an officer in your agency engaged in this behavior and was discovered doing so, what if any discipline do YOU think SHOULD follow?

   | | |
   |---|---|
   | 1. NONE | 4. PERIOD OF SUSPENSION WITHOUT PAY |
   | 2. VERBAL REPRIMAND | 5. DEMOTION IN RANK |
   | 3. WRITTEN REPRIMAND | 6. DISMISSAL |

5. If an officer in your agency engaged in this behavior and was discovered doing so, what if any discipline do YOU think WOULD follow?

   | | |
   |---|---|
   | 1. NONE | 4. PERIOD OF SUSPENSION WITHOUT PAY |
   | 2. VERBAL REPRIMAND | 5. DEMOTION IN RANK |
   | 3. WRITTEN REPRIMAND | 6. DISMISSAL |

6. Do you think YOU would report a fellow police officer who engaged in this behavior?
   Definitely not                 Definitely yes
       1          2          3          4          5

7. Do you think MOST POLICE OFFICERS IN YOUR AGENCY would report a fellow police officer who engaged in this behavior?
   Definitely not                 Definitely yes
       1          2          3          4          5

*Exhibit C.* **Characteristics of the police agency sample**

| Agency Size (number of sworn officers) | Percentage of National Sample | Sample Size | Supervisory Percentage | Percentage Patrol/ Traffic | Mean Length of Service (in years) |
|---|---|---|---|---|---|
| **Very Large** (500+) | 59.9 | 1,937 | 14.8 | 64.2 | 9.18 |
| **Large** (201–500) | 19.7 | 638 | 23.2 | 60.3 | 12.05 |
| **Medium** (76–200) | 9.0 | 292 | 29.9 | 59.0 | 12.29 |
| **Small** (25–75) | 8.5 | 275 | 30.8 | 66.1 | 11.70 |
| **Very Small** (<25) | 2.9 | 93 | 35.9 | 64.8 | 11.29 |
| **Total/Average** | 100.0 | 3,235 | 19.8 | 63.1 | 10.30 |

## Validity of Survey Responses

The validity of the survey's results hinges on the honesty of police officers when responding to the survey questions. Several steps were taken to enhance the legitimacy of the survey results. First, officers were asked only about their attitudes, not about their actual behavior or the actual behavior of other police officers. They also were assured that their responses would remain confidential, although police respondents are naturally suspicious of such promises.

To further allay officers' fears that their identities might be discovered, they were asked only minimal background questions: their rank, length of service, and assignment and whether they held a supervisory position. They were not asked standard questions about age, race, gender, or ethnicity in an effort to assuage fears that disclosing such information, in combination with their rank, assignment, and length of service, would make it possible to identify them.

In addition, at the end of the survey, each police respondent was asked two questions about the validity of the responses. The first was "Do you think *most police officers* would give their honest opinion in filling out this questionnaire?" The second was "Did you?" In answer to the first question, 84.4 percent of police respondents reported that they thought most officers would answer the questions honestly, and 97.8 percent reported that they themselves had done so. The responses of the 2.2 percent of police officers who reported that they had not answered the questions honestly were discarded when the survey results were analyzed.

The survey questions also were designed to minimize any temptation for officers to manipulate responses to create a favorable impression on the public or on their supervisors. Some officers, for example, might have been inclined to report that certain types of misconduct were more serious than they actually thought them to be. At the same time, however, these officers would be unlikely to report that misconduct should be punished more severely than they thought appropriate because of the possibility that they might one day be subject to such discipline, if administrators believed that they were recommending it.

Furthermore, if any substantial manipulation of answers had occurred, it would have been evident in differences in correlation coefficients among the questions about seriousness, discipline, and willingness to report. In fact, the rank order correlation between all six questions is extraordinarily high. Indeed, one could predict with great accuracy the ranking of a scenario on any one of the six questions by knowing the ranking for any other.

To measure how officers perceived the fairness of discipline, the scores on the "discipline *would* receive" scale were subtracted from the scores on the "discipline *should* receive" scale. A difference of zero was interpreted to mean that the respondent thought the discipline was fair. If the difference was greater than zero (positive), the respondent thought that the discipline was too lenient. Conversely, if the difference was less than zero (negative), the respondent thought that the discipline was too harsh.[2] In 7 of the 11 cases, the overwhelming majority of police officers in the sample thought that the discipline that would be imposed was in the "fair" range. But in the remaining four cases, including three that officers considered not serious—Case 2 (accepting free meals and discounts on the beat), Case 4 (accepting holiday gifts), Case 8 (coverup of police DUI), and Case 10 (excessive force on car thief)—more than 20 percent of police officers believed that the discipline administered by their agencies would be too harsh.

**Parameters of The Code.** An examination of the parameters of The Code of Silence, as revealed in the responses of police officers in the sample, indicated that the majority would not report a police colleague who had engaged in behavior described in the four scenarios considered the least serious. At the same time, a majority indicated that they would report[3] a fellow police officer who had engaged in behavior they deemed to be at an intermediate or high level of seriousness.

## Agency contrasts in the culture of integrity

Measurements of the inclination of U.S. police to resist temptations to abuse the rights and privileges of their occupation are likely to prove useful for academic, historical, and cross-cultural studies of police.[4] For police administrators, however, measurements of the culture of integrity of individual police agencies are more relevant than national averages, which often mask significant differences among agencies.

Exhibit 1. **Police officers' perceptions of offense seriousness, appropriate and expected discipline, and willingness to report, ranked by officers' perceptions of case seriousness***

| Case Scenario | Seriousness | | | | Discipline | | | | | | Willingness to Report | | | |
|---|---|---|---|---|---|---|---|---|---|---|---|---|---|---|
| | Own View | | Other Officers | | Should Receive | | | Would Receive | | | Own View | | Other Officers | |
| | Score | Rank | Score | Rank | Score | Rank | Mode | Score | Rank | Mode | Score | Rank | Score | Rank |
| Case 1. Off-Duty Security System Business | 1.46 | 1 | 1.48 | 1 | 1.34 | 1 | None | 1.51 | 1 | None | 1.37 | 1 | 1.46 | 1 |
| Case 2. Free Meals, Discounts on Beat | 2.60 | 2 | 2.31 | 2 | 2.13 | 2 | Verbal reprimand | 2.37 | 2 | Verbal reprimand | 1.94 | 2 | 1.82 | 2 |
| Case 4. Holiday Gifts From Merchants | 2.84 | 3 | 2.64 | 3 | 2.53 | 3 | Verbal reprimand | 2.82 | 3 | Written reprimand | 2.36 | 4 | 2.28 | 3.5 |
| Case 8. Coverup of Police DUI Accident | 3.03 | 4 | 2.86 | 4 | 2.81 | 4 | Suspend without pay | 3.21 | 4 | Suspend without pay | 2.34 | 3 | 2.28 | 3.5 |
| Case 10. Excessive Force on Car Thief | 4.05 | 5 | 3.70 | 5 | 3.76 | 6 | Suspend without pay | 4.00 | 6 | Suspend without pay | 3.39 | 5 | 3.07 | 5 |
| Case 7. Supervisor: Holiday for Tuneup | 4.18 | 6 | 3.96 | 6 | 3.59 | 5 | Written reprimand | 3.43 | 5 | Written reprimand | 3.45 | 6 | 3.29 | 6 |
| Case 6. Auto Repair Shop 5% Kickback | 4.50 | 7 | 4.26 | 7 | 4.40 | 8 | Suspend without pay | 4.46 | 8 | Suspend without pay | 3.95 | 8 | 3.71 | 8 |
| Case 9. Drinks to Ignore Late Bar Closing | 4.54 | 8 | 4.28 | 8 | 4.02 | 7 | Suspend without pay | 4.08 | 7 | Suspend without pay | 3.73 | 7 | 3.47 | 7 |
| Case 11. Theft From Found Wallet | 4.85 | 9 | 4.69 | 9 | 5.09 | 10 | Dismissal | 5.03 | 10 | Dismissal | 4.23 | 10 | 3.96 | 10 |
| Case 3. Bribe From Speeding Motorist | 4.92 | 10 | 4.81 | 10 | 4.92 | 9 | Dismissal | 4.86 | 9 | Dismissal | 4.19 | 9 | 3.92 | 9 |
| Case 5. Crime Scene Theft of Watch | 4.95 | 11 | 4.88 | 11 | 5.66 | 11 | Dismissal | 5.57 | 11 | Dismissal | 4.54 | 11 | 4.34 | 11 |

* Scores are based on officers' responses to the integrity-related survey questions.

To uncover these differences and allow comparisons to be made, a system was devised for ranking the responses of officers in each agency. To determine an agency's overall ranking on how its officers perceived the seriousness of a particular offense, the mean score of all responses by officers in that agency to each of the 11 case scenarios was compared to the mean scores of the remaining 29 agencies. The agency was then awarded 3 points if its mean score placed it among the top 10 agencies on any question, 2 points if it scored in the middle 10, and 1 point if it scored among the lowest 10. These scores were then totaled for all 11 case scenarios. Using this scaling system, an agency's score on its officers' perceptions of the seriousness of the offenses could range from 11 (if it ranked in the lowest third

of agencies on all 11 cases) to 33 (if it ranked among the highest third of agencies on all 11 cases).[5]

These summary scores formed the basis for placing agencies in rank order from 1 to 30 (with 1 being the highest integrity rating), making it possible to say that an agency ranked "*n* out of 30" in its officers' perceptions of offense seriousness. This procedure was used to calculate a summary score and an integrity ranking for each agency's responses to each of the six questions about offense seriousness, discipline that should and would be received, and willingness to report the offense. Exhibit 2 summarizes those rankings.

**The environment of integrity in two agencies.** To illustrate how environments of integrity differ across U.S. police agencies, it is useful to contrast the responses of officers from two of the agencies in the sample. Agency 2, which ranked 8th in integrity of the 30 agencies surveyed, and Agency 23, which ranked in a 5-way tie for 24th place, are both large municipal police agencies. Agency 2 has a national reputation for integrity, is extremely receptive to research, and is often promoted as a model of innovation. Agency 23 has a long history of scandal, and its reputation as an agency with corruption problems persists despite numerous reform efforts. Although a local newspaper once dubbed Agency 23 "the most corrupt police department in the country," six other agencies in the sample appear to have integrity environments that are as poor or worse.

In both agencies, the correlation of the scores' rank ordering among the categories was very high, as it was for all 30 agencies surveyed. For every agency, the mean rank order of officers' responses to the six integrity-related questions was nearly identical. Furthermore, the rank ordering of the scenarios differed little among the agencies.

Although differences in the rank ordering of the scenarios were minimal, both within and between the two agencies, discrepancies in the agencies' absolute scores reflected significant differences (see exhibits 3 and 4). Estimates of offense seriousness were consistently higher for Agency 2 than for Agency 23. The differences were especially large (between 0.5 and 1.0 on a 5-point scale) for three scenarios: Case 6 (auto repair shop kickback), Case 9 (drinks to ignore late bar closing), and Case 10 (excessive force on car thief). Police officers from Agency 2 evaluated each of these cases as substantially more serious than did officers from Agency 23.

The mean scores for discipline indicate that, in almost every case, police officers in Agency 2 not only expected more severe discipline than did officers in Agency 23, but they also thought that more severe discipline was appropriate. The differences in perceptions of discipline were especially great for the most serious types of corruption, such as the scenarios described in Case 3 (bribe from speeding motorist), Case 5 (crime scene theft of watch), and Case 11 (theft from found wallet), as well as for Case 10 (use of excessive force). While officers in Agency 2 thought that dismissal would result from the four most serious cases, officers in Agency 23 expected that dismissal would follow only one scenario, Case 5 (theft from a crime scene).

Exhibit 2. **Composite scores on seriousness of offense, discipline, and willingness to report, rank-ordered by agency**

| Agency Number | Own Opinion of Seriousness | Other Officers' Opinions of Seriousness | Discipline *Should* Receive | Discipline *Would* Receive | Own Willingness to Report | Other Officers' Willingness to Report | Summary Score/ Integrity Ranking |
|---|---|---|---|---|---|---|---|
| 1 | 3 | 3 | 3 | 3 | 3 | 3 | 18/1 |
| 3 | 3 | 3 | 3 | 3 | 3 | 3 | 18/1 |
| 4 | 3 | 3 | 3 | 3 | 3 | 3 | 18/1 |
| 6 | 3 | 3 | 3 | 3 | 3 | 3 | 18/1 |
| 10 | 3 | 3 | 3 | 3 | 3 | 3 | 18/1 |
| 17 | 3 | 3 | 3 | 3 | 3 | 3 | 18/1 |
| 30 | 3 | 3 | 3 | 3 | 3 | 3 | 18/1 |
| 2 | 3 | 2 | 3 | 3 | 3 | 3 | 17/8 |
| 18 | 2 | 2 | 3 | 3 | 3 | 3 | 16/9 |
| 7 | 3 | 2 | 2 | 2 | 3 | 3 | 15/10 |
| 11 | 3 | 3 | 2 | 2 | 2 | 2 | 14/11 |
| 12 | 3 | 3 | 3 | 1 | 2 | 2 | 14/11 |
| 5 | 2 | 2 | 2 | 3 | 2 | 2 | 13/13 |
| 19 | 3 | 2 | 2 | 2 | 2 | 2 | 13/13 |
| 20 | 3 | 2 | 2 | 2 | 2 | 2 | 13/13 |
| 29 | 2 | 3 | 2 | 1 | 2 | 2 | 12/16 |
| 26 | 3 | 2 | 2 | 2 | 1 | 1 | 11/17 |
| 27 | 2 | 2 | 2 | 1 | 2 | 2 | 11/17 |
| 24 | 2 | 2 | 1 | 1 | 2 | 2 | 10/19 |
| 21 | 1 | 1 | 2 | 3 | 1 | 1 | 9/20 |
| 22 | 1 | 1 | 2 | 2 | 1 | 2 | 9/20 |
| 9 | 2 | 1 | 2 | 1 | 1 | 1 | 8/22 |
| 16 | 1 | 1 | 1 | 1 | 2 | 2 | 8/22 |
| 13 | 1 | 2 | 1 | 1 | 1 | 1 | 7/24 |
| 14 | 1 | 1 | 1 | 2 | 1 | 1 | 7/24 |
| 15 | 1 | 1 | 1 | 1 | 2 | 1 | 7/24 |
| 23 | 1 | 1 | 1 | 2 | 1 | 1 | 7/24 |
| 25 | 1 | 1 | 1 | 2 | 1 | 1 | 7/24 |
| 8 | 1 | 1 | 1 | 1 | 1 | 1 | 6/29 |
| 28 | 1 | 1 | 1 | 1 | 1 | 1 | 6/29 |

The most systematic and dramatic difference between Agencies 2 and 23, however, is evident in their attitudes toward The Code of Silence. In both agencies, few officers said that they or their police colleagues would report any of the least serious types of corrupt behavior (Cases 1, 2, 4, and 8). Officers from Agency 2 reported that they and their colleagues would report the behavior described in the seven other cases. In Agency 23, however, there was *no* case that the majority of officers indicated they would report. In sum, while The Code is under control in Agency 2, it remains a powerful influence in Agency 23, providing an environment in which corrupt behavior can flourish.

8

Exhibit 3. **Agency 2 vs. Agency 23: Officers' own perceptions of seriousness of misconduct, discipline warranted, and willingness to report offense**

| Case Scenario | Agency 2 (A2) vs. Agency 23 (A23) Perception of Seriousness | | | | Agency 2 (A2) vs. Agency 23 (A23) Discipline *Should* Receive | | | | Agency 2 (A2) vs. Agency 23 (A23) Willingness To Report | | | |
|---|---|---|---|---|---|---|---|---|---|---|---|---|
| | A2 | A23 | Difference | t test | A2 | A23 | Difference | t test | A2 | A23 | Difference | t test |
| **Case 1. Off-Duty Security System Business** | 1.57 | 1.36 | 0.21 | -2.82 $p<.05$ | 1.47 | 1.24 | 0.23 | -3.60 $p<.001$ | 1.57 | 1.22 | 0.35 | -4.78 $p<.001$ |
| **Case 2. Free Meals, Discounts on Beat** | 3.04 | 2.85 | 0.19 | -1.80 $p<.01$ | 2.50 | 2.31 | 0.19 | -2.48 $p<.01$ | 2.42 | 1.75 | 0.67 | -6.67 $p<.001$ |
| **Case 3. Bribe From Speeding Motorist** | 4.94 | 4.78 | 0.16 | -3.72 $p<.001$ | 5.02 | 4.44 | 0.58 | -6.28 $p<.001$ | 4.67 | 3.02 | 1.65 | -16.09 $p<.001$ |
| **Case 4. Holiday Gifts From Merchants** | 3.07 | 2.79 | 0.28 | -2.47 $p<.01$ | 2.73 | 2.59 | 0.14 | -1.35 NS* | 2.74 | 2.05 | 0.69 | -6.24 $p<.001$ |
| **Case 5. Crime Scene Theft of Watch** | 4.97 | 4.79 | 0.18 | -4.21 $p<.001$ | 5.85 | 4.90 | 0.95 | -12.64 $p<.001$ | 4.92 | 3.36 | 1.56 | -15.97 $p<.001$ |
| **Case 6. Auto Repair Shop 5% Kickback** | 4.58 | 4.02 | 0.56 | -6.74 $p<.001$ | 4.41 | 3.74 | 0.67 | -6.47 $p<.001$ | 4.38 | 2.71 | 1.67 | -15.63 $p<.001$ |
| **Case 7. Supervisor: Holiday for Tuneup** | 4.16 | 4.05 | 0.11 | -1.24 NS* | 3.58 | 3.51 | 0.07 | -0.72 NS* | 3.68 | 2.66 | 1.02 | -8.68 $p<.001$ |
| **Case 8. Coverup of Police DUI Accident** | 3.16 | 2.68 | 0.48 | -4.32 $p<.001$ | 2.85 | 2.57 | 0.28 | -2.69 $p<.05$ | 2.67 | 2.03 | 0.64 | -5.66 $p<.001$ |
| **Case 9. Drinks to Ignore Late Bar Closing** | 4.68 | 3.77 | 0.91 | -9.96 $p<.001$ | 4.10 | 3.17 | 0.93 | -10.45 $p<.001$ | 4.21 | 2.48 | 1.73 | -16.02 $p<.001$ |
| **Case 10. Excessive Force on Car Thief** | 4.45 | 3.49 | 0.96 | -10.12 $p<.001$ | 3.97 | 3.15 | 0.82 | -8.30 $p<.001$ | 4.02 | 2.53 | 1.49 | -13.42 $p<.001$ |
| **Case 11. Theft From Found Wallet** | 4.94 | 4.55 | 0.39 | -6.85 $p<.001$ | 5.42 | 4.13 | 1.29 | -14.17 $p<.001$ | 4.74 | 2.95 | 1.79 | -17.41 $p<.001$ |

* Not significant.

## Conclusions and implications

Redefining the problem of police corruption (i.e., the abuse of police authority for gain) as a problem of police integrity—the normative inclination among police to resist temptations to abuse their authority—enables the direct measurement of the major propositions of an organizational/occupational theory of police integrity. The research reported in this Research in Brief demonstrates that police attitudes toward the seriousness of misconduct, the discipline that should and would result, and the willingness of officers to tolerate misconduct in silence can be measured. Moreover, the measurements reported in this national sample are relatively easy to collect. At the same time, they demonstrate substantial differences in the environments of integrity in U.S. police agencies.

The ability to measure environments of integrity in police agencies holds great potential for academic studies of police and for practical police administration. For researchers, quantitative cross-cultural, historical, and national comparisons that were previously unthinkable have now become feasible.

Equally important, such measurements have direct implications for practical police administration because each of the propositions of an organizational/occupational theory of integrity implies a specific administrative response. If officers do not know whether certain conduct violates agency policy or what disciplinary threats the agency makes, administrators have a clear responsibility to communicate this information to officers. If officers do not regard certain misconduct as sufficiently serious, if they regard discipline as too severe or too lenient, or if they are willing to tolerate the misconduct of their police peers in silence, administrators have an obvious obligation to find out why. A police administrator can take specific actions to deal with each of these problems.

The survey instrument used in this study was designed to assess only one aspect of police integrity. In all case scenarios but one—the use of excessive force—the misconduct described was motivated by personal gain. In discussing environments of integrity,

Exhibit 4. **Agency 2 vs. Agency 23: Officers' perceptions of how most police would assess offense seriousness, discipline that offense would receive, and whether most police would be willing to report offense**

| Case Scenario | Agency 2 (A2) vs. Agency 23 (A23) How *Most Police* Regard Seriousness | | | | Agency 2 (A2) vs. Agency 23 (A23) Discipline *Would* Receive | | | | Agency 2 (A2) vs. Agency 23 (A23) Whether *Most Police* Would Be Willing To Report | | | |
|---|---|---|---|---|---|---|---|---|---|---|---|---|
| | A2 | A23 | Difference | *t* test | A2 | A23 | Difference | *t* test | A2 | A23 | Difference | *t* test |
| **Case 1. Off-Duty Security System Business** | 1.52 | 1.31 | 0.21 | -1.61 NS* | 1.70 | 1.33 | 0.37 | -5.08 $p<.001$ | 1.52 | 1.31 | 0.21 | -3.12 $p<.05$ |
| **Case 2. Free Meals, Discounts on Beat** | 2.53 | 2.57 | -0.04 | 0.41 NS* | 2.77 | 2.51 | 0.26 | -3.27 $p<.05$ | 2.07 | 1.74 | 0.33 | -3.83 $p<.001$ |
| **Case 3. Bribe From Speeding Motorist** | 4.82 | 4.60 | 0.22 | -4.25 $p<.001$ | 4.90 | 4.45 | 0.45 | -5.06 $p<.001$ | 4.23 | 2.90 | 1.33 | -13.89 $p<.001$ |
| **Case 4. Holiday Gifts From Merchants** | 2.73 | 2.61 | 0.12 | -1.10 NS* | 3.07 | 2.88 | 0.19 | -1.94 $p<.01$ | 2.49 | 2.03 | 0.46 | -4.65 $p<.001$ |
| **Case 5. Crime Scene Theft of Watch** | 4.93 | 4.62 | 0.31 | -6.16 $p<.001$ | 5.73 | 4.93 | 0.80 | -10.33 $p<.001$ | 4.63 | 3.25 | 1.38 | -14.99 $p<.001$ |
| **Case 6. Auto Repair Shop 5% Kickback** | 4.31 | 3.75 | 0.56 | -6.28 $p<.001$ | 4.45 | 3.91 | 0.54 | -5.35 $p<.001$ | 3.92 | 2.64 | 1.28 | -12.51 $p<.001$ |
| **Case 7. Supervisor: Holiday for Tuneup** | 3.85 | 3.85 | 0 | 0.04 NS* | 3.24 | 3.52 | -0.28 | 2.78 $p<.05$ | 3.34 | 2.60 | 0.74 | -6.80 $p<.001$ |
| **Case 8. Coverup of Police DUI Accident** | 2.80 | 2.54 | 0.26 | -2.61 $p<.05$ | 3.33 | 2.83 | 0.50 | -4.92 $p<.001$ | 2.40 | 1.95 | 0.45 | -4.55 $p<.001$ |
| **Case 9. Drinks to Ignore Late Bar Closing** | 4.32 | 3.44 | 0.88 | -9.13 $p<.001$ | 4.11 | 3.29 | 0.82 | -8.92 $p<.001$ | 3.79 | 2.35 | 1.44 | -13.89 $p<.001$ |
| **Case 10. Excessive Force on Car Thief** | 4.01 | 3.22 | 0.79 | -8.00 $p<.001$ | 4.11 | 3.46 | 0.65 | -6.86 $p<.001$ | 3.44 | 2.38 | 1.06 | -9.98 $p<.001$ |
| **Case 11. Theft From Found Wallet** | 4.83 | 4.24 | 0.59 | -8.53 $p<.001$ | 5.24 | 4.25 | 0.99 | -10.79 $p<.001$ | 4.38 | 2.74 | 1.64 | -16.20 $p<.001$ |

* Not significant.

therefore, this survey makes no observation about abuses of discretion in arrests, order maintenance, discourtesy to citizens, or other police misconduct not usually motivated by temptations of gain. A second generation of this survey will explore those problems.[6]

## A final note

This survey does not measure the extent of corruption in any police agency or institution. Rather, it measures the culture of police integrity—the normative inclination of police officers to resist the temptations to abuse the rights and privileges of their office. The survey does not identify either corrupt or honest police officers; nor does it provide any evidence of abusive or dishonest practices—past, present, or future. The survey findings do describe, in a fairly precise way, the characteristics of a police agency's culture that encourage its employees to resist or tolerate certain types of misconduct.

## Notes

1. Goldstein, Herman, *Police Corruption: Perspective on Its Nature and Control*, Washington, DC: Police Foundation, 1975; and Goldstein, H., *Policing a Free Society*, Cambridge, MA: Ballinger, 1977. See also Sherman, Lawrence W., *Scandal and Reform*, Berkeley: University of California Press, 1978; Marx, Gary, *Surveillance*, Cambridge, MA: Harvard University Press, 1991; Punch, Maurice, *Conduct Unbecoming: The Social Construction of Police Deviance and Control*, London: Tavistock, 1986; and Manning, Peter K., and Lawrence Redlinger, "The Invitational Edges of Police Corruption," in *Thinking About Police*, edited by Carl Klockars and Stephen Mastrofski, New York: McGraw-Hill, 1993: 398–412.

2. Note that the notions of "greater than zero (positive)" and "less than zero (negative)" are merely shorthand for discipline perceived as too lenient and too harsh, respectively. In other words, because the data are ordinal, positive or negative differences will not be used in any algebraic context. Rather, these differences will be used solely as indicators to classify respondents into three groups—those who perceive discipline to be fair, too lenient, or too harsh.

3. The frequency distribution of responses to the question about officers' own willingness to report a particular offense was analyzed. The five-point scale of offered answers ranged from 1="definitely not" to 5="definitely yes." A cumulative frequency above 50 percent for 1 and

2 was interpreted to indicate that police officers would *not* report the offense. A cumulative frequency above 50 percent for 4 and 5, on the other hand, was interpreted to indicate that the police officers *would* report the offense.

4. See, for example, Haberfeld, Maria, Carl Klockars, Sanja Kutnjak Ivkovich, and Milan Pagon, "Disciplinary Consequences of Police Corruption in Croatia, Poland, Slovenia, and the United States," *Police Practice and Research, An International Journal* 1 (1) (2000): 41–72.

5. An alternative summary ranking system could, of course, be based on the full range of 30-point rankings for each of the 11 scenarios. This type of system would create a scale that could range from 330 (for an agency that scored the lowest of the 30 agencies on all 6 questions for all 11 scenarios) to 1,980 (for an agency that scored the highest of all 30 agencies on all 6 questions for all 11 scenarios). Such a scoring system would, however, magnify small and primarily meaningless differences in mean scores, creating a false sense of precision. The ranking system developed for and employed in

this research intentionally seeks to blunt any false sense of precision by allowing agencies to score, in a sense, only "high," "middle," or "low" on any given question.

6. A summary of the status of progress with this next generation of measures of police integrity can be found on the videotape of the Research in Progress seminar "Measuring Police Integrity," presented by Carl Klockars at the National Institute of Justice in January 1999. Copies are available through the National Criminal Justice Reference Service at 800–851–3420. Please refer to NCJ 174459.

Carl B. Klockars, Ph.D., is professor in the Department of Sociology and Criminal Justice at the University of Delaware. Sanja Kutnjak Ivkovich, Ph.D., is a doctoral student at Harvard Law School. William E. Harver, Ph.D., is assistant professor of social science in the College of Arts and Sciences at Widener University. Maria R. Haberfeld, Ph.D., is assistant professor in the Department of Law, Police Science, and Criminal Justice Administration at the John Jay College of Criminal Justice, City University of New York.

The study reported in this Research in Brief was supported by the Office of Community Oriented Policing Services and NIJ through NIJ grant number 95–IJ–CX–0058.

Police administrators interested in applying the approach used in this study to measure the environment of integrity in their own agencies are advised to contact Professor Carl B. Klockars, Principal Investigator, Enhancing Police Integrity Project, Criminal Justice, University of Delaware, Newark, DE 19716.

Findings and conclusions of the research reported here are those of the authors and do not necessarily reflect the official position or policies of the U.S. Department of Justice.

*The National Institute of Justice is a component of the Office of Justice Programs, which also includes the Bureau of Justice Assistance, the Bureau of Justice Statistics, the Office of Juvenile Justice and Delinquency Prevention, and the Office for Victims of Crime.*

**This and other NIJ publications can be found at and downloaded from the NIJ Web site (http://www.ojp.usdoj.gov/nij).**

**NCJ 181465**

---

## Quick Access to NIJ Publication News

For news about NIJ's most recent publications, including solicitations for grant applications, subscribe to JUSTINFO, the bimonthly newsletter sent to you via e-mail. Here's how:

- Send an e-mail to listproc@ncjrs.org
- Leave the subject line blank
- Type subscribe justinfo your name
  (e.g., subscribe justinfo Jane Doe) in the body of the message

Or check out the "Publications and Products" section at the NIJ home page: http://www.ojp.usdoj.gov/nij or the "New This Week" section at the Justice Information Center home page:
http://www.ncjrs.org

11

# APPENDIX VII:  UNCONSTITUTIONAL POLICE SEARCHES AND COLLECTIVE RESPONSIBILITY

**University of Chicago Law School**
**Chicago Unbound**

Public Law and Legal Theory Working Papers | Working Papers

2004

# Unconstitutional Police Searches and Collective Responsibility

Bernard E. Harcourt



### Recommended Citation

# CHICAGO

PUBLIC LAW AND LEGAL THEORY WORKING PAPER NO. 66

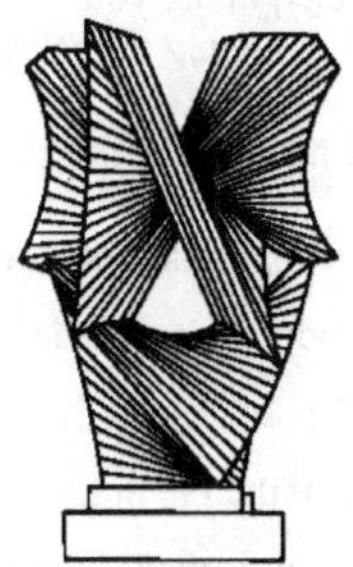

# UNCONSTITUTIONAL POLICE SEARCHES AND COLLECTIVE RESPONSIBILITY

*Bernard E. Harcourt*

THE LAW SCHOOL
THE UNIVERSITY OF CHICAGO

June 2004

Forthcoming, *Criminology and Public Policy*, 2004
The working paper can be downloaded without charge at
http://www.law.uchicago.edu/academics/publiclaw/index.html
and at The Social Science Research Network Electronic Paper Collection:
http://ssrn.com/abstract_id=554642

Draft: May 23, 2004
Comments welcome at bharcourt@law.uchicago.edu
© Bernard E. Harcourt

### Unconstitutional Police Searches and Collective Responsibility:

Then the police officer told the suspect, without just cause,
"I bet you are hiding [drugs] under your balls. If you have drugs
under your balls, I am going to fuck your balls up"[1]

Bernard E. Harcourt[2]

Jon Gould and Stephen Mastrofski document astonishingly high rates of unconstitutional police searches in their groundbreaking article "Suspect Searches: Assessing Police Behavior Under the U.S. Constitution" published in *Criminology & Public Policy* (2004). By their conservative estimate, 30 percent of the 115 police searches they studied—searches that were conducted by officers in a department ranked in the top 20 percent nationwide, that were systematically observed by trained field observers, and that were coded by Gould, Mastrofski and a team including a state appellate judge, a former federal prosecutor, and a government attorney—violated Fourth Amendment prohibitions on searches and seizures.

The vast majority of the unconstitutional searches—31 out of 34—were invisible to the courts, having resulted in no arrest, charge, or citation. In fact, the rate of unconstitutional searches was highest for suspects who were released—44 percent versus 7 percent of arrested or cited suspects. Focusing exclusively on stop-and-frisk searches, an even higher proportion—46 percent—were unconstitutional. Moreover, 84 percent of the searches involved black suspects. The searches were conducted and observed in the early 1990s in the midst of an ongoing war on drugs, during a period of increased police discretion nationwide. The study paints a troubling picture of police practices and raises a number of difficult questions about discretionary policing.

Gould and Mastrofski's findings have a disturbingly familiar ring to them. In a somewhat analogous context—stop-and-frisk searches conducted in New York City during

---

[1] Jon B. Gould and Stephen D. Mastrofski, "Suspect Searches: Assessing Police Behavior," Appendix—Sample Search Narratives and Coding, *Criminology & Public Policy* __:__ (2004) (this is an excerpt from field notes recording a conversation between a police officer and a suspect).

the late 1990s—research similarly revealed high levels of unconstitutional searches. New York Attorney General Elliot Spitzer, in conjunction with Jeffrey Fagan and Columbia University's Center for Violence Research and Prevention, reviewed documentation of more than 15,000 NYPD stop-and-frisk reports, and found that, citywide, 15.4 percent of the reports contained factual bases that were not sufficient to justify a stop and another 23.5 percent stated inadequate factual bases to allow a supervisor to determine whether there were sufficient facts to justify a stop—for a total of approximately 39 percent questionable searches.[3]

To be sure, Gould and Mastrofski have raised the evidentiary bar with their article *Suspect Searches* by drawing on one of the first studies to conduct systematic physical observation of police searches. Rather than being based on written police reports—which raise clear issues of reliability—their new findings are drawn from the field notes of trained observers who accompanied and directly observed police officers on patrol. Any bias in this method—specifically, reactivity effects from direct observation of police practices—would likely tend to minimize a possibly higher real rate of unconstitutional searches.[4] Nevertheless, Gould and Mastrofski's empirical findings corroborate overall Spitzer's conclusions: about a third of police discretionary searches are constitutionally suspect.

The public policy debates that Gould and Mastrofski's article are likely to ignite will also, in all probability, have a familiar ring to them as well. The debates have been rehearsed in a number of policing controversies—not just stop-and-frisk policing on New York City streets,[5] but also racial profiling on the nation's highways[6] and drug-courier profiling at

---

[2] Professor of Law, The University of Chicago.

[3] *See* Civil Rights Bureau, Office of the New York Attorney General, *The New York City Police Department's "Stop & Frisk" Practice: A Report from the Office of the Attorney General* (December 1, 1999), at pp. 160B170.

[4] In addition, Gould and Mastrofski bent backwards to minimize the risk of overstating the rate of unconstitutional searches by reading any factual and legal inferences in favor of the police while coding and consistently giving the police officers the benefit of any doubt in the coding process. *See* Gould and Mastrofski 2004:*19.

[5] *See* United States Commission on Civil Rights, *Police Practices and Civil Rights in New York City* (August 2000); New York Police Department, *NYPD Response to the Draft Report of the United States Commission on Civil Rights—Police Practices and Civil Rights in New York City* (2000); Heather MacDonald, "America's Best Urban Police Force," *City Journal*, Volume 10, No. 3 (Summer 2000).

[6] *See* Jerome Skolnick and Abigail Caplovitz, "Guns, Drugs and Profiling: Ways to Target Guns and Minimize Racial Profiling," in *Guns, Crime, and Punishment in America* (Bernard E. Harcourt, ed.) (New York: New York University Press 2003); Samuel R. Gross and Katherine Y. Barnes, "Road Work: Racial Profiling and Drug Interdiction on the Highway," *Michigan Law Review*, 101(3):____ (2002); John

airports and borders.[7] Civil-liberties-attentive law enforcement officials will probably call for more dialogue and research "in the best spirit of public policy discussion—without rancor or recrimination,"[8] as Attorney General Spitzer recommends in the NYPD context. In this vein, there will also be calls for more "robust scholarly discussion and debate" over topics such as the "training of managers, supervisors, and line officers regarding 'stop & frisk'" and the "methods for supervising officers who apply the technique on the street."[9]

Staunch law-and-order advocates will challenge the findings and place them squarely in the larger context of *crime reduction*. As Heather MacDonald of the Manhattan Institute suggests in the New York City context, these types of studies and the press more generally "specialize[] in blissfully ignorant innuendos about stop and frisks to tar the [police]."[10] Or, as former New York police commissioners William Bratton and Howard Safir argue in the NYPD context, any apparent problem with unconstitutional searches can be attributed to sharply increased rates of civilian-police contact associated with heightened discretionary policing and growing police forces. On a per contact basis, the numbers are very low.[11]

Civil rights organizations, such as the United States Commission on Civil Rights, the ACLU, and Amnesty International, will call for an end to unconstitutional searches and racial profiling, enhanced monitoring and training, better recruitment, and increased resources for the Civilian Complaint Review Board.[12] Progressive academicians may call for an outright ban on discretionary stop-and-frisk policing or its replacement with mandatory randomized searches, and other more radical scholars will question the very idea of criminal profiling.[13]

---

Knowles, Nicola Persico, and Petra Todd, "Racial Bias in Motor Vehicle Searches: Theory and Evidence," *Journal of Political Economy*, 109(1): 203B229 (2001). For an overview and assessment of the empirical studies and policy arguments, *see generally* Bernard E. Harcourt, "Rethinking Racial Profiling: A Critique of the Economics, Civil Liberties, and Constitutional Literature and of Criminal Profiling More Generally," *University of Chicago Law Review*, 71: _____ (forthcoming Fall 2004).

[7] For discussion of the drug courier profile and its public policy implications, *see generally* Bernard E. Harcourt, "From the Ne'er-do-Well to the Criminal History Category. The Refinement of the Actuarial Model in Criminal Law," *Law and Contemporary Problems*, 66(3):99B151 (2003).

[8] Civil Rights Bureau 1999:175.

[9] Civil Rights Bureau 1999:176.

[10] MacDonald 2000.

[11] *See* William Bratton with Peter Knobler, *Turnaround: How America's Top Cop Reversed the Crime Epidemic*, 291 (New York: Random House 1998); *NYPD Response to the Draft Report* 2000:7.

[12] *See, e.g.,* United States Commission on Civil Rights 2000:82B39B40, 80B84, 107B108.

[13] My colleague at the University of Chicago, Tracey Meares, is working on a paper that argues against discretionary policing and in favor of non-discretionary type searches, such as mandatory road

These positions in our public policy debates are familiar. If anything, a bit too familiar. In this essay, I would like to reframe the debates and in the process destabilize these positions. To make them a little less comfortable, a little less sanitized. To start to expose the real stakes. To begin to explore our own responsibility as observers, as social scientists, as commentators, as policy makers, and, yes, as public citizens. In effect, I would like to probe *our own participation* in these police searches. Buried in the Appendix to Gould and Mastrofski's article is a field note about one particular police-civilian encounter that raises especially troubling questions about social science, public policy, and citizenship. Let's start, then, with this field note in the Appendix.

I.

The lead police officer is described in very generic terms. He is a "white cop in his late twenties." Three other police officers are assisting him on the scene, only one of whom is identified, also in generic terms, also as a "white male in his late twenties." The officers have stopped a suspect who was riding a bike. The suspect is identified in the field notes, not surprisingly, as "a black male in his late twenties." The police have searched his pockets, his person, his backpack. They have not found anything—no drugs, no gun, no contraband. No evidence of crime. Nothing. But they decide to search a little further. They decide to look a little deeper. They decide to check under his testicles.

According to the trained field researcher physically observing the encounter, the young white police officer tells the young black suspect: "I bet you are hiding [drugs] under your balls. If you have drugs under your balls, I am going to fuck your balls up."[14] The police officer then tells the young black suspect to "get behind the police car, and pull his pants down to his ankles." The white police officer puts on "some rubber gloves." He then begins "feeling around" the black suspect's testicles. Again, he comes up empty handed. No drugs. No contraband. Just a black man's testicles. So he decides to search even further.

And he says to the black man, now with even less valid suspicion: "I bet you are holding them in the crack of your ass. You better not have them up your ass." The black

---

blocks. For a paper challenging the very idea of criminal profiling, *see* Bernard E. Harcourt, "Rethinking Racial Profiling," (2004).

   [14] Gould and Mastrofski 2004.

man, at this point very compliant, "bent over, and spread his cheeks." The white cop, still with his rubber gloves, then "put his hands up C1's rectum." [C1 is the anonymous code for the suspect—as in "Citizen 1" or C1 for short]. But the white cop finds nothing. No drugs. No contraband. Just a black man's empty rectum.

The citizen pulls his pants back up. The first cop on the scene tells him that he matched the description from a tip the police had received. [Note: "there was simply no evidence elsewhere in the report that the officers had ever received the call to which they referred," Gould and Mastrofski observe. "Moreover, even if they had, an anonymous tip does not in itself justify a body cavity search (*Florida v. J.L.*, 2000)"]. "Besides," the officer adds, "you are so nervous, I would bet that you have some drugs on you too. But then again, I would be nervous too if I was surrounded by four cops."

The citizen repeats, for the fourth or fifth time, that he does not have any dealings with drugs, that "he didn't use or sell drugs." When he is told that he can leave, the citizen says "thank you" and takes off on his bike. For his part, the researcher walks back to the patrol car with the first cop on the scene, whose last words are "I know he had some drugs."

II.

It may be worth stopping here for a moment to experience this encounter in real time. On a conservative estimate—assuming, for instance, that the police officer had rubber gloves right handy—the strip and cavity search took at least ninety seconds. That is a very conservative estimate, and yet it is a long time in which to ruminate, day dream, think, desire. What must have been going through the officer's mind when he started putting on those rubber gloves? Do you think that he felt bad that he was asking a grown man to drop his pants in public in order to feel his testicles? Do you think he was thinking to himself, "Man, I hate this job! I can't believe I have to stick my hand up this guy's ass." Or did he feel entirely self-righteous, proud that he was so selflessly promoting the public interest? Or alternatively did he experience a genuine moral dilemma about having to employ dirty means to achieve good ends—what we might call, after Carl Klockars, "The Dirty Harry

Problem"[15]? Or was he just so convinced of the suspect's guilt that he put all thoughts aside, that he wasn't even thinking?

Did he feel guilty in any way about the racial dimension of the encounter? Did he feel embarrassed about being white and putting his hands up a black man's rectum? Or did that excite him? Do you think he experienced some pleasure at the idea of penetrating a black man? Of course, we do not know what he was thinking or feeling. We can only speculate. Do you think that he felt a spark, a *frisson*, some power, a feeling of domination when the citizen bent over in public and spread his buttocks cheeks for him? Do you think the cop experienced any sexual pleasure? Did he give it a good look? Was it a gentle caress or a punishing grip? Was he acting out some kind of fantasy? Was he hoping that the citizen might be complying out of a hidden desire to be dominated? Or instead, was the cop disgusted by the whole thing? Was it his disgust that attracted him to it? Was he punishing the black man? Was he intentionally trying to hurt him? (After all, wouldn't it hurt to have someone stick a rubber glove up your rectum like that?) Was the cop inflicting this on himself—or on the citizen? Who was he punishing?

What about the three back-up police officers? What were they thinking as they watched their white supervisor, their fearless leader sticking his hand up the black man's rectum in public? Were they taking mental notes—"Okay, so this is how you do it. Let's see now. Okay. Then you put your fingers up his ass." Were they wondering to themselves whether their supervisor was nuts? Or a sexual pervert? Were they thinking of intervening and suggesting that there was no valid basis for further searching the suspect? Were they concerned that intervening might hurt their careers? Or were they envious—jealous that the supervisor got to penetrate the black man and not them. Were they bonding, as males, as delinquents? Was this some kind of initiation ritual? Was it any different than a gang initiation rape? Or was it a heroic act—after all, who wants to stick their hand up someone's rectum to wage war on drugs? Or was this so routine that they didn't even pay attention? Was it a cigarette break? A safe moment during an otherwise dangerous day? Or was it a moment of comic relief? Was it just some good old-fashioned healthy fun and games?

---

[15] *See* Carl B. Klockars, "The Dirty Harry Problem," 428B438, in *Thinking about Police: Contemporary Readings*, ed. Carl B. Klockars (New York: McGraw-Hill Book Company 1983); *see also* Stephen D. Mastrofski and Craig D. Uchida, "On Dirty Hands and Definitions: A Rejoinder," *Journal of Research in Crime and Delinquency* 30(3):354B368 (August 1993).

What about the citizen, what on earth was he thinking and feeling? Do you think he felt humiliated about having to drop his pants in public? Or did he just think to himself, this is simply part and parcel of being a young black man in America today? What did he mean when he said "thank you"? Did it hurt? Could it possibly feel good? Had he done this before? Had anyone told him before what you are supposed to do if four cops stop you and tell you to spread your cheeks? Was he angry? Sad? Depressed? Forgiving? Vengeful? Understanding? Did he think to himself, "One day, white man, your time will come. I will get you back—when you least expect it"? How did he feel when he got home that night? What did he tell his kids? What did he do to his sex partner?

What about the trained social scientist, the observer, the researcher there on site, taking field notes, conducting systematic observation? What was s/he thinking as s/he observed the police officer "put his hands up C1's rectum"? Did s/he take a good look? Was s/he curious as to how a police officer searches someone's balls? Or did s/he close her/his eyes and think "My God, what is going on here?" Did s/he experience anger? Attraction? Repulsion? Arousal? An adrenaline rush? Did s/he try to intervene and tell the police officers that there was no evidence of a tip? Or that a tip would not justify such an intrusive search anyway? Was s/he concerned that this would jeopardize the data collection? Or was s/he projecting being the police officer, having the power, taking control, putting a hand up C1's rectum?

III.

The questions abound. And they all tend toward one central inquiry: to what extent are these various actors *responsible* for the cavity search? Of course, the lead police officer bears much responsibility. It is interesting to note, in this respect, that Gould and Mastrofski conducted qualitative review of the worst offenders and found that "None appeared to be angry, cynical, or the composite of a disillusioned officer with an axe to grind." "All were well regarded by their peers and supervisors and expressed a desire to establish strong bonds with neighborhood residents and to treat all citizens, including suspects, with a respectful demeanor."[16] (We might ask here whether the police officers had voluntarily segregated into these cohesive units and whether their strong peer bonds actually hid sharp tensions along

---

[16] Gould and Mastrofski 2004:*35

other dimensions. In the policing context, for instance, there is a lot of voluntary racial segregation of police units).

What about the responsibility of the other police officers watching? Should they have said something to defuse the situation—something like, "Hey, Sergeant, there ain't nothing here! Let's let the guy go! We'll get him next time!" Why didn't they intervene? Were they worried about getting fired? What was their rank? How much job security did they have? What would lead them to place their own self-interest over the welfare of the citizens they are sworn to protect? At what point and at what cost did they lose their ideals?

And did race play a role in the decision of the three back-up police officers not to intervene? Gould and Mastrofski surprisingly minimize the racial dimensions of these searches. They bend backward to emphasize the lack of a significant statistical relationship between race and the unconstitutionality of searches. "The absence of significant effects for wealth and race deserve special note, inasmuch as other research has shown these variables to influence justice outcomes," Gould and Mastrofski write.[17] But the fact is that *eighty-four percent* of their sample—96 of the searches studied—involved black suspects. Although we do not know the exact demographic breakdown for Middleberg, the fictitiously-named medium-size American city where the study was conducted—all we do know is that "many of the city's residents were African American, and many experienced concentrated disadvantage"[18]—it is hard to believe that the police could reach 84 percent searches of black suspects without some racial profiling. Might that have played a role or contributed in any way to the passivity of the three other police officers?

What about the social scientist who is witnessing, observing, and documenting this incident—taking notes, making a recording, memorializing the interaction? Is s/he responsible in any way for this incident? Does the social scientist have any obligation to step out of the scientific role and actively intervene? To breach the code of social scientific objectivity and prevent the search? Or to report it? Let's put aside personal ethics for a minute and focus on the more formal institutional duties that the researcher may have had. There are, aren't there, some legal responsibilities that attach here? Among social scientists, it might be worth pausing here for a moment and exploring the question.

---

[17] Gould and Mastrofski 2004:*32.
[18] Gould and Mastrofski 2004:*12.

Without doubt, the actions of the police officer involve bodily harm to the suspect. They are physically injurious, dehumanizing, and degrading at least with regard to one of the subjects of the research. In fact, the police conduct may well constitute a felony. In a number of jurisdictions, sexual battery includes anal penetration of another by any object without that person's consent.[19] This is precisely the statutory definition in Florida for instance, *see Fla. Stat.* '794.011(1)(h) (2004), where it is specifically designated a felony in the first degree "when the offender is a law enforcement officer. . . and such officer . . . is acting in such a manner as to lead the victim to reasonably believe that the offender is in a position of control or authority as an agent or employee of government." *Fla. Stat.* '794.011(4)(g) (2004). In Florida, it is punishable by a term of imprisonment of up to 30 years for a first offense. *Fla. Stat.* '794.011775.082(3)(b) (2004).[20]

Given that the actions of the lead police officer cause bodily harm—and may amount to a felony—the social scientist may very well have an obligation to report the incident to the university and to law enforcement officials.[21] First, with regard to the university, the field observation study underlying the Gould and Mastrofski article undoubtedly required human subjects committee (IRB) approval at the university level. A project such as this, even though it involves only "observation of public behavior," would not ordinarily be exempt from review because the disclosure of information beyond the research community "could reasonably place the subjects at risk of criminal or civil liability or be damaging to the subjects' financial standing, employability, or reputation."[22] This is straight from the Code of

---

[19] It will depend on the jurisdiction, of course, and we are not told where the fictitiously-named city of Middleberg is actually located. I have chosen Florida purely hypothetically.

[20] In Florida, consent is defined strictly. Consent requires "intelligent, knowing, and voluntary consent and does not include coerced submission." *Fla. Stat.*§794.011(1)(a) (2004). For prosecutions against police officers under (4)(g), "acquiescence to a person reasonably believed by the victim to be in a position of authority or control does not constitute consent, and it is not a defense that the perpetrator was not actually in a position of control or authority if the circumstances were such as to lead the victim to reasonably believe that the person was in such a position." *Fla. Stat.*§794.011(9) (2004).

Another example would be California. Under the California Penal Code, Chap. 5, §289, forcible acts of sexual penetration include, at section (k)(1), "the act of causing the penetration, however slight, of the genital or anal opening of any person . . . by any foreign object, substance, instrument, or device, or by any unknown object." When the act "is accomplished against the victim's will by threatening to use the authority of a public official to incarcerate, arrest, or deport the victim or another, and the victim has a reasonable belief that the perpetrator is a public official," then it is punishable by imprisonment in the state prison for a period of three, six, or eight years. Cal. Penal Code §289(g) (2004).

[21] I have no idea whether the researchers did or did not report this incident. I can only assume that they did, but I have no knowledge whatsoever.

[22] This is from the Manual of Procedures of the University of Arizona Human Subjects Protection

Federal Regulations concerning the protection of human subjects by the United States Department of Health and Human Services (DHHS) and is usually incorporated *verbatim* in university IRB protocols.

As a result, the actions of the lead police officer would likely have to be reported to the university committee. The typical university approval requires as much. Here, for instance, is the actual text from a letter granting approval for a research project from the human subjects committee at a top American research university:

> Approval is granted with the understanding that no further changes or additions will be made . . . without the knowledge and approval of the Human Subjects Committee and your College or Departmental Review Committee. *Any research related physical or psychological harm to any subject must also be reported to each committee.*[23]

The failure to comply with these requirements could very well lead to academic discipline.

As an aside, it is worth remembering that the regulation of research concerning human subjects is no trivial affair. It had its origins in the Nuremberg trials. As the *IRB Guidebook* of the Office for Human Research Protections of the DHHS explains:

> The modern story of human subjects protections begins with the *Nuremberg Code,* developed for the Nuremberg Military Tribunal as standards by which to judge the human experimentation conducted by the Nazis. The Code captures many of what are now taken to be the basic principles governing the ethical conduct of research involving human subjects. The first provision of the Code states that "the voluntary consent of the human subject is absolutely essential." Freely given consent to participation in research is thus the cornerstone of ethical experimentation involving human subjects. The Code goes on to provide the details implied by such a requirement: capacity to consent, freedom from coercion, and comprehension of the risks and benefits involved. Other provisions require the minimization of risk and harm, a favorable risk/benefit ratio, qualified investigators using appropriate research designs, and freedom for the subject to withdraw at any time. Similar recommendations were made by the World Medical Association in its *Declaration of Helsinki: Recommendations Guiding Medical Doctors in Biomedical Research Involving Human Subjects,* first adopted by the 18th World Medical Assembly in Helsinki, Finland, in 1964, and subsequently revised by the 29th World Medical Assembly, Tokyo, Japan, 1975, and by the 41st World Medical Assembly, Hong

---

Program, Part 4.(2), but it is lifted directly from the Code of Federal Regulations concerning the protection of human subjects from the United States Department of Health and Human Services. *See* 45 C.F.R. Sec. 46.101 (b)(2).

[23] This is the actual text from a letter of approval for research at the University of Arizona.

Kong, 1989. The Declaration of Helsinki further distinguishes therapeutic from nontherapeutic research.[24]

Now, in addition to the university IRB, the researcher who observed the improper cavity search may also need to report the incident to law enforcement authorities.[25] In a number of states, it is a misdemeanor to fail to report a crime that exposes a victim to bodily harm. In Florida again, a person who "has reasonable grounds to believe that he or she has observed the commission of a sexual battery" and who has "the present ability to seek assistance for the victim or victims by immediately reporting such offense to a law enforcement officer," but fails to seek assistance, is guilty of a misdemeanor of the first degree punishable by a term of imprisonment of up to a year for a first offense. *Fla. Stat.* ' 794.027 and '775.082 (2004).

Should the social scientist observer have intervened or later reported this incident?[26] If s/he did not, was it because it would interfere with the research? Because it might have jeopardized this data collection? Because it might have prevented any further cooperation from this police department? Because it might discourage other police departments from allowing systematic observation in the future? Because it might impair our ability, as social scientists, to collect this information? Is the cavity search just the collateral damage inevitably associated with social science—the cost of knowledge? The cost of increasing our collective awareness about police practices? Did the researcher just sacrifice this black man for the betterment of social science and public policy?

Naturally, these questions raise a host of issues regarding the potential conflict of interest that the researcher may have experienced during the cavity search—issues close to, though somewhat distinct from the "dirty hands" dilemma that Stephen Mastrofski, Carl

---

[24] *Protecting Human Research Subjects: Institutional Review Board Guidebook,* "Introduction" (available at http://ohrp.osophs.dhhs.gov/irb/irb_introduction.htm).

[25] Here, for instance, is the actual text of a letter from a district attorney regarding a request for immunity for a research project:

> We have reviewed your request for confidentiality in your interviews with research subjects for the above study. We agree to such confidentiality except where information may come to light about homicides, other serious crimes or crimes involving serious injury to others.
>
> Therefore, if your research subjects should admit to homicide or other serious offenses as listed in [the state's penal code] or one involving serious injury to another, should this information be disclosed to us in any way, we would be required to act on the matter as we deem appropriate and proper.

[26] Again, I have no knowledge whether s/he did. I am discussing this as a pure hypothetical matter.

Klockars, and others have debated.[27] The "dirty hands" dilemma, in its purest form, presents a challenge when the social scientist makes public policy recommendations. It emphasizes that the researcher is responsible for any harm that the policies may produce. Here, we are dealing with a slight variation on the theme, one that focuses on an earlier point in time. The question here is whether the research *itself* presents a moral dilemma. Does the collection of data require complicity with the delinquent police conduct? Do we have to dirty our hands and not intervene *so that* we can obtain the data? And at what price? Do we self-censor our questions, our analyses, our *conclusions* so as not to alienate the police officer or the police department? Do we have to "get in bed" with the police so that they allow us to ride along and observe their daily practices? Did the researcher here stop her or himself from intervening precisely in order to maintain credibility with the police? And will this affect the way the social scientist goes about doing research in the future? Is this the cost of getting this data?

And what about us—me the author and you the reader? What is our responsibility as consumers of this research, as users of this social science? What is my accountability as author of this essay discussing Gould and Mastrofski's article? Am I taking advantage of the black suspect? Here we are, debating the study in an academic journal, gaining reputations as thoughtful scholars, taking positions as policy advisers—but are we just observing sexual humiliation and taking advantage of it? What are *we* feeling as we read the narrative? Are we shocked, amused, disgusted, angered, satisfied, pleased? Do we feel guilt about the racial dimensions? Does it confirm what we suspected? Or is there cognitive dissonance? Is it incredible? Unbelievable? False? Unfair? Do we take responsibility for the actions of the

---

[27] There are, in reality, three "dirty hands" problems that we need to distinguish. The first is the "Dirty Harry Problem" that Carl Klockars writes about (Klockars 1983). This first problem concerns the use of dirty means by a police officer to promote a good end. Then, second, there is the moral dilemma of the social scientist making policy recommendations: the fact is that the policy recommendations may create some harm, and in that sense the social scientist will have "dirty hands." As Lawrence Sherman explains, there are moral dilemmas when we apply social science to policy analysis. "These dilemmas make social science a morally 'dirty' means to a just and good end—a less violent world. It is a 'dirty' means because recommendations based on it may do some harm, even though the odds are against it." Lawrence W. Sherman, "Dirty Hands and Social Science," *Journal of Research in Crime and Delinquency* 30(3):362B364 (August 1993). This is the "dirty hands" problem that Mastrofski writes about in his rejoinder (Mastroksfi and Uchida 1993). The third is the one I am interested here: how police researchers may have to "get in bed" with the cops in order to obtain their data—how they might have to self-censor their questions and analyses for fear of being shut out of the data. This is another form of "dirty hands" that has even more detrimental effects on the social science and policy analysis because it corrupts before anyone has the opportunity to formulate policy proposals.

police officer? Or do we assume that he was right—that the suspect probably had drugs on him, somewhere, maybe deeper?

Are we—*you and me*—responsible in any way for this body cavity search?

## IV.

The answer is "yes". Inevitably. We are responsible. We have chosen this cavity search and others like it. It is ours. After all, it does not come as a surprise, does it? It is not completely unexpected, not even surprising that the police would bend the constitution from time to time when conducting discretionary policing. We know it. We expect it. Discretionary policing comes at a cost—and we knew it from the beginning. It was embedded in the very idea. Recall the original *Broken Windows* essay. How was it, after all, that the police dealt with the disorderly? "In the words of one officer," James Q. Wilson and George L. Kelling wrote, "'We kick ass.'"[28] As Wilson and Kelling explained elsewhere in *Broken Windows*, the police "rough up" young toughs, and arrest on suspicion.[29] George Kelling adds, fourteen years later:

> Another officer in Chicago described in similar terms how he dealt with gang members who would not follow his orders: "I say please once, I say please twice, and then I knock them on their ass." The officer meant it: although a courteous and generally congenial man, he had grown up in Chicago's public housing developments and was not prepared to stand by and watch gangs terrorize his family, friends, and neighbors.[30]

Order-maintenance policing comes with a heavy price tag. Stephen Mastrofski was one of the first to point this out. Writing as early as 1988, Mastrofski emphasized that "One of the most recent attempts to assess the impact of aggressive order maintenance indicated that it contributed to increased criminal victimization and citizen dissatisfaction, while fear of crime and residents' perceptions of disorder remained unaffected."[31]

---

[28] James Q. Wilson and George L. Kelling, "Broken Windows: The Police and Neighborhood Safety," *Atlantic Monthly*, March 1982, 29B38, at p. 35. For a lengthy discussion of this, *see* Bernard E. Harcourt, *Illusion of Order: The False Promise of Broken Windows Policing* (Cambridge MA: Harvard University Press 2001) at pp. 127 et seq.

[29] Wilson & Kelling 1982:33.

[30] George L. Kelling & Catherine M. Coles, *Fixing Broken Windows: Restoring Order and Reducing Crime in Our Communities* (New York: Free Press 1996), at p. 166.

[31] Stephen D. Mastrofski, "Community Policing as Reform: A Cautionary Tale," 47B67, in *Community Policing: Rhetoric or Reality*, eds. Jack R. Greene and Stephen D. Mastrofski, (New York: Praeger 1988), at p. 54.

In this sense, we choose our forms of disorder. We choose our crimes. By engaging in an aggressive war on drugs through discretionary stop-and-frisk strategies, for instance, we are choosing this sexual battery and others. We can estimate how many there will be. We can predict, using actuarial models, how many C1's will have to drop their pants and spread their cheeks in public. It is a form of collateral damage that we can come to expect. What we want most, of course, is to keep it out of sight and out of mind. To deliberately *not* know it. To *not* see it, *not* hear it, *not* think about it. It is, after all, extremely uncomfortable—especially for the tender-hearted among us. But it is predictable. It is to be expected.

In the end, *we* are responsible for this sexual battery. By setting our law enforcement priorities and opting for robust discretionary policing, we are choosing to have more of these cavity searches. We can effectively regulate these assaults—more so than other forms of deviance such as drug use or gun-carrying over which we have a little less control. Here we can regulate the amount. We can turn on more discretionary policing, and with it, more unconstitutional searches. We calibrate the amount of this crime. It happens under our watch. It is the product of our choice. *We* put our hand up C1's rectum.

The great illusion is that all we are doing is fighting crime. That crime is out there, that we know what it is, that we simply go after it. This is the deepest fallacy. The fact is, we *make* crime. We decide what to criminalize and enforce and in the very process we allow other forms of deviance to flourish. Unconstitutional police searches are, tragically, but one perfect example. We set our scope on the drug war, we let loose discretionary policing, and we inevitably produce a certain amount—a predictable amount—of improper searches, of sexual batteries, of bodily injury. Sure, we can try to limit them with improved training and more civility. But still, we know they are going to happen. We can even predict how many will happen.

Discretionary policing involves a trade-off—a trade-off that we make with full knowledge. The most important thing in the public policy debates, then, is to decide, with eyes wide open and brutal honesty, how much unconstitutionality we are prepared to live with—how many sexual batteries of black suspects we are willing to perform. We get to decide. *You* get to decide. *You* choose *our* crime. So, how many of these cavity searches will you tolerate in order to pursue the goal of getting drugs off our streets? To get guns off our streets? And remember, you can't say "none" *if* you want the police to engage in proactive discretionary policing. You would be lying to yourself.

428

## Bibliography

Bratton, William, with Peter Knobler. 1998. *Turnaround: How America's Top Cop Reversed the Crime Epidemic* (New York: Random House).

Civil Rights Bureau, Office of the New York Attorney General. 1999. *The New York City Police Department's "Stop & Frisk" Practice: A Report from the Office of the Attorney General.*

Gould, Jon B., and Stephen D. Mastrofski. 2004. "Suspect Searches: Assessing Police Behavior," *Criminology & Public Policy __:__*.

Gross, Samuel R. and Katherine Y. Barnes. 2002. "Road Work: Racial Profiling and Drug Interdiction on the Highway," *Michigan Law Review*, 101(3):_____.

Harcourt, Bernard E. 2001. *Illusion of Order: The False Promise of Broken Windows Policing* (Cambridge MA: Harvard University Press).

Harcourt, Bernard E. 2003. "From the Ne'er-do-Well to the Criminal History Category: The Refinement of the Actuarial Model in Criminal Law," *Law and Contemporary Problems*, 66(3):99B151.

Harcourt, Bernard E. 2004. "Rethinking Racial Profiling: A Critique of the Economics, Civil Liberties, and Constitutional Literature and of Criminal Profiling More Generally," *University of Chicago Law Review*, 71: _____ (forthcoming Fall 2004).

Kelling, George L. and Catherine M. Coles. 1996. *Fixing Broken Windows: Restoring Order and Reducing Crime in Our Communities* (New York: Free Press)

Klockars, Carl B. 1983. "The Dirty Harry Problem," 428B438, in *Thinking about Police: Contemporary Readings*, ed. Carl B. Klockars (New York: McGraw-Hill Book Company).

Knowles, John, Nicola Persico, and Petra Todd. 2001. "Racial Bias in Motor Vehicle Searches: Theory and Evidence," *Journal of Political Economy*, 109(1): 203B229.

MacDonald, Heather. 2000. "America's Best Urban Police Force," *City Journal,* Volume 10, No. 3.

Mastrofski, Stephen D. 1988. "Community Policing as Reform: A Cautionary Tale," 47B67, in *Community Policing: Rhetoric or Reality*, eds. Jack R. Greene and Stephen D. Mastrofski, (New York: Praeger)

Mastrofski, Stephen D. and Craig D. Uchida. 1993. "On Dirty Hands and Definitions: A Rejoinder," *Journal of Research in Crime and Delinquency* 30(3):354B368.

New York Police Department. 2000. *NYPD Response to the Draft Report of the United States Commission on Civil Rights—Police Practices and Civil Rights in New York City.*

Sherman, Lawrence W. 1993. "Dirty Hands and Social Science," *Journal of Research in Crime and Delinquency* 30(3):362B364.

Skolnick, Jerome, and Abigail Caplovitz. 2003. "Guns, Drugs and Profiling: Ways to Target Guns and Minimize Racial Profiling," in *Guns, Crime, and Punishment in America,* ed. Bernard E. Harcourt (New York: New York University Press).

United States Commission on Civil Rights. 2000. *Police Practices and Civil Rights in New York City.*

United States Department of Health and Human Services. *Protecting Human Research Subjects: Institutional Review Board Guidebook* (available at http://ohrp.osophs.dhhs.gov/irb/irb_introduction.htm).

Wilson, James Q. and George L. Kelling. 1982. "Broken Windows: The Police and Neighborhood Safety," *Atlantic Monthly*, March 1982, 29B38.

Comments should be addressed to:

Bernard E. Harcourt
University of Chicago Law School
1111 East 60th Street
Chicago, IL 60637
          bharcourt@law.uchicago.edu

**University of Chicago Law School**

**Public Law and Legal Theory Working Paper Series**

1. Cass R. Sunstein and Edna Ullmann-Margalit, Second-Order Decisions (November 1999; *Ethics,* v. 110, no. 1).
2. Joseph Isenbergh, Impeachment and Presidential Immunity from Judicial Process (November 1999; forthcoming *Yale Law and Policy Review* v.18 #1).
3. Cass R. Sunstein, Is the Clean Air Act Unconstitutional? (August 1999; *Michigan Law Review* #3).
4. Elizabeth Garrett, The Law and Economics of "Informed Voter" Ballot Notations (November 1999, *University of Virginia Law Review,* v. 85).
5. David A. Strauss, Do Constitutional Amendments Matter? (November 1999)
6. Cass R. Sunstein, Standing for Animals (November 1999)
7. Cass R. Sunstein, Culture and Government Money: A Guide for the Perplexed (April 2000).
8. Emily Buss, Without Peers? The Blind Spot in the Debate over How to Allocate Educational Control between Parent and State (April 2000).
9. David A. Strauss, Common Law, Common Ground, and Jefferson's Principle (June 2000).
10. Curtis A. Bradley and Jack L. Goldsmith, Treaties, Human Rights, and Conditional Consent (May 2000; *Pennsylvania Law Review* v. 149).
11. Mary Ann Case, Lessons for the Future of Affirmative Action from the Past of the Religion Clauses? (May 2001, *Supreme Court Review,* 2000)
12. Cass R. Sunstein, Social and Economic Rights? Lessons from South Africa (May, 2000).
13. Jill Elaine Hasday, Parenthood Divided: A Legal History of the Bifurcated Law of Parental Relations
14. Elizabeth Garrett, Institutional Lessons from the 2000 Presidential Election (May 2001).
15. Richard A. Epstein, The Allocation of the Commons: Parking and Stopping on the Commons (August 2001).
16. Jack Goldsmith, The Internet and the Legitimacy of Remote Cross-Border Searches (October 2001).
17. Adrian Vermeule, Does Commerce Clause Review Have Perverse Effects? (October 2001).
18. Cass R. Sunstein, Of Artificial Intelligence and Legal Reasoning (November 2001).
19. Elizabeth Garrett, The Future of Campaign Finance Reform Laws in the Courts and in Congress, The William J. Brennan Lecture in Constitutional Law (December 2001).
20. Julie Roin, Taxation without Coordination (March 2002).
21. Geoffrey R. Stone, Above the Law: Research Methods, Ethics, and the Law of Privilege (March 2002; forthcoming *J. Sociological Methodology* 2002).
22. Cass R. Sunstein, Is There a Constitutional Right to Clone? (March 2002).
23. Emily Buss, Parental Rights (May 2002, forthcoming Virginia Law Review).
24. David A. Strauss, Must Like Cases Be Treated Alike? (May 2002).
25. David A. Strauss, The Common Law Genius of the Warren Court (May 2002).

26. Jack Goldsmith and Ryan Goodman, U.S. Civil Litigation and International Terrorism (June 2002).
27. Jack Goldsmith and Cass R. Sunstein, Military Tribunals and Legal Culture: What a Difference Sixty Years Makes (June 2002).
28. Cass R. Sunstein and Adrian Vermeule, Interpretation and Institutions (July 2002).
29. Elizabeth Garrett, Is the Party Over? The Court and the Political Process (August 2002).
30. Cass R. Sunstein, The Rights of Animals: A Very Short Primer (August 2002).
31. Joseph Isenbergh, Activists Vote Twice (November 2002).
32. Julie Roin, Truth in Government: Beyond the Tax Expenditure Budget (November 2002).
33. Cass R. Sunstein, Hazardous Heuristics (November 2002).
34. Cass R. Sunstein, Conformity and Dissent (November 2002).
35. Jill Elaine Hasday, The Principle and Practice of Women's "Full Citizenship": A Case Study of Sex-Segregated Public Education (December 2002).
36. Cass R. Sunstein, Why Does the American Constitution Lack Social and Economic Guarantees? (January 2003).
37. Adrian Vermeule, *Mead* in the Trenches (January 2003).
38. Cass R. Sunstein, Beyond the Precautionary Principle (January 2003).
39. Adrian Vermeule, The Constitutional Law of Congressional Procedure (February 2003).
40. Eric A. Posner and Adrian Vermeule, Transitional Justice as Ordinary Justice (March 2003).
41. Emily Buss, Children's Associational Rights? Why Less Is More (March 2003)
42. Emily Buss, The Speech Enhancing Effect of Internet Regulation (March 2003)
43. Cass R. Sunstein and Richard H. Thaler, Libertarian Paternalism Is Not an Oxymoron (May 2003)
44. Elizabeth Garrett, Legislating *Chevron* (April 2003)
45. Eric A. Posner, Transfer Regulations and Cost-Effectiveness Analysis (April 2003)
46. Mary Ann Case, Developing a Taste for Not Being Discriminated Against (May 2003)
47. Saul Levmore and Kyle Logue, Insuring against Terrorism—and Crime (June 2003)
48. Eric Posner and Adrian Vermeule, Accommodating Emergencies (September 2003)
49. Adrian Vermeule, The Judiciary Is a They, Not an It: Two Fallacies of Interpretive Theory (September 2003)
50. Cass R. Sunstein, Ideological Voting on Federal Courts of Appeals: A Preliminary Investigation (September 2003)
51. Bernard E. Harcourt, Rethinking Racial Profiling: A Critique of the Economics, Civil Liberties, and Constitutional Literature, and of Criminal Profiling More Generally (November 2003)
52. Jenia Iontcheva, Nationalizing International Criminal Law: The International Criminal Court As a Roving Mixed Court (January 2004)
53. Lior Jacob Strahilevitz, The Right to Destroy (January 2004)
54. Adrian Vermeule, Submajority Rules (in Legislatures and Elsewhere) (January 2004)

55. Jide Nzelibe, The Credibility Imperative: The Political Dynamics of Retaliation in the World Trade Organization's Dispute Resolution Mechanism (January 2004)
56. Catharine A. MacKinnon, Directions in Sexual Harassment Law: Afterword (January 2004)
57. Cass R. Sunstein, Black on Brown (February 2004)
58. Elizabeth F. Emens, Monogamy's Law: Compulsory Monogamy and Polyamorous Existence (February 2004)
59. Bernard E. Harcourt, You Are Entering a Gay- and Lesbian-Free Zone: On the Radical Dissents of Justice Scalia and Other (Post-) Queers (February 2004)
60. Adrian Vermeule, Selection Effects in Constitutional Law (March 2004)
61. Derek Jinks and David Sloss, Is the President Bound by the Geneva Conventions? (March 2004)
62. Derek Jinks and Ryan Goodman, How to Influence States: Socialization and International Human Rights Law (March 2004)
63. Eric A. Posner and Alan O. Sykes, Optimal War and *Jus Ad Bellum* (April 2004)
64. Derek Jinks, Protective Parity and the Law of War (April 2004, abstract only)
65. Derek Jinks, The Declining Significance of POW Status (April 2004, abstract only)
66. Bernard E. Harcourt, Unconstitutional Police Searches and Collective Responsibility (June 2004)

APPENDIX VIII:  NIJ:  CONTROLLING POLICE USE OF
FORCE:  THE ROLE OF THE POLICE PSYCHOLOGIST

U.S. Department of Justice
Office of Justice Programs
*National Institute of Justice*

# National Institute of Justice

### *Research in Brief*

Jeremy Travis, Director

October 1994

ACQUISITIONS

# Controlling Police Use of Excessive Force: The Role of the Police Psychologist

### by Ellen M. Scrivner, Ph.D.

Police departments have used the services of psychologists for more than two decades. In the 1980's, police psychology began to be recognized as a distinct field, with psychologists' activities expanding beyond screening job applicants to include a broader range of psychological support services. These included counseling to help officers cope with the unique stresses inherent in police work, training in human relations and general stress management, debriefing after traumatic incidents, and such operational interventions as forensic hypnosis and assistance in negotiations with hostage holders or barricaded persons. Psychological support services for officers who used lethal force were more prevalent than interventions for managing nonlethal, excessive force.

Control of excessive force by police officers is a major challenge for the departments they work for, and it will be increasingly important to the success of community policing initiatives. In two of the most recent examples, excessive force triggered riots in Los Angeles and has been associated with charges of police corruption in New York City. In controlling the problem, the police psychologist can play a key role. This Research in Brief discusses that role and presents ways in which psychologists

### Issues and Findings

*Discussed in the Brief:* The role of police psychologists in identifying officers at risk for excessive force and in preventing its use; the factors that contribute to use of excessive force.

*Key issues:* Police psychologists were surveyed to examine the types of services they provide and how those services are used to counter police use of excessive force. The psychologists were also asked to characterize the types of officers who abuse force and to suggest psychology-based intervention strategies that could help police managers reduce excessive force. Of particular interest is whether police departments should rely almost exclusively on preemployment screening to identify violence-prone candidates.

*Key findings:*

♦ Psychologists' services consist of counseling and evaluation more than training and monitoring of police behavior. Counseling is more likely to be a response to excessive force incidents than a preventive step.

♦ Not one but several distinct profiles were created on the basis of the psychologists' descriptions of officers at risk. The multiplicity of profiles belies the popular stereotype of a few "bad apples" being responsible for most excessive force incidents.

♦ For periodically evaluating incumbents, psychologists supported using methods other than routine psychological tests. They recommend increasing behavioral monitoring and providing better training.

♦ Excessive force needs to be considered a result not only of individual personality traits but also of organizational influences. It is symptomatic of a systemwide problem that implicates administrative policies as well as such human resource components as selection, training, and supervision.

♦ Current screening methods to evaluate police candidates are limited almost exclusively to psychological tests and preemployment clinical interviews.

New screening technologies could enable psychologists to examine such areas as a candidate's decisionmaking and problem-solving abilities and quality of interaction with others. These dimensions are important for resolving situations without using excessive force and are particularly relevant to hiring officers who will work in community policing.

*Target audience:* Police officials and administrators, police psychologists, private security firms' staff, researchers.

can identify officers at risk and create remedial interventions, both at the individual level and the department level, to prevent the use of excessive force.

This article summarizes one of the studies sponsored by the National Institute of Justice as part of a Justice Department effort to identify additional means to control police use of force.[1] The beating of Rodney King that precipitated the Los Angeles riots was the event that prompted the Justice Department initiative. On the basis of input from psychologists working in police departments in the Nation's largest cities, profiles of officers who abuse force were developed. The study also identified the functions of psychologists that had relevance to officers' mental health, specifically their use of excessive force, and presented their recommendations on how best to predict, remedy, and prevent excessive force.

The highly experienced police psychologists interviewed for the study had worked a long time either as salaried employees or as consultants to police departments. One out of four were on police command staffs, a measure of the extent to which police psychological services had become established in law enforcement agencies.

## A shift in police department focus

Attention by researchers and psychologists to police use of nonlethal excessive force represented a change in emphasis. For the first two decades in which police departments employed psychologists (see box, "History of Police Psychological Services"), the use of lethal force was the prime concern. Shootings by police were traumatic incidents that created strong emotional reactions from the officers who did the shooting. The need

to provide psychological support for these officers was clear. Departments gradually recognized the need to provide such services immediately following these incidents.

That same level of concern did not generally carry over to the use of nonlethal excessive force. Officers who used excessive force in making arrests or handling prisoners might be evaluated for their fitness for duty, but psychological support services were not widely available.

Over the past few years, however, greater attention has been given to the issue. Recent research has identified multiple determinants of the use of excessive force, raising questions about whether police departments should rely exclusively on preemployment screening to identify violence-prone candidates and predict future officer performance. In fact, two reports that followed the Rodney King beating—the 1991 report of the Independent Commission To Study the Los Angeles Police Department and the 1992 Los Angeles County Sheriff's Report by James G. Kolt and staff—questioned the effectiveness of existing psychological screening to predict propensity for violence.

## Profiles of violence-prone officers

Psychologists interviewed in the NIJ survey were asked about the characteristics of officers who had been referred to them because of the use of excessive force. Their answers did not support the conventional view that a few "bad apples" are responsible for most excessive force complaints. Rather, their answers were used to construct five distinct profiles of different types of officers, only one of which resembled the "bad apple" characterization.

The data used to create the five profiles constitute human resource information that can be used to shape policy. Not only do the profiles offer an etiology of excessive force and provide insight into its complexity, but they also support the

---

### History of Police Psychological Services

Psychologists began to work with police agencies in the late 1960's, following urban riots in several major cities. The 1968 National Advisory Commission On Civil Disorder Report called for screening methods that would improve the quality of the police officers hired. These recommendations, and the availability of discretionary funds through the Law Enforcement Assistance Administration, encouraged police departments to seek the expertise of psychologists to help them select emotionally stable candidates with personal characteristics suitable for police work.

Thus, one of the first police psychology functions involved preemployment screening of applicants, using psychological tests and assessments, a fairly traditional responsibility for psychologists but one that was new to police. Later, clinical services were requested and, by 1980, psychologists were not only screening applicants but

also counseling officers on how to cope with the stress of policing.

Psychologists brought new sets of skills to police agencies in areas such as critical incident response for police shootings, hostage or barricade negotiation, criminal profiling, and forensic hypnosis. They also offered training in how to manage the personal stress unique to law enforcement.

The use of police psychologists' services continued to grow. By the latter part of the 1980's, according to one survey, a substantial proportion of police agencies were using these services. Psychologists were screening police recruits, counseling officers for job-related stress and personal and family problems, and conducting training in human relations.

Currently, although preemployment screening and counseling still command a major share of police psychologists' attention, several departments have adopted a broader role for psychologists, using their services for consultation on policy and planning.

---

2

notion that excessive force is not just a problem of individuals but may also reflect organizational deficiencies. These profiles are presented in the following sections in ascending order of frequency, along with possible interventions.

**Officers with personality disorders that place them at chronic risk.** These officers have pervasive and enduring personality traits (in contrast to characteristics acquired on the job) that are manifested in antisocial, narcissistic, paranoid, or abusive tendencies. These conditions interfere with judgment and interactions with others, particularly when officers perceive challenges or threats to their authority. Such officers generally lack empathy for others. The number who fit this profile is the smallest of all the high-risk groups.

These characteristics, which tend to persist through life but may be intensified by police work, may not be apparent at preemployment screening. Individuals who exhibit these personality patterns generally do not learn from experience or accept responsibility for their behavior, so they are at greater risk for repeated citizen complaints. As a consequence, they may appear to be the sole source of problems in police departments.

**Officers whose previous job-related experience places them at risk.** Traumatic situations such as justifiable police shootings put some officers at risk for abuse of force, but for reasons totally different from those of the first group. These officers are not unsocialized, egocentric, or violent. In fact, personality factors appear to have less to do with their vulnerability to excessive force than the emotional "baggage" they have accumulated from involvement in previous incidents. Typically, these officers verge on burnout and have become isolated from their squads. Because of their perceived need to conceal symptoms, some time elapses before their problems come to others' attention. When this happens, the event is often an excessive force situation in which the officer has lost control.

In contrast to the chronic at-risk group, officers in this group are amenable to critical-incident debriefing, but to be fully effective, the interventions need to be applied soon after involvement in the incident. Studies recommend training and psychological debriefings, with followup, to minimize the development of symptoms.

**Officers who have problems at early stages in their police careers.** The third group profiled consists of young and inexperienced officers, frequently seen as ' hotdogs," "badge happy," "macho," or generally immature. In contrast to other inexperienced officers, individuals in this group are characterized as highly impressionable and impulsive, with low tolerance for frustration. They nonetheless bring positive attributes to their work and could outgrow these tendencies and learn with experience. Unfortunately, the positive qualities can deteriorate early in their careers if field training officers and first line supervisors do not work to provide them with a full range of responses to patrol encounters.

These inexperienced officers were described as needing strong supervision and highly structured field training, preferably under a field training officer with considerable street experience. Because they are strongly influenced by the police culture, such new recruits are more apt to change their behavior if their mentors show them how to maintain a professional demeanor in their dealings with citizens.

**Officers who develop inappropriate patrol styles.** Individuals who fit this profile combine a dominant command presence with a heavy-handed policing style; they are particularly sensitive to challenge and provocation. They use force to show they are in charge; as their beliefs about how police work is conducted become more rigid, this behavior becomes the norm.

In contrast to the chronic risk group, the behavior of officers in this group is acquired on the job and can be changed.

The longer the patterns continue, however, the more difficult they are to change. As the officers become invested in police power and control, they see little reason to change. Officers in this group are often labeled "dinosaurs" in a changing police world marked by greater accountability to citizens and by adoption of the community policing model.

If these officers do not receive strong supervision and training early in their careers, or if they are detailed to a special unit with minimal supervision, their style may be reinforced. They may perceive that the organization sanctions their behavior. This group would be more responsive to peer program or situation-based interventions in contrast to traditional individual counseling. Making them part of the solution, rather than part of the problem, may be central to changing their behavior.

**Officers with personal problems.** The final risk profile was made up of officers who have experienced serious personal problems, such as separation, divorce, or even perceived loss of status, that destabilized their job functioning. In general, officers with personal problems do not use excessive force, but those who do may have elected police work for all the wrong reasons. In contrast to their peers, they seem to have a more tenuous sense of self-worth and higher levels of anxiety that are well masked. Some may have functioned reasonably well until changes occurred in their personal situation. These changes undermine confidence and make it more difficult to deal with fear, animosity, and emotionally charged patrol situations.

Before they resort to excessive force, these officers usually exhibit patrol behavior that is erratic and that signals the possibility they will lose control in a confrontation. This group, the most frequently seen by psychologists because of excessive-force problems, can be identified by supervisors who have been properly trained to observe and respond to precursors of problem behavior. Their

3

greater numbers should encourage departments to develop early warning systems to help supervisors detect "marker behaviors" signifying that problems are brewing. These officers benefit from individual counseling, but earlier referrals to psychologists can enhance the benefit and prevent their personal situations from spilling over into their jobs.

## Steps in prevention

Because the profiles reveal different reasons for the use of excessive force, police departments need to develop a system of interventions targeted to different groups of officers and at different phases of their careers. The types of profiles also reveal that individual personality characteristics are only one aspect of excessive force and that risk for this behavior is intensified by other experiences. Some of those experiences implicate the organizational practices of the police departments in which the officers work. To the extent this is true, it indicates the need for remedial intervention at the department level as well as the individual level.

**Preemployment screening.** The first step in prevention logically entails not hiring officers who would present a problem. Such deselection is the aim of preemployment screening, a function in which the police psychologist has a role. Of the psychologists who perform preemployment screening, almost all rely on fairly traditional assessment tools—psychological tests and clinical interviews. By contrast, they make limited use of more innovative approaches.

There are sound reasons for using the traditional screening tools. They are valid and reliable measurements, and because they are standardized they can serve as the foundation for data bases useful for further analysis. But because the tools are used to prevent problem behaviors, including use of excessive force, screening has become psychopathology-driven. It is focused on identifying the characteristics of "bad" officers, and as a result, less is

known about the characteristics of "good" officers or about how career experiences mitigate or reinforce these characteristics.

Although information about potential psychopathology is essential to making employment decisions for highly sensitive jobs, this focus has dictated the use of a single model, one that screens out. Reliance on this model makes innovation more difficult. The psychologists interviewed made limited use of other screening approaches—risk assessment models, situational testing, or job simulations—even though these approaches could incorporate a wider range of information for making decisions about the best candidates for police officers.

**Innovation on the horizon.** Opportunities for developing new screening techniques that may be better able to predict violence are arising for reasons that have nothing to do with excessive force. In particular, recent developments related to the Americans With Disabilities Act will change screening procedures. According to EEOC enforcement guidance issued in May 1994, some tests administered before a position is offered are now allowable only *after* a conditional job offer has been made. Tests that might detect mental impairment or disorder are included in this category.

As a result of the ADA-driven changes, "preoffer" testing could undergo substantial change, from which will emerge new screening technologies and analytic methods. These will be used to measure how prospective police officers are likely to interact with people under stressful conditions, make decisions, and solve problems consistent with community policing practices. Automated assessment systems, interactive video testing, assessment centers, job simulations, and role playing exercises all hold promise for meeting these goals.

**Testing incumbent officers.** The psychologists were divided on the use of psychological tests to routinely evaluate incumbent officers for a propensity toward violence. Overall, they supported alternatives to testing because the evidence is still not conclusive that all officers at risk for excessive force could be identified. Although significant strides have been made in methods to predict behavior, psychologists are mindful that human behavior is complex; they are cautious in claiming the accuracy of scientific prediction.

Thus, recommended alternatives to testing need to be considered. At the level of the individual, these alternatives should include increased attention to the availability of counseling and support for it.

---

### Innovations in Excessive Force Training

Some of the psychologists interviewed in the study have developed training models that take into account how people function under adverse conditions and in highly charged situations. Components of these models include:

- Cultural sensitivity and diversity.

- Intervention by fellow officers to stop the use of excessive force.

- The interaction of human perception and threat assessment.

- Decisionmaking under highly charged conditions.

- Psychological methods of situation control.

- Patrol deescalation and defusing techniques that not only teach a tactical response but also respond to the fear stimulated by confrontations.

- Anger management programs that use self-assessment and self-management techniques for providing individual feedback to officers on how variable levels of legitimate anger influence judgment.

- Training in verbal control and communication, including conflict resolution.

4

At the level of the department, alternatives should include increased attention to management strategies to improve training, monitoring, and screening.

## Training

Some of the training described by the psychologists interviewed represents innovative and promising trends. The models are based on principles of adult learning that require class participation, using such techniques as patrol simulations and role playing. They emphasize the development of nonphysical skills as well as physical ones in a community policing environment that assumes frequent interaction between citizens and police. (See box, "Innovations in Excessive Force Training.")

For a majority of the psychologists, the excessive force training they offered was in the context of stress management only. To be sure, stress management training is important; it would be difficult to argue that police work in general, and use-of-force confrontations in particular, are not stressful. However, framing excessive force as a stress issue raises several questions, among them whether the notion is supported by research and whether the approach encourages the perception that stress justifies the use of excessive force.

Stress management training in police departments has not been evaluated systematically, and this raises an additional concern. Beyond anecdotal evidence and limited research data, there is little to indicate how stress consistently affects general police performance. A more viable training focus would reflect departmental policy statements that clarify the tolerance limits for use of force and perceive excessive force as a patrol risk that needs to be managed through a range of specialized skills.

First line supervisors received less instruction on excessive force than did recruits. Yet the psychologists indicated that first line supervisors have greater influence on officers prone to excessive force than other police personnel. Police departments may need to shift the emphasis in supervisor training to one that incorporates larger behavioral issues in order to improve the management of excessive force. This level of supervisory training could also incorporate instruction on early warning behavioral monitoring.

## Monitoring

Monitoring of officers' behavior to detect precursors of excessive force was the function used least often by psychologists. (See box, "What Police Psychologists Do.") Although a majority of the police departments represented in the study sample used some form of monitoring, 58 percent did not include the psychologists in these efforts. Computer tracking of complaints appeared to be the most prevalent form of early warning. However, while computer tracking may provide useful management information, it is not as helpful in changing behavior because the behavior is relatively well developed by the time it is flagged by the computer.

Monitoring of police behavior can serve other purposes in addition to early identification and intervention. It can involve a sustained level of contact between supervisor and officer to reinforce policy and training on excessive force. Because it involves supervisors, monitoring can provide valuable information to help police managers evaluate the effectiveness of their policies. Thus it can change the behavior of the organization overall in addition to that of the individual officer.

The evidence showing the current emphasis on referrals to counseling and on fitness evaluations provides further support for increasing the monitoring function. The need for earlier interventions, which monitoring would provide, parallels the metaphor of "broken windows," which in a community are signs of deterioration viewed as forerunners of more serious criminal problems. The metaphor could be applied to human behavior within the police organization. Police managers should pay attention to the signals of deterioration in officer behavior, the behavioral equivalent of "broken windows," *before* it results in excessive force complaints.

---

### What Police Psychologists Do

The survey on which this study is based revealed that psychologists' functions in police agencies fell into the categories of evaluation (preemployment screening and fitness for duty), monitoring of police behavior, training, and counseling. The breakdown is as follows:

- 77 percent provided counseling services.

- 71 percent conducted preemployment screening.

- 54 percent conducted training classes.

- 52 percent conducted evaluations of fitness for duty.

- 42 percent monitored officers' behavior.

The psychologists were also asked what types of functions they directed specifically toward the use of excessive force. Counseling, noted above as the intervention used most often, was also used to respond to excessive force more frequently than were other functions:

- 79 percent counseled officers charged with excessive force.

- 51 percent covered excessive force in stress management training.

- 25 percent conducted training specific to excessive force.

- 23 percent monitored behavior for signs of excessive force.

Of particular significance is the limited amount of training specifically directed to excessive force and the low level of monitoring.

---

## Rethinking the role of police psychologists

The study findings indicate the lack of a coherent strategy to systematically integrate the functions performed by psychologists that are relevant to the use of excessive force. Police departments do not appear to use psychologists as a consistent resource; rather, they use them on an "as needed" basis and as protection against liability from charges of negligence. There should be a greater emphasis on involving the police psychologist in a proactive approach to managing human resources. Screening out potential violators, counseling problem officers, and evaluating them for fitness to perform their duties are critical activities, but there is a strong need for ongoing prevention activities that lead to early identification of problems and timely intervention.

Within this context, the prevalence of excessive force needs to be considered as symptomatic of a systemwide problem that implicates administrative policies as well as key elements of the human resource system: selection, training, and supervision. These services should be integrated into a structure that maximizes the impact on the individual officer and on the department overall.

Simply using a new screening test or trying a new training program will only continue the piecemeal approach. It will not achieve the balance needed in the structure between predicting excessive force and managing it. A more balanced approach encourages attending to the front end of the system (selection) while building in safeguards throughout (monitoring, training, and supervision).

Ellen M. Scrivner, Ph.D., was a Visiting Fellow at the National Institute of Justice. The second phase of her research, now under way, consists of case studies that demonstrate how police departments, working with psychologists, have established model programs to improve their capacity to respond to officers at risk for excessive force. The report of this study will be available through NIJ.

## Note

'The full report of the research discussed in this Research in Brief, *The Role of Police Psychology in Controlling Excessive Force*, can be obtained from the National Criminal Justice Reference Service (NCJRS), Box 6000, Rockville, MD 20850 (800–851–3420). Ask for NCJ 146206.

Findings and conclusions of the research reported here are those of the researcher and do not necessarily reflect the official position or policies of the U.S. Department of Justice.

*The National Institute of Justice is a component of the Office of Justice Programs, which also includes the Bureau of Justice Assistance, Bureau of Justice Statistics, Office of Juvenile Justice and Delinquency Prevention, and the Office for Victims of Crime.*

NCJ 150063

**U.S. Department of Justice**
Office of Justice Programs
*National Institute of Justice*

*Washington, D.C. 20531*

Official Business
Penalty for Private Use $300

# APPENDIX IX:  UNDERSTANDING POLICE STRESS RESEARCH

**Journal of Forensic Psychology Practice**

ISSN: 1522-8932 (Print) 1522-9092 (Online) Journal homepage: http://www.tandfonline.com/loi/wfpp20

# Understanding Police Stress Research

M. Kathrine Abdollahi PhD

**To cite this article:** M. Kathrine Abdollahi PhD (2002) Understanding Police Stress Research, Journal of Forensic Psychology Practice, 2:2, 1-24, DOI: 10.1300/J158v02n02_01

**To link to this article:** http://dx.doi.org/10.1300/J158v02n02_01

## AREA REVIEW

# Understanding Police Stress Research

M. Kathrine Abdollahi, PhD

**ABSTRACT.** Stress in policing has been the subject of volumes of literature for several decades. The overwhelming and inconclusive nature of this literature can make the task of conceptualizing this sub-field inherently difficult. A detailed examination of the police stress literature reveals that several different types of stressors and their effects have been explored. The purpose of this article is to compartmentalize this information into four main categories, providing researchers, practitioners, managers, and policy makers with a clear analysis of the police stress literature. These categories include: (1) intra-interpersonal (i.e., personality-related stressors), (2) occupational (i.e., job-related stressors), (3) organizational (i.e., organizationally related stressors), and (4) health consequences of police stress. The article concludes with implications and suggestions for future research. *[Article copies available for a fee from The Haworth Document Delivery Service: 1-800-HAWORTH. E-mail address: <getinfo@haworthpressinc.com> Website: <http://www.HaworthPress.com> © 2002 by The Haworth Press, Inc. All rights reserved.]*

**KEYWORDS.** Police stress, law enforcement [stress], policing, stressors, stress categories

M. Kathrine Abdollahi is affiliated with The Institute of Psychology, Law, and Public Policy, Alliant International University.

Address correspondence to: M. Kathrine Abdollahi, PhD, Institute of Psychology, Law, and Public Policy, Alliant International University, 5130 East Clinton Way, Fresno, CA 93727.

Journal of Forensic Psychology Practice, Vol. 2(2) 2002
http://www.haworthpressinc.com/store/product.asp?sku=J158


*1*

## *INTRODUCTION*

Over the past several decades, the issue of police stress and its effects on officers has received considerable attention in the academic, trade, and popular press. Attempting to navigate oneself through such voluminous literature can be confusing and overwhelming to the uninitiated. Making the task of exploring this sub-field even more difficult is the realization that the literature is often times disciplinary specific, contradictory, and inconclusive. For example, while many researchers have identified police work as one of the most stressful occupations in existence (Anshel, 2000; Beehr, Johnson, and Nieva, 1995; Brown & Campbell, 1994; Dantzer, 1987), others argue that policing is not at all uniquely stressful (Bar-On, Brown, Kirkcaldy, & Thome, 2000; Brown & Campbell, 1990; Brown & Campbell, 1994; Gulle, Tredoux, & Foster, 1998; Hart et al., 1995; Lefkowitz, 1975). What does seem to be clear from the research is that police stress does cause officers to experience an array of psychological and physical ailments (Ayres & Flanagan, 1994) that contribute to high incidents of absenteeism, burnout, turnover, and early retirement (Brown & Campbell, 1990, 1994; Burke, 1993; Anshel, 2000).

A detailed examination of the police stress literature reveals that it can be compartmentalized into essentially four main categories. The first category is called intra-interpersonal stressors and includes the stress generated as a function of the individual's characteristics and/or from his/her interactions with others. Commonly referred to as the "police personality," personal attributes such as pessimism (Scheier, Weintraub, & Carver, 1986), hardiness (Kobassa, 1979), and authoritarianism are all personality characteristics that are hypothesized to be contributing factors to perceived stress. The second category consists of occupational stressors. These inherent job-related hazards include officer-involved shootings, encountering children who have been the subject of violent crimes, and irregular work hours (Storch & Panzarella, 1996; Brown & Campbell, 1994; Violanti & Aron, 1994). The third category includes the organizational stressors generated by the law enforcement agency. Commonly cited organizational stressors include inadequate support from supervisors (Violanti, 1993; Violanti & Aron, 1993). frequent shift changes (Kroes et al., 1974b), and excessive paperwork (Sewell, 1981). Finally, the fourth category addressed within police stress literature is the physical and psychological health consequences of working in the profession (Anshel, 2000; Brown & Campbell, 1994; Kroes et al., 1974a; Kroes et al., 1974b).

The purpose of this endeavor is to provide the reader with a comprehensive, cross-disciplinary overview of the police stress literature by framing it within the confines of the four categories. In addition, it will provide the reader with a detailed description of the initiatives that have been undertaken thus far, mindful of how such research has contributed to and limited our understanding of the topic. By utilizing this categorical approach and by systematically exploring the different areas of the police stress literature, it is hoped that subsequent studies will advance those issues that have remained ambiguous and unresolved. The review will conclude by tentatively exploring the implications for future research and their potential impact on law enforcement training and practice.

## AN OVERVIEW OF THE FOUR TYPES OF POLICE STRESS LITERATURE

Perhaps one of the most important findings in police stress research is that stress in law enforcement is difficult to measure and can not be attributed to just one factor. In essence, police stress is a complex formula that has many different contributory factors. Symonds (1970) was one of the first researchers to recognize that the causes of police stress could be divided into different types which he described as (1) the stress experienced due to the nature of police work (i.e. occupational stressors), and (2) stress which is the result of the nature of the police agency (i.e., organizational stressors). With the addition of intra-interpersonal and health consequences, these four categories serve as landmarks for the researcher's journey through the considerable amount of literature that has amassed over the past several decades on this topic (e.g., Anshel, 2000; Brown & Campbell, 1994; Crank & Caldero, 1991; Gersons, Carlier, Lamberts, & Kolk, 2000; Kroes et al., 1974; Martelli, Waters, & Martelli, 1989; Storch & Panzarella, 1996; Symonds, 1970).

### Intra-Interpersonal Stressors

Some researchers have proposed that there are certain personality factors that make it difficult to perform the essential functions of police work and they are the key contributors to the experience of stress. The objective of this clinically oriented approach has been to determine if certain personality traits predispose an officer to suffer higher levels of stress than others (Burke, 1989; Beutler et al., 1988; Black, 2000;

Brown & Campbell, 1994; Sarchione, Cuttler, Muchinsky, & Nelson-Gray, 1998; Scogin, Schumacher, Gardner, & Chaplin, 1995). These factors have included, but are not limited to, levels of self-confidence and self-esteem (Hewitt & Flett, 1991; Frost, Marten, Lahart, & Rosenblate, 1990), optimism/pessimism (Alkus & Padesky, 1983; Scheier, Weintraub, & Carver, 1986; Violanti & Aron, 1993), extraversion/introversion (Costa, Somerfield, McCrae,1996; Hart et al., 1995; Krohne, 1996), hardiness (Kobassa, 1979; Li-Ping Tang, 1992), cynicism (Abraham, 2000; Chandler & Jones, 1979; Regoli, Poole & Hewitt, 1979; Wilt & Bannon, 1976), authoritarianism (Coleman & Gorman, 1992; Genz & Lester, 1976; Jensen, 1957), and type A personalities (Davidson & Veno, 1980; Fenster & Locke, 1973; Kirmeyer & Diamond, 1985).

Psychological testing conducted for the purpose of screening appropriate candidates suggests that certain personality aspects are preferable in policing (Murrel, 1998; Murrel, Lester, & Arcuri, 1978). Self-confidence and self-esteem are related but different concepts. The extent to which a person approves of or likes him/herself is defined as his/her self-esteem, whereas self-confidence refers to the level of assurance one has in his/her ability to succeed (Anshel, 2000). Lower levels of self-confidence and self-esteem have been associated with greater job satisfaction in police work (Hewitt & Flett, 1991). Officers who are confident in their abilities to carry out tasks effectively and hold themselves at high regard are generally more satisfied with their profession and in turn feel less stressed (Hewitt & Flett, 1991; Frost et al., 1990). Those who tend to have a more positive outlook on life and feel hopeful about their abilities and their future are generally happier individuals (Scheier et al., 1986). Similarly, officers who have a positive sense of self, tend to be more hopeful about the future and therefore are more optimistic and satisfied in their work (Alkus & Padesky, 1983; Burke, 1989; Violanti & Aron, 1993; Scheier et al., 1986).

A related characteristic that has been associated with stress among police officers is introversion versus extroversion. This trait has been linked to social support seeking (Anshel, 2000), which is a concept that is highly linked to job satisfaction (e.g., Crank, Regoli, Hewitt, & Culbertson, 1995; Kaufmann & Beehr, 1986; Cherniss & Egnatios, 1978). Researchers have found that optimists tend to concentrate on the positive aspects of a situation, they tend to remain stable under pressure, whereas pessimists tend to catastrophize events and feel significantly more bothered by anxiety provoking aspects of situations (Anshel, 2000; Scheier et al., 1986; Scheier, & Carver, 1985; Davidson & Veno,

1980). Optimism has also been related to the concept of hardiness in police officers (Lefcourt, 1992; Li-Ping Tang & Hammontree, 1992).
Kobassa (1979) states that hardiness is associated with one's level of
commitment, perceived control, and the degree to which he/she enjoys
being challenged. Hence, officers who are hardy tend to be more optimistic, have higher self-esteem and self-confidence, and experience
less strain in a stressful event (Lefcourt, 1992; Li-Ping Tang &
Hammontree, 1992; Kobassa, 1979).

Cynicism in police officers has also been identified as prevalent and
problematic (Brown & Campbell, 1994; Lotz & Regoli, 1977). Although cynicism is believed to be unsettling with respect to police-community relations, it has also been recognized as a means of coping with
stressful situations (Anshel, 2000; Brown & Campbell, 1994; Byrne,
1961). Related to this concept is the authoritative personality of police
officers that has been well researched in the literature (e.g., Coleman &
Gorman, 1982; Jensen, 1975). The authoritative officer tends to have
poorer relations with the community and expects adherence to his/her
demands (Wilt & Bannon, 1976). He/she may tend to be more of a per-
fectionist (Frost et al., 1990; Hewitt & Flett, 1991) and experience
greater frustration in stressful events (Anshel, 2000; Brown & Campbell, 1994).

The aforementioned characteristics are consistent with the type A
personality. Although empirically inconclusive, this personality type is
believed to be more prevalent in police officers as compared to the general population (Kirmeyer & Diamond, 1985; Davidson & Veno, 1980).
Those who are classified as type A personalities tend to have higher expectations for themselves, be more competitive, strive for perfection,
and have higher demands (Kirmeyer & Diamond, 1985; Davidson &
Veno, 1980; Friedman & Roseman, 1974). Such individuals are more
likely to experience adverse psychological and physical effects of
stressful situations (Cooper & Marshall, 1976).

Despite efforts to discover the "police personality," research in this
area has yielded inconclusive results. Additionally, studies that have attempted to determine the police personality characteristics contain
some methodological errors (Brown & Campbell, 1994). In his review
of the police personality studies, Lefkowitz (1975) stated that many of
the conclusions proposed in this area are based on subjective interpretations of law enforcement "experts," making the generalizablility and
validity of the research questionable. Several other studies have found
no significant differences between police officers and the general population (Davidson, 1979; Gudjonsson & Adlam, 1983; McLaren, Gollan, &

Horwell, 1998). In addition, there has also been arguments regarding the maladaptiveness of these characteristics. Some have argued that although these characteristics may not be desirable attributes, they are not necessarily the cause of adverse occupational defects (Davidson & Veno, 1980; Reiser, 1976).

### Occupational Stressors

Although personality styles are believed to contribute and/or interact with the inherent demands of police work, resulting in poor work performance and/or burnout; the concerns regarding the stress related directly to the tasks performed as a police officer has led to a second area of police stress research (e.g., Anshel, 2000; Brown & Campbell, 1994; Crank & Caldero, 1991; Kroes, 1979; Kroes et al., 1974a; Kroes et al., 1974b; MacLeod & Paton, 1999; Martelli et al., 1989; Storch & Panzarella, 1996; Stephens & Long, 2000; Symonds, 1970). There is little debate that policing is, at times, traumatic and stressful. The occupation of policing involves various tasks that are potentially harmful and life threatening. What has been the subject of debate is whether or not policing is a uniquely strenuous profession. Nonetheless, officers are often exposed to disturbing images and are forced to encounter circumstances that most other occupations can avoid (Stephens & Long, 2000). Hence, the external stressors that may give rise to the stress of a police officer include a variety of entities. Research has identified a series of work related stressors and some have attempted to rank officer reported stressors (e.g., Kroes, et al., 1974; Stephens, Long, & Flett, 1999; Violanti & Aron, 1994; Violanti, 1994). The most commonly identified stressors in the literature have been classified into six primary factors that will be briefly outlined in the following paragraphs. These stress factors include: (a) dealings with the judicial system; (b) public scrutiny and media coverage; (c) officer involved shootings; (d) encountering victims of crime and fatalities (particularly children); (e) community relations; and (f) encountering violent/unpredictable situations.

Dealing with the judicial system has been identified as a source of stress in police work (Ayres & Flanagan, 1994; Kroes, 1974a; Kroes, et al., 1974b; Stratton, 1978). Officers have reported that court proceedings and dealings with judicial system personnel such as prosecutors and defense lawyers are an aggravating component of the job (Ayres & Flanagan, 1994; Kroes, 1985). Some officers feel that the judicial system is too lenient on certain criminals. They feel that their hard work in capturing a suspect and gathering evidence against him/her is wasted when plea bargains are offered or when suspects are released due to technicalities (Ayres & Flanagan, 1994; Kroes et al., 1974b; Stratton, 1978).

The media has elicited public scrutiny that has also been identified as stressful in policing (Violanti, 1994; Kroes, 1985; Kroes et al., 1974a). Many police departments have had to withstand being publicly humiliated by the media. The Los Angeles Police Department and the New York City Police Department are prime examples of police agencies that are all too familiar with public scrutiny. Distorted reports by the media about incidents of police "disappointments" damages the organization's public image (Eisenberg, 1975). These criticisms by the media causes police organizations to receive a bad reputation and subsequently affects the morale of the institution (Davidson & Veno, 1980; Eisenberg, 1975; Kroes & Gould, 1974; Kroes et al., 1974b; Violanti, 1994).

Officer-involved shootings such as killing someone in the line of duty, a fellow officer being killed, or being shot at by a suspect have all been identified as stressful encounters in police work (Violanti, 1994; Gersons, 1989; Coman, 1987; Coman & Evans, 1991; Stratton, Parker & Shibbe, 1984; Sewell, 1983; Kroes & Gould, 1974; Kroes et al., 1974). As a result of these types of incidents, officers may experience posttraumatic symptoms (Gersons et al., 2000) and other personal problems (Alkus & Padesky, 1981). If these traumatic events are not dealt with appropriately, the officer's symptoms may persist leading to poor job performance and severe psychological or physical ailments (Anshel, 2000; Stephens & Long, 2000; Paton & Smith, 1999).

The nature of police work can, at times, require officers to put themselves in dangerous and unpredictable situations. Officers are frequently dispatched to calls where there is little information available about what is occurring on the scene. As a result, officers must be prepared to face danger, assaultive individuals, or even catastrophes (Blau, 1994). The constant threat of being in danger can be strenuous to the officer (Wells, Getman, Blau, 1988). Officers have reported that responding to a scene where things are unpredictable and the potential for danger is unknown, is even more stressful than actually knowing that there is definite danger awaiting, such as an armed robbery in progress (Blau, 1994; Kroes, 1979; Kroes & Gould, 1974; Kroes et al., 1974b; MacLeod & Paton, 1999; Stratton, 1980).

As a part of their job, officers often have to face difficult situations such as encountering victims of crime. Many officers have reported that they feel a great deal of psychological distress from dealing with victims of crime and fatalities, particularly children (Violanti, 1994; Alexander & Wells, 1991; Duckworth & Charlesworth, 1988; Durham, McCammon & Allison, 1985; Kroes, 1985; Kroes et al., 1974b). Studies have found that officers who encounter these types of situations sometimes experience posttraumatic stress symptoms and often have feelings of guilt (Duckworth & Charlesworth, 1988). Studies have also found more extreme symptoms such as severe anxiety and depression experienced by officers who have been exposed to these types of traumatic events (Alexander & Wells, 1991).

When a crime occurs, police officers are usually the first to be called out to the scene, having to face victims of crime and brutality. Officers have revealed in several studies that encountering victims of crime is difficult for them (e.g., Kroes & Gould, 1974; Kroes et al., 1974b; MacLeod & Paton, 1999; Violanti, 1994; Sewell, 1983). Often times, officers are called out to scenes where they are exposed to abused or injured children (Martin, McKean, & Veltkamp, 1986; Violanti, 1994). Many police officers have reported that encountering victims of crime, particularly the vulnerable, is particularly disturbing (Violanti, 1994). In addition to confronting victims of crime, it has also been reported that officers are anguished by encountering victims of accidents and natural disasters (Duckworth & Charlesworth, 1988; Durham, McCammon, & Allison, 1985). Scholars have argued that repeated exposure to such traumatic events causes the officer to question the notion of a "just world" (Young, 1989), causing grave psychological damage. However, others have argued that police officers do not share the same assumption of a "just world," merely by the nature of their occupation which forces them to witness crime, violence, and injustice everyday (Brown & Campbell, 1994).

Another form of police stress identified in the literature is that of community relations (Brown & Campbell, 1994; Kroes, 1985; Kroes & Gould, 1974; Kroes et al., 1974b; Violanti & Aron, 1993; Violanti, 1994; Wilson, 1968). Police officers report that when the community has negative impressions of them (Kroes, 1985), it exasperates poor relations which makes their work difficult. Figley (1999) describes a phenomenon called "Compassion Fatigue" which is the emotional toll that policing takes on the officer (as cited in Brown & Campbell, 1994). He states that the lack of appreciation displayed by the public towards police officers causes them to become cynical towards the community. With the trend towards community policing, this source of stress becomes particularly important as the officer's interaction with the neighborhoods increase (Brown & Campbell, 1994).

### Organizational Stressors

The third category in which police stress literature can be classified is organizational stressors. Although these types of stressors are commonly cited as contributors to police stress (Ayres & Flanagan, 1994; Crank & Caldero, 1991; Evans & Coman, 1993; Kroes, 1979; Kroes et al., 1974b; Storch & Panzarella, 1996; Violanti & Aron, 1994; Violanti & Aron, 1993), exploration of the topic as an instrumental factor remains limited and relatively underdeveloped. This is in part because those observations that do exist tend to be somewhat cursory, as the topic has not frequently been the focus of research but mentioned as a peripheral contributory factor. Nevertheless, the existence of stressors generated by the police agency is irrefutable and thus warrants a closer examination. The following is a discussion of the most commonly cited organizational stressors in policing.

First, shift work is proclaimed in virtually every study as a major stressor. Because policing is around-the-clock, many officers are forced to work early mornings, late evenings, or swing shifts. Although shift work can be viewed as an occupational stressor, having to work extensively long hours and rotating shifts are enforced by the organization (Ayres & Flanagan, 1994; Crank & Caldero, 1991; Sewell, 1981; Stratton, 1978). Some organizations have implemented 4/10 work schedules (4 days a week, 10 hour days) in an effort to alleviate the stress of five day work week schedules.

Second, officers often report inadequate supervision and poor relationship as stressful. Supervisors who are judged to be unskillful, incompetent, and unfair are identified as variables within the organization that give rise to the stress of subordinates. Unfair practices include negative disciplines, lack of due process, unjustified disciplinary actions, unfair performance evaluations, and unfair promotion practices characterized by little opportunity for achieving higher rank (Ayres & Flanagan, 1994; Eisenberg, 1975; Kroes & Gould, 1974; Kroes et al., 1974b).

Third, lack of input into policy and decision-making is a major source of stress for line staff officers. Unable to provide input regarding decisions that directly affect them and discouraged to express their feeling to their supervisors, these officers feel helpless and stressed (Ayres & Flanagan, 1994; Kroes, 1985; Violanti & Aron, 1993).

Lack of recognition and insufficient administrative support is the fourth area of internal stressors. Officers report feeling unappreciated and unrecognized for good work. They feel that they are only confronted when problems arise. If an incident occurs (i.e., a shoot out), line officers believe that they lack the support of administration and are sometimes used as the scapegoats in the interest of public relations (Ayres & Flanagan, 1994; Kroes, 1985; Violanti & Aron, 1994). Excessive paperwork is another cited organizational stressor. Although many officers understand the need for paperwork, they perceive some of the documentation to be excessive, unnecessary, or feel that there is a lack of clerical support in completing them (Ayres & Flanagan, 1994; Crank & Caldero, 1991; Violanti & Aron, 1994).

Insufficient pay and poor resources are also reported as organizational stressors. Officers have disclosed feelings of frustration in regards to wages and benefits. Moreover, lack of proper equipment and shortage of personnel are present within many law enforcement agencies as contributors to stress (Ayres & Flanagan, 1994; Davidson & Veno, 1980).

Role conflict and ambiguity is also faced by many police officers. The department's goals and objectives may be unclear or contradictory causing doubt and fear for line staff officers while on duty (Ayres & Flanagan, 1994; Brown & Campbell, 1994). Officers are frequently forced to play a double role, that of a law enforcer and a social worker. Many of the calls they respond to each day requires them to counsel either victims or family members, while trying to maintain order. Furthermore, the challenge of facing departmental demands may at times be in direct conflict of the job objectives (Ayres & Flanagan, 1994).

The next widely referenced area of organizational stress is isolation and/or boredom. This is characterized by performance of repetitive work, understimulation as a result of not having enough to do on the job, and physical inactivity (Ayres & Flanagan, 1994; Kroes, 1985; Kroes et al., 1974b). Finally, Reiser (1974) reported the internal discipline structure within a police department as very stressful. A police officer often feels that he/she is in double jeopardy in that he/she is not only liable criminally and civilly for a misdeed, but is also very likely to face punishment within the department. It is almost as though he/she is expected to maintain personal and moral standards at a level higher than would be necessitated for the general public (Reiser, 1974).

The aforementioned findings clearly point to some significant aspects of police work that are related to stress experienced on the job, howbeit the argument that it may or may not exceeds that of other professions. Several studies have attempted to rank the stressors prevalent in police work (e.g., Brown & Campbell, 1990; Crank & Caldero, 1991; Kroes et al., 1974; Kroes & Gould, 1974; Violanti & Aron, 1994). Notwithstanding personality factors and specific job tasks, the literature appears to indicate that organizational components within law enforcement are better predictors of burnout. Storch and Panzarella (1996) found that although some officers report discomfort related to the nature of police work, the key stressors in this profession appear to be more related to organizational factors than to the dangerousness of the work or encounters with human misery. Crank and Caldero (1991) sought to measure stress based on self-report, as it was perceived by a group of officers. They categorized the responses into five "domains of content" and found organizational stressors as most frequently cited.

Using an open-ended questionnaire, Sewell (1981) identified 144 events as stressful in the professional life of a police officer. Many of the commonly reported stressors experienced were related to the organization. Court appearances, writing a routine report, making a routine traffic stop, making a routine arrest, work on a holiday, and changing work shifts were identified frequently. Some of the less commonly reported experiences identified as stressful were death of a partner, dismissal, murder committed by a police officer, taking a life in the line of duty, and suicide of an officer who is a close friend (Sewell, 1981).

Kroes et al. (1974b) conducted a series of semi-structured interviews with the entire police force. Four major questions regarding stress were asked. These questions inquired about: (1) what does the policeman consider bothersome about the job, (2) what the policeman thought was bothersome to other policeman regarding the job, (3) from a list of stressors, what the interviewee found bothersome, and (4) what was it like when the interviewee was last uncomfortable in his/her job. The authors reported that the most significant stressors for the policemen appear to involve those situations or circumstances which produce a threat to his/her sense of professionalism and are highly related to the organization (Kroes et al., 1974b).

### Health Consequences of Police Stress

Police stress may lead to adverse consequences such as physical and psychological ailments at various levels. Routine stressors such as shift work, job overload, and management styles, as well as traumatic incidents such as a death of a partner, officer-involved shootings, or suicide of a colleague are all reported by police officers as being psychologically stressful as well as physically taxing (Brown & Campbell, 1990; Brown & Campbell, 1994; Brown et al., 1999; Crank & Caldero, 1991; Kroes et al., 1974b; Sewell, 1981; Storch & Panzarella, 1996; Violanti & Aron, 1993). Among the psychological problems, diagnosable disorders such as depression, anxiety, drug and alcohol abuse (Dietrich & Smith, 1986; Violanti, Marshall, & Howell, 1985), posttraumatic stress disorder (Carlier, Voerman, & Gersons, 2000; Gersons, Carlier, Lamberts, & Kolk, 2000; Reiser & Geiger, 1984; Robinson, Sigman, & Wilson, 1997), suicide (Arrigo & Garsky, 1996; Baker & Baker, 1996; Cantor, Tyman, & Slater, 1995; Violanti, 1995a; Violanti, 1995b), and personal problems such as high rates of divorce (Terry, 1981) have been reported. The physical health problems reported include an array of illnesses (Milham, 1983; Gularnick, 1963) and higher mortality rates (Violanti, Vena, & Marshall, 1986).

Increasing reports of disease, morbidity, and morality of police professionals are present in the literature (Sparrow, Thomas, & Weiss, 1983; Violanti et al., 1986). Gularnick (1963) found police officers to have significantly greater incidence of heart disease, diabetes, and suicide. Milham (1979) indicated that police officers have an increased mortality risk for diseases such as cancers of the colon and liver, diabetes, and heart disease (as cited in Violanti et al., 1986).

Kroes et al., (1974b) compared a group of Cincinnati police officers with a sample of civilians. Over 32 percent of these officers reported digestive disorders, while 24 percent reported headaches. These numbers are considerably higher than the 14 percent reported by the civilian population. Richard and Fell (1975) examined hospital and mental health center records in Tennessee. They found that between 1972 to 1974, police officers were treated with more health problems such as digestive and circulatory disorders than any other occupation. Grenick and Pitchess (1973) found that police officers had high cholesterol levels and were also more overweight than normal. These findings indicate that police officers have higher risk for developing coronary heart disease (Grencik & Pitchess, 1973).

Franke, Collins, and Hinz (1998) compared cardiovascular disease morbidity among a group of Iowa police officers, comparing them with a cohort of Iowa civilians. After taking into account several conventional risk factors such as tobacco use and age, they found that police officers display higher rates of cardiovascular disease than their counterparts (Franke et al., 1998).

Violanti et al. (1986) conducted a longitudinal study (using archival data from a previous study) involving 2,376 police officers in a large metropolitan area. The researchers found that the overall mortality from all causes of death among these officers are comparable to the expected rate in the country (white male general population). However, the rates of death due to cancer was significantly higher than the general population; specifically, cancer of the digestive (esophagus and colon) organs. Mortality from heart diseases typically increased with increasing years of service for the police officer (Violanti et al., 1986).

It is likely that high mortality rates for cancer and greater risk of death from heart disease among police officers is related to police occupational factors, as well as lifestyle habitations (Violanti et al., 1986). The stress of work environment, irregular hours, poor eating habits, and lack of exercise are not unique to the police officer and these factors clearly contribute to ill health (Violanti et al., 1986). Unfortunately, research is sparse in the area of common physical illnesses and policing. This scarcity makes it difficult to assume that the presence of these disorders among police officers is due to their occupation. Thus, generalization in this area should be made with caution. Nonetheless, research indicates that officers may be at risk for diseases that can contribute to higher mortality rates, common physical illnesses, and the like.

Similarly, another notable factor that has been contributed to the higher rates of mortality among law enforcement is that of suicide. Some researchers argue that the stress endured by police officers often leads to unhealthy coping mechanisms, the ultimate being suicide (Arrigo & Garsky, 1996).

Researchers have argued that the inherent stressors present in police work, the lack of support from administration, and the lack of ample family support are all related to suicide among police (Arrigo & Garsky, 1996). Generally, research has been inconclusive regarding suicide in law enforcement. Violanti (1995b) found that although there may not be higher rates of suicide among police, there is a trend towards increase suicide rates during the past two decades. Baker and Baker (1996) also agree that police are dying more rapidly at their own hands than by the hands of criminals.

On the other hand, Cantor et al., (1995) found that there were methodological errors in studies that have examined suicide among police personnel and concluded that there appears to be a general decline rather than increase of suicide rates. Nevertheless, the issue of suicide among law enforcement calls for great concern.

Some researchers have stated that the effects of duty related stressors on police officers leads to Posttraumatic Stress Disorder (Robinson et al., 1997), which has been one of the leading causes of suicide in law enforcement (Carlier et al., 1997). Posttraumatic Stress Disorder (PTSD) is one of the most researched areas in policing (Gersons et al., 2000; Carlier et al., 1997; Carlier et al., 2000; Carlier et al., 1996; Reiser, 1984; Robinson et al., 1997). In "police officer as victim," Reiser (1984) provided a thorough discussion of posttraumatic syndrome among police officers. After having experienced a highly traumatic incident, a police officer may shift into an altered state of consciousness (Reiser, 1984). This shift can affect all five senses, resulting in tunnel vision, distortion in hearing, hyperawareness, and the individual may dissociate from his/her environment. If these symptoms continue without intervention, the officer may develop posttraumatic stress disorder (Sims & Sims, 1998). Reiser (1984) suggests that police agencies need to understand that officers who have been involved in a traumatic incident will be in crisis. They will be emotionally unstable and depending on the nature of the intervention, they will either improve or deteriorate (Reese, 1982). Thus, police departments need to remain sensitive and treat the traumatized officer as a victim, not a suspect (Reiser, 1984).

Another study examined internal and external risk factors for PTSD symptoms in 262 traumatized police officers at the three- and twelve-month trauma (Carlier et al., 1997). They found that "introversion, difficulty in expressing feelings, emotional exhaustion at time of trauma, insufficient time allowed by employer for coming to terms with trauma, dissatisfaction with organizational support, and insecure job future" (Carlier et al., 1997, p. 498) to be present at this stage. At the twelve-month-posttrauma stage, Carlier et al. (1997) state that "post-traumatic stress symptoms were further predicted by lack of hobbies, acute hyperarousal, subsequent traumatic events, job dissatisfaction, brooding over work, and lack of social interaction support in the private sphere" (p. 498). Virtually all of the studies suggested that intervention techniques offered by the department can greatly reduce the duration and intensity of trauma (Carlier et al., 2000; Gersons et al., 2000).

The misuse of substances, particularly alcohol with police officers, has been extensively examined in the literature as well (Dietrich & Smith, 1986; Violanti et al., 1985; Unkovic & Brown, 1978). These forms of unhealthy coping mechanisms appear to be quite prevalent in law enforcement (Violanti et al., 1985; Unkovic & Brown, 1978). Research has also noted that drinking is not only practiced by off-duty law enforcement personnel, but many officers admit to using alcohol while on-duty (Van Raalte, 1979).

Dietrich and Smith (1986) reported a thorough investigation of the literature pertaining to nonmedical drug use including alcohol among police officers. They found that officers appear to be influenced by a number of factors: the police culture, occupational deviance, occupational demands of the police officer, and coping functions (Dietrich & Smith, 1986). Work cultures such as the police organization appear to foster expectations of drinking, applaud it, and even belie its existence (Fine, Arkabas, & Bellinger, 1983; Dietrich & Smith, 1986). Also, due to the traditionally male-oriented environment of police settings, drinking is excepted for socializing and stress reduction (Babin, 1980; Dietrich & Smith, 1986). Drinking with colleagues is a phenomenon that symbolizes loyalty, trustworthiness, masculinity, and often reinforces the bond members share (Dietrich & Smith, 1986; Van Raalte, 1979). Drinking is viewed as an opportunity to engage in occupational deviance; in other words, a chance to violate rules. This phenomenon is a result of workplace experiences and is often reinforced by peer groups (Barker, 1978; Dietrich & Smith, 1986). Additionally, occupational demands of police work have been identified to relate to alcohol use (Dietrich & Smith, 1986; Van Raalte, 1979; Violanti et al., 1985). Officers often indicate that drinking is regarded as a socially acceptable coping alternative (Violanti et al., 1985; Dietrich & Smith. 1985). Researchers have noted that as officers experience more stress on the job, their tendency to use alcohol as a coping method increases (Violanti et al., 1985).

Van Raalte (1979) conducted an informal survey involving 30 sworn police officers. He found that the evening shift has the highest rate of alcohol consumption, with reasons for drinking varying from social grounds to coping with stress. The results also indicate that many officers drink while on duty. Van Raalte (1979) also gave examples of individuals who have experienced serious repercussions as a result of drinking.

Violanti et al. (1985) state that alcohol consumption among police is underestimated. These researchers sought to discover the relationship between police job demands, stress, coping, and alcohol use, and their impact on the police officer. They measured psychological stress, police job demands (emotional dissonance), and police coping responses (cynicism) of 500 officers. The researchers found that stress has a strong effect on the use of alcohol, while the effects of emotional dissonance and cynicism were small (Violanti et al., 1985).

Relatedly, stress has also been linked to various personal problems within policing. Although research has been primarily inconclusive about divorce rates among law enforcement (Kroes et al., 1974a; Reiser, 1973), many agree that the demands of the job can be taxing on ones family life (Ayres & Flanagan, 1994; Brown & Campbell, 1994;

Violanti, 1981). Studies have indicated that marital problems among police officer's families may be attributed to shift-work and the psychological demands of the job that result in undesirable attributes that contribute to marital discord (Arrigo & Garsky, 1996; Brown & Campbell, 1994).

When dealing with a complex organization such as a law enforcement agency, where multiple factors contribute to the employee's experiences, it is difficult to locate the exact antecedents of stress. In examining the relationship between job satisfaction and psychological burnout, Wolpin, Burke, and Greenglass (1991) agree that the recognition of the specific stressors is the most important factor in successfully dealing with job burnout. As indicated in the above review, this has been a challenging task for scholars of police stress.

## CONCLUSIONS, IMPLICATIONS, AND SUGGESTIONS FOR FUTURE RESEARCH

Police stress has been a well-researched topic for several decades. Researchers have identified stressors relating to intra-interpersonal, occupational, and organizational issues. Furthermore, physical and psychological health consequences of police stress have also been explored. The vast amount of police stress research available is somewhat overwhelming. The purpose of this review was to present the information in a simplistic, precise, and comprehensible manner, mindful of the limitations that exists in this area.

Upon closer examination of this literature, several limitations are revealed. For example, stressors of law enforcement are not clearly defined. Although studies have continuously examined the different "types" of police stressors, most have relied on expert opinion to draw conclusions and/or contain methodological errors within their research, thereby failing to accurately define stressors. Another limitation is that although organizational stressors have been shown to have greater negative health consequences for officers, occupational hazards continue to be the focus of most police stress research. Finally, since its initiation over thirty years ago, police stress research has been conducted in the same manner. It has been exploratory, disciplinary specific, investigative in nature, and lacking a theoretical foundation.

Police stress research has been unpersuasive as to the existence of the unique and adverse police personality characteristics. Likewise, the notion that the nature of police work is inherently stressful and causes psychological and/or physiological damage to police officers is unsettled. Most importantly, investigations regarding organizational factors as contributory elements of police stress have remained unprogressive. As a result of insufficient clarification, research has been limited in moving forward in this area.

At the level of fundamental inquiry, there is a need for future research that seeks to clarify the different types of stress present in law enforcement in a concisely thorough and empirically sound manner. Rather than continually conducting exploratory studies that simply enumerate stressors of law enforcement, research in this area should be theoretically driven. Armed with a theoretical foundation, researchers can better identify strains of policing and offer explanations as to the origins and health consequences of stressors. Only then can stressors be clearly categorized and measured. Furthermore, the undeniable prevalence of organizational stressors within law enforcement also calls for closer examination. Future research must focus on identifying specific organizational factors that may be at the root of police stress. Once this identification is clear, the impact of such stressors needs to be measured. If indeed organizational stressors are the greatest contributors to police stress, a search for remedial plans is warranted.

As Brown and Campbell (1994) have suggested, future efforts should consider the following separate issues:

> (1) Understanding the problem. The questions involved must be teased apart in order to identify the extent of the problem and the key issues involved. (2) Discovering cause and effect. To do this it is necessary to collect and evaluate empirical evidence. (3) Implementing solutions. A full understanding of the issues involved and of the causes and effects of stress will make it possible to decide what mix of primary (preventive), secondary (removal of adverse conditions) and tertiary (damage limitation) remedial measures should be taken in order to tackle the problem. (p. 7)

Adopting this strategy will enable researchers to better understand the police stress phenomenon by shedding much needed light on the origins, antecedents, and effects of this multifaceted topic.

Moreover, as physical and mental health impairments compromise optimal work performance, recognizing and comprehending the manifestation of these conditions as stress-related may be especially important in a career such as law enforcement. In addition, the fact that police officers are charged with a unique task (i.e., serving and protecting the public) and are entrusted with considerable power and authority to do so, attending to their physiological and psychological well-being should be of paramount importance for practitioners, managers, and policy makers. In the final analysis, this level of understanding is vital if the relationship between stress and law enforcement is to be meaningfully addressed and abated.

## REFERENCES

Abraham, R. (2000). Organizational cynicism: Bases and consequences. *Genetic, Social, and General Psychology Monographs, 126* (3), 126-141.

Alexander, D. A. & Wells, A. (1991). Reactions of police officers to body-handling after a major disaster: A before and after comparison. *British Journal of Psychiatry, 159,* 547-555.

Alkus, S. & Padesky, C. (1983). Special problems of police officers: Stress related issues and interventions. *Counseling Psychologist, 11* (2), 55-64.

Anshel, M. H. (2000). A conceptual model and implications for coping with stressful events in police work. *Criminal Justice and Behavior, 27* (3), 375-400.

Anshel, M. H. (2000). A conceptual model and implications for coping with stressful events in police work. *Criminal Justice and Behavior, 27* (3), 375-400.

Ayres, R., & Flanagan, G. (1994). *Preventing law enforcement stress: The organization's role.* Washington, DC: U.S. Department of Justice.

Babin, M. (1980). Perceiving self-destructive responses to stress: Suicide and Alcoholism. *Royal Canadian Mounted Police, 42* (7, 8), 20-22.

Baker, T. E., & Baker, J. P. (1996). Preventing police suicide. *FBI Law Enforcement Bulletin, 65,* 24-27.

Barker, T. (1978). An empirical study of police deviance other than corruption. *Journal of Police Science & Administration, 6* (3), 264-272.

Bar-On, R., Brown, J. M., Kirkcaldy, B.D., & Thome, E. P. (2000). Emotional expression and implications for occupational stress; an application of the Emotional Quotient Inventory (EQ-i). *Personality and Individual Differences, 28,* 1107-1118.

Bartol, C. R. (1991). Predictive validation of the MMPI for small-town police officers who fail. *Professional Psychology: Research and Practice, 22* (2), 127-132.

Beehr, T. A., Johnson, L. B., & Nieva, R. (1995). Occupational stress: Coping of police and their spouses. *Journal of Organizational Behavior, 16* (3), 3-25.

Beutler, L. E., Nussbaum, P. D., & Meredith, K. E. (1988). Changing personality patterns of police officers. *Professional Psychology: Research and Practice, 19* (5), 503-507.

Black, J. (2000). Personality testing and police selection: Utility of the "big five." *New Zealand Journal of Psychology, 29* (1), 2-9.

Blau, T. H. (1994). *Psychological services for law enforcement.* New York: John Wiley & Sons, Inc.

Brown, J. M. & Campbell, E. A. (1994). *Stress and policing.* West Sussex: Wiley.

Brown, J. M. & Campbell, E. A. (1990). Sources of occupational stress in the police. *Work and Stress, 4* (4), 305-318.

Brown J., Fielding, J., Grover, J. (1999). Distinguishing traumatic, vicarious and routine operational stressor exposure and attendant adverse consequnces in a sample of police officers. *Work and Stress, 13* (4), 312-325.

Byrne, D. (1961). The R-S Scale: Rationale, reliability and validity. *Journal of Personality, 29* (3), 334-349.

Burke, R. J. (1993). Work-family stress, conflict, coping, and burnout in police officers. *Stress Medicine, 9* (3), 171-180.

Burke, R. J. (1989). Career stages, satisfaction, and well-being among police officers. *Psychological Report, 65,* 3-12.

Cantor, H. C., Tyman, R., & Slater, P. J. (1995). A historical survey of police suicide in Queensland, Australia, 1843-1992. *Suicide and Life-Threatening Behavior, 25* (4), 499-507.

Carlier, I. V., Lamberts, R. D., Gersons, B. P. (1997). Risk factors for posttraumatic stress symptomatology in police officers: A prospective analysis. *Journal of Nervous and Mental Disease, 185* (8), 498-506.

Carlier, I. V. E., Voerman, A. E., & Gersons, B. P. R. (2000). The influence of occupational debriefing on post-traumatized police officers. *British Journal of Medical Psychology, 73,* 87-98.

Chandler, E. V. & Jones, C. S. (1979). Cynicism–A inevitability of police work. *Journal of Police Science and Administration, 7* (1), 65-68.

Cherniss, C., & Egnatios, E. (1978). Participation in decision-making by staff in community mental health programs. *American Journal of Community Psychology, 6,* 171-190.

Coleman, A. M. & Gorman, L. P. (1992). Conservatism, dogmatism and authoritarianism. *Sociology, 16,* 1-11.

Coman, G. J. & Evans, B. J. (1991). Stressors facing Australian police in the 1990's. *Police Studies, 14,* 153-165.

Cooper, C. L. & Marshall, J. (1976). Occupational sources of stress: A review of the literature relating to coronary heart disease and mental ill health. *Journal of Occupational Psychology, 49* (1), 22-18.

Costa, P. T., Somerfield, M. R., & McCrae, R. Personality and Coping: A reconceptualization. M. Zeidner, N. S. Endler (Eds.). *Handbook of coping: Theory, research, application* (pp. 44-61). New York: NY: John Wiley & Sons.

Costello, R. M. & Schoenfeld, L. S. (1981). Time-related effects on MMPI profiles of police academy recruits. *Journal of Clinical Psychology, 37* (3), 518-522.

Crank, J. P., Regoli, R., Hewitt, J. D., and Culbertson, R. G. (1995). Institutional and organizational antecedents of role stress, work alienation, and anomie among police executives. *Criminal Justice and Behavior, 22* (2), 152-171.

Crank, J. P., & Caldero, M. (1991). The production of occupational stress in medium-sized police agencies: A survey of line officers in eight municipal departments. *Journal of Criminal Justice, 19,* 339-349.

Davidson, M. J. & Veno, A. (1980). Stress and policeman, In C. L. Cooper and J. Marshall (Eds.), *White collar and professional stress.* Chichester, UK: Wiley.

Danzter, M. L. (1987). Police, related stress: A critique for future research. *Journal of Police Criminal Psychology, 3,* 43-48.

T. A. Garrison



Dietrich, J., & Smith, J. (1986). The nonmedical use of drugs including alcohol among police personnel: A critical literature review. *Journal of Police Science and Administration, 14* (4), 300-306.

Duchworth, D. & Charlesworth, A. (1988). The human side of disaster. *Policing, 4,* 194-210.

Durham, T. W., McCammon, S. L., & Allison, F. J. (1985). The psychological impact of disaster on rescue personnel. *Annals of Emergency Medicine, 14* (7), 664-668.

Eisenberg, T. (1975). Labour management relations and psychological stress: View from the bottom. *The Police Chief, 42,* 54-58.

Evans, B. J. & Coman, G. J. (1993). General versus specific measure of occupational stress: An Australian police survey. *Stress Medicine, 9,* 11-20.

Fenster, C. A. & Locke, B. (1973). Neuroticism among policemen: An examination of police personality. *Journal of Applied Psychology, 57* (3), 358-359.

Fine, M, Akabas, S. H., & Bellinger, S. (1982). Culture of drinking: A workplace perspective. *Social Work, 27* (5), 436-440.

Franke, W. D., Collins, S. A., & Hinz, P. N. (1998). Cardiovascular disease morbidity in an Iowa law enforcement cohort, compared with the general Iowa population. *Journal of Occupational and Environmental Medicine, 40* (5), 441-444.

Friedman & Rosenman, R. H. (1974). *Type A behavior and your heart.* New York: Alfred A. Knopf.

Fricke, A. S., & Lester, D. (1999). Suicide among German federal and state police officers. *Psychological Reports, 84,* 157-166.

Frost, R. O., Marten, P., Lahart, C., & Rosenblate, R. (1990). The dimensions of perfectionism. *Cognitive Therapy and Research, 14* (5), 449-468.

Genz, J. L. & Lester, D. (1976). Authoritarianism in policemen as a function of experience. *Journal of Police Science and Administration, 4* (1), 9-13.

Gersons, B. D. (1989). Patterns of PTSD among police officers following shooting incidents: A two-dimensional model and treatment implications. *Journal of Traumatic Stress, 2* (3), 247-257.

Gersons, B. P. R., Carlier, I. V. E., Lamberts, R. D., & Kok, B. A. (2000). Randomized clinical trial of brief eclectic psychotherapy for police officers with posttraumatic stress disorder. *Journal of Traumatic Stress, 13* (2), 333-347.

Graf, F. A. (1986). The relationship between social support and occupational stress among police officers. *Journal of Police Science and Administration, 14,* 178-186.

Graham, J. R. (1993). *MMPI-2: Assessing personality and psychopathology (2$^{nd}$ ed.).* New York: Oxford University Press.

Grencik, J. M. & Pitchess, P. J. The physiological fitness of deputies assigned to patrol function and its relationship to the formulation of entrance standards for law enforcement officers. Law Enforcement Alliance of America (LEAA) Final Report, 1973. As cited in Ayres and Flanagan (1994).

Gudjonsson, G. H. & Adlam, R. (1983). Personality patterns of British police officers. *Personality and Individual Difference, 4* (5), 507-512.

Gularnick, L. (1963). Morality by occupation and cause of death among men 20-64 years of age: United States 1950. *Vital Statistics Special Reports, 53* (3). Bethesda, MD: U.S. Department of Health, Education and Welfare (USDHEW).

Gulle, G., Tredoux, C., & Foster, D. (1998). Inherent and organizational stress in the SAPS: An empirical survey in the Western Cape. *South African Journal of Psychology, 28* (13), 129-134.

Hargrave, G. E. & Hiatt, D. (1989). Use of the California Psychological Inventory in law enforcement officer selection. *Journal of Personality Assessment, 53* (2), 267-277.

Hart, P. M., Wearing, A. J., & Headley, B. (1995). Police stress and well-being: Integrating personality, coping and daily work experiences. *Journal of Occupational and Organizational Psychology, 68* (2), 133-156.

Hewitt, P. L. & Flett, G. L. (1991). Perfectionism in the self and social contexts: Conceptualization, assessment and association with psychopathology. *Personality and Social Psychology, 60* (3), 456-470.

Hogan, R., Hogan, J., Roberts, B. W. (1996). Personality measurement and employment decisions. *American Psychologist, 51* (5), 469-477.

Inwald, R. & Shusman, E. (1984). The IPI and MMPI as predictors of academy performance for police recruits. *Journal of Police Science and Administration, 12* (1), 1-11.

Jensen, A. R. (1957). Authoritarian attitudes and personality maladjustment. *Journal of Abnormal and Social Psychology, 54,* 303-311.

Kaufmann, G. M., & Beehr, T. A. (1986). Interactions between job stressors and social support: Some counterintuitive results. *Journal of Applied Psychology, 71* (3), 522-526.

Kroes, W. H. (1985). *Society's victim: The police officer.* Springfield, IL: Charles C. Thomas.

Kroes, W. H., & Gould, S. (1979). Stress in policemen. *Police Stress, 1,* 9-10.

Kroes, W. H., & Gould, S. (1974). Job stress in policemen: An empirical study. *Police Stress, 1,* 9-10.

Kroes, W. H., Hurrell, J. J., Margolis, B. L. (1974a). Job stress in police administrators. *Journal of Police Science and Administration, 2* (4), 381-387.

Kroes, W. H., Margolis, B. L., Hurrell, J. J. (1974b). Job stress in policemen. *Journal of Police Science and Administration, 2* (2), 145-155.

Kirmeyer, S. & Diamond, A. (1985). Coping by police officers: A study of role stress and type A and type B behavior patterns. *Journal of Occupational Behavior, 6* (3), 183-195.

Kobassa, S. C. (1979). Stressful life events, personality and health: An inquiry into hardiness. *Journal of Personality and Social Psychology, 37,* 1-11.

Krohne, H. W. (1996). Individual differences in coping. In M. Zeidner & N. S. Endler (Eds.), *Handbook of coping,* pp. 381-409. New York: John Wiley.

Lefcourt, H. M. (1992). Perceived control, personal effectiveness, and emotional states. In B. N. Carpeter (Ed.). *Personal coping: Theory, research, and application.* (pp. 111-131)/Westport, CT: Praeger.

Lefkowitz, J. (1975). Psychological attributes of policemen: A review of research and opinion. *Journal of Social Issues, 31* (1), 3-26.

Li-Ping Tang, T. & Hammontree, M. L. (1992). The effects of hardiness, police stress, and life stress on police officer's illness and absenteeism. *Public Personnel Management, 21* (4), 493-510.

Lotz, R. & Regoli, R. M. (1977). Police cynicism and professionalism. *Human Relations, 30* (2), 175-186.

MacLeod, M. D. & Paton, D. (1999). Police officers and violent crime: Social psychological perspectives on impact and recovery. In J. M. Violanti and D. Paton (Eds.),

*Police trauma, psychological aftermath of civilian combat.* pp. 25-36. Springfield, IL: Charles C Thomas.

Martelli, T. A., Waters, I. K., & Martelli, J. (1989). The Police Stress Survey: Reliability and relation to job satisfaction and organizational commitment. *Psychological Reports, 64,* 266-273.

Martin, C. A., McKean, H. E., & Veltkamp, L J. (1986). Post-traumatic stress disorder in police and working with victims: A pilot study. *Journal of Police Science and Administration, 14* (2), 98-101.

McLaren, S., Gollan, W., & Horwell, C. (1998). Perceived stress as a function of occupation. *Psychological Reports, 82,* 794.

Milham, S. (1983). *Occupational mortality in Washington state 1950-1959.* Department of Health and Human Services Publication No. 83-116. Washington, DC: U.S. Government Printing Office.

Mufson, D. W. & Mufson, M. A. (1998). Predicting police officer performance using the Inwald Personality Inventory: An illustration from Appalachia. *Professional Psychology: Research and Practice, 29* (1), 59-62.

Murrell, M. E., Lester, D., & Arcuri, A. F. (1978). Is the "police personality" unique to police officers? *Psychological Reports, 43* (1), 298.

Paton, D. & Smith, L. (1999). Assessment, conceptual and methodological issues in researching traumatic stress in police officers. In J. M. Violanti and D. Paton (Eds.), *Police trauma, psychological aftermath of civilian combat.* pp. 13-21. Springfield, IL: Charles C Thomas.

Reese, J. T. (1982). Life in the high-speed lane: Managing police burnout. *The Police Chief, June,* 49-53.

Regoli, R. M. Poole, E. C., & Hewitt, J. (1979). Exploring the empirical relationship between police cynicism and work alienation. *Journal of Police Science and Administration, 7,* 37-51.

Reiser, M. (1974). Some organizational stresses on policemen. *Journal of Police Science and Administration, 2* (2), 156-159.

Reiser, M. (1976). Distress and adaptation in police work. *The Police Chief, 43,* 24-27.

Reiser, M., & Geiger, S. P. (1984). Police officer as victim. *Professional Psychology: Research and Practice, 15* (3), 315-323.

Reese, & J. M. Horn (Eds.). *Police psychology: Operational Assistance* (pp. 423-433). Washington, D. C.: U. S. Government Printing Office.

Rhead, C. Abrams, A., Trosman, H., & Margolis, P. (1968). The psychological assessment of police candidates. *American Journal of Psychiatry, 124* (11), 1575-1580.

Richard, W. C., & Fell, R. D. (1975). Health factors in police job stress. In W. H. Kroes & Hurrel, J. J. (Eds.), *Job stress and police officer: Identifying stress reduction techniques* (pp. 73-84). Washington, D.C.: U.S. Government Printing Office.

Robinson, H. M., Sigman, M. R., & Wilson, J. P. (1997). Duty-related stressors and PTSD symptoms in suburban police officers. *Psychological Reports, 81* (3), 835-845.

Sarchione, C. D., Cuttler, M. J., Muchinsky, P. M., & Nelson-Gray, R. O. (1998). *Journal of Applied Psychology, 83* (6), 904-912.

Scheier, M. F., Weintraub, J. K., & Carver, C. S. (1986). Coping with stress: Divergent strategies of optimists and pessimists. *Journal of Personality and Social Psychology, 51* (6), 1257-1264.

Scogin, F., Schumacher, J., Gardner, J., & Chaplin, W. (1995). Predictive validity of psychological testing in law enforcement setting. *Professional Psychology, Research and Practice, 26* (1), 68-71.

Sewell, J. D. (1983). The development of a critical life events scale for law enforcement. *Journal of Police Science and Administration, 11,* 109-116.

Sewell, J. D. (1981). Police stress. *FBI Law Enforcement Bulletin, 50* (4), 7-11.

Sims, A. C., Sims, D. (1998). The phenomenology of post-traumatic stress disorder: A symptomatic study of 70 victims of psychological trauma. *Psychopathology, 31* (2), 96-112.

Sparrow, D., Thomas, H. E., & Weiss, S. T. (1983). Coronary heart disease in police officers participating in the normative aging study. *American Journal of Epidemiology, 118* (4), 508-513.

Stephens, C. & Long, N. (2000). Communication with work supervisors and peers as a buffer of work-related traumatic stress. *Journal of Organizational Behavior, 21,* 407-424.

Stephens, C., Long, N., & Flett, R. (1999). Vulnerability to psychological disorder: Previous trauma in police recruits. In J. M. Violanti and D. Paton (Eds.), *Police trauma, psychological aftermath of civilian combat.* pp. 65-77. Springfield, IL: Charles C. Thomas.

Stratton, J. G. (1980). Psychological services for police. *Journal of Police Science and Administration, 3,* 31-39.

Stratton, J. G. (1978). Police stress: An overview. *The Police Chief, 45* (4). 58-62.

Stratton, J. G., Parker, D. A. & Snibbe, J. R. (1984). Post-traumatic stress: Study of police officers involved in shootings. *Psychological Reports, 55* (1), 127-131.

Storch, J. E., & Panzarella, R. (1996). Police stress: state-trait anxiety in relation to occupational and personal stressors. *Journal of Criminal Justice, 24* (2), 99-107.

Symonds, M. (1970). Emotional hazards of police work. *American Journal of Psychoanalysis, 30* (2), 155-160.

Scheier, M. F. & Carver, C. S. (1985). Optimism, coping, and health: Assessment and implications of generalized outcome expectancies. *Health Psychology, 4,* 219-247.

Scheier, M. G., Weintraub, J. D., & Carver, C. S. (1986). Coping with stress: Divergent strategies of optimists and pessimists. *Journal of Personality and Social Psychology, 51* (6), 1257-1264.

Terry, W. C. (1981). Police stress: The empirical evidence. *Journal of Police Science and Administration, 9,* 61-72.

Unkovic, C. M., & Brown, W. R. (1978). The drunken cop. *The Police Chief, April 1978,* 18-20.

Van Raalte, R. C. (1979). Alcohol as a problem among officers. *The Police Chief, Feb,* 38-39.

Violanti, J. M. (1995a). The mystery within understanding police suicide. *FBI Law Enforcement Bulletin, 4,* 19-23.

Violanti, J. M. (1995b). Trends in police suicide. *Psychological Reports, 77,* 688-690.

Violanti, J. M., Aron, F. (1993). Sources of police stressors, job attitudes, and psychological distress. *Psychological Reports, 72,* 899-904.

Violanti, J. M., & Aron, F. (1994). Ranking police stressors. *Psychological Reports, 75,* 824-826.

Violanti, J. M., Marshall, J. R., & Howe, B. (1985). Stress, coping, and alcohol use: The police connection. *Journal of Police Science and Administration, 31* (2), 106-110.

Violanti, J. M., Vena, J. E., & Marshall, J. R. (1986). Disease risk and morality among police officers: New evidence and contributing factors. *Journal of Police Science and Administration, 14* (1), 17-23.

Weiss, W. U., Serafino, G., Serafino, A., Willson, W., & Knoll, S. (1998). Use of the MMPI-2 to predict the employment continuation and performance ratings of recently hired police officers. *Journal of Police and Criminal Psychology, 13* (1), 40-44.

Wells, C., Getman, R., & Blau, T. (1988). Critical incident procedures: The crisis management of traumatic incidents. *The Police Chief, 55* (1), 70-74.

Wilson, J. Q. (1968). *Varieties of police behavior: The management of law and order in eight communities.* Cambridge: Harvard.

Wilt, G. M. & Bannon (1976). Cynicism or realism: A critique of Niederhoffer's research into police attitudes. *Journal of Police Science and Administration, 4* (1), 38-45.

Wolpin, J., Burke, R. J., Greenglass, E. R. (1991). Is job satisfaction an antecedent or a consequence of psychological burnout? *Human Relations, 44* (2), 193-209.

RECEIVED: 12/05/01
REVISED: 12/05/01
ACCEPTED: 12/05/01